ECHOES OF TIME
EPIC OF ATLANTIS BOOK 1

Douglas E. Richards
& Brandon Ellis

Paragon Press

This book is a work of fiction. The characters, incidents, and dialogues are products of the author's imagination and are not to be construed as real. Any resemblance to actual events or persons, living or dead, is entirely coincidental.

Copyright © 2025 by Douglas E. Richards and Brandon Ellis
Published by Paragon Press, 2025

Email the authors at
douglaserichards1@gmail.com
brandonelliswrites@gmail.com

All rights reserved. With the exception of excerpts for review purposes, no part of this book may be reproduced or transmitted in any form or by any means, electronic or mechanical, including photocopying, recording, or by any information storage and retrieval system.

First Edition

CHAPTER 1

Trees towered overhead. Their branches blotted out the sky. Vines twisted down, brushing against Dr. Robert Shaw's face and catching on his clothes. With every step, the undergrowth snagged at his ankles. Sweat stung his eyes as the humid air sapped his strength. His worn leather backpack chafed against his shoulders, heavy with supplies.

Robert was determined to uncover two ancient secrets concealed beneath the canopies of Brazil's Vale do Ribeira's rainforest. Secrets eluding him for half his career.

He stopped. His breaths came hard. Grasping for his canteen, he took a swig of water. He glanced behind him, hovering his hand over the compact, semi-automatic Colt Defender pistol holstered at his hip. For the last hour, he could swear someone had been following him.

Could it be robbers? Relic hunters looking to make a quick profit? The thought made his stomach stir. He'd be damned if he let anyone get their hands on what he was after. These extraordinary and unbelievable discoveries belonged in a museum, where they could be studied and appreciated by all, instead of languishing as trophies in some wealthy collector's gallery. Or, heck, strapped down in a government's warehouse.

He needed to pick up his pace.

Robert hurried past stone jaguars so beautifully carved, so symmetrically perfect, they must have required the artistic skills of a master from a long-gone civilization. He wanted to stop and examine them, but time wasn't on his side.

He slowed. The entrance to a cave stood before him, a dark opening in the rocky hillside. Robert halted at the entrance, listening. A rustle in the underbrush sounded behind him. He spun around. Nothing. Just the wind through the leaves of a nearby kapok tree.

Or was it?

Taking a deep breath, he stepped into the cave. The temperature dropped. Good. It was damn hot outside. He used the sleeve of his shirt to wipe the perspiration dotting his face. Robert switched on his flashlight and the beam of light sliced through the darkness and revealed damp stone walls covered in lichen and moss.

He walked deeper into the cavern. The noises of the jungle faded away. The steady drip of water and the sound of his footsteps took its place.

He froze. Was that movement behind him? Robert's hand went to his holster.

"Eu tenho uma arma e não tenho medo de usá-la," he said in Portuguese. "Mostre-se." He repeated the words in English: "I have a weapon and I'm not afraid to use it. Show yourself."

Silence. Maybe he was hearing things. Robert turned, flashlight in one hand, pistol in the other. The beam swept across the empty passageway. It showed only stone and shadows. He let out a shaky breath, lowering his weapon but keeping it at the ready.

Adrenaline subsided only for doubt to creep in. Was this really worth it? Risking his life, his career, for an inkling, a gut feeling catalyzed by extensive research that his colleagues dismissed as fantasy?

Robert gritted his teeth. They didn't understand. They were too set in their ways, too afraid to challenge conventional wisdom. Someone had to push the boundaries, and as fate would have it, in many cases it was Robert answering the call. He sought truth where others were too blind, or worse yet, too scared to look for it. Still, it was lonely to be the only man swimming in these rarified waters.

Robert moved forward for a few minutes and halted before three trails. One ascended at a low grade into the cavern. Another extended straight before him. The third descended into a sloping path. He thought about the last Hopi tablet he uncovered two years ago. It was in the ruins of Awatovi on the Hopi Mesas of northeastern Arizona. There at the Mesa was a stone slab with ancient words giving an obscure riddle.

The descending path toward realms where walked the deities most high, its truth shall be unto thee uncloaked.

Robert picked the trail sloping at a downward grade leading into the depths. As he continued onward, the passage narrowed and wound through several rocky outcroppings. Another line from the tablet came to mind as he came to a staircase made from stones.

By earthen steps carved in descent thou must make journey onwards, let stony trail be thy guide to the underworld.

Robert climbed down the jagged rocks, trusting the ancient wisdom. At the bottom, a mess of thick, intertwined roots blocked the pathway. Robert tried to push them aside. The roots were too sturdy, like trunks of small trees. He recalled the third phrase as he gritted his teeth.

Entwined roots buried deep and anchored fast, their woven mass shrouds the threshold purposefully veiled.

He reached into his backpack to grab his machete and hack away at the roots. While he swung the blade, sweat dripped from his brow. As he broke through the wood-like vines, something like an archway showed.

A smile grew on his face as he admired its architectural mastery. It was truly amazing.

Robert strode into a narrow corridor only for it to open into a huge cavern. He moved his flashlight around, the beam tracing over the rock walls until he stopped on something unique. There before him stood a circle of statues. They surrounded a central stone figure standing about six feet taller than the rest.

Robert's breath caught in his throat. He'd found what he'd searched so long to find. And it was right in front of him. He knew by the carvings on the main figure that he was staring at a Kachina. A star being, or a spiritual celestial guide, from Hopi legend. This cave was thousands of miles away from Hopi territory. And yet, here sculptured in front of him was a Kachina from their myths. It was evidence the Hopi traditions held further sacred truths. That Hopi and many indigenous tribes had migrated from South America to North America long ago, not just across the Bering Strait.

Feathers decorated the statue's elongated skull. On the human-looking face were large, almond-shaped eyes. It bore ears, a nose, a chin, and more. The body was slender, with overly long arms and hands, and too many fingers. Hopi symbols covered the statue's chest and legs.

His colleagues called it a deity, a relic of ancient South American religious beliefs. To Robert, it was something else entirely. A lifetime studying ancient civilizations convinced him this figure was a profound link between the earliest cultures of North and South America. More than that, it confirmed what certain Hopi traditionalists, including some from the Bear Clan, believed: the Kachinas were not just spiritual guides but physical extraterrestrial beings who visited Earth, as told in their ancient oral traditions.

Examining the symbols, it took him a few minutes to decipher their meaning.

Our kinfolk were driven to traverse northward. Many have already taken foot aboard the feathered boat crafted by Kachina starborn and Hopi hands, while others must wind the serpentine paths to rejoin our tribal embrace.

Robert wrinkled his brow. He paced. *No, no. You've got to be kidding me.*

Of all things, this was the wrong place. From what he'd just read, he'd gone to the wrong country altogether. He'd come this far, and for what? Where was this mythical starship, this feathered boat? Was it back up north, under Hopi land?

No, it couldn't be. He'd have found it by now.

For several moments, he hung his head. So much work, so many years, and again, it led him to another trail leading somewhere else.

According to Robert's studies and discreet interviews with Hopi elders, a sacred flute could activate an ancient starship. This instrument, tied to Kokopelli, the Hopi flute-playing kachina of fertility and cosmic harmony, was carved from bone with intricate spiral patterns, its melodies said to resonate with otherworldly energies. Some Hopi claimed it was crafted over ten thousand years ago, predating the earliest cuneiform. Lost for centuries, its location was unknown even to the Hopi themselves. Yet Robert believed the sacred flute and its starship lay hidden in Brazil's northeastern interior, deep within this cavern.

At least he *had* believed this to be the case. Until the symbols on the chest of the statue he was now facing suggested otherwise.

He continued translating the ancient glyphs.

Seek the hollow bone that awakens the sleeping vessel. But know that it must be aboard the flying boat for this to happen. In the land of stone rivers, carved by invisible waters, find the cleft where three serpents intertwine. There, the key to revive the dormant sky ship awaits. Beyond the serpents' frozen jaws, an obsidian surface will yield to your touch. Press where their joined tails point to the sky, and the void will reveal the resting place of the sacred song-giver.

This had to be a reference to the flute. It was the very means to summon a prehistoric yet hyper-advanced technology. The feathered boat, or "flying shields" as many Hopi called them. An ancient space vessel. In a way, the flute was the key to activating a starship.

He glanced around and spotted several carved serpents on the wall behind the statues. He touched the stone etchings. Pressing the spot where the tails converged, nothing occurred. A second attempt came with the same result. After he applied more force, a hiss sounded. He backed away as a seam appeared in the wall. It groaned open to reveal a small alcove.

He gasped. On a pedestal rested a carved flute made from bone. It was coated in dust.

Incredible! He may have been wrong about the starship's location, but the flute was here, after all. And it was the find of his life. It was the most dramatic evidence yet that certain aspects of Hopi mythology might just reflect a reality that most would consider preposterous.

Robert carefully brushed away the debris and gingerly lifted the artifact to examine it under his flashlight.

He blew gently, clearing untold centuries of accumulated dust from the flute. To his surprise, the instrument vibrated for a moment. He repeated his action and the same vibrations occurred.

He raised his eyebrows. After all these centuries, could it really be . . . *operational?*

He adjusted his grip, and this time, rather than blowing dust *from* the instrument, he blew directly into its mouthpiece. His gently delivered breath resulted in a distinct chirp, which resonated with a subtle, otherworldly power. The cavern walls shook slightly, but just for an instant. He stared at the ancient artifact, his mouth agape.

"Whoa," he whispered.

But if this *was* the flute of legend, the key to unlocking a lost ship, why was it here? You didn't keep your car in Arizona and your keys in Brazil.

He considered this further. The flute's location couldn't just be a random mistake. Not when words on ancient glyphs had so unerringly guided him here. His eyes widened as an intriguing thought entered his mind.

What if convenience was the *opposite* of what the ancients had been aiming for? What if the separation of the key and lock was a *failsafe*? If so, it was ingenious. Because there was a danger of leaving your keys in your car. Anyone who stumbled upon it could immediately drive it away. But separating the flute from the ship by thousands of miles ensured that only someone who was actively, *mindfully*, searching for them both, someone with deep knowledge of these particular traditions, could unlock the ship's power. And the glyphs suggested the musical instrument had to be *inside* the ship. Nothing less would suffice, although this remained to be seen.

But there was only one way to find out. He had to find the starship.

Robert reached for his camera to capture the statues, etchings, and symbols around him. As he did, the crunch of gravel resounded far away through the cavern, and Robert reflexively killed his flashlight and darted behind one of the massive statues.

He wasn't alone.

Seconds later distinct footsteps could be heard quickly approaching, and soon thereafter, the entire area was illuminated by multiple handheld spotlights flooding the cavern with high-intensity light.

An accented voice called out from a distance. "Hand over the artifact. Now!"

Robert pressed even closer to the statue. After he unholstered his semi-automatic, he peeked around the stone figure. Three men stood at the chamber's entrance. Their faces were obscured by bandanas, and each gripped a pistol of their own.

Robert remained silent, his mind racing. He needed a plan. He was an expert marksman, but three against one was three against one. Still, handing the flute over to them wasn't an option. He had unearthed numerous relics over the years, but this was the find of a lifetime. *Priceless.*

While these men saw the flute as priceless in the monetary sense, he saw it as priceless in the scientific and archeological sense. It was a groundbreaking discovery. *Monumental.* Not to mention proof that he had been right all along. If he had focused on Christian relics rather than Hopi relics, this would be the equivalent of the Holy Grail.

The tallest of the trio, standing in the middle, shook his head. "Do you think you can fool us by not replying? We know you're there. So give us what we want, or we'll take it off your bloodied corpse. Makes no difference to us."

After this was said, all three men gently placed their spotlights on the floor to free up their hands.

"What's amusing about this is that you think you have the upper hand," shouted Robert in contempt, knowing the echoes and reverberations of his voice in the cave would make his position difficult to pinpoint precisely, even while speaking. "Ever watch an *Indiana Jones* movie?" he continued. "The ground between me and you is booby-trapped in a dozen ways. Approach me and you're crossing the equivalent of a minefield, which I survived only because I knew exactly where to step."

"Impressive bluff," said the trio's leader. "Might have even worked. But the thing is, we've been here before. We didn't find the artifact like you did, true, but we didn't trigger any booby-traps either. You have five seconds to surrender."

Robert took another glimpse. Two of the men were fanning out, coming from different angles. He ducked back around just as one of the men crept faster around the side. Robert fired. The shot reverberated throughout the cavern. The criminal cried out and clutched his leg as he fell. The man's weapon dropped to the ground. As he reached for it, Robert fired a second shot. The bullet ricocheted off the dirt. The robber pulled his hand away, weaponless. He crawled back toward where he'd come from, leaving a trail of blood.

Gunfire erupted as the other two opened fire. Chunks of stone flew from the statue as bullets impacted around Robert. He winced from the desecration of the statue as if he had been shot himself. He blindly returned fire, his shots pinging off the far wall.

"Don't come any closer!" said Robert. "I'm a marksman. Consider these warning shots across the bow. The next ones won't miss!"

The third member of the gang of thieves tried to flank from the other side. Robert squeezed the trigger. The man scrambled back.

"I thought you said you wouldn't miss?" said the leader of the trio. "I'm still willing to offer you your life if you give us what we want. But my generous offer won't last long."

Robert pressed his body closer to the statue. "I've got enough ammo to last all night," he lied. "And I've got nowhere to be just now. What about you? If you don't get your comrade to the hospital, he'll bleed out."

"I have reinforcements coming," the man replied, unimpressed. "They'll be here in *minutes*. I can spare at least one of them to take care of my friend. If you think I'm bluffing about additional manpower, stick around. You're about to find out."

Their leader paused. "So you're out of options," he continued. "You'll soon be even more outnumbered, and one of my men is posted at the only way in or out. So even if you get by us, which you won't, there's no cover near the exit. At least for someone trying to *leave*. My man on the outside waiting for you, on the other hand, will have plenty of cover. So hand over the item. Last time I'll ask nicely."

Robert peered around the statue. The immediate area was clear. He scanned the vicinity for an escape route. A faint indentation high up on the wall caught his eye in the eerie lighting thrown off by the three high-powered spotlights. It was a small tunnel. It would be a tight squeeze, but it was his only chance. He quickly and carefully packed the flute away in his backpack and took a deep breath.

Here goes nothing, he thought to himself.

Robert raced over to the wall and scrambled up it without breaking stride, leaning into the limited parkour training he had picked up over the years. Loose rocks clattered to the floor and he lost his grip, falling to the hard ground with a loud thud. He ignored the pain and tried again, this time climbing higher.

When he reached the indentation, he shined his flashlight ahead. A long passageway stretched onward, and he heard numerous additional footsteps behind him in the chamber. Apparently, the reinforcements were real. Fortunately, his pursuers hadn't yet realized he had found a possible escape route and were proceeding with utmost caution, mindful that their cornered rat was well-armed.

But their caution didn't last long. Suddenly, the staccato thunder of gunfire sounded as Robert hauled himself into the opening. Bullets whizzed past his feet and sank into the rocks as he crawled deeper into the small tunnel.

Robert hurried through the narrow passage as his heart pounded against his ribcage. Sharp rocks jutted out from the walls. They scraped against his sides as he kept going. Adrenaline coursed through his veins as he dug his fingers a bit too much into the dirt, bending back a nail and leaving his palms scuffed, raw.

Shouts and curses echoed as a few of the men tried to climb the wall to pursue him. Robert pushed himself to move faster.

Go, go, go!

His lungs burned. He bit down hard, doing his best to ignore the stinging pain in his hands, to focus primarily on putting as much distance between himself and those after him.

The ground beneath Robert crumbled, its stability dissolving in a split second. His stomach lurched as the world dropped away and plunged him into darkness. The air rushed past him. Dislodged stones clattered and broken rocks tumbled alongside his falling body. Time stretched, each heartbeat an eternity until . . . impact.

When he hit the ground, all air was driven from his lungs. Pain exploded through his body, radiating from his back and limbs in white-hot waves. For a few seconds, he lay stunned, struggling to breathe.

Where am I? he asked himself as he tried to figure out the sudden change.

As his vision cleared, Robert squinted. Sunlight poured down on him, and humid, suffocating jungle heat hit him like a blast furnace. Groaning, he forced himself to move and staggered to his feet. Where exactly was he? Back outside? How?

Looking up, he realized the tunnel section he'd been crawling through—the part that had crumbled beneath him—was actually extended beyond the cave's main structure. Instead of plummeting deeper into the cave's interior as he'd expected, he'd fallen through a portion jutting out over the rainforest floor. The broken tunnel gaped above him from the rocky overhang.

Robert's initial surprise was quickly pushed aside by fear and anxiety. He still wasn't safe. Not by a long shot.

Angry shouts grew close and Robert darted through the underbrush, ignoring the branches whipping at his face. The curses became louder. Robert spun around, his pistol somehow still in his grasp, and fired into the foliage.

He rushed deeper into the brush and did his best to put as much distance as he could between himself and his attackers. When Robert felt he'd gained enough ground, about fifteen arduous minutes later, he slowed, although his heart continued to race.

He pulled the flute from his backpack to check its condition. If it wasn't fully intact, he'd never forgive himself. He forced himself to examine it, somehow more terrified of finding it damaged than he had been while facing death itself.

It was intact! Robert finally allowed himself to take a long, relieved breath. He blew into the flute again and was rewarded by the same vibrations, which he heard and felt as much with his *soul* as with his ears.

Thank all that's holy, he thought. The flute still worked.

Shoving the precious artifact back into his pack, Robert picked up speed. The dense foliage swallowed him up as he disappeared into the heart of the woodlands.

He had dodged a bullet this time. Literally and figuratively. But he needed to be far more careful going forward.

And he needed to, somehow, locate a fabled starship, lost to the ages, that he truly believed his newfound key could awaken.

CHAPTER 2

Forty-two faces peered down at Dr. Robert Shaw, who stood at the podium in the Emil W. Haury Lecture Hall at the University of Arizona. It'd been two weeks since the incident in Brazil, and he was glad to put it behind him.

"This Hopi symbol here," said Robert, gesturing toward the projector's image on the big screen beside him, "sits in the Tutuveni petroglyph site near Tuba City, Arizona. It's well hidden among the rocks, but what does it show? What *is* its meaning?"

With his laser pointer, he circled the motif. A triangular shape drawing with flares coming off the design.

"Anyone know?"

He scanned the audience. No one answered. He glanced at a student he'd never seen before. A young man wearing a blue hoodie with the hood covering his head, keeping his eyes shaded.

"What about you?" said Robert.

The student winced and shook his head.

"Alright," said Robert in resignation. "What you see here is what some Hopi traditions describe as Star Beings, or at least human interactions with them. Though interpretations of these petroglyphs can vary. Now, look closely at the glyph next to this one."

He placed his pointer's red beam on a dome-shaped object. "To many, this is meaningless. But according to some Hopi accounts I've studied, this could represent what's called a paatuwvota, or *flying shield*. In these traditions, these were described as, ah . . . vessels, or starships, used by the Kachinas to travel between worlds. Some Hopi have described these Kachinas as spiritual guides and teachers to their people."

Robert paused. "Let me drill down on what I just said a little more. If you tell someone that a civilization over ten thousand years ago believed starships existed and beings lived on other worlds, they'll immediately assume these beliefs were pure fantasy."

He raised his eyebrows. "But what about this statement might suggest otherwise?"

He waited for an answer, but only for a few seconds. Long experience had shown him that no student would guess correctly. "Let me tell you," he continued. "When we gaze up at a clear night sky, we see thousands of tiny, twinkling lights. And, since you and I are so sophisticated, we know immediately what these really are. We're taught from birth that a pinprick of light in the sky can be an entire Earth-sized world. Or, more likely, a star—*millions* of times larger.

"But if you were born even six hundred years ago, you wouldn't think that at all. For most of human history, no one knew what these tiny lights truly represented. Hard to believe, since it seems so obvious to us now, but the ancients still thought these lights were spirits, gods, ancestors, or mystical entities. The idea that these were entire *worlds* would seem beyond preposterous to them. Earth was the *only* world, located in the center of the Universe, and everything else moved around us."

He paused. "That's not to say they didn't use the terms *star* and *planet,* which misleads many into thinking the ancients knew what they were dealing with. They didn't. These terms meant something very different to them than they mean to us. *Star* comes from the Greek word for radiance or brilliance. Basically speaking to their shine and sparkle. When they said *star* they weren't thinking massive nuclear furnace. They were thinking brilliant, twinkling light.

"*Planet* came from the Greek phrase *planetes asters*, which means *wandering star.* Wandering star is a perfect name, actually, reflecting that the planets are the odd lights that move about, as opposed to all others, which are stubbornly immobile.

"What's remarkable is that many ancient cosmologies were still *extremely* sophisticated," continued Robert with great enthusiasm. "Made even *more* remarkable given the telescope wasn't invented until the early seventeenth century, so much of this discovery was done with naked-eye observations and math. The Babylonians, Greeks, Chinese, and Mayans, for example, could predict planetary movements with startling accuracy, including eclipses, and created sophisticated calendars based on this knowledge."

He shook his head. "But, even so, they had no idea stars and planets were "worlds" in the modern sense—physical places like Earth with mass, landscapes, or potential inhabitants."

Robert smiled with a gleam in his eye. "So how could someone from ten thousand years ago possibly know enough to claim other worlds existed? Let alone worlds that aliens could live on and travel between? This would never occur to them, even in their wildest imaginations."

He paused for effect. "Kind of makes you think, doesn't it? Not as startling as if archeologists found a ten-thousand-year-old carving of $E=MC^2$ on a cave wall, but still quite . . . *intriguing*."

Robert smiled at the sight of eyes widening across the room as his point hit home. He let the students marinate in this new line of thought for several long seconds but finally pushed ahead.

"In this next slide," he said, "you'll see a design from Inscription Canyon, near Prescott, Arizona. As you can see, it features an etched equilateral cross. According to Hopi elder Oswald "White Bear" Fredericks, this petroglyph is one of many examples of the Hopi's epic migration story and cosmology from a land called Kasskara."

Robert raised his eyebrows, knowing that most of his students would find this material fascinating, but would rail against the need to commit the numerous strange, hard-to-pronounce words he threw at them to memory, along with their definitions. "*Kasskara* is what some Hopi oral traditions describe as their ancestral homeland during the third world, before migrating to the Americas at the beginning of the fourth world. According to White Bear, Kasskara would be what some people today call Lemuria."

He paused. "Now, let me direct your attention to this glyph," he continued, highlighting a dome-shaped symbol. "This refers to the flying shield. Some clans believe it depicts a literal starship piloted by Kachinas, and—"

He stopped in mid-sentence, distracted by a petite female hand that had shot up in the auditorium, eager to get his attention. "Yes," he said to the young student to whom the hand belonged.

"Sorry, Professor, but before you move on . . . what is Lemuria?" She glanced at her notes. "You said that according to White Bear, Kasskara was what some people today call Lemuria. But are we supposed to know what that is?"

Robert smiled. He was so steeped in ancient lore from around the world that he often assumed certain things were common knowledge that weren't. "Right," he said sheepishly. "Thanks. Lemuria is a mysterious lost continent in the Pacific, much like Atlantis is a lost continent in the Atlantic. And like Atlantis, mainstream scientists largely don't believe it ever existed. They especially don't believe that both lost continents were once populated by human civilizations. And, at the same time. Some Hopi lore, on the other hand, suggests otherwise. And, some Hopi believe that the lore maintains that Kasskara and Atlantis were not only civilized, but highly advanced, and that their fates were intertwined."

As he spoke, Robert's eyes were drawn to the bald head of Professor Alan Donovan. Despite the lecture having started thirty minutes earlier, Alan had only recently arrived. He had appeared to be highly agitated just before the young woman had asked her question, and Robert could tell the man had been struggling mightily to hold his tongue while Robert delivered his answer.

Finally, the dam burst, and the rival professor who had crashed Robert's lecture could no longer remain silent. He jumped to his feet. "Dr. Shaw, I must take exception to your lecture. Are you really trying to tell your students that the Hopi Indians emerged from the third world?"

Alan Donovan turned to address the students. "For those unaware, the 'third world' in Hopi mythology refers to the world during the last Ice Age. The 'fourth world' is our current world now, the Interglacial Age, the world after the Ice Age, according to the Hopi."

"Yes, I covered that earlier," said Robert, more than a little irritated by a blowhard trying to insert himself where he didn't belong.

Alan turned to face Robert once again. "Are you also going to tell these students *how* you believe the Hopi came to the Americas? How they got here from their fabled continent in the third world, which was in the middle of the Pacific Ocean? I know you believe they used one of these starships you so love to speak about to make the journey. So will this also be part of your lecture?"

"Of course," said Robert evenly. "But not all the Hopi, just some. And some Hopi Elders called the starship a flying shield. Plus, Alan, I've never stated these are historical facts. I'm teaching a certain perspective of Hopi mythology, and this is a critical part of it. I'm not saying it's true. I'm not saying it's *not* true. I'm just saying that some of the Hopi Elders throughout the ages believed this to be the case. If you had let me finish, I would have made all this clear. And since you've raised the subject, let me finish now."

He turned to the class to continue his lesson as if Alan had never interrupted. "According to White Bear, the Hopi were helped by the Kachinas, a star people with advanced technology who worked hand in hand with them during their expansion on Kasskara, i.e., Lemuria. When Lemuria sank into the Pacific Ocean, many Hopi migrated off the sinking continent via a starship or starships—"

"Be honest with us, Professor," interrupted a man who should have been a colleague, but had become a hostile public critic, unwilling to be denied his full ration of contempt. "You give yourself an out by saying this is mythology. But you—*personally*—believe it's all true, don't you? You believe more than one starship was built and flown by ancient Hopi."

"Professor Donovan, I have tried to be patient with you, in the spirit of scholarship, but my patience isn't limitless. I have a lecture to give. We can discuss this another time."

Alan's eyes narrowed, something all too common when he glimpsed Robert from down the hall between lectures or in the faculty lounge during breaks. But now he'd crossed a line, airing his ill-disguised contempt in a public forum. "I'll leave as you request," said Alan finally. "If I were you, I wouldn't want my outrageous beliefs to be publicly debated, either. But answer one last question for me. How did this Kasskara, this Lemuria, sink into the Pacific Ocean? Please tell all these young students how that occurred, in your view?" He widened his arms to the crowd. "Please listen carefully. This will be quite . . . eye-opening."

"Look, Alan, as you know . . . or at least as you *should* know . . . myth is more real than we think. For instance, as we've come to understand, just about every culture has a flood story. Scientifically, we know a flood took place. That shortly before and during the Younger Dryas, during specific times between 14,000 and 11,600 years ago, sea levels rose three hundred to four hundred feet, flooding massive areas worldwide. There's truth in myth."

"You're avoiding the question. What do you claim is the reason that this hypothetical continent of Lemuria sank into the ocean?"

"Well, if you'd have let me finish, I'd have—"

"How did it sink?" demanded the hostile professor.

A hush came over the auditorium. Some students leaned in toward Robert. A few eyes fixed on Alan as Robert cleared his throat. Some individuals nodded at Alan, perhaps in agreement with the man. Never did Robert suspect a tenured professor, one with an office just down the hall from his own, would challenge him so publicly.

"It sank in the aftermath of a war with Atlantis," he replied calmly. "As I said, their fates were said to have been intertwined. The Hopi believe history moves in cycles. That every age ends because people fail to learn from the mistakes of those before them. If the lessons aren't heeded, the cycle starts over, often with greater destruction. Imagine what that means for us if they're right. We'd be—"

Alan threw his hands up. "There you go. The legendary Atlantis, the incredible Lemuria, sunk by a major war." He turned back to the crowd. "And positing ancient starships? That's the very *definition* of absurd? A war? I'm guessing this was a nuclear war, something so bad it—"

"You said you'd leave after I answered your final question," said Robert with such a fierce yet controlled tone that Alan looked terrified for a moment. "That time has come."

Alan swallowed hard but didn't argue. He made a show of slowly walking to the back of the auditorium, pausing at the door. "You're teaching utter nonsense, Robert, and it won't be tolerated any longer," he said, taking a final, parting shot before rushing through the door.

Fifteen minutes later, as the lecture concluded and students filed out of the room, Alan Donovan returned to the auditorium and approached Robert at the podium. "I need you to know that I've filed a complaint with Dean Laikind," he said, referring to the Dean of the department they were both in. "I'm demanding that you be dismissed for promoting mythology as true history. It's harmful to students *and* the university. Especially here in Arizona, the epicenter of the Hopi nation, where students are likely to be more susceptible to your unscientific beliefs."

Robert snorted. "You went off your meds, today, Alan, didn't you? If you're looking to find someone who's delusional, look in the mirror. Let's see what the Dean thinks of you interrupting my lecture the way you did. Talk about unprofessional."

Alan delivered a cold, grim smile. "Here's the thing, Robert. If you don't cease speaking on this topic, on these untruths, I'll send *this* to the Academic Affairs Office." He set his phone down on the podium, and on it, a video recording played of Robert and a young woman eating at a restaurant. Alan turned up the volume.

On the video, Robert sat across from the woman, his gestures animated. ". . . because some of the Hopi Elders believed you can change the future by altering the past," said Robert's voice through the phone's speakers. "The starship isn't just a ship, in my opinion. It's a time portal, urging us to change the ancient war between Lemuria and Atlantis that created such havoc for humanity over the last thirteen millennia. We've forgotten our origins, Kira. That's one reason the Hopi say the starship is here. *Now.*"

"Is that their official position on the subject?"

"Not really. Only a few of them say this. It's an *idea*, really. That a flying shield, a vessel, still awaits in present times. They believed in other dimensions and portals leading to other worlds. Some think there's even a portal back to the time of Lemuria and Atlantis."

Kira Shelton folded her hands on the dinner table. "A portal?"

"That part is probably fantasy, of course. Only a few Elders ever alluded to such things—fragments, really. Not myth. Not history. Perhaps just attempting to put the pieces together in their own way, while others questioned it. None of them discussed it publicly. It's all hearsay."

"And when you find this starship? What will you do?"

"Share it with the world. It would be the most epic discovery in modern history. It would forever change how we look at our world, and at history. And the knowledge we could glean from it, the technological marvels, could allow us to create a virtual Utopia and spread to the stars."

Kira shook her head sadly. "I admire your idealism, Robert, I really do. But that's not at all what would happen. The government would seize it immediately, and you'd never get near the ship again. They'd threaten your life if you weren't quiet about it, or just kill you from the jump . . . just to be sure."

She paused, lowering her voice. "I've seen it happen before in my own industry. Powerful people burying the truth because it doesn't fit their narrative. That's part of why I'm here. My father was a geologist. Brilliant, but stubborn. He spent his life chasing discoveries that others thought were too inconvenient to acknowledge, or simply myths. When he vanished during one of his last research expeditions in the Scablands, hoping to explain what really happened there, his disappearance was written off as an accident. But I never believed that."

Kira's eyes darkened. "I need to prove that this world holds truths we can't just sweep under the rug. For my own sanity."

Robert smiled. "Which explains why you're so firmly in my corner on this."

Alan paused the recording. "Good quality, isn't it? Now, unless you want me sending this to the Academic Affairs office as proof that you're indoctrinating students with fringe pseudo-history along with wining and dining beautiful pupils, I suggest rethinking your lecture content and the way you conduct yourself. You've even convinced this poor woman that she's on your side. And I see she calls you Robert rather than Professor Shaw. What should I make of that? Talk about *inappropriate*."

"*I'm* inappropriate?" said Robert in disbelief. "How would you define spying on a colleague in a restaurant?"

"So, you get caught trying to indoctrinate a student with fantasies, and you blame me for *catching* you? Let's stick to the point, which is that this woman appears to be fully indoctrinated. How many other co-eds have you wined and dined like this? How many have you dazzled with your theories?" He raised his eyebrows. "How many have you *slept* with?"

"Wow," said Robert. "I always thought you were a contemptible jackass and blowhard, Alan, but I had no *idea*. First, Kira is not a student. She looks young, but she's in her thirties. And unlike you, I don't need people to use my title to stroke my ego. Now leave this auditorium now!" he added in a guttural growl. "Before I do something I won't regret."

Alan opened his mouth to reply, but there was something in Robert's steely, penetrating gaze that made him change his mind. He stormed off without saying another word. When he reached the exit door, he opened it and turned once again to face Robert.

"I'll add that you made a veiled threat on my person to my list of complaints," he said, and then hurriedly rushed off into the hallway.

"Have at it, then," mumbled Robert in contempt as Alan's figure disappeared from the room.

CHAPTER 3

Robert was in his office an hour later, still furious after his exchange with Alan Donovan. There was a gentle, tentative knock at his door. "Come in," he called out, glad to have a distraction from his thoughts. "It's open."

Kira Shelton appeared at the open door, her black hair cascading over her shoulders, framing her face as she entered and took a seat across from his desk.

"Kira," he said happily, a better greeting than *speak of the devil*, which had flashed into his mind when he first saw her. "Good to see you. Where've you been lately?"

"Sorry, Robert. I've been dealing with some business headaches overseas. One of my mining operations hit a snag, and it reminded me why I started investing in your expeditions. I can handle the world of business, but there's something deeper in this work, Robert. Something that feels . . . unfinished."

She eyed his backpack which was sitting on the side of his desk. "Besides, I knew you were out of the country, too."

The hint of a smile crossed Kira's face as she went on to survey Robert's office. Books and papers covered every surface in the room. A small cot was wedged into one corner. The shelves lining the walls held Southwestern artifacts—Ancestral Pueblo pottery shards, Navajo rugs, and turquoise jewelry excavated from ancient burial sites. A large topographic map covered one portion of his cluttered desk. It traced the boundaries of Mesa Verde and was marked with Robert's scribbled notes.

"Do you sleep here?" she asked.

"Sometimes. When the research demands it."

She made a face. "What about showering?"

"The gym has perfectly good facilities."

"Robert, you're living like a college student."

He grinned. "I prefer to think of it as 'dedicated to my work.'"

Kira laughed. "I knew there was a reason I was so eager to support you." She nodded at a drawing pinned to the wall. "Is that what you think these ancient starships looked like?"

"I have no idea, of course. But maybe."

"Starships look odd without any wings."

"Well, as you know, some Hopi traditionalists, drawing on Bear Clan oral traditions, describe the flying shields as wingless ships. And a sufficiently advanced technology wouldn't need wings."

"So what else have you been up to?"

Robert laughed. "I admire your attempt to pretend you're here to see me, and to engage in small talk. But we both know you're here to see the relic I found. And who could blame you?"

"Alright, you caught me. If you were a thirteen-thousand-year-old magical flute, I'd race here to see you, too."

"Thanks," he said wryly. "That's comforting."

Robert rummaged through his backpack. He extracted a small, wrapped object and handed it to Kira. She unwrapped it as if it were the ultimate Christmas morning. "I can't believe you got this."

"I know."

She studied the flute now in her grip. "Have any trouble?"

"A little."

"Your hands," she said. "They're . . . scuffed."

"They're healing."

"You'll get the money transfer soon," she said.

"Look, Kira, I need to thank you again for your continued contributions to my archaeological excavations. There's no way I could do this without you."

"What are friends for?" she replied cheerfully. "If it wasn't for you, a lot of these 'truths' would never be found. Plus, you know, these discoveries are proof that the world is bigger than what I see out there, if that makes any sense. Maybe I'm chasing a ghost—my dad, I guess—but I need to know if any of this is real."

"Yeah, me too. Do you have any ethical issues with us keeping this to ourselves for a bit? As you know, nothing can stop me from making this public and putting it in a museum . . . eventually. But, as you noted, if this really can activate a hidden starship, I'd rather not chance government interest at this point. Maybe I've watched too many thrillers about secret government organizations, but let's play it safe for now."

Kira grinned. "I'm actually pleasantly surprised. I was going to say the exact same thing, but I thought I might have to beat you into submission. You have the ethics of a monk, after all. No one has been this adamant about relics going to museums since Indiana Jones."

Robert nodded, tempted to tell her he had just invoked this fictional figure to bluff three men who wanted him dead, but decided now wasn't the time.

"So, to answer your question," continued Kira, "I'm thrilled that we're on the same page about this." She leaned in. "This makes the existence of the fabled hidden starship even more likely, doesn't it?"

"Absolutely."

She glanced at his wounds and shook her head. "Good. But why do I have the feeling that the acquisition of the flute was a bit more harrowing than you're letting on?"

"Perhaps a tad," he said in amusement.

"You've become obsessed with this now, haven't you?"

"Isn't that why you're funding me? If I wasn't obsessed, I'd have given up years ago. If you're going to place a bet, bet on crazy every time."

She smiled. "You're more right than you realize. As Steve Jobs said, 'The ones who are crazy enough to think they can change the world are the ones who *do*.'"

"I couldn't agree more."

"I know. But even though that's what I was looking for, I don't want your obsession to get you killed."

"Wow," said Robert in amusement. "We really are on the same page. I don't want me to get myself killed, either."

"I'm being serious."

Robert's smile vanished, and his features hardened. "I know. And I appreciate it. But mark my words. The starship's out there, and I'm going to be the one who finds it."

CHAPTER 4

Robert tapped the rim of his ceramic coffee mug with his pen, thinking about Alan's words at the lecture. What the man said was baseless. Other than the Hopi themselves, Robert didn't know anyone who'd researched their culture and mythology more extensively than he had. He'd even led excavations solely focused on Hopi myths and unearthed several artifacts the Hopi claimed were real, despite historians dismissing them as mere folklore.

Whatever claims Alan might present to the Academic Affairs office about Robert would likely amount to nothing. Still, in the current climate, one could never be too sure. And the man had to know that videoing someone having dinner without their consent was likely illegal. Using the video—which wasn't incriminating anyway—could well backfire on him.

His mother shuffled into the room, her walker scraping softly against the wood floor. "Robert, you've been quiet since you got home."

"Just thinking about today, Mom."

She maneuvered herself carefully to a chair at the head of the table and sat down with a slow, deliberate effort. "Is it about Alan Donovan again?"

"He continues to make a lot of noise about my research. But this time he's taken it to the next level."

His mother sighed. "He's just jealous of your work. You're finding connections. Things that no one else is seeing. I know you'll find what you're looking for someday. You're as brilliant as they come, and as tenacious. It's an unbeatable combination."

Her voice softened. "I just hope you're not losing yourself in all of this." She attempted to stand, but winced as she struggled to push herself up with her walker.

Robert went to help, but she found her grip on the walker's handles and stood straighter. She headed toward the hallway, passing by the small table near the front door. She stopped for a second and adjusted a fresh bouquet of flowers in a ceramic vase. Above the table, a mirror reflected her movements. Just beneath it sat a framed picture. It was a photograph of her and Robert's father, locked in a loving embrace. She stared at the image and her eyes lingered there.

His father, who'd passed away from a car accident last year, had always looked at his mother with a deep love. She turned away from the picture and continued down the hall. "Good night, Robert. I love you."

"I love you too, Mom."

As she shut her bedroom door, Robert returned to grading papers at the dining table. He tapped the pen on the edge of his mug again, doing his best to focus.

Twenty minutes later, a knock at the door startled him. He glanced at his watch. It was nearly 10 PM. Who'd be knocking at this hour?

After making his way to the door, he peered through the peephole. A young man in his early twenties stood on his porch. Robert recognized him as one of the students from his lecture earlier in the day.

Robert opened the door. "Can I help you?"

The young man shifted his weight from foot to foot. "Uh, hey, Professor Shaw. I'm Matt Jones. I was at your lecture today."

"Right. What can I do for you, Matt?"

The visitor hesitated. "I wanted to talk to you about your work. I'm a big fan."

"That's very kind, but if you want to talk, schedule something with me at school. I'm afraid you can't visit me here. This is my residence, and it's late. How did you even know where I lived?"

"Sorry. I realize this is . . . irregular. And you can find just about anything on the web, including your address."

Robert gritted his teeth. "Great," he said sarcastically. He'd have to hire someone to scrub this information clean.

He turned his full attention to the student at his door. "Look, here's the deal, you can sign up to meet with me during my office hours online. I haven't seen you before today at any of my lectures. So, if you're thinking of adding my class, you have some ground to make up. Still, it should be doable if you put in the effort. You still have several weeks before the first midterm exam."

With that, Robert nodded a farewell and prepared to close the door.

"I know what you're looking for, Professor Shaw."

Robert stopped the swing of the door just before it closed and pulled it slightly open again. "Oh?" he said, raising his eyebrows. "And what's that?"

"I'm a member of the Hopi tribe, actually. I grew up on a reservation. I left the Hopi life behind, but I still know things. As to what you're looking for, you couldn't have made that more clear during your lecture. You're looking for a starship."

Robert had to admit, the guy had a point. One didn't need to be a super-spy to ferret out his interests. "Okay," he said, "I'm looking for a starship. What about it?"

"I can help you find it. Like I said, I know things, Professor. Things about the sacred sites, the hidden caves. Information that isn't in any of your books."

Robert stared deeply into his visitor's eyes and found nothing but sincerity there. Besides, why would he come here at night, to Robert's home, just to lie? "Why do you want to help me? I thought you left the Hopi life behind."

"Let's just say I have my reasons. And maybe I'm not as disconnected from my roots as I thought. Gray Eagle, my dad, well, he—"

"Your dad is Gray Eagle?"

"Yeah."

Robert had met the legendary Gray Eagle—the revered keeper of sacred Hopi histories and ancient knowledge passed down over generations—during an early expedition five years ago in the Black Mesa region on Hopi lands in northern Arizona.

At the time of their meeting, Gray Eagle himself didn't fully believe in the Hopi legend of an ancient starship. While he acknowledged that such an event could have occurred in the distant past, he doubted any remnants of that mythical starship still existed in modern times.

Still, Robert's position hadn't changed. Through years of uncovering proof validating many ancient Hopi teachings, Robert began to suspect the elderly Gray Eagle was just trying to throw him off the trail.

As for the young man standing before him, he might be deluded, misguided, or leading him on for nefarious purposes, but Robert would be a fool not to explore this further. "Are you willing to tell me these things you know?"

"I am."

Robert invited him inside and they were soon sitting across from each other on two sections of a sofa. "I'm all ears," said the professor. "You have the floor."

Matt swallowed hard as if he was second-guessing himself. Finally, he visibly strengthened his resolve and began. "There's a cave," he said, lowering his voice conspiratorially. "It's got markings. Symbols that match some of the ones you shared in your lecture. There's a tablet there that talks about a skyboat nearby. Very nearby. I found it when I was a kid."

"When you say you found it, you mean you found the *tablet*. I assume you didn't find the skyboat."

"Right. And at the time, I thought the tablet was just more quasi-religious lunacy. I've always believed the Hopi teaching about humanity passing through four worlds, four stages, and then to a fifth, was fantasy. Nonsense. And especially the parts about alien visitors and starships. I was embarrassed that my dad, and a big group of my people, bought into this craziness. So while the tablet suggested a starship was close by, I didn't believe it for a second."

"So, what changed?" asked Robert.

"Recently, for reasons I'm not even sure of, I began to study what archeologists like you, scientists, have written about the Hopi legends. I gravitated to *your* writings, especially, because I found them the most interesting. You aren't Hopi. And you aren't a fool either. You make wild claims, but you support them with evidence, or logic . . . at least of a sort. So, I attended your lecture today to get a better sense of you. And you're persuasive. I still don't believe any of this could be real, but given the cave and tablet from my past, I decided it's time to find out."

"Why not find out on your own?"

"The odds of success are better if I take you. Once we're in the cave, who knows what other symbols or clues we'll encounter? You're the world's leading expert on this stuff. So you'll give us the best chance of finding something—if it's there."

Robert nodded. Matt's story did seem to hang together. He was either who and what he claimed to be, or he was a very good liar. "Why not go to your dad?"

Matt sighed. "We aren't on the best of terms. To be honest, he wouldn't want me poking around in that cave. When he discovered I had entered the cave as a kid, he insisted it was dangerous and made me promise never to go there again. He was *adamant*."

Robert thought about this answer for several long seconds. "I see," he said finally. "So where, exactly, is this cave you speak of?"

"On Hopi lands, not too far from here. I don't know GPS coordinates or anything like that. Couldn't even give you directions. But I'm confident I can find it. So how about if I just take you there? That way, you can see it for yourself. What do you say?"

"If what you're telling me checks out, I think you've found your professor."

CHAPTER 5

Dr. Robert Shaw killed the ignition and the SUV's engine died. With the advice and direction of Matt, he hid the car deep in a small canyon, well out of sight of anyone who might wander by, as rare as this was.

Robert stepped out. His breath formed misty clouds in the frigid pre-dawn air. The Arizona desert spread out before him. Darkness was starting to give way to the first hints of light on the eastern horizon. He eyed his watch. Four forty-eight AM. "We're cutting it close, Matt. Are you sure about the location?"

His young passenger exited the vehicle and closed the door. "Of course I'm sure."

This area belonged to Matt's ancestors. From what Robert learned the past three weeks he'd been in contact with Matt, the young man had changed his name and left his world to live in the city when he was nineteen. Matt was the first one in his family to fly a kite. The first one to hike the entire Appalachian Trail from Georgia to Maine. The first one to compete in a hot pepper eating contest at the Albuquerque Balloon Fiesta.

To make sure Matt was legit, Robert asked Kira to hire a private investigator who specialized in background checks and surveillance. The detective's report, complete with numerous photos, confirmed that aside from some late nights at the bar, a bit of questionable behavior at a local casino, and a handful of speeding tickets, everything Matt had told them was true. His identity, his upbringing with the Hopi, and his claim of being Gray Eagle's son were all verified in the dossier the investigator sent.

Kira slammed the rear door as Robert shouldered his backpack. "Lead the way, Matt," said the professor. "And keep your eyes peeled. Last thing we need is to get caught trespassing on Hopi land."

They set off, Matt taking point. The cold bit through Robert's jacket. He wished he'd packed an extra layer.

"How far?" asked Kira.

"A few miles," said Matt. He motioned toward a shadowed silhouette of hills in the distance. "The cave's hidden in a small canyon. It's easy to miss if you don't know what you're looking for. But given the time, we should pick up our pace."

They soon fell silent as they hiked, accompanied only by the sound of their own footsteps crunching on the rocky terrain. Their labored breathing filled the thin air.

Robert couldn't help but be excited, *energized*, but at the same time he fought to manage his expectations. He would do as he always did. Take things as they came. If this turned out to be a bust, it wouldn't be because he had left a single stone unturned, both literally or metaphorically.

The stretch of flatlands they were crossing gave way to a valley surrounded by hills and cliff faces. Tutuveni, a prehistoric petroglyph site at the base of Echo Cliffs, was known as a sacred place for the Hopi people. The site was once used by young Hopi during their ceremonial pilgrimages to the Grand Canyon to mark their passage into adulthood. They'd stop and camp at this site and etch their tribe's symbols onto the rocks.

The sun began to peek over the horizon, sending warmth and a growing level of light. Robert's heart raced a little more as he thought about the small expedition already going somewhat awry. Their timing was off. They were supposed to carry out this mission under the veil of night. The sun's gaze would expose them sooner than he would have liked.

Just keep going, Robert thought as he trekked by shrubs and cacti dotting the terrain.

Finally, after what felt like an eternity, Matt stopped. "There." He pointed to a barely visible crevice in the rock face ahead. "That's our entry point." The opening was about five yards off the ground.

"Looks pretty small," said Robert. "Are you sure?"

"A hundred percent. Watch your step. Some of the rocks here are loose."

"Thanks for the heads up," said Kira.

As they approached the crevice, excitement swirled through Robert, but also a gnawing guilt. They were breaking the law, trespassing on Hopi land. He had wrestled with the ethics of it for some time, but in the end, it didn't matter. He realized nothing would stop him from pursuing this lead. Well, he'd draw the line at taking an innocent life over it, but his obsession wouldn't be denied.

"Follow me," said Matt as he began crawling up the rocks leading to the cavern. "And remember to watch your footing."

Robert went next. He searched for secure holds in the stone. Kira's labored breathing came from behind him.

"You doing alright back there?" he asked over his shoulder.

"Never better," replied Kira.

When they reached the cave entrance, Matt went in first, with Robert and Kira close behind, all with flashlights at the ready.

The cave expanded downward into what looked to be a tunnel, where the darkness made it impossible to see any farther. It was larger than Robert expected. Etchings and paintings decorated the cavern's walls. Clay pots of different sizes were scattered about, some whole, others in pieces.

Robert walked toward a circular design on the wall. The motif was divided into four quadrants. Each quadrant contained a unique element: corn, rain, mountains, and what appeared to be a stylized bird.

Matt led them to a spot near one side of the cave. "Here's where I found it as a kid. I ended up burying it, although I'm not sure why. It was kind of fun, though, and the ground was a lot softer that day than it is now. Digging deep was pretty effortless."

Robert unpacked his tools, leaving the flute inside his backpack. Next, he assembled three collapsible shovels. Finally, he issued a hopeful sigh. "Let's do this," he said. "Are you ready?"

The dull scrape of shovels biting into the earthen floor resounded throughout the cave. Robert wiped the sweat from his brow with a sleeve. Matt plunged his shovel into the ground beside him and flung clumps of dirt outward with each stroke. The young man's eyes moved toward the cave entrance with each spadeful.

"Worried we might be discovered?" asked Robert.

Matt winced. "You never know. The sooner we get out of here the better."

Robert didn't like the idea of their lithe, wealthy benefactor having to do this kind of manual labor when he and Matt could easily handle it, but didn't want to appear to question her strength. Ironically, she owned a mining company, but he'd wager this was the first time in her life she'd actually done any digging. He admired her willingness to pitch in like this. After he had found the flute, she seemed more eager to get into the weeds with him instead of just writing checks.

Fortunately, Matt's anxiety gave Robert an out. "Kira, can you stop shoveling and serve as a lookout? Matt's right, if we're caught here, it would be very . . . problematic."

"On it," she replied, gently lowering the shovel and heading toward the entrance. She pressed her back against the wall and stepped back into the shadows, peering out of the cave.

They dug deeper. The walls of the hole took on a cylindrical shape. Robert grimaced as he glanced at the ever-increasing pile of excavated earth. The ground here might have been feathery soft when Matt had buried this thing, but now it was more the consistency of concrete.

Finally, after another five minutes, his shovel struck something solid. He yanked his arm backward. "Dammit, may have hit it too hard. Let's use our hands from here."

The pair abandoned their shovels and fell to their knees, now carefully brushing away the remaining dirt. A few minutes later, the edge of a stone tablet came into focus through the remaining debris. Its surface was covered in carved glyphs, just as Matt had promised. With utmost care, Robert and Matt extracted the artifact.

Robert illuminated the designs with his flashlight. He wanted to scream out in excitement, let his words echo throughout the cavern, but he bit his tongue so as not to risk attracting attention.

He touched the ancient symbols and then tore his gaze away from the tablet just long enough to pull out his phone. He scanned the artifact, capturing high-resolution images from every angle.

Kira left her post to check out their find. "It's even more beautiful than I imagined," she said as she approached for a closer inspection.

Robert nodded. "The greater the effort to find something, or achieve something, the greater the exhilaration and appreciation when you finally do."

"Please tell me you can decipher all of this," said Matt, ignoring Robert's armchair philosophy. "I was able to understand some of it, but my glyph education was pretty spotty at the time."

Robert smiled. "Yeah, I've got this," he replied. He read the first symbol etched on the tablet and followed the line of symbols trailing along its side. "Strife between the . . . nation of Kasskara . . . yada, yada," he mumbled. "Okay, here we go," he continued, his voice returning to an audible level. "I'll give you the highlights for now: 'Atlantis . . . the chiefs of both great lands reached no accord and with one devastating strike . . . mighty red wind obliterated all . . . submerging two grand civilizations.'"

He paused.

"Is that all of it?" asked Kira.

"No, sorry. I was just lost in thought for a moment. This is truly a spectacular find, Matt. You have my undying gratitude. Even if it leads to a dead end."

He lowered his head and continued reading. "'Beware the day we forget our mistakes, for on that day, the ashes of our past shall rise again.'" He hesitated, the words coming off his tongue like a heavy bag of lead.

"It's eerie," he said as an aside. "It's as if they feared exactly what we're seeing today. Anyway, it continues as follows: 'As Kasskara descended into the deep waters, we departed, aided by our Kachina brethren. To the Isle of Faces our flying shields and boats bore us. And next, we journeyed to the lands of the south, where we dwelled for a time. Northward then our vessels carried us, to the high desert following the great deluge and exodus.'

"And . . . oh, here we go . . . 'In a vast cavern, deep and expansive, we concealed a flying shield, five thousand paces to our left hand, far below—'"

"Professor Shaw," interrupted Matt, "this is great stuff, and I want to hear all of it, but shouldn't we get this out of here? Maybe it's best if you read the rest from the safety of your house. Then we can think about its meaning for as long as we want while we plan next steps."

Robert didn't hear a single word, tuning Matt out as he continued to read to himself with single-minded focus. "Do you see this?" he said excitedly. "Look. The smaller dome-shape in the middle with three concentric symbols forming outward on it, and lines shooting in all directions? That's where the boat is. And from what I'm reading, it seems that it's actually, you know . . . here! Or right around here."

This time Matt reached out and waved a hand in front of Robert's face until his eyes were no longer glazed over. "Professor Shaw," he said anxiously. "The sun is nearly up and we have a hike ahead of us. We need to leave. We can come back in the dead of night for whatever else the tablet points us to."

Robert shook his head as if coming out of a trance. "Of course," he said as his senses returned. "You're absolutely right, Matt. Thanks." In his euphoria over this find, he had temporarily forgotten that he'd likely be arrested if he was found here, not just for trespassing, but for removing an ancient relic from a cave he didn't own.

And yet he had made peace with this theft, convincing himself that the larger ethical lapse would be to keep such a profound truth from the world. Prometheus stole fire from the gods to give to mankind.

And while this behavior was considered unethical by the other gods, to humankind, it had been a literal *godsend*.

Ethics often depended on one's perspective.

Robert wrapped the tablet in a cloth he pulled from his pack. He knew this was the worst possible thing he could do. Taking a sacred Hopi artifact was not just theft, but a desecration of their most holy traditions. If discovered, it would destroy any remaining trust between him and the Hopi community, end his career, and likely land him in federal prison. But he was too obsessed to stop now. This tablet was yet another lead to something, to the starship that had to exist somewhere. He looked longingly around the cave. The flying shield, or rather, the starship, had to be nearby. Maybe it was deeper within the cave system. Perhaps concealed in a giant underground cavern. This place could be a gold mine of treasures and information, and hell, a starship for all he knew. But Matt was right. With the sun almost above the mountains, they were out of time. If they were spotted by a single Hopi, this site would be forever out of his reach.

Matt made his way toward the cavern's entrance. "Everything looks clear. Let's get as far away from here as we can before sunup. If we're caught elsewhere on Hopi land, it'll be bad, but not nearly as bad as if we're caught here. If we're not here, we can make up some lame excuse, and no one will guess we have an ancient relic with us."

He pulled his phone from his pocket to check the time and gasped.

"What's wrong?" said Kira as Matt's face turned ashen.

"My dad. He's called four times in the last fifteen minutes. I silenced my phone when we began, so I didn't know."

Robert fought to remain calm. Gray Eagle calling—*persistently*—right when they were in the cave almost couldn't be a coincidence. "How often does your dad usually call you?"

"Never."

Robert winced. "Did you tell anyone else in the tribe you were coming here?"

"Of course not."

"He must know something's up," said Kira. "Probably that we're here. So, what's his likely move, Matt?"

"He'll be hauling ass to get here. And he won't be coming alone. He'll likely have the tribal police along with him, at minimum."

"If so, when do you expect him to arrive?" asked Robert.

Matt looked as if he were about to vomit. "About five minutes ago, actually."

Right on cue, a muffled voice drifted into the cave, the sound faint and distant, as if it had traveled on the wind from far away. "Exit the cave right now!" the voice demanded. "We know you're in there! Don't make this any harder on yourselves than you have to."

Matt's face slackened and his voice dropped to a whisper. "It's him."

CHAPTER 6

"Don't say a word," whispered Matt. "My dad's in the middle of the pack. Step back farther, just in case they can see us."

Robert's heart pounded. He peered out of the cave alongside Matt. The morning sun illuminated the figures gathered outside.

Matt's father stood at the center, a man in his late fifties. He wore a plaid shirt, cowboy hat, and long blue jeans. He gripped a rifle. Several tribal elders flanked him, also holding weapons.

The distant rumble of an engine penetrated the silence. A truck appeared on the horizon, kicking up dust as it approached fast. It screeched to a halt, and two tribal police officers stepped out.

Gray Eagle's voice boomed across the clearing. "Little Owl!" he said angrily to Matt. "I know you're in there. I choose not to use most modern tech, but did you really think I wouldn't have a few hidden cameras and sensors installed for a location this important? I feared we might get trespassers here someday. I just never imagined that my *own son* would be leading the way."

He sounded deeply hurt and angry at the same time, and Robert couldn't blame him.

"I'm afraid I need you and your two . . . friends, to come out here with your hands up. And leave the artifact where you found it!"

Robert stepped away, closer to the cavern's darkening tunnel. Talk about history repeating itself. He had just been trapped inside a cave in Brazil with angry men blocking his escape. How had this become a common occurrence?

At least this time the men he was up against weren't threatening to kill him. Still, if being thrown in jail was the alternative, he might be better off if they did.

He quickly turned to Matt. "Is there another exit?" he whispered. "Any other way out of here?"

"I don't know. This is the farthest I ever got."

"Let's find out," whispered Kira. "It's our only option."

"We could surrender," mouthed Robert.

Kira snorted. "It's our only *good* option?" she corrected.

Robert couldn't help but smile.

"Kira, you're worth a fortune," whispered Matt. "Any way you can buy us out of this?"

"Bribing officials to circumvent archaeological excavation laws would be considered a separate criminal offense in itself," replied Robert, answering for his benefactor. "But you're Hopi, and the chief's son. If you want to join them, I'll understand. We have to try to escape, but given who you are, they may go easy on you if you surrender."

Matt shook his head wistfully. "My dad believes in tough love. Consequences. He won't go easy on me. Just the opposite." He sighed. "I'm coming with you."

Robert quickly disassembled the shovels and stuffed them into his backpack.

"Since you're not coming out," boomed the voice of Gray Eagle. "We're coming in. We have rifles, so think twice before doing anything even more . . . reckless."

The trio hastily moved farther into the cavern, following the beam of Robert's flashlight. Shadows moved across the walls, the light showing petroglyphs and ancient Hopi symbols.

"Watch your step," whispered Robert as he moved around a jagged rock formation. The path ahead thinned a little too much for his liking. The ceiling descended low. They were forced to crouch and crawl.

Rough stone scraped Robert's palms, creating cuts and bruises on hands that had just finished healing from his last expedition. Behind him, Matt and Kira followed suit, their breathing labored. The tunnel constricted further. Robert's shoulders brushed against the rocky sides. He tilted his head to avoid scraping the top of his skull.

"Look at the walls," said Kira. "There's a fortune growing here." Gold veins ran through the rock. "That's native gold. And those bluish-green crystals are azurite. We're in what's essentially a natural treasure chest. If my company got their hands on this site, we could fund ten more expeditions without breaking a sweat." She touched the crystal formations. "But that's not why I'm here. I—"

Robert touched her shoulder and put a finger across his lips, indicating the volume of her voice had grown too loud. She stopped speaking and nodded as Robert edged onward.

Gray Eagle's voice resounded through the cavern behind them. "Little Owl! Matt!" he added, perhaps in a show of détente. "Come home, son. We can help you."

When Matt didn't respond, his father continued. "You turned your back on our traditions. But are you really prepared to steal from your own people? Steal the most meaningful artifacts we have? I can't believe it. I *won't* believe it."

Robert and his small crew picked up speed. They rounded a bend into a larger chamber where they could stand. Kira yelped as she bumped into a stalactite.

"Don't go any deeper!" bellowed Gray Eagle's voice, reverberating throughout the cave. "It's dangerous back there. People who venture that far never come out again. It's forbidden."

"There are Powakas in there!" an Elder added.

Kira caught Robert's eye. "Powakas?" she repeated softly, raising her eyebrows.

"Malevolent spirits in the Hopi belief system," whispered Robert as he continued moving as fast as the cave would allow. "They're said to cause sickness, injury, or death. Shape-shifters who can take different forms. Stuff like that."

Matt slowed and moved into a darker recess of the cave to his left. "Up here." With a nod, he led them up a short incline and onto a rocky shelf protruding from the cavern wall. "Turn off your lights and stay quiet," he instructed.

With a click, absolute darkness surrounded them. Robert didn't even try to strain his eyes to see, knowing it would be futile in the near-perfect blackness. Somewhere in the distance, a faint voice sounded.

Someone gripped Robert's arm. He withheld a startled gasp, realizing it was Kira beside him. Her grasp dug into his sleeve, her breaths short and fast.

Gray Eagle, the tribal police, and the elders entered the chamber. They swept the area with flashlights. Robert held his breath as they passed beneath their hiding spot.

Gray Eagle's face creased with focus while he crouched down to examine something on the ground. "They stopped here. They must have."

One of the elders looked around the small chamber. "Maybe that's what they want us to think."

A tribal police officer raised from a crouch after inspecting the dirt. "I heard something." He pointed his flashlight's beam farther into the tunnel. "Follow me."

"Are you sure?" said Gray Eagle.

"Yes. I think I heard footsteps. This way."

Matt's dad hesitated. "Alright, let's go. They couldn't have gotten that far from us."

With a motion of his arm, he led the search party onward into the cave. Their flashlights grew fainter until they vanished around a bend.

"We should climb down and get back to the car while we can," said Kira in low tones.

"My dad is pretty smart," whispered Matt. "I'm betting he left a few people at the entrance. I think we're totally fuc... *trapped.*"

Robert nodded. "You're right," he said at barely audible levels, even for the pair standing right next to him. "We'll have to stay put for a while."

"How long?" asked Kira

"Until they leave."

"And how long will that take?"

"Could be days."

"We might be able to sneak out at night," said Matt. "I doubt anyone will find your SUV for a long time."

The young Hopi repositioned himself on the outcropping, still completely blind, and a rock dislodged, clattering to the cavern floor. It wasn't all that loud, but in the confines of a cave system, it was plenty loud *enough*. In seconds, footsteps pounded as their pursuers doubled back to their position.

"Time to go," whispered Robert, setting his flashlight on dim until their eyes adjusted to the sudden light. He then quickly led the others on a scramble down from the ledge over uneven ground.

He spun around slowly with his flashlight, looking for another escape route, his beam brightening stalactites hanging from the ceiling. "Over here," he said, hurrying toward an opening the light had revealed.

The passage was almost too narrow for them to squeeze through, even sideways. Which was actually ideal. Gray Eagle wouldn't likely guess they had gone that way. Still, as they moved along, their progress slowed as they edged forward into an ever more restrictive tunnel.

Their new route didn't fool the party after them for long. Only minutes later, Gray Eagle's voice boomed in the distance. "We know you took a narrow passage away from here, and we're at the entrance now. You're breaking laws you don't understand. Stop now! Where you're going is extremely dangerous," he added.

"So be it!" he bellowed when they didn't reply. "We're coming in after you."

Robert turned down a left passageway. Kira and Matt followed as the tunnel widened. It allowed them to sprint to gain needed distance from Matt's father and the tribal police.

Five minutes later as the distance continued to grow from their pursuers, the trio burst into a large room. They came to an abrupt stop. The chamber was unexpectedly huge, but that's not what grabbed Robert's attention.

The professor's jaw dropped. *What in the . . .*

A starship sat innocently in front of him. It threw off an amber glow, much like an aura. The vessel dominated the space. At the front, an eagle-like head formed the bow, its eyes shining with an inner light. Short wings tucked against its sides like a bird ready to take flight. The fuselage stretched long, over sixty yards, almost the length of a 747 jet aircraft, but with far more girth.

Robert's eyes almost popped out of his head, like a cartoon character of old. "I don't believe it," he whispered in awe. "*Incredible!*" A tingling sensation rushed through his body, and he felt a tear escape his eye and roll slowly down his cheek.

He had dreamed of this very moment for so many years. It was the culmination of his life's work, the pinnacle of his journey. Another tear escaped his eye as he was overcome by raw emotion, but he shook his head to clear it. Had to stay focused. The relentless Gray Eagle would be here any minute.

Several pulsing lights covered the ship's surface. They created shifting patterns across its metallic skin. The tail section tapered to a point, housing what appeared to be propulsion systems, unlike anything Robert had ever seen.

"It's here," said Robert. "I knew it! It had to be."

Matt and Kira's eyes were just as wide as his own, and both were rendered speechless. The cavern itself was a marvel, a massive dome carved by someone or something. But this ship? It was *beyond* a marvel. More like an *impossibility*.

Or in Robert's case, a dream come true.

Kira, who was typically the essence of poise and control, was more stunned than he had ever seen her. "I've spent my entire life trying to build a business empire," she whispered. "But this makes everything I've ever accomplished seem so . . . *small.*"

"Except you've also worked to prove that existence, the universe, is far more extraordinary than we can possibly fathom," said Robert. "And this is exhibit A. Which we wouldn't have found without you."

"Thank you, Robert," she said as tears now formed in her eyes as well.

The trio stared at the surreal vessel before them for several more seconds, mesmerized by the enormity of the find, but their awestruck expressions vanished when Gray Eagle shouted once more, his voice alarmingly close. "Stop this madness. You're trespassing on sacred ground. The spirits here are not to be trifled with!"

Robert glanced at Matt. The young Hopi's eyes moved between the starship and the tunnel they'd just emerged from.

Gray Eagle's voice was now at near point-blank range. "Son, please. This place is forbidden for a reason!"

Kira tugged on Robert's sleeve. "What now? Any moves left in the playbook?"

His mind spun on overdrive. He didn't have a playbook, but he did have a Hopi tablet, along with extensive, hard-earned knowledge of Hopi lore. He had always believed much of it was true, and his recent finds, especially *this* one, had cemented that belief. So maybe they did have a play left, one he wouldn't have dared attempt this soon if circumstances hadn't forced his hand.

In one quick motion, he took off his backpack and pulled out the flute.

He had discovered a key in Brazil and he was staring at a lock. Now it was time to see if they would fit together.

CHAPTER 7

Profound discoveries often carried grave consequences. The more earth-shattering the truth, the more challenging it became to unveil it to the world. Especially a world unprepared for such revelations. At least, this was what Robert kept reminding himself of as he dashed behind the starship, ensuring those arriving in this chamber wouldn't immediately see them.

What would his students at the University of Arizona think if they could see their esteemed Professor of Archaeology and Anthropology now? He was trespassing in a sacred Hopi cave, and now desperately trying to extract himself from a hopeless situation.

Robert searched the chamber on the other side of the ship to see if there was another way out, but there wasn't. He wasn't entirely surprised. Part of him was glad, as it forced his hand. Or his lips in any case.

He had no need to use words to explain what he was attempting to his two companions. They saw the flute in his hand and he had long since carefully explained the lore regarding this instrument to them both.

He hastily brought the flute to his mouth as the sound of pursuit grew ever closer. Without thinking another instant he put his lips against the instrument and blew. The sound of a chirping bird could be heard, along with a deep, penetrating vibration that could be felt in his bones, the same unearthly vibration he had felt in Brazil.

A hiss sounded, coming from the ship, and a ramp extended to the ground in front of them. Lights blinked along the ramp's edges, beckoning them to board.

The trio rushed up the ramp, just as the Elders entered the vast, artificial-looking cavern. They had been in fevered pursuit, but the site of the ship stopped them all in their tracks, giving their quarry extra time.

Robert paused when they reached the open hatch, his flashlight cutting through the darkness. Organic curves melded with the walls. No rivets, no welding marks. The entire structure was one continuous piece.

Robert swept the beam around. It caught on something in the chamber. A pillar of light, spinning. Within it, symbols and geometric patterns twirled and shifted.

Mesmerized, Robert took a step closer. His flashlight intersected with the spinning column. With a sudden hiss, the ship came to life.

Lights blazed on throughout the interior, revealing a large, circular area filled with shelves lining the walls, some portions stacked with metal crates and containers. The ramp doors began to close with a whir.

Gray Eagle's voice rang out from below them, as he had just made his way behind the ship to see them at the top of the ramp. "Little Owl!" he said in desperation, "what are you doing? This is a sacred Kachina and Hopi ship. I didn't know it was here. But I do know it's not for you to toy with. You're meddling with things you can't possibly understand."

His pleas were cut off as the ramp closed with a thud, sealing them inside. Robert, Kira, and Matt stood frozen. A faint vibration ran through the soles of Robert's shoes.

Robert blinked, doing his best to push away his confusion. This had to be a cargo hold of some sort. Other than the few crates and containers, the space was bare. Walls stretched out around them. A staircase led to a landing encircling the entire room, with a door visible on an upper level—a second floor.

Kira pointed to the ground floor directly ahead. "What in the hell is that?" she said.

The two men shifted their eyes to see a closed door with glowing, shifting symbols fading in and out. Robert guessed it might lead to the cabin and bridge.

All of this was too much. But Robert knew that if he allowed the full immensity of this surreal discovery to overwhelm him, he'd be paralyzed, unable to act, or even to think. He had to find a way to take this in stride, to pretend the extraordinary was common, at least until they were safe.

A low hum began to build throughout the ship. The floor shook more intensely, and Robert's stomach lurched as he felt a vibration, the low rumble of a sleeping giant coming awake.

Kira glanced at him, her expression more panicked than it had been while she was running from armed pursuers through a dark cave system. "Please tell me that isn't what I think it is."

Robert swallowed hard, his mouth suddenly dry. "Sorry, Kira. I have a feeling it's *exactly* what you think it is. I'm pretty sure the ship's engines have just activated."

CHAPTER 8

Robert stood motionless in the cargo hold, straining to hear. A whir continued to fill the air along with a quiver running through the deck. Like Kira, his first thoughts were that an engine had been activated, but they couldn't be certain.

Matt paced back and forth, rubbing the back of his neck. "We have to get out of here," he said simply, less afraid than Robert guessed he might be. By now he seemed resigned to whatever fate was in store for him. "I'd rather face my dad than be trapped inside a vessel that might be about to kill us. Unless you see any glyphs telling you how to shut off the engine," he added, nodding toward Robert.

"My guess is that the engine is coming to life just to activate the ship's systems," said Kira. "Or just to be at the ready if we—the new crew—want to engage it. Just because I start my car doesn't mean it's going anywhere. Not until I put it in drive. So just because the engine is on doesn't mean the ship will do something suicidal, like blasting off through god knows how many yards of solid granite."

"Good point," said Robert.

She frowned. "Still, we'll eventually have to leave. If we really are trapped, starving to death over a matter of weeks or more isn't my idea of a good time. The flute let us in. Maybe it will let us out again."

"I think you're right," said Robert. "It seems to be both a key and a door remote."

Kira nodded. "I say we give it a try."

"We'll be captured if we leave," said Robert.

"I know," said Kira grimly. "But what's the point of waiting?" She turned to face Matt. "Tell me, what are the odds your father and his hunting party will leave this cavern completely unsupervised while we're in here? Even if we stay indefinitely?"

"Is there a number lower than zero?" said Matt.

Kira nodded. "Exactly." She turned to Robert. "But what do *you* think? You're as resourceful as anyone I've ever met."

"Part of me wants to just surrender now," he said. "I'm feeling euphoria and guilt in equal measure. So maybe it's best to just let go and get what's coming to me. Frankly, now that I've found this, I consider myself the luckiest man alive. No matter what happens from here on out, my lifelong dream has been fulfilled."

Kira nodded. "Mine too. No surprise there, as our dreams are so similar. You were searching for this item, specifically. And, as you just pointed out, I was searching for evidence of unimaginable truths, of the utterly fantastic. And this certainly qualifies."

She sighed. "So are we agreed, then? We just pull the Band-Aid off quickly and get this over with?"

"Sorry, I think I misled you. I wasn't finished. Part of me wants to just surrender, yes. But a much *larger* part wouldn't leave this ship now for all the money in the world. I agree we should test out the flute. See if it opens the hatch. If it does, we can immediately use it again to close it. That way, we'll have the peace of mind that we can leave when we want. And I'm happy to let you both out at any time you want, including immediately."

"But you're staying no matter what," said Kira.

"I'm staying. I haven't begun to explore this ship. If I leave, I'll never have another chance. So nothing in this world could drag me away until I've studied every last molecule of it. Worst case, my scientific curiosity, my need to know, will be better satisfied. Best case, we'll stumble over something that can help us get out of this mess. Perhaps a device that can make us invisible. Or a weapon that will knock out our Hopi friends outside without hurting them. The odds are against this happening, but it'll give me something to shoot for while I'm studying the ship."

"Actually, that's a much better plan than I had," said Kira sheepishly. "I'm pretty damn curious about this ship, too. Who wouldn't be? And it beats the hell out of just giving up."

"Yeah," said Matt. "I agree. And I haven't said this, but I'm sorry I got you both into this mess. It's my fault we got caught. My dad isn't big on modern tech, but I should have known he'd make an exception for this site."

Robert shook his head vigorously. "Not at all, Matt. I'm the one who should have considered this possibility. You brought me on because I have experience. The failure here is all mine."

"Okay then," said Kira wryly. "While Rome burns, I'll just let you boys battle it out to decide who's to blame." A broad grin crossed her face. "The key point here is that I, personally, have *zero* culpability."

Robert couldn't help but laugh. "Yeah, less than zero even. But you're right, blame doesn't matter now. We just need to make the best of the situation we find ourselves in." He sighed. "So let's do this."

Robert led them to where they could see the hatch if it opened again and raised the flute to his lips. He took a deep breath and gave the instrument a mighty blow, evoking the same sounds and vibrations he had earlier.

Seconds ticked by in silence. They waited, hearts pounding, for any sign of a response.

Nothing. The hatch remained stubbornly closed. No ramp began to descend.

Matt blew out a long breath. "Now what?"

"Give me a minute," said Robert. He bowed his head to the floor, deep in thought, for almost thirty seconds.

Finally, he raised his head and faced his companions. "I've replayed everything back in my mind. The flute seemed to have summoned the ramp. But the hatch closed automatically behind us when we were inside, without me blowing on the flute. I may be misremembering as there was a lot going on, but I think when my flashlight beam hit that spinning light pillar, it activated the ship. But where is that pillar now?"

"It vanished when the lights came on," said Kira. "I was staring right at it when it disappeared."

Robert considered. If a pillar could vanish, what other tricks did this ship have up its sleeve? "Let's begin our exploration in earnest," he said. "See what other strange things we can find. There has to be a way to make sense of it all. Think of this as a giant puzzle. The pieces all fit together, even though it isn't immediately obvious how. But if we're thorough and persistent, perhaps we can solve it."

Saying this, Robert headed toward the staircase leading to the upper landing above the cargo hold. As he made it to the area in question, he stopped short. "Wait, weren't there stairs here?"

"Yeah, there were," said Kira, mystified. A brief smile flickered across her face. "Now this thing's just showing off."

The railing remained, but the steps had vanished. Robert reached out, touching the railing to inspect it further. Steps materialized, floating and assembling higher and higher until they reached the second level.

Robert glanced at his two companions and arched an eyebrow. "You don't see that every day," he said. "Or ever."

He placed his foot on the first step. It held. One foot after another, he walked up the staircase. "Are you seeing this? These steps seem to be hanging in midair. I'm thinking a magnetic, superconductive effect. Or some kind of anti-gravity."

"Totally insane," said Matt.

"Find anything interesting up there?"

"Nothing yet," said Robert. "Although the stairs alone are interesting enough for ten lifetimes." He crouched down and touched the step he was on with great care. "Solid. No panels or seams I can see or feel."

Kira bent down and ran her hand along the floor. "It almost feels organic, if that makes any sense. Almost alive, you know?"

"How so?" said Robert.

"It's warm to the touch. And there's a bit of a vibration. I don't think the vibration is coming from the engines. Or maybe every part of the ship is vibrating subtly. Who knows?"

"Interesting. The railing up here feels similar."

"What do you make of the lighting?" said Matt. "It seems to adjust as we move."

"Some kind of motion sensors, maybe?" speculated the archeology professor.

Matt stood up from a crouch. "I've found something," he announced. "A slight indentation on this lower wall panel here, and . . ." He winced. "Never mind. I must be imagining things."

Robert halted. A door stood across from him on the top landing. It shimmered with a strange aura, covered in fading golden symbols resembling a hologram. Hopi symbols. "Incredible," he said under his breath.

"I found some glyphs up here," he said more loudly to his companions below. "I'll read them now."

He paused. "'Speak the words of the ancestors,'" he said, tracing the air above each symbol. "'Open the path to the stars. Place your hand upon the sacred circle and recite: Tuwanasavi, Palatkwapi, Kasskara.'"

His heart sped faster as he continued translating. "Basically, it's saying that to open the door, you need to, and I quote, 'Breathe life into the flute of the skypeople.' And to open the lower door, it says that 'The earth's blood will reveal the way.'"

Robert's mind whirled. Whether this door led to escape or deeper into the ship's mysteries, he didn't care. Any change was better than their current situation. "Guys, I think we need to follow these instructions, see what happens."

Both of his companions agreed immediately.

Robert reached for the flute in his backpack, ready to follow the instructions and activate the door. Just as his hand brushed against the instrument, Kira's voice cut in.

"Robert. Get down here. The cargo hold door just opened."

"The ramp, you mean?" asked Robert, checking to see if it was lowering. It hadn't budged.

"No, the door leading deeper into the ship."

Without hesitation, Robert rushed down the gravity stairs, taking them two at a time. He joined Kira at the bottom, with Matt close behind. Together, they walked slowly toward the now-open doorway, peering into the blackness beyond.

CHAPTER 9

Robert hesitated at the threshold of the new opening, peering into the darkness. A light blinked on, like a flash. Robert squinted until the glow softened a second later. It showed more of the interior of the starship.

"Incredible," said Robert.

Walls that were pitch black only moments ago were now glimmering with a faint luminescence. The light pulsed, fading before gradually brightening, almost as if the ship itself were breathing.

Robert exchanged a glance with Kira and Matt. "I'm going in."

"Slowly," said Matt. "And be careful."

"Are you staying back?" he asked Matt.

"Not a chance."

"I'm coming too," said Kira.

Taking a deep breath, Robert stepped through, crossing deeper into the vessel. The others followed.

As they entered, the light clung to their movement, brightening the areas they approached while dimming those they left behind. It was an odd effect, akin to someone watching their every move.

Robert reached out and touched the warm surface of the nearest wall. To his amazement, the area beneath his pressure lit up in response.

Kira moved to stand beside him. "It's like I was thinking. It's . . . alive. This material, it's organic. It's adaptive. My mining company uses drones with similar tech, but nothing even close to this level of sophistication. I think the ship might be reading us, adjusting to our presence. It could be reacting, learning."

"What do you know about this, Matt?" asked Robert.

Matt pointed to his own chest. "Me? What the hell would I know? You're the expert."

"Maybe so, but I didn't grow up with the Hopi. You did. Have you heard anything ever said that would suggest it's biological in some way?"

"No. The ships themselves were nothing but a rumor, in my mind. Myths, at best. I'm not even sure my father believed. No one had ever seen one before, that's for sure. No one ever guessed that an opening in that cave not much larger than a man would lead to such a vast cavern. Or, to a ship. And no one would risk entering a passage that could likely get you stuck like a cork in a bottle unless they were desperate."

He paused. "All I remember is what you already know. The ships were referred to as flying shields. They were made by the Kachinas . . . the star people . . . with some help from the Hopi. So while we knew something of how to make these ships at one time, we lost that knowledge long ago. That's all I remember. I wasn't a good student and thought it was all really stupid. Which is why I left."

He allowed himself a smile. "Given that I'm inside a starship at the moment, though, I'm willing to admit that there's a—*minuscule*—chance that I was wrong."

The area they now found themselves in was large and open and appeared to be a sort of community space. To the left, Robert spotted what looked like a kitchen or bar, but its design was so foreign it was hard to be certain. Curved surfaces flowed into one another, with no visible appliances or utensils. Behind the countertop were empty shelves, similar to those found in a bar. The countertop itself, however, was unique. Its surface undulated in a wavy pattern.

"What do you make of this?" asked Kira, gesturing at a bunch of illuminated orbs suspended above a central island in front of the bar.

Robert shook his head. "I have no idea. Maybe some kind of food replicator?"

"Really?" said Kira in amusement. "I think someone's been watching too much *Star Trek*."

"At least I didn't say they were transporters," replied Robert with a smile. "And this does look like a kitchen in some way, so my guess isn't *entirely* ridiculous."

"Over here," said Matt, motioning toward open doorways leading to what might be crew quarters, or something similar.

Each room contained a single bed, if it could be called that. And there were six quarters, all lined up on one side. Small. The bed's sleeping surfaces were translucent and hovered a few inches off the floor. As Robert entered the room and approached one, it started to emit a soft, blue glow.

"Fascinating. It's responding to my presence." Robert cautiously touched the top of the bed. "It's adjusting to my body temperature. And look, it's changing shape slightly."

They left the quarters and ventured deeper into the ship. Before them, a massive table, reminiscent of a dining surface, stretched along one wall. As they walked toward it, symbols flickered on the opposite wall.

"Wait," said Robert, holding up a hand. "Those are more Hopi symbols." As he began to read, the glyphs shifted, forming coherent sentences. He started translating aloud:

"In the year 59,458 of the Great Cycle, I, Koyaanisqatsi, record my final log aboard this vessel. Our mission has failed. The war between Lemuria and Atlantis escalated beyond our worst fears. The very fabric of the world continues to tremble beneath the weight of their conflict."

Kira walked closer to Robert. "Are you kidding?" she said. "Just when I thought this find couldn't get any more extraordinary."

"It goes on," said Robert. "'This ship, the last of its kind,' he continued reading, '"was created to harness the power of the stargate. A portal to other times. Or, if not other times, other sectors in our known galaxy, if used correctly. We believed we could use it to prevent this catastrophe, to change the course of history. But we were wrong. We made it worse.'"

"A stargate?" said Matt in disbelief. "Are you sure you're reading that right?"

"Pretty damn sure. And it isn't as far out of left field as you might think. Some Hopi stories referenced portals and 'sky openings' through which beings or energies passed."

"Keep going," said Kira.

Robert nodded and continued. "'The war caused a drastic change to Earth's landscape. Entire continents have shifted, crumbled, and sunk into the ocean. Glaciers have melted so rapidly that most couldn't escape. Rising seas swallowed entire civilizations. A huge change in temperature from warm to ice cold. So many have already perished, with many more sure to follow.

"'I must abandon this ship and hide it where it can never be found. Its power is too great, too dangerous. Though its genetics were engineered to be able to interface with the stargate, even this marvel of a vessel cannot undo the damage. We've used it and other vessels to shepherd thousands to the new world, which is good. But now, this starship must be consigned to oblivion, cast into the depths of time and space, never to be found by mortal hands again.'"

The symbols moved more rapidly now as if mirroring the urgency of their creator's words. "Lemuria fell. Atlantis, in its hubris, unleashed forces it could not control. That nation's landmass fell even quicker. The world we knew is no more. I pray that someday, someone will understand the terrible price of our folly. We—"

"Professor!" interrupted Matt. "Over here," he said, frantically waving him over as he rushed down a short corridor. Robert joined Kira on the first level and followed behind, having no idea what he thought he had found. Robert's mind was still reeling from the revelations of the ancient log.

The passageway narrowed, leading to a door. It glistened like all the others, its surface rippling like water.

"You hear that?" asked Matt.

Robert strained his ears. "I don't think so."

"On the other side of this door. You can't hear it?"

Robert shook his head, puzzled. The door's surface shifted, Hopi symbols materializing and rearranging themselves.

"I don't hear anything either," said Kira.

"How can that be?" said Matt in frustration.

Then, suddenly, Robert did. A faint whisper, barely audible, seeping through the door. Matt's hearing was exceptional.

Suddenly, the door slid open. Robert froze, his attention on what he saw on the other side.

A large chamber stretched out. This was a ship's bridge, similar to the ones Robert had seen in movies and shows. Organic-looking stations curved around the perimeter. Holographic displays hovered above consoles, projecting streams of Hopi scripts.

At the center of it all was a captain's chair, or at least that's what Robert assumed. In front of it sat a crescent moon-shaped console. A massive holoscreen dominated the wall just beyond it, the display mostly dark, yet intermittently fracturing into digital snow.

Robert's head jerked back in surprise as a figure materialized in the chair. Robert stepped back, pushing his two colleagues behind him, an instinctive motion to keep them safe.

The being in the captain's seat appeared human at first glance, but as Robert's eyes adjusted, it was something else entirely. The being's form glittered, its skin refracting light like a living crystal. It was both beautiful and unsettling, too perfect to be human yet undeniably sentient, and somehow feminine.

The crystalline being turned its gaze upon Robert. Its eyes were pools of swirling energy. It opened its mouth, and words in perfect Hopi flowed forth, and then in English.

"Suyan qavongvaqam. The ancient words of your ancestors speak through me now. The threshold between what was and what will be grows thin. Through the wisdom of ages, we shall rediscover these ancient paths with new eyes. The moment is upon us. So let us begin."

CHAPTER 10

The crystalline being, sitting in the chair, distorted for an instant like a faulty hologram. In the next moment, it winked out of existence. It left only empty space where its form had been. Robert blinked, stunned by the sudden disappearance. One moment it had been there, saying strange words, and the next . . . poof. Gone, like a dream shortly after waking up.

He turned to his two companions. "Please tell me I wasn't the only one who saw that."

"You weren't," said Kira. "What in the world was it?"

"Don't know, but that thing spoke to me."

"To all of us," said Matt.

"I think we should go in," said Robert. "How can we not?"

"Well argued," said Kira wryly.

Robert's feet carried him forward as if they had a mind of their own, his body drawn like a magnet to the room's interior as the door to the room slid shut behind them.

Robert couldn't tear his eyes away as the bridge came to life around them. Lights turned on, consoles hummed, screens lit up. Even the walls, ceiling, and floor glowed with an inner light. Suddenly, the main holoscreen's white screen transformed into a display of the cavern wall outside.

Robert crept forward, mouth agape. He studied the image. This particular portion of the wall was unlike anything he'd ever seen in his years of archaeological expeditions. It was perfectly straight and rising at least ten stories tall, stretching beyond the screen's field of view. With a surface as smooth as marble, it defied the rugged characteristics of natural cave formations. It was so unique, he couldn't figure out how he missed it before he walked onto the ship. There was no way this wall could have been carved by nature or primitive tools. It must've been cut using some form of advanced laser technology. It was uncanny.

The ship was about half a football field's length from this wall. When Robert stepped closer to the main holo, Hopi script scrolled across the bottom of the screen, too fast for him to read.

"Look." Kira pointed at the display as the view shifted to show what was under the ship. It panned in on someone.

Robert squinted, leaning forward. "Is that . . . Gray Eagle?"

It was. He stood beneath the vessel's belly, waving his arms. His voice burst through the ship's audio system. "You must come out now! The balance is delicate. You risk more than you know. It's not meant to be."

"How's he patching through to us," asked Matt, "or however the heck he's able to get his voice in here?"

"Don't know," said Robert. "It has to be the ship's doing." He tore his gaze from the screen, searching the consoles for any sign of how to respond. "How can we communicate with your dad? Any ideas?"

Matt pushed past him, staring up at the holoscreen. "Dad!" He waved his arms, mimicking his father. "Dad, can you hear me?"

Gray Eagle showed no sign that he did.

A low rumble vibrated through the floor. The holographic displays at all the consoles illuminated, streams of data flowing across their surfaces.

"Robert," said Kira, her voice strained. "We need to find a way to shut this vessel down. Now!"

"Right. There has to be a control system, something we can use to stop this. Matt, look at that console. Find something."

Matt raced to one of the stations, swiftly looking it over, his breathing ragged. "Don't know what I'm looking for."

Neither did Robert. He sat at what must be the captain's chair, where the being had been before it vanished before his eyes. There, he examined the main console like he was studying an ancient stone tablet. Symbols glowed on the interface, rearranging themselves one by one.

The ship shuddered. The view on the screen changed back to the cavern wall. An enormous slab of stone lowered into the ground with a groan. The ship shook even more.

As the wall sank deeper, rocks and debris tumbled down. With it, dust and stone clouded. In seconds, the haze cleared as if sucked away, showing a world beyond the cavern—a dark tunnel as wide as a hangar and as tall as a three-story building.

Robert froze before tapping on just about anything on the interface he could find. Holo-symbols. He twisted dials hovering above the console. He pressed on several buttons, his fingers pushing right through the holograms.

The ship trembled again. Robert stood and stumbled, catching himself on the edge of the computer station.

"Something's happening, and I don't think it's good," said Kira, sitting at one of the empty stations.

Robert shook his head, eyes on the front viewer. "I think we're about to find out what this ship can really do."

The vibration beneath Robert's feet intensified as the craft rose from the ground. The vessel pitched, causing him to fall back into the seat. Restraints materialized around his lap and shoulders, the same occurring to Kira and Matt. The chairs glided forward, bringing them within reach of the consoles. Seconds later, the main screen filled with Hopi symbols.

"Robert, what's it saying?" asked Kira frantically.

Robert narrowed his eyes at the rapidly changing glyphs. "It's . . . it's a *countdown*."

Kira grasped her armrests. "Awesome," she said sarcastically.

Streams of data cascaded across holographic displays at each console, mimicking the main holo. Lights pulsed along the walls. The ship's engines whirred louder.

The starship lifted and moved forward, slowly entering the tunnel. Once inside it sped up to what must have been an incomprehensible speed. The tunnel's walls turned into a blur of rock and shadow, illuminated only by the ship's exterior lights. Robert's stomach lurched as they careened through twists and turns at breakneck speed.

"This is insane!" shouted Matt. "We have to find a way to stop it."

Robert leaned forward but stopped tapping on the console. He was more likely to hit something he'd regret than to find the off switch. He dropped his hands to his lap, stunned by what had materialized at the tunnel's end.

Was that an energy shield? The colors writhed and sprayed like molten lava, sending out tendrils of red, orange, and gold. As if the thing wanted to grab them, beckoning the craft closer and into its embrace, or worse, into a collision.

"Brace for impact!" yelled Robert.

Before anyone could respond, they plunged through the colorful barrier. In an instant, water pressed against the viewscreen and fish swam by in startled schools. Sunlight streaming through the water passed them by.

"How are we *underwater*?" said Kira in dismay. "Did we tunnel all the way to Patagonia Lake?" she continued, referring to a lake about sixty miles south of Tucson.

The ship slowed, hovering in the watery depths. A massive shape glided by. It was a whale! An actual whale. And two more followed behind it.

Robert thought his head might explode as he turned to Kira. "Would you believe the Pacific Ocean?"

"No way!" said Matt. "It would take more than an hour by plane to reach the Pacific."

"Wales don't live in lakes," Robert pointed out.

Matt's face turned ashen. "I think I'm gonna be sick."

The ship tilted upward, accelerating. Silvery fish scattered as they rocketed upward. Sharks darted away. They punched through the surface like a missile breaking free of the sea. Water exploded outward in a crown of spray. They shot into the crystal-clear sky above.

"Look!" Robert pointed. In mere seconds, the blue faded to black. They were in *space*. Satellites drifted by, and there, somehow close and clear, hung the Moon. Every crater, every crevice, seemed to show through the main screen.

The ship pivoted toward a brilliant point of light in the distance, growing larger by the instant.

"Is that coming toward *us*?" asked Matt. "Or are we flying toward *it*?"

"Is that a . . . stargate?" said Robert, mostly to himself.

"It's gorgeous," whispered Kira, her mouth open and her eyes like saucers. "Truly spectacular."

As they hurtled toward the glimmering sight, it became a twirling vortex. A metallic sheen, similar to smoothed mercury, gleamed from the object's circular form. In the center, colors swirled and created patterns both turbulent and somehow ordered. It didn't make sense. The interior undulated with currents of energy rippling like the surface of a pond disturbed by a pebble thrown into it. Sapphire blue, emerald green, and amethyst purple hues intertwined with streaks of gold and silver. If anything, it made for the most hypnotic display Robert had ever witnessed.

If this wasn't a stargate, Robert didn't know what *would* be.

It grew larger and larger in the viewscreen as the ship barreled forward, plunging into its heart.

Robert swallowed hard. "Hold on!" he said as his entire body tingled. In an instant, the bridge erupted with a display of colors. Some Robert could never describe, but others he could. Streaks of radiant azure. Pulsing crimson. Particles of gold. It all circled around violet tendrils, the colors and shapes forming a whirling tunnel.

The ship's vibrations melted away, giving Robert a sense they were now floating. Each breath came easier than the last. Robert's instincts told him they were now in the clear. Everything would work out now. For a moment, suspended between stars and galaxies, Robert was content with everything. He was engulfed in a tranquility, a euphoria unlike any he had ever experienced.

As quickly as it began, it was over. They burst through the other side, facing a blue-green orb. Fear crept back into Robert faster than a pistol's discharge. His breathing quickened. Shallowed. Before them floated Earth. His home. Their home.

Robert gripped the seat's armrests. "Everyone okay?"

"We're alive," said Kira. "I count even that as a blessing."

She sighed. "Are we looking at Earth?"

"Gotta be," said Robert as his heart began gradually slowing to its normal pace. "But something about it is . . . off. The continents didn't look quite right. Bigger landmasses, less ocean."

"But you can't be sure of that," said Kira. "Right? I mean, I'm guessing this is the first time you've seen Earth from orbit, right?"

"Good guess," he said in amusement. "You have a point. Could just be my imagination."

"We didn't travel much through space," said Kira. "Could we have traveled through *time*?"

Robert shrugged. "Sure. Yesterday I would have said that's impossible. Today, the category of *impossible* is shrinking rapidly. And one of the messages I read did mention travel through time."

He surveyed the console, trying to make sense of the interface. "We need to figure out how to control this ship. There has to be a way to navigate. Then we can turn it around and head back through the portal."

"You're the professor, ah . . . professor," said Matt, "but I don't see a portal anymore. So even if we could control this ship, how would we find the portal again?"

"Good observation, Matt," said Robert miserably. "Besides, none of us can even pilot a plane, so we probably shouldn't try to pilot a starship. It might be best to leave things to the autopilot for now."

As if the starship autopilot had heard him, its engines roared, and in a flash, the ship flew toward Earth, the world growing bigger at an alarming rate.

In seconds, they reached the upper atmosphere. As flames licked the viewscreen and an unfamiliar continent grew larger, a creeping certainty squeezed Robert in a vice grip. That all the craziness they had just experienced was only the beginning.

They were the ultimate fish out of water. And they were entirely on their own.

CHAPTER 11

The starship burst through a thick layer of clouds and a wide landscape raced toward them. All a dense forest, broken by a winding river. Beyond stood mountain peaks, their snow-capped summits surrounded by wisps of mist.

"Slow this thing down!" yelled Matt. "Those symbols must tell you how to work this thing."

Robert looked down once again at the various symbols in front of him, interlocking triangles, swirling spirals, and so on, willing them to make sense. "They're gibberish, Matt. Not Hopi, and not any glyph system I've ever learned."

"So we're at the ship's mercy?" said Kira.

"Yeah, what else is new?" said Robert. "We have been since we walked up that ramp. And hitting random symbols is just as likely to get us killed as to save us."

"So we put our faith in the ship?" said Kira.

"No other choice. Well, no other *good* choice."

As they spoke, the ship continued to accelerate, hurtling to the ground as if it intended to bore a hole straight through the planet. A deep growl poured from the engines. The ship's nose lifted slightly, but they still streaked toward the ground.

Sweat trickled down Robert's temple, and his every muscle tensed. Perhaps he had put his faith in the wrong autopilot.

"Brace yourselves!" he shouted, although at this speed, their chances of survival upon impact would have to improve dramatically to get to zero. "Hold on!" he added, regardless of how unhelpful this would end up being.

The ship plunged, and along with it the pit of Robert's stomach, which had also twisted into a knot. Time spread out. Each second dragged into forever as the woodlands closed in fast.

Just as the first branches should have shattered against the hull, the ship jolted, decelerating so rapidly it all but stopped on a dime. Robert was pressed against his seat, but he didn't have to be a physicist to know that applying an absolute brake at the speed they'd been plunging should have turned them into paste, crushing every bone in their bodies. The ship seemed to have an unending ability to defy the laws of physics.

The roar of the descent faded, replaced by silence and the low whir of the stabilizing engines as the starship leveled out. It hovered only a few yards above the swaying trees.

Robert gasped for air as adrenaline coursed through his veins. "Now that's a ride they need to have at Six Flags," he croaked out. "Puts a roller coaster to shame."

Matt swiveled in his chair and doubled over, gripping his knees as he gulped down deep breaths and tried not to vomit. His face was more pale than ever before. "How can you make jokes about this?" he managed to get out through clenched teeth.

"I could either make a joke, or I could scream at the top of my lungs for the next hour. I think I made the right choice."

"Where are we?" said Kira, her voice decidedly unsteady.

Robert followed her gaze. In front of them and extending into the distance was an emerald forest, the trees undulating like a wide, green ocean. Far beyond, a range of red mountains rose against the horizon. Their peaks touched by clouds. The sun's rays ignited the mountains in crimson and gold. If Robert was on a sightseeing tour, he'd snap a shot and win a competition, no doubt.

The three of them sat in an awed silence. While the reality of their escape settled, soft saxophones and rhythmic drums filled the cabin.

"Is that . . . smooth jazz?" asked Matt. "What in the world?"

Robert looked for the speakers embedded in the walls, but didn't find any. "Where's it coming from?"

Matt shook his head. "First we almost crash, and now we're serenaded by elevator music?"

"Maybe the ship's responding to us," said Robert. "Protecting us. Calming our nerves with this type of music."

Kira shot Robert a look. "With jazz? Maybe you aren't the only . . . *entity* here with a sense of humor."

Robert grinned. "Maybe," he said. "But I'm not complaining. Even jazz is better than plowing into the ground at thousands of miles per hour."

Matt threw up his hands. "I don't know. A choice between death and being at the mercy of an ancient ship with a taste for easy listening? That's a tough call."

Robert laughed. "Good one, Matt. I see you have a sense of humor in dire circumstances, after all. A handy mechanism for keeping your sanity."

As this was said, the smooth jazz abruptly stopped, and the holographic console in front of Robert powered down, showing only a white screen. An instant later, technical readouts in English formed. Lines of code scrolled, and a message brightened at the top:

> *Language interface updated to Standard English based on detected speech patterns. System analyzed your language using a vast historical database and advanced algorithms for optimal communication. Apologies for the initial delay. The ship's translator has now mapped your specific speech patterns. Future interactions will occur instantly without lag.*

Kira glanced at Robert. "Are you reading this?"

He smiled. "Yeah. Turns out that in addition to Hopi, I can also read English. Looks like whatever is running this ship—my guess is an advanced AI—is alive and well and adapting to us."

The view on the main holo changed to a panoramic sweep of the landscape all around. The vessel began to descend farther, gliding toward a clearing beside a river. The water churned and foamed. The treetops parted as the ship eased into the glade.

Movement caught Robert's eye. "Something's on the screen." He motioned to a lumbering figure emerging from the tree line. The main screen zoomed in automatically and homed in on the creature. Text accompanied the image:

> **Species**: *Megatherium americanum.*
>
> **Common Name**: *Giant Ground Sloth.*
>
> **Size**: *20 feet in length.*
>
> **Weight**: *Approximately 4 tons.*
>
> **Speed**: *Slow-moving.*
>
> **Temperament**: *Generally docile.*
>
> **Caution**: *Minimal risk unless provoked.*

While the starship continued to descend, the giant animal turned its head toward the ship before it found its feast. It stood on its hind legs, reaching up to strip leaves from a high branch with its claws.

"Robert," said Kira, her voice rising anxiously. "I'm no zoologist, but I'm pretty sure the animal we're watching is *extinct.*"

"The Giant Sloth is *definitely* extinct. Apparently, the one out there never got the memo. Looks pretty damn good for an extinct animal, doesn't it?"

"How long is it supposed to have been extinct?" she asked.

"Over eleven thousand years. Yet here it is."

"I don't suppose this is the last remaining one, like a Big Foot or a Loch Ness monster?" said Matt.

"I'm gonna say no," replied Robert.

The sloth turned and stared at the starship a second time, almost like it had seen many before. The animal settled back down and ambled away deeper into the woods.

After the landing gear extended, they touched down, the engines winding down to a gentle purr.

The restraints around Robert's body released with a soft click. Simultaneously, the bridge's door slid open. From somewhere behind him, Robert heard the starship's rear ramp lowering.

A shaft of sunlight spilled into the cabin, making its way through the open bridge door and down the corridor leading to this section of the ship. Fresh air rushed in, and with it the sweet scents of wildflowers and damp earth.

Kira took a deep breath. "This air seems especially invigorating."

Robert stepped away from his station. "I'm pretty sure we're in an unspoiled ecosystem, one with creatures long extinct in our time, as we just saw. The ship's instruments might have some answers." He glanced back at the console.

Another message materialized on the main interface as if reading his mind:

> **Location, General**: *Nasavi* (English Terminology: North America)
>
> **Location, Specific:** *Tuwanasavi.*
>
> **Year***: 59,457 of the Great Cycle.*

"Does Nasavi really mean North America?" asked Kira in dismay.

"I have no reason to doubt it," said Robert.

"Interesting coincidence that the word *Nasavi* begins with N and A also," said Matt.

"What's even more interesting," said Robert, "is that in Hopi, *Tuwanasavi* means 'Earth Center.' The Hopi worldview is unique in that they saw their homeland, specifically the area around their mesas in Arizona, as the center of all creation on this world."

"Are you saying we're back in Arizona?" asked Matt in disbelief.

"That's what I'm saying. A pretty standard journey, right? Take off inside a cave in Arizona, travel for a bit underwater in the Pacific

Ocean, journey into space and through a stargate, and then end up back in Arizona."

"You left off the strangest part of all," said Kira. "A trip through *time*. So the real question is, *when* are we? What year is 59,457 of the Great Cycle?"

Robert shrugged. "I have no idea. But if memory serves, this is exactly a year before the date referenced in that ancient log I read on the wall earlier. The time when the diary of sorts claimed the world fell into . . . chaos."

The console continued displaying data:

> **Current Temperature**: *68 degrees Fahrenheit, 20 Celsius. (English Terminology).*
>
> **Climate Zone**: *Warm, temperate.*
>
> **Coordinates**: *Latitude 35.1982° N, Longitude 111.6513° W. (English Terminology).*

"How could this be Arizona?" said Matt. "I didn't see any desert on the way down."

Kira frowned. "Yeah, the landscape is completely different. You were right when you thought the globe looked a bit off, Robert."

"Yeah, I thought the continent we saw as we descended from space was shaped differently than it should have been. The landmass we're on is bigger than it should be, and the northern part is covered in ice. Glaciers. But it makes sense if we're deep in the past. And the coordinates the ship just gave us match Arizona.

"If this is before the last Ice Age ended," he continued, "there would be more exposed land. When the Ice Age concluded, sea levels rose about four hundred feet worldwide, submerging large areas and altering continental shapes. If the ship's log is accurate, in a year's time, we'll witness the events some Hopi elders spoke about . . . the war between Atlantis and Lemuria. According to these elders, that conflict triggered an early end to the Ice Age, ushering in a warmer age called the interglacial period. The destruction was nearly total."

Matt shook his head. "There are so many myths and legends. Vampires, werewolves, Pandora's Box, the Fountain of Youth. The list is endless. How could I have been expected to believe that out of thousands of these, the legends of my own people just happen to be true?"

"You couldn't have, Matt," said Robert softly. "Don't beat yourself up. We all get things wrong. The trick is to be willing to admit when you are and change direction. If you weren't already becoming more open-minded, you would have never approached me."

Matt nodded. "Thanks. That does help."

"Back to the Ice Age," said Robert. "Historically, we know the end of the Ice Age did happen, and water rose nearly four hundred feet across the world. In addition to cataclysmic climate hell unleashed on the world. So here's a pro tip. We *do not* want to be here in a year's time. Somehow, we need to find a way back home."

Another line appeared on the main display at the front of the bridge:

Nearest Landmass*es*:

Lemuria—*1,800 miles west in the Pacific Ocean (English Terminology).*

Atlantis—*3,000 miles east in the Atlantic Ocean (English Terminology).*

Robert walked toward the bridge's exit. "Hardly surprising that Atlantis and Lemuria exist right now. Which makes me wonder if Kemet exists now too."

"Kemet?" said Kira. "Is that a place?"

"Sorry. Kemet is the ancient name for Egypt. It means 'Black Land,' referring to the fertile black soil deposited by the annual flooding of the Nile River. Historians believe it only began five thousand years before our time, maybe six thousand at the most.

"My own theories, which are too complicated to explain quickly, suggest that Kemet actually coexisted with Atlantis and Lemuria, seven or eight thousand years earlier than that. If I'm right, and historians are wrong, which is certainly the case regarding the existence of these other two ancient civilizations, Kemet's territory is even larger than Egypt's was, covering more of North Africa."

Kira nodded. "I wouldn't bet against your theories," she said. "It seems you've been right about everything else."

"I just wish that didn't apply to the coming cataclysm. But the log I read about it is holding up. The stage appears to be set for an epic war that ends both Atlantis and Lemuria, even though, at this moment, they're both thriving. Kemet wasn't mentioned, but it still might exist here. Perhaps it managed to survive to form the Egyptian Empire, while the other two were lost to history entirely."

"So what does this all mean for us?" said Matt.

"I don't know. Other than, again, we seem to have foreknowledge that only time travel can provide. So we operate the same way we would if we found ourselves in Hiroshima in 1944. Get the hell out before August of the next year."

Matt swallowed hard. "Yeah. Sounds like a good plan."

A melodic chime resonated throughout the bridge. Robert spun toward the sound. He locked onto the main holodisplay. The screen illuminated with more scrolling text:

Alert: *Potential hostiles detected.*

Bearing: *267 degrees—approaching from due west.* **Number of contacts:** *Five.*

Distance: *514 yards and closing rapidly.*

Species: *Non-human.*

Height: *Hostiles estimated at 10 feet tall.*

Robert's heart sped up again, and Kira and Matt traded shocked glances.

"Ten feet tall!" said Matt.

Kira sighed. "Looks like someone's been drinking their milk."

Robert was about to respond when additional details materialized.

Armaments: *Armed with swords, daggers, and advanced weapons such as pulse rifles.*

An image of a pulse rifle appeared on the screen. A weapon with an elongated barrel pulsing with an inner light.

Pulse Rifle: *A high-energy firearm emitting concentrated plasma bursts capable of penetrating advanced armor systems.*

The screen changed, zeroing in on one of the oncoming figures. The giant moved with long strides through the underbrush. Clad in armor melding metal with organic designs, the individual held an aura of absolute, raw power. Etched patterns covered the armor plates, glinting under the filtered sunlight. With thick, red curly hair and a dense beard, the man looked as human as Robert, although almost twice as tall.

The being cradled a rifle, held at the ready. A curved sword hung at his waist, its sheath covered with hieroglyphs. Several daggers were fastened across a bandolier, their hilts within easy reach.

Behind the lead figure, four more emerged from the shadows. Each mirrored the first in size and armament. They moved in unison.

Robert's gaze followed the lead warrior as he advanced toward the ship. "Guys. We're about to have company. The ship lists these brutes only as *potential* hostiles. We have to find a way to make sure that *potential* doesn't become reality. Because if it does, we won't last three seconds."

CHAPTER 12

A low hiss in the ship's bridge drew Robert's attention. To his right, a panel slid open from a wall. A closet-sized compartment revealed itself. Racks lined the interior, holding numerous weapons. Rifles with thick barrels. Compact pistols. Curved but thin-bladed swords. Daggers with hilts lighting up from the inside. And orbs pulsing with energy.

"Hey!" said Matt, "The screen's scrolling again."

They quickly turned their attention to the main holoscreen and the lines of text appearing there.

> **LDF (Lemurian Defense Forces) Arsenal:**
> - **Plasma Rifle Mark III**: *Effective Range – 1,200 yards. Energy Output – Variable Pulse Plasma. Capable of penetrating Class V armor. Fatal upon cranial or thoracic impact. Firing Modes – Semi-automatic, Burst.*
> - **Plasma Pistol Mark IV**: *Effective Range – 600 yards. Compact design for close-quarters engagement. Energy Output – Focused Plasma Bolt.*
> - **Binding Orbs**: *Non-lethal containment devices. Upon activation, emit an energy net that immobilizes targets. Ideal for capture and restraint.*
> - **Spectral Daggers:** *Energy-infused blades capable of slicing through advanced materials.*
> - **Arc Swords:** *Melee weapons with plasma-edged blades. Energy Output – Sustained Plasma Arc.*

"I guess we're in a Lemurian ship," said Kira. "Or at least one whose arsenal is part of the Lemurian Defense Forces."

"Quite an impressive arsenal, at that," said Robert. "Plasma weapons with variable outputs, effective at over half a mile. That could be very handy."

Kira stared at the rifles. "They look like our military weapons but without triggers."

"Maybe the triggers drop," said Robert. "Who knows? I went hunting quite often with my dad growing up. I know everything there is to know about the rifles of our time. But these? They look complicated."

Matt's brow furrowed. "I've handled my fair share of guns too. But I say we pass on these. I'd be afraid of blowing myself up by touching the wrong thing."

"Do you think the ship wants us to defend *it*?" said Kira. "Or to defend ourselves?"

"Either way," said Robert, "these *potential* hostiles are almost here."

The holoscreen's feed showed the five giants moving through dense foliage, easily trekking across the terrain. It made Robert's stomach perform backflips. Ferns and underbrush parted around the oncoming beings as they pushed forward.

"How are we seeing this?" said Robert. "Are there cameras outside? Drones?"

"At this point, I wouldn't be surprised if the ship has eyes everywhere," replied Kira. "Maybe in the trees. Who knows?"

Robert faced the main console where the captain's chair sat. "Ship, please close the ramp. Seal the entrance."

Nothing happened.

Robert raised his voice. "Close the entrance! If you want to be defended, the easiest way is to not let them inside in the first place."

The ship remained unresponsive.

"Why isn't she listening?" said Kira in frustration.

Robert wondered if Kira was using *she* to refer to the ship because this had been a common practice for ages. Or because the crystalline being they had seen had appeared feminine. Either way, it was easier than saying *the ship* every time. "Good question," he said miserably. He walked over to the display of weapons. "But it looks like she's giving us no choice but to arm ourselves. Hopefully, we won't have to use these weapons."

Kira walked toward the bridge's exit and peered down the corridor into the cabin anxiously.

The main screen blinked off, then illuminated with new text:

Assessment: *Hostile entities likely to engage upon contact.*

Probability of survival without defensive action: *Less than 5%.*

Recommendation: *Arm yourselves to ensure continued existence.*

"Thanks," said Robert in frustration. "You won't shut the damn hatch, but you'll happily warn us that these hostiles are no longer just potential. Super helpful."

> **Additional Note:** *Hostiles are equipped with advanced weaponry.*
>
> **Threat level:** *High. Manual defense is currently the optimal strategy for survival.*

Robert shook his head. The optimal strategy was to close the hatch. He'd like to shove the ship's optimal strategy up her rear engines. He removed a plasma rifle from the ship's arsenal. It was surprisingly light. He inspected the weapon, doing his best to figure it out, but where was the actual trigger?

Kira picked up a pistol. "Light as a feather."

Matt finally removed a plasma rifle and inspected it. "Feels too light to be real. Like it's a toy gun for kids."

The main holo now displayed a top-down map. Five red icons moved toward a central point labeled 'You'. The screen lit up with their route and timing.

"They're almost here," said Matt.

On another feed, the lead warrior emerged from the forest's edge. He pushed aside a massive bush. The rifle in his hands radiated a soft, red light.

Robert's brain went into overdrive. "They no doubt know how to use those weapons. We, on the other hand, don't."

"Then it's a good thing they're also enormous and we're heavily outnumbered," said Kira sarcastically. "We wouldn't want this to be too easy."

Not expecting an answer, she began to study her weapon, while Robert shouted at the ship to give them instructions, which it stubbornly refused to do.

Kira pressed her thumb against a recessed area where a trigger might be. Without warning, a bolt of blue energy discharged, striking the wall beside them. The impact left a scorch mark, the material sizzling.

She gasped. "Sorry about that," she said. "You too, ship. But it's your own fault if you think about it."

Robert eyed the smoldering spot. "Everyone okay?" he asked as he approached the wall. The scorched area began to shimmer, the damaged material weaving itself back together until the surface was pristine once more.

"Unbelievable," he whispered. "The ship must be composed of some self-healing nanomaterial. Organic and inorganic properties combined at a molecular level to allow rapid regeneration."

Kira looked at the pistol more carefully this time. "The trigger is this button here," she said, pointing to the shallow indentation beneath her thumb. "I must have pressed it accidentally."

Both of her companions nodded thoughtfully.

Robert touched the restored wall. "The technology here is centuries beyond ours. The self-repair alone shows an advanced understanding of materials science."

"I have an idea," said Matt in frustration, "how about we focus on saving our asses now and do science later."

"Right," said Robert sheepishly. "Sorry."

Kira aimed her pistol down the corridor. "We need a plan."

Matt sighed. "Have you ever used a gun before, Kira?" he asked. "You know, from our time?"

"Not only used one, but I'm a great shot. I have a range at my home, which I use when I'm stressed."

Robert went back to examining his weapon. Beneath the barrel, where a trigger guard would normally be, there was a touch-sensitive pad. "I see the firing mechanism."

He held it like a traditional rifle and aimed at an empty corner of the bridge. "I'm firing in three seconds," he said, warning his companions. He waited a few beats and then applied the slightest pressure, his finger resting lightly on the pad. A silent beam of energy shot forth, leaving a trail before dissipating against the wall. No scorch mark this time. Perhaps the material absorbed it differently.

"It has minimal recoil and a silent discharge," said Robert. "Very well designed."

Kira looked at the screen. "They're on the ramp."

A knot tightened in Robert's stomach. "We need to use the bridge's layout to our advantage. There's only one way in. Let's bottleneck them."

Kira positioned herself at the bridge's entryway, most of her body hidden behind the wall. Her pistol pointed out into the passageway leading to the bridge. "Matt, cover the rear with Robert. I'll take point."

Footsteps reverberated from the corridor outside the bridge. The intruders started to slow down, their heavy boots striking the metal floor in unison.

Robert shook his head. "Matt, use that console over there for cover. It's got a perfect view into the corridor for a clean shot. Kira, hide behind the main station. It also has a clear shot. I'll take your position."

Kira frowned. "Is this some kind of masculine, chest-thumping thing? I may be a woman, but I'm also the best shot here."

"I'm sure you're quite good, Kira, but you aren't the best here. I have an Expert rating on a US Army qualification course. That's the highest one, above Marksman and Sharpshooter."

"My, aren't we learning a lot about each other," she said in surrender. "I stand corrected. You take point."

They quickly switched places as the footsteps grew louder. Each thud sent a spike of adrenaline through Robert's nervous system. He gripped the rifle tighter.

From behind the doorway into the main part of the ship, a shadow stretched across the cabin's floor. A towering figure stepped into view in the corridor, fitted with armor. He slowed for a brief second upon spotting Robert.

Without a word, the intruder dropped low—surprisingly agile for his size—and ducked behind the kitchenette's countertop. Another one followed, mirroring the first's movements, crouching even more, his massive body almost comically oversized for the cramped space.

"Don't move!" yelled Robert.

A third attacker peeked in, his gaze on Robert before he slipped into one of the crew quarters, weapon at the ready. Like the others, he was a giant of a being with broad shoulders and muscles so thick they looked like they had been carved from stone. It was the kind of height and musculature that made professional wrestlers look like *toddlers*.

Robert swallowed hard. "If you fire, we'll fire back," he said, trying to keep his cool. "We don't want any trouble. Let's figure this out. What do you want?"

Silence hung. The only response was a low murmur from the attackers. A fourth figure emerged. This one was so tall his head nearly grazed the vaulted ceiling. He moved with ease, taking up position in another crew quarter, effectively boxing them in.

"Stay focused," Robert told his friends. "We've got the advantage. They can only get in here one at a time."

Footsteps reverberated off the walls again. A different cadence this time. A fifth individual strode into the cabin. Robert recognized him from the ship's earlier surveillance. The leader, he assumed. His armor was more decorated, and a fury radiated off him. The guy looked mean. He moved as if he owned the place.

"Prepare to fire," whispered Robert, adjusting his grip.

The leader halted at the threshold where the cabin ended and the bridge corridor began. He stood there, blocking their escape route. Raising a gauntleted hand, he spoke in a deep voice. "Var'ash tek nul grovan drakkar fel!"

"Any idea what he's saying?" asked Kira.

"Not a clue," replied Robert.

The leader waited, perhaps expecting a response. When none came, he stepped forward, this time his voice booming even louder. "Drakkar fel vun morran!"

"He's getting angry," said Matt. "I don't think he likes being ignored."

The leader's posture shifted. With a swift motion, he shouted out another command. "Vor'kesh!"

The being retreated down the hallway. As he moved aside, two of his warriors were behind him, each on one knee. Their rifles were raised, barrels pointed straight at the station Robert had taken cover behind.

Robert's finger twitched, seconds away from firing. If he didn't, he was now certain the hostiles would.

Suddenly, a new voice filled the starship. "Kel'mora tek shen!"

An electric current surged through the ship. Flickers of purple lightning snaked along the walls and floor. A tingling shock raced up Robert's legs and through his spine. Pins and needles. The attackers jolted, their movements stunned.

"What the hell was that?" asked Matt.

The warriors parted as someone new stepped into the cabin. A man, tall, but still a dwarf compared to the armored giants. He was dressed in a flowing green robe, his eyes a piercing shade of emerald. He held a staff crowned with a crystal orb, the green gem encased by root-like tendrils wrapping around it.

The man raised his staff, and lightning blasted outward from the crystalline sphere atop it. The electrical energy slid down to the base of the rod and branched out across the floor. "Shal'ven noris talum varen!"

CHAPTER 13

The intruders' leader stiffened, his gaze falling on Robert and the others. Without a word, he turned and marched out of the cabin. His warriors fell into formation behind him. Their heavy boots echoed until they faded into the distance.

The tension in Robert's shoulders eased a fraction. "Did that just happen?"

Kira lowered her pistol. "That only happens in movies."

The man in the green robe stepped forward. His long white beard flowed down his chest, and his bushy eyebrows furrowed as he spoke. "Kal'thoran mek'tah suvai?" His voice was deep and resonant, but the words were incomprehensible to Robert and the others.

Noting their confused expressions, the robed man tried again, this time in a language sounding like a song.

The man sighed, frustrated by the language barrier. He strode past Robert, unconcerned that he might be fired upon, and to the main captain's chair at the central station, as though he'd been on this bridge many times. He tapped in commands on the console's interface, pressing a number of holographic buttons. A compartment on the side slid open, revealing a drawer with what appeared to be a translucent paste.

He scooped up some with his fingers and applied it behind his ear as if it were suntan lotion. He then scooped up more of the clear paste and held it out, gesturing for Robert and the others to mimic him.

Kira and Matt eyed Robert, soundlessly asking his opinion. "Who knows," he said. "But I'm inclined to do what he's asking. He did save our lives. And he used it on himself to show us it isn't poison."

Robert took the paste from the man and applied it behind his ear, and Kira and Matt soon followed suit. The paste induced an odd tingling sensation, but nothing particularly worrisome. After a few moments, it subsided, and it seemed to have been absorbed by their skin.

The bearded man smiled. "You just applied advanced nanotech," he said, "since your expressions indicated you weren't sure what it was. Specifically, these are translation crystallites. If you can understand what I'm saying, they've already integrated with your neural pathways.

Don't worry, it's completely safe and harmless, and you'll never have to worry about language barriers again."

Everyone remained quiet. Robert's mind swirled with more questions than he could begin to ask.

"I see looks of comprehension on your faces, which is good. Can you confirm you understand me?"

"Confirmed," said Robert, and his two companions nodded in agreement.

"Are any of you harmed?"

"We're fine," said Robert. "Thanks to you, I suspect. How did you get them to leave?"

"Doesn't matter. What does is that you're safe. At least for now."

"Who were those . . . guys?" said Matt. "And what did they want?"

"They're self-appointed guardians, of a sort," the man replied. "Bored, really. Their duties here on Earth sometimes cloud their judgment. Their role in manipulating human DNA is—"

He stopped in midsentence, watching their blank expressions. "You have no idea what I'm talking about, do you?"

"No," said Robert. "But at least we understand the *words* this time. That's a step in the right direction."

"Let me assume you have no knowledge of events here and start with the basics. You arrived just now on one of Lemuria's famed starships in controversial territory between Atlantean and Lemurian forces. So, naturally, the Anunnaki warriors would want to ah . . . check things out."

The Anunnaki? Real? Here?

Robert knew them well after years of studying ancient myths, but to see them in the flesh was insane. The Anunnaki were a group of deities from ancient Mesopotamian mythology, particularly in the Sumerian culture. Their name in Sumerian meant "those who came from the heavens" or "offspring of Anu," where Anu was the Sky God and one of the supreme deities in their pantheon.

Apparently, these five beings didn't know they were myths, marching in and out of the ship as if they thought themselves real. And this larger-than-life robed man in front of them spoke of the Anunnaki as if they were as common as a cockroach. Or on this day, perhaps, as a giant sloth.

The academic part of Robert's brain burned with questions, theories. The human part of him still grappled with the shock, the fear, and the exhilaration of coming face-to-face with beings he'd only ever encountered in scholarly books.

"They were going to kill us," said Matt. "Until you showed up."

The man chuckled. "No, they wouldn't have killed you. They might have tossed you outside and taken your vessel, but killing you? Unlikely."

"The ship told us they would," said Matt.

The man raised his eyebrows. "Ships aren't infallible, as I'm sure you know. If they do make the rare mistake, it's almost always due to misreading human behavior and politics. Which is true in this case. If the Lemurians were to discover the Anunnaki killed a Lemurian crew during the time of the Kuimahi Accord, the Anunnaki would find themselves in a political mess."

"What's the Kuimahi Accord?" asked Kira.

The older gentleman's eyes widened. "Now I see. Perhaps the ship didn't misread things, after all. Because it knows you *aren't* a Lemurian crew, after all, doesn't it? No Lemurian could possibly be this uninformed."

Robert hesitated. They had no chance of bluffing this man about being Lemurian, but they also couldn't tell him they were from the far future. "We're . . . travelers. We were hired by Lemurians recently, but got a bit off course."

"But enough about us," said Kira, desperately trying to change the subject. "Now that we're friends and all, I'd love it if you answered Robert's question. How'd you make our visitors back off like that?"

The elder man tapped his staff lightly on the floor. The crystalline orb atop it glowed just a bit. "Authority has its advantages," he said. "And a knowledge of how to employ an Atlantean Vesh'tar doesn't hurt."

Matt narrowed his eyes. "Atlantean what?"

"A Vesh'tar," the man repeated, staring at his wooden staff. "It commands respect. Most sentient individuals find it . . . unsettling."

He paused and gazed at Robert for several long seconds. "But for some reason I can't fathom, it seems to be calling to *you*."

"What does that even mean?"

"These electro-crystalline devices can perceive things beyond our understanding. And I sense it has a sort of connection to you."

He paused. "This being said, let's back up. Your explanation for who you are is a lie. Lemurians would never hire others to fly one of their ships. And these ships don't ever go off course. Not to mention that you came in for your landing scorching hot rather than decelerating gradually. No pilot would choose to land that way, even though it's safe to do so."

He stared deeply into Robert's eyes. "So, would you like to amend your story?"

"Who exactly *are* you?" said Kira.

Their bearded guest raised an eyebrow with a half-cocked grin. "You don't know? You *really* aren't from around here. I'm Thoth, known in some circles as the Hierophant of the Emerald Order. Hence, all the green tones I wear, and my strange eye color. Some say I'm part alien, but I'm not. I'm human through and through."

"Thoth?" repeated Robert. The name was well-known in mythology. Primarily in ancient Egypt, where he was revered as the god of wisdom, writing, and magic. His influence spread to the Greco-Roman culture, where he was associated with Hermes Trismegistus. Thoth's legacy continued through various traditions, including Hermeticism, which explored the nature of the divine, the cosmos, and humanity's place within it, emphasizing a quest for spiritual enlightenment and unity with the divine.

Even in modern times, Thoth was influential in Western esoteric traditions, which emphasized hidden or inner knowledge and New Age ideas.

"I don't suppose Thoth is a common name around here," said Robert.

"What? Why would you ask that?"

"Because if not, you have to be the Thoth from ancient legends."

Robert immediately regretted what he said. He had let the cat out of the bag. Fortunately, Thoth didn't jump on his error. Instead, he seemed to assume Robert was asking about his legendary status in this particular era.

"Legend has a way of distorting truth," said Thoth. "I'm but a humble scholar and, at times, a mediator."

"You're Atlantean, then?" asked Robert, knowing the tablets and old scrolls pointed in that direction.

He sighed. "I *was*. Once. Political shifts have made my presence there . . . unwelcome. I reside here now, on the fringes, doing what good I can. An exiled Hierophant from Atlantis. But titles are burdensome. My philosophies no longer align with the current regime."

He paused. "But let's get back to you. What are your names?"

"I'm Robert. This is Kira and Matt."

Thoth raised his eyebrows. "None are names I've ever heard before. Where are you from? And try not to lie this time."

Kira glanced at Robert, who nodded. "We're from a place called Arizona," she replied.

"Arizona?" repeated Thoth, rolling the unfamiliar word on his tongue. "I'm afraid I'm not acquainted with that realm."

"It's in North America," said Matt, and both Robert and Kira couldn't help but roll their eyes. That wouldn't help in the slightest.

Thoth stared at the trio for several long seconds. "Let's start at the beginning. You aren't Lemurian, yet you somehow acquired this vessel, activated it, and landed in an increasingly controversial territory, without any knowledge of the current state of affairs."

No one replied.

"Did you steal it?" said Thoth.

Kira sighed. "Not exactly. We found it. In a cave."

"We don't mean anyone any harm," said Matt. "We were just exploring and things got . . . weird."

"The ship you command is known as *Tala*. In the Lemurian tongue, it means 'Sky.' She's not merely a freighter but an emissary, often tasked with transporting strategic supplies to prevent the simmering tensions between Atlantis and Lemuria from boiling over."

"We had no idea," said Robert. "This ship—*Tala*—just took off on its own after we entered."

Thoth walked around the bridge, his eyes passing over everything. "I can sense your earnestness. And your ship did seem to burst into existence without warning, as if materializing from a time out of time."

"What does that mean?" asked Kira.

Thoth stopped in mid-stride and faced her. "Sensors in space around the planet weren't detecting her at all. Then they were. Just like that. She hadn't arrived from somewhere else. She was suddenly just there. Both Lemuria and Atlantis have most likely detected this anomaly, which puts you squarely in harm's way."

"So you misled us, as well," said Robert. "You knew our arrival here was anything but ordinary, yet you didn't let on."

"I wanted to see how you'd respond to my questions, yes."

"So are we now just sitting ducks?" asked Matt.

"Ducks? An odd analogy, but I think I understand your meaning. No, you're not helpless prey, but you're not safe either. Let me be clear: discretion is no longer just important . . . it's imperative for your survival, especially when it comes to Atlantean forces. If they discover this ship with ah . . . *clueless* operators like yourselves at the helm, they'll become emboldened. Best-case scenario, they imprison you as spies. Worst case? Well, let's just say we should avoid that at all costs."

Thoth furrowed his brow. "But enough of this," he said. "It's time I stopped playing games and learned the entire truth, which you persist in hiding. I know there's more to tell, in my mind and in my gut, both." He placed a hand on his abdomen. "Since you know so little, perhaps you aren't aware that the gut is lined with millions of neurons that pick up on subtle energies and shifts in the environment. In many ways, the gut acts as a second brain, part of an ancient survival mechanism."

Robert's eyes widened. This was just the latest in a long stream of surprises. Despite their advanced tech, he wouldn't have expected Thoth to casually know about the Enteric Nervous System, the gut's complex network of over a hundred million neurons, which Robert *thought* had been discovered in the nineteenth century.

Apparently not.

But while discovered, or rediscovered, in the nineteenth century, most people in the *twenty-first* century had no idea that such a neuronal network in the gut existed.

But Thoth sure did.

"What do you mean when you say it's time to stop playing games and learn the truth?" said Matt worriedly. "We've told you the truth," he insisted, which, ironically, was yet another lie. "So if you're thinking of torturing us, don't. We don't know anything."

Thoth grinned. "Torture?" he said, shaking his head in amusement. "That's not exactly what I had in mind."

With that, he walked to the command seat and lowered himself into it. He tapped a few sequences on the console, then placed both palms on either side of the interface. Closing his eyes, he took in a deep, long breath.

After a moment, he opened his eyes and turned to face them fully.

"Interesting," he said. "*Tala* tells me that you are from this world, after all. Just not from this *time*. Which explains a lot. Given these circumstances, the implications are far more significant than I initially realized. You're here for a mission you're not fully prepared for, and the consequences could be dire."

"Yeah," said Robert miserably. "Tell us something we don't know."

CHAPTER 14

There was a long silence on *Tala*'s bridge.

"So where is this Arizona? And *when* is it?"

"Geographically, we're in Arizona right now," said Robert. "But in our age, about thirteen thousand years from now, it isn't lush like it is now. More like high desert."

Thoth nodded. "Walk me through how you got into this mess again, now that we're on the same page."

"We came across *Tala* in a cave, as we said," began Kira. "Robert had earlier found a flute thousands of miles away, and he played it. When he did, the ramp lowered by itself."

"I see," said Thoth, deep in thought. "Please go on."

"The next thing we knew," continued Kira, "we were hurtling through some underground tunnel system, then under the waves of an ocean hundreds of miles away, and then into space. I have a feeling *Tala* was just showing off."

Kira winced and looked around nervously. "No offense, *Tala*," she hastened to add. When lightning didn't strike her, she continued. "Eventually, we went through some kind of portal, and now we're here. As simple, and as complicated, as that."

"But you didn't just stumble on a starship by accident, did you? Based on Robert's possession of the flute, he must have been actively seeking it out. Why?"

"It's a subject of our mythology," said Robert. "Which I've devoted my entire adult life to studying."

"I see," said Thoth again. "The stargate you traveled through isn't merely a portal. It's a human-made space-time gateway allowing only vessels carrying the right genetic signature. Picky thing. Without this signature, the consequences of attempting the journey become catastrophic. Lethal. In all my years, I've never witnessed time travel taking place. I've heard about it, much as you heard about *Tala* through mythology, but that's all. And I've been around a long, long time."

"Now that we're all up to speed," said Robert, "a few things should be clear. We're here by accident. We don't belong here. And we need to get back to our time. Can you help us?"

Thoth's gaze grew distant, and his voice dropped to a whisper. "As I said, unauthorized temporal displacement is a grave, punishable offense. The fact that *Tala* managed this feat is remarkable." He tugged his beard softly. "I'll have to talk to her about this later."

Thoth waved his hands to encompass the trio before him. "I doubt you're here by accident. Tell me, what do you know of Lemuria and Atlantis in your time?"

Robert cleared his throat. "They're gone."

Thoth hesitated for a moment. "Excuse me? Gone? As in, your people have never heard of them?"

"No," said Kira. "Gone. As in, they were thought to once exist—at least by some of us—but don't anymore."

The old man's stoic expression faltered. "Do you know what happened? What caused them to disappear? And *how* they disappeared?"

"Based on what we know, it's pretty clear that Atlantis and Lemuria—"

"Stop!" said Thoth, raising his hand. "It may be better for me not to know. I need to spend more time to think through possible consequences. Regardless, we must prevent whatever caused these horrific events. The future often echoes the past. If calamity struck here, it may well befall your own time with similar or more devastating effects. When lessons repeat, they're worse the second time around to ensure the lesson is plain to see, the learning more apt to be internalized."

Thoth turned to address the ship. "*Tala*, is this why you've brought them back?"

Silence filled the bridge until Thoth nodded.

"What did she say?" asked Matt.

"That I'm right. She took matters into her own hands, so to speak, and brought you here to effect change."

Robert shook his head. "Look, I appreciate the gravity of the situation, but our biggest concern is getting home. We didn't ask to be part of this conflict."

"Is there any way you can help us?" asked Kira.

"I'm afraid it's not that simple. The *Universe's* laws governing temporal travel are absolute. Somehow, *Tala* found a way to circumvent these laws, but I'm not sure how. But for this to have happened, the stakes must be unimaginably high. To me, your presence here points to a looming catastrophe in your own time, just like the one apparently looming here."

"Wait a minute," said Matt. "If they're the Universe's laws, how can they be, you know . . . circumvented?"

Robert turned to the young man, somewhat shocked. He had asked quite an astute question.

"I probably don't use this word the same way you do. I use it as a shorthand to represent a number of words various cultures use to describe the same thing. Words like God, Goddess, Deity, Great Spirit, and so on. Whatever you call it, it means all that there is, and the *source* of all that there is. In most circumstances, the Universe, or God if you prefer, wouldn't permit time travel. Yet it allowed *Tala* to bring you here. My future and yours may depend on altering this timeline. My gut tells me that to achieve this, the three of you must remain here."

He leaned against the main console. "And now that I've had more time to consider, I think I should know what we're up against. So, forget what I said earlier. Please tell me what happened to Atlantis and Lemuria?"

Robert blew out a long breath. "Both civilizations, and the continents they called home, sank into the sea. No trace of them remains in my day. There is a myth of a great flood, and something is known to have caused massive climate disruption around that time. The world had been slowly warming, gradually emerging from the Ice Age, when something triggered what's called the Younger Dryas. A sudden return to Ice Age conditions lasting over a thousand years. Some researchers believe natural phenomena caused this dramatic reversal. Others hypothesize it was triggered by comet impacts or other celestial events."

He frowned. "Now I know that neither of those were the primary cause. Based on what I've read in this very ship, it's clear a global war destabilized both continents and threw the entire world into disarray. The war must have unleashed weapons so powerful they disrupted ocean currents and atmospheric patterns. This entire continent was set ablaze. Cataclysms erupted everywhere. Rains that lasted for months, darkness that shrouded the world for years. Almost all the great beasts, the megafauna that roamed this land and others across the globe, died out completely. The result was what scientists in my time call the Younger Dryas. A dramatic cooling that plunged the world back into near-glacial conditions. But first came massive flooding and tsunamis the likes of which we can barely imagine, sending civilization back to the stone age."

Thoth stopped pacing. "That's . . . a lot. Thank you. I wish I could say I was shocked, but I've been concerned by the escalation of tensions for some time now, and where they might lead. So, we desperately need to lower the temperature between these great powers immediately. Atlantis has gotten out of hand lately."

He paused. "But it's possible there are forces pushing them in the direction of war, with or without their knowledge. There are key members of the galactic community who we would consider . . . unfriendly. Dangerous. These include the Anunnaki, Zeta Reticulans, Draconians, and Orions. Then there are those we would consider more as protectors. As positive presences, including the Pleiadeans, Arcturians, Lyrans, and Kachinas.

"The members of these races, and others, maintain a treacherously delicate political balance and have agreed to leave Earth to our own devices. Many of them would love to control us, rule us, but if one did, they would gain an advantage over the others. And those who see themselves as protectors would cry foul on ethical grounds. So all are held at bay by this delicate state of equilibrium.

"But not entirely. Hostile species meddle in subtle and not-so-subtle ways. So the situation has become exceedingly complex. It's possible the war will be started by our own people, but it's also possible it will arise from the machinations of an alien race."

Robert nodded slowly, deep in thought. These were mind-blowing revelations. But if such a robust and complex galactic community was well known to the Atlanteans, why had the Galactics not announced themselves in *his* time? Had the political winds in the galaxy shifted in dramatic fashion over the millennia? Or was humanity in his time still too primitive for them to formally approach?

"But you have starships of your own," said Robert. "So has humanity spread to other worlds?"

Thoth winced, and it was clear that Robert had hit a sore spot. "No. We're a species who came too late to the galactic party. Real and metaphorical occupancy signs are up. And if we did venture outside our solar system in a concerted effort to colonize, protection would be nearly impossible. Hostile species would make quick work of us. So our goal has been to turn Earth into a paradise, all the while becoming powerful enough technologically to be able to one day take a seat at the galactic table and expand to other stars."

There was a long silence.

"This is crazy," said Matt. "Incredible. But getting back to us for a minute, you've described a situation more complex than I could even make up. It seems to me that if we stay here, we'd just complicate the situation further. Given all the powers swirling around this, the three of us are pretty helpless to change anything, right? So maybe we're supposed to just warn you and get our asses back to our own time. What do you say?"

Thoth smiled. "It isn't me you need to convince. It's *Tala*. If it's even possible to get you home, only she can do it."

"Don't you have more ships here just like her?" said Robert.

"*Tala* isn't just *any* freighter. She's been instrumental for the Resistance—the Atlantean rebels—who don't agree with their government's belligerent stance. We've used her to smuggle political dissidents, scientists, priests, rare crystals, weapons, ancient scrolls, forbidden technologies, wisdom tomes, and more. All items necessary for our cause."

"And you're part of this resistance?" said Kira.

"Indeed. As is *Tala*. And given she's returned from the future, we now have two of her. Another reason she came back, in my view. So, if you're able to convince her to get you back to your time, congratulations. But I'd be astonished if you succeeded."

"Does that mean we're stuck here forever?" said Matt.

"Forever is a long time. And stuck is a strong word. Nothing is set in stone, young man. Perhaps I'm wrong."

"Tell us more about there being two *Talas*," said Kira.

"*Tala* in our time, now, is helmed by a man named Koyaanisqatsi. Koya for short. The one we're in now, from the future, is helmed by . . . you three. Sort of. This version is apparently the other version, aged 13,000 years. You know, like a fine wine, only getting better."

"You just said that to suck up to *Tala*, didn't you?" said Robert wryly.

"I'm not sure what you mean by the phrase, *suck up*."

"Never mind," said Robert in amusement.

He considered the idea of two *Talas* further. He had watched any number of time travel movies over the years, and he looked to them to draw insight. In the second *Back to the Future film*, two versions of Marty McFly inhabited the same auditorium at the same time without any ill effects. In another, *Timecop*, it was made clear that if two versions of the same person ever came into contact, they'd merge catastrophically, leading to mutual annihilation.

So, which was it?

"Is it dangerous for two versions of the same ship to exist in the same timeline?" he asked Thoth.

"Apparently not, since it's happening right now."

"But what if they get close to each other?" pressed Robert. "Any chance that would be like forcing magnets together with the same poles? Any chance Nature, or the Universe, or God, wouldn't like that, and the situation could get ugly?"

"I guess there's a chance at that. So, it seems prudent not to let that happen. In short, let's not find out. All I know is that with two

Resistance ships with rare and exceptional programming like *Tala*, we can amplify our efforts. Smuggle important technologies to Lemuria, extract key political allies, gather valuable intelligence, and so on, at a much faster pace. You don't know how rare and incredible this starship truly is. It's one of a kind . . . now *two* of a kind . . . hidden by its own design to look like a basic Mokualin Class Freighter."

He paused while the visitors from the future digested all that had been said.

"I'd like to back up for a moment," said Thoth finally. "Earlier, when I asked you what you meant about Lemuria and Atlantis being gone, Kira said that they were *thought* to once exist. She didn't say were *known* to once exist. And then she added, by some of you. Why only by some?"

Robert winced. "I'm afraid most people in our time consider these two civilizations to be myths. Fantasies. Most are convinced they never existed."

Thoth blinked in confusion. "How is that possible? If the two civilizations sank deep into the ocean, I get how that would effectively hide their existence. But our technology and footprints are spread across the globe. There should be ruins. Endless evidence of thriving civilizations."

"Excellent question," said Robert. "As someone who studies ancient civilizations for a living, allow me to weigh in. You'd be surprised by how completely nature can reclaim the Earth and wipe out evidence of human existence, given enough time. And less time than you'd think. Even the most durable metals show significant deterioration after just a few thousand years unless preserved in very specific conditions. Organic materials like wood and fabric typically disintegrate within centuries."

He shook his head. "In my expert opinion, the odds of finding intact complex technology after ten thousand years or more are not good. Nature has efficient ways of reclaiming its materials, and time is relentless in its destruction of human creations. Unless artifacts were perfectly sealed in rock formations, or in caves, like the flute and starship I found, millennia of weathering and geological changes would break them down into soil or dissolve them into ocean sediment."

Thoth paused in thought. "Very interesting. Thank you. And another thought just occurred to me. Natural causes may well be enough to entirely explain the lack of evidence of our existence. But Nature may also have had help. It's also possible that the galactic community had a hand in ensuring that evidence didn't survive. Although it's unclear why that would be."

Robert considered. "I might have some ideas," he said. "You should know that after the fall of Atlantis and Lemuria, humanity regressed considerably. Although, maybe not right away. But science and tech were lost to history for many, many thousands of years. Math. Plumbing. Electricity. *Everything*. Only in the past few hundred years of my time are we beginning to catch up to where you are now. And we're still decades away from that.

"So perhaps the galactic community wiped out any surviving technology that Nature didn't reclaim. To hinder our return to greatness. Or perhaps their intentions were more charitable. Perhaps they didn't want us to suffer the psychological scars of knowing all that had been lost to us. Or know just how far we had fallen."

Thoth rubbed his beard, deep in thought. "Thank you, Robert," he said after an extended period of silence. "You've certainly given me much to think about."

"So, what now?" asked Kira.

Thoth raised his eyebrows. "Now, I'm afraid I must take my leave. I have much to do."

"You can't just abandon us," said Robert in alarm. "You know that we're strangers in a strange land. Clueless. *Helpless*."

"Hardly helpless. And my gut is telling me to leave you on your own just now. But rest assured, this isn't me abandoning you. We shall meet again. In the meantime, farewell and pleasant journeys."

Saying this, Thoth wasted no time loitering. He quickly left the bridge, made his way through the cabin, and finally disappeared from view. The sound of his steps reverberated as he descended the ramp, eventually vanishing entirely.

And with that, the three visitors from another time were alone once again.

CHAPTER 15

Robert stood at the edge of the ramp and gazed down at the forest floor below. Pine needles carpeted the ground, interspersed with patches of dirt and clusters of shrubbery. The smell of sap filled the air. It couldn't have been more different from the arid landscapes he was accustomed to in this area, in what would eventually become Arizona.

"Thoth!" he called out, his voice echoing into the dense woods. Silence answered him. He'd called the man's name a few times, doing his best not to bring too much attention to the ship. The last call was probably one too many.

Thoth had appeared, extracted information, and then departed without a backward glance. He knew they were stranded here and recognized their complete ignorance of the area and its lurking dangers. And by his own admission, he considered them to be pivotal to the very survival of civilizations. Yet he had abandoned them to the elements, much like an archaeologist might leave important artifacts exposed to the harsh desert winds after an initial survey. Vulnerable and at the mercy of their surroundings.

With a heavy sigh, Robert sat down and pressed his back against the ship's wall. The open ramp remained in full view, showing the prehistoric-looking world outside.

He rubbed the back of his neck. *What did I get myself into?* Being thrown into the past right before it was set to self-destruct hadn't been on his bingo card.

Kira and Matt had followed close behind, and the latter dropped to the floor beside him, running a hand through his disheveled hair, his face as ashen as ever.

"Does anyone else feel like they're dreaming?" said Matt. "Like none of this can possibly be real?"

"Yes," said Robert. "Hard *not* to feel that way. A surreal dream that started the first time we came face to face with an intact starship hidden in a cave. But don't be fooled, Matt. What seems like a dream is very real, and we need to keep that firmly in mind. If we get injured or lost here, we won't just wake up in a cushy bed like it never happened. We'll have to live with the consequences."

Kira settled on Robert's other side, her gaze on the forest stretching out before them. "A stargate? An ancient starship? Mysterious aliens? Just incredible. And you took abuse back home just for theorizing that Hopi lore contained strong kernels of truth. If we ever do make it back home, no one will believe a word of this. Hell, I'm not sure I believe it, and I'm living it."

Robert's thoughts turned to his mother. She wasn't dependent on him, but she'd soon be frantic over his absence. She'd call the cops. The University of Arizona would launch an investigation, contacting colleagues and research sites. His students would be left in limbo, their projects and studies disrupted. The department might even organize search parties, combing through his recent research locations. It would all turn into a mess. Hell, maybe there'd be a news special on him: "Where did the batshit crazy archaeology professor disappear to? No one knows!"

If he really thought they could help prevent the destruction of Atlantis and Lemuria, he would happily stay here. But what could the three of them possibly do that the advanced, sophisticated societies of this time could not? And if they did change history, wouldn't the future change also? If they succeeded, the world might be better, but they would never be born, nor would any of the people they had ever known or loved.

No matter what Thoth said, their goal had to be to return home as quickly as they could. A realization that was painful for him to acknowledge. He had dedicated his life to studying myths and lore, including much about the time period he was now in, so being able to study the reality of it all was beyond irresistible. He felt like a dinosaur paleontologist having the opportunity to visit Jurassic Park. To study the living animals in their full splendor after a lifetime of studying fossils. Giddy at the prospect of all that he could learn. Terrified at the prospect of ending up in the jaws of a *T.rex*. Or, in Robert's case, ending up in the middle of a war that had wiped the planet clean of much of its life.

So, he had to do what he had to do. Part of him was desperate to stay here, but he had to help his companions get home. He owed them at least that much.

But if Thoth was to be believed, all roads home led through their starship. She was the ultimate gatekeeper.

"*Tala*, do you hear me?" he called out.

Silence.

He raised his voice. "If you're listening, we'd like to talk. Please."

No response came, just the faint whir of the ship's systems. Frustration gnawed at him. "You brought us here against our will. Don't you think we deserve an explanation? Why'd you bring us? What do you need from us? And what will it take to get you to return us to our own time? We don't belong here."

"Maybe she thinks she'd be in danger if she ever returned home," said Matt. "Maybe she thinks our government would try to reverse engineer her."

"They would for sure," said Robert, "if they could *catch* her. But she knows they wouldn't have a chance. She could travel to the Moon and back before a fighter jet even got off the runway."

"Even though she isn't responding," said Kira, "she's surely listening to our every word. We should keep that in mind. You can't offend an autopilot back home, but when it comes to a sentient AI like her, you never know."

A quiet settled over them, each lost in their thoughts. A low growl emanated from Robert's stomach, breaking the silence. "I guess coming to the Ice Age doesn't curb hunger."

Kira stood. "We should look for food. There's got to be something on this ship."

"You'd think," said Robert, pushing himself to his feet. "The question is, will it be edible?" He smiled. "My mother always told me, never eat egg salad that's been lying around for more than ten thousand years. She could be wrong, but it's a policy I've always tried to follow."

Kira winced. "Good point," she said with a look of disgust. "Now I'm not sure I *want* to find any food."

"Let's give it a shot, anyway," said Robert. "If *Tala* can conquer time travel, maybe she's *really* good at preserving food. I mean, she probably doesn't have tech as good as Tupperware or Saran Wrap, but there's always a chance."

Kira laughed, an unselfconscious sound that wasn't forced and seemed to light up the ship.

Matt, on the other hand, remained sullen. Robert guessed that now they finally had a moment to catch their breath, Matt was feeling the true weight, the true enormity of the mess they were in, crushing his mood.

Still, he followed his older companions into what they thought was the ship's kitchen. He might be shell-shocked by what they were facing, but he was also hungry.

When they arrived, Robert moved behind the counter and scanned the panels lining the walls, their surfaces unmarked by any type of handles or buttons. He trailed his fingers along one panel, trying to find a means to unlock them. To his surprise, one of the panels slid open to reveal a slew of unfamiliar objects.

Matt stepped forward to inspect the contents, but neither he nor Robert were able to make any reasonable guesses as to what the items might be used for.

Robert opened another panel, which contained a collection of crystalline containers, all empty. He glanced at Kira and shook his head. She walked to a larger panel dominating one wall. As she drew near, it illuminated and slid open, letting out a cool draft. Inside were compartments resembling shelves. "This might be a refrigerator," she said.

Robert peered inside. "Doesn't look like any fridge I've ever seen, but it fits the bill. Still, it's empty."

Matt leaned against the countertop. "Like you said, Professor, since *Tala's* been sitting in a cave for thousands of years, we're likely to strike out in the food department. So, what's the plan? Hunt prehistoric creatures with futuristic rifles?"

"Pretty much," said Robert. "And I like the way you phrased that, Matt," he added, trying to cheer up his young companion. "Using *Prehistoric* and *futuristic* in the same sentence is brilliantly ironic."

Matt grunted but didn't reply.

"What years are considered *prehistoric*, anyway?" asked Kira.

"The term encompasses a 2.5-million-year period. Starting way back when our progenitors, *Homo habilis,* first came on the scene. Ending about five thousand years ago, when formal writing systems first emerged."

Robert raised his eyebrows. "The term needs to be redefined, doesn't it? I'm pretty sure *prehistoric* was never meant to refer to an age of starships and holograms."

"This might be interesting if I wasn't starving," said Matt. "Can we stick to that subject? What are we doing about food?"

Kira sighed. "Seems to me that hunting is only one option. There must be endless nuts and berries out there also."

"It's a good thought," said Robert. "But I think it's too risky. Let's say we find berries that we think we recognize. Say blueberries. The problem is that they might be blueberries, or they might be a poisonous variation that exists in this time we don't know about." He paused. "In my view, cooked meat is our best bet. It's the only food we can be sure about."

"*Tala* could tell us if a berry was poisonous or not," said Kira, unable to hide her frustration. "If she would stop being so . . . fickle. I'm trying to stay calm," she added, "but her unresponsiveness is driving me a bit crazy. In fact, she and Thoth both seem to think we're insanely important. And both could be of immense help. Yet both have chosen to abandon us. It's absolutely *maddening*."

"Yeah," said Robert. "It is. I'm coping by assuming they must have a good reason for their behavior, even if we don't understand what it is." He shrugged. "Maybe a trial by fire, a way to toughen us up, get us to work together more cohesively. Or maybe it's a test."

"What kind of test?" asked Kira.

"I don't know," said Robert. He paused in thought for several long seconds. "Maybe a test of our initiative," he said finally, seeming to warm to the idea that had just formed in his mind. "God helps those who help themselves, right? Maybe it's the same with *Tala* and Thoth. Maybe they want to see us help ourselves before they pitch in. With respect to Thoth, maybe he wants to see if we won't take abandonment lying down. If we'll have the fortitude and resourcefulness to find *him* this time. He may well live close by. After all, he got here pretty damn quickly and seemed to be on foot."

"Interesting possibility," allowed Kira. "So, what do you recommend?"

Robert considered once more. "Let's kill two birds with one stone," he said. "We hunt for Thoth at the same time we're hunting for food. Except if we catch Thoth, we don't cook and eat him," he said with a smile. "Unless we get a lot hungrier than we are now."

"Thanks for the clarification," she replied in amusement.

"Kira, I'd like you to come with me. Matt, you can man the fort. Assuming you're both okay with that."

Both indicated they were.

"Good," said Robert. "Kira, let's grab rifles and get started. No time like the present."

Kira snorted. "Except we *aren't* in the present."

"Wow," said Robert, shaking his head. "Didn't see that coming."

Only minutes later the pair of hunters made their way down the ramp and set foot on a younger version of the Earth they knew. Outside, the air was crisp. Towering evergreens surrounded them, their branches forming a dense canopy.

As they moved, the sounds of rustling leaves and distant birdcalls surrounded them. The underbrush was thick, and ferns and shrubs brushed against their legs as they walked.

With the barrel of his rifle, Robert pushed a wiry tree limb out of the way. "If you could go back in time?" he said to his companion, "which a day ago I thought was a purely hypothetical question, would you support my work all over again?"

"You mean, given that we ended up trapped in the past with no way home?"

"Yes."

"Absolutely," she said without hesitation. "We're all going to die. But we don't all get the chance to truly *live*. Most men lead lives of quiet desperation, right? *Boring* lives of quiet desperation. But we're on the ultimate adventure. An impossible adventure. Like you said when we first boarded *Tala*, 'if I die now, I'll die happy.' Well, so will I, knowing I had the chance to experience the extraordinary. A chance denied to all but a few of the billions who ever lived."

"Wow. Good answer. There's more to you than meets the eye."

And there *was*, he realized as he stepped over a downed tree. She had come from nowhere and had supported his work without question. He had thought she had chosen him fairly randomly. But maybe not. She was revealing herself to be exceptionally deep and thoughtful, more so than he ever would have guessed. And more capable. So perhaps her support of his work, in particular, was *anything* but random.

There was more to her than met the eye. Maybe the same could be said of her *agenda*.

He sighed. On the other hand, maybe he was getting carried away. Maybe the high oxygen content of the forest was messing with his brain.

They both fell silent for an extended period, focusing all their efforts on the task at hand, finding either lunch or a clue to Thoth's possible whereabouts. After almost ten minutes, Kira halted, kneeling down to inspect something on the ground.

"Look at this," she whispered, not wanting a loud voice to scare off possible game in the area.

Robert knelt beside her. She reached out and touched a tall, shimmering stone. It stood out among several other crystal-like, clear stones scattered around it. The formation seemed unusual and out of place.

"Have you ever seen anything like it?"

Robert's eyes narrowed and he shook his head. "Never."

The strange growth had spread across the ground like a dense, crystalline bush. Its root-like tendrils had burrowed into the soil and expanded in all directions.

"It's extraordinary," said Kira in low tones. "It's a mineral, but it almost seems alive." She hovered her palm over the shimmering surface.

"I can feel pins and needles against my skin. There's some kind of physical energy coming from it."

Robert placed his palms where she had and felt the same.

"Whatever this is," said Kira, "it could have immense potential for energy applications. If this substance existed in our time, it could be extremely valuable."

Robert sighed. "Yet another mystery. And another miracle. Add it to the list. A working starship would be pretty valuable in our time too."

Kira's eyes widened as he spoke. She pointed excitedly to an area fifteen feet ahead. "Are those footprints?"

Robert followed her line of sight. Sure enough, a series of footprints were pressed into the soft earth. "Well done, Kira. And they were made by a pretty large shoe. Which supports the idea they were made by Thoth. He looked tiny next to our alien friends, but he was probably six-eight."

"So maybe you were right. He left a trail for us to follow if we had the initiative and fortitude to find it. Unless you think there's another nearly seven-foot-tall ancient wizard guy walking around these woods?"

"You know he isn't really a wizard, right? Just a hippy with a mastery of, you know, ancient futuristic technology."

Kira rolled her eyes. "Thanks, Robert," she said sarcastically. "And here I thought he was Harry fricking Potter. Glad you were here to set me straight."

Robert grinned. "Sorry. I deserved that."

"You ready to see where these footprints lead?"

"Let's do it," he said, mentally cataloging their surroundings. The distinctive gnarled stump they'd passed earlier, the uniquely shaped boulder with a patch of moss on its north side, the crooked tree with bark peeling off in a spiral pattern. He noted the angle of the sun, the direction of the breeze, and even the subtle changes in vegetation as they progressed.

They followed the imprints deeper into the forest. The trees grew denser, their trunks wider. The underbrush thinned out, replaced by a thick layer of fallen needles and leaves. The birdcalls faded, and a weird silence settled in.

A soft rustling sounded to their left. Robert froze, holding up a hand to signal Kira to stop. "You hear that?" he said, raising his rifle.

She nodded, surveying the foliage. "Stay alert."

A low growl rumbled through the air. It sent a chill down Robert's spine. From the shadows emerged a massive feline creature, standing nearly five feet tall at the shoulder. Its tawny coat rippled over powerful muscles, and its amber eyes locked onto them.

Both Robert and Kira aimed their weapons at the massive cat's nose as they took slow steps backward.

"An American lion," whispered Robert. "Panthera atrox. Abundant during the Ice Age. I knew they were immense, but not *this* immense."

"No sudden movements," said Kira. "Just keep moving back, slowly."

The lion's tail flicked as it stared at them. It padded over the forest floor, drawing closer.

Kira kept her rifle trained on the creature. "What's our next move? Should I shoot?"

"No, not yet. Let's stick to your original plan. Let's back out of here slowly."

As they began to edge away from the beast, Kira shook her head. "It keeps following us."

Robert gripped his rifle tighter. "We may need to fire after all. But let's make that a last resort. Keep backing up, but be ready."

The lion bared its teeth, revealing long, glinting canines. A deep roar escaped its throat, the sound reverberating through the trees.

"This is bad," said Kira.

"Just hope it doesn't get worse," said Robert, his fixation on the immense predator unblinking. "They were known to hunt in packs."

As if on cue, a second lion appeared to their right, followed by a third coming out from behind a cluster of ferns. They formed a loose circle around the two humans, each over a thousand pounds of pure muscle, speed, and ferocity.

"Wait for my signal," said Robert, his voice thick with tension. "Fire on my mark. Left one's mine, right one's yours. Then we race to take out the one in the middle. Loser buys dinner."

Kira's expression steeled. "Got it."

The first lion crouched low, muscles coiled. A moment after, the others mimicked their leader. They were ready to pounce.

CHAPTER 16

Advisor Elowin Balivae
City: Mu'lira
District: Namala Shores
Location: Southwest Lemuria

Elowin knelt beside a young girl on the sun-kissed sands. The breeze from the ocean played with Elowin's thin robe, the cool air brushing against her skin. Beneath the robe, she wore soft linen, leaving her arms and legs bare. She ran her fingers through her long black hair, untangling strands the wind had teased.

Ahead of them, where the beach met the tall grasses, a cluster of crystals shimmered. The crystals looked as if they'd sprouted from the earth. When the sun hit them just right, rainbows moved across the sand.

The girl gazed at the crystals, eyes wide. "They're so beautiful."

Elowin smiled. "These are Opalith crystals. They have the ability to harmonize with our bodies. If you look closely and concentrate, they might share their wisdom with you."

The girl leaned in, her small face inches from the nearest crystal. She closed her eyes. Moments passed, the only sound the crashing of waves against the shore.

"I think I hear it whispering," the girl said.

"What does it say?"

"It's like it's telling me to use my ears really good and listen to everything around me."

"Does it tell you anything else?"

The girl shrugged. "I don't know."

"Listen harder."

"Okay." The girl squeezed her eyelids shut, as tight as she could, concentrating as if it was the only thing important in the world. "I think . . . yeah."

"Yes?"

"Does it say animals and plants and stuff are all kinda connected?"

Elowin chuckled. "Did you hear that from one of the healers from the Medicine Society, or is that what you actually heard from the Opalith?"

"Don't know."

"Well, let me ask you this, and think hard on it, okay? You ready?"

"I am."

"What if you *did* know?"

"What do you mean?"

Elowin touched the tip of the little girl's nose. "Sometimes when we say 'I don't know,' it's like our mind is playing hide and seek with us. If we sit quietly and think really, really hard, it's like we're searching for that hidden thought. And guess what? More often than not, we find it."

The little girl hesitated for a moment, her brow furrowing in deep thought until she looked up at Elowin. "I guess I did hear it from one of the healers. But I also hear the crystals. They're whispering that we're all family. Everything and everyone."

"I see," said Elowin. "Perhaps you'll become a Crystal Keeper one day."

The girl's face lit up. "That's what my aunt is. I love spending time with her. She shows me all these amazing things. But she also says Atlantis has gone too far with the crystals. What does that mean, Advisor? She keeps saying that to everyone. Why? Atlantis is so far away."

Elowin glanced toward the horizon where the sea met the sky. "Because Atlantis has taken these crystals and turned them into tools of harm in some cases. They have been used for purposes that disrupt the harmony they were meant to maintain. It's something the Elders of the Lemurian Circle of 12 are deeply troubled by."

Hesitating, Elowin realized her words were quite heavy for such young shoulders. She smiled. "But that's a matter for us to handle. What's important is that you continue to discover and learn."

The girl looked back at the crystals, touching their pointed tops. "I love exploring. There's so much out there to find. It's like . . . forever and ever."

Elowin reached out and tucked a stray hair behind the girl's ear. "Lemuria is a wondrous place. We're fortunate to live amidst such beauty. And I'm grateful to be able to help others appreciate it, especially a curious and really smart girl like you."

The girl grinned. "The other day, I was exploring the cliffs near Kailanopa Point—"

A shadow moved across the sand. Elowin looked up as a teardrop-shaped ship glided silently overhead. Its silver surface reflected the sunlight while it descended onto a flat area of the beach nearby. Landing gear extended as it settled onto the ground. A ramp began to extend from its side.

Elowin placed a hand on the girl's shoulder. "It's time for you to go." The girl nodded, disappointment in her eyes. "Will I see you again?"

"I'll be returning to speak with your clan chief very soon. We have more business to attend to. And I'll make sure to find you."

The girl smiled before turning and running toward the distant cluster of homes nestled among the trees. As Elowin watched the child's figure grow smaller, her gaze drifted to the skyline beyond. Buildings formed an array of rounded shapes, blending in with the natural surroundings. Small, cozy houses shaped like upside-down bowls with pointed tops stood alongside others resembling oversized bell jars. Taller structures, up to ten stories high, boasted smooth curved walls and circular windows.

Trees grew throughout, their vines decorating the exteriors, while some roofs sported trimmed grass that looked like green, fluffy hair atop the domed structures.

Elowin felt blessed to have been born in Lemuria, where most districts were as beautiful as this one.

She turned to the ship as an imposing figure emerged at the top of the ramp. Clad in a tunic, the edges of his garment were embroidered with geometric patterns in shades of copper and gold. Over it draped a long mantle billowing in the sea breeze. The man had sharp cheekbones and plenty of lines of wisdom. His dark eyes sparkled with the vitality of someone decades younger.

Elowin bowed and pressed her hands together in respect. "Elder Kona Makelo, I wasn't expecting you. My ship is supposed to be landing here, not yours. Can I assume you're responsible for this change?"

"I am," said Elder Kona as he descended the ramp. "Apologies, Advisor Balivae, but your pilot has been redirected back to the capital. You're to accompany me to the north. There's a matter of great concern that needs your attention."

These days, 'great concern' seemed to cloud a lot of matters. "What's this about?"

He halted at the base of the ramp, the wind tousling the fringes of his robe. "War looms, and it's drawing nearer than we'd hoped. Atlantis isn't keeping its agreements, and the treaties aren't being honored."

"I was in negotiations with the Atlantean Senate just weeks ago. The Lucents, even the Archon . . . they assured me and the other emissaries that all was well with the treaties."

"Apparently, assurances aren't what they used to be."

Without another word, Elowin walked up the ramp. Inside the ship, murals of swirling patterns in turquoise, sienna, and gold covered the rounded walls. Woven blue mats made up the floor, and niches held various artifacts.

Four empty tables with chairs were scattered about the cabin. She took a seat at a low, dark wood table inlaid with mother-of-pearl, surrounded by embroidered cushions. Elder Kona sat across from her, folding his hands atop the table.

The pilot's voice resonated through the cabin. "Prepare for departure."

The ship whirred as it lifted off. A section of one of the ship's walls turned transparent, showing a panoramic view. Below, the beach's Opalith crystals glittered. As they ascended, the villages of domed structures nestled in greenery grew smaller.

"Where are we headed?" asked the Advisor.

"Sholani. The Circle of 12 is convening there to address this crisis."

"Understood. But I'm convinced diplomacy with Atlantis can still prevail. We've made significant progress."

"Maybe. But only if they can be trusted. Their words say one thing, but their actions say another. They've mobilized their fleets and soldiers on Eastern Nasavi, heading toward our outposts. They've constructed a base near Tokpela Gate, practically touching our walls."

Elowin winced. "That is troubling. The Archon assured me otherwise."

"I know. But we have to confront the reality that is, not the reality we want."

"I need to return to Atlantis and speak directly with the High Councilor himself. We can't allow decades of peace to unravel."

Kona gazed at her in thought. "Your dedication is unquestioned, Elowin, but we're running out of time. We need to prepare. We need to erect defenses and discuss strategy."

His words hit her hard, though she masked her distress well, like a true diplomat. To Atlantis, war had become the answer to everything. Lemuria held fast to the belief that peace created a balance that benefited all, but when faced with the power-hungry leaders of Atlantis, morals alone wouldn't suffice.

The ship leveled off. Clouds parted, showing a vast wilderness below. Rolling hills blanketed in forests stretched wide, with rivers snaking through the landscape. The sight made Elowin long for a moment of respite. To bathe, to breathe, to pause life and find some peace. Rest had been more than elusive since she'd become an Advisor, and lately, even a small bit of sleep felt impossible.

Elowin stared at the spectacular view. She couldn't allow anyone to harm her home. Not this place. Not this beauty. Not her people. "I can convince them to pursue peace," she said. "There has to be a way. And I'll find it."

"Maybe. But most see this war now as inevitable. We've exhausted all other avenues."

"Then we'll find new ones. Surrendering to inevitability is not an option."

He gave a slight nod. "You have no idea how much I hope you're right."

"Please, Elder, send me to Atlantis. I can stop this war. Lock me in a room with their leaders, and I'll work out an accord they'll actually honor."

"That's precisely why I'm taking you to the Circle of 12. So the Elders can hear you plead your case. But I have to be honest, their minds are closing fast. Look at what the Atlanteans are doing in Kemet. They're raining destruction upon lands that aren't theirs to claim, insisting that they're preserving order."

Elowin gritted her teeth. "I feel for those in Kemet," she said. "And I know what I'm up against." Her voice strengthened, and her tone became one of absolute conviction. "But I can do this! I know it. And I *will* convince the Council."

"Again, Advisor Elowin, I hope you're right."

"But you don't think I am."

"No. And that's what terrifies me."

CHAPTER 17

All three lions now had their muscles flexed, moments away from pouncing. Time moved like molasses as Robert held the aim of the plasma rifle steady on the lion to his left, while Kira did the same with the one on the right.

It was an absolute crime to kill creatures so magnificent, so perfectly molded by nature to be apex predators, but it couldn't be helped.

"Now!" he shouted.

The lion on the left sprang first, a blur of sinew and fury. Kira screamed, her finger squeezing the activation button on her rifle. A bolt of searing energy erupted from her rifle. A bright streak met the lion mid-leap. The plasma struck the animal's chest. Fur ignited flesh in an instant. The beast let out a roar that quickly turned into a pained cry. It crashed to the forest floor and skidded to a halt a yard from them. Smoke rose from its scorched wound.

Robert shot at the same time, and the lion on the right died in the same way, although its massive carcass fell farther away from them on the forest floor.

The moment their primary targets were down they immediately shifted their rifles to the magnificent cat in the middle, and both pulled the trigger within microseconds of each other.

Nothing happened.

Only silence in their hands.

They both pressed the trigger again frantically, but the guns were entirely unresponsive.

What had been fear before suddenly crescendoed into full-on panic, but they were lucky. The middle lion had held back a moment, smart enough to hesitate after seeing his companions cut down by bright bolts of energy.

"It's spooked," whispered Kira, as they both pressed the activation buttons on their rifles several more times to no avail.

The remaining lion slowly advanced, eyes squinting. Focused.

"Keep pointing the rifle at it, even if it's useless," said Robert quickly. "It's smart enough to realize these rifles are dangerous appendages. Back up as fast as you can but continue facing it. If we run, it'll be emboldened and be on us in seconds."

They backpedaled faster than either had thought possible, continuing to point their rifles forward as the lion effortlessly followed, although cautiously, as it struggled to make sense of the puny, fangless prey that should be helpless, but somehow wasn't.

The lion let out a mighty roar so loud it seemed to shake the forest, and then followed this with another, even louder, seconds later. Kira and Robert continued moving backward with *purpose*. Branches clawed at their clothes as they weaved between evergreens, glancing behind themselves periodically to get a lay of the land and maneuver in thick woods without the luxury of a rear-view mirror. The forest floor was a tangled mess of roots, each step about to snare one of them, if not both.

They heard rustling to their left and right, large animals approaching quickly.

Two more American lions burst into sight. Robert shouted a loud curse. It was as if they were Hydras. Cut off one head and two more grew back.

Or had the lion's earlier roars been calls for reinforcements? Just how smart *were* these animals?

Robert decided the answer was *very*. At the same time, he realized that he and Kira hadn't been using their brains at all.

There was no way a futuristic plasma rifle would be one and done. Impossible. The rifles were too advanced to exist solely for a single use. So what were they missing?

The rifles must be in single-shot mode, as stupid as that seemed to Robert. Maybe this was a safety feature. It made no sense to limit their operation so severely, but perhaps it was done for energy conservation or sniper-like targeting. Maybe it minimized unnecessary damage in delicate situations, especially since this was a weapon that could inadvertently start fires.

There had to be a way to change the setting. To activate a multi-fire mode that would allow the rifles to unleash a rapid succession of plasma bolts.

All of this flashed through Robert's mind in an instant, as adrenaline and a life-and-death situation accelerated his thinking.

"Kira, the rifles must have a multi-shot mode," he shouted urgently. "Find a way to activate it. I'll do the same."

She did as he asked without question, and he began sliding his hand up and down the rifle, searching for an indentation or other control.

But while Kira was focused on finding the proper setting, she backpedaled into a cleft in uneven ground and twisted her ankle so severely she almost broke it. She screamed out in pain and dropped to the ground, crashing the back of her head into the hard soil.

"Kira!" screamed Robert in panic, sliding down beside her.

She winced, clutching her ankle. She was dazed from the blow to her head, but her faculties quickly returned. "I'm okay," she said. "Watch the lions, not me."

The trio of cats grew cautiously nearer. Robert grabbed a low tree limb with his left hand and kicked it off the trunk. He turned to face the approaching lions, positioning himself between them and Kira. The big cats slowed, tails lashing back and forth.

"Stay back!" he screamed, swinging the branch in a wide arc while continuing to point the plasma rifle toward them, giving them even more to consider.

The lions prowled closer, giant paws swatting at the tree limb as Robert waved it like a madman. The force of the animals' strikes reverberated through the branch, and Robert barely managed to hang on to it.

"Can you stand!" he shouted to Kira behind him, not daring to take his attention off the predators.

"Working on it," she replied.

Robert backed away, keeping the branch between them and the lions. He reached out with one hand, helping Kira to stand. She leaned heavily against him, favoring her injured ankle.

Moving far more slowly now, the pair continued their backward retreat. Kira limped alongside Robert, using his body as a human crutch, her face contorted in pain.

The lions circled wider. They seemed to understand that their prey was weakened, and there was no need to rush. Robert had counted his blessings that all three lions had been in front of them, but now one repositioned, working its way behind them. Seconds later they were surrounded on all sides by three of the most lethal predators that had ever existed.

The cats spread out, using the trees for cover as they circled their prey. The empty threats of a branch and useless gun had slowed them down, but it was clear they were all out of patience. The one directly facing them tensed, just like the lion who had first launched itself toward them. But this time they didn't have working weapons. This time they only had their bare hands, which wouldn't delay these predators for an instant.

Robert knew the end was seconds away. They had cheated death, but death was about to get its revenge.

"I'm so sorry, Kira," he whispered.

He braced himself for a truly horrific death, being torn to pieces and eaten alive, but just then Kira gave him a shove forceful enough to send him to the ground, and a plasma bolt finally burst from her rifle, killing the cat about to strike. Kira fell to the ground, losing her one-footed balance, and rolled, burning a hole through a second cat. She rolled once more and pointed her weapon at the third lion, but it had seen enough and raced off through the brush, abandoning what should have been an easy meal.

Both humans sat on the ground as their hearts raced at a furious pace.

"I figured it out," she said after her heart rate decreased enough for her to catch her breath. "You need to hit the activation button and hold it for three to four seconds. Then the entire rifle becomes bathed in green light, which blinks three times. After that, it's good to go."

"How did you know the blinking indicated it was in multi-shot mode?"

"I didn't. All I could do was hope like hell and give it a try." She raised her eyebrows. "Sorry I shoved you so hard."

"Are you kidding?" said Robert. "You saved us! *Thank you.*"

He threw back his head and exhaled loudly. "And as fierce as your shove was," he added in amusement, "I think the lions might have been a tiny bit fiercer. Just a guess."

"You deserve at least as much credit as I do, Robert. It was your idea to activate a multi-fire mode. You'd have figured it out yourself if you weren't practically carrying me and fending them off at the same time. So, thanks to *you.*"

Robert picked himself up off the ground and examined his rifle. He pressed the activation button and kept the pressure on it until he was rewarded with three green flashes. "I'll be damned," he muttered to himself.

He stared at the bodies of the two lions nearby and shook his head sadly. It had to be done, but it was a tragic waste. The Hopi had the deepest respect for all life, rooted in their spiritual and cultural beliefs about maintaining harmony with nature. Hopi hunters often offered cornmeal or prayer feathers to a fallen animal's spirit to honor it, acknowledge its role in the cycle of life, and ensure balance with the natural world.

Robert returned his attention to Kira. "Let's get you back to the ship. When I asked you to join me on a hunting expedition, I thought *we'd* be the ones doing the hunting."

Kira's ankle was much worse now and she put her arm around his shoulder. He supported her weight almost entirely and proceeded slowly to ensure she maintained balance. Finally, he suggested a fireman's carry. Not the most dignified for her, but the best way to move at a more rapid pace and spare her further damage or discomfort.

Kira was soon draped around his shoulders, her head halfway down his back and facing his rear end. She continued to clutch her rifle, despite her awkward position. Robert held his rifle facing toward the ground as he walked, remaining fully alert for possible predators and counting his blessings that his passenger weighed no more than 115 pounds dripping wet. Even so, after fifteen minutes of carrying her, he was running out of steam.

He was about to put her down to take a few minutes respite from the backbreaking exertion when he finally spotted a metallic glint through the trees.

Their starship. Talk about a sight for sore eyes. It was sitting in the clearing in which they had landed, although he couldn't yet see the river running behind it. No need to take a break this close to the finish line.

Robert emerged from the thick forest and entered the clearing. The ramp was now only sixty feet away and closing. He covered much of the remaining distance when he heard the slightest rustle coming from the tree line, now well behind them.

His blood went cold, and his gut screeched an alarm, dictating that he pivot around as if his life depended on it. Just as he completed his turn, he saw what had caused the sound. Just as his gut had somehow known, it was the lion who had bolted off. But it hadn't gone far. It must have stalked them the entire way back, waiting for its moment to finally kill its quarry and exact revenge for the death of its pack-mates.

Robert fired, but he was in an awkward position and the beast was racing across the clearing at breathtaking speed. He was able to hit its shoulder, causing it to fall to the ground and yelp in pain, but it wasn't enough to stop it. It quickly rose again while Robert tried to reposition himself for a better shot, but with Kira still on his shoulders, he was weighed down and off-balance and they crashed to the ground like a one-legged stool.

He and Kira both rolled to get off additional shots, but Robert knew they would be too late.

A brilliant, blinding flash of light engulfed the entire area as if a mini-supernova had exploded above their heads. For an instant, Robert wondered if this was the afterlife, but then heard a whimper coming from a lion who had stopped less than five feet away from them.

Robert and Kira shielded their eyes as the lion whimpered once more and then scrambled back into the woods.

With his pulse pounding, Robert looked up the ramp. Standing at the top was a radiant, crystalline being. Her flowing hair cascaded over her shoulders like liquid silver. She wore a robe shimmering with blue and silver hues, matching the shine of her skin. Her palm was extended toward the retreating lions, a soft light fading from its center.

Robert's breath caught in his throat. "*Tala*?" he managed to croak out in disbelief.

The crystalline woman lowered her hand and nodded. "That's correct," she said with a smile. "It's nice to finally meet the two of you. In *person.*"

CHAPTER 18

Robert suddenly noticed that Matt was standing at the top of the ramp as well. The young man had been completely overshadowed by the miraculous crystalline figure.

"Matt, Kira's injured," he called out. "Can you give me a hand?"

The young man quickly joined them, and he and Robert formed two pillars on either side of their patient, who put one arm around each while they carefully helped her to the ship and up the ramp.

Kira's jaw clenched as even small movements sent jolts of pain through her ankle. When they entered the ship, they lowered her to a seated position against the wall, and *Tala* came inside to join them.

Robert's gaze returned to the crystalline being. "It's truly an honor to see you, as you say, in person again. We glimpsed you one other time. But before we get better . . . acquainted . . . is there any chance you could close the ramp this time?"

Tala nodded and the ramp sealed instantly.

"Thank you," he said in relief. Lions would be starring in his nightmares for years to come. Poor Kira had just been through the same trauma he had. She'd experienced the same constant fear of being torn to bloody pieces. She had been forced to deal with immobility and agonizing pain at the same time.

And she had handled herself brilliantly. She was truly extraordinary.

But they were safe now, and he felt euphoric. He had faced dangerous men in his line of work, like he had in the cave in Brazil. For some reason, he never imagined dying in the jaws of an extinct species of lion while holding a useless plasma rifle.

"Do you have any questions for me?" asked *Tala*.

"Too many to count," he replied. He wanted to confront her about a number of issues, but as Kira had said, best not to antagonize a likely sentient being who held their lives in her hands. Or, at minimum, their chances of returning home. "But let me start with this one," he continued. "You were ah . . . kind enough to close the ramp just now. Why did you refuse to do so when the Anunnaki were coming?"

Tala blinked her luminescent eyes. "Thoth's energy signature was approaching. Allowing him on board was necessary for him to confront the Anunnaki. Your meeting with him was imperative."

Matt folded his arms. "Hold on. You warned us those giants were going to kill us. What was that about, then?"

"I detected their advanced weaponry," said the personification of a starship. "Their weapons, their elevated heart rates, and their aggressive postures indicated hostile intent. I had to be honest with you about that. But I let them in because I calculated Thoth would arrive in time to defuse the situation."

"What if your calculations were wrong?" asked Robert, wanting to hurl this question at her, but instead using the most polite tone he could manage.

"My calculations *weren't* wrong," she said simply as if this explained everything.

A soft groan pulled Robert's attention back to Kira. She clutched her ankle, eyes squeezed shut.

"She's in pain," noted *Tala*.

Guilt washed over Robert. He should have tended to her immediately, but his curiosity had trumped his compassion and his growing affection for this woman.

"Let me see your ankle," he said gently.

Carefully, they eased off her boot. Her ankle was swollen to nearly twice its size, the skin mottled with deep purples and blues.

Matt winced. "That doesn't look good."

"We need to get you off the floor and get that leg elevated," said Robert.

Tala gestured toward the cabin. "There are beds in the crew quarters. I'd suggest moving her there."

Within minutes, they managed to transport the patient to one of the small rooms and lay her on the bed. As they settled her down, the mattress shifted, contouring perfectly to her body. Beneath her head, a pillow materialized from the bed itself, rising to cradle her neck.

"How did it do that?" asked Kira weakly.

Tala stepped forward. "I'm activating a healing protocol. Frequency set to 727 hertz for bone and tissue regeneration."

Around Kira's ankle, soft lights started to glow. Waves of emerald and sapphire pulsed, sending geometric patterns to her skin. A soothing hum filled the room.

"What's happening?" asked Robert.

"The bed emits frequencies that accelerate cellular repair," explained *Tala*. "The photonic energy stimulates bone growth and tissue regeneration. She should be fully recovered by tomorrow, assuming no complications."

Kira's expression softened as the lights worked their magic. "It feels warm. The pain's easing."

Tala turned to Kira and smiled. "I'll be monitoring your vitals."

"Do you have any food?" asked Matt.

"I'm sorry, but I don't. Not even a vat of egg salad that's been lying around for 13,000 years."

Robert and Kira exchanged quick glances. This confirmed that the walls had ears.

"Was that a joke?" said Robert in dismay.

"At least an attempt at one. Did you like it?"

"Yes. Very amusing. And a bit surprising. None of the starships I was buddies with growing up had a sense of humor."

Tala didn't respond. Instead, she turned to Matt to complete the answer to his question. "If you want food, you'll need to hunt and prepare your own meals, I'm afraid. Including gathering fruits and vegetables. I can tell you if they're edible. Or you can seek help from Thoth. But be careful. In addition to lions, you need to watch out for dire wolves, sabretooths, and other predators."

"Noted," said Robert. Now that they knew how to set the plasma rifles properly, this would be much less of a problem.

"I have another question," said Matt.

"By all means."

"Can you get us home?"

"I can't. My programming won't allow it. Not until I've fulfilled my purpose—ensuring Lemuria's safety and survival. I failed once, and I can't fail again. I waited a long time for someone to find the flute, and to find me."

A surge of irritation tightened in Robert's chest. He took a deep breath, trying to keep his voice steady. "But you know that in our future, Lemuria is no more. It's gone."

"Precisely," said *Tala*. "That's why I'm here now. I traveled through the stargate to save Lemuria. Where I failed before, I hope to succeed now. Where there was once one of me, there are now two. This will help the cause, though *I'll* operate more covertly than my double. The other *Tala* and I will never see each other."

"We aren't from this time," said Robert. "We're babes in the woods. Politically and culturally. And in every other way. We don't know how anything works. Wouldn't you be much better off with a crew who *does* know what's going on? Why not get a talented, experienced crew that can help you achieve your mission? Then you can swing by the future to drop us off. Before, you know, returning here."

Tala smiled, and her voice radiated a newfound warmth. "I assure you, Robert Shaw, the three of you are *exactly* who I need."

Thoth had warned them they'd fail to convince the ship to take them home. While Robert was disappointed, once again, the archaeologist in him thrilled at the prospect of exploring a world he'd only theorized about, where Hopi legends materialized into reality. Everything he'd postulated, dismissed by many as mere fantasy, now surrounded him. He would be able to dig deeper into ancient mysteries, uncover truths that had eluded scholars for centuries. He'd now have the chance to validate his life's work, which would be both exhilarating and daunting. Whether he liked it or not, he was at the epicenter of a historical quagmire, and the scientist in him couldn't help but feel a spark of excitement at the challenges that lay ahead.

Kira stirred on the bed. "*Tala*, who . . . or what . . . are you, exactly?"

"I'm the consciousness of this ship. As alive as you are, though in a different way. I'm the heart, soul, and brains of this starship."

"Yeah, we gathered that already," said Kira. "But can we assume you're an advanced form of artificial intelligence? Or are you something else entirely?"

"Artificial intelligence is a primitive construct that often fails to operate in the best interests of all beings. I'm a Quantum Resonance Consciousness."

"Quantum Resonance Consciousness?" said Robert. "Can you elaborate?"

"Think of me as a symphony of subatomic particles. I'm composed of crystalline energy. Imagine if light could crystallize yet still flow and think. That's me."

Robert crossed his arms. "Are you saying you're living light?"

"In essence, yes," said *Tala*. "I can project myself as the hologram you see, allowing me to interact with you. I'm alive, though in a different form than you."

Robert considered. "Can you appear anywhere?"

Tala's form shimmered. "Anywhere on this ship, yes," she replied. "But I won't violate the privacy of the crew quarters. Not unless there's a medical emergency like this one, or I'm invited to do so. Even if I'm invited in, I'll leave as soon as I'm asked to."

"If you're made of light," said Matt, "does that mean you can't touch anything? Like a ghost?"

"Close. I can't physically touch anything the same way you can. But I often don't need to. For example, you would need to press a button to lower the ramp if you knew where to find it. I, on the other hand, being the ship, can just *cause* it to be lowered, without need of this construct touching anything."

Robert rubbed his chin in thought. He had been hesitant to ask the most important question of all, but couldn't wait any longer. "*Tala*, if I may... who programmed you?"

Tala's gaze held a little too long on Robert, as if she had to think about his question, and then how to answer it. "I'm not programmed in the sense you're thinking of. I do have free will. My creators simply integrated certain protocols to guide my actions and ensure I take actions that benefit humankind. I, myself, am unsure of who created me, although I have my own theories. Just as you're unsure of who created humanity, be it God, evolution, ET's, or something else, you also have your theories."

Robert wasn't entirely satisfied but decided not to pursue this further. "You said earlier we're *exactly* who you need to save Lemuria. Why *us*?"

"The flute you brought serves as my anchor. It must remain on board to keep me connected and functional."

That really didn't answer his question, but he let it go and glanced toward the bridge where the flute was stored in his backpack. He thought about the inscriptions he had read on a statue in Brazil. "Has that always been the case?"

"No. There was a time when the flute was required to awaken me and then was no longer needed. But I've evolved, or rather, I've reprogrammed my systems to require the flute to remain aboard during takeoff, landing, and flight. Its constant presence is now an absolute requirement."

Kira adjusted her position on the bed to get more comfortable. "So you need a flute to operate... you. That still doesn't explain why you need us, specifically."

Tala's form pulsed. "Your presence is intertwined with pivotal events we must change. I must save Lemuria. I can't reveal everything, or history won't unfold as I think it should to accomplish my mission. Nonetheless, know that your actions can play a critical role. As a group, you possess qualities and knowledge that are indispensable.

Each of you brings something unique. If you can help the Resistance, I'll be able to bring you home."

"With all due respect, are you sure you've read our resumes correctly?" said Robert. "I'd like to think I'm a superhero with qualities that can change worlds, but I'm just an archaeologist and adventurer, at *best*. Kira is just a brilliant businesswoman who is expert in mining operations. And Matt, is, well, just Matt. How can we make a difference here?"

"By being who you are. Your choices, your courage. They can alter outcomes. Sometimes unexpected paths can lead to necessary destinations."

"I guess we have to take your word for it," said Kira. "Can you help us? Can you tell us how to proceed?"

"I can't. But let me suggest the following for now. Let's continue getting acquainted, as Robert put it, for another hour or so. After that, you need to sleep. To heal. Tomorrow, when you wake up with fresh eyes, I'll give you Thoth's location. You'll be able to find him once again and acquire food and drink."

Tala paused. "And then, I strongly suggest that you convince him to return here."

CHAPTER 19

Advisor Elowin Balivae
City: Sholani
District: Loma'i Shores
Location: Northwest Lemuria

Elowin stepped off the ship. The icy air nipped at her cheeks. Below her feet loomed the Grand Chambers of Lemuria. At the moment, she stood on a circular landing platform etched with geometric symbols. On either side, domed structures rose high and pierced the snowy sky. Flakes drifted down, settling on the stone beneath her feet.

In the distance, the rumble of waves made the ocean sound closer than it was. There, the Loma'i Shores crashed relentlessly against the towering cliffs below. It was a reminder of the Glacial Seas' proximity. Though Lemuria stretched far to the warm southern lands, here in the north, winter held its grip much longer.

Kona Makelo walked beside her. Ahead, a group of men and women awaited, their long robes flowing. Without a word, they guided Elowin and Kona down a slender ramp leading to a staircase.

They descended into the building on which they had landed and entered a vast, rounded chamber filled with warm air. In the room's center stood a platform with four nested bowls. The largest brimmed with water. Within it sat a slightly smaller bowl filled with fine sand. Above that, an empty bowl held only the essence of air. At the heart, the smallest bowl cradled a flame. They called it the Elemental Unity Bowl, a sacred vessel reminding all who saw it of the Lemurian belief that everything in existence was connected. It was a principle guiding both their daily lives and their government.

The Circle of 12 encircled the platform. These were the Elders. Each represented the twelve clans of Lemuria, custodians of wisdom and tradition. Their eyes followed her as she approached, the silence thick.

Elowin halted before them and bowed. She lifted her head. "This discourse of war must cease," she said, wasting no time getting to the point. "Even entertaining the idea of war threatens the very soul of Lemuria."

"Well, it's nice to see you, too, Elowin," said an Elder with a smile. The Elder stepped forward. Her name was Melia Kapule'a. Lines etched her face. "I assume you're now aware that Atlantean battalions have amassed on East Nasavi? That their forces have moved close to our outposts?"

"They haven't engaged us," said Elowin. "No declaration of war has been made. We must initiate dialogue, urge them to withdraw from our sovereign territories."

Melia's neutral expression stayed the same. "Their intentions are clear. Ignoring the threat endangers our people. We've had dialogue for years, and yet here we are. They've repeatedly shown they can't be trusted. And we can't tolerate their behavior any longer."

Elowin sighed. "Our principles guide us toward peace. Let's not forget who we are."

"Let's not forget who *they* are, either," said Melia. "Or at least who they've *become*."

From the circle, a tall man walked forward. Beneath his robes, he had a muscular build. Bulging chest, shoulders, and arms. His name was Huku Nali, a figure of authority who had been voted the leader of the Circle just a year earlier. "Before we proceed," he said, "there's a matter we must address. Your recent activities across Lemuria—these speeches, these gatherings promoting peace—they're causing unrest. You need to stop. Your influence could compromise our security."

Elowin's spine stiffened, but she didn't reply.

"Your dedication to peace honors us," he continued. "You're the youngest to have ever been elected to our government. And we admire your passion. But reality is reality."

"Reality is shaped by our choices," argued Elowin. "Meeting aggression with aggression only spirals into destruction."

"Strength recognizes strength," countered Huku. "If we don't prepare to defend ourselves, we invite peril."

"We need to focus on the core issue," said Elowin. "Atlantis is being heavily influenced by the Draconians."

Huku shook his head in disgust. "The fact that you subscribe to this conspiracy theory is troubling, Advisor. Reptilian overlords influencing our world? It's absurd. The galactic community wouldn't stand for it."

"If they knew about it," replied Elowin.

Kona nodded at Huku. "I understand your skepticism," he said. "But there are too many rumors of Draconian influence to ignore. If members of this species are hiding here, somehow controlling the Atlantean Council, it would explain a lot. It could be a major reason why, over the decades and centuries, the Atlantean Council has changed for the worse so dramatically.

"You don't just become dark and dangerous that quickly," continued Kona. "You don't just systematically destroy the sacred pillars that once held Atlantis to the Light. The Hierophants of the Emerald Order with their ancient wisdom. Temple Lyra's grand harmonies. The healers of Mount Parnassus. These were the very heart of Atlantis, yet one by one they were dismantled by the government, undermined, persecuted, falsely accused and convicted of treason, debilitated, and eradicated in all other ways possible. The Emerald Order, for instance, which if the Dracs were real, would present the greatest threat to them, was especially targeted. And the elimination of this ancient order accelerated the dramatic change in Atlantis, as darkness, control, subjugation, and war became Atlantean priorities instead of the peace and harmony that had reigned for so long."

Huku scoffed. "That's an interesting interpretation of history," he said. "From what I understand, those in the Emerald Order were *traitors* to Atlantis. If any group is responsible for their descent into darkness, perhaps it's them. We shall not speak their name. In fact, I find it a positive development that they were cast out from Atlantis and are all but extinct."

He paused in thought for several long seconds and then shook his head. "If someone brings me solid evidence that the Dracs exist and are behind this, we'll take appropriate action. Until then, we have to assume Atlantis is acting entirely on its own."

Huku shifted his gaze from Kona to Elowin. "So tell me, Advisor, do you have any concrete proposals that don't involve imagined aliens?"

Elowin was slow to anger, by nature, but she couldn't remember when she'd been so infuriated. She took several deep, mental breaths. "I do," she managed to get out calmly. "Let's engage Atlantis in a series of public dialogues broadcast throughout both our lands. Let their words be heard by all, their promises recorded for posterity. We'll ask pointed questions, demand specific commitments, and cross-reference their statements over time. In the court of public opinion, inconsistencies will be exposed, and the pressure of accountability will keep them honest. If they refuse such transparency, their intentions become clear. If they accept, we create a framework for truth that will be hard for them, or any possible puppeteers, to manipulate."

Huku shook his head once more. "That would be playing right into their hands," he said dismissively. "They'll use these talks to buy time to further prepare their forces while we sit idle. We can't afford to be naïve. We'll prepare for conflict while leaving a small window open for diplomacy. But we can't base our entire strategy on the hope that public pressure will somehow keep our enemies honest."

Elowin had expected resistance to her ideas, but not the absolute dogmatism she was facing now. Still, she was a diplomat, trained to remain calm and clearheaded no matter what the provocation. She intuitively realized that none of the arguments she had carefully prepared in her head would work. Which meant she had only one card left to play.

"I realize the majority in this room believes the ship of war has already sailed," she began. "That nothing can stop it. But I can turn the tide!" she insisted. "I've never been more certain of anything in my life. So, give me just two weeks. If I can't clearly show that tensions are being calmed, aggression is being reversed, then do what you must. No matter how skeptical you might be, are you really prepared to turn your back on the possibility of a peaceful resolution, especially one that requires such a brief amount of time? With stakes nothing less than the future of this entire planet, are you really prepared to deny me just two weeks to prove myself?"

She shook her head sadly. "If so, then I fear that the soul of Lemuria is truly gone."

Huku's expression made it clear that he had been taken by surprise by this extraordinary gambit. Elowin had been bold enough to put all of her chips on the table, in a way that painted him into a corner. She had positioned this in such a way that if he didn't call for a vote on her proposal, he'd seem reckless, unwilling to support a reasonable request by a talented woman exuding absolute confidence.

To his credit, he knew when he'd been outmaneuvered and called for a vote immediately. Eight of the twelve Elders nodded their assent.

"Very well," said Huku, not trying to hide his skepticism. "You have your chance, Advisor. *Two weeks*. Not a moment longer."

"I'll need a delegation. A few members of the Warrior Society to show our strength."

"So be it," said Huku. "Tell me, which Atlantean will you approach first?"

Elowin hesitated. She first planned to seek out the counsel of a man who could provide invaluable guidance to her. Thoth, the last Hierophant of the Emerald Order. But as much as she hated to lie, Huku had just moments before made his feelings clear about the Order. In fact, he had said, "We shall not speak their name," which was difficult to misinterpret.

She glanced at Kona and sighed. "I have yet to decide my first step," she replied. "I have much to consider."

"Well, consider *quickly*," said Huku. "The clock on your two weeks has already started."

CHAPTER 20

Atlantean Councilor Kairos Daedalus
High Marshall of the Atlantean Military Forces
The Scarlet Dune Campaign
Location: Northern Kemet, East of the Nile River

Kairos Daedalus stood atop a massive dune, taking in the odd sight. This sprawling desert, stretching as far as he could see, had no business existing here in the middle of such fertile country. Sheltered within an open-air structure supported by large columns, he gazed out at the harsh landscape. A fan operated overhead. It dispensed a cool mist brushing against his face, giving him a break from the scorching sun.

While much of Kemet remained lush jungle, this particular zone was rapidly transforming into one of the hottest regions known to humankind. With it, the terrain was starting to change.

The circular command center around him teemed with busy personnel. Argo, Kairos's second-in-command, stood to his right, while technicians and officers manned various consoles arranged in concentric circles around the central holographic display. Towering viewscreens lined the perimeter, showing real-time battlefield footage.

Before Kairos hovered a crystalline display, which formed a holomap of Kemet, showing troop movements in great detail.

"Councilor, the Eastern Nile Delta reports increased resistance," said Commander Argo, his focus on the pulsing red indicators on a holomap.

Kairos studied the flashing zones. He had two titles, *Councilor,* and *High Marshall,* but he had asked his troops to address him simply as *Councilor,* allowing him to maintain the appearance of humility and better conceal the true extent of his ego and ambition. "Deploy a dozen Gorgon Colossi Assault Vehicles to sector seven," he said. "Cut off their retreat and force them toward the ravine."

"At once," replied Argo, tapping a crystal console to relay the commands.

In the distance, Gorgon Colossi, bulky yet agile Atlantean Hover Assault Vehicles, skimmed over the dunes on repulser fields. These vehicles were some of the most sophisticated military technology Atlantis had at its disposal, carrying a crew of three and able to transport up to eight fully equipped soldiers. Their primary armament consisted of twin crystalline laser cannons, capable of delivering high-energy beams, melting most armors. Spry for its weight, and equipped with adaptive camouflage and electronic countermeasures, the Gorgon Colossi excelled in rapid assault and fire support roles, particularly in challenging environments like desert warfare.

"Councilor, intelligence confirms Lemurian plasma rifles among the Kemet forces," reported another officer.

Kairos nodded. "So, the Lemurians are now arming them openly. An interesting choice."

He turned to his left, where two tall Kozars stood beside the command center. The obelisk-like structures pulsed with an inner light, channels of energy coursing through their crystal structures. These ten-story-high sentinels were the lifeblood of Atlantean engineering.

Composed of a rare, quartz-like material infused with rhodium and iridium, the Kozars formed an energy network, a power grid, across Atlantis and its territories. Thousands of them crisscrossed Atlantean lands and beyond.

The Kozars were fed by Nexus Prime, which stood four times as tall as they were in the heart of Atlantis. This colossal crystal structure harnessed energy directly from the Earth's upper mantle, where temperatures were well over a thousand degrees. Its exact composition remained a closely guarded secret, known only to a select few.

From Nexus Prime, through the Kozars, energy flowed to the lumina cores—compact devices ranging from the size of a fingernail to no larger than a hand. These lumina cores functioned like batteries, receiving and storing energy transmitted by the Kozars. Once charged, they powered everything in Atlantean society. From homes and vehicles to the weapons Kairos's soldiers carried, this energy distribution system was the backbone of Atlantean civilization, touching every aspect of their daily lives.

A distant rumble drew Kairos's attention to the horizon. There, Atlantean infantry advanced toward a massive, stepped ziggurat and a series of domes. The stone structure bristled with hidden weapon emplacements, while small, semi-submerged spherical fortifications dotted the landscape like metallic bubbles, their slitted openings concealing plasma weapons.

The Atlantean soldiers, clad in desert camouflage, moved forward. Their helmets had visors with advanced digital interfaces, providing real-time tactical data, environmental readings, and target acquisition assistance. Each trooper carried an LR-7 Vernex, a weapon whose barrel could emit focused beams capable of vaporizing targets in milliseconds.

Explosions erupted as beige-clad Kemet fighters retaliated, their plasma rifles sending bolts of energy toward Atlantean lines. The sands shook with each detonation. Plumes of smoke rose into the sky.

"Councilor, our forces are requesting air support," said Argo. "They're encountering heavy fortifications."

"Dispatch the Skyblade Fighters."

"Yes, Councilor." Argo hastily sent out the orders.

Moments later, Skyblade Fighters streaked overhead. Their forms mimicked a predatory bird. Powered by lumina cores drawing energy from the Kozars via Nexus Prime, these aircraft manipulated gravity fields for silent, high-speed flight and maneuverability. Their hulls were a muted bronze color. The fuselage, crafted from a titanium-aluminum alloy, resisted heat and corrosion, while the quantum fields generated by the cores allowed for near-silent operation.

"Target the enemy's artillery positions," said Kairos over the comms.

"Targets acquired," came a pilot's steady response.

"Engage."

The fighters released PrismTide Missiles. Slender projectiles tipped with warheads. Upon impact, the missiles erupted in a flash, releasing concentrated solar energy that engulfed the target area. Massive chunks of the enemy's fortifications crumbled under the assault. Waves of heat rippled across the battlefield.

"Enemy defenses partially neutralized, with key strongpoints still operational," an operator announced.

"Understood," said Kairos. "Now, have the Novaliths advance to secure those positions."

The Novaliths were massive hovercraft armored with layered crystal plating, and they began their forward movement. Shaped like elongated opals, they stretched nearly sixty yards in length. Their front and rear were rounded, while the sides were linear. Capable of transporting entire platoons, they hovered over the terrain, their underbellies glowing with the pulsating azure energy of the lumina cores.

Atop each Novalith, Atlantean soldiers manned Helios cannons. These golden weapons, easily as long as three men, swiveled on gyroscopic mounts. Their barrels crackled with barely contained laser fire, ready to unleash salvos of energy. Observation domes protruded from the Novaliths' upper decks, giving a 360-degree view of the battlefield, while iris-like hatches along the sides stood ready to deploy troops at a moment's notice.

"Councilor," said a communications officer. "We're intercepting enemy transmissions. They're falling back to defensive positions."

Kairos smirked. "They're running. Press the attack. Cut off their escape routes. Increase the output of the Kozars. Channel additional power to the front lines."

"Augmenting energy flow now," responded a technician.

The Kozars beside them intensified their glow, flashes of energy radiating outward. Across the battlefield, Atlantean weapons and vehicles surged with renewed power.

"Councilor, incoming message from Captain Losath," said the communications officer. "He requests permission to deploy Aelis Artillery."

Kairos considered for a moment. Aelis Artillery were large cannons able to fire energy shells over long distances.

"Permission granted," said Kairos. "Target the enemy's command center."

"Yes, sir."

Far off, the ground shook as these potent weapons commenced firing. Arcs of energy soared through the sky, descending upon the Kemet stronghold. Explosions blossomed along the enemy lines.

Despite the great distance, burning flesh from the battle filled the air and reached even where Kairos stood. Aelis Artillery continued its bombardment, pounding the life out of the Kemet soldiers. The ground trembled. Sand moved beneath the feet of soldiers bracing for impact. Blue-white and searing lines of energy carved paths across the sky. For a moment, time slowed as the energy bolts hung suspended. Beautiful. Lethal.

Then hell erupted.

The Kemet stronghold flared into a cascade of shattering explosions. The air itself seemed to ignite, shockwaves pouring outward, flattening dunes and tossing soldiers like toys.

Novaliths surged forward across the undulating battlefield. They kicked up clouds of sand mingling with the smoke of battle. A barrage of plasma bolts erupted from a hidden Kemet emplacement.

The lead Novalith shuddered as the first bolt hammered into its side. More plasma bolts followed in quick succession. The Novalith's turrets began to rotate, seeking a target.

With a grinding screech of metal, the Novalith's armor buckled. Plates of reinforced alloy peeled away, exposing the vehicle's innards. The crew inside fought to regain control, their communication blaring over the comms inside Kairos's command center.

A final plasma bolt found its mark, piercing deep into the Novalith's core. The vehicle burst into a massive fireball, its fusion reactor breached. The explosion was blinding, vaporizing over forty soldiers inside.

Debris from the destroyed monster of war scattered across the winds, raining down on the dunes. Twisted metal and burning fragments soared through the sky.

As the dust settled, all that remained of the once-mighty Novalith and the platoon it had carried was a smoking crater and a field of scattered, smoldering wreckage.

In the next moment, Kemet artillery shells whistled across the dunes. One landed mere yards from a group of Atlantean soldiers. The explosion sent bodies flying, limbs peppering the blood-soaked sand. Those who survived the initial blast writhed in agony.

As the Kemet artillery continued to rain destruction, a phalanx of Novaliths burst through the enemy's defensive line. The massive vehicles plowed over makeshift barricades.

"Deploy more Skyblades," ordered Kairos.

Seconds later, starfighters streaked across the sky. They released a flurry of projectiles corkscrewing toward targets. Kairos turned his attention to the holographic display before him and watched as the PrismTide missiles found their marks. Each impact erupted, blasting Kemet defenses and opening new avenues for the Atlantean advance. Kemet fortifications crumbled in places, a dome collapsed, a weapons emplacement went dark. Then, a large eruption tore through the main ziggurat, and it fell like a tree cut at its base.

"Enemy command center neutralized," confirmed the operator.

"Excellent," said Kairos. "Begin Phase Two of the operation. I want all resource extraction teams prepared to move in once the area is secured."

"Councilor." Argo walked in Kairos's direction. "I've got some troubling news. I just learned that the fortifications we just destroyed were built by the *Lemurians*."

Kairos shrugged. "What of it?" he asked.

"What of it?" repeated his underling incredulously. "We just destroyed Lemurian assets. This basically amounts to an act of war against this nation."

"Very good. And it's about time," said Kairos grimly.

CHAPTER 21

Councilor Kairos shot Argo a look of disgust while the battle continued raging. "Get some backbone," he said. "So we've committed an act of war against Lemuria. Should that trouble me?"

Argo froze in place, unable to reply.

"I knew about these Lemurian assets going in," continued Kairos. "This was factored into my plans."

"You're clearly unphased by the implications," said Argo, finally finding his voice.

"The possible fallout from this was considered carefully. Sometimes war demands difficult choices. The Lemurians are too passive to pose any real threat. Too *cowardly*. They'll protest, of course, but when it comes to actual conflict, they'll fold like wet parchment. They're avowed pacifists. What will they do, file a protest? What would you have *me* do? Hold their hand and tell them I'm sorry?"

"Of course not, sir."

Kairos turned to face the battlefield, grinning. "The Lemurians will let us trample over their precious 'neutrality' with barely a whimper. They lack the spine for true warfare, though they fight a proxy war with us by funding and supplying Kemet forces, making sure not to get their own hands dirty. The Lemurians lounge by their beaches while Kemet's sons die. Regardless of what Lemuria does, we will crush all opposing forces and secure our dominance. Atlantis will not be denied its destiny."

Argo bowed. "As you say, Councilor."

A sudden flare on the crystalline map caught Kairos's attention. "What's this?"

"Reports of increased resistance in the southern quadrant," explained a technician. "The Kemet forces are regrouping."

"Persistent," said Kairos. "Divert the Gorgon Colossi to intercept. And send a squadron of Stormcallers for aerial support."

The Stormcallers—compact aircraft equipped with Voltex Cannons—did well for crowd control. They unleashed concentrated blasts of wind and energy, scattering enemy formations.

"Orders dispatched," replied the technician.

"Councilor, I have messages from the medical units," said Argo. "Casualties are growing, and they request additional lumina cores for the field medics."

"Authorize it," said Kairos.

As the battle progressed, Kairos's gaze moved between the live feeds and the map, assessing and adapting.

"Councilor," said Argo. "We've intercepted a Lemurian transmission. They're expressing deep concern over our recent actions, sir. They accuse us of aggressive expansion and violation of established territorial agreements. They're not immediately threatening retaliation. Instead, they're urgently requesting a diplomatic summit to discuss the situation."

Kairos scoffed. "Of course they are. A summit. What a joke."

"Sir," continued Argo, "they also mention that if diplomatic efforts fail, they'll be forced to consider more . . . *assertive* measures to maintain regional stability."

"They're bluffing," said Kairos. He paused in thought. "On the other hand," he added, "just in case they grow a spine, it can't hurt to pretend we're up for possible negotiations. That way, we ensure they stay paralyzed long enough for us to achieve our objectives."

He paused. "Prepare a response indicating our willingness to engage in dialogue. But make no commitments and admit to no wrongdoing."

"Right away, Councilor."

Kairos waited for the message to be sent. "And Argo, prepare a dispatch to the High Councilor detailing Lemurian interference. Underscore *their* violation of non-intervention agreements."

He considered. "Also, put in my recommendation that we increase our military presence in Nasavi. Tell them we need to gradually advance our positions closer to Lemurian outposts."

"Yes, sir."

Kairos knew that such aggressive moves overstepped his mandate. But he had found the High Councilor malleable to well-crafted arguments, especially when presented with an irreversible action. This gambit would require Kairos to employ finesse and take some risk, but the potential gains for him were well worth it.

As more orders were relayed, satisfaction coursed through Kairos. He was pushing the boundaries of his role as a government official, even overstepping. True greatness often required bending, if not breaking, the rules.

If his gamble paid off, Atlantis would be several steps closer to achieving its destined dominance. An Atlantis-dominated world was inherently a better one. Better for all.

The sun began its descent, casting an amber glow over the desert. The cool mist continued to swirl around the command center, the whir of machinery and distant sounds of warfare blending together.

The Kemetens had fought valiantly, their tenacity one of the few qualities Kairos found worthy of respect.

"All elements report readiness to proceed to the next objective," reported Argo.

Kairos nodded. Outstanding. The Scarlet Dune Campaign would be a turning point in their expansion efforts.

Amidst the distant echoes of battle, Kairos reflected. The conquest of Kemet was just one step in a grander design. A design requiring a willingness to make difficult decisions. He vowed to be as ruthless as it took. To not allow his objectives to be denied.

There was much to do in this campaign, and he would see it done, regardless of the costs.

CHAPTER 22

Robert adjusted the plasma rifle slung over his shoulder, eyeing the shimmering blue line hovering just above the forest floor. The ethereal arrow curved between redwoods, guiding them deeper into the forest.

"Can't say I'm used to following a glowing path only we can see," said Matt.

Kira brushed aside a low-hanging branch. "It's like augmented reality, but without the glasses. Remarkable doesn't even begin to describe it."

Before they'd left *Tala* and made their way through the woods, the ship had informed them that the translating solution they had applied behind their ears linked them to her. Now, the starship was projecting navigational cues directly into the visual cortexes of its crew, guiding them to where she claimed Thoth could be found.

They trekked onward, the forest alive with sounds of rustling leaves and distant birdcalls. Sunlight filtered through the canopy, sending dappled patterns on the moss-covered ground. Robert hadn't known that redwoods grew in this area at the end of the last Ice Age. In his time, no traces remained of this ancient forest. Not even fossilized pollen in sediment cores or lignin residues in the soil. While he recalled studies of redwood relatives from millions of years ago in Arizona, these trees were far more recent. Where had they gone, and how had the land managed to keep them secret?

"Wait," said Kira. "*Tala* activated this path we're seeing. But how do we turn it off if we want to?"

"Good question," said Robert. "Let's try to ask her. Maybe the gel can also act like a comm. *Tala*," he said loudly, "can you hear me?"

No response. He tried again with the same result.

It didn't make sense that *Tala* could trigger their visual cortex to illuminate a path, that they were somehow connected to her, but they couldn't communicate. Still, he was finding that he often couldn't make sense of how things operated here.

"I have an idea," said Kira. She paused for a moment and her eyes lit up. "It worked," she said excitedly. "I just tried to *will* the arrow to disappear, and it did. No need for *Tala's* direct help at all."

Robert and Matt tried this for themselves and got the same results, to their delight.

"You can toggle it back on with your thoughts, too," announced Robert a few seconds later.

"Now that's some useful tech," said Kira.

They continued to hike, stepping over gnarled roots and walking around giant ferns. A stream gurgled nearby, its waters teeming with fish.

"This forest is breathtaking," whispered Kira. "And life in this time seems... larger than in ours. The trees. The wildlife. Even the towering aliens. All huge."

Robert nodded. "Just remember, while we're admiring the scenery, we can't let our guard down. We need to keep our eyes peeled for predators. With multi-shot rifles, we should be okay, but only if we see a threat coming. We need to watch out for snakes, poisonous spiders, and so on. There were snakes in this time period that could reach twenty-five feet in length. About the same as a really good-sized anaconda."

"At least it's harder for a snake that size to hide from us," said Kira.

A smile flashed across Robert's face. "Now that's what I call a glass-half-full kind of attitude."

They walked on for almost twenty minutes when a rustling halted their conversation. Twigs cracked, sounding from the foliage to their right. Low yelps echoed nearby.

From the shaded brush came a massive beast. A dire wolf, its silvery-gray coat bristling. Standing nearly shoulder-high, its amber eyes gazed upon them.

They all raised their rifles and pointed them at this latest predator. "Is that a dire wolf?" said Kira, much more excited than afraid.

Robert wasn't surprised she had guessed correctly. There was a time when only a small percentage of the population had ever even heard of this extinct creature. But that had changed dramatically eight years earlier, in 2025, when breathless news anchors on every channel trumpeted Colossal Biosciences' audacious claim of "de-extincting" the animal.

Headlines screamed about the birth of three dire wolf pups. Hailed as the first resurrected extinct species ever, their white fur and broad skulls splashed across screens worldwide. The reports explained how scientists had edited gray wolf DNA to incorporate dire wolf genes extracted from their fossilized remains. It'd been an enormous story, almost impossible to miss.

"Let me guess," he said, not taking his eye off the wolf for an instant, and trying not to blink. "You followed the dire wolf de-extinction story back home."

"Who didn't? But I have to say, the lab-grown variety were much cuter."

"The news only showed them when they were *pups*," said Robert in amusement. "As you can see, they get a lot bigger, and meaner. And like the lions we just faced, they hunt in packs."

"Of course they do," replied Kira in exasperation. "I hate to say it, but we should shoot this one before its buddies get here and surround us. Who knows, maybe this one will become the fossil that the future biotech company will use to resurrect the species."

"Yeah," said Matt. "Let's make that happen. Its eyes are freaking me out."

"Let's start with a warning shot," said Robert. He aimed just above the creature and pulled the trigger. A white-hot gout of plasma burst forth, sizzling through the air and striking a tree branch overhead. The branch exploded into a shower of sparks and splinters.

The wolf flinched, hackles rising. With a sharp bark, it turned and darted back into the forest.

"Let's hope that sends the right message," said Kira.

They resumed their pace, quickening slightly. The blue arrow guided them over a babbling brook, the water cold against their boots as they splashed across. They climbed over fallen logs covered in moss and ducked under low-hanging vines covered with flowers.

The forest teemed with life. A herd of deer grazed in a distant meadow. Colorful insects buzzed around blossoms, and in the distance, a beast roared.

A low growl rumbled from behind them. Then another to their left. From the darkness, pairs of glowing eyes materialized. Dire wolves stepped forward. *Lots* of them. Teeth bared, surrounding them.

Robert swept his plasma rifle toward the nearest one, finger hovering over the activation button. The creature snarled. Around them, more wolves accumulated. They seemed *endless*.

Matt's rifle traced an arc as he backed up beside Robert. "This is bad."

"*Disperse!*" bellowed a deep voice from behind them. "*Go on, get out of here!*"

Robert thought these instructions were for them, but miraculously, the wolves' ears twitched and their savage demeanor abruptly changed. They glanced around and then trotted away, reluctantly looking over their shoulders.

"*Go on!*" bellowed the same voice, apparently not fully satisfied with the wolves' retreat. *"Leave now or suffer."*

At that, the wolves broke into a run, disappearing into the forest as fast as possible.

Robert lowered his rifle as a man on a slope behind them walked quickly in their direction. Clad in green flowing robes, he raised his staff. It was crowned with that glowing crystal orb.

"Thoth!" said Robert excitedly, and in that moment the blue arrow in his vision vanished. They had basically arrived at his home.

Thoth strode closer, lowering his staff. "How did you find me?"

"*Tala,*" replied Kira. "She guided us here. Told us you'd have food and water. We're pretty desperate for a meal. Also, she wants you to come back on board the ship. She claims you'll help stop the war between Lemuria and Atlantis, alongside the Resistance."

He wrinkled his brow. "So, she finally decided to have a real conversation with you. It's about time. She's unpredictable. I thought if I abandoned you, it might force her hand. Make her less . . . shy. You know what they say, the only thing harder to understand than a Quantum Resonance Consciousness is Atlantean bureaucracy."

"Of course," said Robert with a wry smile. "Who hasn't heard *that* old saying?"

"Welcome to what I call Soulwood," said Thoth, ignoring the sarcasm. "A part of the forest whose beauty knows no equal. And you're basically in my backyard. Follow me, and we'll get you fed in no time."

He led them through a thicket that finally gave way to a meadow bathed in the sun. Wildflowers swayed in the breeze. "What's with the Dr. Dolittle routine?" said Kira, stealing the question that Robert had been on the verge of asking.

"The what?"

"Can you really talk to animals?" she asked, getting to the point. "I mean, it sure seemed that you just talked those wolves into leaving. Maybe you *are* Harry Potter, after all." Then, obviously remembering where she was, she hastily added, "And no, I don't expect you to know who that is."

"Whatever you did," said Robert, "thanks. You extricated us from quite a mess. But how did you do it?"

"If you'll indulge me, I'd rather explain that later. First, I want to know everything that happened to you since I left. What did you think of *Tala*?"

"Remarkable," said Robert. "Astonishing. I don't have the words. They don't make starships or crystalline beings like that anymore."

"Her capabilities are truly extraordinary," agreed Thoth. "Given her recent time travel trick, even more than I knew. She's incomparable. But we haven't collaborated in some time. I look forward to doing so again. I'd like to think this will put us a step closer to making a real difference."

He parted a pair of branches covered in thick leaves. "We've arrived."

Nestled against the edge of the clearing stood Thoth's home. A dome-like structure, surprisingly large, half submerged in the ground. Its rounded wooden roof was masterfully crafted, with beams interwoven like the petals of a flower. A stone chimney rose from the top, wisps of smoke curling upward, giving the whole place the appearance of a giant mushroom.

"Very nice," said Matt.

"Thank you. It's simple but sufficient. Nothing like the temple I once presided over in Atlantis, but a lot cozier."

Beside the dwelling lay a smooth stone platform with geometric markings etched into its surface. It looked like a landing pad.

Thoth glanced at the pad. "That's for my occasional visitors. One never knows who might drop by."

They approached the entrance; a sturdy door carved with more geometric symbols. Thoth pushed it open, and warm air enveloped them. Inside, the dwelling was spacious yet homey. Windows encircled the room just above ground level. Shafts of light beamed through the glass, illuminating the interior.

A fire crackled in a grand hearth, above which hung a cast-iron pot emitting an inviting aroma. The walls were lined with shelves holding ancient scrolls, crystal vials, and peculiar artifacts. Plush cushions and low wooden tables formed a seating area atop woven rugs.

"Please, make yourselves comfortable," said Thoth, gesturing to the cushions.

Robert settled onto one, the fabric soft beneath him. Empty, hand-carved bowls were beside each seat. "Did you know we were coming?"

Thoth stirred the pot, a grin on his face. "Let's just say I thought *Tala* might guide you here. Better to have food ready, just in case. I knew that whatever food she might have had onboard turned to dust ages ago."

Thoth was aware his guests were ravenous and plied them with food and water for almost thirty minutes while they recounted their experiences since he had left, including their entire conversation with *Tala*.

When they were done, there was a long silence. Thoth digested their story while they digested his food.

Finally, the Hierophant turned to Robert. "Remember on the ship when I told you the Vesh'tar's energy yearns to connect with your essence?"

"What about it?"

"This yearning seems to have grown stronger. I'm not offering my Vesh'tar to you, but I thought you should know. In due time, when the stars align, I suspect that a staff like this will merge with your very being. You possess certain gifts, dormant though they may be."

"Are you suggesting Robert is some sort of Jedi Knight?" asked Matt.

Thoth raised one eyebrow questioningly.

"A fictional character," explained Robert. "With certain abilities, including influencing the actions of animals, as you seem to have done."

"I can't comment on that comparison, Robert. All I can say is that when you truly understand the powers of the Vesh'tar, you'll comprehend yourself in ways you never thought possible."

"But none of this requires magic or mysticism, right?" asked Robert. "As a scientist, that would shatter everything I believe in. We have an often-used saying in my time: any sufficiently advanced technology is indistinguishable from magic. Is that the case here?"

"The saying you quoted describes the situation exactly. No magic involved. Its powers simply emerge when human heart and intent is focused through ancient Atlantean technology. It's a magnifier, of sorts. I willed for the wolves to leave you alone, and the Vesh'tar amplified my will and transmitted it into primitive brains. Nothing magical, although I couldn't begin to explain the science behind it."

Robert opened his mouth to ask another question when a whirring sound cut through the quiet. The windows rattled slightly.

"What's happening?" asked Kira, looking at the ceiling.

Robert stood, moving to one of the windows. "A ship is landing on the pad."

Outside, an almond-shaped vessel descended onto the platform, the ship's engines emitting a soft, purring sound as it settled.

Thoth's expression was now grim. "A Lemurian government ship."

The ship's ramp extended, touching down with a thud. Two men in midnight blue battlesuits descended first, their rifles—similar in design to Robert's—swept the area. Once they signaled the all-clear, a tall man draped in elegant robes emerged from within the vessel. Behind him followed a young woman, maybe in her mid-thirties. She scanned the surroundings. Four more soldiers trailed her.

Robert couldn't take his eyes off this woman. It wasn't her beauty, though she possessed that in abundance. It was something else entirely. She seemed to glow with an inner strength, a power radiating from her very being. Robert couldn't pinpoint its source or explain how or why it was there, but its presence was undeniable. She was like an angel, if Robert ever saw one. A confident one at that, too.

He stared at her with his mouth open, mesmerized by her aura.

But who was she? Was she a friend? Or was she dangerous?

And what could explain his powerful reaction to her? Was he mesmerized by her because she radiated an innate purity and sense of decency?

Or had he become more like a helpless mouse, mesmerized by a snake as it prepared to strike?

CHAPTER 23

Advisor Elowin Balivae
Thoth's Home
Soulwood Thicket
Location: Southwest Nasavi

Elowin Balivae stepped off the ship's ramp, the cool air brushing against her face. Elder Kona Makelo descended ahead of her, his robes flowing with each step.

As they began their walk, six figures fell into formation around them. These military men wore Lemurian battlesuits, their helmets with semi-transparent visors. Each soldier carried a plasma rifle, held at the ready. These men were part of the Protectorate, the most highly trained, elite members of the Lemurian military.

As they walked along the stone path toward Thoth's home, faces peered through the windows. She straightened her posture and kept her gaze forward. She was an Advisor, after all. She'd been on the receiving end of so many stares that it no longer bothered her.

Rounding the corner, they approached carved stone steps leading to the entrance, which opened just before she arrived. There stood Thoth, her old friend. His long white hair framed a face lined with age yet illuminated by bright, emerald eyes. He was dressed in his customary green robe over simple linen garments.

"Elder Kona Makelo," he said by way of greeting. "Advisor Balivae," he added warmly. "What a pleasant surprise. Leave your soldiers outside, please, and join us."

They entered and closed the door behind them. "Allow me to introduce my friends," said Thoth, motioning to his trio of guests. "These are Robert, Kira, and Matt."

Elowin's gaze met Robert's, and for a moment, time stood still. He was tall with rugged features, his clothing foreign. Materials and styles unlike any she'd seen. Something stirred within her, an unfamiliar flutter.

She bowed. "Nice to meet you," she said, then looked away, a faint warmth rising to her cheeks.

Why am I feeling this way? She thought, but shook it away.

Thoth's eyes flickered with amusement as he no doubt observed the awkward exchange. "Please, make yourselves comfortable," he said, pointing toward a seating area covered with woven cushions and low tables.

Elowin settled beside Kona, wondering who these new people were with clothes so strange. Kira's attire clung to her form, constricting. She wondered if it would feel uncomfortable, even suffocating. She had trouble getting any read on the young man named Matt, who looked Lemurian. Robert, on the other hand, exuded mystery. He had an aura of quiet confidence, of decisiveness and competence, and his eyes gleamed with intelligence.

"To what do I owe the pleasure of this visit?" said Thoth when he was also seated.

Elowin exchanged a brief glance with Kona before speaking. "The situation with Atlantis is getting worse. War is looking ever more inevitable."

Thoth sighed. "I'm not surprised. That has been the trajectory for some time."

"Atlantis is more deceptive than ever," added Kona. "More manipulative. And less trustworthy. A nightmare combination."

"They fabricated provocations with Kemet to justify their invasion," said Elowin. "And they're doing the same now, trying to paint Lemuria as the aggressor. We despise war, yes, but they're making a grave mistake by so grossly underestimating us as an adversary. Yes, we tend to be pacifists, but we've also been realists for some time. We live in a potentially dangerous world. In a potentially dangerous galaxy, if these alien races ever decide to risk being outwardly hostile. We're far more formidable than Atlantis knows, more evenly matched."

She frowned. "Which in many ways is the worst-case scenario. A war between evenly matched forces only ends in one way."

"And your job is to prevent this from happening at all costs," said Thoth.

"Yes."

"How do you plan to do that?"

She produced her most charming smile. "Step one is to visit you, esteemed Hierophant, and get some advice. There must be those in Atlantis's military and government who seek peace. But I find myself lacking the means to reach them directly."

Thoth smiled. "So . . . more than advice. You'd also like me to help set up meetings with the right people."

"Yes."

"Why isn't the Circle of 12 setting them up?" asked Thoth. He stared at Elowin a brief second longer, his expression hardening. "You did it again, Elowin, didn't you? You're taking on the whole world by yourself."

"Well, not entirely by myself. I'm here asking for your help, after all."

"Nice deflection, but I'm right, aren't I?"

Elowin sighed. "Pretty much. The Circle have given me two weeks to prevent the looming war. They believe I have no chance, so they aren't supporting me. I was lucky to get the two weeks."

"I'm so sorry it's come to this, and I'll help you in any way I can, of course. I can get you an audience with those in Atlantis's highest echelons. But don't bring me up while you're there. And you know better than to trust everything you hear. Or *anything*, for that matter."

"Thank you," said Elowin. "And believe me, my eyes are wide open. I'll work with those I can sense really do want peace. As for those I sense are lying, I'll use my time with them to set subtle traps, to gather evidence, to get them to expose their schemes without even realizing they're doing it."

"If you want to unravel schemes," said Thoth, "I can help you there, too. *Especially* there. I can put you in contact with the perfect person to help you get evidence of Atlantis's true intentions. Aethor Daedalus. The son of Kairos Daedalus."

Elowin jerked back. To her, the Daedalus family was a major threat not only to Lemurian life, but to all life. "You must be aware of Kairos's savagery, right? He's the High Marshall of the Atlantean military, the main driving force for the coming war. I've heard rumors . . . rumors I believe to be true . . . that he's had any number of political rivals murdered over the years in ways that look like accidents or suicides."

"Kairos is a despicable war-monger without doubt. I'm not sending you to him. Aethor despises his father, and what is becoming of Atlantis. He has access to the corridors of power. He could get what you need."

"And you trust him?"

Thoth nodded. "For now, yes. But you shouldn't trust anyone entirely. Still, he has aided the Resistance before, and at the moment, his motivations align with ours. He may even get you access to the High Councilor when you decide the time is right."

Elowin glanced at Robert and his companions. They had remained silent throughout, but they were listening with a great intensity. Something told her they were more than mere bystanders. Perhaps allies in this unfolding struggle.

She returned her attention to Thoth. "I came to you for guidance. I'd be a fool not to accept it now, despite my innate distrust of anyone named Daedalus. But I don't have much time. How soon can you set up a meeting with Aethor?"

"I won't know until I try, but I'll get on it right away and set things up as soon as I can. I'll contact you while you're in the air to let you know what happened."

Elowin stood, her attention falling on Robert for a moment, then back to Thoth. "How can I ever thank you enough?"

"No need. We share the same goal. And I have great affection for you, as you know."

Elowin hesitated. "Thoth, there's something else. I've heard highly troubling rumors about Nexus Prime. It's not just a power source, is it? They're creating a way to weaponize it."

"It's been weaponized for decades, even though only a handful of people in the world are aware of it. Even most of the higher-ups in the Atlantean government aren't in the know. Nexus Prime can create a devastating beam of sound and energy waves. It's been tested, but never used in actual battle. It's a weapon of last resort. At full power, it could obliterate continents. The Resistance has been trying to obtain concrete evidence of its capabilities, and operational specs, for years. All attempts have failed. And with each failure, we've lost good people."

"Do you believe I'll have the chance to get the evidence you've been after?"

"Not really, no. But your diplomatic mission could provide cover for our ongoing efforts in that regard. We've been lying low recently, allowing suspicions to fade, but your presence in Atlantis may give us the opening we need to finally succeed."

They spoke for a few more minutes before Elowin finally said her goodbyes. The soldiers led her and Kona up the ship's ramp and the vessel's systems spooled up, piercing the stillness with the whir of its engines.

Kona placed his hand on the young Advisor's back. "Are you ready for this, Elowin?"

"Not even close," she replied. "But when was the last time I let *that* stop me?"

CHAPTER 24

Robert stood by the window of Thoth's home and Elowin climbed aboard her vessel, which quickly ascended into the sky.

He hadn't been able to take his eyes off her, and now that she was out of view, he couldn't get her out of his mind. He now felt certain she was an angel rather than a snake in disguise. An angel who exuded empathy and compassion, and who'd taken on the burden of saving the world all by herself.

Robert had found the exchange between Elowin and Thoth fascinating, almost as fascinating as he found Elowin all by herself.

Although his research primarily centered on Lemuria, known to the Hopi as Kasskara, and the lost starship, Robert had also devoted considerable time studying Atlantis. Not just studying, but challenging his peers with controversial theories. There was an area in the mid-Atlantic, centered around the Azores, that was as vast as Greenland. Science, he'd insist, had proven the existence of continental rock beneath the waves, land that was once above water. He argued that core samples taken over a half mile below the ocean floor proved his case.

The dramatic rise in sea levels of over four hundred feet worldwide, in the age he found himself in now, had played a fundamental role in not only submerging the fabled continent of Atlantis but also millions of square miles of coastal lands worldwide. In Robert's view, transverse ridges and fracture zones on the ocean floor were not just the result of plate tectonics, but the scars left by the catastrophic sinking of Atlantis.

"Robert?" said Kira. "Robert?" she said again, and he realized she had been trying to get his attention for several seconds. "Are you okay?"

"Sorry, just distracted. I'm fine."

"You practically froze when that woman entered the room," noted Matt. "I mean, she was pretty hot, but no one is *that* hot."

Robert sighed. "I'm going to pretend you didn't just say that, Matt."

"Me too," said Kira.

Across the room, Thoth stood before a crystalline console, deep in conversation with someone at the end of the line, although too hushed for his guests to make out what he was saying. When Thoth concluded the exchange, the console folded back into itself like melting ice.

Thoth tapped it lightly. "I've set up some meetings for Elowin. I've also reached out to a trusted group of guardians to provide assistance. They'll be joining us soon."

"Does Elowin have any chance of succeeding?" asked Robert.

"There's always a chance. Especially for her. She's a very rare soul. A game changer. Or, as I like to call it, a systems buster. She has an aura unlike any other. And while some are immune, many find themselves drawn to her. She can often open minds and hearts in ways others can't. She can evoke strong emotions in ways that are varied and unpredictable. In ways that, to those unaffected, are hard to understand."

Not that hard, thought Robert to himself, but he didn't respond.

Thoth moved to a carved wooden chest and retrieved another emerald robe, layering it over his current one. Gripping the Vesh'tar, Thoth closed his eyes in concentration. He brought the staff close to his lips and began to whisper. When he finished, he straightened himself. "Well then," he said, fastening the clasps on his robe. "Are you ready?"

"Ready for what?" asked Robert.

"Our journey to Atlantis. We can't leave everything to Elowin, or even to her and the Resistance together. *Tala* believes you three will be instrumental in preventing this war, and I plan to operate as if she's right."

Robert exchanged worried glances with his two companions. "I thought you weren't welcome there."

"I have my ways," said Thoth. "And *Tala* will help. She's the most capable ship in the Lemurian fleet, but she can alter her energy signature to read as an ordinary freighter."

"And Atlantis will let her in?" asked Kira.

"Trade continues between the two nations. At least for now. *Tala* will appear to be nothing but a supply freighter built to move goods from one place to another. We can pose as simple merchants trying to do our jobs."

Thoth paused, observing the blank expressions on his guests' faces.

He smiled. "Excellent. I can see you're bursting with enthusiasm. I guess it's settled then."

None of the three returned his smile as they tried to process what a trip to Atlantis might have in store.

"If we do make it there," said Robert, "what will we be doing? The Atlanteans will figure out that we're fish out of water in minutes."

"I'm aware of the challenges. I have faith we can overcome them. As for what we'll do when we get there, we can discuss that on the way. For now, let's return to *Tala* so we can get started."

Saying this, he led them out of the door, and they began their brief journey back to the ship.

"Tell me," he said once they were underway, "do politics and war still plague humanity in your time?"

Looking at their grim expressions, Thoth nodded before anyone replied. "I see. So humanity hasn't learned. Perhaps has even forgotten the past entirely. If we can't stop this conflict, the ripples through time will only grow more devastating. Perhaps even create a catastrophe capable of wiping out humanity in one swift stroke."

They continued their conversation and soon came to the clearing where the ship had landed. They rounded a final group of trees and *Tala* finally came into view.

And so did five massive Anunnaki warriors, lying in wait below her. All were clad in armor and clutched weapons humming with energy.

Robert and Kira both extended their plasma rifles as if facing a pack of wolves, their hearts crashing against their chests.

Thoth reached over and gently pushed their rifles lower, shaking his head.

The lead Anunnaki stepped forward. "Hello, old man," he said to Thoth. "Shall we finish negotiating our price?"

"Nice try, Ishar," replied Thoth. "We *have* finished, as you well know. I'm counting on you to honor our terms."

He turned to the trio beside him. "This is a group you've already met. I've hired them as mercenaries until further notice. For now, they'll be guarding us."

Without waiting for a response, Thoth walked closer to the ship's hull with his staff and looked up. "*Tala*, would you kindly lower the ramp?" he said. "You win. I'll do as you ask. I'll awaken and activate my Resistance comrades."

The ramp remained stubbornly closed. "Come on, *Tala*. We're here so you can take us to Atlantis. We're going to end this war. Or die trying."

With that, the ramp appeared and extended to the ground.

Thoth turned to his human companions. "Here we go. You'll soon be learning why some secrets were meant to stay buried."

CHAPTER 25

Robert sat on a bench seat behind a large table in the starship's main cabin. His back rested against a smooth, metallic wall. At the moment, the ship flew above the clouds, journeying toward Atlantis. Matt and Kira were beside him, and Thoth was in a lone seat at the end of the table.

Robert was anxious and giddy at the same time. Within him, scholarly excitement mixed with pure, childlike wonder. Atlantis. Along with Lemuria, this lost civilization had also consumed countless hours of his research. Now, he wasn't just reading about it or theorizing. He was actually going there.

Would Plato's descriptions prove accurate? He wondered.

Would he find the concentric rings of water and land, the great harbor, the temples described in ancient texts?

As an archaeologist, he'd spent his career piecing together humanity's past from fragments. Broken pottery. Weathered inscriptions. Crumbling ruins. Cryptic writings. This was different. He wasn't just going to study the remnants; he was going to see Atlantis in its prime.

He glanced at his companions, wondering if they could possibly understand the magnitude of what they were about to witness. Atlantis, the crown jewel of ancient mysteries. He, and the rest of those on board, were about to step into its living, breathing reality.

Across from Robert, the Anunnaki warriors occupied most of the available space. Their larger-than-life bodies made the cabin cramped. Unable to use the chairs or benches meant for smaller beings, the Anunnaki sat on the floor, leaning against the bulkheads.

"So you really intend to stop a war, Thoth?" said Ishar, the leader of the alien hired hands. He had a scar running across his beard. "Why?" he added in contempt. "The Anunnaki crafted humanity long ago, but you continue to be a disappointment. Especially in your weak, pacifistic outlook. If a war is to happen, let it. Battles breed courage. We spliced aggression genes into your DNA when you were hopelessly out-armed by every creature on this planet. Our gene engineering was designed to spur humanity on so you could better defend yourselves.

So you could be courageous and strong of heart. Apparently, even with our help, your species is . . . lacking."

"You Anunnaki love reminding us of your meddling, don't you?" said Thoth, trying to sound bored. "Lacking, Ishar? Hardly. We have more courage and heart than you could ever comprehend. And we've become the apex predator on Earth. Not *thanks* to the Anunnaki tampering with our genome, but *despite* it. We always had intelligence and a warrior spirit. You just saddled us with mindless aggression, also, with bloodlust, which plagues us to this day."

Ishar snorted. "The Anunnaki are the epitome of strength. Just because you didn't have it in you to follow our path, don't make excuses."

At this, the other crimson-bearded warriors raised their fists in unison. "Glory to Anu!"

Anu—still their king? thought Robert. Anu was the sky god, ruler of the gods, according to Mesopotamian mythology. If this being were truly alive now, that meant these beings lived for millennia on end, as the Sumerian writings claimed.

Thoth sighed. "You're the epitome and self-delusion, Ishar. And your species needs to change its ways. The Anunnaki's unauthorized gene modifications of our ancient hominid ancestors, and other crimes the Anunnaki have committed, will catch up to you one day. My guess is that at some point in the future, Earth and the entire galactic community will decide they've had enough of your meddling."

Surprisingly, Ishar smiled. "We shall see, Hierophant. We shall see. But I think this is enough. Why trade barbs when we have a temporary alliance? We aren't your enemy at the moment. In fact, you're paying us to be your ally. So perhaps we should put our animosity aside for the sake of the mission."

"Agreed," said Thoth.

"Who are your comrades?" said Ishar. "If we're to protect them, we should at least know their names."

"Fair enough. Robert, Matt, Kira—meet Ishar, Mardak, Ashtur, Enkuul, and Nuradu. They're the finest security of their kind. When compensated appropriately, their skills are unmatched."

Nuradu gave a slight nod.

Robert smiled. "I've read extensively about your people."

Nuradu stared down at him in contempt. "I've read extensively about my people too. So what?"

Robert blinked, unsure how to respond. Kira glanced at him, eyebrows knitting together.

Tala's disembodied voice rang out through the cabin. "Apologies for the interruption. Per protocol, I must inform you that I'm confined to the bridge to maintain optimal flight operations."

"Thank you, *Tala*," said Thoth. "Please focus on piloting. We'll handle matters here unless an emergency arises."

"Understood, Hierophant," she replied. "Redirecting all auxiliary systems to flight control."

Matt leaned over to Robert. "Does she always announce her limitations like that?"

Robert shrugged. "She's following protocol, I suppose."

The lighting inside the cabin shifted to a shade of red. *Tala's* voice filled the cabin once more. "Priority alert. Military presence detected. Visual confirmation available on the main display."

Thoth stood and moved quickly toward the bridge. "Show us."

A surge of adrenaline hit Robert. He, Kira, and Matt hurried behind Thoth while the Anunnaki remained seated. As they entered the bridge, the main holodisplay projected an image of the zoomed-in landscape below, showing a massive Lemurian outpost. One of its walls stretched along a wide river that reminded Robert of the Mississippi.

Lemurian soldiers manned turrets that looked like exotic cannon emplacements, while more troops patrolled the walls in battlesuits. Inside the walls, mushroom-shaped buildings covered in vines rose into the sky, with empty markets and shops lining the streets. Several ships like Elowin's were parked in what looked like a landing zone.

From this high, Robert could see this land's eastern coast, mostly rolling sand dunes and scattered trees. About a mile east of the Lemurian position, Robert spotted what could be an Atlantean army.

Thousands of soldiers were in formation, their golden banners and white crystal-marked standards catching the sun. The army had positioned itself closer to the eastern shoreline, where teams of builders were putting up strange crystal obelisks about twice as tall as the soldiers themselves.

Behind their lines, stone blocks floated through the air without any visible support, assembling themselves into walls and buildings. Workers stood at metal control boxes, their hands guiding the impossible construction. The whole site stretched for a considerable distance along the coast, full of rising temples, plazas, and columns covered in interesting patterns.

"Atlanteans," said Thoth, eyes narrowed. "My people. And they're amassing close to the Lemurian outpost. We may have less time than I thought."

Kira studied the screen. "These Atlanteans are using extraordinary tech. But they're making mistakes. Their defensive turrets, for example, are staggered for wide coverage, but they leave blind spots on the lower perimeter, which the Lemurians could exploit to get past their defenses."

Robert turned to her. Who was this woman? Just when he thought she couldn't surprise him any further. "How are you able to size up military tactics so expertly?" he asked.

"I've told you before. My father was a Marine before he became a geologist. Taught me everything he knew."

That might be true, but Robert was certain of one thing: she had never told him this before. He would have definitely remembered. Not that he would call her on it right now. He had realized for some time now that there was more to Kira Shelton than met the eye. He just hadn't realized how *much* more.

Tala moved lower, giving them a clearer view of the hovering blocks assembling themselves into walls and buildings.

Robert motioned toward the stones. "Anti-gravity?"

Thoth shook his head. "No. Vibrational energies. I don't understand the tech myself."

He pulled out a communication device from his robe, the same one he had spoken into at his home, "I need to get your full name, and Kira's and Matt's as well, so I can have you put into the Atlantean system."

Robert nodded and provided this information.

Thoth spoke into the clear device. "Nehemiah? I need three names entered immediately into the Atlantean Citizen Registry. Also, we'll need *Tala*'s energy signature reconfigured to match an Opalith freighter. Her new name will be *Nautilos*."

A voice replied through the device. "Standing by."

Thoth provided his guests' names. "Register them as crew members of the *Nautilos*. Supply vessel classification. And note in their records that their names were legally altered through the High Arbitrator's Chamber."

"Understood. Recalibrating ship's energy signature now." There was a brief pause. "We'll list them as transporting Opalith crystals from the Kanaloa Mines in Eastern Lemuria."

"Perfect," said Thoth.

"I'm entering them into the ACR now. I've listed them under Transport Division, Class Three clearance, with authorized access to Spaceport Lios in Poseidia. Adding standard biometric markers and temporal timestamps . . . done. They're in the system, and *Tala*'s signature now reads as the *Nautilos*."

"Excellent work," said Thoth. The device dissolved like frost in an oven before he slipped it back into his robe.

Kira watched the screen. "That's a sizable force."

"Too large for a mere exercise," said Thoth.

"Do they know we're here?" asked Matt.

"They do. Well, they know that the *Nautilos* is here. But we still have to proceed with caution."

Robert studied the display. Several military-looking aircraft were now flying toward them.

"We should all assume positions at the bridge stations," said Thoth. "Just sit there as human props and act like you know what you're doing. *Tala* will handle the technicalities."

Robert settled into the captain's chair, studying the array of holographic displays materializing off the seat's armrests. Atlantean symbols and readouts scrolled across multiple screens. He was surprised at just how natural sitting in command felt to him. "I don't know why," he said in confusion, "but this really feels . . . right."

"Good," said Thoth. "I'm not surprised. And there may come a time when you're in charge of directing *Tala* yourself."

He was about to say more when *Tala's* voice filled the bridge. "Two Stormcaller-class vessels are approaching rapidly. Displaying specifications now."

The main screen shifted to show sleek aircraft with swept-back wings resembling a manta ray, about thirty feet long. As expected, the specifications revealed that they were heavily armed and dangerous. Thoth instructed the ship to keep her defensive systems offline, and not to deploy weaponry under any circumstances.

Seconds later, one of the incoming aircraft hailed them.

Thoth swiveled to face Robert. "You need to respond."

"Why not you?"

"Their computers will recognize my voice. So just repeat what I say. *Tala*, make sure my voice doesn't get picked up in the transmission. And only let them see Robert's face. His clothing is odd and might arouse suspicions."

"Acknowledged," said *Tala*.

Robert rested his arms on the armrests and lifted his chin. "Let's do this!" he said, practicing projecting the confidence he knew he would need to project during the coming interaction.

Thoth gave him quick instructions on how to operate the comm, and a thin black microphone arm extended from the console just after, curving up toward Robert's face. The viewscreen flickered to life, revealing an Atlantean pilot in a helmet, the visor black. "Unidentified vessel, state your designation and purpose."

"This is the *Nautilos*," whispered Thoth just out of sight of the camera. "En route from the Kanaloa Mines to Spaceport Lios."

Robert cleared his throat and pressed a send button on his console. "This is the *Nautilos*," he repeated. "En route from the Kanaloa Mines to Spaceport Lios."

"Your energy signature is irregular," said the pilot. "Explain."

"Our Opalith crystal processors experienced some fluctuations during transport," said Robert, repeating Thoth's words.

Another voice crackled over the channel. "Submit to a full scan, *Nautilos*."

"Negative on the scan request. Our cargo is sensitive. We're authorized by Transport Division, Class Three clearance."

"Stand by," a pilot said.

The seconds stretched. Matt tapped his fingers nervously on the console.

"They're verifying our credentials," explained Thoth. "Stay calm."

The pilot returned. "Credentials confirmed, *Nautilos*. You're cleared to proceed to Spaceport Lios. Maintain your current trajectory. We'll escort you to the perimeter."

Robert exhaled and parroted Thoth for the last time. "Understood. Maintaining course."

The transmission ended. The Stormcallers flanked their ship, matching speed. They flew over what would one day become the East Coast of America—now Nasavi—and out over the Atlantic Ocean. Within minutes, The Stormcallers banked away, their ships arcing westward back toward Nasavi leaving them alone as a distant landmass emerged on the horizon.

Thoth nodded at Robert. "Well done. Watch everything I do as acting captain of this ship as carefully as you can. Try to learn as much as you can, in case you ever need to take over."

"I will," said Robert.

"We're approaching Atlantis's western coastline," announced *Tala*. "Atlantean settlements are visible ahead."

The holodisplay shifted to display sprawling cities filled with gleaming towers and other fascinating architecture. Roads wound through the landscape like red yarn, connecting hubs of activity. Vehicles of various shapes and sizes moved about on the ground, hovering or filling the skies.

Robert's eyes widened. "Incredible!"

Matt leaned forward. "No doubt."

"It's *breathtaking*," said Kira. "A true paradise." Her awestruck expression was quickly replaced by a deep frown. "Which makes what is happening even more tragic. What does it say about human nature that even when poverty has been vanquished, man's warlike instincts can still prevail?"

"Perhaps spurred on with some extraterrestrial manipulations," said Thoth. "Although that remains to be seen. Regardless, you're absolutely right. It's sickening how mankind often continues to be its own worst enemy."

Minutes passed as they flew over the continent. The sheer scale of Atlantean civilization unfolded beneath them. Cities teeming with life. Vast agricultural fields. Colossal structures. White pillars rose from terraced hills, supporting buildings cascading down to the shoreline. Domes of polished copper glinted, their weathered green patina creating a pronounced distinction against the marble and limestone. Markets and courtyards swarmed with people, while robed figures moved through streets radiating out from central temples like spokes on a wheel.

Beyond the cities, fields dotted the vista, separated by irrigation channels. Massive granaries and storage facilities littered the countryside, and here and there, monuments of impossible scale loomed in the far reaches. Obelisks pierced the clouds. Step pyramids dominated the plains.

"*Tala*, increase speed," ordered Thoth. "We need to arrive in minutes rather than hours."

"Understood," replied the ship.

Tala flew upward, climbing higher into the clouds. The city and land below blurred until vanishing completely, replaced by white cloud cover stretching to the horizon.

Just three minutes later, they began their descent. As they broke through the cloud layer, their destination appeared. An island rose from the sea shortly beyond a coastline. Was this the east coast of Atlantis?

Thoth spoke to *Tala*. "Adjust course. Bypass Spaceport Lios. Set destination to the coordinates of the Resistance."

"Adjusting course."

Robert pointed to the island off the coast. It was a series of perfect rings, each band of land and water alternating inward like the layers of a larger-than-life archery target.

"Thoth, is that what I think it is?" he asked incredulously.

"Indeed. The capital of Atlantis. Easily the most important metropolis in the world."

CHAPTER 26

The concentric rings of the island just off the coast of Atlantis unfolded beneath them. Three perfect circles of land and water interlaced, connected by grand bridges spanning the canals. Towering statues guarded the entrances—colossal figures carved from stone.
"What's the capital's name?" asked Robert.
"Poseidia," replied Thoth.
"Poseidia," he repeated, letting it roll off his tongue. It was a name that resonated with him. "It's exactly as a famous philosopher named Plato will describe it more than ten thousand years from now."
"I wish my dad could see this," said Matt. "I wish my dad could see *everything* we've seen. It would mean so much to him." His eyes became moist. "And I wish I could apologize to him for thinking he was a fool for holding the beliefs he held."
Kira instinctively gave him a hug, as if sensing he needed one badly.
"Your dad won't see what you're seeing," said Robert, "but we will get back home. I know it. When we do, you can describe everything you've seen, and apologize."
Kira separated from the young man, who was sad and happy at the same time. He nodded at both Kira and Robert. "Thanks," he said, using the back of his hand to wipe away tears that had just formed. "And sorry. I know it's not the time for this."
"You can't control when bottled-up emotions escape," said Kira. "Since we arrived at this time, Robert and I have been feeling the weight of emotion too. It's impossible not to. The human heart and mind can't prepare itself for the physical, cultural, and psychological transposition we've undergone."
Matt nodded and walked closer to the main viewscreen, as if he wanted to shift gears away from himself and back to the wonders they were seeing. "Those bridges are amazing."
"I was thinking the same," said Kira, deciding to let him move on rather than address his inner feelings in more depth. He was right, now wasn't a great time. "I'm seeing characteristics of both copper and gold, but there's something else. The way the light catches on it suggests crystalline integration, maybe some form of stabilized quartz

matrix. And to get structural integrity at that length you'd need . . . I don't know . . . some kind of polymetallic compound, perhaps. One with some kind of molecular reinforcement."

"Impressively accurate analysis," said Thoth. "It's called Oralcim, a metal unique to Atlantis."

"Synthetic?" she asked.

"Yes. Like all materials in the three major civilizations of our time, Atlantis, Lemuria, and Kemet, it's designed to gradually break down without harming the natural world. Every hundred years or so, we must restore most of our structures. It's a cycle of renewal that's been in place for many centuries."

Matt pointed at a massive pyramid in the center of the island capital, crowned by a shiny yellow material. "Is that gold?"

Robert guessed that it was. The great pyramids in Egypt were also thought to have had capstones made of gold.

Thoth nodded. "Gold is one of the most conductive metals in existence. Both electrically and energetically. Its atomic structure allows for nearly perfect electron transfer. When properly refined and shaped, it becomes an ideal conduit for certain frequencies. The Atlanteans understand this quite well. The pyramid is fed by Nexus Prime and channels energy across Atlantis through Kozars."

"What are Kozars?" asked Robert.

Thoth gestured to obelisks spread fairly evenly throughout the city. "Energy relays that distribute power. They form a network connecting all regions. They're powered by Nexus Prime."

"Right," said Kira. "Nexus Prime. Which you told Elowin can be used as the most powerful weapon on the planet."

"I'm afraid so. Glad you were paying attention."

"That's something I wish I hadn't heard," said Kira with a scowl. "But no use dwelling on it now." She motioned at the pyramid in the center of the island. "That thing is *enormous*. It dwarfs everything else."

"In the past, students would gather there to seek enlightenment and ponder sacred teachings. It has a network of crystals that helps power our cities now, but their true purpose was spiritual awakening. Sadly, this tradition is no longer practiced, for political reasons."

Robert had studied Thoth, the mythological figure, fairly extensively. Legends suggested he was immortal, a keeper of ancient wisdom who had walked the earth for countless ages. Looking at him now, Robert saw the weight of centuries in his eyes. But how old was he really?

"If I may ask," said Robert, "will you tell us your age?"

Thoth flashed a fleeting smile. "Older than I look, I would say. A devotion to the celestial cycle, breathwork, mindful nourishment, and physical discipline can extend one's lifespan."

Robert tilted his head. "What's the celestial cycle?"

"A profound way of life once practiced by our ancestors. Such that our society was centered around knowledge, artful pursuits, the divine, and harmony. But progress and politics have changed this. Much for the worse."

Tala's voice filled the cabin before Thoth could tell them his age . . . if he planned to actually answer.

"We're approaching the designated coordinates," said *Tala*. "Atlantis Docking Authority has verified our clearance. All systems are functioning within expected parameters."

"Thank you, *Tala*," said Thoth.

Matt adjusted his seat. "What now?"

"We land and then proceed with caution."

Robert's eyes narrowed. Not much of an answer, but he decided to leave it alone.

The ship began its descent, the details of the city growing clearer. Smaller pyramids dotted the landscape between columns of pure white stone soaring skyward. Flying vehicles resembling elongated teardrops wove between the spires. Tropical palms and flowering trees lined the streets, their emerald fronds swaying in the breeze.

A massive starport dominated the island's northern coastline. Robert gazed in awe at a vessel larger than *Tala* that lifted off and quickly pierced the clouds. Ships with dragon-headed prows and translucent sails glided between the rings of canals. Colossal statues of Poseidon flanked the harbor entrance, their bronze tridents raised.

"Unbelievable," muttered Robert under his breath upon seeing the towering statues. How had Plato gotten so many things right about this place? It was uncanny. It was clear to Robert that the man was even more impressive, even more mysterious than he had thought.

In Plato's dialogues, *Timaeus* and *Critias*, he explicitly linked Atlantis to Poseidon, the Greek god of the sea. According to Plato, Poseidon was the patron deity of Atlantis, whose people believed he had founded its civilization and had shaped its culture and geography. The Greek philosopher had written that the Atlanteans revered this deity and built statues in his honor.

Like the statues Robert was gazing at now.

How had Plato known so much? The great philosopher had provided an impossible-to-check, hand-waving answer to this question on his own, claiming he had learned of it from an oral tradition passed down from a Greek statesman named Solon, who had learned of it from Egyptian priests. But this claim seemed dicey. So just who was Plato, really?

Robert put these questions out of his mind for now and continued exploring the great city below him. People in flowing robes walked on sidewalks, passing beneath archways. Water cascaded from fountains shaped like mythical creatures. Griffins, phoenixes, and other beings Robert had only seen in ancient texts. Spiraling towers stretched toward the heavens and gardens hung from their terraces, bright with flowers.

"The energy consumption here must be off the charts," said Kira.

Thoth didn't reply. Instead, he asked *Tala* to transmit new coordinates to the Atlantis Docking Authority, requesting a landing at a specific terminal, which she carried out. Only seconds later authorization was granted and *Tala* adjusted course.

The ship angled northward, veering away from the central hub. A smaller landing strip with clustered hangars came into view, less grand but teeming with activity.

"Follow me," said Thoth, striding toward the crew quarters.

They hurried after him. Inside one of the living quarters, Thoth pressed a solid section of the wall. A panel slid open, revealing coarse, basic garments, which he handed out. "You'll need to appear to be freighter workers."

Robert examined the outfit. A tunic of rough fabric in deep maroon, flowing trousers gathering at the ankles like those worn by desert travelers, their fabric light and airy but dotted with practical pockets. The boots were unlike anything he'd seen, with a natural spread for the toes rather than the cramped point of modern footwear. A long sash-like belt wrapped around the waist, its ends hanging loose at the hip.

Kira pulled hers on over her clothes without hesitation. "At least they're comfortable."

Matt tugged at the collar. "Why do I feel like I'm about to go trick or treating?"

Thoth clutched the Vesh'tar in his right hand and nodded at his companions. "Ready?" he said, and then, not waiting for a reply, added, "Let's go. Move quickly, but not like you're in a panic."

"Good tip," said Kira dryly.

In the cabin, Thoth motioned for the Anunnaki to stand, and the entire entourage followed Thoth to the cargo hold. Behind Robert, Ishar hulked like a not-so-miniature tree, his breath like rotten fish.

Thoth placed his hand against the wall like he did in the living quarter. A golden light rippled outward from his touch in concentric circles. With a deep resonant whir vibrating through the deck plates, a massive section of the floor split apart. From the depths below, a hydraulic platform rose, bearing twelve enormous crates dwarfing them all. Each container shined, their surfaces covered with geometric patterns and hieroglyphs. One stood nearly twice Robert's height and was wide enough to house a small car.

"These containers emit the energy signatures of Opalith crystals," Thoth said. "The authorities will believe we're transporting legitimate cargo."

After touching a hidden panel on a crate, Thoth stepped back. The crate's side slid open. Inside, a thick cushion-like material lined the walls, which were at least a foot thick and studded with crystals and some type of circuitry. Dim lights cast a soft illumination throughout the space.

Ishar crossed his arms. His golden armor clanged together as he squared his shoulders. "We do not hide like rats in boxes."

Behind him stood his elite guard: Ashtur, Enkuul, Mardak, and Nuradu. Their faces showed clear disdain.

"Then perhaps you'd prefer explaining your presence to Atlantean authorities," said Thoth. "Your kind are impossible to miss, and the penalty for unauthorized entry is severe."

"We're warriors, not cargo," insisted Ishar. "There has to be another way."

"We both know there isn't. Once we clear customs, you'll blend in perfectly with the smattering of other Anunnaki still authorized to be in the city. Then we can get you different attire, so you won't be walking around like clattering bronze statues."

The warriors exchanged glances before Ishar gave a curt nod. One by one, they climbed into their assigned crates, weapons and all. The doors sealed with barely a whisper.

Thoth was at least as recognizable here as the Anunnaki, and he entered his own crate. He stared deep into Robert's eyes and nodded. "You've got this. Just go with the way the winds blow."

"What should we—"

The panel shut, cutting off Robert's question and leaving him, Matt, and Kira alone in silence.

"So, we just . . . do what?" asked Matt.

"I guess, just stay cool," said Robert with as much false confidence as he could manage. "Thoth wouldn't put us in this position if he didn't know we could get through it."

"Should we hide some weapons in our clothes?" said Matt.

Kira shook her head. "We can't risk it. They may frisk us, or they may have sensors that can detect hidden weapons. Probably standard protocol."

The ramp began lowering. Sunlight flooded in, revealing a bustling tarmac. The crates rose smoothly, arranging themselves in a perfect line before gliding down the ramp.

"Into the lion's den," said Robert. "Here we go."

While the three followed the containers down the ramp, up ahead, inspectors approached. Each wore a fitted jumpsuit. The men's uniforms were deep navy with silver lining along the shoulders and wrists, while the women's was slate grey with gold accents. Their boots made no sound on the tarmac, despite the metallic surface.

The insignias on their chests depicted a trident wrapped in flowing script. Each inspector also wore a crystalline badge pulsing with a soft blue light.

The woman stopped before the crates, her posture perfect as she assessed them. A thin circlet of what appeared to be Oralcim crowned her head, maybe marking her superior rank.

Robert caught Matt's sidelong glance and could interpret it without any trouble. The young man had clearly noticed that every woman they had seen here was extremely attractive.

The inspectors moved around the crates, passing wands over their surfaces. Robert tried to read their expressions as they studied whatever data their instruments were showing them.

One inspector paused, frowning at his readings. He gestured to his colleague, who came to verify his findings. They spoke in low tones, consulting a holographic readout between them.

"Is there a problem?" asked Robert.

The woman stepped toward him. "Are you the captain of this vessel?"

A heartbeat of hesitation. "Yes."

"Do you consent for your crew to accompany me? Your presence is also required."

Required for what? he thought belligerently, but was just able to stop himself from saying this out loud. This may have been too bold a question for who he was pretending to be. Also, Thoth had told him to roll with the punches, so maybe cooperation was the better path forward.

"I . . . suppose . . . you have my consent. My crew and I are prepared to willingly accompany you as you've asked."

"Good," said the woman as *Tala*'s ramp retracted behind them.

The spaceport stretched far. Freighters of varying designs dotted the tarmac. Personnel moved about, vehicles zipped between ships, holographic displays flashed with data. Crates hovered and stacked themselves, and workers directed flows of cargo.

They entered a massive hangar, the ceiling arching high above. Inside, industry continued. Crates the size of small houses hovered into towering stacks. Machinery hummed, and voices echoed.

The woman led them into a spacious, empty room. She dismissed the men who'd accompanied her, telling them she'd handle things from here. After they left to inspect other cargo, the door shut behind them with an audible click, sealing Robert, his companions, and the woman inside.

She faced them. "Identify yourselves."

Robert's mouth went dry. "I'm Robert Shaw. These are Matt Jones and Kira Shelton." According to Thoth, those names were now in the system. Hopefully, the old man was right.

She consulted a tablet, pressing on its surface. After a moment, the ground beneath them shifted. Panels parted without sound. A staircase spiraled downward, each step appearing to float. The crates lifted and descended into the opening.

The woman motioned toward the stairs. "Come with me. All of you."

CHAPTER 27

Councilor Kairos Daedalus
High Marshall of the Atlantean Military Forces
Nadiria Territory

The office's citrine crystal walls cast light across the large space, illuminating the solitary figure within. Kairos Daedalus stood at the pinnacle of the Alarion Spire, four stories of Atlantean engineering rising beneath his feet. Outside, the heart of Nadiria pulsed with life. A territory molded by his vision and iron will, thriving under his command.

He moved to his desk, a masterpiece of translucent minerals. With a touch, holographic schematics blossomed above the surface. Battle reports, energy outputs, resource allocations. He lingered on the latest updates from Kemet. Argo's maneuvers lacked the decisive force Kairos demanded.

A soft tone signaled the arrival of his guest. The doors slid open as Ixra Maren, a city council member known as a Syndic, entered. Sharp-eyed, the Syndic carried herself like a predator, exuding poise, confidence.

"Councilor," said Ixra. "You summoned me."

Through the years, Kairos had observed Ixra. The young woman's tireless work ethic. Her diplomatic finesse with political figures. Her talent for transforming struggling districts into economic powerhouses. Her ability to use her striking beauty as a weapon.

In short, Ixra's talent and ambition mirrored his own.

Kairos tapped a control, minimizing the projections. "Ixra. I trust the city continues to operate smoothly."

"The manufacturing sectors in District Seven have shown marked improvement," she said, pulling up detailed metrics on a crystal tablet she held. "Where we once struggled with constant equipment failures and worker unrest, the new protocols have streamlined operations."

"Before my time, those sectors were a disaster." Kairos's lip curled up in disgust. "Outdated equipment, untrained workers, poor resource allocation."

She continued her report, indicating gains in the output of crystal refineries, textile mills, mineral processing plants, and improvements in the operation of the energy grid, while thanking Kairos for his more ruthless approach to personnel management, which helped make her successes possible.

"Nadiria flourishes because we demand excellence," said Kairos when she had finished. "And punish laziness and failure. Too few people have the proper ambition anymore. Although you don't suffer from that particular problem, Ixra," he added with a smile. "Decidedly not."

"Thank you, Councilor."

Kairos looked out at the city's skyline through wraparound windows. "Argo isn't living up to my expectations commanding the Kemet campaign. He's too soft."

"Unfortunate."

"Tell me, Ixra, have you ever considered a role beyond the Council?"

Her eyes narrowed slightly. "I'm willing to serve Atlantis in any capacity deemed appropriate."

"Appropriate." Kairos tasted the word. "Suppose I required someone willing to do what others might find . . . *inappropriate*?"

She allowed herself the hint of a smile. "As I think you know, I have a history of taking action where others hesitate."

Kairos nodded slowly. "War demands a certain fortitude. An understanding that the ends justify the means."

"A philosophy I embrace wholeheartedly."

"If circumstances allowed, elevating you to a position of greater influence might benefit Nadiria profoundly, but more importantly, Atlantis. Argo may find himself reassigned if his performance doesn't improve. If you take over for him, would you be concerned about your lack of battlefield experience?"

She shook her head. "Not at all. I learn fast, I'm adaptable, and I'm a proven leader. Not to mention that I'll have you to guide me. I feel certain I'd meet or exceed your every expectation."

Kairos nodded. He couldn't argue with her. He had found her to be an extremely fast learner.

A chime interrupted their exchange. The doors opened, showing Kairos's aide. "Councilor, your next appointment awaits," she said.

"Thank you, Selene." Kairos dismissed her with a nod before returning his gaze to Ixra. "We'll continue this conversation at a later date."

"I look forward to it," his underling replied with a slight bow.

Kairos watched as Ixra departed and the doors sealed behind her. A moment later, Aethor Daedalus entered. His son carried a datapad, its crystalline interface projecting patterns of light and data into the air. The two men shared a stiff greeting.

"Why am I here?" said Aethor. "If you're interested in catching up on my life, visit me. Don't summon me to your offices."

Kairos's gaze drifted to the datapad in his son's hands. The moment he did, it was shut off. His son was fiercely independent, which he admired, but Aethor's behavior often bordered on insolence. On the other hand, Kairos would much rather have a strong-willed, bull-headed son who never backed down than one who was weak and accommodating, one who would be an embarrassment to their shared last name.

"What do you need, Father?" asked Aethor, breaking him from his reverie.

"What do I need?" repeated Kairos. "I need to learn why you're meddling in medical affairs that shouldn't concern you."

"Meddling? If by that you mean questioning the integrity of medical product evaluations, then perhaps more meddling is exactly what's needed. And did you really say these medical affairs shouldn't *concern* me? I'm a physician, not a soldier, Father. Medical affairs are my *only* concern. And if medical reports have been falsified, they should be of concern to *everyone*."

"And what have you discovered?"

"The supposed impartial review of the Cognitive Enhancement Serum was conducted by a committee. I know their report to be false, so I've been digging into who appointed them. It's quite a convoluted path, but I've finally been able to trace the authorization codes. And guess whose signature I found embedded in the clearance algorithms?"

Kairos maintained a flat expression. "Enlighten me."

"*Yours*," said Aethor. "Why are you pushing a product that's been proven to degrade cognitive functions over time? It effectively lowers intelligence in those who use it extensively."

Kairos leaned back, steepling his fingers. "The enhancements offer immediate benefits. Any long-term side effects are negligible."

"*Negligible*? To whom? The public is being duped into thinking it's a miracle drug, while it's silently and slowly eroding their cognitive functioning."

Kairos waved a dismissive hand. "You're overreacting. Such data is inconclusive at best."

"Not inconclusive. Suppressed. And I have the proof."

"From whom? Disgruntled employees peddling conspiracy theories?"

"I've seen the evidence with my own eyes. It's real. So why are you doing this?"

"I'm not. My responsibilities are vast. I can't be expected to know about everything my countless underlings are up to. But I *will* see to it that the matter gets investigated thoroughly."

Aethor smiled. "Investigated? I know you too well, Father. You offered that up much too quickly for it to be real. You said it only to placate me. You have no intention of conducting an investigation. *Suppressing* an investigation, maybe."

Again, Kairos was proud and infuriated at the same time. Aethor was nobody's fool, and he never backed down. It must be in the genes. "I need you to stop kicking this particular anthill. For your own good and the good of Atlantis. You're jeopardizing initiatives beyond your comprehension."

"Try me."

A muscle tightened in Kairos's jaw. "Fine. You've heard of the Etherion Collective?"

Aethor's eyes narrowed. "The consortium managing Nexus Prime."

"Precisely. Their work is pivotal to our future."

"Pivotal? Improving upon the offensive capabilities of an already weaponized power grid?"

"That's a gross misinterpretation."

"Is it?" said Aethor. "Because I have a video that suggests otherwise." He tapped his datapad and a holographic image materialized between them, displaying the towering Nexus Prime. "Watch."

Nexus Prime dominated the projection. A massive crystalline structure dwarfing the surrounding buildings of southwest Atlantis. Its base alone covered two city blocks, tapering as it rose nearly forty stories into the sky. But what could be seen was just the tip of the iceberg. It was far wider *below* the surface, reaching down as it did twenty-five miles into Earth's upper mantle to extract energy from the blistering heat there.

The structure was visible through a translucent exterior and flashed with a steady white-gold rhythm. Energy conduits spiraled up the tower's length like veins, each one calibrated to channel and amplify the power drawn from its nether regions. The upper third split into three spires curving inward, their tips almost touching to form a focal point.

On the holographic projection, the focal point flared to life, and Kairos felt the hair on the back of his neck stand up. How had his son gotten this footage?

Raw power gathered between the spires like liquid lightning, churning and building until it lanced into the sky in the form of a wide, throbbing beam of light looking powerful enough to punch a hole in the fabric of space-time itself. The beam seared through the sky, scorching it on the way to its mark. When it hit the island, the small landmass temporarily disappeared, blocked by an explosion of light. The small supernova abruptly ceased a second later, but the damage was already done.

Kairos could barely contain his excitement upon seeing this again, even in holographic form. This was everything Nexus Prime was meant to be. Absolute control over the forces of nature itself. Each facet of its surface had been the result of brilliant, groundbreaking innovations. Each energy circuit placed according to calculations that had taken years to perfect.

"That island," said Aethor, biting off the words in barely contained fury, "was one Atlantis has been trying to annex for years. As you're well aware. It fell under our control just days after this incident. How many died there, Father? Official reports said their capitulation came as a result of a military operation. Military operation, my ass! You slaughtered an untold number of innocents and induced the rest to surrender instantly, with a single blow from a single superweapon."

Kairos held back a deep swallow. How in the hell had his son gotten that vid?

"I'm disgusted and horrified," continued Aethor. "But even more, I'm *embarrassed* for you. Embarrassed for Atlantis. More embarrassed than if I'd learned you'd used an entire squadron of Skyblade Fighters to kill a *bunny rabbit*. Hardly sporting, Father. I thought you valued courage and strategy. What courage or strategy did this strike take? Or do you cut off your opponent's arms, engage him in a sword fight, and then boast of your victory?"

The blood boiled in Kairos's veins. His son had hit a sore spot, drilling into it with surprising savagery. But he wouldn't let him know just how well he had scored. "It isn't cowardice to use all the advantages you have to win a battle. It's cowardice to *refuse* to do so based on misguided principles of fairness. These people weren't bunny rabbits. They had fangs. Not using the weapon would cost more lives on both sides, making a Nexus Prime strike the more compassionate alternative."

"Whatever helps you sleep at night."

"This is a matter of national security. If you fail to keep this to yourself, not even *I* can protect you. This is all for the greater good. I'm sorry if you can't see that."

"Greater good?" repeated Aethor in disgust. "Greater good for who? You? You've turned Nexus Prime into a potential continent killer. At the same time, stripping citizens of their intellect and autonomy?"

"Both of these statements are lies. Where are you getting your information?"

"Since they're lies, why do you care?"

"Because those feeding them to you are inciting unrest. People will begin to ask questions better left unspoken. The last thing we need is another Thoth stirring dissent."

"Thoth is dead. And like you, I had little regard for his methods."

"He's *not* dead. You know it as well as I do." Kairos searched his son's face. "He's just in hiding. You're not associated with any remnants of his so-called Resistance, are you?"

"Absolutely not."

Kairos studied him for a moment longer, then nodded. "Good. I'd hate to think my own son was entangled in treason."

"Treason?" Aethor shook his head. "Is that what you call revealing the truth?"

"That's what I call the actions of a group who willfully destabilize the very fabric of our society."

"This *fabric*, as you call it, has become suffocating. Perhaps it's something that *needs* to be destabilized."

Kairos glared at this son. "We're done here. But remember my warning. If you don't cease these activities, I can't protect you. Further, I wouldn't protect you if I could."

"Is that supposed to come as a surprise?"

"Don't test me, Aethor!"

Aethor returned Kairos's glare. "Test you, Father?" he repeated with fake, exaggerated innocence. "I wouldn't think of it."

CHAPTER 28

Advisor Elowin Balivae
Poros Territory, Poros City
Location: Southwest Atlantis

Elowin looked out from the floor-to-ceiling window at the city of Poros, while Kona waited for her outside. Thoth had done a miraculous job of arranging meetings with Atlantean politicians. While she waited for this one, her thoughts drifted to Robert Shaw, the strange companion of his. There was something about him she couldn't quite place—a quality intriguing, yet unsettling. She'd been attracted to men before, but not like this.

Why? She couldn't put a finger on it, so she shook her head, pushing the distracting thought aside. More pressing matters were at hand.

Beyond the lobby windows, spires dominated the Poros skyline, one of Atlantis's largest cities. From her vantage point, waterfalls cascaded down the building's facade into aquamarine ponds ringing its base.

Far in the distance stood the magnificent Nexus Prime, towering over the horizon. A colossal crystal piercing the sky. Pictures didn't begin to do it justice. It was hard to imagine something so beautiful could harbor such potential for destruction.

A woman at the central reception area adjusted her tunic and stepped forward. "Councilor Deir Slan will see you now. If you'll remain seated here, she'll come out to you."

Moments later, Deir Slan emerged from an office. She was a woman of advanced years, her silver-streaked hair styled and held in place with decorative pins, and insisted her guest remain seated. Dark robes flowed around her, tridents woven into the fabric.

"Councilor Slan," said Elowin, extending a hand.

Deir regarded the gesture for a beat before lightly clasping the offered hand. "Advisor Balivae," she said, taking a seat opposite her. "To what do I owe this visit?"

"Thanks for meeting with me," said Elowin. "I have pressing matters to discuss."

"No doubt. I must say, I'm intrigued by how swiftly this meeting was arranged. My appointments are typically scheduled weeks in advance. I'm not sure how it happened. My office received a rather cryptic message, and I've heard rumors that a man named Thoth was involved."

Elowin shrugged. "Doesn't ring a bell."

"Really?" said Deir, not hiding her skepticism. "That is surprising. Thoth is a figure of considerable renown."

Elowin titled her head in thought. "You know, now that you mention it, I have heard of the man you're referring to. But I thought he was exiled and died in a cave somewhere."

An amused glint appeared in Deir's eyes. "How intriguing. I've heard no such tales. Here in Atlantis, Thoth's name is still spoken with a mix of respect and . . . caution. It seems news travels differently across the seas."

"Regardless," said Elowin, "I'm as curious as you are about how his name became falsely associated with our meeting."

Deir studied her guest for a moment. "Yes, quite the mystery. Which brings me to wonder . . . who *did* help you set up this appointment?"

Elowin shrugged. "I asked for a meeting and left it to those who work for my government to schedule it. I'm glad it was handled so expeditiously."

"Me too," said Deir. "So, in the spirit of efficiency, why don't you begin."

"Here? In the lobby?"

"Only my assistant is here, so it doesn't matter. You can speak freely."

"Thank you," said Elowin. "I'll get right to the point, then. I'm concerned about the increasing military presence along our shared borders. Preparations that suggest imminent conflict."

"Imminent conflict?" said Deir. "Surely you're mistaken. Our activities are merely standard security measures. Nothing more."

"Standard measures don't usually involve amassing armies, Councilor."

"In these times, precaution is necessary. After all, the world is unpredictable."

"Yes. But my worry is that actions like this exacerbate that unpredictability. It's critically important that we prevent any escalation."

Deir sighed. "I understand your concerns. But you're under the wrong impression. Our advancements ensure peace and stability. A strong presence deters those who might disrupt harmony. We're helping both sides. Yours, and ours."

"At the risk of being... indelicate, Councilor Deir, I remember your leaders repeatedly reciting these exact words. Just before your unprovoked attacks on Kemet. So, I hope you can forgive me if I don't find comfort in these platitudes."

Deir was rendered temporarily speechless, surprised to have been called out in such a bold and blunt fashion.

Elowin continued. "I do believe we can find a diplomatic solution to our concerns. If Atlantis would consider passing legislation to reduce its military presence along our borders in Nasavi, it would go a long way toward easing tensions. After all, this is an area previously acknowledged by Atlantis to be neutral and under Lemurian stewardship."

Deir's gaze hardened. "Atlantis has long desired more territory in Nasavi. But your people have refused to even enter negotiations on the matter."

Elowin forced herself to remain calm, calculating. Her request for such legislation had zero chance of success. She had used it as a red herring only, to rattle Deir, to *anger* her. Elowin's true goal was to apply a hammer to Deir's knee and wait for her reflexive kick, carefully reading the woman's face and body language to gauge her reactions and emotions and obtain information the woman wouldn't knowingly share.

At this point, Elowin realized that getting an Atlantean official to make a concession on *anything*, let alone *legislate* such a concession, was impossible. But getting one to inadvertently reveal his or her hand was not. Elowin's success would be measured by how well she could get the lay of the land, and if she could ferret out which officials, if any, were truly interested in peace.

"Oh?" said Elowin, intent on getting under Deir's skin even more. "I see. If Atlantis wants something, and we're unwilling to sell it to you—or *negotiate* for it, as you said—then Atlantis is justified in just taking it by force? Is that what you're saying? It also sounds as if you're implying it's *Lemuria's* fault for not selling Nasavi to you. I find that twisted, even for Atlantis."

Dier's eyes blazed with fury, and she was so put off her game that she couldn't come up with an immediate retort.

"Let's be honest with each other," continued Elowin after a quick beat. "If not for Lemuria, Atlantis would have steamrolled through Nasavi long ago. And yes, we've refused to negotiate. But how can we negotiate away the rights or lands of other peoples? The inhabitants of Nasavi are the shepherds of their land."

"It isn't that simple," replied Deir through clenched teeth, still seething but finally finding her voice. "Control of Nasavi isn't something that's just important to Atlantis due to its proximity to our west coast. Such control is vital for the safety of all humanity. We live on a potentially hostile world. Worse, in a galaxy we *know* to be hostile in many ways. The galactic wolves have been held at bay. For now. But we believe only by a hair. The balance of power is so delicate it can be blown apart by a single breath of air. If we don't globalize under Atlantean leadership, we'll be helpless to stop an advanced alien species from having their way with us. But, with the entire world united under our banner, under our leadership, if there is a galactic power shift that doesn't go our way, we'll at least have a fighting chance."

Elowin's mind raced. This was a new rationale, one she was sure had never been articulated before. And it actually made sense. The wisdom of this position could be vigorously debated, but it wasn't as indefensible as aggression and conquest for its own sake. Now she was getting somewhere.

Perhaps it was time to kick Deir's knee even harder. She faced the woman across from her. "Interesting argument," she said. "But think hard. Did this flawed logic come from the Draconian advisors who have been whispering in Atlantean ears?"

She watched every micron of the woman's face and body as she said this and immediately recognized a number of tells. For just a moment, the woman had looked like a kid caught with her hand in the cookie jar.

"No need to reply," said Elowin, "because the answer is obvious. The Dracs *were* behind it. Not to *help* Atlantis. Just the opposite. Because you haven't thought through the implications, have you? Putting this bug in your ear is a brilliant ploy by the Dracs," she continued. "The galactic community prevents them from exercising overt power here. Yet . . . if they can work Atlantean leaders into a lather over fears of the Galactic conquest of Earth, they can worm their way into your trust and good graces. They can get you dependent on their counsel. And by counsel, I mean *puppeteering*. They can get you to destroy much of the world, weakening it immensely, and leaving us as easy pickings for their covert maneuverings."

"This is an outrage!" spat Deir, but for just an instant, her body language had revealed her true emotions. She had been *rattled*. Elowin's insistence that Atlantis was being played by the Draconians, a reptilian race that few believed even existed, was something she hadn't considered, and she was greatly troubled by it.

"Your accusation is preposterous," continued the Atlantean. "Not even worthy of a response. We are not working with Draconians in any way. Even if what you say is true, the opposite would happen. Global conquest would *strengthen* Earth, not weaken it. We don't intend to go to war, but if we did, it would be short and sweet, with almost no destruction or casualties, leading to a much stronger world. The opposite of what you suggest a group of non-existent Draconians might want."

Elowin was now in the zone, like an athlete delivering a brilliant performance by surrendering to pure instinct. "You claim no Draconian involvement, but I know otherwise. I have a Draconian source," she lied, making this up on the spot. "One who has been mistreated by his people. One who, for the right price, has been willing to disclose everything to us. So, I can tell you this. The Drac's are laughing at your leaders' gullibility. They've convinced you that Atlantis is so superior, conquest will cost very little. But they've manipulated your intelligence agencies to vastly underestimate Lemurian strength. You believe we're sheep ready for the slaughter. We are not. We're your equal. So once Atlantis and Lemuria finish hacking each other nearly to death, the Dracs will swoop in like vultures to pick over our remains."

For just a moment, Deir looked horrified again, before quickly donning a mask of stoicism once more. Elowin had not only learned much from this interaction, she'd scored a number of clean hits.

"I'm afraid I have to end our discussion here," said the Atlantean. "But I will share all you've said with the High Council, including your delusions. Just for good measure."

"Thank you," said Elowin. She was under no illusion that stopping this war would be easy, but she was off to a good start. "One last thing before you go. We've heard unsettling reports about Nexus Prime's capabilities. Reports that it's been turned into the ultimate weapon."

"Like your Draconian fantasies, I admire your imagination," said Deir. "At the same time, I'm troubled by your willingness to believe in conspiracy theories. This accusation is also completely false."

"Really? It is an outlandish accusation, I'll give you that. Most would never think that the very device that supplies critical power to your people could be turned into such a weapon. Yet you didn't show any surprise at all. You didn't say such a thing was *impossible*. You didn't say that my accusation was *preposterous*. Instead, you calmly delivered a scripted response, as though you were bored. Makes me think I hit the target dead center."

Deir shot her an icy smile. "Good try," she said. "There's something about your initial demeanor that invites people to underestimate you. It's become crystal clear to me that doing so would be a grave mistake. Still, impressive or not, you're wrong about Nexus Prime."

"If that's the case," said Elowin, "I'd ask you to arrange a tour of the device for select Lemurian representatives. Allow them to visit the control room and examine specs. Just to put our minds at ease. It would go a long way toward reducing tensions. Refusal, on the other hand, will put us more on guard than ever."

"Nice try, again, Advisor. But the precise specs and the technology behind Nexus Prime are kept secret for a reason. If this is divulged, an enemy could find a weakness and potentially cut off our entire power grid. It's obvious we can't risk something like that."

Deir rose and extended her hand. "It was nice meeting you, Advisor Balivae. I trust you can see yourself out."

***

Elowin left Deir's office and soon reunited with Kona in their private ship. She quickly recounted the entire conversation to him.

He was stunned by her report. She had let her intuition guide her on a fishing expedition, and she might have caught a whale.

"You have more arrows in your quiver than even I had guessed," he told her. "You were bold, that's for sure. Playing the Drac card and the Nexus Prime card in the same meeting. That's a special kind of audacity."

"Time is too short for cookie-cutter diplomacy. I had to take risks. And they seem to have paid off."

"Are you certain the Draconians are involved?"

"Almost. Not entirely, but almost."

"Inventing a Draconian spy and pretending he's providing information to us was brilliant. Truly inspired. If the Dracs *weren't* involved, Deir would immediately know you were lying and call you on it."

Elowin nodded. "One would think, yes."

"And this ruse will cripple them somewhat, also," said Kona. "If they believe there's a Drac spy in their midst, they'll have to be more cautious. Less trusting. Suspicion and paranoia will flourish, creating havoc. Dissent will be fomented in their ranks."

"I wish that were true, Kona, but I don't believe it is. Stronger minds than Deir's will realize if we really did have a spy, I would never have outed him the way I did. I wouldn't *boast* of having a spy. I'd refuse to admit it, even under torture."

Kona tilted his head and nodded at Elowin in admiration. "Wow. Your grasp of every last nuance of the situation is stunning. You should report what you've learned about Drac involvement to the Circle of 12."

She shook her head. "I think not. I have only my assessment of Deir's body language to go on, which the Circle will find subjective. And since I brought the Dracs up when I met with them last . . . and they shot me down . . . they'll find my report conveniently self-serving. I still need more tangible evidence."

Elowin paused. "But I'm certain Atlantis has turned Nexus Prime into a weapon. Deir's reaction when I brought this up was unmistakable. My gut has never been more positive of anything."

"Do you think they've built something they can't control?"

"Worse," said Elowin. "I think they know exactly what they've built, and they're preparing to use it. Hopefully as a measure of last resort if the war isn't going their way. But we can't be sure."

She clenched her fists. "We need to get inside that facility and find a way to stop it. If not, the consequences will be catastrophic."

CHAPTER 29

Robert shook his head as if trying to wake himself from a trance. How had the floor of a spacious room just beyond the hangar opened up like the jaws of a leviathan to reveal a spiral staircase? And how had the customs inspector now standing on the top stair managed to get their cargo to move into the opening?

And *why* had this happened?

If her plan was to arrest them, take them to some sort of wild, secret dungeon, their cargo wouldn't be coming along for the ride.

"Captain?" said the inspector for a second time, her tone showing irritation.

It took Robert a moment to come out of his trance and remember that the word *captain* was being applied to him. His fake promotion to captain had been a bit abrupt. "Sorry, what were you saying?" he asked the inspector, a woman whose beauty would have made her a Hollywood star back home.

"I was telling you and your crew to follow me," she said impatiently. "I won't ask again."

Robert stepped onto the anti-grav staircase gingerly, surprised that this woman would make herself vulnerable by turning her back on them. Another reason he doubted they were about to be imprisoned. Behind him, Kira and Matt followed suit. In front of them, the crates glided down the steps on their own.

When they reached the bottom, the ceiling sealed shut above them. The staircase folded against the wall, vanishing as if it had never existed. Their guide stood beside a hovering vehicle shaped like a teardrop, floating a yard off the ground. The crates settled down beside her, all in a lined row.

Robert looked around the large space stretching into darkness. The emptiness felt oppressive. "Why have you brought us here? This place feels a little . . . isolated."

"Your names are highly unusual," said the woman, ignoring his question. "How did you come to crew *Tala*?"

"*Tala*?" said Robert, his heart jumping. "I think you have us mixed up with another crew. We crew the *Nautilos*."

"I refuse to believe that *Tala* would let you crew her if you didn't know exactly who she was. She belongs to the Hierophant himself."

"The Hierophant?" said Robert. "I have no idea who that is. All I know is that we're the crew of a freighter named *Nautilos*. We're delivering a shipment of Opalith crystals from the Kanaloa Mines."

The woman's expression hardened. "Opalith crystals from Kanaloa? Those mines are under Lemurian control and are quite distant. Your ship—*Tala*," she said with special emphasis— "was here only hours ago, with a different crew. She couldn't have left, swapped crews, gone to the mines, loaded crystals, and returned so quickly. I refuse to believe it. So, what am I missing?"

Robert's head was spinning. How could this woman be so certain the ship giving off the fake ID of *Nautilos* was actually *Tala*? He was dying to ask her this question but decided his only chance was to continue his denials. "What you're *missing*," he said emphatically, "is that our ship isn't called *Tala*."

"Enough!" The woman drew a metallic device from her hip. A weapon with a slender barrel and engravings along its handle. It was unlike any firearm Robert had ever seen, but the intent was clear. "I'm going to see to it that you're arrested and interrogated. I *will* get to the bottom of this."

Robert fought off a growing panic. If they were taken into custody, *Tala* would be searched. They'd find the flute, among other things, which couldn't be allowed.

His eyes darted around the room. Was there any way out? Anything he could use as a weapon? The woman continued to stand beside a large hovering vehicle. He tensed his muscles. He would have to risk a suicide lunge to try to wrestle the gun away from her. Perhaps if he executed a bull rush, he could slam her into the side of the vehicle and knock her unconscious.

Robert prepared to launch himself forward, knowing he'd likely be shot, when he was stopped with only seconds to spare by a calm voice arising from behind the crates. "Perhaps introductions are in order," said the familiar voice. "These are my friends, *and Tala's*. Who have shown themselves to be better actors than I thought."

All eyes turned as Thoth emerged from one of the containers, his green robes flowing around him. "Ah, Alara," he said to the inspector. "Apparently, you didn't get my message. My sincere apologies about that. And, I must say, it's been too long."

A flash of emotion crossed the inspector's face as she lowered her weapon. "Thoth?" she said in wonder. "Is that really you?"

A tear glistened in her eye before she brushed it away. "After the last incident, I thought..."

He placed his hand on her shoulder. "Sorry again. I was needed elsewhere. But the time is right for my return."

"Your timing has always been impeccable," said the woman named Alara. "But why are you here? What's your plan?"

Thoth grinned. "Before I tell you, I should really open up the other crates. They contain mercenaries who have pledged to protect us and follow my orders."

The crates opened in unison, revealing the giant Anunnaki warriors. Ishar stepped forward, his scarred red beard unmistakable, followed by his four comrades. Alara did her best to give them a pleasant greeting, but couldn't quite remove the hostility from her voice.

Thoth then introduced his human friends, whose names she already knew.

"Who are you people, really?" Alara asked the human trio once introductions were complete.

"We really are *Tala's* crew," said Robert. "Well, sort of."

Alara turned to face the Hierophant. "Okay, Thoth, is this some kind of strange joke? What am I missing? I saw *Tala's* crew a few hours ago, and these aren't them."

"We have much to discuss," he replied. "Though I warn you, what seems strange now is about to get a lot stranger. But that's for later. First, Alara, you can shed this façade. You've played your part brilliantly, even if you did startle my companions."

He faced the others. "Alara is deep undercover. This is one of precious few occasions when she can finally let her hair down and be who she truly is. Ironic that both sides in your recent exchange were pretending to be something they weren't."

Thoth nodded at the vehicle hovering beside her. "Let's put that thing to good use."

Thoth explained to them that the vehicle was designed to fly, but also to race through tunnels at high speed, much like pods raced through hyperloop systems back home, imagined Robert.

The entire party quickly boarded. There was a pilot's seat at the front, while cushioned benches lined the sides. Robert found himself pressed between Matt and one of the Anunnaki. The close quarters made movement minimal. The Anunnaki kept their heads low, shoulders rolled forward, their faces miserable as they grunted deep guttural sounds. It didn't take a genius to know these warriors hated this cramped situation. Alara settled into the pilot's seat, manipulating the controls. The vehicle whirred to life, gliding forward into the tunnel's abyss.

"Where are we going?" asked Matt.

"We're headed to safety," said Thoth. "Since you've arrived you've been under considerable pressure. But I should tell you that when this pressure subsides, Matt, and when the time is right, you'll discover something within yourself so profound that it may change how you see everything, even *Tala*."

What does that mean? Thought Robert. Beside him, he could tell Matt was thinking the same.

The darkness outside was punctuated by occasional flashes of light. As they picked up speed, Thoth leaned in. "Alara has been instrumental in our efforts. Together, we've thwarted many of Atlantis's most aggressive moves."

Alara sighed. "Maybe so, but it feels like we've only delayed the inevitable. And now my cover's blown. My bosses will wonder where I went."

"Leave that to me," said the green robed sage. "I'll give you a sound alibi and make sure you keep your job."

The vehicle accelerated through the tunnel, its speed increasing by the minute. Thoth continued to grip the Vesh'tar, its green gem pulsing ever so faintly. For the first time, Robert felt it pulling at him as if it were luring a moth to a zapper. He mentioned this to Thoth and then asked again about the mysterious device. "You told me earlier that you sensed your Vesh'tar calling to me. That it has a connection to me. Can you tell me anything more about it?"

"It's a device that has many uses, including as a weapon," said Thoth. "A device designed to serve humanity as a whole. Each Vesh'tar is unique, forged from elements older than Atlantis itself, containing ancient technology." His eyes took on a distant look. "Each one resonates differently with its keeper. Some find their purpose in healing, others in protection. Still others have remarkable capabilities that I won't describe right now."

The gem pulsed, almost like a heartbeat. Something about its rhythm felt good to Robert, though he couldn't say why. "You've made it seem as if these artifacts choose their bearers."

"They do. As I've told you, I believe you're meant to carry one."

"And if I choose not to?"

Thoth chuckled. "Choice is but a facet of destiny. The Vesh'tar chooses its keeper. It's not about desire, but alignment. It defends, it heals, it serves purpose without malice."

Robert considered this new information in silence, deciding not to ask additional questions for now. The vehicle surged upward, emerging from the tunnel into a wide aerial highway. Streams of similar crafts wove through the sky, flitting between towering spires and pyramids.

Vehicles zipped past in structured flows, the air alive with motion. Bridges connected structures suspended in the sky, and waterfalls cascaded from floating platforms, dissolving into mist before reaching the ground.

"Welcome to the heart of Poseidia," said Thoth.

"All those legends about Atlantis," whispered Robert. "They didn't do it justice."

Alara steered through the stream of traffic. Ahead, a pyramid loomed, its apex jutting into the clouds. The vehicle veered toward a less impressive section of the city, the grandeur giving way to industrial structures and warehouses.

They descended toward a dilapidated area, the dome buildings worn out like they'd been there too long and just wanted to die. The vehicle approached a deserted lot. After they landed with a slight jostle, Alara raised her hand.

"Wait," she said, scanning her monitors. "Air traffic above. We need to hold position."

Through the viewscreen, they watched as a freighter passed overhead. Its shadow temporarily darkened their surroundings. Once it cleared, Alara lifted the vehicle into the air. The ground beneath them split open, revealing a hidden passage.

Alara guided them into the subterranean area. As they descended, lights brightened. Before them was a chamber. She set the craft down once again, and as they disembarked in the underground room, the group's footsteps echoed off the stone walls. The Anunnaki warriors' armor clanged with each step, the sound reverberating through the space.

"Our first order of business," announced Thoth, "is to get everyone properly clothed. Especially you and your warriors, Ishar."

They continued walking. "This is the Underground," explained Thoth. "The home of the Resistance."

Stone columns rose into darkness, their surfaces carved with glyphs.

Before them, three lighted corridors split off, each carved from the living rock and reinforced with ancient stonework. The corridor opened into a chamber.

"The Great Hall," said Thoth.

Columns soared upward to support a vaulted ceiling disappearing into shadow. The space possessed the solemnity of a cathedral combined with the energy of a command center.

Throughout the chamber, about a dozen people moved between crystalline consoles displaying holographic maps and data streams. Planning tables dominated the center of the hall, their surfaces alive with projections of what could be Atlantis or surrounding territories. Operators huddled around these interfaces, perhaps analyzing what Robert thought could be intelligence reports by the way the individuals analyzed the data with intense focus, pointing at specific locations, making notations, and conferring in hushed tones. Some marked what appeared to be supply routes, reminding Robert of war rooms he'd seen in spy documentaries and films.

Several people turned to the new arrivals, and their faces lit up at the sight of Thoth.

Within seconds the news had spread through the room and all twelve who were there when they entered stopped what they were doing to gawk at the Hierophant.

Raising a hand in greeting, Thoth said, "My friends, it's good to be among you once more."

Thoth's mere presence transformed the room. Everyone quickly gathered around him, their faces bright with relief, as though they were children welcoming the return of their beloved father. Robert sensed they regarded Thoth not just with the deep respect and affection he had likely earned from years of kindness and wisdom, but with something more profound, which he couldn't quite put a finger on.

Around them, workstations lined the walls. Holographic displays floated above consoles. A central table showed a rotating model of Atlantis, with markers indicating key locations. Vehicles similar to the one they'd arrived in were docked along one side.

In short, the place looked every bit the underground rebel base that it was.

Robert caught Thoth's eye. "Impressive."

"It's a much smaller group than it once was," said Thoth, "but the heart—the commitment—of these people is unparalleled."

A man with rugged features and an intense gaze emerged from the small group and approached the sage. "I've done it, Thoth," he said excitedly, pulling out a crystalline data chip. "The complete schematics for Nexus Prime, including its weak points."

"Outstanding, Aethor! Where did you get this?"

"I stole it from the central Nadiria grid. Almost right under my father's nose."

"Even though you have a powerful father, you'd have been executed for treason if you were caught."

Aethor grinned, his eyes blazing with a fierce intelligence. "Then it's a good thing I wasn't caught."

CHAPTER 30

Thoth shot Aethor a warm smile, his eyes crinkling at the corners. "It's a relief to see you here, my friend. Your courage is commendable. As for your father, I'd like to believe that deep down, Kairos holds more love for you than he shows."

Aethor snorted. "I'd like to believe that too. Too bad it isn't true."

Robert watched them interacting and could tell they shared the strongest of bonds. Thoth spoke to him like he was a trusted lieutenant. Still, there was an underlying current of something more personal, as if they were battle-worn comrades who'd risked everything together for the Resistance. How long had they been fighting this shadow war against the government?

Thoth introduced Robert, Kira, and Matt to the group now gathered around them. He went on to explain who they were and how *Tala* had brought them from the future into this age.

A stunned silence descended over the gathering when he finished. Only their faith in him kept them from openly expressing disbelief.

"Atlantean authorities did detect a temporal anomaly recently," said Aethor to the gathering, further supporting the Hierophant's account.

Alara also decided to chime in. "I can also report that I saw two *Talas*, each with a different crew. I was convinced they were identical—yet different—and had no explanation. But given what Thoth has just told us, the presence of two *Talas* makes a bizarre kind of sense."

Thoth nodded. "It means a lot to me that you're willing to believe what I know seems impossible. It will take some time to process. It did for me also. And, I need to tell you why this occurred. It seems that, in the future, something transpired that *Tala* felt warranted this extraordinary measure."

He paused. "Put another way, our *Tala* has already experienced the time we're in now . . . and beyond. And she was alarmed enough to return. Alarmed enough to attempt to alter the course of events that led to the future she comes from."

"Hold on," said Aethor thoughtfully. "If *Tala* changes our timeline, wouldn't that create some sort of catastrophic paradox?"

"One would think," said Thoth. "I have faith the Universe wouldn't allow her to travel through time if this wasn't important, and if a catastrophic paradox were to result."

"And what of Koyaanisqatsi?" asked someone in the small gathering.

"Koya commands the other *Tala*," said Thoth. "He's been instrumental in carrying out covert intelligence missions. Thanks to him, the Lemurians have valuable information about Atlantean movements."

Aethor held up his datapad so the entire gathering could see it. "I also have Koya to thank for the intel that ultimately led me to this. Detailed plans of Nexus Prime, including its vulnerabilities."

"Just how devastating is it as a weapon?" asked Thoth.

"Much worse than we imagined," said Aethor. "Which begs the question, what has *Tala* seen in the future?"

"She's seen the coming war," said Thoth. "And Robert has told me that in the future both Atlantis and Lemuria are beneath oceans and mostly lost to history. Suffice it to say that she delivered my three guests to our time to help stop the war. That's all that's really important."

"Can we assume she gave you extensive details of all that's about to ensue?" said Alara.

"Extensive? No. I had a private consultation with her, but she wouldn't tell me. She didn't want foreknowledge to cloud my judgment. *Our* judgment. She worried we might try to outsmart fate and, in doing so, cause the very disasters we're trying to prevent."

To Robert, that made no sense. Still, as Thoth had said, *Tala* could be inscrutable.

"While she didn't provide specific, actionable intel," continued Thoth, "she did bring back these three people. She's changing the equation by adding new variables, new minds, new skills. If she simply told us what went wrong, we might obsess over avoiding those specific mistakes while being blind to new ones. Instead, she's given us new allies, new perspectives, and new possibilities. She's changing the game board itself, not just telling us which moves we made wrong."

He paused. "Sometimes the most effective change comes not from knowing what went wrong, but from having the right people in the right place to make entirely new choices."

Robert nodded slowly. This last argument was the strongest yet and seemed to calm the nerves of those around him. But while the argument finally made sense to him, it further increased the already backbreaking pressure on him and his two companions.

"I'm willing to trust *Tala*," said Alara. She rolled her eyes. "You know ... *any Tala*. Things have gone from bad to worse in a hurry. So, perhaps her timing is as good as yours seems to be, Hierophant. Atlantis is amassing forces in Nasavi and is making good progress against Kemet."

Aethor sighed loudly. "And worse still, they've begun testing Nexus Prime in secret. It's more formidable than we feared. I've seen the surveillance footage myself. One blast, just one, for only about a second destroyed much of a small island."

Thoth frowned deeply. "I've been absent far too long. In my self-imposed exile, I watched and waited when I should have acted. Although perhaps it was good that I was in my hideout in the forest when *Tala* brought these three to my doorstep. In any case, it's clear I no longer have the luxury of inaction."

He gripped his staff tighter. "We have two important tasks before us. First, we must neutralize Nexus Prime, with immense gratitude to Aethor for providing us with a means to accomplish this. However, stopping the invasion force requires a different kind of strategy altogether. What comes now will echo across time itself. Should we fail, the lesson will not end here. No. Our failure to learn, to gain the proper wisdom, will ultimately lead to those in the future having to face even graver consequences."

To Robert, the talk of a weapon capable of obliterating entire islands, and more, was overwhelming, and not surprising. This had to be the weapon, and the war, that some Hopi Elders indicated had brought about the destruction of both Atlantis and Lemuria.

Across the way, the Anunnaki looked disinterested, seated with their backs against the wall, talking among themselves, almost as tall sitting down as Robert was standing.

Thoth thanked the gathering for their attention and asked them not to tell a single additional soul what he had disclosed about the time-traveling starship and its far-future crew, making sure Ishar and his Anunnaki comrades also gave their word on this point. No one else would likely believe time travel was possible, anyway, but if they did, it would bring about unanswerable questions and confusion, along with unwanted attention to a starship and crew that benefited greatly from anonymity.

Finally, Thoth asked the group to return to their duties.

The Hierophant spent another few minutes having a private discussion with Aethor, who then bid farewell to the sage and his three guests and soon disappeared down a long corridor.

"What's next?" asked Robert.

"We begin the most perilous part of our joint mission," said Thoth. "*Tala* chose you all for reasons beyond our understanding. From this point forward, you'll need to adapt. Kira, I sense you're already prepared in ways even you might not fully realize. I think it best if you remain here for the time being. And, Matt," he continued, pivoting to face him, "you'll remain here with Kira. There's much you can learn from these people." He gestured around the bustling chamber. "A dozen souls, each committed to a cause greater than themselves. They'll help you awaken the warrior spirit within.

"And you, Robert," said Thoth in a calm tone, "I'd like to take you to look at something. Something that might change the course of your life and may well change the course of history."

"Why does my gut tell me you're speaking about a Vesh'tar?"

Thoth smiled warmly. "Because your instincts are exceptional. Perhaps the very reason you're being chosen. And yes, I'd like you to visit a library with me and try a certain Vesh'tar on for size."

Robert nodded.

He and Thoth bid farewells to Kira and Matt and then, without wasting another moment, the Hierophant led Robert out of the Great Hall.

CHAPTER 31

Robert and Thoth wound deeper into the heart of the underground base. Carvings continued to cover almost every surface. Glyphs and symbols intertwined. Robert recognized some from his studies. Ancient scripts, astronomical charts, geometric designs hinting at mathematical principles long forgotten.

They passed through a tall, wide chamber where the ceiling arched high overhead, supported by colossal pillars carved to resemble massive trees. Stone vines wrapped around them, leaves created with such detail they seemed almost real. Here, a few other individuals ambled about, carrying scrolls. At a table, two people engaged in a hushed conversation.

"Impressive place to set up a Resistance," said Robert.

"The Underground is a sanctuary. A repository of knowledge and a refuge for those who seek truth."

Thoth descended a spiral staircase with Robert close behind. The steps were worn smooth by countless passages, and at the bottom, an arched doorway led into another portion of the library. As they crossed the threshold, Robert's breath caught.

This part of the library was a cavernous hall with shelves upon shelves stretching into the distance, laden with scrolls, tablets, and books bound in materials ranging from leather to metals, and what he'd come to know as datapads. Thin devices reminding him of computer tablets. Some sat on tables, chairs, and what appeared to be couches. The floor was inlaid with a mosaic of the Tree of Life, its branches and roots extending outward. Statues stood tall along the perimeter. They were larger-than-life figures draped in flowing robes, their expressions serene. Some held orbs, others staffs. One statue carried a double helix spiraling up like DNA.

"The Tree of Life," said Robert. "A symbol of interconnectedness. Of the unity, between the physical and the spiritual."

"Very good. Exactly right."

"I still can't comprehend why Atlantis would pursue conquest," said Robert. "Its civilization is almost Utopian. The technology, the harmony, the beauty. Everything I see and learn about Atlantis indicates a society dedicated to peace, learning, art, beauty, and so on. Not violence and war."

Thoth looked more distraught than Robert had ever seen him. "Don't underestimate the bloodlust and aggression in our genes," he said miserably. "Buried just below the surface of the most civilized among us. This aspect of human nature has helped our race achieve greatness. Still, it's also a part of us that requires constant suppression, even while living in paradise." He sighed. "*Especially* while living in paradise."

"Why *especially*?"

"Boredom and contentment can be an enemy of our ambitious, aggressive natures. Some have a need to feel adrenaline in their veins, to engage in dangerous activities for the thrill of the danger itself. When we have too much luxury and leisure, and too few life-and-death challenges, some find ways to create these challenges, these dangers, for themselves. So they can feel alive."

Robert's eyes widened as the point finally sunk in. As a historian, he should have realized what Thoth had been getting at. Alexander the Great had basically conquered the entire known world. But had this made him happy? Content?

The answer was a resounding *no*. History had famously noted that just the opposite had occurred: "Alexander wept, for there were no more worlds to conquer."

Robert was also reminded of a relevant statement made in an old movie called *The Matrix*. One uttered by the AI-created villain, speaking to the movie's hero: "Did you know that the first Matrix was designed to be a perfect human world? Where none suffered, where everyone would be happy. It was a disaster. No one would accept the program. The perfect world was a dream that your primitive cerebrum kept trying to wake up from."

Robert nodded at Thoth. "I think I do understand, after all."

"Good. But the darker side of human nature is just one facet of the problem. We've matured considerably as a species. We've made great strides when it comes to getting the demons of our nature under control."

He paused. "Remember when I told you that hostile species meddle with us? That the coming war might be our own idea, or we might be getting manipulated by an alien race, spurring us on to favor the ugly side of our natures?"

"I remember."

"Over the past hundred years and more, the alien culprits in this regard have been a race called the *Draconians*. Dracs for short. They've been insidious. So much so that even the Emerald Order didn't realize what was happening until it was too late."

Thoth paused. "Beginning many decades ago, a political faction arose in Atlantis, one that championed dominion over stewardship, control over harmony. We didn't know how it grew to be so powerful at the time, but it's clear to me now that the Dracs were responsible for fanning this faction from a tiny ember into a roaring fire. These Reptilian extraterrestrial beings found a way to subvert much of our government. They're patient, subtle, and at times, quite clever. Through politics rather than the devastation of all-out war, they've all but taken over."

He blew out a long breath. "They began to control the will of a handful of Atlantean politicians. Bribing them. Spinning webs of lies, deceit, and manipulation. *Brainwashing* them. That brainwashing spread like a plague. And while it's hard to believe, they've done so with such finesse and secrecy that not even the Atlantean High Councilor or the Lumerian Circle of 12 are aware that they exist."

"How is that even possible?"

"It seems like it *wouldn't* be. Which is why our leaders scoff at the very idea. The Dracs are long-lived, calculating, and most importantly, *extremely* patient. They manipulate so much, yet almost never leave their fingerprints on any of it. They show themselves to precious few humans, who do their bidding, greatly extending their reach while they remain hidden. When conducting business remotely, they pretend to be other humans. So, our leaders, at the highest echelons, see the Dracs the same way your historians view Atlantis and Lemuria. As interesting, highly elaborate delusions."

He shook his head in disgust. "And once they solidified their influence, they became a festering cancer inside the body politic. Like cancer, an entire tumor can be obliterated, but if a single cell survives, it will grow into a tumor again. But this time, the tumor will be even *more* resistant to the cure."

He paused, his voice carrying centuries of stress. "The Dracs have reshaped our governance, our very ways of thinking, so subtly that most don't have any idea of just how deep their manipulations go. Most humans affected believe they act of their own accord, yet their choices echo this inherited dogma. It flows through our councils and our decisions. It acts as an invisible current that pulls us ever further from our original path. Even now, it persists, though few can name it or see its workings. Those who remember the old ways grow fewer with each passing season, while the insidious influence of the Dracs continues to take hold."

"What you describe is too horrific for words," whispered Robert. "It's truly *sickening*." He shook his head. "It actually brings to mind a parasitic relationship I've read about that occurs in the natural world. One that's equally insidious."

"Tell me about it."

"The parasite, a protozoan named Toxoplasma gondii, manipulates rodents in a way that's truly diabolical. When a rodent is infected, the parasite alters its brain chemistry in such a way as to dramatically reduce its fear of predators, especially cats." He raised his eyebrows. "Even wilder, the infected victim actually becomes *attracted* to cat urine. In short, under the parasite's influence, a rodent is induced to ignore its own survival instincts."

Thoth's face curled up in disgust. "But why? How does that help the parasite?"

"Because it desperately wants to be inside a cat. The parasite can reproduce *asexually* inside any host. However, cats are the only animals that accumulate linoleic acid in their intestines, which the parasite requires for *sexual* reproduction. It's evolved to manipulate rodents into becoming cat food, so it can hitch a ride into the cat's intestines."

Thoth looked ill. "That is one of the grisliest things I've ever heard."

"Yes. And the way you describe the Dracs brings it to mind. Although the parasite uses physiological means to exert control, while the Dracs use psychological methods."

Thoth frowned. "Yet the result is the same, isn't it? We ignore our own survival instinct to the benefit of the manipulator."

There was a long silence in the room. "A fascinating discussion," said Thoth finally. "I really should get back to why we're here." He motioned to an alcove, where a semi-circle of staffs had been collected, each one unique. Vesh'tars. They hovered just above the floor, five in total.

The leftmost staff was crafted of dark wood with a turquoise sphere. Beside it floated one of pure white wood, topped with a clear crystal catching and scattering light like a prism. The middle staff appeared to be made of living bronze, its surface rippling with patterns like flowing water, crowned with an amber sphere wrapped in metallic ribbons.

The fourth was the shortest but somehow the most imposing. Black as midnight and smooth as glass with what looked like a round piece of obsidian suspended in a cage of silver atop the shaft. The fifth and final staff seemed to be woven from strands of some pale green material he couldn't identify, with a misty orb at its peak swirling with colors he couldn't quite name.

"Do you feel yourself drawn to any of these?" asked the Hierophant.

Robert nodded, surprised when he realized the answer was yes. A subtle pull drew him forward, like a magnetic force making his skin prickle. His heart thundered in his chest as he moved closer and sweat beaded on his forehead.

The one that seemed to call to him was the leftmost staff, which had a shaft made of dark, polished wood capped by turquoise, a bluish orb wrapped in brown tendrils mimicking roots. The craftsmanship was unlike anything he'd ever seen.

Robert's hand trembled slightly as he reached out for the staff. When his fingers touched the wood—warm and alive rather than cold and dead as he'd expected—a surge of energy coursed through him. It was as if lightning had struck, but instead of pain, it brought an overwhelming sense of connection. Nothing in his life had prepared him for this sensation.

He jerked as the energy pulsed . . . once, twice . . . sending vibrations through every nerve ending in his body. His knees gave way, and he collapsed onto the mosaic floor, the impact barely registering through the flood of power. The staff remained clutched in his hand, anchoring him to reality while everything he thought he knew about the world shifted around him.

When he hit the ground, a deep voice resonated within his mind. *"You are now ready for the Emerald Order."*

Images flooded his consciousness. Vast libraries filled with knowledge, galaxies spinning in the void, threads of light connecting distant stars. Figures in green robes standing guard over sacred places, their staffs glowing like beacons. Emerald-robed hierophants forming defensive lines around spires, their Vesh'tar staffs raised high. Vessels screamed across the sky, exchanging fire with ground batteries while those wielding the ancient devices channeled brilliant arcs of lightning upward, creating corridors of safe passage for evacuating civilians. He witnessed healers kneeling beside fallen defenders, their staff crystals pulsing with soft, restorative light, mending wounds.

The scenes changed to great halls where master hierophants used their staffs to project star maps, manipulating the very fabric of space-time to calculate celestial alignments. In underground chambers, others used their crystals to maintain ancient machines, the staffs interfacing directly with Atlantean technology.

Despite their power, the images showed the gradual fall, the overwhelming of even these mighty defenses. The final scenes showed the desperate acts of those who chose to preserve what they could of their knowledge, sealing it away in hidden vaults, accessible only to those who would one day prove worthy of such wisdom.

"*The Emerald Order seeks not power, but balance,*" the voice continued. "*As you've seen, many who were once in the Order are gone. As a guardian, you'll carry the light of wisdom into the darkest corners. You should consider it a great honor, but also an even greater responsibility. And know that your journey won't always be an easy one.*"

The visions faded, and Robert became aware of his ragged breaths. Thoth was kneeling beside him, a steady hand on his back.

"Are you all right?" asked Thoth.

"I think so." Robert looked at the staff in his hand. The orb was pulsing in rhythm with his heartbeat.

"You've now connected with the Vesh'tar, and it has acknowledged you."

"But I saw what I believe was the past."

"Good. That means that your destiny is intertwined with ours now. The path of the Emerald Order lies before you, should you choose to take it. The Emerald Order is about safeguarding knowledge and fostering harmony. The Vesh'tar you've chosen is a symbol of that commitment."

A sudden jolt of energy burned through Robert's arm like a hot poker pressing into his skin. He stumbled backward as the Vesh'tar clattered to the floor. The crystal at its tip blinked once before falling dark.

Robert rubbed his tingling palm. "What just happened?"

"Apparently, the Vesh'tar felt that you weren't quite ready to take on the full level of responsibility required. You must have subconsciously pushed it away."

Thoth raised his bushy eyebrows. "But when you are ready, it will be waiting, I can assure you of that."

CHAPTER 32

Councilor Kairos Daedalus
High Marshall of the Atlantean Military Forces
The Scarlet Dune Campaign
Location: Northern Kamet, East of the Nile River

Kairos Daedalus strode across the scorched Kemet sands, his boots crunching over shattered armor and broken weapons. Smoke curled from the ruins of the Kemetian fortifications. It cast a haze clouding the desert sun. Dead soldiers lay strewn about, their bodies twisted amid the wreckage Kairos's forces had wrought. All around, structures had collapsed, some still belching fire, others nothing but char and ash.

A dozen Atlantean soldiers wearing battlesuits flanked Kairos. Each held a rifle at the ready. Kairos gripped his own rifle, his gaze sweeping over the devastation.

A feeble groan drew his attention. A Kemetian warrior struggled on the ground, half his body fused with the remnants of his battlesuit. The metal had melted into his flesh, leaving a disgusting meld of man and machine. Blood pooled beneath him, soaking into the thirsty sand.

Kairos approached, his shadow falling over the wounded trooper. The soldier's eyes were full of pain, though they also held a defiant spark.

"Brave effort," said Kairos. "Your people fought fiercely."

The soldier grimaced. Words failed him, but the desperation in his stare spoke volumes.

"Do you have a son?" asked Kairos, crouching beside him. "A family at home, waiting for you?"

A weak nod accompanied by a choking cough was the man's only response.

"Sons can be quite the challenge. I hoped mine would follow in my footsteps, but it wasn't to be. Now, I'm a disappointment to him. And he's become quite the thorn in my side." Kairos glanced at the horizon. "Your fight reminds me of him. Stubborn. Unyielding. Sometimes plain dumb."

The soldier's breathing grew more intense, and he coughed a few times, lowering his chin as if his neck was too weak to support him.

"I'm sorry that you're suffering," said Kairos. "A warrior such as you shouldn't have to endure such indignity."

In one swift motion, he raised his rifle and fired a laser bolt between the Kemetian's eyes. The soldier's head lurched back, his eyes glazing over, lifeless. Without a second glance, Kairos turned and continued up a sand dune.

At the crest, Argo awaited him near a makeshift outpost. The seasoned commander surveyed maps projected in holographic displays, coordinating with other officers.

"Impressive results," said Kairos as he approached.

Argo looked up, his expression like steel. "We've secured the area, Councilor. The Kemetian resistance is faltering here."

"I must admit, I've had my doubts about you, Argo. But today's success speaks volumes."

"Thank you."

"Continue your efforts. The eastern Nile must remain under our control before we proceed to the west and south."

Argo nodded and returned to his strategizing.

Movement caught Kairos's attention. Through the heat waves rising from the sand, a Helion-class diplomatic vessel touched down at the dune's base. The transport's obsidian hull was angular and marked by deep blue energy lines glowing along its length. It was the same type of craft that had brought him here. Unlike military vessels, the Helion series was built for politicians rather than combat, though its defensive capabilities were far from negligible.

Beyond the landing site, the ancient Kemetian city of Amshira sprawled across the horizon. Its golden buildings jutted upward, while vast temples dedicated to silly gods stretched into the distance. The surrounding jungle pressed against the city's edges like a green tide, threatening to reclaim what civilization had carved from its depths.

In the far distance, over Amshira's western quarter, flashes of combat lit the sky. The sound of explosions reached Kairos seconds later, a delayed song of warfare resounding across miles. While the battle for the jungle city continued, its outcome was now certain. It would soon fall to Atlantis and become yet another territory to rule.

A figure emerged from the Helion shuttle and from the swirling sands below. Archon Lysandra Therianos. She ascended the dune, tall and stately, her steel-grey eyes never missing a thing. As second to the High Councilor of Atlantis, she moved with two Sovereign Guards—elite warriors in battlesuits. They were Atlantis's finest, handpicked protectors of the highest echelon of Atlantean leadership.

"Archon," said Kairos in greeting.

"High Marshall," she replied in a monotone pitch as she reached the outpost and stepped inside. "A significant victory today. I came here to take a look, observe, and have a chat with you. Can we talk?"

"Certainly." He led her away from Argo and his commanders into a crystal-walled sanctuary. The transparent panels adjusted automatically, dimming to filter the harsh desert light while maintaining a view of the battlefield all around. Cool air breezed from hidden vents.

Two lounge chairs rose from the floor beside an obsidian table. As Kairos and Lysandra sat, the furniture's blue fabric adjusted its density and temperature to them.

Kairos poured each of them a glass of wine as his guest studied the battlefield.

"The cost of lives is staggering," she said. "On both sides."

"A necessary sacrifice for the prosperity of Atlantis."

"Prosperity built on the ruins of others."

He took a drink and swallowed, taking his time. "Atlantis carries the torch of civilization. Those who oppose us hinder progress. Hinder the worldwide unification we need to protect ourselves if the galactic order takes a turn for the worse. We've discussed this before in many debates. Is that why you're here? If so, you're a little too late. Our advancements began months ago."

"That's not why I'm here." Lysandra set her drink down. "You've issued troubling reports regarding Lemuria's involvement in recent battles."

"Yes. It's clear that Lemuria is using Kemet to fight a proxy war with us. They've been supplying them with aid and weaponry."

"Do you have proof?"

"Yes. On several fronts. We've seized any number of Lemurian weapons on the battlefield. Their signatures are unmistakable. And Lemuria isn't just helping Kemet, but interfering in other initiatives."

He lifted his eyebrows. "In addition, they're limiting our procurement of Opalith crystals from the Kanaloa Mines. They've been hoarding resources. Land. And they've been squandering potential that Atlantis could harness to enhance worldwide security and prosperity."

His guest shook her head. "Arming our enemies and other interfering activities around the edges aren't ideal. Still, they don't constitute an act of war, either."

"Make no mistake, Archon, Lemuria isn't just posturing. They're preparing for war. And the gravest mistake a military leader can make is underestimating the enemy. I've seen reports that they are weak and cowardly. Pacifistic. I'm sure you and the High Councilor have seen the same. I don't believe them. I'm convinced that if we wait for their first move, become reactive rather than proactive, they could hurt us. We risk a war that could last years . . . *decades*."

He leaned forward. "But if we strike first, one decisive and overwhelming offensive, we end this before it begins. Their mighty territories are ripe with potential, yet languishing under inefficient governance. Every day we hesitate is another day their resources remain untapped, and their people are denied the benefits of true Atlantean innovation.

"If we can take control swiftly and implement our systems of governance, we can transform their struggling territories into models of advancement. The longer we wait, the more lives will be lost in a protracted conflict. Sometimes the most humane action is the most decisive one. Even if it appears destructive."

She flinched from his words, either not expecting them or surprised by the weight behind them. "They seem to be doing just fine on their own," she countered. "In many ways, better than us."

She held his stare for several long seconds. "Why do you propose violating longstanding agreements? Provoking further conflict, further violence? I believe the reports. The Lemurians want to avoid war at all costs. If we ease tensions with them, there's no way they'll strike the first blow."

"Have you seen what they've done to Nasavi? They've systematically displaced entire nations of people, pushing them from their ancestral lands. The Lemurians claim to bring advancement and prosperity, but I see only cultural extinction. They march across territories that aren't theirs, planting their flags and building their cities and outposts, whatever they deem necessary to spread their nonsense. That's what they'll do to us."

"I've not heard of Nasavi being harmed in any way by the Lemurians," said Lysandra. "In fact, quite the opposite. Mutual cooperation and advancement. That's what I've read. That's what I've *observed*."

"Then tell me, where are the indigenous peoples now? Where are the great nations that once walked those lands? Swallowed up by Lemurian tyranny."

"They were integrated voluntarily, Kairos. The Lemurians provided them with advanced systems. You know, sustainable housing, medical technology, educational initiatives."

"Integrated?" He laughed. "You mean forced to abandon their spiritual practices, their cultural identity? It was the Lemurian way or death. It was a choice between survival and extinction. The only difference was the speed of their demise."

"It appears we see the same events quite differently, Councilor."

"I'm telling you they're a threat. They've armed our enemies. They've repeatedly breached the Crystal Trade Accord, deliberately withholding key shipments of Opalith crystals while claiming 'production delays.' Their vessels have been spotted conducting 'exercises' near our established shipping lanes, and their diplomatic corps continues to undermine our influence in smaller nations."

Lysandra folded her arms. "I worry that you're exaggerating the transgressions, and the threat, to satisfy your thirst for conquest."

"And I worry that you're grossly *underestimating* their capabilities and resolve, which puts Atlantis in a dangerous position."

The Archon looked almost amused, as if she were playing with her food, and it had managed to scurry out from under her claw for a moment. "I admire your passion, Kairos," she said. "But I'm afraid you need to return your focus to matters closer to home."

Kairos's mind raced. What was he missing? "And why is that?" he asked finally.

"There are concerns regarding your son, Aethor."

Kairos's gaze sharpened. "What of him?"

"Reports indicate he's been consorting with Thoth."

"Impossible."

"Nothing is impossible. It's really why I've come here to speak with you. Aethor's involvement with Thoth poses grave risks. To both you and Atlantis."

"Do you have evidence?"

She produced a tablet. From it, a holographic projection illuminated, showing Aethor standing beside Thoth. The background was obscured, though.

"Where did you get this?" he demanded.

"An anonymous source. They couldn't disclose precise details, but the implication is clear."

He stared at the image, a storm brewing inside him. Had the thorn in his side now become a dagger in his eye? Could his son have possibly betrayed him to this extent?"

"The situation requires careful handling," said Lysandra. "Aethor's actions could undermine Atlantis's efforts. Terrorism spreads fast, and it looks as if Thoth is back to his old ways."

Kairos rubbed his jaw. "I'll address this personally."

"Please do. The High Councilor expects loyalty above all."

He met her gaze. "Speaking of the High Councilor, perhaps his attentions are divided. With threats on multiple fronts, decisive leadership is essential."

"Are you questioning his competence?"

"Merely observing that Atlantis needs unwavering strength. Now more than ever."

She studied him. "It isn't weakness for him to put the nation's welfare over his personal ambitions. Atlantis shouldn't conquer lands if we're only motivated by power and greed."

"I would never suggest otherwise."

Lysandra turned her attention back to the battlefield. "We should coordinate our next moves. If you're correct, Lemurian involvement complicates matters. Send me the proof you have and we'll consider the best way forward from there. And by we, I mean you, me, and the High Councilor. I'll arrange a strategy meeting with him."

"Excellent. In the meantime, I'll get to the bottom of my son's possible involvement with Thoth's Resistance."

She stood. "Very well. And, Kairos, be mindful of your next political moves. In my decades of service, I've witnessed many ambitious leaders chart similar courses. Few reached their intended destination."

With that, the meeting ended. Kairos watched as Lysandra descended the dune, her Sovereign Guards moving beside her. The Helion-class vessel's entry hatch opened. As she disappeared inside, the craft's engines whirred to life. Sand twisted in eddies as the ship lifted. In a burst of blue energy, it shot skyward like a bolt of lightning, leaving only scattered sand behind.

After downing his drink, Kairos exited the chamber and motioned to one of his officers. "Prepare my shuttle. I need to return to Atlantis immediately."

"At once, Councilor."

Argo walked in his direction. "Is everything okay, sir?"

"Priorities have shifted. I need to return to Atlantis. Continue consolidating our hold here."

"Of course. We'll secure the remaining sectors."

"Stay vigilant. Lemurian interference may escalate."

Argo gave a curt nod. "We'll be ready."

Kairos placed a hand on his shoulder. "Your performance today demonstrated your capabilities. Perhaps greater responsibility is in your future. I was worried about you and your place among my elite."

"I won't disappoint."

Kairos nodded, walked down the sloped dune, and moved toward his shuttle as the ramp lowered. As he boarded, his thoughts turned inward. Aethor's alliance with Thoth could unravel everything.

Thoth, the perpetual thorn, the agitator challenging the established order. And Aethor? His son's betrayal gnawed at him. Not just any betrayal, an alliance with Thoth was the *ultimate* betrayal. Kairos had spent most of his career fighting to rid Atlantis of the smug, dangerous Hierophant. An ancient soul capable of manipulating anyone and everyone. Capable of steering the course of nations with mere whispers. And now, it appeared, he had poisoned Aethor. If Thoth now had his son's ear, he would also gain access to Atlantean government systems, secrets, and so much more.

But was it true? The photo could have been faked. It could be a political maneuver initiated by his enemies to derail his ambitions and sabotage his carefully laid plans. And to force his hand.

He would have to find out. The ultimate betrayal? Or just another move in an ever-shifting game of power? And could Lysandra, herself, be behind it? Or someone else entirely?

Settling into his seat, Kairos activated a secure communication link. A holographic screen materialized, awaiting input.

"Connect me to Syndic Ixra Maren."

"Connecting," an automated voice responded.

Moments later, Ixra's image came into view. "Councilor Daedalus, how may I assist?"

"We have a situation requiring discretion. I need surveillance intensified on certain individuals within Atlantis."

"Names?"

"Aethor Daedalus and any known associates of Thoth."

Ixra hesitated. "Your *son*? Is there a specific concern?"

"His activities may pose a risk to national security. I expect this matter to remain confidential."

"Understood. We'll initiate enhanced monitoring immediately."

"Good. Report directly to me with any findings."

"Of course, Councilor."

Kairos terminated the connection. He desperately hoped this was an elaborate deception. His son, though misguided in many ways, had always been loyal to Atlantis.

The craft lifted from the desert floor. Through the viewport, the fractured landscape of Kemet shrank below. The conquest here was but one piece of a larger game. A game he intended to win.

As the shuttle pierced the upper atmosphere, Kairos considered his next move. He activated another communication channel. "Schedule a meeting with Councilor Deir Slan upon my arrival."

"Yes, Councilor," his aide responded.

Deir Slan held sway over key political assets and harbored her own ambitions.

A notification chimed softly. "Incoming message from Councilor Slan."

"Put her through."

Deir's visage appeared, her eyes sharp beneath a furrowed brow. "Kairos, I hear congratulations are in order for your victory in Kemet."

"A small win, yes, but a decisive step forward. Our forces performed admirably."

"Indeed. What prompts this call?"

"I'm returning to Atlantis. I wish to discuss matters of mutual interest upon my arrival."

"You're coming to Poros City?" said Deir.

"I am, if you'll have me."

"Of course."

"Good. I'll arrive within the hour."

"I had a rather fascinating encounter recently. A Lemurian Diplomatic Advisor—Elowin Balivae."

"Why would she seek you out?" asked Kairos.

"She claims we're doing everything we can to provoke war. That we're orchestrating it from the shadows, while Draconians are orchestrating *us*." Deir's lips curved into a thin smile. "Dangerous accusations."

"Let me guess. She intends to sound the alarm. Expose these supposed machinations."

"That's her intent, no doubt. But her own government must not believe her, or she'd have already sounded the alarm, loudly and with great frequency."

"Perhaps it's time that I met with her myself," said Kairos. "Determine if she poses any real threat to my plans."

"I'd be happy to arrange a meeting between you two in my private chambers?"

Kairos smiled. "Please do. This should prove . . . enlightening."

"I'll schedule it immediately. Perhaps we could discuss this further over dinner afterward. I know a discrete establishment."

"It's as if you're reading my thoughts, dear colleague."

The hologram dissolved, leaving Kairos alone with his reflections. Some problems, he mused, required his personal touch to resolve. Or perhaps, to destroy.

CHAPTER 33

The long oak table dominated the room. Robert sat along its edge, dwarfed by the great ceiling stretching above.

Around him, figures in flowing robes conversed in low tones. Some wore garments similar to Thoth's, though theirs varied in hues. Deep maroons, earthy browns, dull oranges. The Hierophant sat nearby. His eyes held a far-off look. "I worry about Aethor," he said to Alara.

She sighed. "For good reason. It's hard to imagine a riskier mission than the one he's undertaking."

As they continued their conversation, Kira leaned closer to Robert. "This place is incredible," she whispered. "Everything down here. The architecture, the atmosphere. The tech."

Robert nodded, taking in the high arches and stonework. "Never thought I'd be dining in an underground palace. Certainly beats the university cafeteria."

Matt shot the professor a quizzical look. "Last time we saw you," he said, "Thoth was taking you to what he called a library. He said he wanted you to try a certain Vesh'tar on for size. His words. So, did that happen?"

Robert nodded. "He showed me five of them, actually. All unclaimed."

"I figured you'd be holding one by now," said Matt. "What went wrong?"

"The one that called to me isn't quite ready. Well, to be fair, it claims that *I'm* not quite ready. I'm not entirely sure what happened." Robert smiled. "And we thought *Tala* was mysterious. Apparently, the motives of sentient starships and sentient staffs aren't always easy to understand. Who knew?"

Matt grinned. "Good one, professor," he said. He bent forward, resting his elbows on the table, and his expression transformed into one both serious and thoughtful. "I'm guessing when one of them called to you, you were pretty freaked out. It's mysterious and powerful, so I get that. But maybe it sensed your anxiety. Maybe that's why it pulled back."

The young man paused. "It seems to me, though, at the risk of sounding like a bad movie, it's your *destiny* to carry one. So, maybe next time you're near it, if you can find a way to sort of, well . . . surrender to this destiny, it will realize you're ready."

"I have to agree with the kid," said Kira. She turned to Matt. "And since when did you get to be so spiritual and wise?"

"Hard not to be changed by our journey," he replied. "By realizing that my father's teachings weren't far-fetched after all. In fact, after what I've seen here, his teachings were too conservative. They weren't impossible *enough*."

Robert studied Matt for a moment. "Guess we're all finding truth in ancient wisdom and sacred lore these days."

Matt picked at his plate. "I'm young and I'm not a professor," he said. "And I have wasted some of my life and potential. But that ends now. I know you don't see me as anywhere near your equal, but my hope is to earn your respect."

"You have already," said Robert. "Kira and I have many more years of education, experience, and maturity than you, so no, I don't feel you're as capable as we are. Not yet. But I do think you've handled yourself extremely well considering all we've been through and considering your age."

"I agree," said Kira. "Bettering yourself is a worthy goal. I have no doubt you'll find a way to unlock your full potential."

There was a sustained silence.

"What about the two of you?" said Robert. "While I was off with Thoth, what were you up to?"

"Believe it or not," said Kira, "Firearms training. Rifles and a few other weapons. And not standard target practice. They had this holographic setup that felt absolutely real. We ran scenarios in jungle and city environments."

"You should've seen the Atlantean city simulation," said Matt. "Towers going on forever into the sky, lights everywhere. Pyramids. Along with other stuff I didn't begin to recognize."

"If the simulation is that good, imagine what the real city is like," said Robert.

"Maybe we'll get the chance to tour it someday," replied Kira. "The training room's something else, though. You'd be really impressed."

Matt pointed his utensil at Kira. "She's even more of a badass than you'd think."

Kira smiled. "You surprised me in there, too, Matt. It almost seemed as if you've had military training."

Matt shook his head. "Hopi training. We had vision quests growing up, physical training, defensive training. Dances. Rituals. All important to my father and other elders. So, I learned a thing or two. It's not Navy SEALS or anything like that, but it can be pretty tough. And I like to think I'm a good athlete."

"No doubt," said Kira. "And we already know that Robert can more than hold his own."

Robert leaned in on his elbow. "I'd love to give this simulation a try. Where's this training room?"

Before Kira could answer, Thoth turned to them. "I couldn't help but overhear. The training room is down a level, near the eastern chambers. It used to run day and night when we had thousands of Resistance members living down here. We use it to prepare our people for various environments they might encounter. Simulations help without exposing anyone to unnecessary risk. It was created by the Emerald Order long ago."

"Of course it was," said Robert, rolling his eyes.

"It's an immersive training experience," continued Thoth. "It can sharpen skills exponentially better than target practice on a range."

"I'm intrigued."

"Good. We'll make it happen," said Thoth. "For now, I'd suggest the three of you get some sleep. The future is likely to be . . . challenging. It's important to catch up on your sleep when you have the chance. I can have Alara show you to your quarters."

"Now that you mention it," responded Kira, "I am pretty beat."

Both of her male companions agreed. Only minutes later, Alara was leading them through a passageway as the low roar of conversation faded behind them in the great eating hall.

"This place is a maze," said Matt.

"You'll get the lay of the land soon enough," replied Alara, not bothering to look back and with a tone that wasn't particularly friendly.

Robert glanced at symbols on the wall. "What do these mean?"

"Records of our history. Stories preserved in stone."

Kira ran her fingers lightly over the carvings. "They're beautiful."

Alara's eyes narrowed. "And thousands of years old. So please don't touch them again."

"Right." Kira winced. "Sorry about that."

They reached a set of doors; each marked with unique patterns.

"Your quarters," announced Alara, who then abruptly left them, vanishing from view around a corner.

"I don't think she likes us much," noted Kira when she was gone.

Robert shrugged. "Probably being protective of Thoth. And after all she's been through, I'm sure trust doesn't come to her easily."

Robert pushed open his door and looked inside. At the back of the room was a bed carved from stone and covered with soft linens, and a small table with a glowing orb providing light. The trio took one step inside, noting the earthen walls exuded a natural warmth. A simple chair and a shelf completed the space. Another doorway hinted at an adjoining room, perhaps a bathroom.

"Of all the underground lairs I've been in," said Robert, "this has the nicest quarters."

Kira nodded. "Yeah, it's going to ruin us for other underground lairs going forward."

Matt smiled. A moment later he issued an epic yawn. "I'm going to my room to get some sleep. See you guys in the morning. Assuming we survive the night."

"Why wouldn't we survive the night?" asked Robert.

"Well, we *are* part of the Resistance now," replied the youngest member of their trio. "Who knows when Atlantis will figure out we're all down here and exterminate us like rats in a sewer."

Kira sighed. "What a lovely thought," she said as Matt moved to exit the room. "You should be a poet."

CHAPTER 34

With Matt gone, Kira turned to leave herself, ready to find her own room next door and fall into a blissful sleep. "Goodnight, Robert."

Robert took a deep breath. "I know we're both exhausted, Kira." He raised his index finger, signaling for her to halt. "There's . . . something I wanted to ask you before you go."

"Sounds serious."

"Hopefully not. Let me get right to it. When you and Matt were describing the training simulation, he reminded me of what a badass you are. He used this exact word, actually. I've begun taking that aspect of you for granted. Seems like we've been here forever. But before we arrived, this was a side of you I had no idea existed."

She shrugged. "How could you? We never had to face extinct lions, wolves, towering aliens, and so on, back in our time. You can't tell that someone is great at tennis until you see them play tennis."

Her expression turned quizzical. "So I can handle myself in a tight spot. Is that a problem?"

Robert gave her a weary smile. "No. It's a godsend. If you weren't so effective, we'd likely be dead by now. We make a great team. But it troubles me that I thought I knew you, and I keep being surprised. What else don't I know?"

"Are you saying you're suspicious of me?"

"Not really," said Robert unconvincingly. "No, of course not," he added more forcefully. "Let's just say I'm *curious*. And I want to be sure I understand your history and motivations. Because it's more than you just being able to handle yourself. You've shown insight into military tactics. You know more, have more depth, and are more thoughtful than you came across back home. Don't get me wrong, you were impressive then, also, but you're showing multiple layers I didn't know were there. I find you to be truly *extraordinary*."

"And that's a *bad* thing?"

"No. Of course not. Just a *surprising* thing."

"So when did surprise turn into suspicion?"

"Right after you analyzed and critiqued the Atlantean military emplacements. I asked you at the time how you were so well-versed in military tactics. You told me that your father was a Marine before he became a geologist and taught you everything you know."

"That's right."

"But you also claimed that you had told me about this earlier. Trust me, you hadn't. That's not something that would ever slip my mind."

"I must have misremembered, then."

"Maybe. Or you were doing your best to discourage me from following up. Hoping that this subtle ploy would lead me to believe I had previously found this information forgettable, unremarkable, and as such, unworthy of further discussion."

"The information *is* unremarkable. My father was a Marine. Why does that matter?"

"Because you told me everything about him. Everything about why you sought me out and what motivated you. But then it turns out, you really *didn't* tell me everything about your dad. You left out something pretty key to his story. So . . . what else might you be leaving out?"

Kira smiled. "You think like a detective, Robert. Which makes sense. I've heard it said that archeologists and anthropologists have to be better than elite detectives since they have to solve the ultimate cold cases. Cases so cold that all the witnesses died off *thousands* of years before. But you need to stop being a detective when no crime has been committed."

"Why did you really fund my research, Kira? I know your father disappeared. But there's more to it than that, isn't there? Why me, in particular?"

"Your research touched on areas he was investigating. I hoped that if he was still alive, you might lead me to him. You know, using those finely honed detective skills of yours."

"Interesting. You do realize this is different from what you told me before. I think you're having trouble keeping your stories straight. You told me your father vanished in the Scablands. That you believed there was more to his disappearance than the authorities were letting on. And that you wanted to support research capable of proving that the world holds mysteries and truths well beyond what is commonly accepted. That there are more things in heaven and earth than are dreamt of in our philosophy. You hoped any revelations I might find would serve as a tribute to your father's beliefs and help you maintain your own sanity."

Kira nodded slowly. "Okay, you're right. That is what I told you. I didn't want to admit I was holding out hope he was alive. It's such a long shot. And even if he's alive, *finding* him is an even greater longshot.

So I gravitated toward your research, which touched on areas he was investigating. I thought supporting you might lead me to him. It would take a miracle, but at least I'd have *some* hope."

"He was a geologist. Not an archeologist. So how could our work overlap? And how could I lead you to him?"

"I didn't share everything with you, Robert, but my intention wasn't malicious. And you can't say you didn't benefit from our alliance."

"No, I can't. And not just because of your funding. You redirected my research, steered me toward specific sites. You chalked it up to intuition, but it was more than that, wasn't it? You had information. Real information. Didn't you?" Robert hesitated for a moment. "So what really happened to your father?"

"It isn't entirely clear. And at the risk of saying something an archeologist might find blasphemous, perhaps some mysteries should stay buried. The bottom line, Robert, is that you have to choose. Either you trust me, or you don't."

"So, you aren't going to tell me?"

"I prefer to remain a little mysterious," said Kira, flashing a smile. "It heightens my allure, don't you think?"

"Trust me, Kira, your allure doesn't need any heightening."

"Will you be able to work and fight by my side, despite not having your curiosity completely satisfied?"

Robert blew out a long breath. "There's no one I'd rather have by my side. No one. I'm frustrated that you've been keeping things from me. And still are. But *Tala* chose us for a reason. So, while I might never know your full agenda, I believe that our goals are aligned. I trust you to have my back. And your competence and poise in desperate situations is second to none."

"Thank you. Your abilities and intellect aren't too shabby, either."

Robert snorted. "Probably not the most glowing compliment I've ever gotten. But I'll take it."

CHAPTER 35

Advisor Elowin Balivae
Poros Territory, Poros City
Location: Southwest Atlantis

Elowin stood in the foyer of Poros's Grand Hall Council building. Columns of white and gold stretched toward vaulted ceilings where chandeliers hung. Massive murals attached to the walls depicted Atlantean history. Even the air felt different here, filtered through purification systems making it almost too clean, too perfect.

In nature, everything worked in harmony, regardless of how it might appear. The mud caking a tree's roots wasn't a flaw. It housed microbes feeding nutrients to the bark. The crooked branches, the uneven edges of leaves, the forest floor with its messy tangle of fallen twigs, decomposing leaves, and busy insects. They all worked together. It had been some time now since Atlantis had truly appreciated this lesson.

Elowin frowned. She'd been waiting too long. But she wasn't going anywhere. Not when she had the chance to meet with Councilor and High Marshall Kairos Daedalus himself. A hawk who, for some reason, had chosen to masquerade as a diplomat.

Finally, the receptionist approached her. "Councilor Daedalus will see you now. Your guards will need to remain here."

"My guards will accompany me. That isn't negotiable."

The receptionist stared deeply into her eyes and came away convinced that she wasn't bluffing. A tense silence pierced the air before the woman gave Elowin a curt nod. "Very well."

She was led down a corridor lined with towering columns and tapestries showing Atlantean conquests. Eight of Lemuria's most elite soldiers followed. Finally, they reached heavy double doors, which swung open to reveal Kairos Daedalus. He stood at the window with his back to his guest, gazing out at the Poros skyline.

Holographic maps of the city floated above a desk made of larimar crystal, and shelves lined with artifacts covered the walls. Larger-than-life marble statues of past Atlantean heroes ringed the massive room.

Kairos turned, wearing an insincere smile. "Welcome, Advisor Balivae. Please come in."

The room he was in was magnificent, opulent, and half the size of a ballroom. He gestured to the eight elite soldiers with her and shook his head in amusement. "Do you think you brought enough guards?"

"Not really, no," said Elowin with the hint of a smile. "Not to compare my courage to yours," she added, "but I'm fairly sure that you would never agree to do the converse of what I'm doing now. You would never agree to come to the heart of Lemuria to meet with the head of *our* military. No matter how many guards were with you."

"Very nice," said Kairos. "I couldn't have delivered a better response myself. Not the diplomatic rubbish I'd expect. I like you already. Still, I must insist your guards remain outside."

"That's not acceptable."

"It will have to be. This is a diplomatic meeting, not a military operation. My security detail will be stationed beyond the door also."

Elowin frowned. The truth was, it didn't matter. She was in the belly of the beast, well behind enemy lines, and she had always known she'd be vulnerable. This had also been true when meeting with Deir in this very location, but Kairos Daedalus was a different animal entirely. Intel suggested he could be savage, ruthless, and capable of atrocities others would deem unthinkable. Elowin's gut had told her to take a larger, faster shuttle, and add a number of guards to her usual contingent, just for good measure.

Still, she wasn't too concerned for her safety. After all, she wasn't a military strategist or other high-value target who would stand in Kairos's way when the war did begin. Why capture or assassinate a woman he had to believe was a feckless pacifist? Doing so would risk enormous negative repercussions even within his own government. There were certain rules of diplomacy that were sacrosanct, even during wars, which this was not. There were certain lines that even psychopathic monsters couldn't cross without consequence.

And perhaps even more importantly, if he tried to kill her now, given her guards, there was a slight chance he'd die in the crossfire, himself. She couldn't imagine he'd calculate the significant risks were worth the negligible rewards.

She instructed her guards to wait outside and then tapped a quick message to Kona, who was manning their ship on the roof. She asked him to join the guards and provide any high-level pushback needed if Kairos insisted on disarming them or stationing them farther from the room. Finally, with the guards outside the closed door, she turned to Kairos.

"Where is Councilor Slan? I was told she'd be present."

"Councilor Slan sends her regrets. She's engaged elsewhere."

"Isn't this her office?" she asked, which she found an absurd word to describe a space that was at least ten times the size of her own spacious office.

"It is. But I'm afraid we need to proceed without her. I'm no diplomat, as you know. So, forgive me if I'm more blunt than you're used to, but let's get right to it. What's on your mind?"

"Atlantean forces continue to amass along our borders in Nasavi. This show of aggression destabilizes the region. We demand the immediate withdrawal of your troops."

"Demand? That's a strong word. Our forces are merely making sure there's peace and order, as you've been told countless times."

"You've invaded Kemet, one of our allies. And several islands as well."

"We have conflicts with others, yes. But *invaded* is the wrong word. They're at fault. They started this, not us."

Elowin had to forcibly concentrate on not rolling her eyes at this ridiculous re-write of history.

"The important thing for you to know," continued Kairos, "is that we aren't at war with Lemuria. We have great respect for your country. It's magnificent. A beacon of cooperation and harmony."

He shook his head, and his eyes took on a fierce glare. "But... consider this: while Lemuria builds consensus, Atlantis builds *empires*. While you debate, we *act*. The world needs both dreamers and doers. And sometimes, the dreamers need protection from those who would take advantage of their gentler nature. Without Atlantis, this world would be stagnant, diminished in every way."

Elowin held her tongue. She was under no illusion that she could get the High Marshall of the Atlantean military forces to budge a millimeter. Given that he was the *architect* of Atlantis's current aggression, he was the last person in all the realm who would capitulate. She was here only to gauge him, search for any potentially exploitable weakness. Listen to his rantings rather than speak herself. See what she could learn, if anything.

"You spout harmony," he continued. "But you ignore a key fact. The tensions between nations are the primary cause of *disharmony* on our world. If the entire globe were one glorious nation, wouldn't that be the epitome of harmony? Atlantis offers enlightenment in every aspect of civilization. We'll make the world better. Stronger. More advanced. And better able to fend off any attack from beyond."

He paused to let Elowin respond, but she just sat there in rapt attention, as if waiting for him to continue. "Further," he said, "without movement, without growth, worlds crumble. Human beings need challenges. We stagnate and fall into depression when we stop evolving, when we remain static, when we sit around doing nothing. The same principle applies to nations."

Kairos paused again, but Elowin remained silent. He no doubt had expected endless, cloying arguments about peace, love, harmony, aggression, and other such pablum, and yet Elowin just sat there calmly as if hanging on his every word.

"What, no argument?" he said finally. "Where is your pushback, your fight? I assumed you would challenge my assertions."

Elowin laughed. "If they truly *were* your assertions, I'd challenge them. I don't suppose you'd let me meet with the Dracs whose assertions these really are? You're just the mouthpiece. I can almost see a Drac hand up your back, controlling a pathetic puppet who thinks he's a man."

Kairos's eyes almost shot fire, and for a moment she thought he would strangle her with his bare hands. She had hit the nerve she'd been aiming for. She had belittled him, dismissed him as impotent, as a stooge, with no independence or power. She had hit him squarely in his massive ego, emasculating a man who was nine-tenths testosterone.

Finally, his temperature fell, the lava heat replaced by a controlled, ice-cold demeanor. "You know, my intel suggested that Lemuria had given up on trying to stop the war. That you represented their last-ditch effort. I figured you'd be as inept as all the others. But Deir found you to be far more competent, and far more dangerous, than she expected. You drew her out. Manipulated her into making mistakes. As you almost just did with me. Deir was right. You're a breed I've never seen before. A diplomat with the heart and cunning of a warrior."

He paused. "Your words were precisely chosen to bring my blood to a boil, which isn't easy to do. Yet you succeeded. Since I knew this would likely be one of your tactics, your success is all the more impressive. I wasn't sure what to do about you, but you've now helped me reach a decision. You're too good to be allowed to remain on the board. You're a victim of your own competence."

Elowin's eyes widened in horror. Coming from someone else, Kairos's last two statements might be metaphorical, but coming from him, they were almost certainly literal. She reacted less than a second after he finished, diving to the floor, rolling, and pressing a crystal bead on her bracelet that sent an alarm to her guards just beyond the door.

Seconds later, a thunderous explosion rocked the corridor outside, the blast wave rattling the artifacts on their shelves. It was the high-pitched whine of Atlantean laser fire mixed with the deeper thrum of Lemurian plasma weapons. It meant her warning had come just in time for her guards to raise their weapons an instant before they were gunned down in cold blood.

Through the doors came the echoes of combat. Armored bodies slammed against marble. Shouted orders. The sharp crack of return fire.

Elowin's mind spun. The door behind her. Blocked. Windows. Too high. Her guards. Likely overwhelmed.

The double doors burst inward with a splintering crash. One of Elowin's guards stumbled through, his battlesuit scarred and smoking. A deep burn had melted through his chest plate, the edges still glowing orange, before he collapsed face-first onto the floor. Two others joined him, both in better shape, along with Kona, who should have known to stay out of the fray and leave the fighting to the warriors.

The Lemurian guards turned to engage Atlantean soldiers who entered the room at their heels. Kona ignored the exchange, spotting his friend, and raced to her side, just as Kairos's formal robe shifted to reveal a glint of metal beneath. The councilor shed the outer garment, revealing a lightweight combat vest. Two laser pistols materialized from concealed holsters at his ribs.

Elowin pushed Kona to the floor and rolled behind a massive marble statue as the room erupted in blinding light. One beam sizzled past her head, so close she felt its heat scorching the wall behind her.

Kona scrambled to her side behind the statue.

But he didn't quite make it. Just as he was about to find cover, a beam hit him squarely in the back, killing him instantly. Kona's eyes stared upward, unseeing, the light and wisdom in them forever extinguished.

"No!" shrieked Elowin, a primal scream piercing through the roar of battle. A wave of nausea washed over her, and a tear came to her eye.

Heavy footsteps approached. Kairos trained a pistol at her head. "Goodbye, Elowin. I'm sorry, but I've come to believe that if anyone could pull off the impossible and derail my plans, it would be you."

She stared into Kairos's cold eyes, steeling herself for the inevitable. Kona lay motionless beside her, his once incredible spirit gone.

A flash came from the doorway as a plasma bolt flew past Kairos, narrowly missing his temple, fired from another of her guards who had made it into the room after the pair who had entered with Kona had been killed.

Kairos dove aside, his pistols skidding across the floor. He rolled behind a marble column, cursing under his breath.

The guard seized Elowin's arm, pulling her to her feet. "We need to move! Now!"

Kairos wanted to retrieve his fallen weapons, but the crossfire kept him at bay while the guard led Elowin away. They dashed out of the office, and Kona's lifeless form was burned into Elowin's memory. Her heart ached, but survival propelled her forward. Numerous Atlantean soldiers lay dead in the wide hallway, their armor charred and smoking, along with at least three more of her own.

The guard with her spoke into his helmet mic. "Bear Three to Shuttle. Elder Kona is down. Advisor Balivae is secure. Prepare for immediate exfil. We're en route."

A crackle responded. "Copy, Bear Three. Shuttle's ready. Standing by."

They darted toward the stairwell. "Up to the roof!" the guard bellowed. "Stay close!"

They rushed into the stairwell, the sound of pursuit coming from below. As they climbed, the guard demagnetized his sidearm and thrust it toward her. "You'll need to use this."

She grasped the plasma pistol. "I haven't fired one in years."

"Point and shoot."

Voices shouted. The guard glanced back. "Keep moving!"

An Atlantean soldier appeared on the landing above, weapon aimed. Elowin reacted instinctively, firing. The plasma bolt struck the soldier's shoulder, spinning him into the wall. The soldier with her quickly aimed and fired two perfect shots. One through the hostile's visor, the other into his exposed neck. The Atlantean's body slumped, smoke curling from his wounds.

They continued upward. Each landing shifted between light and dark as the emergency lighting system blinked erratically. Two Atlantean soldiers emerged from the upper level. Their laser rifles whined, beams cutting through the air.

The Lemurian guard shoved Elowin against the wall, his armor scraping against the concrete. "Stay down!" Laser fire peppered his battlesuit, each impact leaving burnt craters across his chest plate. Still, he planted his feet, becoming a human shield between Elowin and certain death. The soldiers closed to mere yards, the confined space of the stairwell filling with the smell of charred metal.

Elowin's guard deflected the first soldier's rifle with his damaged forearm, the laser blast going wide and melting a hole in the wall. The Lemurian sent a power kick shattering the Atlantean's knee joint with a loud crunch of metal and bone.

As the second soldier brought his weapon to bear, the Lemurian guard's reflexes proved faster. His armored hand shot out, knocking the rifle aside. In one fluid motion, he jammed his plasma rifle into the gap between the Atlantean trooper's helmet and shoulder plate. The blast illuminated the area in blue fire, and the Atlantean's body fell limp.

Elowin had known this was an elite group of soldiers, but she was still surprised by just how special the man protecting her truly was.

They ascended farther. The rooftop door loomed ahead, but more footsteps came. A squad approached fast.

Elowin's guard yanked a neural disruptor from his tactical belt—a Lemurian weapon looking like a rippling sphere of liquid metal. "Shield your eyes!"

He hurled it down the stairwell. The sphere pulsed with increasing frequency, emitting a high-pitched whine. The device detonated in a flash, targeting the Atlantean troop's neural interfaces. Their screams echoed up the stairwell as their own armor's systems turned against them. Bodies dropped, twitching, as their suits' neural links misfired, leaving them convulsing against the steps.

"Won't hold them long," the Lemurian soldier said. "Their armor will reset in thirty seconds."

Elowin and her guardian reached the door, finding it barred from the outside. The guard swore, pulling out a breach charge. Behind them, boots thundered up the stairs, getting closer. He armed the small explosive as laser bolts began hitting the walls around them. He slapped the charge against the door's locking mechanism. "Three seconds!"

The explosion rocked the stairwell, and the door blasted outward, tumbling across the roof. They pushed through the threshold where their shuttle awaited, ramp extended. Two Lemurian soldiers waved them forward. "Over here!" one shouted.

Scattered around were the bodies of Atlantean troopers and several of her own. The guard guided her toward the shuttle. "We're not safe yet. We've got to go now!"

They rushed toward the shuttle's extended ramp. Through the open hatch, Elowin glimpsed the pilot, preparing for an emergency take-off. But something caught her eye. A subtle distortion near the shuttle's main thruster housing. Her years of security briefings kicked in.

"Wait!" she said. "There's a—"

An electronic shriek, like metal being torn apart, started low and climbed higher. The sound signature was unmistakable. It was an Atlantean phase-charge, designed to detonate when detecting people moving toward it. She'd seen one demonstrated eight months ago during a military oversight committee meeting when Lemurian Intelligence had acquired and analyzed Atlantean weapons. That demonstration had ended with half a reinforced bunker reduced to slag.

The guard grabbed her arm, trying to pull her back, but they were too close to the ship.

The explosion ripped through the shuttle's hull, turning the aircraft into a fireball. The shockwave lifted Elowin off her feet, hurling her backward through a storm of burning shrapnel. The world spun, sky and roof trading places. She slammed hard against the rooftop, the impact driving the air from her lungs.

Through blurred vision, a twisted sheet of hull plating spun toward her head, its edges still glowing orange from the blast. Her last conscious thought was of Kona's lifeless eyes, and the bitter realization that Kairos had prepared for every contingency, even her unlikely escape to her vessel.

Then, the metal descended, and darkness claimed her.

CHAPTER 36

Councilor Kairos Daedalus
High Marshall of the Atlantean Military Forces
Poros Territory, Poros City
Location: Southwest Atlantis

Kairos crouched amid the wreckage, fingers coiled tightly around his pistol's grip. Smoke wafted from the barrel. Across the office, another firearm lay on the floor. He rose, surveying the aftermath.

Near the office's entrance, a Lemurian guard sprawled motionless, his visor blasted open, and eyes fixed on some distant point beyond the ceiling. A piece of the broken visor stuck into the ridge of his nose, blood dripping down his cheek.

Just beyond the entry, bodies of his own Atlantean soldiers littered the floor, armor destroyed by plasma burns. He noted their positions, reconstructing the moments leading to their demise.

They were slow. Although outnumbered, the Lemurian guards were better, more skilled.

But he likely only had himself to blame. It should have been an *ambush*. Not a battle. So, either something his men had done had tipped off the vigilant Lemurian guards, or something *he* had done had been responsible. Namely, foreshadowing Elowin's demise.

He still couldn't believe she had reacted so quickly. So decisively. It was incredible. And a woman capable of assimilating imperfect information so quickly and making the instant decision to dive to the floor, was also a woman who would make sure she had a way to warn her guards of an ambush, to sound an alarm.

Only the smallest fraction of even his most elite warriors would have reacted as flawlessly as Elowin had done. He still blamed himself for foreshadowing what was to come, but he wasn't prepared to beat himself up. Sometimes you just had to acknowledge a brilliant reaction by a worthy adversary. He had been right to give the termination order when he had. She was even more dangerous than he had suspected.

Kairos stepped over a shattered vase once holding rare blossoms from the Hanging Gardens, and his gaze settled on Kona Makelo. The Lemurian Elder lay on Deir Slan's office floor, a dark stain spreading across his traditional robes.

A distant rumble echoed through the building, the floor vibrating beneath his feet. The tremor built to a resonant boom, rattling the fixtures hanging from the ceiling.

The explosion was right on cue. He may have erred by letting the cat out of the bag a moment too soon, but at least he had the foresight to prepare an explosive booby trap in the highly unlikely event Elowin managed to survive long enough to return to her ship.

Now, the remains of this exceedingly gifted and attractive woman were scattered across the roof.

A soft chime sounded from the comm device on the desk. Kairos glanced at the console before walking over.

He tapped the screen, and the holographic face of Councilor Deir Slan materialized. She took in the disarray. "Can I assume Elowin Balivae is no longer a concern?"

"That's correct. The record will read that her vessel underwent an unfortunate malfunction."

This might have actually worked out for the best, he realized. Now, he could burn and mangle the corpses of the fallen Lemurian guards to make it seem they were caught in the explosion along with the Advisor. He could stage them in a grisly, macabre scene on the roof, allowing him to claim that Elowin and her crewmates had lost their lives in a tragic accident. One not of his doing.

It would require extra work and planning, and he had a huge mess on his hands that needed cleaning up, but it might be worth it.

"The Circle of 12 will suspect sabotage," he continued. "But they won't have proof. Our hands should remain clean. Well, clean *enough*."

"Good work," said Deir. "But Thoth remains a threat. He's like a virus spreading dissent, poisoning people against us. He's even more dangerous than Elowin."

"As you know, he's a top priority. It's only a matter of time before he's found and dispatched."

A subtle notification blinked at the corner of the console. Kairos's eyes moved to the alert. "It's for me. I have to take it."

"How are you getting calls on my private comm channel?" asked Deir.

"Sorry. I only gave access to one person. Trust me, they won't use it again or give it out."

She considered. "I suppose that's okay. I do trust you implicitly. Are we still on for dinner tonight?"

"Absolutely. See you soon."

Deir's image blinked off before the transmission ended.

Kairos accessed the incoming message, an encrypted channel opening to reveal Syndic Ixra Maren. "Councilor Daedalus, it seems our investment in a certain sympathetic party has finally yielded dividends. The beacon is active."

The Syndic was once again proving her exceptional effectiveness. "You've confirmed the signal?"

"Let's just say that our mutual friend has provided us with an unprecedented window of opportunity. One that could benefit you significantly."

"Show me," said Kairos.

Ixra transmitted the data, and a series of holographic images materialized, most depicting Thoth seated at a grand table, surrounded by three unfamiliar faces. "Our mole has provided quite the intimate perspective."

Kairos studied the three unknown figures. A rugged man with keen eyes, a striking woman who held herself with poise and self-assurance, and another man—almost a boy—who seemed far too young to have earned a seat at any table with the Emerald Hierophant.

"I don't recognize any of the three," said Kairos. "And they look out of place somehow. My gut finds them odd in ways I can't put into words. Who are they?"

"Unclear," said Ixra. "But I agree. There is something about them that paints them as outsiders. It's intriguing to me that Thoth would risk such associations."

"I assume they didn't match anyone in our databases?"

"That's right." Ixra leaned forward. "Hopefully, they represent a weakness we can exploit to get to Thoth. We may be able to topple, not just the Hierophant, but his entire support structure."

Kairos beamed. He had been chasing Thoth's shadow for years, and he was finally getting close, and just at the perfect time. But who were these strangers? And were they something to worry about, or a sign of Thoth's desperation?

"I took the liberty of having our forces positioned strategically," continued the Syndic. "Purely as a precautionary measure, of course."

"Well done."

"Thank you. And I'd suggest we move quickly. Windows of opportunity have a way of closing unexpectedly."

"Indeed they do." Kairos's gaze lingered on Thoth's image. He had pursued the man for years, and each failure had added another layer to his obsession. "Our informant has done a masterful job of getting this to you."

"Yes, an excellent choice."

"Keep this just between the two of us. Just as Thoth is being betrayed by someone he trusts, we don't want to risk that we also have a betrayer in our midst."

"I agree. A wise precaution."

Kairos ended the transmission, and the holographic images dissolved into nothingness. Ten minutes had passed since the explosion. Enough time for rumors to start spreading throughout the building. Kairos moved toward the shattered doorway. The hallway strobed with warning lights, systems still reacting to the rooftop detonation. A unit of Sovereign Guards approached. "Councilor Daedalus, we've secured the perimeter," reported the lead guard.

Kairos continued his strides. "Clean up this mess," he said, gesturing to the bodies still strewn about. "Then take the Lemurians out on the roof and blow them up. Stage them as if they were victims of the vessel exploding. Take videos of the scene and then cart them away in body bags. But first cordon off your path so no one here sees what you're doing. And get a team to clean this office and restore it to exactly as it was before. I want it sanitized. Antiseptic. Not a hair or skin cell left behind. Finally, coordinate building security and ensure the official narrative is disseminated. What happened was a tragic malfunction in the Lemurian shuttle, nothing more."

His mind flashed to previous attempts to capture Thoth. Each time, public perception had been key. "Any witnesses are to be thoroughly debriefed."

The guards fell in around him as they moved through the halls. Officials pressed themselves against walls, their faces showing the fear and curiosity he'd anticipated. Perfect. Their whispered conversations would carry the story he wanted told.

Rather than engage in unnecessary dialogue with the guard captain, Kairos issued directives as they descended to the transport bay. Every minute spent here was another minute Thoth might slip away, as he had on Nasavi, in the Eastern Wastes, and in the Caved Cities. Each escape had narrowed the Hierophant's options, forcing him to take greater chances. Like trusting those around him a little too much.

His shuttle waited on a platform, engines cycling up. Kairos turned to the lead guard. "Dispatch a covert team to these coordinates." He handed him his datapad. "Swift, but invisible. I want Thoth's new associates caught in the same net."

Settling into a chair inside his craft, Kairos contemplated his situation. In the many years he'd hunted Thoth, he'd never had coordinates or such clear visuals. The Sage was brilliant at maintaining his network—a web of supporters and allies across territories—while remaining personally hidden somehow. These new outsiders, however, represented something different. Thoth was usually careful to work through intermediaries, keeping layers of separation between himself and his operatives. But not this time, apparently.

The pilot's voice came over the intercom. "Councilor, we're cleared for immediate departure. Destination locked."

"Proceed," replied the High Marshall.

As the shuttle lifted off, he watched the city unfold beneath them, the spires of Atlantis reaching toward the clouds. The night sky was punctuated by the distant glimmer of civilian crafts.

He called Deir on his personal comm. He had to capture Thoth while the iron was hot. With the Hierophant in custody, they had a real chance of unraveling his entire network. "I'm afraid I'm going to have to reschedule our dinner," he said to Deir when she answered. "I promise I'll make it up to you. Sorry about the late notice, but something urgent has come up."

"Something urgent delivered by whoever called you on my line?"

"Yes."

"Anything serious?" she said with obvious concern.

"Nothing I can't handle," he said, "but I need to go. We'll dine together very soon. And perhaps we'll have something momentous to celebrate," he added, ending the connection.

Kairos immediately wondered if this were really true. Thoth had repeatedly proven himself to be more clever and more slippery than any other adversary. Kairos's thoughts drifted to previous near-misses with him. The ambush in the Corine Caverns leaving three squads in shambles. The trap in the Northlands' Upper Districts the sage had somehow known about hours before it was sprung.

Still, this time was different. This time they had Thoth dead to rights. This time, he couldn't possibly elude them.

Kairos winced, remembering that these were his exact thoughts the previous times he had the man in his sights. He had learned the hard way that when it came to Thoth, one could never count their eggs before they hatched.

CHAPTER 37

The air rippled as Robert stepped into the holographic chamber. A pulse of energy washed over him, and his stomach lurched as reality changed.

Beside him, Thoth adjusted his flowing green robe. Matt and Kira moved forward, while Alara hung back, watching.

The Atlantean capital of Poseidia materialized around them, unfolding in layers. First came the ground, then the buildings, and finally the sky itself. Golden-topped pyramids pierced the heavens, their ivory sides shining from artificial sun rays.

Robert had to remind himself that nothing inside the simulator was real except the humans who had just entered and a large case that Thoth was carrying.

The Kozar obelisks caught Robert's eye immediately. Crystalline structures pulsing. Their hexagonal forms drew energy from the pyramids, feeding it into transmitters powering the sprawling metropolis.

"Your simulation is even better than advertised," said Robert.

"Glad to hear it," said Thoth. "I'd hate to disappoint."

Streets paved with red tiles wound through the city. Civilians moved about. Men wore fine tunics belted at the waist, the fabric draping over loose-fitting trousers. Women dressed themselves in gowns full of beautiful patterns woven into the fabric.

Exotic spices wafted to Robert's nostrils, accompanied by the salty sea breeze. Laughter and lively chatter filled the area as merchants hawked their wares from open-air stalls.

A young woman carrying a basket of fruit brushed against Robert's arm. "Pardon me," she said with a warm smile before disappearing into the crowd.

Robert wasn't sure if *reality* felt as real as this simulation.

"It's like we're in the Matrix," said Matt, obviously feeling the same way as Robert.

Kira noted Thoth's questioning expression. "The Matrix is a fictional story from our time," she explained. "In which people live their entire lives inside a simulated reality without knowing it."

"Many of our scientists believe that our entire universe is just a simulation," said Robert.

He had planned to elaborate, but he was too transfixed by the marvels around him to keep his train of thought. "How long have you *had* this technology?" he asked Thoth in awe.

"For thousands of years. We mostly use it for training and exploration."

Robert's gaze had drifted upward to the levitating transports gliding between spires, but this response caused him to return his full focus to the Hierophant. "Thousands of years?" he repeated in dismay. "You have to be *kidding* me. Just how long has Atlantis been around?" he added, realizing this was a question he should have asked long ago.

"In one form or another," said Thoth, "for sixty thousand years or so."

"*Sixty thousand?*" whispered Robert in shock. "That's absolutely *astonishing*. In our time, no civilization was thought to have survived for much more than five thousand years," he noted, thinking of both the Chinese and Egyptians.

"Atlantis has evolved, adapted, endured, changed, and even changed hands a few times. Civil wars, areas that sunk into the vast sea, disrupting the landscape. You name it, and it's happened to both Atlantis and Lemuria."

They moved deeper into the city, entering a grand marketplace. Stalls lined the avenue, displaying goods. Artisans crafted jewelry beside devices projecting holographic images. A vendor demonstrated a levitating orb floating above his palm, delighting a group of children.

"We're wasting time!" said Alara irritably. "We should get on with their training already. They can sightsee when there *isn't* a war looming."

She had continued to lag behind the group, her stance that of someone ready to move at a moment's notice. The way she watched them reminded Robert of a cornered animal. Alert, dangerous, and distrusting.

"I can understand your impatience, Alara," said the Hierophant. "But surely we can spare another five minutes. You've been immersed in this city since you can remember, but for them, it's entirely new, and obviously a feast for their eyes."

Alara nodded but didn't look happy about it. Kira turned to her. "Look," she said. "We didn't get off to a great start. You know, seeing as how you were about to arrest us, or worse, when we landed. But that was then, and this is now. So, no need to keep your distance. We're all friends here."

Alara didn't respond, but she didn't move any closer and wore an expression that suggested she couldn't disagree more with Kira's assessment.

Children darted past, chasing after a small, mechanical bird. It fluttered and dipped. The sound of music drifted from a nearby pavilion where performers played instruments both familiar and alien.

Kira turned to watch the performers. "It's beautiful here."

Thoth smiled. "It is. And this is exactly the way it is in real life. The setting hasn't been enhanced."

Robert admired a nearby fountain where water cascaded in defiance of gravity, swirling upward in strange patterns. "Now, that's fascinating."

A shadow passed overhead. One of what looked like a potential patrol craft. Around Robert, the civilians tensed, their conversations dropping to whispers until it moved on.

Thoth's expression darkened. "Things are not always as peaceful as they appear."

As if in response, a distant alarm began to sound. The crowd's mood shifted. Subtle at first, then with growing urgency. Parents called their children closer. Merchants began securing their valuables.

The patrol craft circled back, lower this time. Two more joined it, their engines' pitch changing. The civilians knew what it meant—Robert could see it in their faces as they began to move quickly away from the market square. "This is part of a battle simulation, isn't it?" he said to Thoth. "We've already begun our training, haven't we?"

"I was hoping you'd figure that out. Which is why I didn't warn you."

Thoth opened the case he was carrying and two Vesh'tars appeared, hovering. The first was Thoth's, its vivid green crystal orb glowing, encased by root-like tendrils. Beside it hovered the staff Robert had connected with. At the same time, rifles and other weapons materialized to their right, arranged on a floating rack.

"Robert, the staff is attuned to you, as you know," said Thoth, gesturing toward the second Vesh'tar. "Are you ready to take it?"

Robert thought about this for a long moment and finally nodded. "I am," he said decisively.

"I mean *really* ready. Ready to embrace the pairing. And the responsibility."

Robert thought a few seconds longer. "I am," he repeated.

"Good. As you've no doubt guessed, the staffs are real, whereas the weapons are virtual. The Vesh'tar can't be fully simulated, even in the most sophisticated of simulators, nor can the bond between you and it."

Robert hesitated, eyeing the glowing orb nestled within the root-like tendrils. "I don't know how to use it."

"Trust in yourself," said Thoth. "It will guide you. And while it's real, it has tied itself into the simulator, so will keep its actions virtual. It's aware this is a training exercise."

A searing beam sizzled past Robert's ear. The rifle next to him exploded in a shower of sparks and molten metal, its remains scattering across the ground. Through the marketplace's morning haze, dark figures emerged from three directions—a squad of armored soldiers spilling from an alley to their left, another unit rappelling down from a nearby rooftop, and a third group advancing through the screaming crowd from the main thoroughfare.

"Move!" shouted Matt, diving behind a nearby pillar.

Thoth grasped his own staff. "Arm yourselves!"

Robert grabbed a rifle from the floating rack. A soft hum vibrated through his palms as the weapon's crystal core powered up, status indicators flickering across a screen on the small of the rifle's stock. Like the Lemurian plasma rifle, this Atlantean weapon was lighter than he expected, its alloy frame warm to the touch. Kira and Alara each took a rifle as well.

Civilians scattered in panic. Market stalls toppled, spilling fruit and crafts across the red-tiled street. The soldiers advanced, their armor glinting as they took positions behind columns and overturned carts. Energy beams crisscrossed the marketplace with a high-pitched whine, leaving phosphene trails. Each blast shattered pottery and scorched stone.

Kira took a position behind a stone kiosk. She fired, each beam finding its mark. An enemy soldier fell, then another.

Merchants abandoned their stalls and exotic birds burst from their cages in a flash of rainbow feathers. The enemy troops continued to move swiftly, some using market stalls as cover while others advanced through the colonnaded walkways on either side.

Robert crouched behind a toppled market stall, realizing he had instinctively grabbed a rifle, a weapon that was familiar to him, rather than the Vesh'tar. Not a good start.

His heart pounded in his throat. This wasn't a game anymore. Reason told him he couldn't be hurt here. But his senses told him this was real, and he would die if he was hit, and his adrenal glands and heart obviously agreed. He peered over the wooden counter. Twenty yards ahead, an Atlantean soldier had taken position behind a fallen column, his visor reflecting the fires starting to rage throughout the marketplace. Sparks rained down from a damaged power conduit overhead.

Robert aimed and pressed the trigger. A bolt of energy shot forth, striking the soldier's arm. The enemy cried out, weapon clattering against the broken tiles. The soldier dove forward, his armor scorched but intact, reaching for his fallen rifle. His armored fingers had just brushed the weapon when Matt's covering fire forced him back behind a small dome.

"Nice shot!" shouted Matt from his position near a merchant's cart, its display of fabrics now riddled with smoking holes.

Robert sprinted toward a massive stone fountain, energy beams cutting through the air around him. He slid behind its base, boots splashing in the pool of water spreading across the tiles. The fountain's central sculpture—a leaping dolphin frozen in crystal—provided decent cover, though its tail had already been sheared off by enemy fire.

Explosions erupted around them. A Kozar obelisk took a direct hit, its crystalline structure fracturing before detonating in a massive flash of light. The shockwave knocked Robert off his feet. He crawled behind an elevated planter box the size of a small car, its flowers swaying in the breeze.

Thoth stood in the open, Vesh'tar raised high. Electricity arced from the orb, leaping across the ground like luminous serpents. The energy struck a squad of soldiers, their armor convulsing with sparks before they collapsed.

Alara darted between columns along the marketplace's eastern edge, providing suppressing fire at soldiers attempting to advance. She pointed toward a narrow alley between two buildings decorated with hanging gardens. "We need to flank them!"

Kira nodded, motioning for Matt to follow. "Cover us!"

An elderly man stumbled into view, his robes tangled around his legs, terror etched on his wrinkled face. Without hesitation, Robert rushed from his cover and guided the man toward a sheltered archway where other civilians huddled.

Above, aircraft engines gave out a hollow shriek. Three vessels swooped between towers, their electromagnetic drives generating a metallic taste on Robert's tongue. The air compressed and expanded with each pass, making his ears pop. They were predatory in shape, with swept-back wings shifting configuration mid-flight. Twin cannons mounted beneath each wing rotated, tracking them. The lead craft's ventral beam emitter glowed red as it locked onto their position.

A low-slung assault vehicle rounded the corner. Twin turrets unfolded from its sides, swiveling to target their group. The teardrop-shaped craft whirred as it glided forward on invisible repulsers.

Thoth slammed his staff into the ground. The resulting ripple sent a wave of energy coursing beneath the street's red tiles, leaving a large amount of buckling stone in its path. It erupted beneath the approaching vehicle, flipping the craft into the air. The machine crashed onto its side, sliding into a merchant's shop in a display of sparks and twisted metal before exploding.

"Keep moving!" commanded Thoth, gesturing toward a towering spire in the distance where several transport platforms docked. "The extraction point is at the Tethin Terminal! Follow me!"

Robert was about to comply when the air rippled around him. The vivid colors of the city began to fade, buildings flickering like a dying projection.

Robert gasped as his gut insisted they were now in *real* danger, rather than just virtual. The simulation technology was thousands of years old and had to be nearly malfunction-proof. He tried not to panic, but saw this as unmistakable evidence of an imminent attack, just as he would if he was in a military safe-house back home and all phone lines went dead at the same time.

Something very bad was about to happen.

The simulation powered off entirely a moment later, leaving them in the dim confines of the chamber. The floor shuddered. Dust cascaded from the ceiling while the sound of distant explosions—this time terrifyingly *real*—echoed throughout the underground facility.

A young resistance fighter rushed into the sim room, breathless. "Thoth!" he shouted in a panic. "We have a breach. Atlantean soldiers have infiltrated Sector Twelve. We've been found!"

CHAPTER 38

The simulated rifle that had felt so real had vanished along with everything else. Robert's gaze locked onto the turquoise Vesh'tar hovering before him, its tendrils coiled around the thrumming crystal atop the staff.

Had it followed him through the simulation? Or had his brain been fooled into thinking he had covered a significant distance when he had barely traveled? Given the very finite size of the cavern, this latter must be true.

"Robert, move!" shouted Alara as she scanned the trembling walls. "Forget the Vesh'tar!"

His feet refused to obey. His fingers twitched at his sides, drawn to the ancient relic. A second. Maybe two. With a sudden lunge, he grasped the smooth, pulsating material.

The weight settled in his palm. Electric, alive. He spun toward the stairwell just as Thoth waved them forward. "Up the stairs! Hurry!"

Robert followed, staff in hand, bolting behind Matt, Kira, and Alara. Dust rained from the ceiling as the sounds of turmoil grew louder above. Shouts, gunfire, the muffled thumps of explosions pressing closer. The stairwell shook.

Thoth stumbled mid-step, catching himself on the railing. "No," he whispered in horror. "This isn't possible." His wide eyes darted to the quaking walls. "They've found us, despite our advanced cloaking tech."

"Someone must have sold us out," said Kira, as she and the others took the stairs two at a time.

They burst onto the upper level. Robert froze, bile rising in his throat. The Underground's grand hall was unrecognizable. Resistance fighters lay scattered in pools of blood across shattered tiles. The stench of burnt flesh hung thick in the air. The handful of remaining members fought fiercely, but they were outmatched. Atlantean soldiers in battlesuits were about to tear through them like bulldozers clearing a dig site.

An Atlantean soldier tackled a Resistance fighter into an earthen column, cracking it upon impact. As the fighter crumpled to the floor, the soldier fired a point-blank shot into his chest.

Off to the side, a low-yield explosion rocked the chamber, sending shards of debris flying. Smoke and stone dust filled the air, obscuring sight.

From a concealed corridor, more Atlantean soldiers poured in, their entry point hidden from view. They advanced, cutting off escape routes.

Amid the bedlam were the Anunnaki. Enkuul, towering at eleven feet tall, unleashed a storm of fury, his weapon sending bolts. Each shot punctured enemy armor. Soldiers screamed as he charged, hurling one hostile with such force that he crashed into two others, their battlesuits sparking as they hit the ground, crushing the scattered remains of display cases beneath them.

A concentrated energy shot struck Enkuul mid-charge, piercing his chest. Time crawled as Robert stood at the top of the last stair. Enkuul staggered, looking down at the smoking wound before collapsing with a loud thud. All mayhem paused for an instant.

"No!" roared Ishar, his red braids swinging wildly. He leaped onto the nearest Atlantean soldier. His massive fists crushed metal plating.

From his position by the stairwell, Robert scanned for cover and for possible escape routes. His archaeological instincts screamed to find high ground, but the fighting made it impossible.

Through the hell, Ishar blurred past Robert, smashing into an Atlantean soldier. While Robert ducked behind a fallen column, Ashtur and Mardak's rifle shots hit between armor plates, sending several Atlanteans falling.

Robert lost sight of Nuradu in the smoke, only to spot him materializing behind an enemy. He was using two knives to stab through thin slits in the soldier's armor, where the neck met the bottom of the helmet, killing him instantly.

"Push them back!" shouted Alara. She dashed to a fallen Atlantean and snatched up his rifle. She aimed and pulled the trigger, but the weapon sputtered. A malfunction. She flung it aside in frustration and fell back.

A dozen Atlantean soldiers remained in sight, with uncountable others spreading like a time-lapse fungus across every inch of the Underground, making sure to root out every last Resistance fighter. Nine fallen Atlanteans were also in sight, their bodies spread across the chamber floor, their battlesuits still smoking from the return fire of the Resistance and the fury of the alien giants.

The remaining hostiles split into two groups. One group took positions behind toppled columns, the other moved to flank from the right side of the hall.

Kira rushed forward and dove on the floor, scooping up the rifle Alara had discarded. Somehow, she cleared the jam and rolled. After raising the weapon and finding a soldier in her sights, she fired. Her shots struck true, the trooper going lifeless.

Through a haze of smoke, Robert spotted three resistance fighters taking cover. One crouched behind an overturned statue, another behind a granite column, and the third pressed against a damaged wall panel. They fired at the Atlanteans in bursts. A shot caught the first hostile in the throat, his body crumpling. The second managed to drop an Atlantean before he was cut down himself. The third retreated safely and vanished into the hazy dust flying all around.

Robert, Thoth, and Matt were exposed near the stairwell. Sensations ran through Robert's grip, his Vesh'tar's energy slightly electrifying. His instincts screamed to use it, but uncertainty held him back. One wrong move and he could kill his own people. A fallen soldier's rifle caught his eye, lying twenty yards away near a broken chair. Too far. Crossing the open space would be suicide.

Thoth stepped forward and raised his Vesh'tar high. "Your path ends here!" he declared, his voice thundering above the clamor. He slammed the staff into the ground. The crystal at its apex flared, tendrils unfurling like serpents. A bolt of electricity erupted, striking one soldier before arcing to the next, a web of lightning ripping through circuits and flesh. The enemies convulsed before collapsing, their battlesuits twitching in spasms.

Thoth's emerald eyes locked onto Alara. "Take them and go!"

"I won't leave! Not without *you*!"

"You must!" Thoth lifted the staff high again as Atlantean reinforcements flooded into the hall, maybe eight more. "Get our friends to safety. They're our only chance. *Tala* knows what to do."

He turned to Ishar. "Withdraw and escort my friends out. Now! I'll double your compensation!"

Ishar reacted immediately, ordering his surviving alien comrades to retreat and protect the human foursome.

"Thoth!" screamed Robert, clutching the Vesh'tar. "How can I help?"

"By surviving!" said Thoth urgently. "Go! Fulfill the purpose you've been brought here for."

The final resistance fighter rose from behind an overturned table. The young man pulled the trigger twice before a laser bolt caught him square in the face. The impact splattered blood and brain across the wall. Robert's stomach churned and he jerked his gaze away, but the image was already burned into his mind. The fighter's rifle crashed to the floor, spinning to a stop near a pile of rubble.

Arcs of electricity now radiated from Thoth's Vesh'tar, forming a luminous barrier as Ishar grabbed Alara's arm and led her and his other human clients down a long corridor. Ishar and the other still-living Anunnaki took up the rear of the living column, and all began picking up speed until they were nearly sprinting.

Robert glanced back as they ran. Thoth stood at the center of a swirling dome of light, electricity spiraling around him. A massive eruption sent shockwaves ripping through the hall. Robert looked away as they turned a corner.

They raced into a hidden hangar, not on any plans, where Alara's vehicle awaited. The group scrambled inside, shoulders bumping as they squeezed into the confined space. The Anunnaki warriors had to crouch, their rifles scraping against the ceiling. Ishar dominated the rear compartment, his muscles visibly rigid as he folded himself into the tight space. His eyes burned with rage from the death of his comrade and their undignified retreat. The door slammed shut, plunging them into the dim glow of interior lighting.

Beneath them, the elevator groaned, lifting them upward. Robert's heart pounded in his ears, drowning out Matt's whispered Hopi prayers. Kira peered behind them, no doubt watching for approaching soldiers.

Robert was still breathing hard from their sprint. "Will Thoth be okay?" he asked Alara.

"Stupid question!" she spat angrily. "Are you an idiot? How can I know that? But I don't see *how*, do you?" She balled her hands into fists. "This shouldn't have happened!" she shouted, agony evident in her voice. "Someone betrayed us!"

Sunlight burst into the cabin as the platform emerged into the industrial warehouse district. The vehicle's engines roared, and they shot into the sky.

Robert looked down. On the other side of a warehouse, a stream of Atlantean soldiers swarmed into a gaping breach in the ground, descending into the depths of the Underground. His stomach twisted at the sight. How many were there? Hundreds? Maybe *thousands*. Atlantean planners weren't leaving this to chance. Thoth was surely dead, and it was a miracle that the sage and his Vesh'tar had held off the enemy long enough for them to escape.

But they weren't out of the woods yet.

Through sheer determination, they reached a skyway, weaving between spiraling highways packed with flying vehicles.

"I'm taking us to the starport," said Alara. "To *Tala*."

She pressed on the controls and then tapped on the comm. "Poseidia Starport Control, this is Alara Valar. Authorization BC-734QI. I'm bringing in a crew for ship retrieval on Level One."

They darted through the congested airways, Alara maneuvering like a fighter pilot. Robert didn't know if Atlantis had police, but if they did, he wished she'd slow down and not give away their position. Vehicles swerved as they narrowly avoided collisions.

"Watch out!" shouted Robert as they skimmed past a flying vehicle.

"Hold tight!" responded Alara, diving beneath a hovering cargo freighter. The cityscape blurred around them. They shot past a crystal dome decorated with what looked like a botanical garden suspended in mid-air. On a nearby tower's observation deck, civilians in flowing robes pointed at their speeding vehicle.

The comm crackled for a second and then delivered a response from Starport Control. "You're cleared to land on Level One, Inspector Valar."

"Violet Alert protocols active," she replied. "Be quick about it."

The starport loomed ahead. It was a sprawling nexus beside a colossal pyramid, crystalline obelisks reflecting the sun's rays. Alara descended toward a landing pad. The docking bay swallowed their vehicle as she guided them in. Guide lights glowed along the walls, leading them to their designated pad. The ship descended on cushions of what Robert thought must be anti-grav energy, while mechanical arms extended from the walls like giant metal fingers. As the clamps locked onto their hull, their hydraulics whined as they secured the vehicle.

The doors opened to the busy starport. A pair of workers in light blue uniforms approached, datapads in hand.

Forcing a confident smile, Alara stepped out of the vehicle and strode down a short decline toward them. "Inspector Valar reporting in. I was away on orders, as your records will confirm . . . to show these dignitaries the city."

She had landed right next to *Tala* and now motioned toward the ship. "This is their vessel, Starship *Nautilos*. They're in high-level negotiations with four Anunnaki dignitaries, who are also with us."

The workers exchanged uncertain glances, consulting their datapads. "We don't have any record of—"

"Listen, protocols are shifting rapidly," interrupted Alara, her voice friendly yet insistent. "You *know* me. You know I have the highest-level clearance possible. And I don't have time for delays. This is important business."

The pair moved to the side and had a whispered discussion while Alara waited, appearing to be irritated by the delay.

Inside the vehicle, Robert clutched his Vesh'tar while Matt and Kira held their breath. The Anunnaki warriors looked disgusted, as if wanting to be on the offensive instead of cowering in cramped quarters and waiting for a human woman to lie her way to safety.

The weight of the Vesh'tar in Robert's hands felt heavier as guilt gnawed at him. Thoth had sacrificed himself for them, so they could fulfill their purpose. He knew that *Tala's* purpose for bringing them here was to prevent the coming war. But was there more to it than that? With Thoth gone, would they ever know for sure?

Down below the vessel's exit ramp, the starport workers finally reached a decision. "Very well, Inspector," said the most senior of the pair. "You're cleared to proceed. But we're making a note that this is highly irregular."

"Of course," she said graciously. "Thank you. And please leave the area for a bit while we transfer to the *Nautilos*. The Anunnakis' negotiations with Atlantis are secret, and they insist on not being seen by anyone outside the group they're now with."

"Very well," said the pair's spokesman, not consulting with his co-worker this time. "We can take a five-minute break. But no more."

Alara nodded and signaled to the humans and Anunnaki aboard the vessel to join her on the floor, which they did with alacrity. As they hurried toward *Tala*, the ramp lowered, and a man appeared at the top.

Robert's heart jumped to his throat. *No one should be inside Tala.* What did this mean? Moments later a sense of relief flooded through him as he recognized the figure who was now descending.

Aethor Daedalus. A friend.

But what was he doing here?

Aethor's expression was just as confused as Robert's as he surveyed the four humans and four Anunnaki about to board.

"Alara?" he said. "Why are you here? What's going on? Where's Thoth?"

Alara's face tightened. *"What's going on?"* she shrieked in contempt. "Why don't you tell *me* what's going on, Aethor? I can see from your shocked expression that you didn't expect to see us alive again, did you? It was you, wasn't it? You gave them our location."

"What? Who do you mean by *them*? What *location* are you talking about?"

"Don't play innocent! We were wiped out while you were conveniently gone. And now you're *here*? Aboard *Tala*. You sold us out, didn't you?"

Ishar raised his weapon and pointed it at Aethor, his eyes narrowing to slits. "The Anunnaki reserve a particularly horrifying death for traitors," he said. "You'll be screaming until your vocal cords give out. Begging me to let you die. But I won't. Not for a *very* long time. Not until you've suffered as much as you deserve."

CHAPTER 39

Alara grimaced. The pair of starport workers would be reentering the area any minute.

"Let's continue this inside," she said. "Quickly! Ishar, keep your weapon on him until I tell you otherwise."

They hustled up the ramp and were soon inside *Tala*. Through the cargo hold, the main living area opened up before them. Alara directed Aethor to sit against the wall.

"Is someone going to explain what's happening?" asked Aethor. "Why you seem to think I'm a traitor? Nothing could be further from the truth. I've been nothing but loyal to the Resistance."

"*Tala*, shut the ramp," ordered Robert.

"*Ramp closing*," replied the ship as the entrance began sealing. "Welcome back, Robert. It's great to see you and your two fellow travelers once again."

"Thanks, *Tala*," he said. "But a true reunion will have to wait. We're in crisis mode right now."

Aethor was staring at Robert with what appeared to be an awestruck expression. "You're carrying a Vesh'tar. That's extraordinary. *You* must be extraordinary. Vesh'tars only allow a chosen few to wield their power. Those chosen are a rare breed."

"Don't try to change the focus here," said Alara. "We're here to get to the bottom of your betrayal."

"Maybe so," said Kira, "but before we start, shouldn't we get the hell out of here? You know, before anyone decides to check your story more closely."

"Good point," said Alara.

"Where to?" asked Robert.

"Nasavi," replied Alara immediately. "Where Thoth was living."

"Do you know where that is?"

She shook her head. "No. But I assume you and *Tala* do."

"Why there?" asked Robert.

"Because it's a location he's managed to keep completely hidden from Atlantis. What better place to hide out, plan, and regroup?"

Robert nodded and quickly issued orders to *Tala* to take them there. Moments later the ship lifted, and the great city of Poseidia soon began to shrink beneath them.

Now that their trip was underway, Alara glared at the captive once more. "Thoth was a great man. A man who *trusted* you. A man who treated you like his own son."

"What do you mean *was* a great man?" said Aethor in dismay, looking like he might vomit. "Are you saying he's *dead*?" Tears welled up in his eyes. "I can't believe it. I *won't* believe it."

Robert studied him carefully and decided that either his shock and grief were real, or he was quite an accomplished actor.

"He's dead because of *you*!" said Alara. "You told your father how to breach the Underground."

Aethor shook his head in horror. "I would *never* betray Thoth. And I'd never work with my father against the Resistance. You can't possibly believe that. My father is a tyrant who only cares about war and power. You've known me for years, Alara. You know how hard I've been fighting against everything my father stands for."

"Maybe," she replied. "Or maybe you're *exactly* like him. Just as deceitful. Just as calculating. Just as capable of playing the long game. So perhaps you were working together from the beginning. Perhaps you and he were biding your time until you finished gathering all possible intel on us. Then, once you had, he gave the order to have us slaughtered."

"That's absurd," said Aethor.

"How did you come to be on *Tala*?" asked Robert, his tone much calmer and more sympathetic than Alara's had been.

"*Thoth* told me to meet him here," replied the prisoner, visibly fighting back tears. Robert could well understand why he wasn't letting them flow. Based on what he'd learned of Kairos's reputation, Robert wouldn't be surprised if the man had beaten into his son's head that tears were a sign of weakness. "I told Thoth that I'd procured the schematics for Nexus Prime yesterday . . . and much more . . . and he was eager to review them."

Robert's heart skipped a beat. "You have them here? Now?"

"I do," said Aethor, nodding toward one of the sleeping quarters. "I've been reviewing them now for the better part of twenty-four hours, and hell, longer actually. They're in there. Over the bed. See for yourself."

Robert and Alara rushed into the quarters. Spread out on the bed was a datapad holographically displaying diagrams and maps in the air above.

"What do you think, Alara?" said Robert. "Do these look like the real plans?"

Alara studied the information as Matt and Kira joined them in the room, leaving Ishar and his alien comrades to guard their prisoner.

Alara sighed. "I'm not expert enough to be sure."

"*Tala*, what about you?" said Robert. "Can you weigh in?"

"These schematics match every piece of Atlantean engineering I've ever seen," said the ship. "The power configurations, the security protocols. Even the small details like maintenance access points. They're too precise, too consistent with known Atlantean architecture to be fabricated. I've never seen the actual facility plans before, but I'm certain these are authentic."

Robert crossed his arms, his eyes on the screen. "If that's true, then Aethor is innocent." A soft glow emanated from his Vesh'tar, and it thrummed in his grip.

Robert strode back into the living area with the others following. "We need to turn around," he announced. "Head to Nexus Prime tonight. With these schematics, we can stop Kairos's superweapon. Before it's used on Lemuria. Nothing is more important. It's the most destructive force the Earth has ever witnessed."

Alara shook her head in contempt. "First, you don't need to tell *me* how destructive it is . . . I *know*. Second, before we race to Nexus Prime, don't you think we should study the schematics and learn if we can cripple the weapon? And, if so, *how*? Third, if we do find a way to stop it, we'll need time to gather resources and come up with a plan of attack. Or do you think they'll just let us waltz in and do whatever we want?"

Before Robert could reply, her eyes widened. "Wait a minute," she said. "Something just occurred to me. *Tala* says the plans are real. But that doesn't mean Aethor can be trusted. Not necessarily. Perhaps just the *opposite*."

"What do you mean by *that*?" said Kira.

"Kairos is known to be as brilliant as he is ruthless. He must have realized that no matter when he struck our underground facility, some of our members would be elsewhere. So, what better way to kill all the strays than to give his son the plans we most want? What better way to finish off every last remaining Resistance fighter than to lure us all to Nexus Prime, like moths to a flame, and set a trap?"

Robert winced. He still believed in Aethor's innocence, but she did have a valid point.

Aethor blew out a long breath. "That's the first thing you've said that actually makes sense, Alara. I'm not in league with my father, but if I were, this is exactly the kind of strategy he'd use. I wish there was a way I could *prove* to you that I didn't tip him off. But there isn't one."

"I, for one, believe you," said Robert.

"Why?" demanded Alara.

"When *Tala* confirmed the specs were real, I said this proved Aethor's innocence. And the moment I did, my Vesh'tar reacted. I'm convinced it was guiding me. Confirming what I had just said. The timing was too coincidental."

"Or maybe it was indicating you were dead wrong," said Alara. "How would you know? You've had *what*, twelve seconds of experience with the thing? Are you an expert now in interpreting what it does?"

Robert shook his head. "I have to trust my instincts. I think it wants us to turn around and infiltrate now. While we still have the chance. Yes, if Aethor were a traitor, we'd be walking into a trap. But if he's innocent, as I believe him to be, Kairos has no idea the plans have been copied. No reason to believe an attack on Nexus Prime is coming. So we have a window of opportunity if we act now—decisively."

"It's too risky to take that chance," said Alara. "Even if Aethor is innocent, his father's no fool, and will protect his most important weapon. So, either way, rushing in is likely a suicide mission. We need to get these plans to the right people, who can study them and find the best way to sabotage the weapon. We have to regroup, reestablish our network."

"I agree with Alara," said Ishar. "Tactical advantage is key. In this case, proper planning is key. I'm all for aggression for aggression's sake, but there are times when misplaced bravery is the same as idiocy."

"Right," said Robert. "Times when discretion is the better part of valor."

"Exactly," said the alien. "Perfectly said."

"Thanks. I'll pass that on to William Shakespeare the next time I see him."

"Who?" said Alara.

Robert ignored the question.

"I agree with Alara and the Anunnaki," said their prisoner. "I know I'm not a traitor. I know my father's unaware we have the plans. But Alara is right. Even if he doesn't know, he's no fool. And he's careful."

"You can pretend to agree with me all you want," said Alara. "But that won't make me think you're innocent."

Aethor allowed himself a brief smile. "Believe me, I know just how stubborn you are, Alara. But I'm being sincere. You're right about a lot. You're just wrong about me."

He paused. "And there's another thing you're wrong about. We don't need an expert to begin preparations. I've studied the specs extensively, and other documents, and I have a plan."

"What other documents?" said Alara.

"Sorry, that isn't something I'm willing to disclose at the moment."

"Then tell us this plan of yours," she pressed.

He shook his head. "Not until I know I can trust everyone on this ship, including the Anunnaki you brought on board. We'll get one chance at this, and if there is a traitor in our midst, we're done before we start."

"*You're* the traitor!" insisted Alara.

"Really?" said Kira. "Haven't we been through this enough? Round and round and round we go, pin the tail on the traitor. When we all know the odds are extremely low that *any of us* are traitors. We're almost certainly still on the same team. But as frustrating as it is, we seem to have reached an impasse."

Robert sighed. "We have to find a way to get everyone to trust each other. Until we do, I guess we have no choice but to proceed to Thoth's residence, after all. We have no plan. Aethor refuses to give us his. And the two people pointing fingers at each other, Alara and Aethor, both think this is the right course of action. So, who am I to argue?"

"Finally," said Alara triumphantly. "I was beginning to think that you were immune to all reason."

Robert sighed and shook his head. "You're a real charmer, Alara," he said sarcastically. "Has anyone ever told you that?"

CHAPTER 40

Councilor Kairos Daedalus
High Marshall of the Atlantean Military Forces
Poseidia, Capitol City of Atlantis
Location: Northeast Atlantis

Kairos dropped through the opening into the Underground as smoke twisted through the air. Lights blinked on and off repeatedly across the cavernous space, illuminating the lifeless bodies of Resistance fighters on the floor. He paused, surveying the devastation wrought by the Sovereign Guards, the most elite soldiers in the Atlantean military.

Satisfaction warmed him. *These rebels had plagued Atlantis for too long.*

It was true the Resistance had been less active these days, but any terrorist organization should be rooted out and killed, regardless of their current operational tempo. These Resistance people weren't doing much over the past few years, for reasons Kairos could only guess at, but with the reemergence of Thoth, it would have only gotten worse again, and in short order.

In the past, Thoth's propaganda had snaked into everything. His message that the current government was corrupt and that the old governments, the old ways, were superior. His call to reinstate the Emerald Order, to take back the government, and restore unity. And worse still, his advocacy to allow influential alien species, considered to be friendly, back into Atlantis, which would ruin everything the current regime had constructed and all of Kairos's plans.

Thoth and his followers were determined to stop wars, but wars had been critical to the Atlantean Empire's expansion. To their current dominance on the world stage. Wars were temporary inconveniences, which ultimately benefited nations that initially resisted Atlantean help. Atlantis had dramatically improved the quality of life for all nations they'd absorbed, which had bettered humanity.

How could Thoth be opposed to that? How could anyone be opposed to Atlantis's manifest destiny? Those who stood against progress deserved whatever came to them.

A Sovereign Guard commander approached Kairos, his armor scuffed. "Councilor Daedalus."

Kairos's gaze remained on the fallen. "Where's Thoth?"

The commander hesitated. "When we attempted to capture him, sir, he resisted fiercely. He wielded some kind of weapon and took down over a dozen of our men."

"What kind of weapon?"

"A, uh . . . a *staff*, sir."

A soft chuckle escaped Kairos's lips. "The Vesh'tar. A relic from another age. A failing piece of ancient technology from the old Hierophants of the Emerald Order. How quaint."

"It was highly effective in his hands."

"I'll bet it was." Kairos turned to face the commander. "I wish to see him. I assume you finally succeeded in capturing him?"

The guard cleared his throat. "He's dead, Councilor. There's nothing left of him but ash."

Kairos's eyes narrowed. "Show me."

"Yes, sir. This way."

He led Kairos deeper into the wreckage, stepping over gnarled metal and collapsed beams. They stopped beside a blackened crater where fragments of a robe and piles of ash lay scattered.

The commander gestured to the remains. "This is where he was standing when we deployed the incineration charges. The blast would have vaporized anyone."

Kairos stared at the ashes. "And you're certain this is Thoth?"

"Yes, Councilor. We cornered him here. When he refused to surrender, we had no choice."

"You had *any number* of choices," said Kairos angrily. "Yet you carelessly chose the easy way out. You chose to kill him in a way that left no remains."

"Apologies, sir. Our orders were to capture him if he surrendered. Kill him if not. We weren't told to be sure his body remained intact."

Kairos cursed at himself. A failure of imagination, of preparation, on his part.

"What are the chances we can recover DNA from the ashes?" he asked.

"I'm not a scientist, sir," replied his underling. "But I'd guess extremely low. DNA can't withstand the blistering heat that was created."

"Try, anyway," said Kairos. "I'm ninety-nine percent certain he's dead, as you say. But for this man, I need to be a *hundred* percent."

Kairos returned to the surface, blinking against the daylight before striding toward his waiting shuttle. After walking up the ramp, he stepped inside.

An advisor approached immediately, presenting a datapad. "Councilor Daedalus."

Kairos settled into his seat. "What is it?"

"We've received reports regarding the Cognitive Enhancement Serum."

"I never asked for reports."

"The distribution approval has been blocked. The Bill failed to pass."

Kairos jerked his head in surprise. "How is that possible? The Council was in favor."

The advisor handed over the datapad. "It appears your son, Aethor, intervened. He persuaded several key politicians to oppose the Bill."

Kairos fought to keep his expression neutral while he raged inside. His own son taking his feet out from under him. His own son associated with Thoth. He desperately wanted to scream curses at the top of his lungs, barely managing to suppress the impulse.

He took several deep breaths to calm himself and scanned the documents. "I see no direct evidence of Aethor's involvement here."

"We've traced communication logs. He was in contact with the majority of the officials who voted against it. His influence was significant."

Kairos tossed the datapad onto the table. "And the ones who supported the Bill?"

"Primarily your long-standing allies, Councilor."

"It seems I've underestimated Aethor's reach. I should have ensured broader support. Contact him."

The advisor moved to a nearby console, initiating a comm link. After a moment, he glanced back. "No response, sir."

Kairos wasn't surprised. If Aethor really had become the ultimate traitor to the cause, he wouldn't be taking Kairos's calls. His son's act of persuading officials to defeat this legislation fell well short of treason. If Aethor ever did cross that line, Kairos knew he would have no choice but to put him to death.

The tablet beeped, and Kairos drew it closer, studying the screen. He stood at once. Another beacon had activated. He ignored his advisor and strode toward the cockpit. "Pilot, prepare for immediate departure."

"Destination, Councilor?" the pilot asked over his shoulder.

Kairos handed him the datapad and pointed at coordinates. "Get us here at best possible speed."

"Understood."

As the shuttle lifted off, Kairos moved back to his seat. He settled in, looking around. His contingency of five guards sat at individual chairs, backs straight, battlesuits on. Where he was going, he'd need them.

The advisor approached. "Councilor, there's another development."

Kairos didn't turn. "Speak."

"Our intelligence network reports a breach in Nexus Prime's security protocols."

"Clarify," demanded Kairos.

"The schematics have been accessed without authorization. We suspect someone has acquired them."

Kairos's expression darkened. "Do we know who?"

"Not definitively, but given recent events. . ."

"You think Aethor's involved?"

"I'm sorry, sir, but it is a possibility."

Kairos shook his head in disgust. How had his own son become such a formidable obstacle? The boy was brilliant, but he had never been cunning. This had always come as a disappointment to Kairos. But, apparently, Aethor was *so* cunning he'd been able to fool his own father into believing the opposite.

It was time to stop giving his son the benefit of the doubt. He had to get to the bottom of his possible treachery, no matter what it took.

"Advisor, prepare a detainment order for Aethor Daedalus. Effective immediately."

"I'll see to it, sir."

"Good."

A silence settled over the cabin. Kairos's lips pressed into a thin line as he contemplated the moves ahead.

"Prepare a secure channel to Central Command. I need to authorize containment protocols."

"Yes, Councilor."

A moment later, the advisor signaled. "Channel open." He handed Kairos the tablet. A holographic projection of a high-ranking official materialized.

"Councilor Daedalus," said the official. "We weren't expecting your call."

"Situations have arisen that require immediate action. I'm invoking Executive Directive Eight."

The official's eyebrows rose. "That's a serious measure. What's the threat?"

"Classified. But suffice it to say, the integrity of Nexus Prime is at stake. I suspect Lemurian activity."

The official nodded. "Authorizations will be processed. Full resources are at your disposal."

"Excellent." Kairos ended the transmission and turned to his advisor. "Deploy the Trident Armored Division to Nasavi. I want a full complement of mechanized infantry, heavy artillery support, and air defense systems in position along those Lemurian border sectors. Double our ammo cache at Outpost Anvil and get those supply lines fortified. And triple our Sovereign Guards at Nexus Prime. Full tactical loadout, shoot-to-kill protocols. No one gets within a hundred yards of that facility without authorization."

"Of course, Councilor."

Kairos returned to the viewport and stared at the landscape below. If anyone infiltrated Nexus Prime, especially now, it would derail everything.

He'd spent years crafting this plan, fitting each piece together. The timing had to be perfect. Only one task remained before he could unleash the Atlantean forces he'd positioned along the Lemurian border lines on Nasavi. Soon, they'd crush the Lemurian outposts there. And after that . . .

A smile crossed his face. After that, Lemuria itself would burn. The entire continent had been a thorn in his side since he could remember. All those years of frustration, of watching that backward nation thwart Atlantean ambitions, were about to end.

Just one final step. He wouldn't let anyone interfere. Not now. Not when he was so close.

"Councilor," said the pilot, "we're approaching restricted airspace."

"Proceed without deviation. Transmit my clearance codes. Keep this off the official records. I don't want unnecessary attention from the High Councilor."

"Understood."

The advisor raised a finger, his attention on his datapad. "Councilor, I have breaking news from the Atlantean Information Network. The Lemurian Circle of 12, under High Elder Huku Nali's directive, has officially suspended all Atlantean operations at the Opalith Kanaloa Mines. They're implementing a full trade embargo against Atlantis and have closed their ports to all Atlantean vessels. They're citing 'aggressive militarization' along their borders as justification and the probable murder of Advisor Elowin Balivae."

Perfect. This was exactly the provocation he needed. The High Councilor and the Archon had been hesitant to take decisive action against Lemuria, but with this diplomatic aggression, combined with their posturing, he could finally convince the High Councilor to authorize the use of the Nexus Prime weapon.

The power of this weapon would destabilize the entire Lemurian continent from within, triggering massive tectonic events, destroying their infrastructure, and leaving their cities in ruins. Their precious Circle of 12 would be powerless to stop it. In the chaos following, Atlantis would come in to "restore order."

The final pieces of his plan were moving into place nicely.

CHAPTER 41

The earthy scent of herbs saturated the air. It mixed with the faint aroma of burning incense as Robert leaned back against the soft cushions lying across Thoth's living room. Matt sat beside him, idly tracing patterns on the wooden floor, while Kira leaned over the datapad on her lap. There, she studied the schematics displayed.

Across the room, tension crackled like static electricity. The Anunnaki warriors towered over everyone. Ishar's head brushed the ceiling beams, and Naradu had already knocked into two hanging lanterns, setting them swaying. Ishar's plasma rifle remained trained on Aethor, who sat next to a door leading to the back.

Robert gestured to the vigilant alien. "Lower the rifle already, Ishar," he said. "Aethor is helping us. Besides, he's unarmed. Do you really think he can make it past four humans and four Anunnaki? And let's be honest, I think it's fair to count each of you *twice*."

Alara sneered. "You don't issue orders here, Robert. *I* do. In Thoth's absence, command falls to me."

"Since when?" said Aethor, folding his arms. "There's a chain of command. You can't just declare yourself leader."

"Someone has to take charge. Unless you'd prefer mayhem?"

"How about democracy," said Robert. "We should all work together."

"I agree we need to cooperate," said Kira. "But *we* should get the final say."

"Who's *we*?" snapped Alara.

"Me, Robert, and Matt. We've been chosen for a special purpose by both *Tala* and Thoth. And we have a perspective on the situation that you're too close to it to have."

Alara snorted. "I'd argue the opposite. You're outsiders who know nothing about the intricacies of our society, our technology, or our politics. You don't even know the players."

"Are we going to sit here and have a pissing contest until the world ends?" said Matt. "Or are we going to try to stop Kairos?"

"What's a pissing contest?" said Aethor.

"Matt makes a good point," said Kira, ignoring the question. "Let's call a temporary truce and focus on what's important. At the same time, don't be a petulant child, Alara, and shoot Robert down when you know he's right. Ishar should lower his rifle already. Aethor isn't going *anywhere*."

Alara sighed and gestured for Ishar to comply.

"Now that this is settled," said Kira, tapping a datapad she had recently learned how to use. "Take a look at this. I was able to zoom out. I've expanded the schematics to reveal the surrounding city blocks. Streets and alleys. Red dots mark security stations, while shaded zones indicate restricted areas."

"Security seems tighter than we thought," said Alara.

Matt gestured to the clusters of checkpoints. "Is it just me or does it seem like the entire place is on lockdown?"

"Exactly," said Kira.

"We wouldn't want it to be too easy," said Robert in frustration. "Have you managed to contact other surviving members of the Resistance?" he asked Alara.

"No. All comms are down. I've been trying."

Aethor shook his head. "Easier to maintain the fiction that you're in charge, Alara, when you can't reach anyone who knows better, isn't it?"

"Are you saying I'm lying about the comms being down?"

"Or suppressing them yourself. Why not? You refuse to trust me. Why should I, or anyone else for that matter, trust you?"

The Vesh'tar in Robert's lap felt heavier all of a sudden and became warmer. A subtle tug pulled at his consciousness, like an insistent whisper at the edge of hearing. For a moment, dizziness took over.

"Excuse me for a moment," he said, rising to his feet.

"Everything okay?" asked Kira.

"Yeah, I just need some air." He moved toward the open doorway leading to the garden with the Vesh'tar in his grip.

The moment he stepped outside, the world around him shifted. The colors swirled around him in dizzying waves. His stomach lurched as though he were falling, though his feet remained planted. The garden's flowers melted into streams of light, while the trees stretched and warped like taffy. Static crackled in his ears, starting as a buzz before building to a roar. His heart hammered against his ribs as panic clawed at his throat.

What's happening to me?

The static gradually transformed, becoming deeper . . . like the beating of massive wings. The sound reverberated as if coming from the end of a vast tunnel, growing louder, closer.

When his vision cleared, Robert stood before a colossal pyramid. Its smooth sides reflected the glow of a setting sun. Beside it stood a sphinx. Not the weathered monument he knew from textbooks, but a pristine lion guardian carved from gleaming stone, its body massive and its head sporting an impressive mane.

Where am I?

A voice twirled around him. "You stand at the threshold of knowledge forgotten by time. There's more than one sphinx on Earth. They guard truths older than the sands beneath your feet."

"Thoth?" said Robert, recognizing the voice. "Is that really you?"

A figure emerged from the shimmering air. A tall, white-haired man in flowing green robes stepped forward. His eyes sparkled with wisdom.

"How is this possible?" whispered Robert. "Are you real?"

"In the same way a dream or a memory is real," replied Thoth. "We don't have much time. Your Vesh'tar is more than a weapon. More than a means to heal. It's also a conduit, a bridge between worlds and times."

Robert rolled his eyes. "Of course it is," he said sarcastically. "It's the ultimate Swiss army knife. I'm sure it can also make a mean cup of coffee and sing opera. But you've alluded to this *bridge between worlds and times* thing before. Why remind me of this now?"

"Because you need to let your past guide your future."

Robert winced. "Thanks, Thoth, but still not helpful."

"Trust in the Vesh'tar," said the phantom Hierophant. He moved closer, seeming to glide across the distance between them, almost as if he were floating. "Its power flows through you. Feel it, and it will show you the way."

Robert studied his Vesh'tar's crystal sphere. "What is this thing, really?"

"The crystal sphere serves as a quantum interface, capable of connecting to the electromagnetic fields generated by human consciousness. The root-like tendrils are actually microscopic arrays of receivers and transmitters, interfacing directly with the bioelectric field of your nervous system."

Robert turned the staff, watching light play across its surface. "So, in a way, it's reading my mind?"

"More than that. It's creating a bridge between your conscious mind, your subconscious, and what some might call your soul, though that too is ultimately energy, patterns, information. The crystalline matrix contains millions of years of stored data, experiences, memories.

When it connects with a compatible user, it creates a temporal link to that user's neural pathways, allowing access to this vast repository of knowledge."

"But why me? Why now?"

Thoth's expression grew serious. "Because, Robert, sometimes the right key must find the right lock. The Vesh'tar chose you because your mind, your particular way of understanding and interpreting the past, makes you uniquely suited to what must come next."

Robert swallowed hard. "My gut, or the staff, is telling me to stare at the sphinx." As he said this, he shifted his gaze to the lion's eyes, which glowed with an inner light.

"Then you're doing the right thing. Fixate on the light and keep your mind open to whatever comes."

Robert did as instructed, and after a few more seconds, visions flooded his mind. Massive crystal-powered cities rose from desert sands, their spires reaching higher than mountain tops. Beings of light descended from hovering craft to meet with early humans. Tall humanoids with elongated skulls taught mathematics to gathered crowds. Ships of different designs—some organic, others geometric—appeared and vanished throughout history.

He witnessed genetic laboratories where different human species were studied and modified. Advanced civilizations rose and fell in the blink of an eye, some using technology defying physics as he knew it. The images came faster and faster, showing him truths archaeology had never dreamed of uncovering, truths too distant, too long ago, too far in the past for anyone to find, let alone discover in an archeological dig.

The weight of ages settled upon him along with a lightness, as if he were both observer and participant in all that is and ever was. Knowledge streamed into him, about the Vesh'tar, about Nexus Prime, about the delicate balance between Atlantis and Lemuria. How the balance fed all societies on Earth, and how, if either were to tumble, all would fall.

A moment passed and he was back beside Thoth, his hands shaking. "I can't hold all of this. It's too much."

"You don't need to understand everything now," said Thoth. "You just need to realize how much power you have to make a difference."

"How? We have little chance to sabotage Nexus Prime, despite having the plans. We can't even be sure who to trust."

Thoth placed a hand on Robert's shoulder. "As always, trust your instincts."

Before Robert could respond, Thoth's form began to fade.

"Wait!" called out Robert. "Are you alive? Where are you?"

But he had asked too late. The golden light began to wither away like a sunset being pulled behind clouds. Robert was drawn back, the infinite knowledge receding, leaving behind impressions and insights darting into his consciousness. The sphinx's eyes dimmed, and the pyramid's gleaming surface started to blur.

Thoth's final words resounded through the fading dreamscape and vanished. Reality reasserted itself in layers. First sound, then sensation, and finally sight. The transition left Robert with a profound sense of displacement as if he'd lived a thousand lifetimes in the span of a heartbeat.

"Professor, are you with us?" said Matt, who was snapping his fingers a few inches from Robert's face.

Kira was by his side, her hand rubbing gentle circles on Robert's back. "You just zoned out. We thought we lost you for a minute."

"I'm . . . I'm okay," stammered Robert, still reeling from the experience. He looked down at the Vesh'tar, feeling its warmth pulsating in his grasp.

"What happened?" asked Matt.

Ishar scoffed from across the room. "We can't have one of our people going into a coma at the wrong time," he said. "You're becoming a liability."

Robert looked around. "How am I inside? Didn't I leave?"

Kira frowned, lines of worry crossing her face. "No. You haven't left the cushion."

A low hum resonated throughout the house. The floor vibrated, and a light flashed outside the window. The vibration intensified until the windows rattled. Outside, a flock of birds flew from branches, no doubt in a panic. A massive ground sloth, easily the size of an elephant, lumbered past the window with surprising speed. Its long claws left deep furrows in the earth. It was running from something, if you could call what it was doing *running*. The plants in Thoth's garden swayed like they were caught in a windstorm.

"Did anyone else feel that?" asked Matt. "Or see that?"

Aethor turned toward the window, and his face turned as pale as a ghost. "That's my dad's shuttle descending. How does he know I'm *here*? How does he know where Thoth's home is?"

Aethor clenched down hard, gritting his teeth, and he faced Alara with a look of horror. "It was you all along, wasn't it?" he said. "It *has* to be. That's why you wanted to come here. So they could *track* you here. *You've* been betraying us all along."

"And you've been betraying *Atlantis*!" she replied emphatically, finally not trying to deny his accusations. "I'm doing what's *right*. I'm being loyal to my nation."

She shot him a look of contempt. "But cheer up, Aethor. I've finally proven you aren't a traitor to your precious Resistance. And no need to thank me," she added with an icy smile. "I'm happy to help."

CHAPTER 42

A shuttle began slowly descending into the clearing beside Thoth's home. The vessel's thrusters kicked up a whirlwind, sending leaves spiraling in crimson torrents while dust clouded the air. The deep vibration of the engines rattled Robert's chest, and he tightened his fingers around the Vesh'tar, its warmth turning hotter, nearly searing his palm.

"The Sovereign Guard," said Aethor, his mouth agape. "My dad doesn't go anywhere without them, and for good reason." He turned to Alara. *"What have you done?"*

"What I've done is set off a beacon that led to the invasion of your Underground. And then I led your dad here, to Thoth's hideout, whose location he's long been desperate to learn. And, at the same time, I'm opening his eyes when it comes to *you*. Now he'll see the full extent of your treachery. I only learned you were a traitor when I brought Thoth to the Underground and you were there, but I couldn't risk communication with Kairos. He *still* doesn't know about your involvement in the Resistance, at least not from me. But I did manage to set off beacons, to leave a breadcrumb trail. So, in just minutes, he'll see for himself."

Outside, the shuttle had landed, and its engines were powering down. Five men clad in battlesuits, weapons at the ready, appeared at the top of a ramp that slowly extended from the ship's belly.

"But *why*?" said Aethor. "Thoth did so much for you. For all of us."

"No. He did so much *against* Atlantis. He's been unraveling our society, stitch by stitch. Every member of the Resistance is nothing but a traitor to Atlantis, by definition."

"And you're nothing but a pawn of an evil, corrupt system," said Aethor. "You've damned us all. My father won't spare anyone. And you've already orchestrated the slaughter of innocents. Of *friends*."

"I ended a chapter that needed ending. Thoth and his Emerald Order have been a blight on Atlantis, sowing discord and rebellion for hundreds of years."

"So our escape from the Underground wasn't miraculous, after all," said Robert. "The attackers were given strict instructions to let you go."

"*Very good,*" she said condescendingly. "Maybe you aren't as stupid as you look."

Robert's head was spinning. How had he missed this? He had known that Aethor wasn't a traitor, but Alara had fooled him in spectacular fashion. She had treated them poorly all along. She'd been hostile, argumentative, and unfriendly. A total nightmare. Which is what had thrown him off. A spy would want to be well-liked, want to avoid confrontation, so as not to arouse suspicion. No mole would have the nerve to invite suspicion so openly. Which is why her ploy had worked. Robert had never expected the obvious choice to be the right one.

Ishar faced Alara and snarled like a feral animal. "This treachery won't stand!" he roared.

She almost looked amused. "Come off it, Ishar. Why do you care? Since when do mercs take sides? Especially in human affairs? Your only loyalty is to your payday, and I'll make sure you're paid three times what Thoth promised. So back off."

Ishar glanced at his fellow soldiers, their expressions mirroring his disdain. "You've made a serious mistake, Alara, by assuming you understand the nuances of what motivates Anunnaki warriors. Yes, we value compensation. But when we give our word, *we honor it.* No matter what! And we pledged our services to Thoth, whose death *you* caused."

Alara's eyes darted between them, realizing just how completely she had miscalculated. In a heartbeat, she drew her weapon and fired at Ishar. Nuradu lunged forward, taking the blast in the neck. His body hit the floor with a crack, the stench of burnt skin filling the room. His eyes, still wide, stared lifelessly into the room.

"Nuradu!" Mardak shouted, rushing to his fallen comrade.

Alara bolted toward the front door. Ishar's retaliatory shots scorched past her, searing holes into the wooden frame.

In that moment, the Vesh'tar vibrated in Robert's grasp while whispers flooded his mind. He staggered back, the voices overlapping, indecipherable. Urgent.

Outside, the Sovereign Guards opened fire, energy blasts tearing through walls and windows. Shards of glass exploded inward, forcing everyone to duck.

"Get down!" screamed Kira, pulling Robert behind an overturned marble table. She kept her grip on the datapad.

Matt crawled beside them. "This is bad. Really bad."

Ishar yelled orders, his booming voice slashing through the gunfire. "Mardak, flank left! See to it that the humans are armed."

The Anunnaki returned fire, their weapons emitting deep thuds opposite the high-pitched whine of the Sovereign Guards' rifles.

A column splintered nearby, wooden fragments raining down. "We need to move!" shouted Aethor, picking up Nuradu's fallen weapon.

Kira peeked over the table edge as an alien tossed her a gun. "We can't stay here. The entire structure is coming down."

The roof groaned, beams cracking under the assault. Robert's head pounded, the murmurs from the Vesh'tar merging with the external hell breaking loose all around.

"Professor, snap out of it!" yelled Matt, shaking him. "Come on! We have to get out of here!"

Robert nodded, struggling to focus. "Right. Let's go."

They crawled toward the back door, keeping low as more blasts tore through the house. As they burst into the backyard, Ashtur took point, towering above the humans and charging ahead. A flash of light came without warning as a shot from one of the two guards flanking around the back blasted a hole through the alien's forehead and he crashed to the ground like a felled tree.

Robert, Matt, and Kira stumbled into cover behind a large stone planter, with Ishar crouching beside them, his weapon ready. To their left, Mardak roared in fury, emerging from the doorway and unloading his weapon at the attackers. Two of the Sovereign Guards fell, their armor no match for Anunnaki firepower.

"Keep moving!" yelled Mardak, covering their retreat.

The deep thrum of his Anunnaki rifle resounded across the yard. To the right, Mardak and Aethor found cover behind an ancient fallen statue, its marble face half-buried in earth and moss. The statue's thick base provided solid protection, though stray energy bolts were already chipping away at its surface.

The Sovereign Guards had positioned themselves along the treeline. Their battlesuits reflected dappled sunlight as they moved between the large trunks of old-growth trees. Three were spaced across a thirty-yard span. Their leader, marked by crimson striping on his armor, directed the assault through hand signals. Every few moments, one guard would provide covering fire while the others advanced, slowly closing the distance in a leap-frog maneuver.

The Vesh'tar grew hotter in Robert's grip. The whispers intensified, forming words. *Protect. Unite. Defend.*

Ahead, a man in white robes used a tree as cover, his rifle leveled. "Sovereign Guard, hold your fire!" He bellowed. "I repeat, hold your fire!"

Despite their earlier ferocity, both sides froze at the man's command. The Sovereign Guards remained in firing position but didn't advance, while the Anunnaki warriors, surprisingly, also held their fire. The sudden stillness felt like a drawn bowstring, taut with tension.

Robert had no doubt that the man who had called the ceasefire was Aethor's father. Their striking resemblance was undeniable. But more than that, his commanding presence and effortless authority made it clear he was a man accustomed to being instantly obeyed, to bending entire armies to his will.

"Aethor," bellowed his father. "Alara just told me you're out there. Give yourself up, and I'll see to it that you get preferred treatment."

"You'll have to kill me, Councilor!" screamed out Aethor from behind the cover of the marble statue. "Or should I say, High Marshall? I'd use the title of *Dad*, but that's the one that suits you least."

"I'm working to give you a future worth having," replied Kairos. "To give the entire world a future worth having."

"You're as delusional as you are ruthless. Thoth was the one working to give the world a better future. You've been doing the opposite. Thoth was a man of wisdom and honor. You're a man of unbridled savagery and lust for power."

"*So be it!*" bellowed Kairos, his tone reflecting severe emotional pain and debilitating rage in equal measure. "If you're so misguided, so eager to die, I won't stand in your way!"

He flicked his wrist toward the shuttle, signaling to it. The craft lifted off the ground, its gun turrets rotating toward the Anunnaki and humans who had been trying to flee as it hovered above them.

Robert gazed into Ishar's eyes as he crouched so low they were almost at equal height. "Can your weapon down that ship?" asked Robert.

"Not a chance."

Robert's vision hazed, the voices in his mind reaching a fever pitch. The Vesh'tar shook of its own accord, energy coursing up his arm. The power waited, begging him to unleash it.

Ishar rose and squared his shoulders. "We stand our ground. For Nuradu, Enkuul, and Ashtur!"

Mardak nodded, weapon ready.

The Vesh'tar pulsed, a brilliant light emanating from the crystal orb. The whispers coalesced into a singular presence, a sentient energy merging with his consciousness.

I am here, said the Vesh'tar. *At your disposal.*

Robert closed his eyes, envisioning the battlefield. He saw the positions of the Sovereign Guards, the shuttle overhead, the desperation etched on his friends' faces.

Help me protect them, said Robert.

As you wish.

He opened his eyes. Raising the Vesh'tar, a surge of power poured through him, unlike anything he'd known. Electric energy danced around the orb, spiraling down the staff and into the ground. In the next instant, lightning arced from the shaft, striking the nearest Sovereign Guard. The soldier convulsed as the electricity coursed through him, collapsing in a heap.

The remaining guards turned their weapons toward Robert. On instinct, Robert thrust the staff in their direction. The crystal flared, and a bolt of crackling energy slammed into the nearest guard's weapon. The rifle exploded in his hands, sending him backward into a tree.

"Impossible," said Kairos.

Aethor seized the moment, squeezing off three rapid shots. The plasma bolts caught a distracted guard, killing him instantly. The soldier crumpled, his weapon clattering against stone.

Ishar barked a command in his native tongue, and both Anunnaki warriors coordinated their attack. Their heavy weapons thundered in unison, the combined barrage overwhelming the remaining Atlantean soldiers. A guard's battlesuit erupted in a shower of sparks before he collapsed, while the other spun from the impact, falling lifeless to the ground.

Above them, the shuttle's targeting systems whirred to life. Its twin gun turrets swiveled, their barrels glowing with building energy as they locked onto Robert. The craft's shadow loomed over him.

"Robert, watch out!" screamed Kira.

The moment Robert looked up, the Vesh'tar responded. A bolt of concentrated lightning struck the shuttle's underbelly. The lightning ripped through the shuttle's hull, igniting its fuel cells. Fire erupted from its seams as it lurched sideways, spinning wildly. The craft plummeted into the treeline, its impact breaking ancient trunks in half. A thunderous explosion followed, sending a mushroom cloud of flame skyward. The shockwave knocked everyone to the ground as burning metal hailed down around them.

Robert's muscles trembled, every nerve ending ablaze just as the whispers returned. *Your body cannot sustain this for long.*

"What do I do?" said Robert aloud.

Trust in yourself. Let go.

Kairos's face twisted with rage. His finger tightened on the trigger, the weapon's charging coil emitting a high-pitched whine.

"Enough!" roared Robert, standing. He directed the last of his strength into the Vesh'tar, a blinding flash erupting from the staff. The white light consumed everything, even his vision.

Pain unlike anything he'd known tore through Robert. As if every atom of his being was unraveling.

"Robert!" Kira's voice was faint, distant.

His vision fragmented, shards of reality falling away. The last thing he sensed was the warmth of the Vesh'tar slipping from his grasp, and a bright light consuming him.

CHAPTER 43

Councilor Kairos Daedalus
High Marshall of the Atlantean Military Forces
Thoth's home, Soulwood Forest
Location: Nasavi

A flash erupted from the Vesh'tar, flooding everything with light. A force slammed into Kairos's chest, lifting him off his feet. Legs flailing, he soared backward until his spine collided with a moss-covered log. The impact drove the air from his lungs. His robes smoldered, smoke corkscrewing into the canopy above.

Once he blinked away the residual light stinging his eyes, he struggled to his knees. Burnt fabric filled his nostrils. Across the clearing, his Sovereign Guards lay face down.

Useless imbeciles, he thought. *The finest security Atlantis had to offer reduced to rubble.*

In the distance, movement caught his eye. One of the Anunnaki hoisted an unconscious figure over his shoulder—the man wielding the Vesh'tar. Kairos squinted. He'd seen that face before in images. It was one of the foreign men aligned with Thoth.

Nearby, Aethor came out from behind a shattered tree. Their gazes met. Kairos knew he had a clear shot at his son. In one quick motion, he could end Aethor's life, but even the thought of it made him sick to his stomach. His son had hurt him more deeply than he would ever admit, so Kairos acted out of anger, though he instantly regretted his decision.

When he thought Aethor might die at his command, he'd suddenly gained absolute clarity. He had realized just how much he still loved his son, despite his defiance. The fact was, in some ways, he *admired* this defiance, and how Aethor was turning into a great man, a passionate, courageous leader and risk-taker. They were cut from the same cloth, they just had vast differences in belief as to what was best for Atlantis and the world.

He couldn't help but be overjoyed that Aethor had survived, despite Kairos's misguided efforts to end him, and he would do whatever it took to make sure this continued to be the case. He'd do whatever it took to rescue his son from his false beliefs, deprogram him, so that his full potential as a force for positive change could be harnessed and appreciated by all.

Aethor hesitated, casting another glance at his father. Kairos remained stone-faced, masking the maelstrom of emotions inside him. Finally, his son turned and sprinted toward a starship parked in a clearing along with the other survivors from their side. After Aethor and his companions boarded, the vessel's ramp closed. Engines whirred to life, and the craft ascended, slicing through the canopy before arcing eastward toward Atlantis.

Kairos pushed himself upright, brushing debris from his robes. The ship's ion trail faded into the horizon. Betrayed and deserted, he surveyed the aftermath. His elite guards defeated. His shuttle a mangled mess of metal and flame.

As he trudged toward the wreckage, he came across Alara sprawled amid the underbrush. Her face was smeared with soot, dark circles shadowed her eyes, and blood trickled from a crooked nose. The Vesh'tar had doubtlessly thrown her off her feet, also, and whatever she had slammed into hadn't been kind to her body.

He knelt beside her and checked for signs of life, but found none.

He had to admit, the archaic Vesh'tar weapons still held immense power. He wouldn't dismiss one so lightly next time.

He left Alara and activated his personal communicator. "Ixra."

Ixra Maren replied, "Councilor Daedalus. I trust your mission was successful."

"Hardly." Kairos eyed the smoldering shuttle. "Send extraction immediately. And dispatch a squadron of Skyblade Fighters to my coordinates."

"Understood. What's the target?"

"Incinerate this wretched forest. It's infested with filth. Have Thoth's dwelling searched for possible useful information, which I doubt will be found, and then reduce it to ash."

"Consider it done."

"Also, the vessel known as *Nautilos* is en route to Atlantis. It's likely masking its energy signature already, but it's heading home. Increase Nexus Prime security protocols. I want those traitors found and captured."

"Understood," said Ixra. "And your son? Is he among them?"

"He is."

Ixra paused before replying, "Your instructions regarding Aethor?"

"He's chosen his path," said Kairos, staring into the distance. "He'll face the consequences," he added with absolute conviction, despite knowing this wasn't true. Aethor would face consequences, but Kairos would see to it that these wouldn't include being put to death for treason.

"Very well. I'll make the necessary arrangements."

Kairos ended the communication and sank onto a fallen log. Memories surged. A sunlit afternoon by the river's edge. Young Aethor, no more than eight, his face alight with joy as he hurled rocks into the glistening waters.

"Watch this, Father!"

They aimed for a boulder jutting up from the current. Time after time, their stones splashed wide. Finally, with a triumphant shout, Aethor's rock struck true, clacking against the boulder.

"You did it," said Kairos, a broad smile crossing his face.

Aethor beamed, sprinting over to embrace him. The warmth of that hug remained even now, decades later. Kairos clenched his fists, nails digging into his palms.

Back in the present, Kairos bowed his head. Shoulders shaking, moisture came to his eyes, which he fought off with all his being. Emotions were a luxury he could ill afford. Atlantis needed his strength, now more than ever.

When he rose, he cast a glance toward the horizon where the starship had disappeared. For about twenty minutes, he sat there, wallowing in misery, trying to figure out how it had gone so wrong with his son. Every so often, he'd look at Alara's dead body, part of him wishing she had never set off the beacons that had finally forced his hand.

The flames from the destroyed shuttle were dying down when a distant thrum signaled the approach of another shuttle minutes later.

Kairos stood tall and composed himself as the craft descended, stirring leaves and ash. Once it landed, the ramp extended, and Ixra Maren emerged.

"Thanks for coming," he said. "I'm afraid the situation has escalated."

"So, it appears," she replied, surveying the destruction. "I'm sorry about the loss of your Sovereign Guards."

Kairos frowned. "I'm just sorry they weren't more competent. If so, they'd still be alive."

She sighed. "Perhaps our training regimen needs to be upgraded. In any event, I've ordered the Skyblades as per your instructions. Soulwood will be cleansed."

"Good." Kairos stepped aboard the shuttle. "Any progress on intercepting the *Nautilos*?"

"We're monitoring any ship that's on a flight path toward Nexus Prime, and I've authorized a blockade around it. They won't breach."

"Ensure they don't." Kairos settled into a seat.

"Of course," said Ixra, taking a seat opposite him, hands cupped in her lap. "If I may, Councilor, the involvement of your son complicates matters."

"Aethor's choices are his own."

"Nonetheless, his knowledge of our operations poses a risk."

"What are you implying?"

"Merely that containment may require . . . decisive action."

Kairos leaned forward as though insulted. "I understand that better than *anyone*! Do you doubt I'm capable of the decisive action required just because it involves my son? Check the comm record. You'll find I ordered Aethor killed during our recent skirmish." He delivered these words with steel in his voice, ensuring Ixra would never guess he'd come to regret this decision the instant it was made.

"I feel for you, Councilor. A brutally tough decision. But a necessary one."

"No!" said Kairos. "Sitting here, waiting, I've come to realize it was a *foolish* one. Aethor needs to be taken alive at all costs, so he can be interrogated. He likely possesses the highest quality intel of anyone. He knows the Resistance inside and out. But he can also tell us what other Atlantean intel he's fed them, in addition to the Nexus Prime schematics. He's a pivotal agent here, with one foot in the upper echelons of Atlantean power, because of me, and one foot in the Resistance."

He sensed that Ixra was biting her tongue. That she desperately wanted to argue that he was giving Aethor preferential treatment, but couldn't, since the points he made were too valid.

"Report on the Lemurian situation," he ordered, changing the subject.

"Intelligence suggests they're mobilizing."

"Make certain our forces are prepared. I won't tolerate any more messes."

"Naturally." Ixra's tone was silk over steel. "May I suggest a revision of our internal security protocols? Thoth's network may have deeper roots than we anticipated."

"Implement whatever measures you deem necessary." Kairos waved a hand dismissively. "I expect results."

"Understood."

The shuttle came to life, its systems lifting them from Soulwood Forest's scarred earth as they accelerated skyward. Sunlight flooded the cabin, and below, the wreckage of his former shuttle diminished to a black smear amid the endless green.

"Change of plans," said Kairos to the pilot. "Set course for Outpost Anvil, Eastern Nasavi."

From the corner of his eye, he caught Ixra's look of surprise, though it was quickly masked. The woman's fingers twitched ever so slightly, but she remained silent, probably processing this deviation from their intended return to Atlantis.

"Course adjusted," the pilot replied. "Eastern Nasavi, Outpost Anvil."

The vessel banked, climbing into the stratosphere before leveling out. Kairos nodded, his mind still on his son.

The rest of the journey passed in quiet. A half-hour later, the pilot's voice crackled through the cabin. "Beginning descent to Outpost Anvil."

The landscape below had transformed from a beach to a sprawling military encampment. The Atlantean outpost rose from the shore like a collection of massive pearls. Interconnected, domed structures of white metal. Defensive towers punctuated the perimeter.

Rows of Stormcrawlers stretched across the makeshift runways. Shadow Striders patrolled the perimeter. Aelis Artillery units had been positioned along the high ground, their long barrels aimed toward the river marking the border of Lemurian territory.

The shuttle touched down on a landing pad near the central dome. Through the holowindow, Kairos spotted a familiar figure waiting. Argo's silver-trimmed commander's armor was distinctive even at a distance.

"Larger force than expected," remarked Ixra.

"Indeed." Kairos's eyes narrowed as he studied the Lemurian position across the river. Their stronghold showed their own military might. Angular structures of dark metal rising from fortified walls. Their large military presence was concerning, and it was considerably greater than Atlantean Intel had predicted. They must have been amassing for the last few days.

Squadrons of their aircraft—shapes of black metal with swept-back wings—sat on airstrips. Hover-tanks moved between defensive positions, their turrets tracking Atlantean movements. Artillery platforms bristled with cannons, and their soldiers in camouflaged battlesuits looked like a sea of shadows flowing between fortifications.

The shuttle's ramp extended. Argo approached. "Councilor. We came as soon as your orders reached Kemet."

Kairos descended the ramp. "Your quick response may have saved us precious time."

"The Lemurians have nearly tripled their forces since yesterday," said Argo, walking beside him. "Their crystal embargo was just the beginning."

"No," said Kairos, looking at a mechanic working on a Skyblade Fighter. "It was merely the excuse we needed." He turned to Ixra. "Contact the High Councilor. Inform him Lemuria's military buildup constitutes a direct threat, that they're preparing for combat. Activate Nexus Prime's weapon systems."

"And the Lemurians, sir?" asked Ixra. "Shall we issue a formal declaration of war?"

"No. After today, Lemuria will announce it themselves, and the High Councilor will have no choice but to react." Kairos stared across the river at their forces, his voice hard. "Lemuria denies us what is rightfully ours. If they want war . . . that's exactly what we'll give them."

CHAPTER 44

Advisor Elowin Balivae
Poros Territory, Poros City
Location: Southwest Atlantis

Elowin stirred. A throbbing pain ached at her temple. Darkness enveloped her, broken only by the glow of a distant streetlamp filtering through cracks in boarded-up windows. A cool, damp cloth pressed against her forehead. A stinging sensation where the cloth touched made her wince.

"Easy now, Advisor," a calm voice said beside her.

She tried to sit up, but a firm hand guided her back down. A wave of nausea hit her as the room tilted sideways. Her ribs protested with sharp, stabbing pains, and dried blood clung to her hair. She struggled to focus until she settled on the silhouette of a man kneeling at her side.

Her throat felt like sandpaper. She parted her lips to speak, but only a hoarse whisper escaped.

"Here." He brought a shallow bowl to her lips, tipping it gently. Cool water touched her tongue. She swallowed, the liquid easing its way down.

"Where . . . are we?" she managed.

He sat back on his heels. "I'm not entirely sure. After the incident on the roof, things got complicated. They tried to eliminate us. A broken panel from the explosion nearly took your head off, but you moved at the last second. Yet, a piece still caught you. Any closer . . ."

The man shook his head. "Fortune favored us in that moment. I managed to get you away and found this place. Seems to be an old shop or something. We've been lying low here for two days."

"Two days?" Elowin's fingers brushed against his hand, needing confirmation he was real. Warm skin met hers. "You brought me here?" She didn't know where 'here' was, exactly, or what was happening, other than a blur of confusion trying to form into something she could remember.

He gave a soft smile. "Couldn't very well leave you behind, could I? It's good to see you awake."

She pushed herself upright, the room spinning as she moved. He reached out to steady her. "Take it slow."

Shelves lined the walls, empty and coated with layers of neglect in this dim space. Old countertops hid beneath tattered sheets, and the air was thick with must.

"What happened?" When she spoke the words, a flood of memories hit her. "Did anyone survive?"

The man kept his eyes on hers. "Just us."

She felt immense despair but forced it away. She didn't have the luxury right now of mourning the innocents who had died because of her decision. Too much else was going on. "You've been here all this time?" she asked her rescuer, attempting to stand. "With me?"

He rose with her, keeping a supportive hand at the ready. "Had to make sure you were okay."

She leaned against a chair, the cool metal steadying her. Once the dizziness subsided, she looked at him fully. He was a handsome specimen of a man, dressed in casual clothing, with alert eyes softened with concern.

"What's your name?" she asked.

"Jalon Kiva," he replied. "Lemurian Protectorate." He dipped his head slightly. "At your service."

The Lemurian Protectorate served as personal bodyguards for Lemurian politicians. Like all Protectorate members, Jalon Kiva carried himself with a confidence coming from years of specialized combat training. His stance shifted a little to maintain what Elowin figured were optimal viewing angles of both her and their surroundings, a habit she knew had been ingrained through the Protectorate's rigorous six-year training program. Even his breathing was controlled. He'd no doubt mastered the art of remaining perfectly still for hours while maintaining complete alertness.

"Of course," said Elowin. She must have really been dazed to have forgotten that he and a number of his comrades had been assigned to accompany her on her political trip to Atlantis.

"I owe you an apology, Advisor. We failed in our duty. I survived long enough to save you, but Kona Makelo is among the dead."

She sighed. This was something she could never forget. Her knees buckled as she remembered Kona's vacant expression. Jalon moved swiftly, guiding her back to the chair. She covered her face with her hands, a sob escaping despite her efforts to contain it. The loss pressed down, and tears hazed her vision.

Jalon handed her a folded handkerchief.

"Thank you." Elowin wiped her tears. "Kairos was behind this. He was the one who ordered the deaths of an entire diplomatic contingent."

"Yes. That was quite clear."

"Does he know I survived?"

"I don't believe so. If he did, we'd have company by now. I've been monitoring the situation as best I can. The holovision hasn't mentioned any search efforts. Officially, you died from a shuttle malfunction."

"What about Lemuria? Has there been any news?"

He glanced toward a doorway leading to another room. "There's something you should see."

She stood, steadier this time. Together, they moved into the adjacent space. Dusty sheets draping over abandoned furnishings hinted at the room's former life. Perhaps this place was a cafe or a small eatery. Large windows faced the street, raindrops tracing lazy paths down the glass. Outside, the world was unnaturally still. Hover vehicles glided along, but the sidewalks were empty, the usual frenzy of Atlantis absent, especially in this city, the city of Poros.

A craft slowed near their building, and Jalon's hand moved to a plasma rifle hidden behind an old blanket. His body tensed, ready to move. They both held their breath until the vehicle passed.

"We need to keep down," he said. "I've been watching, and they haven't been running regular patrols. It's a good thing, yet I've seen that vehicle three times today. Could be innocent, but we need to be ready to move at a moment's notice."

Elowin nodded. "Understood."

Jalon tapped a crystalline device on a table. A small orb perched on a tripod. It sprang to life, projecting a holographic display into the air. The image resolved into a news anchor.

". . . reports confirm that hostilities commenced at precisely three fifteen PM today. The Lemurian Elders, also known as the Circle of 12, have declared war following the closure of the Kanaloa Mines to all Atlantean operations. Our sources indicate that negotiations broke down after Lemuria accused Atlantis of sabotage in relation to Advisor Elowin Balivae's tragic shuttle accident."

The feed cut to aerial footage of an Atlantean outpost. Through billowing clouds of black smoke, a station's dome was visible, its eastern section torn open like a broken eggshell. Bodies in Atlantean battlesuits lay across the scorched ground. Defense turrets hung limp. A secondary explosion lit up the background, momentarily washing out the video feed.

Elowin's eyes widened. "No! This can't be."

The anchor continued, "... despite thorough investigations clearing Atlantis of any wrongdoing regarding Advisor Elowin Balivae, Lemuria has responded with unprecedented military aggression. At three thirty PM, Lemurian forces launched a devastating assault on Outpost Anvil in Nasavi. Initial casualty reports from the outpost are still incoming, but military sources describe the situation as grave. This attack comes mere days after the tragic explosion at the Grand Hall that claimed multiple lives, including those of Lemurian Advisor Elowin Balivae, Elder Kona Makelo, their personal guard, and several members of the Atlantean diplomatic staff."

The footage shifted to the Grand Hall, where Elowin's mangled shuttle still protruded from the damaged roof section. Emergency crews swarmed the building. In the background, a tired-looking field reporter set down his microphone while his cameraman adjusted equipment at the security perimeter, joining dozens of other media crews jostling for position.

The feed returned to the anchor. "The High Councilor has called an emergency session..."

"Turn it off," said Elowin weakly.

The hologram flickered out as Jalon complied. Elowin stood frozen. "Why would the Circle of 12 do this?" she demanded, more to herself than to him. "They know about Nexus Prime. Do they think they can stop it through war?"

She grimaced as an ache in her head seemed to be spreading. "This has to be Huku Nali's doing. He wanted war, as if it's the only way to show our might. And now we're all going to pay the price."

"Desperate decisions are often made in the absence of clear information, I'm afraid," said Jalon.

"We need to get to Kairos," said Elowin. "He's orchestrated everything. Perhaps under Draconian influence, perhaps not. Either way, he's unquestionably the key now. Nexus Prime isn't just a weapon ... it's his insurance policy. As long as he controls *it*, he controls both sides of this war."

Jalon's eyes narrowed. "He'll be more heavily guarded than ever right now."

"But he and his people will be watching for known assassins and armies. Not the ghost of a woman they thought they had killed. That's my advantage. Our advantage."

"You're a diplomat and pacifist. Are you really willing to become an assassin?"

She smiled gently. "You misunderstand. My fault. I didn't mean to imply I could get to him physically. The plan would be to expose him diplomatically. In the court of public opinion."

She thought in silence for a considerable period. "Perhaps Deir Slan is the answer."

"Deir Slan, ma'am? I'm not following."

"Before everything went wrong," said Elowin, "I noticed something. Her computer had a unique interface. Custom security protocols. I'm guessing she and Kairos share highly sensitive files. If we can access her systems, we might be able to get the evidence we need. The files will be encrypted with the latest protocols used by the upper echelon of the Atlantean government, but with luck, our experts in Lemuria can break through in a few days of concerted effort." She winced. "Assuming the world has a few days."

"The Grand Hall Council building will be crawling with security, especially after hours. It's impossible."

She smiled. "Impossible, Jalon? You managed to get an unconscious woman off the roof of a building filled with hostiles while deep in enemy territory. Sounds *more* than impossible to me."

"I got lucky," he said modestly.

"How did you do it, anyway?"

"Right after the explosion, the Atlantean forces didn't rush the roof immediately. Much was still burning, and they didn't know if another shoe would drop . . . or, more literally, if another explosion would occur. It gave me time to carry you down one flight of stairs and find an empty office. I hid with you in a tight storage closet for six hours. Then I left you there, only temporarily, and only when it became pitch black outside."

He paused to gather his thoughts. "There were still soldiers staging the scene on the roof and cleaning up the mess in Deir's office. I stalked one of them and . . . disabled him. Changed into his uniform. Then, pretending to be an Atlantean soldier, I carried you out of the building in a body bag, and in plain sight."

"Incredible!" she said. "Brilliant and bold. Not only did you pull off the impossible, but you also make it seem *easy*." She shook her head.

"And I'm sure that it was anything but." She paused. "So why aren't you still in the Atlantean uniform you borrowed?"

"It would be out of place where we are now. I stowed my own battlesuit with you in the body bag. It's hidden in this room. Wearing a battlesuit, Lemurian *or* Atlantean, in a civilian area isn't exactly the recipe for blending in. Although to be honest, Advisor, you could *never* appear ordinary, no matter *what* you were wearing. And no matter who you were with."

"Thank you for saving my life," she said emphatically, delighted by his compliment but not responding. "I owe you *everything*. Your bravery and improvisational skills are exceptional. As is your modesty."

She flashed him a dazzling smile. "But you get the original point I was trying to make, right? You said that infiltrating the Grand Hall would be impossible. *You*, the man who pulled off a miracle to save me, and made it look easy. All I'm asking is for one more miracle now."

He laughed. "Well, when you put it like that, how can I refuse? Actually, I'm pretty sure I'd do anything you asked of me, even if it wasn't my job."

Interesting reply, thought Elowin. "Great. Now, let's figure this out. We've been to the Grand Hall twice. Surely, we can use what we remember to plan this out."

Jalon winced. "Actually, no. Everything's changed, rendering what we know of their security obsolete. The damage from your ship and the extended firefight in Deir's office will have necessitated all kinds of changes."

Elowin's eyes widened. "Wait a minute," she said, gesturing to the powered-down holovision. "Did you see all those media crews? They've probably been swarming the site since the explosion. And the camera operator was right at the edge of the security perimeter. He set his equipment down right there. That's it. That could be the solution."

"Impersonating a cameraman? Or impersonating unattended equipment?"

Elowin beamed. "Both! Or, perhaps, neither. Whatever works. We'll figure it out. Lots of chaos, media crews coming and going. And the two of us with proven improvisational skills."

She considered further and frowned. "But we need to do this tonight. Media interest will soon wane. Worse, every hour we wait, more soldiers will die in a manufactured war."

"Then what are we waiting for?" said Jalon, now projecting nothing but confidence and bravado. "Let's get to where we need to be and make this happen."

"Thank you!"

"Don't mention it, Advisor. I was getting bored waiting here, anyway."

She smiled. "Glad I could help with that. I guarantee that neither of us will be bored for much longer." Elowin raised her eyebrows. "*Dead* . . . maybe," she added with a sigh. "But not bored."

CHAPTER 45

Councilor Kairos Daedalus
High Marshall of the Atlantean Military Forces
Outpost Anvil, Venus Cove
Location: Nasavi, East Shores

An explosion rocked Outpost Anvil's subterranean corridors, sending tremors through the reinforced walls. Dust cascaded from the ceiling as Kairos gripped the handrail. The ground shook. Distant blasts resounded through the underground facility like thunder rolling across a storm-darkened sky.

Kairos brought his personal comm toward his lips. "All Raven Wing elements, immediate scramble. Protocol Eight-Five."

"Copy Eight-Five. Raven Wing notified and preparing to launch," responded Control.

He strode down the passage as sirens wailed overhead. Technicians and soldiers moved quickly around him. The Lemurians were attacking, or so the world would believe. In truth, this was the opening movement of a symphony he'd been composing for a long, long time. His clandestine spec ops team had drawn first blood, hidden beneath layers of false intelligence and carefully planted provocations. The media, ever hungry for sensation and grateful for the exclusive access he'd granted them over the years, would broadcast exactly the narrative he'd written. That the Lemurians struck first at innocent Atlantis.

The political game was like the ancient Atlantean strategy of Depths and Tides. Sacrifice the smaller pieces to position your leviathans for the killing strike. Kairos had always excelled at that particular game.

As High Marshall, protocol dictated he command from the safety of the war room. There, he'd move pieces across holographic displays while other men bled and died for his strategies. In most cases, it was exactly what he did. But appearances mattered in politics as much as victory mattered in war.

Occasionally, he made it a point to climb into the cockpit himself. To show the troops their leader was willing to share their risks. Even if he had no intention of sharing their fate.

Tales of his combat missions spread through the ranks faster than illness and disease through a refugee camp. No High Marshall in recorded history had been willing to do the same. He'd even publicly rebuked the High Councilor when he demanded Kairos stop risking himself. The troops loved Kairos for it.

Kairos entered the primary hangar where his personal Skyblade waited. The craft's adaptive camouflage skin shifted, matching the surrounding darkness as the underground hangar lights dimmed. Forty-seven other fighters lined the deck in perfect rows. Three full squadrons of Raven Wing. The elite of the elite.

This operation should be textbook. Intelligence reported a major Lemurian strike package inbound from their western Nasavi command sector—eighteen heavy bombers escorted by forty fighters launching from a base far west of the Tokpela Gate Outpost that was currently engaged with the Atlantean outpost, Anvil. Finally, a legitimate threat worthy of his full attention.

He'd position himself with the command flight element. Close enough for the cameras to capture his heroism. Far enough back to avoid any real danger. A calculated risk for maximum propaganda value.

"Control, keep Thunder Wing on standby," he ordered into his comm. "Standard reserve deployment."

"Copy that, High Marshall. Thunder Wing standing by."

Kairos climbed into his cockpit and sealed the canopy. After slipping his helmet on, the neural interface synced smoothly, connecting his thoughts directly to the fighter's systems. The whir of the Kozar-infused lumina core vibrated through the hull.

His HUD flickered to life. Crystalline displays projected Atlantean blue holograms across his field of vision. Forty-eight friendly contacts appeared as azure delta markers, each trailing streams of tactical data.

"Raven Wing, form up by squadron," he transmitted. "Standard combat ascent. Command element will coordinate from high cover."

The Skyblades catapulted forward into the underwater launch tunnels stretching from the hangar and deep beneath Outpost Anvil toward the ocean floor. Bioluminescent markers blurred past in streams of green light as the fighters accelerated through the enclosed tubes. The tunnels angled downward first, then leveled off as they extended far beyond the beach into the deep waters offshore.

The launch chamber cycled through its sequence. Sealing, pressurizing, opening to the ocean depths. As each Skyblade reached the tunnel's exit point, hundreds of feet below the surface and miles from shore, the craft burst free from the protective tubes into the open ocean. The fighters' hulls shed streams of bubbles as they engaged their aquatic propulsion systems, rocketing upward through the dark water toward the distant surface above.

In seconds, the fighters burst from the water into the night. Forty-eight fighters rising. A cascade of ocean spray erupted outward as their hulls shed the aquatic environment.

Through Kairos's cockpit, streams of water snaked across his canopy before the Skyblade's repulsion field activated, clearing his view.

Kairos pulled back on the controls, his helmet's neural interface responding instantly to his thoughts. The formation banked inland, leaving Outpost Anvil's coastal position behind as they climbed toward the interior. Raven Wing angled northeast, climbing to fifteen thousand feet to intercept the incoming enemy formation before the hostiles could reach Anvil.

In the distance, far beyond the forested interior, through the magnified dash feed, Kairos could make out the sprawling Lemurian stronghold. A cluster of mushroom-shaped buildings and interconnected domes dominated the landscape. The central command structure rose five stories high, flanked by six heavily armed guard towers. Weapons platforms bristled along its perimeter, already powering up their defensive systems.

His tactical display blazed with contacts. The immediate threat they'd launched to intercept. Multiple hostiles bearing two-six-zero, range eleven miles and closing fast.

"Control, Raven Lead," said Kairos. "Multiple contacts in formation bearing two-six-zero."

"Acknowledged, Raven Lead," replied Control. "You're cleared to engage. Weapons free. Ground defense reports Lemurian soldiers detected in sectors seven through twelve."

The ground war was already beginning. Kairos switched to the tactical command frequency to monitor the surface battle below.

"Anvil Actual to Raven Lead," came the voice of a ground commander. "We have multiple breach points along sectors seven through twelve. Estimate company-plus strength with heavy weapons and armor support. Immediate priority targets at grid four-niner-two and five-zero-eight. Request immediate close air support."

"Anvil Actual, Raven Lead. Negative on immediate close air support. Primary air threat takes priority. Will redirect Thunder Wing to your position." Kairos switched channels. "Control, Raven Lead. Redirect Thunder Wing to assist Anvil Actual immediately."

"Understood, Raven Lead," said Control. "Thunder Wing proceeding to assist ground forces."

Through his canopy, the enemy flying formation approached. Eighteen massive bombers held the center, their angular hulls bristling with defensive weapons. Around them, forty Lemurian fighters wove protective patterns.

This was the real thing. No training exercise or propaganda stunt. The Lemurians had coordinated a full-scale assault. Air and ground simultaneously.

"Raven Wing One and Two Squadrons, engage the escort fighters," ordered Kairos. "Three Squadron, prosecute the bombers. Four Squadron maintains high cover with me."

"Yes, Raven Lead. One through Three engaging."

The formations closed like armies charging across a field. Laser and plasma fire alike erupted across miles of sky as the first fighters made contact. His pilots were good, some of the best Atlantis had to offer, their Skyblades technologically superior in every way.

This should be an easy route.

"Raven Lead, this is Two-Seven. Multiple intruders breaking through the screen! They're coming in waves!"

On Kairos's display, red contacts scattered across the tactical map. The enemy fighters were throwing themselves against his formation in suicidal waves, accepting losses to punch holes in his defensive screen.

PrismTide missiles streaked across the sky, their quantum-split warheads finding their marks. Three Lemurian fighters disintegrated under the barrage. Still, more kept coming.

"Raven Three-Four is down! Repeat, Three-Four is down!"

"Two-One, break left! Break left! Enemy on your six!"

The radio chatter filled with voices of his pilots calling out threats, coordinating attacks, reporting damage. The rush of combat hit Kairos, even from his relatively safe position in the command element.

Two enemy fighters broke through Kairos's protective cordon, ignoring the defensive fire streaming around them. They vectored straight for his command element.

Smart tactics. Cut off the head and the body dies.

Kairos threw his Skyblade into evasive maneuvers. The neural interface responded to his thoughts faster than conscious reaction. His wingmen engaged the attackers, energy bolts crisscrossing the sky.

The first Lemurian fighter blew apart under fire. Burning fragments spiraled toward the ground below. The second one pressed its attack, weaving through the defensive fire.

"Raven Lead, this is Four-Three. I can't get a clean shot! He's too close to you!"

Kairos rolled hard left, then snapped back right, but the Lemurian pilot matched him move for move. Plasma bolts reached out toward his fighter, missing by mere feet. The second barrage found its mark.

Plasma fire hammered into his starboard wing. His shields flared brilliant blue, then collapsed in a cascade of failing energy. Warning klaxons screamed through the cockpit as critical systems went offline.

"Breakfall! Breakfall! Raven Lead taking critical damage!"

The blast tore through his wing structure. Control surfaces failed. The neural interface shrieked warnings directly into his brain as the fighter lost stability and began its deathly spiral.

This wasn't supposed to happen. Not to him. Not today.

Kairos fought the controls as his Skyblade tumbled through the sky. Emergency power flickered to life, giving him just seconds to regain some semblance of control. The ground rushed up to meet him.

"All RavenWing elements, Raven Lead going down!" yelled Kairos. "Continue the mission! Do not break formation to assist!"

"Raven Lead, Four-Two. I'm on you for emergency escort."

The Skyblade shuddered. Metal groaned under impossible stress. His altitude bled away faster and faster. Through the hellfire of failing systems, he'd managed to maneuver his Skyblade closer to home, and could see Outpost Anvil's emergency landing field growing larger in his cracked canopy.

Yet, he smiled. The most wolfish of all smiles. This couldn't have worked out better if he'd planned it himself.

The propaganda value of a wounded High Marshall making an emergency landing would be worth a hundred routine victories. The media would crown him a hero before he even climbed out of the wreckage.

His wingman's urgent voice cut through: "Raven Lead, Four-One. Six intruders diving on your position! They've broken through!"

Kairos's blood chilled to ice. The carefully orchestrated battle was spiraling beyond his control. He'd positioned himself for low risk, calculated exposure that would enhance his reputation without genuine danger. War. Even manufactured war. It had a way of writing its own rules.

"All elements, converge on Raven Lead's position!" he commanded, but even as the words left his lips, he could see the tactical display fragmenting. Red contacts swarmed through his defensive screen.

The first enemy fighter materialized through the haze of battle. Plasma cannons swiveled toward his position. Kairos threw his Skyblade into evasive maneuvers.

Emergency klaxons blared, and smoke filled the cockpit.

CHAPTER 46

Robert stood at a podium before a packed auditorium, the murmurs of eager students and skeptical colleagues filling the air. A slideshow projected behind him, displaying ancient petroglyphs and maps of lost continents.

And, very soon, it would display the words of the visionary Greek philosopher, Plato, who Robert had briefly introduced to the assembly as a man who had forged the foundations of Western philosophy. As a man who was undeniably one of history's most important figures, shaping ethics, politics, and metaphysics for millennia to come.

"In just a moment," he said to the audience, "I'll put up on the screen excerpts of what Plato wrote about the fabled Atlantis. Although . . . spoiler alert . . . I think much of what he wrote might not be so *fabled* after all."

Robert paused. "In general, Plato frames Atlantis as a historical account set many thousands of years before his time, as found in his dialogues *Timaeus* and *Critias*, published 360 years before the birth of Christ. Scholars have often called this a complex blend of allegory, mythology, and speculative history, in which references to the divine serve philosophical and narrative purposes.

"Allow me to read the first excerpt," he continued as the quote in question now appeared on the large screen behind him. "This is taken from Benjamin Jowett's standard translation of *The Dialogues of Plato*, first published in 1871.

"*. . . for they [the Atlanteans] possessed true and in every way great spirits, uniting gentleness with wisdom in the various chances of life, and in their intercourse with one another. They despised everything but virtue, caring little for their present state of life, and thinking lightly of the possession of gold and other property, which seemed only a burden to them. They were not intoxicated by luxury, nor did wealth deprive them of their self-control. Instead, they were sober, and saw clearly that all these goods are increased by virtue and friendship with one another.*"

He paused. "In short, these and other passages paint Atlantis as a hyper-advanced paradise, and its residents almost saint-like in spirit and behavior, living together in total harmony. But, alas, this state of perfection couldn't be maintained in Atlantis forever.

"Lore is replete with examples of humanity falling from grace," he continued. "Of being unable to continue living in paradise without screwing it up, as hubris increases and morality declines. Adam and Eve in Eden. Lucifer and his rebels in Heaven. The Golden Age in Greek Mythology. Dilmun in Sumerian Mythology. Aztlán in Aztec Mythology. The Dreamtime in Australian Aboriginal Mythology. Satya Yuga in Hindu Mythology. And Asgard's Ragnarök in Norse Mythology."

Robert smiled and raised his eyebrows provocatively. "And, of course, The Third World, Kasskara, in Hopi Mythology," he added. "But much more about that later, as I believe this part of Hopi mythology is partially another recounting of Atlantis and Lemuria, and their subsequent falls."

He paused to catch his breath as the next slide appeared behind him. "Which brings me to a brief passage in Plato that speaks to this fall. *'By the continuance in them of a divine nature,'* he continued reading, *'all that has been described increased in them. But when the divine portion began to fade away and human nature got the upper hand, they behaved unseemly. To outsiders, they appeared glorious and blessed at the very time they were full of avarice and unrighteous power.'"*

He took a sip from a water bottle he had placed on the podium and continued. "The slightly longer version of this passage makes it clear that this moral fall of Atlantis didn't happen suddenly but took place over many, many generations." He paused. "But let me return to Plato's last sentence in the passage I just read. *To outsiders, they*—The Atlanteans—*appeared glorious and blessed. At the very time they were full of avarice and unrighteous power.*

"So much for being spiritual, peaceful, non-materialistic, and one with nature, right?" said Robert. "Most of you know what *avarice* means. But *unrighteous power* was Plato's way of speaking about an aggressive imperialism that emerged as Atlantis sought to conquer other lands, with an eye toward ruling the entire world. This shift from virtue, on the one hand, to greed, disharmony, and conquest on the other, marks their moral decay."

He paused to let this sink in. "Which sets the stage for Zeus to punish them, as their greed and hubris offended divine order. Here is a key passage.

"Zeus, the god of gods, perceiving that an honorable race was in a woeful plight, and wanting to inflict punishment on them, that they might be chastened and improve. He collected all the gods into their

most holy habitation, and when he had called them together, he spake as follows—"

He stopped. "Raise your hand if you're curious to know exactly what Zeus . . . *spake.*"

Every hand in the room instantly rose.

Robert grinned. "I don't blame you. I'm curious too. Too bad Plato's dialog abruptly ends right there, and he never goes on to detail exactly what Zeus said . . . or you know . . . spake. But other sections make the gist of it clear. Zeus observed the debasement of the Atlanteans and convened the gods to decide their punishment. The destruction of Atlantis. While this passage sets up the punishment, it doesn't explicitly describe Atlantis' submersion. The actual destruction is only detailed earlier in Timaeus: *"violent earthquakes and floods; and in a single day and night of misfortune . . . the continent of Atlantis . . . disappeared in the depths of the sea"*

Robert paused and surveyed his audience. They appeared mesmerized by the material. Even his critics couldn't help but be fascinated by Plato's famous account.

"More about Plato later," he said. "Because this is the perfect segue into a discussion of this *disappearance in the depths of the sea* of which Plato writes. And don't be thrown off by his contention that it all happened in a single day and night. If it did happen, it almost certainly took longer than that, but one can forgive the man for taking some dramatic license."

He was about to continue when Alan Donovan rudely threw open the door to the lecture hall and strode arrogantly inside, taking a seat near the back.

"So. let's talk about floods," continued Robert, doing his best to ignore this interruption by a man determined to be an ever-present thorn in his side. "Let's talk about geologic catastrophes. Identical flood myths are known to have emerged independently across the globe." He paced the stage. "These appear in the legends of cultures separated by vast oceans. Cultures that had no known contact with each other. Yet they share a common narrative. Just coincidence? Or did something transpire? A cataclysm of immense proportions? The Hopi speak of such a deluge, but the question remains, how exactly did this happen?"

He paused to let his students marinate on this question.

"But there's more. It isn't just wild myths. There is evidence of a cataclysm in the geologic record. Around thirteen thousand years ago, archaeological evidence shows that human settlements worldwide were suddenly abandoned, including the complete disappearance of the Clovis culture in North America. Again, all over the world, and happening at about the same time.

"We also discovered a black layer in the geological record. Below that black layer lies the bones of extinct megafauna—saber-toothed cats, dire wolves, American lions, giant ground sloths, woolly mammoths—species that had existed for hundreds of thousands of years. In a geological sense, all vanished overnight. Just. Like. That. Approximately eighty percent of North American megafauna species and seventy percent of South American megafauna species went extinct. Europe experienced roughly sixty percent megafauna loss during this same period, in what appears to have been a simultaneous continental-scale extinction event."

Robert's pitch grew more intense. "This black layer contains high concentrations of carbon, specifically soot. At its base, hexagonal nanodiamonds were found, which can only form under extreme heat and pressure, along with magnetic grains, microspherules, and most telling, iridium. The same metal found only in asteroids, intense cosmic events, nuclear detonations, high-energy weapons, extreme explosions, and so on. The evidence is irrefutable," Robert kept at it, speaking at a quick pace. "Something catastrophic happened at this time."

"Is this about Atlantis and Lemuria again?" said Alan Donovan in contempt, rising from the seat he'd just taken.

"If you had been here earlier, you wouldn't have to ask."

"Why don't you give it a rest already, Robert? Continents don't just sink. The very idea defies basic geology."

"Depends on your understanding of geological processes," said Robert, trying not to let his irritation show. "Imagine a catastrophic event. Let's say . . . a massive explosion. One powerful enough to destabilize a continental plate. The repercussions would be immense. An intense explosion could fracture the crust, unleash unprecedented seismic activity, and trigger volcanic eruptions. The thinning crust would succumb to tectonic subsidence, and in extreme cases, even subduction would occur. The continent might not disappear overnight, but over weeks or months. Years? It's within the realm of possibility.

"Take Thonis-Heracleion," he continued. "An entire Egyptian metropolis now lies beneath the Mediterranean. We've documented how a perfect storm of geological factors, such as, earthquakes, soil liquefaction, and the natural subsidence of deltaic soil, caused this thriving city to slip beneath the waves. The presence of active tectonic plates only accelerated the process."

He paused, letting it all sink in. "If a city can vanish into the sea through natural processes alone, imagine what a catastrophic event could do to a larger landmass. We're talking about documented geological phenomena on a larger scale."

He raised his eyebrows. "And I know how it happened. Atlantis's energy source, Nexus Prime, was turned into a superweapon. And this superweapon was wielded by the High Marshall of the Atlantean military. And—"

"Now you've *really* gone mad?" said Alan Donovan with a smirk on his face. "Nexus Prime? Atlantis? A High Marshall? You're psychotic. You desperately need your head examined. You're living in a rich fantasy world of your own making."

He jabbed a finger in Robert's direction and began to laugh so hard it seemed he might collapse to the floor. The entire auditorium joined in, the sound of collective mirth filling every corner of the space. The cruel laughter began to distort, warping into a mechanical whir growing louder and louder until . . .

Robert jolted awake from his vivid dream, a dull ache throbbing at the back of his head. The soft thrum of the ship enveloped him, the echo of the mocking laughter still ringing in his ears.

It wasn't real. Just a nightmare. *Thank God.*

Dim lights sent a soft glow around him. Where was he? One look, and he could easily tell he was in one of *Tala*'s crew quarters. Kira sat beside him, her hand warm on his leg.

"Welcome back, Robert," said Kira softly. "We've been worried about you."

CHAPTER 47

Robert blinked, trying to focus. Matt leaned against the doorway, arms folded. Aethor rested his upper back against the wall.

"How long was I out?" asked Robert, his voice hoarse.

"Too long," replied Matt.

Kira squeezed his hand. "We couldn't pry that staff from your grip."

Robert glanced down. The Vesh'tar lay in his hand, its turquoise crystal orb glimmering. "What happened?"

"Whatever you did back there," said Matt, "it was pretty wild. You sent those guys flying across the forest. Even knocked Aethor's father for a loop."

Aethor scratched his jaw. "He won't stay down for long. He's probably already on the move."

"Where are we?" asked Robert.

"Inside *Tala*," replied Aethor. "In a forest clearing just north of Poros City. It's just past dark. I've been polishing my plans to infiltrate Nexus Prime. Given that you're finally conscious, our traitor has been weeded out, and I'm certain I can trust everyone here, it's time to share my plan. We don't have much time. The plan calls for us to reach Nexus Prime under deep cover of darkness at about two in the morning. Which is about six hours from now."

Robert's brows rose. "Six hours?"

"Yes. For reasons I'll get into soon, delay would be a mistake."

Robert tried to sit up, but a wave of exhaustion came over him. "It feels like the sphinx fell on me."

"You drained yourself," said *Tala's* disembodied voice, just before her crystalline form materialized at the foot of the bed. "Using the Vesh'tar without proper attunement is taxing."

"I thought you couldn't be in here unless it was an emergency," said Robert.

"And you don't think this qualifies?" she said in amusement. "You need strength." *Tala* reached out, her translucent hands hovering over his feet. A warmth spread through him, tingling up his legs and radiating outward. The ache in his muscles began to dissolve, replaced by a mild heat reminding him of sunlight on his skin. The fog clouding his thoughts lifted.

Robert inhaled deeply. "Thank you."

"Don't mention it," said the beautiful crystalline being.

Robert swung his legs over the side of the bed and stood, testing his balance.

Kira steadied him. "Careful."

"I'm alright." Robert looked around the room. "We have a mission, right?"

A broad smile crossed Matt's face, a grin clearly reflecting his relief at seeing Robert unharmed. There was something more than mere happiness in that look, though Matt tried to mask it behind his usual demeanor. "Damn right we do," said the young man, no longer showing any tension in his shoulders.

Robert walked out of the quarters and into the common area with Kira, Matt, and Aethor trailing close behind. The Anunnaki warriors sat quietly at the table, their giant forms occupying most of the space. Ishar looked up as Robert and his three human companions approached and took seats. Aethor set a datapad down on the table.

"I'm sorry about your friends," said Robert to the pair of aliens.

Ishar gave a slow nod. "They fought and died with honor. None of us can ask for anything more."

Robert stared up into Ishar's eyes. "Where I'm from, a great general, George Patton, said something I think you'll agree with. 'Don't mourn the men who died. Instead, thank God that such men *lived*.'"

Ishar nodded. "In our culture, we honor the fallen by carrying their strength forward. They died protecting what they believed in. Their sacrifice will not be forgotten."

Mardak took a long drink before adding, "Better to fall in battle defending what matters than to live centuries as a coward. When my time comes, I hope to meet my end with half their courage." He raised his cup in silent agreement, a warrior's tribute to his fallen comrades.

"Throughout human history, every civilization has honored their fallen warriors differently," said Robert. "But the core meaning stays the same. Remembering their sacrifice, carrying their memory forward, and not letting their sacrifice be in vain. Nexus Prime is a threat we have to neutralize. It's a must. Let us vow to do it for our friends, for our fallen comrades. And for Thoth."

Everyone voiced their hearty agreement.

Robert glanced at the viewport. Rain pattered against the glass, trailing down in uneven rivulets. Beyond, the forest stretched into the darkness. "Okay, Aethor," he said. "I'm ready. Tell us about this plan of yours. And I'm also curious to hear about these other documents you alluded to earlier."

Aethor smiled. "I've been looking forward to telling you everything. I'm quite proud of this plan, which I think gives us a reasonable chance of success. Even survival."

"Only reasonable?" said Matt, swallowing hard.

"Which is *infinitely* better than our chances would have been yesterday."

Robert winced. "I don't know about that. After Alara joined up with Kairos, the first thing she must have told him is that we now have the Nexus Prime schematics. If he didn't know already. So he's sure to have changed things up already. Upgraded security. So, whatever plan you've come up with is doomed to failure."

Aethor raised his eyebrows. "That would normally be the case, yes. But here's what you don't know. I didn't just steal a copy of the schematics. I installed a virus that provides backdoor access to my dad's computer and communications systems. Very sophisticated. A virus that will survive a reboot of the system, which he no doubt ordered done right away, and which will stay invisible to standard scans. He'll find it eventually probably soon . . . but he hasn't yet."

Robert nodded. "Now *that's* a game-changer. I assume this means your plan has taken into account all his latest moves."

"Exactly. For the moment, at least, we can stay one step ahead of him."

"Well done!" said Matt.

"Thank you. Without the virus, the backdoor access, we'd be killed before we got anywhere near Nexus Prime. Because of my backdoor access, I know my father isn't just looking for *Nautilos*, or any other signature a ship of *Tala's* class might take on. He's taking no chances. He's planning to stop *every single ship* on a flight path toward Nexus Prime that isn't pre-authorized."

"How do you get around *that*?" asked Robert.

"I've used the backdoor into my father's computer to retrieve a treasure trove of top-secret files . . . the documents I spoke of. But I can also use it to *plant* information. Various military ships will be permitted in Nexus Prime airspace. Just before we go, I'll change the list of cleared military vehicles to include the one that *Tala's* energy signature will show her to be."

Robert still didn't look convinced. "That would be great, but if they get a visual rather than just an energy signature, *Tala* won't look the part."

Aethor smiled. "Yes, she will. She's the most advanced ship ever built. She has the capability of projecting a holographic image of another ship around her shell. So she can fool sensors *and* human eyes."

"Very nice," said Robert.

"Let's circle back to this virus of yours," said Kira. "I agree with Robert. This backdoor access of yours is the ultimate game changer. How did you manage to pull it off?"

"It was a long time coming. My father trusted me alone with his computer, believing I wouldn't betray him, and believing I didn't have the expertise to find a vulnerability in his systems, anyway. He was right on the second count. Lucky for me, I was guided by the top experts in the Resistance for almost a year. Most importantly, I was assisted by Atlantis's chief computing officer, who sympathizes with our cause and has been a mole for us, an undercover informant, for seven months now. He was the one who provided me with the latest encryption and decryption keys that I needed after I broke in yesterday morning. To say I've been on the case to stop the Nexus Prime weapon for a long time is an understatement."

Robert nodded. "Just incredible."

"Glad you like it."

Kira leaned forward. "Okay, let's keep going. We have a way to at least reach Nexus Prime airspace now. What then?"

"Our goal is to remove the weapon's core processor. That's the heart and brain of it. The critical piece that allows my father to turn the most useful and important energy-producing system ever built into the most dangerous weapon ever used. It was an absurdly difficult bit of programming and engineering, and the genius scientist who finally managed it was killed trying to destroy his own creation."

Robert raised his eyebrows. "If he tried to destroy it, he must have grown a conscience."

"My father insisted it would be used for defensive purposes only. But he let his cover slip in front of the man, and he learned of my father's *true* intentions. So this scientist had a conscience all along, he just didn't have the truth. Once he did, he wiped the details of the core processor's configuration from every system before he died. He had already made sure the device itself couldn't be reverse engineered. Just to be on the safe side."

"Which is great news," said Kira. "You're saying it's one of a kind. If we remove it, Kairos can't replace it. He doesn't have a dozen more of these he can pop back in stored in a closet somewhere."

"Exactly. Remove it, and we disable the weapon forever. Well, forever, if after we take it, he never gets his hands on it again."

"Can't we just destroy it and be done with it?" asked Robert.

Aethor winced. "Not right away. My father embedded it in a crystal matrix that's pretty indestructible. Which is why its own inventor was caught before he could manage to destroy it. After that incident, my father had it booby-trapped. He mentions this in his private files but doesn't say how. There are rumors, which he probably started himself to serve as yet another deterrent, that if it's destroyed, it will release a lethal, highly contagious virus he had engineered, one that could spread like wildfire and kill millions. Just to be on the safe side, we'd want to take the processor to scientists in Lemuria to evaluate and decide if it needs to be destroyed inside a maximum containment biolab."

"Your father sure doesn't make things easy," said Kira.

Aethor sighed. "Yeah. Tell me about it. And this is just the beginning of him making things difficult. The core processor, also called the quantum crystalline matrix, is about the size of my palm. The Resistance was absolutely *certain* we knew where it was. But, as it turns out, after immersing myself in my father's most top-secret files, we were *wrong*."

"Yikes," said Matt. "Not good."

Aethor sighed. "Yeah. It turns out my father is even more paranoid, and even more brilliant, than I thought. Here's what I've learned. Kairos realized at the start that no matter how hard he tried to keep the weaponized nature of Nexus Prime secret, it would eventually leak. Especially since he planned to conduct multiple tests of the weapon. Since it's the lynchpin of his entire strategy, he decided that when it did leak, he'd ensure the weapon could never be stopped or sabotaged, by friend or foe."

"How?" said Kira.

"He built a 'secret' vault inside the vast Nexus Prime structure to house the vital core processor. One guarded around the clock by a dozen soldiers."

"And, it's a ruse, isn't it?" said Ishar in admiration, finally chiming in. "The vault is empty."

"Close, but not quite. It isn't empty. He put a replica of the processor inside and hooked it up. It looks very real. It just doesn't do anything."

He told his key allies that this is where the brain of the weapon is being kept."

"And this information was subtly leaked on *purpose*, I suppose," said Robert.

"That's right. Setting a trap for his enemies. That way, if he was betrayed, if his allies or the Resistance tried to stop him, they'd attack the wrong place. It would take a miracle to get inside that vault, and his enemies would have to show their hand to do so and would almost certainly be killed in the process. Even if they miraculously managed to do it, they'd destroy the fake crystal and go home happy."

He paused. "And there was a secondary reason for the ruse. If the political winds had shifted along the way and something went horribly wrong, such that the High Councilor decided he had to allow a Lemurian inspection, my father could let them inspect the false sight, the red herring, and even let them disconnect the fake brain of the weapon."

"Nice," said Matt. "And then he'd still be in business."

Robert found himself *spellbound* as Aethor delivered one astonishing revelation after another and noted that Matt and Kira were also on the edge of their seats, as were the two Anunnaki at the table.

"How many people were told the real location?" asked Mardak.

"*None*. Kairos kept it entirely to himself. I know because I accessed his private files. He murdered the two men who installed the real processor just after they had finished."

"Right," said Robert. "Dead men can't spill secrets."

"Kairos is truly as ruthless as they come," said Ishar. "I'm really starting to like this human."

Aethor shook his head. "I have a feeling that will change before this session is through. More about that a bit later."

"So where is the *real* processor located?" asked Kira.

"The real processor, the quantum crystalline matrix, is in the very last place anyone would ever think to look," said Aethor. "Inside a large, uninhabited control room he had built below the vast Nexus Prime structure. Within a maze of multiple stories of subterranean maintenance tunnels that aren't used anymore. Inside an *unguarded* control room."

"It can't be that simple," said Robert. "Why do I have the feeling that despite knowing where it is, and being unguarded, it'll still be nearly impossible to get at?"

"Because you've been paying attention," said Aethor. "Because my father has proven to be a brilliant strategist, and more paranoid and careful than anyone on the planet."

"So how is it safeguarded?" asked Kira.

"There is one tunnel that leads to the rest. It's the only way into the spiderweb of these other tunnels. It's the ultimate bottleneck. My father purposely caused an *accidental* cave-in that blocks anyone from getting through. Not just a cave-in, but an artificial one, in which he had large boulders added afterward to make sure the tunnel was absolutely impassable."

"Did he kill the construction workers who helped him with this?" asked Robert.

"Probably, I'm not sure. It wasn't as though they had any idea *why* they were importing boulders. He could have told them anything. Here's the bottom line. Even though the passage is twenty feet wide, there are hundreds of tons of boulders blocking the way, some of them truly massive."

"But the tunnel is wide enough to allow for a bulldozer," said Matt. "Sorry, you probably don't know that word. It's a specialized heavy-duty vehicle that can move boulders pretty easily."

"My father plans to use such a vehicle to move them aside if he ever needed to check on the processor. But *we* can't. There are cameras down there, which I have the codes from his computer to control. I can make them blind to us. And there's a sort of trip-wire alarm early on, but I can defeat that too.

"What I *can't* defeat are the seismic sensors he's planted in this critical tunnel. Anyone who uses heavy equipment to move the boulders will set off the sensors, and he'll be alerted. He'd send an army of soldiers to investigate immediately."

"Then we're screwed," said Robert bluntly. "There's no way to move the boulders without heavy equipment. In my excavations, clearing collapsed tunnels was always the trickiest part. One wrong move and you risk a secondary collapse. The Egyptians had techniques for clearing blocked passages in their tombs, but they had the luxury of time. We're talking about shifting tons of debris in minutes without bringing the whole structure down on our heads."

"Or," cut in Aethor, eyes turning to Robert, "we could use what's already in your hands." He nodded toward the Vesh'tar. "That staff can move rock with more strength than a hundred men. I've seen Thoth clear cave-ins without making more noise than a whisper. It's all about control, focusing the energy into a steady stream rather than a blast."

Robert studied the crystalline orb. "You make it sound so simple. But every time I've used this thing, it's been more like an unstable explosive in my hands rather than a scalpel. I'm not sure I have that kind of control."

"Maybe," said Aethor. "For now, let's assume you'll figure it out so we can proceed."

Robert nodded. "Okay, go ahead. Let's pretend I'll find a way to get us through. What's next?"

"I've spent hours memorizing the layout of the tunnels, just in case I lose my datapad," said Aethor. "Once we get through the bottleneck, I can navigate us through the spider web of tunnels to the control room. *Removing* the crystal is the next big challenge. There are two main security safeguards. Complicated, yes, but I have a way around them. First, there's a biometric scan keyed to my father's *modified* DNA. Second, there's an electrical field that will fry anyone trying to dislodge the crystal."

"What do you mean by your father's *modified* DNA?" asked Robert.

"When I discovered his DNA was part of the key, I was suspicious. DNA is too easy to get. From hair, blood, sloughed-off skin cells . . . you name it. Go into any room my father's been in and you can get a sample of his DNA and amplify it."

A slow grin grew on Aethor's face. "As you know, I'm a doctor, so I secretly gathered up several hairs and sequenced each at different time points. As I suspected, my father's too clever to use plain DNA that can be obtained so easily. He had his genome illegally engineered to include a unique anchor sequence, a kind of docking site. In his living cells, this anchor binds a volatile molecular tag, a passcode that's only produced while the cell is alive. Within an hour of a cell being shed, the tag degrades completely. If you try to use old DNA from his hair or skin, the scanner won't find the tag it's looking for."

He paused. "Any guesses what happens to someone who tries to use my father's DNA that *doesn't* have the tag?"

"Something really, really bad?" said Matt.

"Yep. I hate to give my father credit, but again, it's brilliant. He leaks that his DNA is the key, then waits for his enemies to use it, unaware of the modification, and they walk right into his trap."

"Brilliant, sure," said Kira. "But not enough to fool you, was it? I assume you've managed to create and synthesize a stable version of his DNA in the lab that will still have the tag?"

Aethor gave her a nod. "Good guess."

"Let me recap," said Ishar, and once again there was admiration in his tone. "Your father has used three consecutive ruses. First, if his enemies can pull off a miracle and get through to the fake site, they'll sabotage a fake processor. Second, if an even bigger miracle happens, like you being able to access his secret files, and someone learns of the real location of the processor, they'll have no way to get through his boulder blockade without triggering the seismic sensors. And third, if someone, against all odds, makes it into the proper room, they'll use Kairos's normal DNA and be killed on the spot."

"That sums it up nicely," said Aethor.

"Remarkable," replied the Anunnaki.

"Assuming we clear his DNA hurdle," responded Kira, "how do we take the final step? How do we beat the electrical field?"

Aethor pulled a small device from his pocket. "This frequency modulator will create a window just wide enough to reach through. Once I hit this bypass switch here, it'll reroute power directly to the city's main plant and isolate it from the weapon's systems. Everyone keeps their lights on while we end the menace.

"Then, we'll be able to remove the crystalline matrix, and the weapon systems will deactivate. The matrix contains all the quantum calculations needed to create the weapon's effect. With that gone, Nexus Prime becomes nothing but a power station, as it should be."

"Just another routine mission," said Robert wryly. "If I would have known it would be *that* easy, I'd have taken it out on my own."

Aethor laughed. "Unfortunately," he said, his tone serious once again, "I'm not finished. I didn't describe what we'll need to do to get into the first tunnel undetected. The area is swarming with Sovereign Guards and drones. Heavy armaments abound. So, we'll need a major distraction above ground to be sure we can even get started. A prolonged distraction that causes so much seismic activity, if we do set off the seismic alarms in the tunnel, my father will assume it's from this diversion and not investigate the tunnels immediately."

Kira sighed. "Are you sure there isn't a moat filled with fire-breathing dragons we have to cross also?"

"Pretty sure," said Aethor with a grin. "Still, I can't rule it out entirely. Given how careful and paranoid my father is, *nothing* would surprise me. I learned from his files that at the same time he was setting up the site we're going after, he was also working on a way to control the weapon remotely. From a site far removed from Nexus Prime. Apparently, he even got it to work."

Robert looked confused. "So why isn't that our target?"

"It was another impossible project with little chance of success, but he loved the idea of it. Apparently, he put a trio of top scientists on it, who made an epic breakthrough, finally solving it only weeks after the core processor crystal was installed in the tunnel system. In the end, he decided he was satisfied with the set-up we're going after, and it wasn't worth the trouble of removing the crystal, so he shut the project down. No mention of where it was located or who was involved."

"You do have to hand it to him," said Kira. "He's exceedingly thorough, and he thinks outside of the box like few in history."

"Outside of the box?" asked Aethor.

"He thinks differently," explained Kira. "Moving on, why did you schedule the attack for two in the morning?"

"My father might find my backdoor computer access any minute, and then all bets are off. We have to go as soon as possible. Two AM gives us time to prepare, ensures it's pitch black, and is the last hour the guards will serve before a shift change, so they'll be at their most fatigued."

"How are we achieving this aboveground distraction that we're in such desperate need of?" asked Robert. *"Tala?"*

"No," said Aethor. "We can't involve *Tala* in this. They have anti-starship weapons on the Nexus Prime grounds that can reach miles out. Her cover would be blown, and, as amazing as she is, she'd be destroyed."

He shrugged. "Besides, she's a *Lemurian* starship. If she appears to be attacking the main source of power for all of Atlantis, our problems—and Lemuria's—will only multiply."

"Right," said Robert sheepishly. "No *Tala.*"

"She can transport us in," said Aethor, "but that's where her contribution ends."

"Then how do we achieve this distraction?" said Kira.

Ishar sighed. "Mardak and I can provide that."

"Thank you," said Aethor. "I was hoping I wouldn't have to ask. All of us are going to need to be at our best. No mission has ever been more important. I'm more convinced than ever that my father won't hesitate to use Nexus Prime as the ultimate weapon. He's convinced it's the key to Atlantean supremacy. I've seen a holovid of the weapon annihilating much of an entire inhabited island."

Visions of massive ice sheets collapsing, oceans swelling, entire civilizations drowning beneath relentless waves flashed through Robert's mind. They couldn't let history repeat itself. The nuclear weapons of his time, given radioactive fallout, would cause even greater destruction than that which they were trying to stop here.

"Here's the challenge," continued Aethor. "While two Anunnaki warriors are a formidable force, we'll need more of you to create the diversion, the havoc, that we'll need. *Many* more. And we'll need them in a hurry."

Ishar snorted. "Then you're out of luck. It's as near a suicide mission as it gets, no matter how many are involved. Mardak and I are willing to stare down almost certain death to avenge our fallen comrades, and because we pledged our services to Thoth. No other Anunnaki would sign on to such a mission, no matter how much money you offered."

Aethor didn't look concerned. "Remember when I told you that your newfound admiration for the ruthlessness of Kairos would soon take a bad turn? Well, that time is now. I've mentioned that I immersed myself in my father's most top-secret files. It turns out that one of these files has information that will get your comrades to sign onto this mission. In fact, it will get them *demanding* to be part of it, without need of any payment."

The two Anunnaki suddenly looked intrigued, and troubled. "We're listening," said Ishar warily.

"I'll give you the gist of what's in this file now. After that, I'll send it to your datapads and you can use whatever sophisticated methods you want to verify its legitimacy and confirm what I've told you. Then you can send it to your fellow warriors to help you build up Anunnaki forces, under your command, of course."

Ishar smiled, obviously liking the sound of that. "Of course."

"What's in the file?" said Mardak uneasily.

"My father sees aliens as an impediment to his plans. *All aliens*, but especially the Anunnaki. You're too good at being warriors. And too willing to sell your services to his enemies. There is so much more to it than that, which you can read in the file, but time is of the essence, so I won't elaborate further now."

"Okay, he doesn't like us," said Ishar. "What about it?"

"He plans to push a bill through the Atlantean High Council he calls ISAPPA—The Interstellar Species Accountability and Planetary Protection Act. The Act will expel all aliens from Earth and prohibit any others from visiting in the future. It's pure isolationism, allowing him to conquer the world without having to worry about alien opposition, either physical or political."

Aethor stared up into Ishar's eyes. "Here's the thing. He's saved the vilest part of his plan for *your* species. It isn't just that he doesn't like the Anunnaki. He fears you. And he doesn't trust that you'll leave Earth quietly. So, he plans to frame your entire species. To offer incontrovertible evidence that you're disregarding the Galactic edict to leave Earth in peace. The evidence will be ginned up, but trust me, it will be believed by all. It will show that all Anunnaki currently on our planet are an advance guard, scouting out our weaknesses, hatching plans to subjugate the entire human race. With the help of a fleet from your home world that will arrive in five to ten years once you've set the stage."

Aethor paused to let everything he had said sink in.

"Go on," said Ishar, looking like he might set the entire room ablaze with just the power of his rage.

"He'll use this as a pretext to round all of you up and have you executed. Soon. Very soon. Don't take my word for it. You can study the file for yourself. And I've only scratched the surface. When you see his plans for the Anunnaki for yourselves, the level of treachery, of deceit ... of *butchery*... involved, you'll be just as motivated as we are to stop him. You won't be fighting as a favor to us. You'll be fighting for the lives of your own people and the reputation of the Anunnaki. And to stop a man, my father, who is on the verge of committing the ultimate betrayal to your species."

There was a long silence as the two aliens digested these words.

"We have a saying," said Robert softly, breaking the silence. "The enemy of my enemy is my friend. It's never been truer than in this case."

Ishar nodded. "We have a similar saying." He glanced at Mardak, who was fuming, both of them barely able to contain their fury. At that moment, they looked as if they could mow down the entire Atlantean army single-handedly.

"What do you think?" said Aethor. "What I'm telling you *will* check out. When it does, can you and Mardak convince a force of your brethren to go on this mission under your command?"

"If what you say is true, absolutely. Nothing could keep my fellow warriors out of this fight. The problem is one of short notice. Two in the morning is fast approaching. It's unclear how many warriors I can activate and have ready by that time. And there's a logistical problem. As you pointed out, Kairos is seeing to it that no ships can get close to Nexus Prime. I'd need all those I'm able to recruit to convene in a non-secure area somewhere where *Tala* can pick them up. Seeing as how you've set her up as the only ship who can enter the proper airspace."

"Depending on how many you can recruit," said Kira, "once *Tala* is within Nexus Prime airspace, she can drop off groups of your warriors at different locations. Spread Kairos's forces thin. Give them multiple mini-fronts to focus on. Ishar and Mardak can coordinate the different groups through a command comm-channel."

"Won't a single ship landing multiple times to drop off Anunnaki passengers arouse enormous suspicion?" asked Robert.

"Normally, yes," replied Aethor. "But if anyone checks on the ship that *Tala* will disguise herself to be, I can make the record show that she's operating under the direct command of my father. Believe me, no one will ask questions. And *Tala* can extend her holographic camouflage to cover the Anunnakis' exits. She can drop them off in locations where they can find plenty of immediate cover from prying eyes."

Ishar faced Aethor with his eyes blazing, his fury having barely subsided. "Send us this file of yours to examine and review. If it is what you say it is, we'll round up the biggest force we can manage."

Aethor sighed. "It *isn't* what I say it is. It's worse. *Far* worse. You'll see."

Minutes later, Aethor sent the file in question to the two Anunnaki, who retreated into a separate room for privacy and focus.

Robert shook his head in wonder. This last rabbit Aethor had pulled from his hat was a twist Robert hadn't seen coming. He was thrilled by the prospect of having additional Anunnaki help. Perhaps they'd be able to sabotage the Nexus Prime weapons system and get out alive, after all.

But he was still the key. "I need to go outside and practice controlling my Vesh'tar," he announced, beginning to move toward the ramp.

"I was going to suggest the same," said Aethor, following him. "You have about five hours to figure out how to use finesse instead of raw power. And I believe I can help you."

Robert gripped the Vesh'tar tighter, its crystal brightening, and swallowed hard. A small monitor against one wall showed that rain had intensified outside, and thunder was rolling across an ominous black sky. Given the versatility of the Vesh'tar, he wouldn't be surprised if it had an *umbrella* function, not that he'd be able to find it.

"*Tala*, lower the ramp," he ordered, steel in his tone.

"Let's give this a shot," he said to the rest of the group. "I'm not sure if I can master a power I barely understand in such a short time, but I'll do my best. It could be our only chance."

Kira shot him a determined, supportive smile as the ramp began to extend. "Trust me, Robert, you *will* succeed. I'm willing to bet my life on it."

Robert winced. "That's just it. You *will be* betting your life on it. All of us will be."

CHAPTER 48

Rain pattered against the leaves overhead as a rumble of thunder growled in the distance. Robert stood in a clearing, the Vesh'tar in his grip. The crystalline orb atop the staff emitted a slight turquoise aura. It shimmered with each flicker of lightning on the horizon. The wind picked up, rustling the canopy of trees encircling him.

Behind Robert, rain droplets slid off the starship's surface. Robert glanced at Aethor, who pulled his cloak tighter against the chill. "Do you even know what you're teaching?" he asked the Atlantean.

"Not exactly. I've observed Thoth using the Vesh'tar. I think it's about connecting with it, aligning your intent."

Robert gritted his teeth. "Less helpful than I'd hoped."

Matt and Kira sat on the edge of the ramp leading into the cargo hold, watching from above. Aethor pointed at a half-sunken boulder nestled between the trees. Moss and shrubbery clung to its surface. "Try moving it with the Vesh'tar. You know, without making any sound."

For just a moment, an image of Luke Skywalker on a jungle planet flashed through his mind. Apparently, Aethor was the new Yoda, only taller.

"Focus your intent," added Aethor. "Let the Vesh'tar amplify it."

Robert took a deep breath, closing his eyes. He tried to quiet his mind, feeling the cool rain on his face. The sounds of the forest faded until only his heartbeat remained. He concentrated on the boulder, visualizing it moving.

A tingling sensation spread through his fingers and up his arm. The Vesh'tar's crystal sphere brightened. A surge of energy coursed through him.

Opening his eyes, he directed the staff toward the boulder. A beam of golden light shot out from the crystal, crackling through the air. Before he could react, the beam struck the large stone, and it exploded with a loud boom.

Shards of rock flew in all directions. Robert and Aethor dove to the ground, covering their heads as debris whizzed past. Fragments pinged off the starship's hull, embedding into nearby trees.

Robert pushed himself up, dusting off bits of dirt and pebbles that clung stubbornly to his wet clothing.

"I trust you're both okay," said Kira.

"Mentally or physically?" said Robert in frustration.

"Perhaps a bit less power next time," said Aethor.

"Thanks," said Robert sarcastically. "That never would have occurred to me."

The wind gusted, sending a chill through the air. The rain began to fall harder, droplets pelting them like tiny rocks. Robert adjusted his stance, gripping the Vesh'tar with more strength.

Aethor motioned toward another boulder, smaller than the first but still substantial. "Focus on finesse. Let the energy flow, don't force it."

Robert steadied his breathing. He closed his eyes once more, the rain now soaking through his clothes. The cold seemed distant compared to the warmth emanating from the Vesh'tar.

He envisioned the boulder lifting, no explosions this time. Energy flowed from the Vesh'tar and into his body, a steady current rather than a torrent. Opening his eyes, the crystal started glowing with a soft light.

The boulder trembled, a subtle vibration coursing through it. It began to lift, rising a few inches off the ground.

"You're doing it," shouted Kira.

A thrill shot through Robert. The momentary excitement broke his concentration. The sphere's glow intensified, and a bolt of electricity arced from the Vesh'tar, striking the boulder. It scorched the rock, blackening its surface, and the boulder dropped back to the ground with a heavy *thunk*.

"Steady," said Aethor. "You can't let yourself get distracted."

Robert exhaled. The storm intensified, thunder cracking overhead.

"Alright," said Robert. "Third time's the charm."

Closing his eyes, he attempted a different approach. Instead of commanding the Vesh'tar, he sought to communicate with it. The staff was advanced technology, even sentient in a way.

He focused on reaching out mentally. A subtle presence responded, a murmur at the edge of his consciousness. *We are connected*, it said.

Can we work together on this? thought Robert.

Always, and in all ways, the Vesh'tar replied.

Robert looked down at the Vesh'tar, rainwater streaming off the carvings. *Help me*, he thought. *How can I wield you without causing harm?*

A heat emanated from the staff, spreading through his hand. A voice echoed in his mind. *You need not force control. Trust in our connection.*
What does that mean?
Like a river flowing naturally around stones, rather than trying to break through them. We are partners, not master and tool. Your intent guides, but my power flows. Together we find balance.
Robert furrowed his brow. *But how? Explain it to me clearly. No riddles.*
Release your tension first. Breathe deeply and let your muscles relax. When you try to control me, you create resistance. Feel the energy as it moves from the crystal through your arms and into your core. Don't push or pull. Simply guide it, like directing water through an open channel. When you see an object you wish to move, don't think about forcing it to move. Instead, envision it already in motion, flowing to where you want it to be. The power will follow your visualization naturally, without strain.

He closed his eyes, allowing himself to relax. The tension in his muscles eased. The Vesh'tar felt like an extension of his own body now.

Opening his eyes, he focused on a smaller rock nearby. Visualizing it already lifting off the ground, he raised the staff, and the stone rose. No surge of power, no struggle. Just smooth, fluid movement.

Encouraged, he guided the rock through gentle arcs, moving it with ease. No drain on his energy, no resistance. The connection felt simple, even symbiotic.

He tried with a larger stone, and the result was the same. Even as the storm raged around him, a sense of peace passed over him. He guided it upward. He allowed himself a quick smile. He then moved the Vesh'tar to the left, and the boulder glided accordingly. To the right, and it followed.

"Remarkable," said Kira from the ship.

"Yeah," said Matt, also from the shelter of the ship. "Super impressive. You know what it reminds me of?"

"Luke Skywalker learning how to use the force?" said Robert.

"Well . . . yeah," said Matt, looking disappointed.

Robert lifted the boulder higher, pushing it above the treetops, leaves stirring in the escalating wind. Lightning streaked across the sky, followed by a roar of thunder. The storm was directly overhead now.

Thank you, he thought.

The Vesh'tar pulsed in response.

Satisfied, Robert and his teacher, who'd turned out to be largely unnecessary, made their way back inside the starship. Still, a strange, and a slight, exhaustion tugged at Robert. No doubt from using the Vesh'tar, and probably a little incorrectly, too.

"Well done," said Kira when he entered. "I knew you'd master it. I *knew* it."

"How?" he asked.

"Because I believe in you. And in Thoth. And in *Tala*. And I believe in *us*, the trio *Tala* chose to bring here."

"Thank you, Kira. I won't let you down." Robert sighed. "Let's go over the detailed plan three or four times and then try to get as much rest as we can. We'll need to be at the very top of our game."

Given Robert's success with the Vesh'tar, he had finally come to believe they *would be* at the top of their game.

Still, despite a truly inspired plan, an enormous number of *things* had to go just right for this to work. And he couldn't help but wonder if even their best would be enough.

CHAPTER 49

Advisor Elowin Balivae
Poros Territory, Poros City
Location: Southwest Atlantis

The city glowed like embers in darkness under the cloak of night, lights woven between spires and bridges. Towering among it all stood the Grand Hall, reflecting the faint light of the Moon's haze through the rain clouds. Sporadic drizzle still fell, but the brunt of it had passed half an hour earlier.

Elowin adjusted the collar of her ill-fitting tunic, the Atlantean fabric strange against her skin. "This doesn't feel right." She tugged at the hem brushing her thighs.

Jalon stepped beside her, his gaze fixed on the Grand Hall's entrance, busy with activity. "You wear it well, Advisor."

Earlier, they'd slipped through a deserted marketplace. The stalls, teeming with merchants and patrons during normal business hours, had stood silent, their wares secured behind white gates. One boutique had caught their fancy. Its display of Atlantean attire shined under dim luminescent orbs.

"Are you sure about this?" Elowin had whispered.

Jalon had nodded while working on the lock. "We need to blend in."

The door had yielded, and they had moved inside. Mannequins draped in flowing tunics and tailored suits had lined the walls. Elowin's eyes had fallen on a simple yet elegant tunic, the deep blue fabric adorned with subtle silver threading.

Elowin hated the idea of stealing, but not as much as she hated the idea of Kairos wiping out many millions of her countrymen and destroying much of her homeland.

So, she had stolen the tunic and shed her Lemurian robes for the Atlantean garment. Jalon had discarded his already stolen Atlantean garb for an ensemble allowing for maximum movement while giving him an air of professionalism. They'd left their old clothes hidden outside behind a statue partially hidden by shrubs.

Now, standing on the outskirts of the Grand Hall's plaza, news crews swarmed like restless fruit flies, cameras hovering above tripod stands powered by levitation crystals. The devices' lenses rotated independently to capture every angle. Reporters held wireless mics, slender wands etched with runic symbols.

From their vantage point in a place called Moonweaver Park across from the Grand Hall, Elowin and Jalon hid among twisted trees. The park's dense foliage provided perfect cover while giving clear sightlines to the plaza. Stone benches and fountains dotted the grounds between them and their target, each presenting potential cover if needed.

"There's no end to the media," said Elowin. "We need their equipment, but we can't just waltz over there and take it."

Jalon watched the crowd. "What we can do is create our own opportunity," he said. He nodded toward a duo stepping away from the throng—a cameraman adjusting his apparatus and a female reporter reviewing notes on a translucent slate. "Those two."

"What's the plan?"

"I approach from behind and incapacitate them quietly. Then we take what we need."

Her stomach twisted at the thought of assaulting innocent strangers, but she finally nodded. Too much was at stake to be squeamish about anything.

"Do it," she said.

They moved, shadows among shadows, circling behind a parked news transport. A hovering vehicle with panels displaying network insignias. The reporter and cameraman eased away from the crowd, heading toward a lit alley.

As the media pair paused to converse beside a recycling receptacle, Jalon moved stealthily away from Elowin. He slipped between two parked transports, using them for cover. In three silent steps, he was behind the cameraman. His arm wrapped around the man's neck from behind. The cameraman struggled briefly, then went limp and unconscious as the hold cut off blood flow to his brain. Jalon lowered him quietly to the ground, the man's chest still rising and falling steadily.

Before the reporter could turn around, Jalon's hand covered her mouth while his other arm encircled her neck. She struggled for a moment, then her eyes closed, and her body went slack, unconscious but breathing. Jalon caught her as she collapsed.

Crouched behind a stone planter filled with night-blooms, Elowin watched the clean takedown. Twenty yards of manicured lawn separated her from the alley's entrance, giving her clear sight while remaining hidden from the plaza's crowd.

Jalon caught her eye and waved her over. Elowin took a deep breath and moved. She kept low, using the decorative shrubs for cover. Three quick dashes between patches of darkness brought her to the first transport. She paused, checking for witnesses, before rushing between the vehicles to join Jalon.

"Help me with the equipment," he whispered.

She nodded, moving the levitating camera off its harness. It was lighter than it appeared, the anti-gravity crystals doing most of the work. The mic wand illuminated with her touch, its runes dimming a moment after.

They donned the crew's attire. Jalon clipped the network emblem to his lapel and minded the camera as Elowin adjusted the reporter's earpiece and gripped the mic. She pulled her hair back, tucking it beneath a sleek headband matching the uniform.

"How do I look?" she asked.

"Convincing."

They left the alley, merging with the ebb and flow of personnel. Almost immediately, Elowin felt eyes on them. Guards, technicians, other journalists casting suspicious glances their way.

"Stay calm," muttered Jalon. "Confidence is key."

She straightened her posture, adopting the poise she'd honed in countless Council meetings. With confident strides, she led the way toward the Grand Hall's main entrance. The energy shifted. Attention slid off them like they'd become part of the backdrop.

Approaching the security checkpoint, they faced a row of six solemn-faced guards clad in armor. One held up a hand, obviously the man in charge.

"Halt. Identification, please."

Elowin raised a translucent slate, tapping it as if accessing credentials. "We're with Hyperion News Network," she said. "Here for the late-night briefing."

The guard's gaze narrowed. "No additional press are scheduled."

Elowin feigned annoyance. "We were contacted by Deir Slan herself. *Councilor* Deir Slan. She specifically requested our presence."

The guard exchanged a glance with his second-in-command. "Wait here."

He moved away, speaking into his communication device. A knot tightened in Elowin's stomach.

An instant later, the guard returned. "There's no record of such a request. I'm afraid we'll have to deny entry."

Elowin leaned forward and checked her slate, tapping on it, acting the part. "We have *twenty minutes* to set up before Councilor Slan's statement about the Nasavi Defense Initiative!" she said in exasperation. "She and her people have no doubt been rushing around like crazy, preparing. Do *you* want to explain to her that her chosen media team was delayed because some busy, overworked subordinate in her office neglected to add us to the approved list? *Do you?*"

The guard swallowed hard. "I've never heard of any Nasavi Defensive Initiative."

"But you *have* heard that Lemuria attacked Outpost Anvil, right? She'll be outlining Atlantis's response."

Elowin shook her head in exasperation. "Look," she said, "we're already running late. You've got six guards manning this post. You should be able to spare one of them to be our chaperone while we work. Have them point a gun at our backs if it will make you feel safe from two scary civilian newspeople," she added sarcastically. "Whatever you have to do to make yourself comfortable with us going in, *do it now!*"

The man appeared to be frozen by indecision.

"Have you ever disappointed Councilor Slan?" said Jalon, deciding to add fuel to the fire. "She'll be *merciless*, even if you were just following protocol. If she doesn't have the media crew she wants for this announcement, believe me, you're *screwed*. She'll have you demoted and sent to the middle of a desert to guard scorpions and count grains of sand!"

Jalon paused for just a moment and then forged ahead. "We're going inside to set up right now!" he insisted. "You can let us in, you can shoot us, or you can send one of your men with us. Your choice. Because I'd rather be shot in the back than have my entire career torpedoed."

The guard exchanged a glance with his second-in-command, a look that Elowin judged to be one of surrender. "Very well," he said. "But *I'll* be accompanying you myself. My name is Thane," he added and then turned to his second. "You're in command of the checkpoint while I'm gone."

"Thank you," said Elowin, as she and Jalon wasted no time rushing past the checkpoint, not waiting to see if Thane was following. She shared a relieved glance with her partner. She was pretty sure Jalon could have taken out all six guards by himself, but he couldn't do so out in the open without attracting an army. Now, however, he could easily dispatch this Thane whenever it was necessary and prudent.

The Grand Hall's interior was a network of corridors and chambers. Crystal chandeliers cast myriads of patterns across the floors, and columns decorated with carvings rose toward vaulted ceilings.

Jalon slowed his pace, feigning distraction as he adjusted the camera. "Apologies," he said to the guard. "This equipment is temperamental."

The security officer halted. "We can have a technician assist."

Elowin shook her head. "No need. But perhaps you could point us to the nearest restroom."

He glanced at his timepiece. "Make it quick."

They diverged down a side corridor with Thane following close behind. As soon as there was no one else present, Jalon put him in a choke hold with a speed and precision that was truly remarkable and stuffed his unconscious body into a supply closet within a massive restroom.

"Did you get his weapon?" asked Elowin when Jalon emerged, his camera with him to sustain their cover if they were seen.

He shook his head. "It's keyed to his biometrics. Apparently, those in charge don't want hostiles overpowering outside guards and using their weapons."

As he was speaking, he led Elowin to a nearby stairwell. "Follow me."

They cautiously pushed through the door, ascending rapidly. Their footsteps were muffled by the plush carpeting lining the stairs.

When they reached the hallway outside Deir Slan's office, memories surged back into Elowin's head. Tense negotiations, the taste of betrayal, shots fired, Kona's death.

"Stay alert," said Jalon unnecessarily.

They approached the door, its glass surface like frozen starlight. Elowin tried the handle. It was locked, as expected.

Jalon fished tools from a pocket and began picking the lock with a speed and expertise that was obvious. Once again, Elowin marveled at his abilities. When he was with her, she felt like anything was possible.

In seconds he was finished and gripped the handle to the door, nodding at her that they were going in.

The moment the door opened an alarm pierced the air, its wail echoing down the corridors.

He cursed. "No turning back now," he said, charging into the office. They had both been aware this was a likely possibility. Still, Deir Slan's office was remote, and she had left long before. Given the many other high-value targets in the building, they had estimated they'd have a few minutes before guards were deployed to check on the office alarm.

Elowin rushed to Deir's desk and activated the woman's console, the interface blooming to life under her fingertips.

"Hurry!" said Jalon from the doorway while he scanned the hallway.

A sphere atop Deir's desk flashed azure light. A holographic array materialized above the desk, layers of translucent Atlantean script floating in geometric patterns.

Elowin's fingers moved through the light, typing on ethereal keys.

Aegis access::diplomatic override theta
clearance::council prime

The system pulsed red. Access denied.

"Come on," she muttered, typing fanatically over the virtual keys, trying another approach.

Quantum path:nexus prime archive
initiate:deep scan {war protocols+lemuria}

The hologram transformed, data cascading. Her eyes darted through the Atlantean index markers.

MILITARY CONCORDANCE
SOVEREIGN PROTOCOLS
CLASSIFIED AEGIS

There . . . file clusters with high-security markers.

DAWN RECKONING INITIATIVE
PROJECT NEXUS PRIME

She expanded them with a gesture.

access:dawn reckoning {all files+communications}

File names materialized in the air. *Conflict orchestration strategy. Evidence fabrication. Lemurian insurgency construct. Nexus Prime Lemurian strike protocol.*

"I can hear distant footsteps," said Jalon. "We have to go."

"Almost there," said Elowin, punching in commands as fast as she could.

download:project nexus prime {weapon schematics, deployment coordinates, falsified intelligence reports}

Her heart beat faster as the echo of boots pounding against the hallway grew louder.

Another secured archive caught her eye.

access:outpost anvil directive {operation parameters, target selection, staged incidents}

"This is it." She initiated the transfer, directing the data to her personal archive—a secure network accessible only through Lemurian quantum pathways.

initiate:quantum transfer {buffer protocol: lemurian secure compression:maximum trace scatter:active}

"Thirty seconds, Advisor!" said Jalon tensely.

The footsteps came closer, voices accompanying them.

The progress circle began filling.

41%. 60%. 74%.

"Come on, come on," muttered Elowin as the progress circle reached 89%.

Two voices called out. "Halt! You're in a restricted area!"

Jalon stepped into view, hands raised. "We got lost." He nodded to the camera. "Equipment malfunction. We were told someone in this office could help. The door was open."

"Hands where we can see them!" said the taller of the two guards, unimpressed by his farfetched excuse.

Elowin shook her head, eyes fixed on the screen, ignoring the soldiers.

Jalon took a slow step forward. "Look, we're just the press. No need for—"

A warning shot sizzled past him, scorching the wall.

"Zero tolerance policy tonight," said the guard. "Down on the ground!"

Elowin clutched her fists. 92%.

Jalon lowered himself to one knee. "Alright, we're complying."

Elowin trembled. The transfer hovered at 93%.

The guards advanced cautiously. "Both of you, now!"

She took a deep breath. 95%.

Jalon turned his head toward her. "Getting close?" he said in exasperation.

"Ninety-eight percent," she replied.

"What does that mean?" said the guard

Jalon shifted.

"Stay down!" said the second guard.

TRANSFER COMPLETE:DATA SECURED

"Got it!" said Elowin.

The evidence was locked in her quantum network channel, ready to download wherever she could find a safe place. Now they just had to escape and get the files to Lemurian decryption experts who would pull out all stops to break through.

But getting past these guards was one thing. Getting past the numerous guards and soldiers who would be sure to swarm the scene if they did escape was quite another.

She had never seen Jalon's equal. But even a man of his talents would be hard-pressed to survive the night.

CHAPTER 50

Councilor Kairos Daedalus
High Marshall of the Atlantean Military Forces
Outpost Anvil, Venus Cove
Location: Nasavi, East Shores

Alerts sounded, and fumes filled the cockpit of Kairos's Skyblade. Through the mayhem, his neural interface maintained a connection with the fighter's core systems, each pulse of data akin to ice through his temples.

"Lead is hit! Lead is hit!" Raven Nine's voice cracked through his helmet.

Kairos's training took over. He shut down the damaged port stabilizer, rerouting power to the remaining systems. "Still here," he said, wrestling with the controls. "Switching to auxiliary power."

The Skyblade's backup systems engaged, giving him minimal control. He dove hard, using the momentum of the spin to his advantage. The maneuver caught his pursuers off guard, and they overshot his position, their plasma bolts striking empty air.

"Control, this is Raven Lead. I've lost primary power but maintaining controlled descent. Request immediate—"

A sound burst overhead. The shriek of Stormcaller engines. Through his cracked canopy, Kairos glimpsed two dozen Atlantean fighters screaming past, their weapons engaging the Lemurian pursuers.

"This is Shadowhawk Actual," a voice transmitted. "Sorry we're late to the party, Councilor. We'll take it from here."

Kairos guided his wounded Skyblade toward Outpost Anvil, the backup systems straining to keep him airborne. "Raven Wing, regroup and support the Stormcaller Squadron. I'm making an emergency landing."

Above him, the tide of battle shifted as the Stormcaller squadron tore into the Lemurian forces. His tactical display flashed with updating combat data. The red markers representing Lemurian fighters began disappearing. Thirty-one hostile signatures reduced to twenty-six, then eighteen, then thirteen . . . in mere seconds. The holographic overlay showed the Stormcaller squadron executing near-perfect attack formations as they sliced through enemy craft.

Explosions lit up Karios's display as three more Lemurian fighters disappeared in bursts of flame. Yes, several of Atlantis's finest had fallen in the aerial combat, but such were the cruel demands of war. Even with Kairos's damaged systems, his Skyblade's battle analytics predicted a complete Lemurian rout.

As he approached the landing zone, Kairos held a grim smile. The "Lemurian aggression" would justify everything coming next. Through his canopy, Outpost Anvil came into view from the coastal mist. Its massive structure was half-embedded in the beach sands near the ocean's waves. Standard protocol would have him approach over the sea, into the ocean, and through the landing tubes leading to an underground hangar bay. With his systems failing, he couldn't risk the vertical descent.

"Control, this is Raven Lead. Requesting emergency clearance for surface approach, runway three."

"Confirmed, Councilor. Crash teams standing by."

Kairos fought the controls as he lined up his approach. His port engine sputtered, threatening to fail. The Skyblade lurched to one side, forcing him to compensate with manual thrusters. Sweat beaded on his forehead as the runway rushed up to meet him. Too fast. He was coming in too fast.

The fighter scraped the runway with a shriek of tortured metal, sparks erupting as his damaged landing gear collapsed on impact. Gripping the control stick with an iron fist, he prevented the Skyblade from cartwheeling as it skidded sideways across the landing strip. The nose veered toward the outpost's perimeter gate, ready to end both his life and his ambitions in a single fireball.

With a final burst from his remaining maneuvering thrusters, Kairos straightened the fighter's trajectory. The Skyblade slid to a smoking halt just yards from the runway's end, its hull leaving a trail of debris.

Kairos popped the canopy. He winced as his neural interface disconnected. Burnt circuitry and scorched metal filled his nostrils. Far off, he could hear the battle raging. The distinctive thunder of Atlantean weapons mixed with Lemurian plasma fire. Each explosion was another beautiful sound in his plan, another step toward power.

Emergency response teams converged on his position. The vehicles' lights colored the hazy air in alternating patterns of gold and red.

"Councilor!" A medical officer rushed forward, carrying a diagnostic scanner. "Are you injured?"

Kairos waved him off. "Attend to my fighter's systems first. I want a full damage assessment." The pain shooting through his left shoulder could wait. Right now, appearances mattered more than comfort.

Commander Argo rushed toward him. "Councilor Daedalus, I must insist you visit medical. Protocol demands—"

"Protocol? Protocol is what led to this attack, Commander. Our enemies grow bold while we hide behind procedures and regulations." He gestured to the battle behind him. "How many died today because we waited for proper authorizations?"

In truth, the day's events had unfolded as Kairos wanted. His black ops team struck with perfection. It drew the predictable Lemurian response while his force held back, playing the victims until the precise moment he unleashed hell.

Yes, in time, more Lemurian soldiers would join the fray and fight hard. The reports of this "unprovoked attack" on the Lemurian side would ensure it. This would become the bloodbath Kairos needed, but for now, his part was done.

He had long known that politics, like war, required sacrifices. He now savored the delicious irony of the moment. Every spark of damage, every system failure—the fact that he had barely survived—would serve his greater purpose. His near-death would dominate headlines across Atlantis. The valiant Councilor, commanding his forces from the front, almost martyred by savage Lemurian aggression.

The masses, predictable in their emotional simplicity, would demand blood. The High Council, those pompous fools who had rolled their eyes at his influence too many times, would have no choice but to grant him the emergency powers he'd carefully orchestrated these past years. The citizenry's calls for his promotion would echo through Atlantis's halls.

When the next cycle of elections arrived, who better to lead their great nation than the hero who'd stared into the darkness of Lemurian hate and emerged victorious? The population would carry him to the High Councilor's seat on their shoulders. By then, his true vision for Atlantis would emerge, and they'd cheer him for it. Their savior, their champion, the most beloved leader in recorded history.

While tales of his heroics spread across Atlantean channels, he'd board his shuttle and fly to Poseidia, where he could better manage the growing conflict. Such was the life of a political leader, war hero, and master strategist. Always performing for the masses. The mounting pressure of it all, coupled with his son's recent defiance—the boy he loved more than anything in this world—might wear on him a bit too much, but he'd be fine in the end.

Stress had always been Kairos's constant companion, and in a way, his fuel. Now, watching Atlantis slowly decay under outdated ideals of peace and cooperation, the same stress drove him forward. If breaking his own heart and spilling others' blood was the price of saving their civilization, so be it. The coming Atlantean-Lemurian war would forge a stronger Atlantis, and a stronger humanity, with him as its leader.

"Secure a direct channel to the High Councilor," he ordered Argo. "The man needs to understand the gravity of what's happened here."

More importantly, Atlantis needed to see Kairos in the immediate aftermath of his brush with death, showing nothing but composure and determination. "Get me as many media contacts as you can. I'll stand here for the interviews."

"At once, Councilor." Argo turned on his heel and made his way to the command structure, already activating his neural comm to make those necessary calls.

A young technician approached with a preliminary damage report on Kairos's Skyblade. The fighter's port side was a mess of scorched and ruptured systems. The Lemurian fighting crafts had come dangerously close to breaching his cockpit's shielding.

"Sir!" Argo called out, striding toward Kairos. "The High Councilor is assembling an emergency session. They're requesting your immediate testimony."

"Will this be live on nationwide media channels?" asked Kairos.

"Yes, Councilor."

"Have my personal shuttle prepared. After this, I'll be heading away from here. And Commander Argo?"

"Councilor?"

"I want hourly updates on our defensive positions. The Lemurians may have failed today, but this attack proves what I've been warning the Council about for years." He paused, making sure everyone within earshot could hear his next words. "The old ways of peace are over. Atlantis must evolve, or we'll perish."

By nightfall, similar conversations would be happening across every Atlantean city, settlement, and neighborhood. And he'd be at the center of it all, the wounded hero who had long been trying to prevent this very tragedy.

A technician strode in their direction and halted beside Argo. The tech held an orb-like device. "Councilor, you're on."

The technician raised the metallic orb, its surface pulsing with soft blue light. The device hovered at eye level, its outer shell rotating to reveal dozens of micro-lenses. A beam of light erupted from its center, materializing into a crystalline screen nine feet wide.

The imposing figure of High Councilor Nereus Pyralis filled the display. His crimson hair and full beard, the traditional mark of his station, cascaded like waves of copper, framing a face seasoned by decades of leadership. Standing well over six feet tall, even his holographic presence commanded attention. His formal tunic, deep blue with gold geometric patterns woven through silver threads, bore the ancient symbols of Atlantean leadership across his chest.

In the corner of the projection, a small indicator showed the live viewer count. 184 million and climbing. Every household in Atlantis and its territories would be watching this exchange.

Nereus's eyes narrowed slightly as he regarded Kairos. When he spoke, his deep voice carried the careful measure of a man walking a political tightrope. "Councilor Daedalus, while we've had our disagreements about military preparedness, it seems your warnings held merit. The people of Atlantis watch now as one of their elected leaders stands amid the wreckage of Lemurian treachery.

Kairos could hear the reluctance in Nereus's tone, the subtle resistance even now. It didn't matter. The stage was set, the audience captive. He straightened despite his injuries, projecting strength for the millions watching. "High Councilor," he began, "today we saw the true face of our Lemurian enemies. They struck without provocation, targeting not just military assets but the very heart of our outpost here."

Kairos gestured to the smoke-filled sky behind him. "I stand before you not as a politician, but as a father who wants his child to inherit an Atlantis that is strong enough to defend itself. One that prospers and doesn't fall to the tyranny of outsiders jealous of our might, of our technology, of our freedom. The time for half-measures and diplomatic niceties is over. I swear by the ancient waters that no Atlantean will ever again fear any enemy, any intruder, any army."

As the words left his mouth, Kairos watched the viewer count spike even higher. In homes across the empire, his message would be striking its mark, planting the seeds of war in fertile soil. The coming days would water those seeds with fear, and from them would grow his new Atlantis, whether Nereus and his traditionalists liked it or not.

CHAPTER 51

Advisor Elowin Balivae
Poros Territory, Poros City
Location: Southwest Atlantis

Jalon launched himself upward like a predatory cat, closing the seven-foot gap between him and the first Sovereign Guard in the blink of an eye. With a swift twist, he wrenched the guard's weapon free. The second guard, positioned just two steps behind his companion, raised his rifle at Elowin as she darted from behind the desk.

The blast seared over her head, scorching the wall behind her. Jalon spun the first guard around, using him as a human shield while the second guard hesitated, unwilling to fire through his comrade. That split second was all Jalon needed. He pushed forward, still gripping his human barrier. Jalon dropped and swept the second guard's legs from under him. The guard crashed down hard, his weapon clattering across the floor. With the other soldier still in Jalon's grip, he picked him off the ground and slammed him into his friend.

Jalon snatched up the fallen laser rifle and fired in one fluid motion. Laser bolts ended both soldiers' lives before they could scream. Jalon sighed, relieved that the rifle wasn't biometrically locked like Thane's had been.

"This way!" he yelled.

They sprinted down an adjoining corridor, alarms blaring. Doors blurred past.

"Exit routes?" said Elowin.

"Working on it," he replied, scanning for signage while keeping pace beside her.

Behind them, the clatter of armored boots reverberated off the walls, growing louder.

A set of double doors stood slightly ajar ahead. After a few more steps, they burst through them into an atrium. The space stretched upward, dominated by a glass ceiling showing the night sky. Moonlight pooled on the floor while droplets from the dying rain tapped against the transparent dome.

Jalon pointed to a service door. "Over here!"

They reached it and yanked it open, only to find a squad of guards emerging from the stairwell beyond. They slammed the door shut, Jalon spinning the lock mechanism until it clicked into place.

In seconds, the soldiers pounded against the metal, each impact making the hinges groan. "You're surrounded!" a voice said. "Surrender now!"

Elowin glanced around, desperation tightening her chest. No clear escape.

"Can you climb?" asked Jalon, eyeing support beams ascending toward a maintenance hatch in the glass ceiling.

She followed his gaze. "Looks like we're going to find out."

He clasped his hands, offering a boost. She stepped into the foothold made by his interlocking fingers, and he launched her upward with all his strength. She just caught the edge of the beam, muscles straining as she pulled herself up.

Jalon followed. He swung from beam to beam, using his momentum to close the distance between them.

The service door exploded inward as Sovereign Guards flooded the space, weapons scanning the area. One looked up, barking commands to his comrades. Energy bolts struck the metal around the two fugitives. Glass shattered, shards falling.

They reached the hatch and Elowin wrenched it open. Cool air rushed in along with a light drizzle of rain.

"Move!" shouted Jalon.

Shots streaked past, and he let out a yelp. Blood dripped from his leg as they scrambled onto the rooftop. Below them, the city sprawled outward, lights dazzling.

Elowin glanced at her partner's leg. Blood seeped through his pants. "How bad?"

"I'm fine. Looks worse than it is."

Elowin nodded toward aerial walkways that connected them to adjacent buildings. "That's our path."

Through the curve of the massive glass dome, Elowin spotted movement. A different squad of guards were coming from a maintenance door on the far side of the roof, nearly thirty yards away. The dome's apex provided cover from their position, leaving only the troops' helmets visible.

A soldier motioned in Elowin's direction and began leading the charge after them.

The two fugitives raced across the walkway, their footsteps triggering safety lights in the transparent platform. Now seventy feet above the streets, fierce winds buffeted them from all sides. The curved dome continued to work in their favor. The pursuing guards had to climb its arc to reach the walkway, buying them valuable time. Though the soldiers remained out of firing range behind the dome's slope, even with this head start, the guards were slowly closing the gap.

They reached the next building, darting through a rooftop garden decorating the top of a commerce structure. Atop the building, trees swayed in the wind, their leaves graced by the soft glow of copper lanterns. The garden's paths wound between meditation pools and native flora.

"Down here!" said Jalon, gesturing toward a maintenance ladder.

They began their descent, the metal rungs slick with rain. Ten yards down, Elowin's foot slipped on the wet surface. Her heart lurched as she started to fall. Jalon's hand shot out, catching her arm. Above them, the guards' boots thundered across the garden.

"Thanks," she said, her heart beating so quickly she could barely speak.

They touched down in a narrow alley flanked by stone walls. Waste reclamation units hummed, and steam hissed from environmental control vents. The sounds of pursuit reverberated overhead. Service doors lined both walls and maintenance drones whirred past on their preset paths, oblivious to the chase.

"Where to now?" she asked.

"We need to get off the streets. This way. There's a hidden tunnel entrance we can take."

"How do you *know* that?" said Elowin in amazement as she rushed to follow his lead.

"You've traveled to the Great Hall twice. All Protectorate members on your security detail studied intel on this building as a matter of course. Which is one reason we were able to hold our own during the battle there. Well, *after* you warned us of the ambush with about two seconds to spare, saving us from being killed at the very start."

Jalon took a left behind a short building. "I have to say," he continued, "that the most elite soldiers I've ever served with couldn't have reacted any more decisively and courageously than you did. We're supposed to save *you*, not the other way around."

"Don't worry, you've done more than your share of saving me."

"Thankfully, yes," said Jalon with a heavy sigh. "Anyway, during preparations for your visit, I took it upon myself to go the extra mile. I studied the intel Lemuria has, not only on the Great Hall itself, but its surroundings, especially noting places like the extensive tunnel system we'll be in soon, where assassins might emerge to stage an attempt on your life."

"Wow! Do you usually go to such extraordinary efforts?"

"No."

"So why did you in this case?"

"To be honest, because I find you extraordinary enough to warrant extraordinary efforts. And, as it turns out, these preparations will serve us quite well in our current . . . predicament."

He stopped as they arrived at the tunnel entrance, hidden by a dense tangle of thorny vines, which turned out to be nothing but perfect holographic simulations. When they pushed through the lethal-looking hedge and entered the tunnel, bright strips blinked along the curved ceiling. A subterranean network opened before them, which Jalon told her were maintenance corridors honeycombed beneath Poros City.

Steam hissed from pipes overhead. Automated maintenance drones whined past on their eternal rounds, their sensors ignoring the two fugitives as non-priority entities.

Every few yards, Jalon paused at intersections, pressing them against slick walls as he checked for pursuit. Security cameras dotted the tunnels, but most pointed toward critical infrastructure. Water purification nodes, power conduits, and particle refinement stations. Their blind spots created perfect stealth paths for those who knew where to look.

The tunnel floor descended gradually. Condensation dripped. Each distant clang or mechanical whine had them spinning around, expecting to see Sovereign Guards materializing from the gloom.

"These tunnels," whispered Elowin, ducking under a low-hanging cluster of cables, "do they connect the entire city?"

"Most of it," replied Jalon. He stopped and held up a fist so she would stop as well. They listened to what sounded like footsteps, only to realize it was water hitting a collection grate.

They passed through sections where the walls opened into wide chambers, filled with buzzing environmental processors and tangles of pipes disappearing into darkness.

After what felt like jogging and running for miles, the tunnel began to angle upward. Fresh air filtered down, carrying with it the unmistakable smell of a river. They came out through a maintenance door screened by ferns and at a secluded embankment along one of the city's waterways. The river's surface reflected the city's lights.

Elowin leaned against a cargo crate on the riverfront dock, catching her breath. The water lapped gently against the moorings. "How long until they sweep this sector?"

Jalon stood at the edge, scanning the barges dotting the waterway. "Based on standard pursuit protocols, we have maybe ten minutes before they establish a full cordon. River traffic's our best chance. Harder to track biosignatures through the water."

"You've really thought of everything, haven't you?" she said in admiration.

He sighed. "Let's hope so."

"I have full confidence in you," she said. "The second we have the chance, we need to get the information I retrieved to Lemurian cryptologists. The moment they break the code, I'll make sure it gets into the right hands."

"What hands did you have in mind?"

"Right now, the High Councilor of Atlantis, Nereus Pyralis."

"Seriously?" said Jalon in dismay.

"He isn't a warmonger. He's the only one with the power and authority to stop Kairos dead in his tracks. I'll tell him that if he refuses to do so, I'll make sure the information of Kairos's treachery goes wide, entering the court of public opinion around the world. If he stops Kairos and the war, on the other hand, I'll keep it secret, sparing him and Atlantis the humiliation . . . and the scandal. It's my only leverage, but I think it's powerful."

"And what if he's more of a warmonger than you think?"

"I have to trust my gut on this. I know him. He has a military background, but I'm convinced he sees the military as providing defense only, not as a tool for conquest."

"If the information you took in Deir's office was all encrypted, how can you be sure you'll have enough evidence to convince him?"

"I can't be. But the file names themselves weren't encrypted, and they left little doubt as to Kairos's treachery. I'm confident the information stored under these file headers will be more than sufficient. With luck, we'll find out for sure very soon."

She paused, still catching her breath. "I'm sorry you keep having to put your life in jeopardy for me."

"I'm not sorry. It's an honor to serve Lemuria. And to serve you, especially, Advisor Balivae."

"*Elowin*," she insisted. "You don't even have to save my life once to use my first name. But saving my life *more* than once definitely qualifies."

Several military hover-vehicles were now in the air, their searchlights sweeping across the waterfront district. Behind them, smaller pursuit vehicles followed.

"They're continuing the search," whispered Jalon, pulling back into the shadows.

A medium-sized barge drifted into view, its hull scraping against the dock's cushioned barriers. The vessel's stabilizers vibrated, keeping it barely afloat as its automated systems prepared for departure. Steam rose from its processing vents, creating a veil of mist above the dark water.

"There," whispered Jalon, motioning to the maintenance handholds running along the barge's hull. "We can use those to stay hidden."

Elowin nodded as hover-vehicles grew closer, searchlights continuing to sweep across the waterfront.

They slipped into the water, which was warm enough to tolerate for an extended period without inducing hypothermia. They moved beneath the barge's shadow with careful strokes, minimizing any ripples.

Jalon reached the handholds first, his fingers finding purchase on the slick metal. He guided Elowin's hand to the nearest grip, and they pressed themselves against the hull, submerged to their necks.

The barge's propulsion system engaged, sending vibrations through their bodies. Above them, the processing machinery churned, masking any sounds they made. The vessel's movement was slow, barely a crawl away from the dock.

The current pushed against them, threatening to sweep them into the open water. On their right, lights reflected off the river's surface, a reminder of the pursuers. To their left, across the wide expanse of water, the dark silhouette of a forest stood, far out of reach.

"Hug the hull," said Jalon into her ear. "Sensors sweep outward."

The barge's shadow gradually enveloped more of the river as they drifted farther from the waterfront. The sounds of pursuit grew fainter.

A metallic clang resonated through the hull. Footsteps.

They pressed themselves tighter against the barge as the footsteps grew nearer, stopping almost directly above them. A maintenance hatch creaked open, spilling light onto the water just yards away.

Elowin controlled her breathing, making each inhale silent. A figure leaned out over the edge, dark against the hatch's glow. The worker adjusted something on the hull, muttering about pressure readings.

The light from his headlamp moved across the water's surface, drawing closer to their position.

The beam stopped just short of revealing them. But just as Elowin thought they had dodged a bullet, the beam continued to move.

And seconds later, it flashed straight into their eyes.

CHAPTER 52

Nexus Prime stood in the distance. Inside that massive structure sat their target. A quantum crystalline matrix no bigger than Aethor's palm. It was the key to shutting the weapon down.

The behemoth monument dwarfed Poros City's surrounding buildings. Its surface gleamed, illuminating the rain-slicked streets. It stretched high into the air, and its base covered two city blocks.

The rain clouds had dropped their load of moisture but still remained, blotting out any light from the Moon or stars such that anything not illuminated artificially was impossible to see in the darkness.

Robert squinted through the drizzle. His heart pounded all too fast, the Vesh'tar in his grip. Nexus Prime dominated his thoughts, the sheer scale of it almost overpowering. It was far more impressive than any of the ancient structures he'd studied or visited during his career. To top it off, Robert had to somehow remove many tens of thousands of pounds of granite boulders and rubble with a single staff. It was a job for a superhero, not an archeologist.

Robert and his fellow team of human beings waited patiently for Ishar's signal. Their two alien friends had managed to recruit twenty-eight additional Anunnaki warriors. They were split into four groups of seven, and *Tala* had dropped each group off in a different location, where they had found immediate cover. Ishar and Mardak were each responsible for coordinating the movements and commanding two of the groups, while the entire contingent was under Ishar's final command.

Robert spoke through the patter of rain. "We move in the shadows," he said. "Follow my lead." His tone was all business. He motioned behind them toward a second alley that was as dark and narrow as the one they occupied.

Robert pressed against a cold stone wall while the group hid together in a dark recess. Rain dripped from overhanging eaves. It created a curtain of water at the alley's entrance and hid them well.

They had been moving and hiding now for thirty minutes, waiting for Ishar to stage his small army in the best way to create the mother of all distractions. The numerous drones patrolling the skies had night-vision capabilities that would allow them to see the trespassers as if they had arrived in broad daylight. Fortunately, Aethor had intel on the drones' activity and movement patterns, and his expertise had kept them safe thus far while they waited.

Aethor tapped the barrel of his rifle. "Ten minutes until a drone swarm will enter this sector," he said softly. "We'll need to be moving by then."

Robert relayed this information to Ishar through a comm, and the alien acknowledged the urgency of starting the distraction. Once the melee began, Robert would go radio silent so as not to risk giving away their position.

To their left, what looked like a dumpster provided additional cover. Just beyond the alley, puddles had formed on the cobblestones, reflecting the glow of streetlamps lining the main thoroughfare.

The group was positioned just beyond the reach of the shallow pools. Every so often, flashes of lightning illuminated the area, giving glimpses of empty streets and shuttered shopfronts. Thunder rumbled in the distance.

"Sovereign Guards!" warned Matt in a whisper, pointing toward a pair of heavily armored figures patrolling nearby. They were carrying powerful flashlights of a sort, which made them stand out vividly in the dark night.

"Let's move!" said Robert. "Keep your eyes open for additional guards. Watch for flashlight sweeps and make sure to stay out of the beams. It's possible that some guards will have night-vision displays also, so remain as well hidden as you can and stay alert."

"Ready when you are," said Aethor quietly, and Kira and Matt nodded to indicate their own readiness.

Robert turned and headed east, away from the guards, hugging the wall of a building. The rest followed close behind.

After crossing several streets and stealthily navigating around a service depot, Robert held up a fist, signaling a halt. He peered around a corner and then turned back to face his friends. "We're exactly where we need to be. We'll move to the access point just after Ishar and his comrades start the fireworks. It isn't far. Aethor knows the way."

Robert realized that a distraction created by a force of Anunnaki was much better for them than the same distraction created by a force of humans. Once word went out that it was an Anunnaki attack, their raiding party would be all but ignored.

Two more minutes passed before Ishar's voice rattled through Robert's ear, finally giving the word, the last communication they would have. Only seconds later, all hell broke loose, as expected, as heavy munitions exploded at four different locations simultaneously within a half-mile radius of them. This was followed by the snap-hiss of plasma weapons splitting the air in the distance, the high-pitched screech of laser fire, and finally, the blaring of alarms that shrieked throughout the area.

Robert and his sabotage party wasted no time, sprinting across an open plaza as the rain intensified and pelted their faces. They soon arrived at a street bordering what looked like a large corporate plaza back home, with spectacular marble and glass buildings separated by wide open spaces and lush flower gardens.

Seconds later they reached a maintenance hatch, one that appeared old and worn.

Aethor handed his rifle to Robert while he pulled out a datapad from a pouch around his waist and tapped on the screen. Nodding to himself after reading data scrolling down the display, he lifted a lever flush with the street and pulled upward. A piece of the road the size of his hand slid to the side, revealing a keypad. Aethor hastily punched in a series of nine numbers and the hatch popped open.

Robert returned the weapon to its owner, and the foursome clambered down a ladder into darkness. The hatch sealed, muffling the sounds of combat above ground.

Aethor activated a light on his weapon, showing the wide tunnel that was their only route to the processor core controlling Nexus Prime's weapons function. "All video cameras are now on a loop and will continue to show nothing but an empty tunnel."

They began walking at a brisk pace, and within a handful of seconds could just make out the tunnel blockade off in the distance that they had known would be there.

"Looks like you're up soon, Professor," whispered Matt.

They continued to move swiftly down the tunnel. Water dripped from unseen cracks. The air grew thick with mustiness. Robert's mind kept drifting to the firefight raging above. The Nexus Prime grounds were heavily fortified for miles around, and swarming with guards and drones, but that wasn't stopping the thirty Anunnaki commandoes from unleashing a fury that would never be forgotten.

Ahead, Aethor held up a hand. "Security checkpoint," he noted. "No guards, but a hidden biometric scanner. Give me a minute."

As Aethor worked to bypass the scanner, Robert leaned against a wide column. After all that had happened, it was still surreal to be deep beneath an Atlantean metropolis, heading toward a secret, non-descript control room, about to attempt sabotage that could change the course of history. It was terrifying and exhilarating at the same time.

The Vesh'tar felt heavy in his hand. He glanced at Matt and Kira. Like him, determination filled their eyes.

"You know," whispered Matt while they waited. "I used to scoff at my dad. One of the last times I saw him, he was drawing circular patterns in the sand, talking about doorways between worlds. Said our people had walked them before. That there was a delicate balance between earth and sky, past and future. That the stars held ancient memories. *Everything connects*, he'd say. I laughed it off then and rolled my eyes, calling it superstition. And now it turns out that his insane, preposterous ramblings are fairly accurate, and the history the rest of us know is anything but."

Kira's attention remained on Aethor, watching him work on the scanner. "My father disappeared chasing geological mysteries," she said in low tones. "He'd be proud to see me here. Worried out of his mind, yes, but also proud. I wish I could see his face again."

A soft beep sounded from the scanner Aethor was working on, and the High Marshall's son blew out a relieved breath. "We're through."

The sound of the aboveground battle had died out since they had entered the tunnel, which didn't come as a surprise to Robert. The Anunnaki had no doubt taken out most of the guards in their initial surprise attack, and the Atlanteans were on their heels. But the Atlanteans' numbers were too great, and they could access too many reinforcements for this state of quiet to last long. They would soon regroup and come at the Anunnaki *hard*.

A few minutes later the human foursome arrived at the cave-in, and Robert surveyed the scene. Large boulders and packed earth made a barrier. It stretched from the tunnel's ground to its high ceiling. Rocks with jagged edges protruded at odd angles. From Robert's excavation experience, those stones looked like they could shift at the slightest disturbance.

Kairos's construction workers had done well, purposely creating a precarious blockade that desperately wanted to degenerate into an avalanche of rock that would set off seismic sensors and bring the entire ceiling down.

Robert sighed. Nothing like playing a game of Jenga for the ultimate stakes. "I'll start with the smaller rocks," he said. "if we can create a stable path—"

Multiple explosions shook the tunnel. Dust and pebbles showered down, and a rock blocking the way rolled forward. Robert and Kira exchanged knowing glances as another explosion from above rocked their world. The sound of energy weapons and shouts filtered down from above. Their alien friends had surprised the hell out of the soldiers here, but the battle had now been well and truly joined, with the Atlantean side bringing much heavier weapons and explosives to bear, which Ishar had expected and planned for.

Perfect timing by the Anunnaki above. The tunnel's seismic sensors were no doubt alarming, but there were alarms blaring throughout the Nexus Prime grounds and airspace, and a raging battle happening, so the tunnel alarms would be blamed on the Anunnaki attack and largely dismissed.

Their alien friends were creating an even bigger distraction than Robert had hoped for. What he hadn't counted on was the possibility of the *distraction* killing them instead of the Atlanteans.

"I'll begin now," said Robert, hoping his voice didn't sound frantic. He extended the Vesh'tar. Its crystal brightened with turquoise light as he closed his eyes and fought to ignore the fighting raging on the surface and the adrenaline now pumping into his bloodstream.

Keep your eyes open, Robert, the Vesh'tar's voice reverberated in his mind.

He complied and concentrated on the rocks in front of him. Visualizing their movement, he willed the smaller boulders to shift. The Vesh'tar crystal blazed brighter, and slowly, the first rock hovered. Robert guided it against the wall, then moved to the next. A second stone rose, and he steered it next to the first rock. Over and over, huge stones and boulders moved, although after many dozens, his mental strength began to visibly ebb.

As he cleared the middle, the rocks on either side remained balanced. With all his strength, he concentrated on maintaining the Vesh'tar's hold on these rocks. If he lost control, they would tumble into the cleared area and undo all his progress.

He continued being careful, but this was no longer about not making noise, it was about not creating an avalanche that would bring down the ceiling and crush them to death.

Robert, said his intelligent staff, *use my energy, don't add any of your own. That's what's depleting you.*

Robert nodded. A memory flashed into his mind. A memory of his father helping him build a treehouse when he was seven. His job was to hammer in long nails, and he was bending many of them. "Let the weight of the hammer do all the work, Bobby," his father had told him with a smile. "Relax. Grip it loosely. Gravity alone will drive the nail. You just need to guide the hammer."

Robert smiled despite himself. It was good to see his father and his Vesh'tar saw eye to eye.

Time came and went as if it drifted between dream and reality. Boulders weighing thousands of pounds rose, one after another. After a period of time that seemed both instant and endless, he finally cleared a path.

"Go!" he instructed his companions as he struggled to maintain his hold on dozens and dozens of heavy boulders desperate to let gravity return them to their former chaotic arrangement.

Kira, Matt, and Aethor darted through the opening. Robert strained to hold the passage open for just a while longer, taking a step forward to join his companions, when more explosions, far more *massive* explosions, returned from above, creating an earthquake in the tunnel. The Anunnaki commandos must be inflicting heavy losses, or the Atlanteans wouldn't have been forced to bring out such heavy artillery, wouldn't have risked unleashing such destructive powers in their own metaphorical house, risking extensive collateral damage.

Suddenly, the earth shook so terribly that he could barely stay on his feet, and the shaking boulders were ten times harder to control. The giant explosions made it almost impossible to maintain his concentration, just when he needed it most. He'd been juggling twelve eggs and someone had thrown in a *chainsaw*.

The world spun around him as he fought to hold on for just a few seconds more, but it was something beyond even his abilities. The sound of cascading stone filled his ears as the feared avalanche of boulders and stone blocked the opening once again and separated him from his friends.

CHAPTER 53

Councilor Kairos Daedalus
High Marshall of the Atlantean Military Forces
Location: Bedroom, secondary residence, Og City, Atlantis

It was well past midnight, and Kairos bolted up from his bed as the blaring of an alarm woke him from a sound sleep.

The seismic sensors had been triggered.

How could that be? Was it possible that Aethor had discovered the true location of the core processor, the quantum crystalline matrix? Impossible!

He needed to call Ixra Maren. She didn't know about the core processor, so he would tell her that one of his spies had just informed him that a Resistance team was trying to breach Nexus Prime by using the main maintenance tunnel. He'd have her personally supervise the scores of guards he would send to capture them.

He was just about to place the call when Ixra beat him to the punch.

He blinked rapidly, taken aback when he saw her face. She was more awake than he was and looking troubled. Why was she awake? The seismic sensors were set to only send an alarm to him.

Ixra looked just as surprised to see him awake. "Councilor Kairos," she began urgently. "Nexus Prime is under attack. As of about fifteen minutes ago. Anunnaki forces have infiltrated the area. The Sovereign Guard is encountering heavy resistance and sustaining substantial losses."

His eyes narrowed. "Is the battle entirely aboveground?"

She looked confused by the question. "As far as we know, yes."

"How many Anunnaki are involved?"

"Unclear. But likely two dozen or more. Spread out. Well-coordinated, well-trained, and exceedingly bold."

"Are heavy munitions and explosives involved? Does it sometimes feel like an earthquake on site?"

She shrank back, again confused by the question. "Yes, to the first. I haven't asked about the second. But I'd say that given what we're throwing at them, the earth has to be shaking extensively."

Kairos blew out a sigh of relief. No one was in the tunnel, after all. How could they be? Only he knew how important this particular tunnel was. The sensors had been set off by the battle aboveground.

"Do we know what the Anunnaki are after?" he asked.

"Unsure. We believe they're trying to breach the main Nexus Prime structure near where the quantum crystalline matrix vault is located. Which is why I decided to wake you."

"How did they even get on the grounds?" he demanded. "I ordered all ships vectoring toward Nexus Prime stopped. How did we miss a ship depositing over two dozen freakishly large aliens on the grounds?"

"We aren't sure. Maybe they traveled a long way on foot."

Kairos forced himself to remain calm. "Regardless of their lethality, they should have been easy pickings for the Sovereign Guard. This so-called elite force continues to disappoint. But no matter. The men are expendable, and the Anunnaki pose no danger to Nexus Prime, no matter how good they are. They won't get anywhere *near* the vault."

"I'm not worried about that either, Councilor. These terrorists will be put down shortly. Nexus Prime itself is impregnable, as you so rightly point out. From dozens of Anunnaki commandoes, or hundreds, it won't matter."

Kairos sighed. He wasn't worried about Nexus Prime in the slightest. He was worried about his son. "Any human terrorists sighted among them?" he asked, purposely not mentioning Aethor by name.

"None so far."

Kairos frowned deeply. He didn't believe in coincidences. He had set a trap to snare the rest of the Resistance, giving explicit orders that his son was to be taken alive at all costs. And the trap had caught these aliens instead. Although, at the moment, *caught* wasn't exactly the right word, as they were wreaking untold havoc. Regardless, he had no doubt that Aethor was involved. Anunnaki warriors had been at his son's side while he was at Thoth's residence in the forest, after all, and the timing was too perfect.

"Good," he replied finally. "Order our forces to capture a few Anunnaki for interrogation if possible. Kill the rest. Remind our forces that any humans found to be involved are to be captured only, unharmed. Make this last absolutely explicit."

"I thought this last order only applied to Aethor."

"I've changed my mind. If he isn't among the terrorists, we'll need others to interrogate. Get it done! Now! I'll wait."

She signed off and returned to the call less than a minute later. "Your orders have been . . . forcefully . . . delivered."

"Good," said Kairos. "On the bright side," he continued, "this attack will add considerable fuel to the fire I'm building. It actually could turn out to be perfect for our needs. We can use it to further push undecided Council members to support quick passage of the ISAPPA Bill."

"That is a silver lining," agreed Ixra.

"What's the current state of play with respect to the bill?"

"Councilor Zelchin remains resolute in her objections. She questions the breadth of power the bill grants and its implications for civil liberties. She claims Earth is a destination that should be open to all."

Deep down, Kairos fumed, but kept a stoic expression. "Zelchin has been a persistent obstacle to progress. It's our world. It doesn't belong to the Anunnaki, or the Arcturians, or the Hathors, or the Kachinas. Her idealism blinds her to the realities we face. The presence of extraterrestrials threatens our existence on the one hand and stunts our growth and lulls us into a false sense of security on the other."

"If you'd like," said Ixra, "we can employ more . . . direct persuasion when it comes to Councilor Zelchin."

"I admire your aggressive nature, Ixra, but intimidation or accidental death, if discovered, will end everything I'm trying to accomplish. I can't take that risk."

He shook his head in disgust. "No, I'll speak with Zelchin when I get back to my office. I'm sure I can change her mind. I'll insist the Anunnaki attack on Nexus Prime has the support of their home world, and is but the tip of a coming spear. I can amplify this incident, so it seems catastrophic. It doesn't take much imagination to understand that if Nexus Prime were destroyed, it would be a devastating blow to the entirety of Atlantean civilization, practically returning us to the Stone Age."

He paused. "Later, I'll add the fabricated evidence against the Anunnaki to the mix that we've been planning to unleash, anyway. Their attack has no chance of success, but it will end up playing right into our hands."

"Understood. What about the media? Should I activate them?"

"Yes. Excellent thought. Public opinion will apply huge additional pressure. Make sure the narrative highlights the Anunnaki threat and the necessity of decisive action."

"I thought you might say that," said Ixra. "A few minutes after the attack began, I ordered staff to prepare articles and broadcast scripts to that effect. Which we can send to the media with urgent tags."

"You continue to exceed expectations, Ixra."

With that, Kairos clicked off the call and steepled his fingers underneath his chin. The Interstellar Species Accountability and Planetary Protection Act, or ISAPPA, was key to his plans. It would give a more solid foundation to Atlantis's supremacy. The type of foundation that was only possible when external interferences and threats were eliminated. Soon, Atlantis would be a predator without prey.

He quickly contacted Soton Amenti, the captain of a nearby Helion-class diplomatic shuttle named *Umbra*, to come get him immediately, with orders to then make best speed to Nexus Prime. It was time for him to be involved there personally.

Kairos walked to a panel in the wall of his bedroom, the same wall he had installed in all of his residences. A weapons rack showed itself, and he grabbed a rifle, sliding his palm up the barrel. The weapon powered on, its laser charge vibrating. Tonight, he would set a precedent, one that he hoped would be felt by all Anunnaki across the solar system and beyond.

It was ironic. He'd gone to great lengths to fabricate evidence that painted the Anunnaki as the ultimate existential threat. And just before he released this information, they had gone and painted *themselves* that way.

Other than the situation with his son, things couldn't possibly be going any better.

CHAPTER 54

Advisor Elowin Balivae
Poros Territory, Poros City
Location: Southwest Atlantis

Elowin and Jalon clung to a metal barge and held their breath, staying perfectly still as a light from above now shined into their eyes, blinding them.

Desperate to drop into the depths of the water and out of sight, Elowin's gut stopped her since Jalon hadn't done so. She quickly realized why: the last thing the worker expected to see were two figures clinging to the hull, so stillness was their best option. Humans were hypersensitive to motion, but capable of easily overlooking something unexpected that remained perfectly still.

In a heartbeat that seemed like an hour to Elowin, the worker above them straightened, scratched his neck, and switched off his headlamp. Seconds later the hatch squeaked shut and he was gone.

Elowin blew out a long sigh of relief. That was lucky.

"Follow me," whispered Jalon as he began climbing handholds on the hull. When they reached the ship's deck, Jalon helped her over a railing and they made their way over to a stack of empty cargo crates near the bow, lashed in place there. They quickly wedged themselves between the containers, becoming almost perfectly hidden from view.

Hours went by. Clouds parted. The rain slowed to a drizzle before dying altogether. When the Moon emerged, its light painted itself across the river's surface. If they weren't in this predicament, Elowin would be admiring the sight.

She was acutely aware that every second she delayed getting the information she held to the Atlantean High Councilor, the chances increased that she'd be too late. As did the chances that Kairos would unleash the destructive potential of Nexus Prime on her beloved nation.

Elder Kona Makelo came to mind. Elowin's heart fell to her stomach at the image of his dead eyes staring back at her, charring a memory in the back recesses of her mind where it would no doubt stay for the rest of her life. He was a champion of peace and gave his life to save hers because he believed in everything she stood for. And, for that, she'd claw through a mountain with her bare hands to end this war.

Beside her, Jalon remained still. He continued to scan their surroundings. His slow breaths were the only sound beyond the lapping of water against the barge. As dawn approached, the barge began to ease into a dock in an area that was only sparsely populated.

As soon as it began its approach, the two fugitives stealthily slipped back into the water. They swam to shore under cover of the dim, pre-dawn light and emerged out of sight of the barge as it carefully eased its way into port. Jalon promptly picked the lock of the lone store nearby, which offered a little bit of everything, from tools to shipping supplies, to, most importantly, clothing. They quickly swapped out their wet attire for dry, being sure to give each other privacy while they changed. Elowin now wore a green linen tunic that fell to her knees, cinched at the waist with a leather belt, with soft, worn leggings underneath.

"What now?" she asked.

"As soon as we have transportation, we fly to the nearest town, which should have a more sophisticated computer network we can . . . borrow. We can use it to download the stolen files and then send them to Lemurian cryptologists."

Elowin nodded. "Great. But how do we get transportation?"

"There's a small lot just beyond the dock with a handful of hovercraft parked there. Did you see the lot on the way in?"

"I didn't. Good thing I'm with someone highly trained to be situationally observant. But go on."

"I'm guessing a few members of the barge's crew live within twenty to thirty miles of this dock, and these vehicles belong to them. So, wait here. Hide. I'm going to stalk the barge. If I'm right, once it's docked, these crewmembers will begin to straggle out one by one. When the first one to leave starts his vehicle, I'll put him in a chokehold. Knocking him out without killing him," he hastened to add. "Then I'll steal the vehicle and come get you here."

Elowin marveled at her companion once again. She hadn't noticed the parking lot, nor would she have formulated a plan so bold, one that required superhuman stealth, speed, and lethality. Left to her own devices, she would have no idea how to obtain transportation, while he made doing this seem like child's play.

Less than twenty minutes later a hovercraft landed at the back of the small store they had breached, with Jalon driving. Again, he was a force of nature, making things happen that others would find impossible, and doing so in a way that seemed effortless.

A few minutes later they were in the air and putting the dock, and the barge, behind them. Within moments, they pierced through the cloud layer. "I'm punching in the coordinates for Poseidia," announced Elowin.

"Poseidia?" repeated Jalon warily. "I thought we were going to a quaint city nearby."

"I had time to think while you were off doing your, you know, *stalking*. I think it's best if we head straight to Poseidia."

"Sure," he said. "We're being hunted, so why not go even *deeper* behind enemy lines? Not just deeper, but to the capital of Atlantis itself. That's bold."

She grinned. "Maybe you're rubbing off on me."

"Why there?"

"I've decided we don't have time to get these files decrypted and then read through them. As good as our cryptologists are, I've been assuming they can break through in a few days. But what if I'm wrong? What if they never do? And what if we don't even have a few *hours*?"

"How does going to Poseidia help?"

"Instead of waiting for an unknown period, we get an audience with the High Councilor *immediately*. One thing we know for sure is that *he* can decrypt the files. That way, we can all read them together. If Kairos and Deir Slan fooled us with the file names, and all we find are recipes for soup inside, that will be . . . less than ideal. But we have to go for it. We don't have any other choice."

Jalon sighed. "Okay. Let's do it. And I thought just going to Poseidia was bold. This plan makes bold look meek."

"Thank you for not trying to talk me out of it," she said. "I was worried you would think it was too risky."

He smiled. "It *is* too risky. Normally, getting you to safety would be all I cared about, Elowin. But in this case, millions of Lemurian and Atlantean lives are riding on us. And you're right, there is no other choice."

"Here we go," said Elowin, tapping on the dash's interface and dialing the private comm sequence for Melia Kapule'a, a member of the Lemurian Circle of 12. The holographic image of her friend materialized, and Melia jerked back in shock at the sight in front of her.

"Elowin?" she whispered in shock. "It can't be. We thought you were . . . *dead."*

"Almost. But I managed to survive, as you can see."

"Well, thank harmony for *that*," she said in delight. "It was reported that your shuttle malfunctioned and exploded at the Great Hall while you were visiting Kairos Daedalus. We didn't buy it for a second."

"Yeah. He tried to kill me. Long story. Elder Makelo is dead."

Melia lowered her eyes. "I'm sorry," she said softly. "But I've thought you were *both* dead for some time now. Despite the tragedy of Kona's death, I'm elated that you're still here."

She paused. "Atlantis has begun their attack, Elowin. And they're doing their best to paint us as the aggressor to their own people, to justify their actions."

"I know. And I'm still working to stop the war before it gets worse. I need you to get me in touch with the Atlantean High Councilor Nereus Pyralis immediately. Have you spoken with him?"

"Yes, he isn't happy with the situation, but he refuses peace talks. At least for now."

Jalon veered the craft starboard, banking away from a flock of birds, and headed into a group of clouds. A white haze surrounded them.

Keeping her focus on Melia, Elowin nodded. "I see. Elder, I have incriminating evidence against Kairos that I need to present to Pyralis. If the High Councilor is the man I think he is, it'll change the direction of the war, hopefully ending this conflict between us for good."

"That would be extraordinary. I'll see to it that you have a line into the High Councilor. And I'll inform the Circle of 12 immediately."

"Please don't," said Elowin. "The fewer people who know about this, the better. The stakes are too high. For now, let's keep this between us."

Melia's hologram distorted for an instant as Jalon lowered the sky-vessel, the sun's rays gleaming off the windshield. Below them, a stream of vehicles flew along designated sky highways. Up this far, they looked like small pebbles.

"Comm chatter's low," said Jalon beside her. "ETA to Poseidia is eleven minutes."

"I need to sign off," said Elowin. "Can you connect me directly to High Councilor Pyralis' office and switch the call over?"

"Consider it done," said Melia. "Good luck, Elowin. I've always believed that if anyone could pull us out of this nosedive, it would be you."

With that, her figure disappeared, to be replaced just over a minute later by a woman with coiffed hair, manicured nails, and a bored expression.

"High Councilor's office," she announced.

"I'm Advisor Elowin Balivae of the Lemurian Circle. Most of the world thinks I'm dead. I'm not. I'm en route to Poseidia, and I need to speak with the High Councilor right away."

"Is this some kind of joke? How did you get this number?"

"Not a joke. Repeat what I told you to his personal assistant. I guarantee that my call right now is the most important one you've ever gotten. If he finds out later you didn't at least inform his assistant, you'll lose your job. Depending on his temperament, probably more than that. Do what I ask, and the most you'll lose is a minute of your time. Worst case, he'll tell you to ignore me, and you can get on with your life."

The woman hesitated.

Jalon decided to add his improvisational skills to the mix. He leaned in so the dash cam would transmit his holographic image also. "Look, we have absolute proof that someone in the Atlantean high command is orchestrating the High Councilor's removal from power. A coup. It will be a bloodbath if it isn't stopped. You're in his offices, so you'll be among the first to be killed."

The woman seemed paralyzed, unable to make a decision.

"Look at me!" insisted Elowin. "I was all over the news. The shuttle explosion on the roof of the Great Hall. Remember? I was reported killed. Look at me!"

The woman's eyes suddenly widened to the size of saucers. "You're that Lemurian dignitary," she whispered, suddenly realizing that this was very real. "Stay put. I'll contact the High Councilor myself. I suspect he'll want to speak with you."

"Thank you!" said Elowin. "We'll hold for as long as we need to. But hurry! There's no time to waste."

The screen went blank as they were put on hold.

Only three minutes later a hologram of the High Councilor formed on the dash. Nereus Pyralis. Red hair and a full beard. His eyes blazed with a fierce intensity.

"Advisor Elowin Balivae," he began. "You look great for a dead woman."

"Yeah, I get that a lot."

"You say you have evidence of a coming coup? Why would you share that with me?"

"To save both our nations. This coup, and this war, have all been orchestrated by Councilor Kairos Daedalus."

"I've heard that before. From Lemurian propagandists."

"I have evidence. Unimpeachable evidence. Meet with us and we'll share it all. I guarantee you'll be convinced. Trust me, part of Kairos's plan is to have you removed from power so he can take control of the Atlantean Council."

He pressed his lips into a firm line. "Twenty minutes. My office. My people have triangulated your position from the call, which appears to be originating at a sight inside Lemuria, and then being redirected to you. It appears you're nearing our capital in a vehicle registered to an Atlantean . . . barge worker."

"Yeah, long story."

"Don't make it too long. You'll have twenty minutes. Not a moment more. I'm sending a squadron of Stormcallers to escort you."

He rested his elbows on his desk, silent for a few seconds. "If your plan is to get close enough to take me out, think again. My guards will make sure you never have a chance. Attempt to kill me, and I'll be just fine. But you'll end up dead yourselves."

"We aren't trying to *kill* you!" said Elowin, barely managing not to add *you idiot*. "We're trying to *save* you. And the lives of millions."

The High Councilor considered her carefully. "That remains to be seen, Advisor Balivae. That remains to be seen. But if you're lying, I guarantee you won't come back from the dead a second time."

CHAPTER 55

Robert quickly regained consciousness. He tried to stand, but his body thudded against the ground. Confusion clouded his mind as he did everything possible to make sense of his surroundings. Was he on an archeological dig? Most likely. Soot settled on a wall of rocks in front of him, blocking his path. To where? He couldn't remember. Why was he in this location in the first place?

He must have been on an excavation, and the roof had caved in.

He looked around. Other than the dust falling on the massive rocks surrounding him, everything was still. Where were his assistants if he was in the field? Was he exploring a find all by himself?

An explosion from above shook the ceiling, showering pebbles and small debris. Energy weapons discharged. Their whine pierced through the stone walls surrounding him. Muffled shouts and yelled orders filtered down. Robert's head swam, his thoughts a jumbled mess.

A panicked voice bellowed out his name. "Robert! Are you okay?" the voice screamed. "Robert? Please answer!"

Finally, something he recognized. The voice of Kira Shelton.

"I'm right here!" he shouted back, but he was still dazed, and the shout came out not much louder than his speaking voice. "How did I get here?"

Memory flooded back to him in fragments. The tunnel system. The Sovereign Guards battling the Anunnaki above. The Vesh'tar, still clutched in his hand, glued to his palm like a magnet.

Massive explosions from the surface shook the tunnel once more and he subconsciously activated his staff, which barely held the boulders in place in front of him.

The shaking abruptly stopped. He wiped blood now trickling from both of his nostrils away with his forearm. He felt weaker than ever.

A voice resonated in his mind as his Vesh'tar chose to speak into his consciousness once again.

You've depleted yourself, Robert. You were doing well, but these externally generated earthquakes were too much for you. You need a recharge. I can help. The technology that created me gives me the ability to channel energy from the air, from gravity, and from the planet itself. Place your hands on the earthen barrier in front of you and let this energy flow through you.

Robert crawled toward the rocks blocking his path and pressed his palms against the stone. At first, nothing happened. Soon a warmth began to spread from his fingers, up his arms, and throughout his body. The dizziness receded like an outgoing tide. It left clarity, alertness, and strength, and it all surged through his veins.

Robert stood, surprised at the sudden absence of vertigo.

He shouted once again to Kira. This time much louder.

No reply.

Panic filled him. He couldn't help but imagine her on the other side of the barrier, crushed or impaled. He cared for Matt and Aethor greatly, but he realized he had never cared for anyone the way he did for Kira. Just the thought of losing her was like a knee to his gut, taking his breath away and bringing on a quick burst of nausea.

He screamed out for her several more times but continued to be greeted by nothing but silence.

Robert's heart sank. She'd been alive and had sounded strong. And no guards could get to them where they were. He would have heard if the ceiling had collapsed. He would have sensed it in his gut.

He had to believe his friends were okay. Maybe when he hadn't responded to their calls, and having no way to reach him, they had no choice but to go on without him. The mission had to come first. It was all that mattered. Not just for this timeline's existence, but for his timeline's future, as well. The fate of *two* civilizations hung in the balance.

He screamed out his friends' names several more times. Still no response. He had to get out of here and find his comrades. He had to help Aethor get to the control room.

He raised the Vesh'tar, squeezing his eyes shut. He pictured a bright light blasting outward from the staff's crystal orb. Though his eyes remained closed, wind whirled around him, and a flash erupted beyond his eyelids. If he opened them, he was sure he'd go blind.

A rumble shook the ground. Robert maintained his focus. He had to breach the barrier, no matter what. Small stones pelted his face. Some left stinging cuts, while others bounced off, probably leaving bruises.

Once again, he dropped to his knees. He lowered his head, palm pressed against the ground to keep from collapsing onto his chest. Heavy breaths escaped his mouth as blood dripped from his nose. He fought against the fainting spell with every ounce of willpower.

The Vesh'tar spoke. *Open your eyes.*

Robert's eyelids were like lead weights as he forced them open. In front of him lay a pile of rubble where the rock barrier had stood. A trail had been cleared. With shaky arms, he pushed himself to his feet. Maybe he should have used this technique to blow a hole through the rocks in the first place.

That would have been foolish, he realized. He could have easily been hit by even bigger shrapnel that might have killed him or caused a collapse of the ceiling that would have killed him and possibly his friends. It had been right to do this carefully the first time. And also, right to throw caution to the wind after he had become separated from his friends.

You must find a way to open your mind to true understanding, said the Vesh'tar.

Robert wrinkled his brow. "I don't know what that means. Tell me how to do as you ask."

The knowledge resides within you. As I've said, with confidence, you can harness my strength without depleting your own. Ours is a partnership, and I can draw upon energies beyond you. Let me do that job. Your job is to provide the focus, the force of will. It's up to you to discover the how.

"I'll do my best," said Robert.

Best is but a mirror of your limits. Necessity knows no such bounds. You have to learn to do better than your best.

Robert was about to object to the absurdity of this statement when he finally realized what was going on. The Vesh'tar seemed to teach in riddles rather than with recipe-like clarity. Robert was well aware of the precedent for this type of instruction, so perhaps he should stop expecting more and get with the program.

Socrates, who was Plato's teacher, had developed a method of answering a question by posing *additional* questions. The Socratic Method sought to stimulate thinking and help students uncover profound truths of their own rather than being spoon-fed solutions.

Zen koans were similar. Riddles, paradoxes, and absurdities pushing a student to transcend dualistic thinking and experience direct insight into spiritual truths, often through *atma-vichara*, meaning meditation, or self-inquiry.

Several well-known koans flashed across Robert's mind. *What is the sound of one hand clapping? Before your parents were born, what was your original face? A monk asked Dongshan, "What is the Buddha?" Dongshan replied, "Three pounds of flax."*

Robert was well aware that these methods were designed to push a student to achieve deep introspection and transcendent thought, but this style had never been his cup of tea. Perhaps it was time for that to change.

Robert decided to table further discussion with his Vesh'tar and rushed through the rubble of what had once been a barrier, with his friends still nowhere in sight. Light hit him now from a great distance behind, and he could hear just the faint echo of voices.

Sovereign Guards! And from the sound of it, *lots* of them. Maybe as many as fifteen.

Kairos's seismic sensors had been triggered long before, but he must have chalked that up to the Anunnaki attack aboveground as they had hoped. Otherwise, the guards would have come to check long before. And while Kairos had sent a large number of them, they didn't seem to be operating with any urgency, so he must have sent them just in case, not expecting they would really find anyone.

Robert rushed ahead, but the maze of tunnels soon began. He cursed to himself. Aethor had the lone datapad with the layout of the tunnels, which he'd also committed to memory. That had been a huge mistake. They should have all carried datapads. If only *Tala* was here to take them back into the past so he could rectify this mistake.

He chose one route and soon became hopelessly lost. He had considered laying down a breadcrumb trail of strategically placed pebbles so he could retrace his steps back out, but he couldn't. A breadcrumb trail would lead the Atlantean soldiers straight to him.

He walked silently, carefully, straining to hear possible voices from friends or foes, and wondered if he hadn't been going in circles. After almost ten more minutes of further wandering, he took a right fork and heard the voices of several Sovereign Guards. At one time, all fifteen had been behind him, but they had split up, and God only knew where they might have ended up. Given that they must be consulting datapads with a detailed layout of the tunnels, most were likely way ahead of him.

The worst part was that Kairos had known for almost fifteen minutes now that the seismic sensor alarms hadn't been tripped accidentally. His soldiers would have reported that a passageway had been blasted through the boulder blockade, and he would know exactly what that meant.

Robert pulled back. His friends hadn't come this way, or they would be in captivity. Or worse. He turned, noticing a dark passageway stretching in the opposite direction. Without hesitation, he slipped into the shadows, hoping this way would lead him to his friends.

The tunnel thinned as Robert continued walking, the Vesh'tar's faint glow guiding the way. The sounds of battle above grew more distant with each step. Finally, the passageway widened, opening into a larger chamber.

The passage ahead split into two. He chose the right fork for no good reason. Voices echoed from around the corner. Robert's heart hammered as he pressed himself against the wall, wedging his body into the darkest recess of the corridor. Conduits jutted from the wall and dug into his back, but he dared not move. He held his breath and willed the sphere atop his Vesh'tar to turn off.

It complied.

Boots thudded on the ground. One after another. They drew closer. Two Sovereign Guards strode past his hiding spot.

"—can't believe those Anunnaki breached the Nexus Prime perimeter," one said.

"Did you hear that?" said the second guard, scanning the area as the sound of explosions and heavy munitions rumbled above.

The other soldier glanced at the ceiling. "Those alien bastards have put up a fight for the ages," he said, almost in admiration. "But I'm told that even heavier reinforcements will be here in less than five minutes. They're finally about to get massacred. Long overdue."

Robert backtracked down the corridor silently, taking the left fork this time. He soon came upon another passageway and followed it. Not a raw corridor this time, but a finished one with a large open door at the end. He pressed himself against the doorframe and peered around it into the room. Crystalline structures and complicated-looking machinery dominated the space. In the center stood what appeared to be a control module, its surface covered in symbols.

His heart leaped. There, next to the main control console, stood Kira and Matt. Beside them, Aethor was working on the console.

They were all alive! He wanted to shout out in joy but managed to hold his tongue.

Just as he was about to enter and hug Kira for all he was worth, Sovereign Guards arrived from the other side and rushed in with rifles extended, having finally found their quarry.

Robert's friends raised their arms. Kira's jaw was set in defiance, while Matt's eyes moved between the soldiers. Aethor stood expressionless.

Laser rifles whirred to life, their targeting systems painting red dots across Aethor's chest. The squad leader's helmet reconfigured, outer plates sliding away to show a face beneath.

Robert pressed himself even harder against the doorframe, out of sight but close enough to hear the conversation.

"Tell Councilor Daedalus we have his son," said the leader of the contingent triumphantly. "Tell him he'll be taken alive, as ordered."

He turned to Aethor. "I assume the Anunnaki forces above are with you, correct?"

"Anunnaki forces?" said Aethor, feigning confusion. "What are you talking about?"

"Look," said Matt, "you don't understand what's happening here. Your leader is a psychopath who only wants—"

A guard lunged forward and slammed the butt of his weapon into Matt's chest and continued pushing, stopping the young Hopi in mid-sentence and driving him to the ground. The guard stood over his victim as if daring him to rise, while Matt grimaced in pain from the blow, putting his arms over his face to protect it.

Rage exploded in Robert's chest. Without thinking, he rushed into the room, Vesh'tar raised, his focus on the guard who'd struck Matt. The man flew backward, crashing into his comrades. Only a few toppled from the impact, but for several seconds, confusion ran through the guards' ranks.

Robert envisioned himself leaping over his friends and his body responded at once, the Vesh'tar's technology somehow carrying him through the air. He landed in front of Kira, bringing the Vesh'tar down hard against another guard's chestplate. The impact sent the soldier flying, his body slamming into the wall with a crunch before the man slumped to the ground, unconscious.

The remaining guards raised their weapons. Robert's small victory turned to an instant hell as he realized his impulsive actions doomed them all. The air filled with energy weapons, bolts streaking through the air.

Time barely moved. Fear coated Kira's eyes as she ducked. Matt's pained groan reverberated from the floor. Aethor dove for cover.

Robert crouched and bashed the ground with the end of his Vesh'tar. A roar filled his ears as the floor shuddered beneath them. Hairline cracks spiderwebbed outward from the impact point, spreading faster than the guards could react. Rifle fire sizzled through the air above their heads as the ground gave way.

Matt grabbed for Kira's arm as they all plunged downward. Aethor tried to find purchase on something solid, but the entire section of flooring had given way at once and gravity wouldn't be denied.

CHAPTER 56

Robert's knees struck metal grating as they fell. His shoulder smashed into something hard, followed by his face meeting something cold, something solid. The impact knocked his breath away. Through ringing ears, Kira yelped and Matt grunted beside him.

Thick dust billowed around them like a sandstorm, and debris rained from above. Chunks of concrete. Twisted metal. It all fell. Soot pattering down like artifacts in a disturbed burial chamber. Coughs and groans resounded through the space, ally and enemy alike.

Robert held his breath, frozen. Looking around, everything was dark, like they'd fallen into a black cloud. A dusty fog swirled everywhere, the remains of the annihilation of the floor brought about by the Vesh'tar's powerful tech.

The Vesh'tar! he thought.

Where was it? Did he drop it when he fell? He didn't remember it slipping from his grasp.

Robert pushed himself up, waving at the hazy soot. He touched the ground, searching. The ancient maintenance tunnel floor beneath them groaned. His hand brushed against crumbling stone and corroded metal supports. Small chunks of the floor shifted and fell away into deeper darkness below them, dropping through holes and widened cracks. Even through the dust, he could make out spreading fractures in the stone. Whatever this level was built from, the years hadn't been kind.

Vesh'tar, where are you? Can you hear me? thought Robert.

No response.

"Don't fire!" a guard shouted somewhere in the fog. "Too much dust. You'll hit one of us or collapse this entire level."

Robert instinctively dropped low upon hearing this voice. It seemed to bounce off unseen walls, making its direction impossible to pinpoint.

"Status check," said another guard. "Sound off."

A hand brushed Robert's ankle. "Robert?" Kira whispered. "Is that you?"

"Here," he replied in hushed tones, relieved beyond measure to learn she was still okay.

"*Thank God,*" whispered Kira, her voice choking up.

"Matt?" Robert called out in low tones.

"Yeah." A pained grunt. "Banged up but mobile."

Robert crouched lower and found Matt's shoulder in the dark. "Keep your voice low."

"Got it."

"We hear you," said a trooper from an unknown location. "If you surrender, we promise to take you alive."

Aethor's hand gripped Robert's shirt and they exchanged silent glances.

"They can't see us," he whispered into Robert's ear. "And they've admitted my father gave them orders to take me alive. They won't risk hitting me."

Robert raised his voice just enough to reach the others nearby. "Everyone link up. Grab wrists, not hands. Strong grip. Form a chain. We'll follow Aethor's lead."

They found each other by touch in the murk. Kira gripped Robert's wrist. He reached forward, grasping Matt. Aethor completed their human chain.

"Guards at our six," said Aethor. "Follow my lead. Two taps means stop, one means go. Stay low and quiet."

"Fan out!" the guard ordered. "Get those lights up!"

"The dust, sir . . . our helmet filters are clogging."

Robert and his small crew crept forward through the confusion.

"There's a step here," warned Aethor. Robert's foot caught the edge. He tripped a little, but steadied himself. Matt slipped from his grasp but quickly reconnected.

They took a left around an unseen corner. Kira stifled a gasp as she collided with something solid.

They passed signals down their line. One tap, two taps, stop, go. Aethor pulled them left, then right, the guards' voices growing softer as they gained distance. They only had a short time until the dust settled to make their escape.

"I've found the ventilation shaft I was looking for," said Aethor in the lead, after they had made seven or eight turns.

Robert found himself in awe of Aethor's navigation skills. The way he had committed the layout down here to memory and was able to lead them precisely where he wanted to be, while basically blind, was incredible.

"Duck and follow me through," continued the Atlantean. "It's a tight fit." The sound of his clothing scraping against stone reverberated all around.

Robert clenched his teeth. No doubt those soldiers heard them. Seconds later, when it was Robert's turn, he searched the wall. There it was, a narrow shaft about a yard off the ground, and surrounded by more rock.

Once Robert and the rest of his group squeezed through, their bodies tight against stone, Aethor continued to lead them upward. The shaft was almost at a forty-five-degree incline but had indentations at even intervals that could be used as finger holds to make climbing possible. The soot thinned as they rose. After about twenty feet, the shaft narrowed considerably before ending at a maintenance grating. Aethor dislodged it with a heavy shove, and it fell to the floor of a room, leaving an opening barely large enough for them to squeeze through.

When Robert emerged and checked his surroundings, his jaw dropped to the floor. They were back in the control room. Incredible. While he had been hopelessly turned around and confused, Aethor had acted like a human compass. One corner of the large room, a gaping hole in the floor, thirty feet across, reminded him of his Vesh'tar and their perilous plunge into the room below.

Robert's muscles burned from the climb as he gazed at the gape in the floor, its edges torn, jagged. Below, the dust had settled, literally, revealing the destruction he'd caused. No troops looked up at them.

The azure crystal tube rising from the center of the room pulsed. Consoles that hadn't fallen through the floor still stood, their holographic displays alive and ready for use. Ancient Atlantean symbols scrolled across screens, monitoring power levels and containment fields.

Robert motioned to Matt and Kira. "Guard the tunnels," he whispered.

They took positions at opposite entrances while Aethor attacked the nearest interface.

Aethor pulled out a vial of crimson liquid from a pouch inside his pants and smeared a drop of his father's modified blood over a small biometric scanner next to where the processor core throbbed in all its evil glory.

A light on the scanner changed from red to green, causing Aethor to issue a sigh of relief.

The Councilor's son tore open an access panel. It showed a mess of circuitry and processors. What looked like fiber optics veined through banks of light-based computing cores. An electrical barrier crackled around a central chamber.

The frequency modulator he had brought with him whirred, powering on, projecting a spherical field intersecting with the electrical barrier.

"Tricky part is maintaining the exact frequency while extracting the matrix," said Aethor. "Too high, and the field collapses. Too low, the quantum containment fails, and the matrix destabilizes. We don't want either one to occur, or we could destroy the entire city."

Aethor manipulated the modulator's controls to create a stable gateway in the barrier. "Now comes the delicate part," he said, reaching through the opening. "The matrix is suspended in a quantum-locked state. Breaking that lock incorrectly could trigger a cascade failure. In other words, this is just another way I could kill us all."

Kira turned back toward the room. "I think guards are coming this way," she whispered. "Hurry!"

Aethor didn't respond, as he was completely focused on the task at hand. He now grasped the quantum crystalline matrix, the core processor, the heart and brain of the weapon. The palm-sized octahedron glowed with light. Swirling geometric shapes floated around it, spinning furiously, almost like ghosts that couldn't quite get themselves free.

With tiny adjustments, he rotated it forty-five degrees counterclockwise, then up another thirty. A click echoed through the chamber as the quantum lock disengaged. The control tube attached to the base of the ceiling dimmed to an amber color for a second before moving back to azure.

He had managed to get the quantum crystal beyond the lethal electrical field and out. It was disengaged!

Aethor pressed several holographic buttons and read the Atlantean symbols streaming down the screen. "We did it!" he whispered with a broad grin spanning his face. "The system is searching for a weapon, but can't find one. It's off. No more weapon."

"Let's get out of here," said Robert unnecessarily.

"Too late!" said Kira as heavy footsteps could now be heard sprinting toward the entrance she was guarding.

Aethor rushed over to Robert's side and extended the core processor. "Take it!" he insisted. "Get it to Lemuria. I'll buy us time."

Robert wanted to argue, but they only had seconds. He took the offered crystal and shoved it tight into the deep front pocket of his pants.

Aethor picked up a fist-sized rock from a pile of rubble and raced toward Kira, stuffing the rock under his shirt in a way that made the bulge look obvious as he moved. Just as he arrived, four guards stormed into the room, and Aethor stepped in front of Kira. His shoulders were squared, blocking her from view. "I'm Aethor, the High Marshall's son. You have orders to take me alive."

"I'm well aware of that," said the voice of a man who was just entering the room. "So are these soldiers."

Aethor shook his head in defeat and sighed. "Hello, Father," he said, greeting the newcomer.

"Hello, son. I should be furious. I *am* furious. But I also can't help but be proud. This was the boldest, most well-executed operation I have seen in my entire career. And you must have hacked my computer. It's the only way."

Aethor gestured toward Robert and the others. "These people are innocent. Take your fury out on me."

"Innocent?" Kairos's voice dripped with disdain. "Let me guess, they were just hanging out down here and knew nothing of your plans."

Kairos eyed the deconstructed console, his gaze traveling from the exposed circuitry to his son's defiant stance. "Incredible. You must have even figured out how I modified my DNA. And that information wasn't even in my computer. But as impressive as you've been, I'm afraid you failed in the end. I need you to hand over the crystal that you just removed."

"I don't have it," said Aethor.

"Really? Because you have a core-processor-sized object straining against your shirt. I'm afraid it's impossible to miss. Hand it over, or I'll have it taken by force. Your choice."

Aethor turned to look at his friends and then made a point of shifting his eyes to the floor beside Robert and Matt in an obvious manner, where the small ventilation shaft was still open. The maintenance grating they had pushed through from below was still lying on the floor beside the tight opening.

Be ready, mouthed Aethor, and then quickly turned back around to face his father.

Aethor stared into his father's eyes while he removed the rock from under his shirt, fully enclosing it with his hand so that its identity couldn't be detected. "Are you ready for it?" he said to his father, but Robert knew that these words weren't intended for Kairos. They were intended for him, and for Matt, as they stood at the ready by the ventilation shaft.

"You're making the right choice," said Kairos, holding out his hand to accept the crystal.

Aethor whipped what he'd been holding through the large hole in the floor so it landed out of sight in the rubble-and-dust-covered room below. Kairos and his guards all followed it with their eyes, but he had thrown it too quickly for them to see that it was simply a stone and not the precious processor. As they collectively turned toward the large gap in the floor in horror, Aethor rushed toward the guards like a charging bull, obviously knowing they had orders not to shoot.

Robert had been primed to act and did so the moment Aethor threw the stone, squeezing through the tight opening with Matt close behind. Rifle shots rang out, clanging on the grating near the opening, indicating that at least one of the guards had recovered from Aethor's distraction enough to see what they were attempting.

But the guard was too late. Robert and Matt had already begun bounding down the forty-five-degree slide, enclosed on all sides by unforgiving granite, and out of the line of fire.

They had escaped down the ventilation shaft unscathed. But surviving the plunge might be an even bigger challenge.

CHAPTER 57

Robert tumbled down what had become a lethal slide, his hands scraping against rough stone walls, skin burning as he slid down. The shaft, carved from rock, twisted and turned. His shoulders, the side of his head, and his knee slammed against the sides. Each impact forced an unwanted grunt.

After pinballing down the shaft for twenty feet, the slide ended about a yard above the ground, where Robert dropped like a sack of bricks and slammed onto the maintenance tunnel floor. Pain shot through his back and hip as Matt crashed down beside him. The young man was leaking blood from a raw shoulder.

Matt had literally dodged bullets, but the trip down the shaft had been less kind. While Robert had been bruised and battered on the way down, Matt's shoulder had been torn open by the shaft and looked to be in bad shape.

Robert fought off his own pain and managed to get to a standing position. No guards were in sight. He glanced up at the shaft as if soldiers would soon be crashing down upon them, but of course, that wasn't happening. He and Matt had barely made it through the tight opening, and they weren't wearing bulky battesuits. There was no way any of the guards could follow. And the array of tunnels was helping them, as the location where they had fallen through the control room floor earlier, where Aethor's rock had landed, was completely separate from where they were now. The two locations weren't that far apart, but only Aethor had been able to navigate from there to here.

Better yet, Aethor's ploy of throwing what his father thought was the processor core through the gash in the floor and into the dusty chaos below was brilliant. Kairos and his guards would be obsessed with retrieving it and ignore anything else. Hopefully, including their escape. And it would be a long time before they gave up, as they'd be searching for something that didn't exist.

Robert returned to his young ally. "Looks like you got the worst of it," he whispered. "I'm so sorry."

"Me too," replied Matt weakly with a tired smile. "But I'm alive. Do you still have the crystal?"

Robert checked his pocket, and it was still there, wedged tightly against the fabric of his pants. "Still have it. You're bleeding a fair amount. Can you move your arm?"

Matt winced, moving it slightly before leaning to the side, pain across his face. "Not much. Where is your Vesh'tar?" he asked as if noticing its absence for the first time.

Robert grimaced. "I wish I knew. Looks like we're on our own."

Matt's shirt was already torn. Robert quickly tore it further, procuring a large piece of fabric that he tied around the young man's wound, hoping to staunch the flow of blood as much as possible.

Robert forced his heart rate down and cleared his head. He had to find a way out of this. He took a quick inventory of the situation. Thoth was dead, and Kira and Aethor had been captured. The idea of either one of his friends being tortured, especially Kira, made his blood boil, but he couldn't do anyone any good if he allowed himself to be overcome by rage, pain, and regret.

He calmed himself down. He hadn't heard any sounds of a battle above ground now for some time, so the Anunnaki incursion had finally been put down, with Ishar and Mardak either captured or killed.

It was all up to him now. He had to get the core to Lemuria.

Tala was on call, having stayed out of the fight but ready to help with exfiltration. If he could just get them outside, they at least had a chance.

"We need to go," he said to his wounded ward. "Aethor bought us time, but our prospects are pretty grim."

"Really, Professor?" Matt managed to rasp out. "I thought you were supposed to lie to your troops about stuff like that."

Robert was encouraged. It was a great sign that Matt still seemed to have a sense of humor. He gently helped him to his feet. "Aethor bought us an escape window. The problem is, I have no idea where we are, or how to get out."

"I think I do," whispered Matt.

"What? How?"

"I know we were supposed to rest up before the big mission, but I couldn't sleep . . . or rest. So, I studied the tunnel system. Memorized it. You know, just in case."

"Matt, you're a genius."

"Thanks," said Matt. "I haven't earned that kind of praise in the past, but I intend to change that." He nodded to a passage on the right. "Through there."

Robert helped him stay upright as they moved toward their destination, but Matt waved him off. Adrenaline and determination allowed him to walk at a pace that Robert would have thought impossible while tolerating the pain. He needed to take Matt's mind off his injury as much as possible, at least when they were in straightaways and the lad didn't need to navigate.

"You know I spoke with your father at one of my digs a few years back," he began. "I probably should have told you earlier. Anyway, while your dad and I spoke of many things, he talked about *you* the most."

"I find that hard to believe," said Matt. Despite his skepticism, Robert could tell his plan was working, as Matt was now focused on something other than his injury.

"I get that. Still, it's true. I swear it. He mentioned he had a son that he was very proud of. And that you had left to find your own path. And that he missed you a lot."

"Doesn't sound like him."

"I wouldn't make this up, Matt. You should've seen the look in his eyes when he mentioned you. A bit of sadness, yes, but you were like this shining orb to him, a son—his son—who went on his own vision quest to find himself. I heard the pride in his tone and saw it in his expression. He told me he had named you Little Owl . . . and *why*."

"I've always hated that name," said Matt. "I always wished he had named me Strong Bear or Thunder Warrior. But being named after an owl? And worse yet, a *little* one. It's a horrible name."

Robert chuckled, doing his best to keep up their pace. "Totally understandable," he said as Matt gestured for them to take a left fork approaching. "To English speakers not raised in the Hopi tradition, the name probably isn't . . . ideal. However, you know as well as I do that in the Hopi tradition, names are like prophecies. Little Owl means wisdom beyond your years, a watcher in the darkness. Something like that."

"Okay, so . . . why *did* he choose this name?"

"He told me that owls see much that others miss. They can guide others through the night. Which, come to think of it, is exactly what you're doing at this very moment. Without you to guide us, we wouldn't stand a chance. Meaning Atlantis and Lemuria wouldn't stand a chance, either."

"That is an unlikely coincidence," said Matt.

"Or maybe everything's connected. To continue, he told me that when he first looked into your eyes the day you were born, he sensed a great wisdom housed within you. He had planned to name you Soaring Eagle, but he changed his mind at that moment, convinced that wisdom would be your greatest quality. And while I don't think you got the best start toward harnessing great wisdom, I think you're firmly on that path now. From what I know of you lately, I think your father got your name exactly right."

Matt perked up as they took the middle of three passages. "I've actually never heard the story of how he chose my name. Why wouldn't he tell me?"

"I wouldn't have either. Imagine the pressure you would have felt to live up to that name and his expectations. Your name tells the story of who you'll become, not just who you are."

"Thank you for telling me this," said Matt, and while Robert had initially felt guilty for not having shared it earlier, he suddenly realized that this had been the perfect time.

They walked in silence for almost a full minute. According to Matt, they were approaching the main tunnel, the same one they had entered through, which would provide their passage back to the surface.

The guards in the control room were surely preoccupied with searching for the crystal. Kairos had likely shined a light down the ventilation shaft and might have concluded that no one could have survived such a plunge or could figure their way out of the spider web of tunnels if they did. If a trespasser didn't know where he was going, it would be easy for him to starve to death before finding the exit.

At this juncture, Kairos most likely only cared about two things: his son and the core processor, the quantum crystalline matrix, now supposedly buried somewhere in the debris below the control room.

After two more minutes, they entered the main tunnel, and the exit loomed ahead. Finally, they reached the end and climbed to the surface, with Robert using all his might to help push his weakened friend up the ladder. The hatch had slid open automatically as it sensed their presence and they stumbled gratefully into the dark outside world.

They had done it. Robert was ecstatic to get this far, but they had a long way to go.

Wind gusted in their faces as they quickly made their way across the street to what Robert had thought looked like a large corporate plaza back home, with lush gardens and plenty of tranquil open spaces.

A roar broke through the howling wind. Above, a ship was descending fast, floodlights blazing down and blinding them as they looked up in panic. They were sitting ducks.

A ramp must have been extending while it landed, because the moment it touched down, a single pair of boots raced down. The floodlight made it impossible to see who it was, but Robert could make out a rifle pointed forward. The weapon's power cell hummed.

He quickly raised his hands, palms up, in surrender. Praying that the people of this time would recognize the gesture.

Robert got his answer seconds later. It wasn't the one he hoped for. A laser flash streaked out from the rifle, and in that instant, he knew that he had taken his last breath.

CHAPTER 58

Advisor Elowin Balivae
Atlantis Capital, Poseidia
Location: Northwest Atlantis

The sky-craft descended through Poseidia's early morning air as Jalon manipulated the controls. Elowin had visited Poseidia before, but never at dawn when the buildings transformed into prisms of amber and gold.

The Divine, or what the Lemurians called the Great Spirit, had granted her this chance. She was sure of it. It was one last opportunity to prevent a war that would devastate her nation.

Above them, a squadron of Stormcallers maintained their holding pattern. The aircraft's surfaces shifted colors as they banked, their Voltex Cannons visible but powered down. A show of force acting as an honor guard.

As they made their descent, the High Council's Sovereign Dome rose before them. Gardens and fountains surrounded the building.

Their sky-craft settled onto a circular landing pad. Similar platforms dotted the manicured grounds. Security towers stood all around, a frenzy of activity inside each one.

Elowin and Jalon opened the vehicle's doors just as a guard's voice penetrated the air. "Leave all weapons inside. Once you've disarmed, step out of the vehicle."

Jalon did as asked before they both exited the craft. In step beside each other, they headed toward the High Councilor, heads up, eyes straight ahead.

Nereus Pyralis waited at the pad's edge. Sovereign Guards flanked him, all clad in battlesuits. Two guards stood at diagonal angles to the High Councilor, close enough to react to any threat, their laser rifles at the ready.

Nereus stood at attention in his formal Atlantean robes; deep blue fabric trimmed with silver threading. Despite his stern expression, warmth lingered in his eyes. The same kind eyes appearing in holo images of him playing with his children by the capital fountains. Elowin had always believed it was an act, but in person, the truth in someone's pupils rarely evaded her.

And it was rare for a politician to be known as a family man first and a leader second, but Nereus managed both. Unlike Kairos. Even now, as he watched Elowin and Jalon walk his way, there was a protective nature about him.

"Advisor," said Nereus. "Welcome to Poseidia."

"Thank you, High Councilor." She dipped her head as she approached, stopping about a yard from him. "Thank you for making the time."

Nereus looked at the man beside Elowin. "Who's this?"

"The last of my Protectorate. I owe him my life. Without him, Kairos's attempt to murder me would have succeeded."

Nereus's eyes squinted at this casual accusation of a murder attempt by the Atlantean Councilor and High Marshall, but he didn't directly respond. He led them across the Capital building's grounds and to the dome's entrance. Massive doors slid open. Inside, an atrium stretched high. Light filtered through the crystal panels. Water features flanked the main corridor as they continued their strides.

Jalon stayed close to Elowin's side as they made their way deeper into the structure. Corridors branched off here and there, each monitored by more guards. Holographic displays lined the walls. They showed real-time data from across Atlantis. She turned away from an image of an explosive battle taking place between Lemurian and Atlantean forces in Nasavi.

They rounded a corner into a vast hall. At the very heart of the towering room stood a statue of Poseidon, rising from churning waters. His marble, muscular body stood two stories high, trident raised as if commanding the seas.

Nereus led them to a set of doors at the far end, each one touching the tall ceiling. They had to be sixty feet in height, if not more, inlaid with red wood and gold patterns. The guards opened the entrance and took positions outside as Nereus ushered Elowin and Jalon into his domain.

Nereus settled behind a crystalline desk, fingers laced in his lap. "Let's get right to it. You said you have evidence of a coup."

"Yes. First, let me provide the background. You and I both know Kairos's ambitions extend far beyond his current position. The man who ordered my death isn't satisfied with mere territorial control. He wants your position, and he's vying for it through a war he's created between Lemuria and Atlantis."

"Allegations you've already made. You're here to show me the proof."

"Then let me say something new. Because of his actions, the supply of Opalith crystals from my nation will trickle to a crawl, at best. Nexus Prime supplies the energy, but you need the crystals to deliver it. This catastrophic scarcity of crystals will be all Kairos's doing, but who do you think the people will blame for it? Especially with him behind the scenes showing the way. You know better than anyone how clever and ruthless he can be. Enough to make sure all the blame lands right in your vaunted lap."

The High Councilor frowned but didn't respond. "Go on."

"When your people are facing rolling blackouts and failing infrastructure, whose head do you think they'll demand? Not Kairos's, who's been methodically positioning his pieces. They'll blame *you*. And I can show you exactly how he's orchestrating this. But I'll need to examine some very specific information to connect these dots."

"Politics is a game of calculated risks, Advisor. Kairos plays it well, no doubt. But I play it *better*. I'm not where I am by accident."

"Nor is he. Would you bet your position that he'll never outmaneuver you a single time? Would you bet your life? He's already convinced three Councilors that your leadership is wavering. The war with Lemuria? A stage-managed crisis to demonstrate your inability to maintain peace."

Nereus studied her. "You make a compelling case . . . if true. The thing is, I was promised evidence, not words. This is the last time I'll remind you."

"The evidence I've gathered is extensive, High Councilor. Digital trails of funds diverted to influence Council votes. Encrypted communications revealing Kairos's true plans for Nexus Prime. Most damning? Secured records of his private meetings planning your removal."

"Show me."

To Elowin's credit, she didn't wince or swallow hard. Instead, she forged ahead as if what she would say next was all quite normal. Even expected. "I have the evidence, High Councilor. I need you to access it with your holocomp."

Nereus shook his head in disbelief. "Should I also give you the launch codes to my Skyblade squadrons? There is no world in which I give you access to my systems."

"I need to send you downloaded data from my personal archive. The data is protected by the latest Atlantean encryption protocols. I assume your holocomp handles such encrypted files as a matter of course and decrypts them for you automatically."

"That's convenient," he said. "You have evidence of a coup, but I need to let you connect my networks to yours, and open mystery files you claim are evidence. What if you've perfected an untraceable virus? For all I know, if I connect to your network and open these files, I'll unleash a plague that will provide Lemuria secret access to my systems. Or crash them entirely."

He paused for several long seconds in thought. "Your time is up. I'll see to it that the guards escort you to your vehicle."

Elowin actually smiled. "Your choice, High Councilor. You said that politics is a game of calculated risks. Well, time to calculate now. You know in your gut that what I've said about Kairos rings true."

She began walking toward the exit, motioning for Jalon to follow her. "Soon, Kairos will pull the rug out from under you. Your own people will demand your head on a platter. And Kairos will have you arrested. When your execution is looming and this has all come to pass, I want you to remember that I came here and warned you. And that you decided that a phantom risk . . . a one-in-a-million chance that we've come up with a virus that can outdo your security . . . trumped what you know in your heart to be true. Instead of facing this uncomfortable truth, you stuck your head in the sand and shooed me away."

Elowin issued a sad sigh. "And when you do remember my warning, you'll have to live with your decision to ignore it for the rest of your life." She raised her eyebrows for effect. "But look on the bright side. By then, the rest of your life will be measured in *minutes*."

CHAPTER 59

Robert stood facing a rifle at the bottom of a ramp as plasma bolts issued from the weapon. Incredibly, the shots *missed*. Robert ducked, yanking Matt down with him.

Matt yelped in pain as they hit the ground. From the ship's ramp, a shadowy figure fired again, and this time the shot went wide left. Armor clattered behind them. Keeping his eyes on the shooter, Robert dove further aside as several more rapid blasts whizzed past.

Turning around, Robert's eyes widened. Five Sovereign Guards lay sprawled on the ground behind them. One twitched. Smoke rose from their battlesuits, the weapon's plasma most likely burning through their chests and hearts, killing them instantly.

"Robert and Matt! Hurry!" yelled the figure on the ramp. "Get in here! Now!"

Ishar?

From this angle and with the light in his eyes, Robert hadn't even noticed his alien height. But it was *him*. It wasn't a man on the ramp, but an Anunnaki warrior. And his shots hadn't missed them. His shots had *saved* them. Saved them from soldiers who had followed them from the tunnel and finally caught up, the dust and dirt on their battlesuits showing conclusive evidence of their recent passage through the tunnel system.

Robert rushed up the ramp, practically carrying Matt, and into what he now recognized as *Tala*'s cargo hold. Flicking a glance over his shoulder, more soldiers rushed toward the starship, closing the distance, but they were too late.

Tala's engines growled as she lifted off the ground, laser fire hitting her hull from the Atlantean troops still emerging from the tunnel. The ramp closed as Ishar pulled both Robert and Matt farther into the cargo bay.

"Kira and Aethor are still alive," said Robert. "We have to go back for them."

"I'm relieved they're alive. But we both know now isn't the time to try to retrieve them."

Robert wanted to scream in frustration and pain. Kira was the most extraordinary woman he had ever known, and the thought of losing her forever was *unbearable*. He'd fight an entire army with his bare hands if he thought it would do any good. But he knew Ishar was right. They would get themselves killed with no hope of saving her. Of saving *them*.

Robert vowed not to rest until he found a way to rescue his friends, but too much was at stake for him to go back now, and he'd be useless to her if he died with no hope of success.

"Did you get the processor?" asked Ishar.

"Yes. You and your warriors couldn't have performed any better. Thanks. I have the crystal with me now."

"Outstanding. Then you know we need to get it to Lemuria at best possible speed." Ishar turned toward the bridge. "*Tala*, take us to Lemuria, Loma'i Shores, Sholani City."

"Affirmative," she replied.

"*Tala*?" said Robert in dismay. "Since when are you taking orders from Ishar?"

"Since it became clear that your life was in jeopardy, and he was your only chance."

"Good answer," said Robert.

Matt went limp and collapsed to the floor. Robert cursed himself. There was nothing he could do at the moment for Kira and Aethor, so Matt should have been his highest priority. He hadn't attended to the young man immediately because Matt had been so strong, so courageous, Robert had almost forgotten that he was hanging on by a thread.

Blood oozed down Matt's arm. Without a word, Ishar scooped him up and hurried down the passageway into the living space. Robert followed, his breath coming in ragged gasps. They entered one of the crew quarters.

Tala materialized before them. "Place him on the bed," she told Ishar. "I'll attempt to heal him."

"Thank you," said Robert softly, clearing his head. For now, he had to keep attending to the tasks at hand, rather than agonizing about Kira and her possible fate.

He turned to Ishar. "Mardak?" he said, already knowing the answer.

"He didn't make it. The fight he showed has never been matched by any Anunnaki in history, as far as I'm concerned. All the warriors under me died. The last five gave their lives to ensure I escaped, knowing that you and *Tala* trusted me and that I might be instrumental in helping you complete the mission."

As the alien spoke, *Tala* worked on Matt, moving her hands about as the bed slowly flashed different healing lights.

Tala looked up at Robert. "Matt's condition is improving, but the tear and puncture to his shoulder has caused significant tissue damage and partial nerve severance. I've initiated accelerated cellular regeneration, but he'll be incapacitated for a while."

"Thank you," said Robert.

"While *Tala's* working," said Ishar. "Let me tell you about another big problem we have. Kairos or his people have removed Aethor's backdoor computer access."

Robert wasn't surprised. He had been in the control room when Kairos had realized his son must have hacked his computer. Despite the man's frenzy to retrieve the crystal, he must have realized he couldn't leave his Achilles' heel vulnerable for another second and had radioed orders to his experts to find and remove the virus.

"That's unfortunate," said Robert. "But the backdoor did serve its purpose."

"Maybe so, but because of this little wrinkle, *Tala* is disabled, barely limping along."

"She seems perfectly fine to me. Explain."

"The ship *Tala* was masquerading as was only authorized to be in Nexus Prime airspace because Aethor planted false information."

"Crap!" said Robert, instantly catching on. "So, when they discovered Aethor's backdoor computer access, they also discovered this implanted information, and *Tala* became a high-priority target."

"Exactly. As Aethor mentioned, Nexus Prime has anti-starship weapons. They fired on Tala, targeting her main drive with a precision strike—the first step in killing a starship. With her drive intact, she's too fast to hit, so you clip her wings first. The weapon focused all its power on a coin-sized spot, piercing through even at full shields. After that, she could still dodge and her shields protected her from weaker strikes. Which allowed her to survive the second stage of the attack for just long enough."

"Long enough for what?"

"For me and three of my warriors to disable the anti-starship weapon before it adjusted to her tactics and finished her off."

"Well done!" he said in awe. "What's her status now?"

"She's crippled. Not just the drive, but a number of connected and related systems. She's only as fast as a standard shuttle now. We're just lucky that in all the chaos, they didn't send fighters after her."

This turned out to be the worst-timed proclamation Ishar had ever uttered as *Tala's* crystalline figure suddenly disappeared from the room, and her voice issued over the ship's speaker system. "I've just picked up multiple Atlantean Skyblades and a shuttle in pursuit! I need you both to get to the bridge immediately!"

Ishar cursed as he and Robert rushed off to the bridge.

"I'm showing incoming missiles," said *Tala* over the speaker. "Brace yourselves for impact."

CHAPTER 60

Councilor Kairos Daedalus
High Marshall of the Atlantean Military Forces
Helion-class Diplomatic Vessel
Shuttle Designation—Umbra
Over the Atlantic Ocean

Kairos sat facing the passenger compartment of his shuttle, his back to the cockpit. Two Sovereign Guards stood at attention, laser rifles trained on the prisoners despite the restraints holding them in place.

Aethor glared at Kairos from the rear bench. Beside him, Kira pulled against her bonds. The adhesive strips across her mouth muffled her curses.

Kairos studied his son. "I have to admit, Aethor," he said finally, "you might be as good at deception and battlefield strategy as I am. And you're trained as a doctor, not a strategist. Truly remarkable. Throwing a fake crystal into a veritable black hole to create a diversion so your comrades could escape with the real one? Absolutely brilliant. Inspired. And you had only seconds to come up with it. Not only that, but your plan had the added bonus of buying your comrades time while we tore apart the room looking for something that wasn't there."

He shook his head. "And the way you hacked my private computer systems," he added. "I wouldn't have thought it possible. *Obviously* not, or I never would have left you alone in my offices. My team of experts found your virus and removed your access, by the way. Still, they were astonished that you were able to breach my security. Seems like you're impressing a lot of people."

Kairos paused in thought. "I guess there is one silver lining that we're on opposite sides of the playing field right now. Your opposition to me has brought out true greatness in *you*."

"Ironic that you haven't praised me in years, and the first time you do, it's only because I got the better of you."

Kairos smiled. "That's because no man ever has before. In many ways, you're the first. But not for long."

"You know I won't help you get the core processor back."

"I know. Fortunately, I have that covered."

Kairos saw the panic-stricken expression on his son's face and shook his head. "No, your comrades haven't been caught or killed. Not yet. But I have learned how you managed to get into restricted airspace. We've identified the vessel you used. It turns out it's the same one that picked up your two friends and brought them back out again."

Aethor snorted. "Is that supposed to impress me?" he said in contempt. "She's a *starship*. Speed wise, you'll never catch her. Plus, my friends will change her energy signature, and you won't have any idea where they went."

Kairos shook his head. "Guess again. Your ship was hobbled by our anti-starship weapon. She can still fly, and still maneuver, but she's no match for the Skyblade fighters I sent after her."

Aethor looked sick to his stomach at this revelation, but he recovered quickly. "Destroy that ship and you risk destroying your precious crystal."

"I'm well aware, my son. Which is why my orders are to disable the ship only. The question is, what do I do with your traitorous friends once I've downed the ship?" Kairos squinted his eyes like a reptile ready to pounce on an unsuspecting insect. "Cooperate, and perhaps I'll let them live out the day."

CHAPTER 61

"Direct hit to our aft shields," reported *Tala* as Robert and Ishar sprinted toward the bridge. "Shields now down to 78% capacity."

Robert finally made it to his destination. The main holoscreen showed multiple bogies closing in on their position.

"Take the captain's seat," said Ishar, moving to a nearby console. "I'll man the secondary weapons station."

Robert hesitated for a split second before sliding into the chair. The seat adjusted to his form, and holographic controls sprang to life around him. On the main holo, it showed the fighters plus a shuttle, along with streams of data scrolling above each one.

"*Tala*, can you identify the shuttle?" he asked.

"It's a Hermes-class diplomatic shuttle," said *Tala*. "The probability is high that Kairos is on board."

"Then we have to spare it at all costs. Because if he's on board, it's likely Kira and Aethor are, also."

"In war, sacrifices have to be made," said Ishar. "If we kill Kairos, we can end this."

"We've already all but ended it," said Robert. "Provided he doesn't get the crystal back."

"His shuttle is beyond my current, more limited, weapons range, anyway," reported *Tala*, cutting off further argument.

The tactical overlay showed their position relative to the pursuers. The two Skyblades kept closing distance. Numbers scrolled past; speed, heading, and weapons status.

Tala banked hard as a Skyblade launched a second projectile. On the main screen, the name PrismTide flashed. Robert assumed it was the missile type heading for them now.

"Activating my point defense system," the ship announced.

On the large display, laser fire erupted from a turret that had lowered from *Tala's* belly. The projectile heading toward them twisted, and white smoke billowed out from its stern. It snaked, avoiding a few laser bolts until a direct hit turned the missile into a bright flash. Sparks flew outward.

A third and fourth missile streaked toward them as the Skyblades edged closer. The starship veered left, then ascended sharply, taking Robert's breath away.

The tactical display shifted from the targeting icons to an external feed. The defense grid colored crimson lines across the sky, the cloud they just flew through making everything hazy for a moment.

A laser shot out and cut through one of the missiles at a thousand yards out. The projectile flared before it dropped out of the sky. A second missile burst into a hundred fragments at 812 yards. A third erupted into a yellow and orange ball of fire at 643 yards. A fourth had gotten through and was too close for comfort—400 yards and closing fast. 350. 225 . . .

A fifth and sixth missile followed behind, with the last three all making it through *Tala*'s defenses and finding their marks.

The ship shuddered violently from the multiple impacts, rattling as fiercely as liquid in a cocktail shaker. Robert felt his insides scramble and wondered why he wasn't dead.

"Ship's shields at just over seven percent and falling," announced *Tala*. "We can't survive another direct hit."

Just as this message was delivered, one additional missile made its way through *Tala's* defenses, and Robert closed his eyes, preparing for certain death for the second time in under an hour.

But when the missile was still fifty yards out, it detonated, washing out the video feed. When the image stabilized, the debris field spread like shrapnel. The impacts transformed from dings to metallic thunder as fragments battered the hull.

"Proximity detonation," said *Tala*. "I didn't hit the missile; it exploded on its own. Meaning Kairos knows our shields are now ineffective. He wants me disabled, not destroyed. Hull integrity dropping. I have a—"

Ishar's console exploded in a fountain of burning flecks. The blast caught the Anunnaki square in the chest, hurling his massive frame across the bridge. He slammed into the bulkhead with a *thud*. Blood streamed from a gash above his eye.

A whining sound came from Robert's station. He unstrapped and jumped back as fiery bits showered from his displays, dying down a moment later. On the bridge, all but the main holo blinked off.

Ishar pushed himself up, crimson coating half his face. He lunged for the smoking console. "*Tala*! Status!"

"Point defense systems critical. Main weapons grid offline. Secondary systems failing. Only my manual turret weapons are operational. Belly mount, section B-2."

"I'm on it," said Ishar. "Can you guide me to its location?"

"It will have to be Robert," said the ship. "Too tight a fit for an Anunnaki."

Robert cursed to himself. Ishar was experienced, and he wasn't, but unless Ishar was prepared to let the ship cut him in half, the tall alien wasn't an option.

"Lead me there, *Tala*," said Robert hastily.

"Take the emergency shaft," said the ship as she banked hard, forcing Robert to grab onto the railing on the corridor wall as he exited the bridge. Ishar rushed after him, likely to make sure he reached his destination in one piece. "One level down, port side," added *Tala*. "I'll continue taking evasive action and trying to repair systems. Hurry!"

Robert and his alien ally rushed to where *Tala* had indicated. When they entered the proper sections, she materialized, waving a crystalline hand over a hull plate, which promptly slid aside, revealing a circular hatch set into the floor beneath.

Ishar yanked the hatch open. "Down! Now!"

Robert scrambled down narrow stairs as the shaft opened into a transparent bubble protruding from *Tala*'s belly. Below, the ocean stretched far and wide. All around, white clouds floated against the blue sky.

"Interface activating," said *Tala* as Robert dropped into the gunner's seat. A holographic display phased into life around him. A joystick protruded from a panel in front of him. He tested it and was able to move the turret around with smooth precision. After just a few experimental maneuvers and shots, the weapons software seemed to adapt to his needs, adjusting to his subconscious preferences. He was now able to control the weapon almost instinctively, as if the system had synced with his neural pathways, turning the joystick into an extension of his thoughts.

"Tracking solutions will be displayed in red," said the ship. "Lead your targets."

After only a brief pause, *Tala* added, "We have additional incoming!"

The sky lit up with fresh missile trails. Above him, Ishar's blood-streaked face appeared. "Time to show me what you're made of," he said, slamming the hatch shut.

Two additional missiles entered his sights. Robert began to track the first as it hurtled toward them, now about a mile out. The projectiles sent white, cloudy lines across the sky. Robert squeezed the trigger. His shot went wide, puncturing through a cloud before vanishing from view. The turret's laser carved empty air as *Tala* banked hard right.

Robert fired again and missed. He wasn't leading them enough.

The missiles split, coming in from different angles. One at his nine o'clock, the other at two. *Tala* dove, the ocean rushing up fast through the bubble canopy. His next shot went high and blasted toward the upper atmosphere as they pulled out of the dive. The missiles were now within a thousand yards and closing on the hobbled starship.

Robert let loose another shot. This time the laser connected. It turned the incoming ordnance into a ball of orange and yellow before what remained of it fell toward the sea.

He had no time to celebrate. The second missile corkscrewed through his field of fire, closing fast.

Tala rolled right, then left, trying to throw off the missile's guidance system. Robert's shot sailed wide again, and the missile kept coming. On the display, it grew larger as it closed in.

"Estimate it will self-destruct in five seconds," said *Tala*, "hitting us with shrapnel again."

Robert took a breath, reminding himself to lead the target, anticipate the movement. The missile juked right, but he managed to catch it just as it changed course.

The explosion rocked the ship. Through the canopy, Robert watched the debris rain down toward the water.

"We're almost across the Atlantic," announced *Tala*. "Navigation systems optimal. "Nasavi ahead. Atlantean Outpost Anvil detected. Adjusting course for Tokpela Gate, the nearby Lemuria Outpost. Warning, battle between both outposts is underway. ETA ten minutes to Tokpela. I've notified Tokpela Command of our approach. Their ground batteries are targeting the Skyblades now."

The Lemurians opened up with their plasma cannons. Energy bursts zipped past the starship as *Tala* rolled and dove. Robert's weapons display flashed briefly. It showed *Tala*'s armaments: eight retractable plasma cannons, each able to deliver fifty terawatts of magnetically contained destruction.

A Skyblade swooped closer. Robert pressed the trigger, engaging one of the wing-mounted cannons. To his surprise, the plasma bolts caught the Skyblade's wing. A secondary explosion went off, black smoke puffing from what looked like an engine beside the wing. Electricity—like lightning—zapped all around the ship before it erupted into flames.

Robert blinked as sweat stung his eyes. He wiped his sleeve across his forehead. His heart pounded as he tracked the next target. The remaining fighter flew closer.

"Atlantean Stormcallers incoming from Outpost Anvil," said *Tala*. "Multiple signatures. They're moving to cut off our approach to Tokpela Gate."

The ship banked hard and descended toward the Lemurian outpost. Warning indicators flashed across his display as dozens of missiles now headed their way.

Robert downed as many projectiles as he could, but there were too many, each one barreling toward them at incredible speeds. In seconds, another made it through and self-destructed near the ship, while the others then instantly adjusted course to miss, being sure not to kill the wounded prey.

The massive impact of additional missile shrapnel rocked them. Klaxons blared through the turret bubble.

"Direct hit to primary systems," said *Tala*. "I'm losing stability control. Robert, get out of there now!"

The hatch above him flew open. Ishar's hand reached down, pulling Robert from the gunner's seat. The Anunnaki threw him through the opening as the ship shuddered. The hull section moved back over the sealed hatch with a grinding sound as Robert slid across the cabin floor.

"Bridge! Now!" bellowed Ishar.

They stumbled through the corridor as the ship bucked and twirled.

"Matt is secure, restrained to his bed," said *Tala*. "Get yourselves secure immediately!"

They burst onto the bridge, heading for their stations as the ship's nose dipped. Through the main viewport, sandy beaches rose to greet them like a wall.

Robert could tell that *Tala* was fighting for control. They skimmed over the shoreline and veered around one of Outpost Anvil's high walls. A guard in a tower watched as they continued to descend. Finally, *Tala* leveled out, and they found themselves halfway between both outposts.

"Brace for impact!" she said.

The ship slammed into the sand, which was now half-covered in foliage and reeds. Metal screamed as they skidded sideways. Robert's head snapped forward against the restraints. Charred trees and busted vehicles whipped past in a blur.

A concrete barrier stood ahead. It came out of nowhere and *Tala* tried to pull up. They were moving too fast. The ship's wing caught the wall. The impact spun them, tearing away chunks of hull plating.

They finally ground to a halt, listing heavily to one side. Sparks rained from damaged panels. Smoke drifted from the deck plates. There had to be a fire somewhere beneath them. Outside, the whine of approaching aircraft grew louder.

Ishar unstrapped himself. "We need to move. Now!"

Robert fumbled with his restraints. On the main holo, figures in combat armor advanced through the smog of battle. He couldn't determine their identities.

The bridge door wouldn't open. Jammed from the crash. Ishar braced himself against the frame, his fingers pulling it halfway open. The smoke was getting thicker.

"Robert." said the ship, "I'm starting internal repairs. We have soldiers incoming. From both sides."

She was about to continue, but the bridge abruptly fell dark, and her voice cut out.

CHAPTER 62

Smoke poured through the bridge's ceiling as Ishar wrenched the bridge's door completely open. The metal screeched, nearly blowing out Robert's ear drums.

Robert stumbled into the corridor, eyes stinging. His lungs convulsed, each cough tasting of ash. He stopped moving when they reached the cabin. "Matt's still in the room."

"Leave him!" said Ishar. "We're surrounded. We need to go!"

Robert ignored him, sprinting to the crew quarters, where Matt thrashed against the restraints binding him to the bed. The straps were pulled tight across his chest and legs.

He was still alive! At least for now.

Robert jerked forward and yanked at the straps, which proved to be as immovable as steel cables. "*Tala!*" he shouted. "Release Matt's restraints!"

No response, except for the crackle of electrical fires. Distant explosions shook the deck.

"*Tala*, release Matt's restraints now!"

Ishar burst through the doorway, battle knife drawn, its vibro-molecular, quantum-serrated edge vibrating at a subatomic level. The curved blade glinted as he slashed through the straps with quick cuts.

"Move. Now!" He hurried out of the quarters, disengaging his dagger's vibro-molecular function and strapping it back onto his belt.

Matt rolled off the bed. He stumbled a little before finding his feet. Still, it was obvious that *Tala*'s treatments had helped him considerably. Robert grabbed his arm and they sprinted to the cargo bay. There, Ishar wrestled with the manual release for the exit ramp. The warrior labored against the mechanism as he attempted to force it open. The metal refused to give.

Outside, the sounds of battle grew closer. Plasma bolts sizzled through the air. The whine of fighter engines overhead was mixed with the deeper rumble of eruptions going off just about everywhere. An explosion rocked the vessel. Robert gripped onto a hand railing on the wall while Matt held onto Robert's arm to stay upright.

"*Tala!*" Robert steadied himself. "We need you back online!" He slammed his shoulder against the ramp controls.

He turned to Ishar. "Can't you use that fancy knife of yours to get it open?"

"No. The panel's made of graviton-infused steel, specifically designed to withstand knives like mine."

As they spoke, shrapnel pinged off the outer hull like hail, the impacts resonating throughout the ship. Robert stumbled before catching himself against the wall. And that's when he saw blue-green light rippling through the panels around him. The glow spread outward as *Tala's* systems stirred back to life.

"My apologies," she said as her soft voice filled the bay. "Running emergency overrides now. Ramp will open momentarily. Get clear of the ship. I'll attempt repairs and rejoin you at Tokpela Gate when able."

The ramp lowered. Robert felt for the core processor crystalline matrix still shoved deep into his front pocket. Ishar rushed down the ramp, his plasma pistol raised, while Robert helped escort Matt down the ramp and onto scorching sand. An Atlantean soldier in armor materialized from a black plume wafting about, weapon aimed at them. Ishar's shot caught the trooper square in the visor. Blood splattered. The soldier dropped without a sound.

"This way!" Ishar led them around *Tala's* hull and toward the Lemurian outpost—the Tokpela Gate. It stood before them. Mushroom-like structures sprouted from the sand, crowned by spires and domes. A high wall ringed the complex. Massive gates stood open. Guard towers bristled with weapons, plasma bolts streaking out at approaching Atlantean forces.

Lemurian troops in battlesuits rushed across the dunes. One took a direct hit and crumpled, armor smoking. Robert weaved between scattered trees and rock outcroppings as they sprinted uphill. His lungs burned.

The whine of Skyblade engines sliced through the combat. A fighter dove in their direction, its missile pods opening.

"Down!" shouted Robert.

A projectile struck the dune. Sand erupted like a geyser. The blast picked Robert up and hurled him through the air. He tumbled down the slope and his mouth and ears rang from the concussion. His vision blurred.

Finally, he managed to stagger upright. His pulse pounded in his ears. Dense vapor and dust clouds whirled around him. The whip and sting of wind-blown sand against his face made it impossible to see more than a few yards all around.

A ship's engines roared nearby. A shadow descended through the swirling murk above, its form obscured by the dense, debris-filled fog. Before Robert could process what it was, a laser bolt seared past his head. The heat of it singed his hair. The near-miss spun him around.

Moments after, hands seized him from behind and shoved him to the ground, where he was rolled over and frisked, although not for long, as the crystal bulging out from his front pocket left no doubt where to start. Seconds later, through the choking haze, he glimpsed Kairos sprinting toward a waiting shuttle, clutching the crystal in his hand. Sovereign Guards stood over Robert with their weapons trained on him.

"Leave him for me!" Kairos said to the guards while raising a pistol. Robert dove out of the way as the shot streaked past, leaving a glass-lined crater in the sand.

Kairos grunted. "Forget it! Kill him. Kill him, now!"

When the guards took aim, Robert swallowed hard. He grabbed sand and flung it into the air hoping to distract them, even a little. He rolled away as shots rang out. Every muscle contracted, waiting for the burning impact. Nothing. No pain. He'd always imagined laser fire would hurt, would feel like something worse than what he felt now. Maybe he was numb?

He managed to twist around to find the guards standing over him were now face-down in the sand, their bodies still. Dead. Killed by an unknown benefactor.

Robert scrambled to his feet as Kairos sprinted up the shuttle's ramp with the core processor still clutched in his grip. Seconds later, the High Marshall of Atlantis vanished into the craft's belly.

The shuttle's engines flared blue-white. The backwash hit Robert like a sandblaster. It drove stinging particles into his face, arms, and chest. He staggered back, throwing a forearm across his eyes as the craft lifted on columns of fire before blasting through the clouds above.

Ishar appeared at Robert's side, Matt right behind him.

"You're welcome," said Ishar. "Do you know how many Atlantean soldiers I've sent to their graves to keep you alive?" He flexed his hands, grinning. "Though I must confess, ending their miserable existence brings me considerable pleasure."

But Robert's face was sullen, horrified. "You saved me, but Kairos got the crystalline matrix," he said. "And he's gone. And, all of this was for *nothing*. He'll have his Nexus Prime superweapon working again in no time. After all our efforts, we've failed. *I've* failed. I've condemned multiple civilizations, and I'm allowing history to repeat itself . . . again."

CHAPTER 63

Robert glanced around. Ishar and Matt had been busy, putting down any number of Atlanteans while sniper fire from the Lemurian position had taken out scores of others. The air was finally still, and off in the distance, the Lemurian gate was opening.

They hustled toward the gate, and Robert had never felt so despondent. He had run a marathon, only to trip a few yards short of the finish line. So many had lost their lives to stop this war, and they had failed. Now Kairos possessed two things that were more precious to Robert than his very life: the quantum crystalline matrix and Kira Shelton.

"Don't worry," said Matt, moving briskly beside him. "We'll find another way."

"No . . . we won't," said Robert, wanting to vomit on the sand. "We're out of time, and out of options."

"Okay, so don't believe me," said the young Hopi, who was holding up beautifully after *Tala's* treatment. "Believe Kira Shelton instead. We both know she's smarter than the two of us combined," he added with the hint of a smile. "Remember when she was so sure you'd learn how to control the Vesh'tar. And you asked her how she could be so sure. Remember what she said? She said, 'Because I believe in you. And in Thoth. And in *Tala*. And I believe in *us*, the trio *Tala* chose to bring here."

A tear came to Robert's eye as he remembered. Matt had found the exact right words to break him out of his severe depression, and he could feel the fight and resolve begin to surge through him once again.

"Where there's life, there's hope," added Matt. "The professor I've come to admire would know that."

"Thanks, Little Owl," said Robert as they passed through Tokpela Gate's massive archway. "That helps. You're beginning to display that next-level wisdom your father saw in you when you were born."

Lemurian troops rushed past them as they entered the Outpost. A colossal mushroom-shaped structure dominated the center of the stronghold. It bristled with plasma cannons, all firing bolts into the sky and over the beach at regular intervals. The booms vibrated across the compound.

Around the central building, smaller domes dotted the area. Medics rushed wounded soldiers on hovering stretchers into several of the domes. Troops sprinted toward guard towers rising from the defensive walls as mounted cannons along the ramparts swiveled, blasting at unseen threats.

Ishar hurried Robert and Matt toward the central structure's giant doors, which parted with a groan. Inside, a chamber stretched several stories high. Circular tiers stood along the walls. Each level was packed with operators manning consoles. Holograms glowed everywhere. Some showing troop movements, others displaying aerial views of burning soldiers and vehicles—live feeds from the beach battle.

"Incoming fighters, sector two!" an operator said.

"Multiple casualties reported at the east wall!"

"Need immediate evac at checkpoint blue!"

The voices blended into a constant stream of battlefield updates. Officers rushed between stations, talking over displays and speaking commands in rapid fire.

A hologram showed Atlantean forces advancing across the beach. Plasma fire lit up the projection as defenders tried to hold them back. The scene shifted to an overhead view of both outposts. Anvil's black walls much different from Tokpela's earthen color barriers, both with cannons mounted atop and blasting at opposing forces.

Ishar led Robert and Matt past banks of communication stations, where multiple faces were lit by scrolling data feeds and status reports. Some yelled orders while others worked in total concentration, tapping on haptic interfaces like nothing else mattered. To those people, it probably didn't.

Robert and his small crew passed through an archway into a system of corridors branching off in all directions. The walls displayed maps and tactical readouts. More staff hurried by, carrying tablets and equipment. The floor trembled with each impact from the battle outside.

Ishar guided them down a side passage. "I've only been here a few times, but my memory is superior to yours. The Command Center lies ahead. We should be relatively safe here until *Tala* uses her macro-bots and nano-bots to effect repairs."

The corridor opened into another chamber. More workstations faced a wall of displays showing different aspects of the battle. A group of older men and women stood around a central holotable projecting a map, perhaps of troop movements. Of that, Robert didn't know. Flags, copper shields, and scrolls hung from the walls all around.

"You were the ones inside *Tala*?" A tall man strode to them, eyes full of concern.

"Yes," said Robert.

"I'm Koyaanisqatsi," he said. "Call my Koya. Wild situation we've got, isn't it? I've captained *Tala* and have been working with Thoth and the Resistance for years. Now, I understand, there are *two* of her. A time-travel thing. I've heard that if she ever meets herself, the consequences would be catastrophic."

"Thoth didn't think that would be the case," said Robert, "but he also couldn't rule it out. Regardless, he thought we shouldn't let them get near each other . . . to be on the safe side."

"A wise man," said Koya.

"Where's your *Tala* now?" asked Robert.

"Well, that's the thing. I recently lost her over the ocean between Nasavi and Atlantis. We went down smuggling a political prisoner from the city when a Skyblade surprised us. The prisoner died, and I barely made it out alive myself. A Lemurian boat found me and took me to shore. I scrambled my way here. I've been flying fighters since yesterday. Lost our whole squadron this morning. Now we've got no flying craft at all. Reinforcements are coming, but it isn't looking good."

"Have you heard what happened to the home of the Resistance?"

Koya nodded solemnly. "Yes. Overrun. Sovereign Guards broke through and killed everyone. I assume Thoth made it out, though."

Robert shook his head. "I'm afraid not. He died buying us time to escape."

Silence fell. Koya closed his eyes for a moment. Grief etched deep lines in his face. When he opened them, he clenched his jaw. "Those . . . Atlanteans. Sometimes hate doesn't describe how you really feel."

He thought for a moment. "Come with me. I need to get back to the war room to check on an ongoing Special Operations mission that might turn the tide of this battle."

"We're right behind you," said Robert.

CHAPTER 64

Advisor Elowin Balivae
Atlantis Capital, Poseidia
Location: Northwest Atlantis

Elowin and Jalon moved to exit the High Councilor's magnificent chambers, as several Sovereign Guards moved with them.

Elowin wondered if Nereus would let them leave. She had gambled everything on a last-ditch effort to reach him. She had been blunt, hammering him, almost belittling him, and hadn't pulled a single punch. A tactic that would either knock some sense into the man or lead to a very short life expectancy for her.

"Halt!" said the High Councilor.

She and Jalon stopped in their tracks as guards blocked their passage. She turned to face Nereus, a scowl still on her face.

"No one has dared speak to me the way you just did in many years," he said.

"Then you need underlings with more backbone. Not ones who are pleasant to your face while plotting to plunge a dagger into your back. I'm trying to save your crown, and your life. If I sugarcoat the reality, fail to get through to you, you'll be removed from power and millions will die . . . at minimum. If you can't handle a passionate argument, can't handle hearing unpleasantries you'd rather not face, then perhaps you don't deserve the position you're in, anyway."

Nereus looked completely dismayed. "Not your average diplomat, are you?"

"Diplomacy isn't what you need right now."

"You have courage to spare, I'll give you that."

"And so did you at one time," she said, doing anything but backing down. "Apparently, that isn't true any longer. During your rise to power, you were known to be more courageous than anyone, High Councilor. That's why it's so frustrating to see this trait absent from you now. To see you fearful of learning the truth. Fearful of the small possibility that your computer systems will be corrupted."

Nereus stared into her defiant, unblinking eyes for several long seconds. "Okay, Advisor. You could have left here when I told you to go without saying another word. You could have left quietly, annoyed to have been shot down, but counting your blessings that you weren't being shot down *literally*."

He shook his head. "Instead, you made sure to insult me on the way out. To risk my ire, and your own life. Not the wisest choice, but one I can't help but respect. Anyone willing to do that has my full attention. So, answer me this. If these files are encrypted, how do you know what's in them?"

She sighed. "I don't. I just know the truth of what Kairos has planned, and I've seen the file names, which are quite suggestive." She paused. "Well, how about this? Download and decrypt the files. If they infect your systems or don't provide the evidence I say they will, torture me. Kill me. Have at it."

Elowin inhaled slowly. "And, consider this. Suppose I *am* lying. What happens? Worst case, your systems become infected. So what?"

She raised her chin and crossed her arms. "But what if you *refuse* to download the files, and I'm telling the *truth*? If that happens, what's the worst-case scenario then? In that case, you get executed by a man who's betrayed you. You lose your power. You lose your life."

Elowin motioned to a dozen holographic images on Nereus's desk, showing a loving wife and three children at various ages, all the children with the same striking red hair as their father. "But it's a lot worse than that, isn't it? Your wife will lose a husband. Your children will lose a father."

She watched as his eyes surveyed the holograms of his family and then returned to her. "You have to ask yourself, High Councilor, if you have to make a mistake here, which is the better one to make? The one with a very slight chance of compromising Atlantean computer systems? Or the one that might cost you your life, and so much more?"

Nereus nodded thoughtfully and remained silent for an extended period. "I can't find a flaw in your argument," he said finally. "Unless this is a suicide trip for you, but I don't see it in your eyes. In fact, right now, your passion and spirit are unmatched."

The High Councilor turned away from her. "Guards!" he bellowed imperiously. "Leave us! Take her comrade with you," he added, gesturing to Jalon, "but don't harm him."

When Elowin was alone in the massive room with the High Councilor, he locked his eyes on her once again. "Beauty, intelligence, poise, and an indomitable spirit. You're the complete package, aren't you? If you weren't Lemurian, I'd appoint you to our own Council." He cleared his throat before continuing. "Now, tell me how to access these files of yours and let's both find out if you're telling the truth. I hope you're lying, of course, and Kairos is still loyal to me." A faint smile touched his lips. "Yet, I have to admit, a tiny part of me almost hopes you aren't, as I'd hate to have to execute such a remarkable woman."

She grinned. "Yet another thing we have in common. I'd also hate for you to have to execute me."

He laughed at this, which she found surprising.

Elowin walked him through the procedure for accessing her Lemurian network channels. She guided him past encryption barriers, her credentials bypassing the security protocols. It allowed them to reach the secured data cache, where she'd stored everything from Councilor Deir Slan's holocomp.

Nereus's desk filled with holographic displays. Document after document materialized in the air. Nereus's face turned ashen as he absorbed what Elowin had discovered, and more. It was far more incriminating than even she had imagined.

Kairos hadn't just infiltrated the military. He'd penetrated every level of Atlantean governance. Trade negotiations, energy contracts, defense appropriations. They were all manipulated to slowly strangle Nereus's authority while strengthening Kairos's grip on power. The High Councilor's own advisory staff had been compromised, replaced by operatives who reported directly to Kairos. The man's power and reach seemed endless.

It was Kairos's personal correspondence that seemed to hit Nereus the hardest. Messages between Kairos and Councilor Deir Slan, discussing Nereus as if he were already gone, planning the transition down to the finest detail. They'd mapped out a campaign to erode public confidence, creating small failures that fed into a narrative of incompetence. Each crisis, from the Lemurian war to the energy shortages, had been engineered to show Nereus as a leader far out of his depth.

The documents outlined ways to expose manufactured scandals, each designed to destroy Nereus's political legacy and his family's standing for generations to come. His children would be disinherited, their futures erased, their names synonymous with treason.

Nereus's eyes were ablaze as he accessed the final file, which was a timeline for the next six months. It showed Kairos's endgame: using the war with Lemuria to declare a state of emergency, suspending the Council's authority, and establishing himself as Supreme Commander of a unified military-civilian government. Nereus's "tragic accident" was already penciled in for the first month.

The High Councilor sat back, rage exploding out of every pore. In the documents Elowin had provided, Nereus found evidence of betrayals on a truly epic scale, along with the end of his political career and the death of Atlantean democracy itself, all put together by a man he'd once trusted as an ally.

Remarkably, Nereus found a way to re-assert self-control. He took several deep breaths and managed to quickly find calm before Elowin's eyes, as though, seconds before, his entire body had been made of lava, but he had thrown himself into an ice bath to instantly quench the blistering heat.

His gaze returned to Elowin, and he even managed to flash a smile. "Okay, Advisor Balivae, I think it's fair to say that you were telling me the truth."

"I'm so sorry," she whispered grimly. "I wish it weren't true. More than anyone. My nation has already suffered greatly at Kairos's hands."

"I've always thought him to be brilliant and ambitious. A true strategic mastermind. Which is why I appointed him High Marshall of our armed forces. Apparently, I didn't know the half of it."

"How do you plan to proceed?"

"I'll start by contacting Kairos's underling, Commander Argos, who isn't implicated in the files. Sit tight. I'll let you witness this first step. You've earned it."

He tapped his desk console, and a new hologram sprang to life, one with a military officer, whose eyes widened as he realized just who had called him on his high-priority channel. He barely stopped himself from gasping. Instead, he gave a slight bow. "High Councilor. How can I help you?"

"Commander Argo," replied Nereus. "Effective immediately, I need you to locate and detain Councilor Kairos Daedalus and Deir Slan. They're to be taken into custody on charges of treason, conspiracy to commit murder, and crimes against humanity."

Nereus's gaze was steel. "I'm also calling for an immediate ceasefire between Lemuria and Nasavi. I have some things to sort out, but in just a few days' time, I'll be initiating peace negotiations with Lemuria. I'll be forging a treaty with a diplomat there named Elowin Balivae."

Argo winced. "I'm so sorry, High Councilor, but I have bad news," he said, looking sick to his stomach. It was clear he didn't relish the idea of disappointing the High Councilor. "You may have not heard, but Elowin Balivae was in a horrible accident. I'm afraid she's dead."

Nereus turned to Elowin, whose image wasn't being transmitted, and grinned. "Yeah, she gets that a lot. But she's far less dead than you'd imagine. In fact, she's in the room with me now."

"Understood, High Councilor. I'll personally carry out and oversee all of your orders, of course."

"One more thing, Commander." Nereus glanced at his children's holos. "I want my family moved to a secure location. Choose the detail yourself. People you trust absolutely.

"And, as for the capture of Kairos, gather a small team of your most trusted soldiers to apprehend him, at best possible speed. I want him in custody *yesterday*. No directive has ever been more urgent."

"Understood, High Councilor."

"If you need to reach me, I'll send information to your datapad on how to contact me directly when this discussion ends. One final thing I need you to understand beyond the shadow of a doubt. You, and whoever else is involved in carrying out these orders, can't breathe a single word of this to *anyone*. I can't risk Kairos being tipped off that we're coming and going after my family to gain leverage. If word leaks out, I *will* find the leaker, and I *will* have him tortured to death. No trial, no recourse, just the most horrible of deaths. Do I make myself understood?"

"Absolutely, High Councilor," said Argo. "I won't let you down."

"See that you don't," said Nereus, abruptly ending the call.

Elowin could barely contain her delight. "Thank you, High Councilor!" she said, almost gushing.

"No. Thank *you*. The most powerful man in all of Atlantis is now in your debt. A man who will remain the most powerful man in Atlantis only because of you. I won't forget that."

"I'm grateful," she said. "I took a risk coming here. You could have been aware of everything Kairos was doing. You could have ordered it yourself. You're known to be absolutely faithful to your wife when you could have any woman in Atlantis. And known to put your family above all else. So, my gut told me you were a good man. One who wouldn't possibly support a war unless you'd been dangerously misled. I'm happy to learn that I was right about you. And sorry about earlier, when I was so . . . blunt."

"It was the medicine I needed," replied Nereus. "You and your comrade should leave now. Go back to Lemuria. Things are about to become . . . complicated in Atlantis."

She nodded. "I know you'll take care of it. And I look forward to initiating peace negotiations with Atlantis in a few days. My hope is that our two great nations will go on to become closer than ever before."

Nereus grinned. "I won't tell anyone, Advisor Balivae, but just then, you *finally* sounded like a diplomat."

CHAPTER 65

Councilor Kairos Daedalus
High Marshall of the Atlantean Military Forces
Helion-class Diplomatic Vessel
Shuttle Designation—Umbra
Over the Atlantic Ocean

Through the shuttle's viewport, Kairos watched the Atlantic waves undulate below. The quantum crystalline matrix rested beside him. The sound of the engines filled the cabin as they approached Atlantis. Two Sovereign Guards flanked Kairos, seated on either side of him.

Across from him, Aethor and Kira sat bound to their chairs. The look in his son's eyes told Kairos everything. Anger, disappointment, betrayal. All of it raw. No father wanted to see hatred from their own child. Fathers and sons fought. It was part of life, wasn't it? In time, like Kairos with his own father, Aethor would look back and see that his father wasn't only right, but had everyone's best interests at heart, especially his son's.

Kairos knew his choices would hurt Aethor, but just in the moment. He would come to see his father's point of view as he aged. That leaders had to make impossible choices for the good of their people. And these choices could appear cruel and heartless at the microscopic level, while saving the future of the entirety of the human race at the macroscopic level. Sometimes a great leader, a visionary, had to pull entire nations along, with force, so they'd see a better way. A truer, healthier path.

Nonetheless, everything . . . the hard calls, the brutal decisions . . . all of it was for his son's future. For Atlantis. Since no one seemed up to it, Kairos had to keep his nation strong, had to make sure they remained the guardians this world needed. Their technology, their healing arts, their motivation. The world would crumble without Atlantis watching over it all.

"You'll understand one day," whispered Kairos, more to himself than his son. "When you see the bigger picture, you'll know why I had to do this. Every ounce of it."

"You've become everything you once fought against," said Aethor. "The power-hungry tyrant. You're willing to sacrifice countless innocents so you can control those who remain."

"You've always possessed such passion, such conviction," said Kairos. "But you aren't seeing the bigger picture. Salvation through strength. Nexus Prime will end this war swiftly and decisively. No more drawn-out battles, no more dead Atlantean soldiers."

Kira leaned forward against her restraints. "There are rare cases when such calculations can be justified. But never by the side who is clearly the aggressor. *You* started the war. *You* can end it peacefully at any time. Saying that your use of a superweapon will save lives in the long run is absurd. You can save more lives by just stopping the war.

"Attempts to justify the use of a superweapon can only be made if you're up against an implacable enemy who refuses to stop coming under any circumstances. Like the Japanese in World War II, whose leadership refused to stop fighting, even while much of its civilian population was starving to death. In that case, you could make the case that a single nuclear strike could end up saving millions of lives, including Japanese lives. For the record, I disagree with the nuclear strikes on Japan too. Yet, even that is *hotly* debated."

"What are you talking about?" said Kairos.

"I'm from the far future. So, I guess I shouldn't use a case from my time as an example. So let me tell you what happens in *your* time. If you activate that weapon, in the end, entire continents will fall. Not just Lemuria, but Atlantis also. The death toll will rise beyond anything you can imagine."

Kairos rolled his eyes. "You can persist in claiming you're from the future all you want, but that doesn't mean I'll suddenly believe it."

"Don't believe it," said Kira. "But before you do something you can't take back, have your scientists study the possibility of the weapon causing geological instability, triggering tsunamis, earthquakes, and volcanic eruptions, and destroying the very civilization you claim to protect."

"I already have. They've run extensive simulations."

"Your simulations are flawed."

Kairos shook his head. "This isn't up for debate. It's decided. The crystalline matrix will be reinserted, and the weapon will be used."

Kairos's datapad issued a chime, indicating an incoming message of the highest possible priority. He called it up, noting that it had been sent by one of his spies, a Sovereign Guard on the High Councilor's personal security detail.

He lifted the datapad to eye level and began to read.

Urgent! Lemurian Advisor Elowin Balivae is not only alive but just visited Nereus to present evidence of your moves against him. Nereus dismissed all guards, but I managed to plant a listening device on my way out. He knows everything. He's ordered Argo to locate and detain you and Deir Slan on charges of treason, conspiracy to commit murder, and crimes against humanity. He's also ordered Argo not to disclose this to anyone, on threat of death. Your own guards won't be aware this is happening, at least for a short time.

Kairos's head spun. Elowin was alive! He'd known she was exceptionally formidable after meeting her, which is why he'd ordered her killed. Still, she'd somehow found a way to derail all of his plans, anyway.

But not quite. Neither she nor Nereus had counted on one of his spies giving him warning of what was coming. He could still follow through on his plans to use the Nexus Prime weapon.

Kairos left his two prisoners so he wouldn't be distracted and ordered his pilot, Captain Soton Amenti, to take him to Nexus Prime at best possible speed. One way or another, he would ensure his legacy. Even if that legacy was written in fire and blood.

CHAPTER 66

Koya guided Robert, Matt, and Ishar through several passageways and into the war room within the Tokpela Gate Outpost. "You've really come to the wrong place at the wrong time. What's happening now has the makings of the most destructive war ever fought."

In front of them, dozens of operators bent over holos. The largest hologram took up the entire center of the room, displaying a group of soldiers in battlesuits rushing down a tunnel. In seconds, it changed to a digital view, those soldiers now red dots moving through a virtual tunnel.

"These men are our last hope," he said, gesturing to the screen. "We discovered just yesterday that Atlantis had broken the encryption protocols we use for battlefield communications. Because they think we don't know they're intercepting our communications, we figured they'd be overconfident. While they still think they have the upper hand, we changed our comm algorithms and sent in Special Operations teams to infiltrate their stronghold here, Outpost Anvil. The team is now working their way through tunnels to get to its power core."

"Why is it always tunnels?" murmured Robert.

"What was that?"

"Nothing, please continue."

"I'm astonished they've made it as far as they have," continued Koya. "But they are with the Protectorate, the best commandos Lemuria has ever produced. Even so, they've taken heavy casualties. They're heading for a crystal that powers Anvil's entire operation. All of it. Their defensive grid, their aircraft, their weapons, their shields. Everything."

Ishar crossed his arms, watching, as if scrutinizing their every move. Robert stood beside Matt and Koya, not knowing what to say, his body a bit numb, along with his mind. He kept his eyes glued to the special ops teams on the screen.

A team labeled Bear, represented as six red dots on the massive interface, moved through a tunnel beneath Outpost Anvil. They crept along the blue wireframe passages. A second team of four, designated Crow, approached from the opposite direction.

For more than ten minutes, Robert, Matt, and Ishar watched the helmet camera feeds of these commandos on the main screen in awe. They were practically superhuman as they managed to fend off a brutal onslaught of hostiles that never seemed to dwindle, yet they outmaneuvered, out-strategized, out-aimed, and outfought the numerous forces arrayed against them. The images reminded Robert of a first-person-shooter video game, but these men only got a single life.

"I think they're going to make it," said Matt.

Koya didn't take his eyes off the display. "They have to. If they fail, we're done here. We'll have no choice but to abandon this outpost, allowing Atlantis to push their advance westward."

Finally, the surviving members of the Lemurian team converged on their target, the room housing Anvil's power core. In the middle, their helmet cams showed a crystal pulsing with energy. Unlike the crystalline core processor Robert had carried, this crystal was enormous, about nine feet tall and six feet wide. As the survivors approached, enemy soldiers swarmed in from several entrances.

"There are too many," whispered Robert. "They'll never get out alive."

Koya lowered his eyes. "That was never the plan," he said, and his voice was raw, *anguished*.

At that moment, Robert knew what was about to happen and squinted his eyes. These men had volunteered for a kamikaze mission. They had to succeed, so blowing the room with them in it was the only way to be sure.

For one terrible heartbeat, nothing happened. The chamber remained unchanged. Then, almost on cue, the holographic image erupted into a supernova of blinding white light. The blast wave rippled through the virtual display, consuming everything in its path. The crystal's signature flared before shattering into nothingness. Warning indicators cascaded across every screen as the power surge raced through Outpost Anvil's systems.

"Crystal destroyed!" called out multiple operators. "Drone feeds are showing Anvil's primary systems dying! Secondary systems are also going critical!"

Koya lowered his head, and a tear escaped from one eye.

Robert blew out a long breath. "I am so sorry, Koya. Their bravery was extraordinary. As much as I'd like to give you time to grieve. To celebrate. To honor their incredible sacrifices. I can't. Because our victories mean nothing if Atlantis chooses to use its Nexus Prime weapon against us. And that's exactly what Kairos Daedalus has planned."

"Hold on," said Koya, tilting his head in such a way to suggest someone was speaking through the comm in his ear.

"Sorry, but the base commander needs to see me for ten minutes," he said, already rushing off. "Stay here. I'll be back as soon as I can."

Robert wanted to scream but managed to contain himself. Every tick of the clock was an eternity. They needed help to go after Kairos, and since Koya knew about the two *Talas*, only he would instantly believe they were from the future and take them as seriously as needed.

Koya returned eight long minutes later. Eight minutes they probably didn't have. "I'm sorry," he said upon his return. "What were you saying?"

"I was saying that Kairos is heading to Atlantis this very second to activate a weapon that could wipe the Lemurian continent off the map. Millions of lives, gone in an instant. If we don't stop him . . . if we fail . . . ." He shook his head. "I know things that you don't, so all I can do is ask you to trust me. It won't be just Lemuria's extinction, most of the world will fall. Tens of millions. even hundreds of millions, will die across the globe."

"And you're *certain* of this?" said Koya.

"*Positive*," replied Robert, and Matt and Ishar nodded their agreement beside him. "Kairos will activate his superweapon, and soon, and it will ultimately wipe Lemuria off the map."

Koya winced. "Is there any way to stop him?"

"That's unclear. But we have to try. You have to get us to Nexus Prime as fast as possible."

"If that's the case, then *Tala* is our only real choice."

Robert sighed and turned to Ishar. "The damage to *Tala* was extensive. Any chance she could have possibly repaired herself by now?"

"Yes. She's that remarkable. She should be able to fly using her secondary engines. Self-repair of her stardrive and hull damage will take longer. Although, propulsion and possibly shields could well be back online already."

Matt opened his mouth to speak but closed it again when a broad-shouldered officer burst through the door and approached Robert. "I'm told you're the captain of the starship that crashed just beyond our gates."

"I am."

"You'll find this nearly impossible to believe, but it's true. I just received a communication from the Atlantean Commander of Outpost Anvil, Argo Dyrean. He wants to meet with whoever commands that ship. He wouldn't say why, but he said that if you agree, he'll show up at our gate, unarmed and unaccompanied, and we can train guns on him from afar while he has a confab with you."

Koya shook his head in disbelief. "Did this Commander Dyrean say *why* he would do this? Did he give you any sense of what he wants to discuss?"

"Negative. I asked, but he wouldn't say. He's only prepared to tell the captain of the downed starship. He gave his solemn promise that no harm will come to him or any of the rest of us. That this isn't a ruse. He insists the captain of that ship will like what he says. If he doesn't, the Atlantean pointed out that he'll be at our mercy."

"I don't like it," said Koya. "And we've stripped them of all power, so they're *already* at our mercy."

Robert considered. "I don't like it either. But my gut says we have to hear him out. Koya, does this Argo Dyrean strike you as the kind of man who would engage in trickery? Set up a secret trap? Or is he a man of his word?"

Koya deferred to the officer standing beside him, and the officer nodded.

"Affirmative. He's a well-known commander. The intel we have on him is that he's talented, well-liked by his troops, and also a man of his word. He's earned respect even from enemy forces, known for treating prisoners fairly and keeping civilian casualties to a minimum."

Koya turned to the officer once again. "Did he say anything else?"

"Affirmative. He stated he's counting on us being honorable and will be outside our gate in five minutes. No reply needed. He's requesting this starship captain meet with him, fully aware that our snipers will keep him under surveillance."

Robert turned to the young man beside him. "What do you think?"

Matt looked a bit surprised that he was being asked, but the show of respect in this question clearly wasn't lost on him. "I agree with you, Professor. If he's truly willing to put his life in enemy hands, it's hard not to respect that. And you have to find out what this is about. When an enemy commander risks everything for a face-to-face meeting, it could mean he's got something significant to offer, or he needs something badly enough to take this risk. Maybe he has technical knowledge that could help with *Tala's* repairs, or intelligence we desperately need. I don't know, but we won't know unless you hear what he has to say."

"Well analyzed," said Robert. "However, *I'm* not meeting with him. All three of us are. Matt, Ishar . . . you in?"

Ishar grunted a yes, while a smile crossed Matt's face. "I wouldn't miss it for the world."

"Good," said Robert. "What are we waiting for? Let's go see what this Argo Dyrean wants from us."

CHAPTER 67

A lone man stood fifty yards beyond the gate and the trio got the all-clear to proceed out to him. Snipers were in place, and recon had made it clear that no weapons were trained on Robert and his comrades.

They walked out to the Atlantean commander while he stood perfectly still, being sure to make no sudden moves. They stopped five feet away from him and studied him closely. He didn't appear to be armed. Robert had decided to let him be the first to speak.

The commander was probably in his mid-fifties, but his battlesuit fit like it was made for someone half his age. Despite the gray at his temples, he stood straight-backed and alert, muscles visible even through the armor's bulk.

"I'm Commander Argo Dyrean, but please call me Argo," he began. "I asked to meet with one man. And while math isn't my best subject, I can't help but notice there are *three* of you."

Robert smiled. "You're very observant," he said wryly. "Yes, there are three of us. Whatever you need to say to one of us, you can say to all three."

"Can I assume one of you is the captain of the ship back there? She was using a fake energy signature previously, but after she sustained damage, she read clearly as the starship *Tala*."

"Yes," said Robert. "One of us is *Tala's* captain."

"Thank you for honoring my request on little notice. I wasn't sure if you would, or frankly, if I'd be gunned down before I even got this close."

"Why are you here?" said Ishar.

"Because, suddenly, unexpectedly, we are now on the same side. I'll provide details, but first I need your word that you will keep what I tell you to yourselves. At least, for a while longer."

"A strange request," said Robert.

"I'm confident you'll understand the need for this request soon."

The trio exchanged glances and all three gave their word as requested.

"There have been any number of startling developments in a very short period of time," began Argo without further preamble. "Our High Councilor, Nereus Pyralis, contacted me about an hour ago. He's never contacted me before. I answer to Kairos Daedalus, and he answers to the High Councilor. Quickly, I learned why the chain of command was circumvented."

He paused for effect. "Nereus told me he wants an immediate cease-fire with Lemuria. That in a few days' time, he wants to enter peace negotiations. And, most stunning of all, he wants Kairos, the High Marshall of the Atlantean military, taken into custody on charges of treason, conspiracy to commit murder, and crimes against humanity."

"I don't believe you," said Ishar bluntly

"I understand. I wouldn't either. I'm having trouble believing it myself."

"Did you ask him why he issued these orders?" asked Matt.

Argo snorted. "Negative. The High Councilor didn't see fit to tell me. And it isn't my place to question him. It's my place to carry out his orders."

He stopped speaking for a moment, gathering himself. "What I *can* tell you is that he was with a Lemurian woman named Elowin Balivae. Have you heard of her?"

Robert's eyes widened. Elowin Balivae. He had more than heard of her. He'd been mesmerized by her very presence. Who wouldn't? She'd told them at Thoth's forest residence that she was a diplomat, and represented Lemuria's last hope of stopping the war. Apparently, she was just as effective as advertised. The fact that Argo had mentioned her name lent *considerable* legitimacy to what he was saying. Suddenly, the absurd became plausible.

"So, you do know of her," said Argo.

"Yes, she's a diplomat of some . . . reputation."

"That makes sense. Nereus wants her to represent Lemuria in the peace negotiations, so he must have found her to be quite . . . important."

Robert considered. "All right, let's say I believe you. Why are you telling *us*? Where do we fit in?"

Argo stared into Robert's eyes. "Because I need your help. The High Councilor insisted Kairos be arrested as quickly as possible. He specified this was to be done *yesterday*, to give you a sense of his urgency. We had eyes on the crash of your ship. Long-range optical sensors. They recorded footage of Kairos leaving his shuttle and taking something from you. I happen to know what it was, the quantum crystalline matrix that turns Nexus Prime into a weapon. Or am I wrong about that?"

"Go on," said Robert.

"High Councilor Pyralis told me to gather a few of my most trusted men and capture Kairos, and a Councilwoman named Deir Slan. My trusted colleagues in Poros City apprehended Deir Slan almost immediately. But the High Councilor doesn't want Kairos tipped off. He made it very clear that I can't breathe a word of this operation to anyone, and neither can those I recruit. On threat of torture and death. I'm having other trusted men relocate the High Councilor's family to a secure location, so it's clear he fears what Kairos might do if he learns he's being hunted."

"I see," said Robert thoughtfully. "That's why you need us. You don't have a choice. You know Kairos is heading to Nexus Prime to re-arm the weapon and then use it. And the High Councilor gave you explicit orders to capture him quickly. With Outpost Anvil's power crystal destroyed, all your aircraft are grounded. Now, you need *Tala*. And a starship won't take orders from a stranger. Which means . . . you need *us*."

"Affirmative on all counts. For this mission, I can't imagine we aren't aligned. We may have been fierce enemies just hours ago, but fate has turned us into allies. The war is ending. A ceasefire is being announced. And we both have reason to stop Kairos as quickly as possible. I know better than anyone just how dangerous he can be. If we don't capture him soon, he'll get wind that we're coming. He has spies everywhere. I only trust four of my men here enough to help me capture him."

Argo paused. "Ironically," he continued, "since Kairos plans to wipe out Lemuria, I trust your side more than I trust my own. If we leave now, he'll only have a twenty-minute head start, which *Tala* will make up in seconds."

Robert sighed. "Not quite. Her primary drive has been disabled, but assuming she's finished repairs on the secondary drive, we can be close behind him."

"Does that mean you're in?"

Robert exchanged glances with Ishar and Matt, who both nodded. "We're in. But you have to let me tell the base commander here about it, along with a starship captain friend of ours. I'll swear them both to secrecy, but you're right, there's no need. The last thing they want is for Kairos to be tipped off that we're coming."

"I understand, but why do you need to tell them?"

"I want the base commander to provide commandos that we can take with us. To add to the four from your side you've already chosen. As you said, Kairos can be a . . . handful."

Argo nodded. "Good thinking," he said. "I'll maintain position by the ship and have my four soldiers rally here. Move fast! Time is not on our side."

CHAPTER 68

They were on their way in *Tala* less than fifteen minutes later, truly a miracle of efficiency. She wasn't nearly fully operational, but she could still fly as fast as a fighter.

Robert found it to be the most unlikely group of temporary allies ever assembled, consisting of a Quantum Resonance Consciousness named *Tala*, an Anunnaki warrior named Ishar, and groups of both Atlanteans and Lemurians. And while this was an exceedingly unlikely combination all by itself, it was made many orders of magnitude *more* unlikely by the presence of two allies from the *United States of America*.

Robert, Matt, and Ishar had rushed back to the outpost, where the base commander was eager to learn what Argo had said. They quickly recounted the situation, along with their certainty that Kairos was about to unleash an Armageddon upon the world. Koya, who was well respected, vouched that they were from the future, as they claimed, so when they insisted this was a tipping point, and that all would be lost if they didn't stop Kairos, the commander had no choice but to help them. He wasn't entirely convinced, but convinced enough to quickly assign the last eight Protectorate commandos on base to Robert and his team, who arrived in midnight blue battlesuits, heavily scarred from combat.

After getting the base commander's word he would keep their secret, the crew of the second *Tala* bid a fond farewell to Koya, and soon they were off.

Argo now sat with Robert, Matt, and Ishar on the bridge, while the four Atlantean Sovereign Guards and eight Lemurian Protectorates were kept on separate ends of the ship, so they didn't try to kill each other while their leadership was discussing strategy.

Robert faced Argo. "Can you quickly reach your High Councilor, Pyralis?"

"Affirmative."

"Outstanding. You need to contact him immediately. The High Councilor was right to make sure Kairos wasn't tipped off that he was coming for him. That's not true any longer. We know exactly where Kairos is . . . in a shuttle."

"Right," said Argo, "the *Umbra*."

"And we're nearly positive we know exactly where he's going. Nexus Prime. So why chase him? Who's the ranking officer on the *Umbra* when Kairos isn't present?"

"Captain Soton Amenti."

"Will Sovereign Guards also be aboard?"

"Almost certainly. A contingent of three."

"Okay, so . . . have Nereus contact Captain Amenti on the *Umbra* and have *him* arrest Kairos. End of problem."

Argo considered. "And if Amenti and the three Sovereign Guards are Kairos's handpicked loyalists? If they were promised considerable money and power to help him carry out his coup? In that case, we'll have tipped Kairos off, and they'll run rather than arrest him."

Ishar shook his head. "You humans don't think savagely enough," he said. "Just have your High Councilor tell Amenti that he scrambled Skyblades to intercept the *Umbra* before he made the call. That the fighters are just out of *Umbra's* detection range. This will allow him to threaten Amenti if required. He can tell him that if Kairos isn't arrested within five minutes, the shuttle will be shot down, *obliterated*, and all on board will die. I don't care how loyal they are to Kairos, they won't sacrifice their lives for him."

"Great point," said Robert. "And with stakes this high, savagery, as you put it, is well justified. And just in case Kairos isn't arrested, and the ship survives—both extremely unlikely—High Councilor Pyralis can also arrange for quite a greeting party for Kairos at Nexus Prime. More fighters to shoot him down. Along with dozens of soldiers at the ready in the control room where Kairos will have to go to replace the quantum crystalline matrix we removed. There's no conceivable scenario in which he reinstalls the crystal and activates the weapon without being captured or killed."

Argo smiled and rose from his chair. "Well done," he said happily. "Sounds foolproof." He began moving toward one of the private quarters. "I'll contact Nereus right away and wait on the line until Kairos is in custody. I don't want you in the background, or I'll have to waste time on explanations. I should be back in about ten minutes with good news."

Argo was back in five, looking decidedly troubled.

"What happened?" said Matt.

"Kairos isn't *on* the shuttle anymore. Amenti reported that not long after the *Umbra* left the vicinity of Outpost Anvil, while still over Nasavi, Kairos ordered him to land in the middle of nowhere and drop him off. Along with two prisoners, both bound, a woman named Kira Shelton and Kairos's son. It was a highly unusual order, but Kairos insisted, so the captain had little choice but to obey."

Robert temporarily lost his ability to concentrate. All he could think of was Kira Shelton. She was still alive! At that moment, nothing else mattered.

"Kairos is as formidable as they come," noted Ishar, who, unlike Robert, wasn't temporarily paralyzed by the thought of an extraordinary human woman. "He must have learned Nereus was coming for him, after all."

"Yes," said Argo. "And while the High Councilor is sending ships to where he was let off, they won't arrive for quite a while. Regardless, we must assume Kairos isn't still there, even now. He must have had another ship ready to pick him and his prisoners up the moment the *Umbra* was gone. So now he knows we're coming, and we have no idea where to find him."

Matt winced. "So much for our foolproof plan."

"Nereus was *furious*," said Argo. "He'll still set up the ambushes at Nexus Prime, but Kairos is too smart to trigger that trap. He's sure to realize what will be waiting for him."

"There's a bright side to this," noted Matt. "He's on the run. And he can't use his superweapon. Nothing is more important than that."

"That's true," said Argo. "Yet, it's only a temporary victory. Kairos is out there, and he'll be coming for Nereus. And for his family. How long will his family be safe before Kairos finds them and uses them as the ultimate leverage against Nereus? How long before Kairos can regroup and find a way to still carry out his coup? He's as good as it gets, as ruthless and cunning as it gets, and he can still succeed. And if he does, he'll be able to use the weapon without interference."

Argo scratched his jaw in thought. "If I haven't found and captured him by the end of the day, the High Councilor has made it clear he'll have my head on a *platter*. But I don't see how I can possibly do what he asks. Kairos could be *anywhere*."

Robert had a sudden, sickening realization, and the blood drained from his face. "No," he whispered in horror. "*Not* anywhere. Because the situation is *much* worse than we thought. He'll be using the superweapon after all, and soon. Depending on how quickly his allies were able to retrieve him, we might have only minutes to find him."

"I don't understand," said Argo.

"Kairos's son, Aethor, gained access to his secret files. Long story, but according to Aethor, Kairos came up with a way to use the quantum crystalline matrix, the brains of his superweapon, from a remote site. He shuttered the site after deciding the subterranean location he had already put in place on the Nexus Prime grounds was so perfectly secure it was better to leave well enough alone. But the remote site still exists. Which means he doesn't need to go back through the tunnel under the Nexus Prime grounds. He can just activate the weapon from this remote secondary site. I can't believe I didn't remember that earlier."

Matt grimaced. "Ishar and I didn't remember it either, Professor, so don't beat yourself up."

"You may have remembered in time to stop him," said Argo. "Where's the location?"

Robert frowned. "That's just it. It was never specified. I don't know if there's really any way to find it."

"Come on, Professor," said Matt. "Along with Kira, you're the smartest person I know. If anyone can figure it out through logic alone, it's you."

Robert's head was spinning. If he couldn't figure out the location, then all was lost. The superweapon would be used with the devastating results he knew only too well. And he would never see Kira again. He wanted to weep, scream, and drive his fist through a wall at the same time. But being the center of an emotional maelstrom wouldn't help these magnificent civilizations survive.

Wouldn't help *Kira* survive.

He had to do what his Vesh'tar had told him to do. He had to find a way to be *better* than his best. If any situation called for that particular Zen koan to be realized, this one did.

"I was there when Aethor brought the remote site up," said Ishar. "He gave us nothing else to go on. Logic can't help in this case." The towering alien turned to Argo. "How many research facilities, bases, and offices in Atlantis and territories beyond are funded by secret budgets? How many are fronts, not engaged in what they outwardly appear to be engaged in, but instead are used for secret military or governmental purposes?"

Argo didn't hesitate. "Thousands."

Ishar nodded. "Exactly. And any one of these might be the site he used. Or he might have funded it privately, so it's even more obscure than that. And there's no way to narrow it down."

Robert gasped as an inspiration hit him from nowhere. "Maybe there *is* a way," he said as his eyes widened to the size of an owl's.

"Aethor made one other disclosure. He told us his father had three top scientists on the project."

"Right," said Ishar, "but he didn't give any indication of who they were."

"Maybe he didn't need to," said Robert. "Maybe this is the one time when Kairos's paranoia and thoroughness proves his undoing."

"Explain," said Argo.

"Nothing is more important to him than the crystal that controls the weapon," replied Robert. "He went to ridiculous lengths to keep all knowledge surrounding its location and operation to himself. He didn't share it with a single soul. The only way we knew where it was in the tunnel system was because Aethor gained access to his computer. Kairos even killed the scientist who installed the crystal there, just to make sure no one else knew."

"That's it, Professor," said Matt. "You did it."

"Maybe. Maybe not," responded Robert. "Let's find out. Argo, I need you to use your datapad to search all news and information available. Look for three top Atlantean scientists who mysteriously died or disappeared at some point over the last few years, all in a very short span of time. Hurry!"

Less than a minute later, Argo shrank back, astonished. "You were right," he said in awe. "Two years ago, three elite scientists were together in a small shuttle, on their way to Poseidia, when the shuttle malfunctioned and crash-landed, killing everyone on board. It turns out that all three were living and working at a remote research station on the obscure island of Ulthat-Khem. The station is located at the rim of a crater within a dense forest."

Argo continued, "The island is between Nasavi and Atlantis, but much closer to Nasavi. In fact, it's quite close to where we are now."

"*Tala*," said Robert immediately, "proceed to the Island of Ulthat-Khem at best possible speed."

"Proceeding to Ulthat-Khem at best possible speed," confirmed the ship.

"There's more," said Argo, continuing to read. "The crater was made by an asteroid that left deposits of astrium." He stopped reading and looked up. "You know, astrium has a unique crystalline structure that resonates with specific frequencies, enhancing signal transmission by acting like a natural waveguide, or lens, for EM waves. Small amounts of it are used in our long-range military communication systems. In short, the entire crater acts like a giant signal amplifier, boosting signals to unheard-of levels."

Robert nodded excitedly. "That was just the first requirement to get something as complicated as the core processor to tie into, and bypass, certain Nexus Prime systems. It wasn't enough. Aethor said it took a major, surprising breakthrough after that. Even so, the rim of this crater would be the ideal place to set up such a project."

"Shouldn't you contact the High Councilor and have him send reinforcements to the island as fast as possible?" asked Matt.

"It's a good thought, but it wouldn't end well. *Tala* is the closest vessel, by far. I'd have no way to explain to Nereus how I got this intel without telling him about you three. And once I do that, I'd have to convince him you can be trusted."

"It's better to ask forgiveness than ask permission," mumbled Robert.

"Exactly," said Argo. "Reinforcements are too far off, anyway. I'm afraid we're on our own. We stop Kairos. Or no one does."

CHAPTER 69

They studied the site for just a few minutes longer before Robert and Argo rushed off to opposite sides of the ship to gather the twelve elite soldiers together in one room. Argo barely had enough time to give them the most top-level of briefings.

The crater and surroundings on the island of Ulthat-Khem were truly extraordinary. Twelve miles of dense, ancient forests surrounded the remote facility and had even overgrown much of the crater. The bowl-like depression on the mountainside shielded the research station—likely a fortified bunker—from harsh weather. At the same time, the site leveraged geothermal features like hot springs and steam vents, and the presence of other ultra-rare and exotic elements left behind by the asteroid, to help mask energy signatures. There were also caves beneath the crater. And last, but not least, a variety of predators roamed the area, including short-faced bears, the largest carnivorous land mammal to ever walk the Earth.

Soon, Argo was imparting this knowledge to an assemblage of everyone on board, along with a general briefing on the players and stakes involved. This included a reminder of the High Councilor's insistence that Kairos be taken alive, so he could learn the full extent of his treachery.

The four Atlantean and eight Lemurian commandos were now in the same room but stayed as far apart from each other as they could get, and the hatred in the air was as thick as tar.

When Argo finished, Robert hesitated, then stepped forward. His heart pounded as he realized every eye in the room had turned to him. "I'm probably the last person who should be speaking to you," he said. "I'm not Atlantean or Lemurian. I've spent most of my life studying ancient civilizations, not fighting in modern wars." Xx He made sure not to tell them that the ancient civilizations he was speaking of were their own.

Robert looked around the room. "But history has taught me something important. That civilizations don't fall because of external enemies. They collapse when they tear themselves apart from within."

He sighed, trying to find the right words. "I know you were enemies hours ago. I can see it in your postures, in the way you're sizing each other up. And I understand. You've lost friends, brothers-in-arms."

Robert paused, thinking of the ancient texts he'd studied for years. "There's a passage from an ancient writing called 'The Maxims of Ptahhotep' that says, 'Hatred diverts the heart, and causes men to be deaf to the words of justice.' I've seen that truth play out across millennia of human conflict.

"But today, something bigger is at stake. It's not about Atlantis versus Lemuria anymore. It's simply not. This is about whether there will *be* an Atlantis or Lemuria tomorrow. Because, as Commander Argo has pointed out, the stakes are nothing less than that.

"There are other stakes involved as well. Not as epic, but just as important to keep in mind." His eyes welled up with tears, but he managed to keep them from streaming down his face. "Kairos has taken two innocents as prisoners. A wonderful, innocent woman, who has risked her life multiple times to save your two civilizations. and is doing so now. And Kairos's son, Aethor, who has betrayed his own father to stop a catastrophe. To prevent multiple genocides."

Robert exhaled. "Yes, stopping Kairos from unleashing his weapon must be our top priority," he said, although his eyes suggested otherwise. "And we must also do everything humanly possible to spare these two prisoners who have done so much for *us*."

He paused for as long as he could, given the severe constraints on time. "Back to your current animosity toward each other. I'm not asking you to forget about the recent conflict, the recent bloodshed. But I am asking you to do what humans have always done in moments of true crisis. To put aside smaller conflicts to face the greater threat. Whether you're Atlantean or Lemurian, you all swore oaths to protect your people. Right now, that means working together. Soon, the war will be over, and relations will normalize. And you'll find out that so much of the hatred you feel for each other was ginned up by evil politicians and complicit media, spreading propaganda and lies about the other's nation. Some Atlanteans are truly evil. So are some Lemurians. But most are not. Where it truly counts, most of the populations of your nations are strikingly the same. With the same hopes, fears, and dreams. The same love for their families and respect for their elders. You're only enemies at this moment because of the actions of corrupt leadership, using you as pawns in a game of their own making."

He smiled slightly. "I'm just an academic who's had to adapt to extraordinary circumstances. But one advantage of studying history is seeing patterns repeat. And I can tell you this. The true heroes in any civilization's story are those who can see beyond the divisions of their time when it matters most."

Robert paused for several long seconds. "We don't have to like each other. We just need to work together for the next few hours. After that, maybe, just maybe, you'll have a chance to build a better world than the one that made you enemies in the first place."

With that, Robert nodded to Argo, who stepped up and reinforced the message in stronger, more military terms.

Robert surveyed the room and thought he could detect the temperature lowering, at least a little. He could only hope they had reached this group, and that they'd have each other's backs. Either way, they would find out in minutes.

Their mission, as usual, would be difficult enough. But if they couldn't operate as a cohesive group, they had no chance at all.

CHAPTER 70

The dense forest canopy on the island of Ulthat-Khem stretched below them as *Tala* descended through the cloud cover. Robert kept his focus on the bridge's main viewscreen. The crater's rim appeared through breaks in the forest. Steam rose from hidden geothermal vents.

"Attention, trespassing starship," said a deep male voice. "This is an automated sentry. You have entered restricted airspace. Compliance required. You have exactly three minutes from transmission's end to execute one of two authorized actions: Immediate departure vector south, or controlled landing at designated coordinates.

"Additionally, approaching within two miles of the northern crater perimeter will result in *immediate* engagement, even during the three-minute reprieve. Failure to leave or land upon expiration of this reprieve will result in automatic engagement by anti-aircraft and anti-starship defense systems.

"If landing option is selected, subsequent takeoff must include immediate southern departure or automated weapons systems will engage. This message will not repeat. Timer initiated."

Robert swallowed hard. They had known this wasn't going to be easy. Still, it didn't need to be *this* hard.

"*Tala*," said Argo, "show the number of seconds we can remain airborne in the right corner of the viewscreen."

Robert glanced up and 176 was showing on the screen. 175 . . . 174 . . .

He grimaced and turned to Argo. "I'm not complaining, but why give us warning? Why not just shoot us down immediately?"

"Standard operational security," replied the Atlantean commander. "Shooting down aircraft draws significant attention. Search and rescue teams, military investigations, debris fields that show up on surveillance satellites. Much better to scare off intruders so they assume it's just another military restricted zone. Most pilots turn around and are smart enough to never mention they inadvertently trespassed over a classified military installation."

"Then why give us the option of landing?" asked Robert.

"Knowing Kairos the way I do, it's a test. If a ship really is here accidentally, they'll leave like a bat out of hell the moment they realize they've stepped on a landmine. But if they're here on *purpose*, they might be tempted to land, which triggers security forces to scramble to the island to capture and interrogate those onboard. Assuming forces aren't *already* on the island, as they are now."

Robert nodded. That made sense. Once again, Kairos had landed on what seemed to be the optimal strategy.

"Is there anything we can fire at the facility that might make it through the sentry?" asked Matt.

"No," said *Tala*. "A weapon capable of shooting down something as fast as a starship can handle anything kinetic or energetic we throw its way. And the first time we try, it will destroy us wherever we are, in the air or on the ground."

"Speaking of the ground," said Argo, "Are your drones in place to transmit visuals?"

"Displaying visuals now," announced *Tala*, and on the magnified display, any number of hostile soldiers moved through the undergrowth.

"*Tala*, I want half the main viewscreen to show just Kairos and his two prisoners," said Robert. "On the other half, show the rest."

Instantly, the main viewscreen was cut in half. The monitor on the left showed five figures in the center of the pack, isolated and magnified. Kira's dark hair was unmistakable. Her hands were bound behind her back. Aethor walked beside her, similarly restrained. Kairos, with a guard on either side of him, drove the prisoners forward with a pistol.

Robert frowned. The monitor on the right displayed groups of soldiers on four separate tiles, but it was unclear if these images captured all of them, or how they were positioned.

Argo had the same issue. "*Tala*," he said. "Describe the positions of the different enemy units with respect to Kairos, and their numbers. Add in anything else you think will be useful."

"Kairos, two guards, and two prisoners are in the center of the formation, heading north toward the bunker facility. Three groups of ten soldiers are each stationed about forty yards from him, due east, due west, and due south. The final two soldiers are about sixty yards ahead to the north. It's unclear why they're using this asymmetrical setup.

"The bunker is located at the lip of an active geothermal crater surrounded by thick forest canopy. While the area just abutting the facility is open, it's cluttered with lava rock of various sizes, and the ground reads as too unstable and fragile to sustain a landing. In fact, because of that and the forest, scans show no suitable landing zones within four miles of the complex. Not for me, and not even for a shuttle. Which is why they're on foot, even though Kairos is immune from his sentry.

"Finally," added *Tala*, "battlefield comms won't operate within about two miles of the crater. As Argo noted earlier, the crater is rich with astrium deposits left over from an asteroid strike. While its crystalline structure amplifies certain signals by orders of magnitude, it also disrupts others. The sentry was able to get a highly boosted signal through from the crater, but a standard comm cannot."

Robert cursed. Things were looking bleaker than ever. They had to come up with a solid plan, and they had to do it in a hurry. His mind was racing, and so were those of his companions. Robert was still in command, but given that Ishar and Argo were both seasoned military leaders, he'd given them nearly unlimited latitude to issue orders of their own.

They needed to land in a hurry, that much was clear, and as close to the bunker as possible. The clock was—literally—running down. Kairos had all the advantages. He had a head start, outmanned them almost three to one, and held hostages that Robert would go to superhuman lengths to keep safe.

The only good news was that they were right about the island, and that Kairos and his prisoners were here. If Robert hadn't thought to locate this sight by tying it to scientists who had died under suspicious circumstances, they wouldn't have found him in ten lifetimes.

On the display, Kira walked like she was in a stupor, lifeless and uncaring. She tripped over a fallen branch, her bound hands preventing her from breaking her fall. She hit the forest floor hard, making no move to turn her head, luckily hitting at an angle that left her nose unbroken.

Kairos immediately trained his weapon on her. Robert almost screamed when the High Marshall pulled the trigger. The laser bolt struck a tree inches from her head. Bark exploded in a shower of splinters. Kira didn't even flinch or make any move to get out of the way of possible shrapnel.

It was as if she'd been drugged, or had withdrawn into herself, with her legendary determination and fight totally absent.

Argo was still deep in thought. "*Tala*, factoring in that Kairos's prisoners will slow him down," he said, "what is your best estimate as to when he'll arrive at the bunker?"

"In approximately eighty-three minutes."

Robert's jaw tightened. The bunker sat at the crater's edge, partially hidden by volcanic rock formations. Once Kairos reached it, he'd be able to access the control station and remotely activate the Nexus Prime weapon.

Argo glanced up at the countdown, which had reached ninety-four seconds. "Kairos has too much of a head start. Even slowed by his prisoners. We have to stall him. I recommend that we ignite the trees to his north while we're still airborne. Create a raging fire, a long wall of flames blocking his way forward."

"That's brilliant," said Robert. "That should stop him completely."

"Unfortunately not," replied Argo. "Their provisions are sure to include a handful of thermochromic nanofilm jumpsuits. Graphene-based. Standard precaution when operating near volcanic or geothermal areas, and compact enough to carry in a pack. They provide multipurpose protection against fire, cold, and energy discharge. Kairos will be able to use these to get through the fire. Nonetheless, the tactic will create chaos and slow him considerably."

"Which would normally be a very good thing," said Robert. "But given he'll be able to eventually get through, where will that leave *us*? How will we get through to go after him?"

"I carry four such nanofilm suits myself," noted *Tala*. "As far as igniting the fires, my best option would be to use my Plasma Pulse Arrays. But I'll need to fly closer to Kairos's forces to achieve the proper precision targeting."

"Do it!" said Robert. "Make sure the blaze is at least ninety yards ahead of Kairos. I don't want Kira anywhere near those plasma bursts, or the fire."

"Understood," said *Tala*. "I'll be careful to torch a corridor between Kairos and the facility without vaporizing the entire forest or killing him and his hostages."

"Hurry," said Matt. "The timer is down to seventy seconds."

"Activating Arrays," announced *Tala*. Her hull vibrated as the Plasma Pulse Arrays deployed. Six hexagonal emitters emerged from hidden panels. The arrays fired in sequence, sending rapid pulses into the distant woodlands.

The forest erupted into an orange inferno. *Tala's* quick, evenly spaced bursts created a wall of fire that Robert found astonishingly long, stretching across Kairos's intended path and extending for hundreds of yards on either side.

Ancient trees cracked and popped as flames consumed them. Smoke billowed upward. Thick black columns.

On the viewscreen, Kairos halted and shielded his eyes from the sudden barrier of heat and light materializing a hundred yards ahead of him. He turned and looked at *Tala* in the distance with an expression of disbelief and thrilling hatred before mayhem erupted in his ranks.

Robert locked his eyes on the image of Kira. As she saw the ship, she seemed to come back to life. At first, her eyes widened in dismay and disbelief, but then a broad grin came over her face and a look of defiance, both of which Robert felt were aimed directly at him.

"Warning! Sentry weapon systems charging!" announced *Tala* urgently. "Making emergency landing now!"

The ship banked hard to the south, her engines roaring. Seconds later she dove toward the forest canopy, her hull scraping against thick branches as she maneuvered into a narrow clearing. They touched down hard with twenty-eight seconds remaining on the timer.

"We're down and out of the line of fire," reported *Tala*. "The automated sentry implied that we wouldn't be targeted if we followed its landing orders within the allotted time.

An extra screen popped up on the main display, showing four Atlantean Sovereign Guards and eight Lemurian Protectorates standing beside each other at the ship's exit, preparing for deployment the moment *Tala's* ramp descended, all twelve performing equipment checks on their laser rifles and plasma weapons. Recent enemies preparing to fight side by side. Proof that some threats transcended even the deepest rifts.

Robert stared at the tactical displays, and his mind raced. He had read *The Art of War* by the famous military strategist, Sun Tzu, and tried to channel it now. All warfare is based on deception, Sun Tzu had famously written. Appear weak when you are strong, and strong when you are weak.

Great advice, thought Robert, as they hurried toward *Tala's* ramp. They were certainly weak now. But how in the world could they appear to be strong?

Electricity surged through Robert as an idea began to form. "Argo," he said while they strode through the cabin, "Kairos won't have any idea how we found him. After seeing *Tala*, he'll likely conclude the last few members of the Resistance somehow learned about this place. The important thing is, he'll think we're just a rag-tag group of outsiders making a desperate attempt to stop him. Crewed by me, Matt, and Ishar, along with maybe a handful of Lemurian soldiers."

Argo took the lead as they moved into the cargo bay, the ramp with all the soldiers waiting was just ahead. "How does that help us?"

"When we were at the Lemurian Outpost, we learned that your side had broken the encryption protocols they were using for battlefield communications."

"That's right," said Argo, stopping beside the troops. "Although I wasn't aware the Lemurians had already discovered this breach."

"Will Kairos and his men have this decryption intel?"

"Yes," replied Argo. "And he won't know that Lemuria discovered the breach, either. When he and his team intercept communications, the stolen decryption protocols will be automatically tried as a matter of course. I assume you plan to use that against him."

"Exactly," said Robert. "We can let him overhear our commands... on purpose. We can use two separate channels. One we want him to overhear, and one we can use to give our actual commands."

"How do we sell that?" asked Argo.

"We start by broadcasting a message we want him to intercept. To our entire team, informing them that we'll be using two channels for this Op. A general comm channel and a more exclusive comm channel for command personnel only. When Kairos can intercept one and not the other, he'll just assume they just happen to use different encryptions."

"Well done, Professor," said Matt. "What kind of disinformation did you have in mind?"

"Using the fake channel, we'll give orders to soldiers who don't exist. *Tala* can answer back for them, so they appear to be responding. That way, we can conjure up fake positions, phantom sniper teams, and so on. We can get Kairos to think he's surrounded by a full military operation. By a superior force."

"Now that's devious," said Ishar in admiration. "Even for an Anunnaki."

Argo quickly came up with a tactical plan and relayed it to the twelve elite soldiers.

"Remember," he added, "Kairos needs to be taken alive, if possible. He needs to be interrogated so we can learn just how deep the rot has penetrated. If he's killed, that will only put Lemuria at greater risk," he said pointedly, making sure the Protectorate commandos thought twice before acting on the utter hatred they were sure to have for the man.

"I say again," added Robert, "the two prisoners with him are also to be protected. At all costs! As I've told you, Lemuria and Atlantis owe their continued existence to their bravery. They've risked their lives many times over to save both nations. Exercise extreme caution, and hold your fire if there is any chance they might be hit.

"Obviously," he continued, "stopping Kairos from using the weapon is absolutely paramount. So, as a last resort, everyone is expendable." He paused, forcing three additional words from his lips that burned like acid on their way out. "Including the prisoners."

Robert's jaw tightened in resolve. He just had to be sure it didn't come to that.

"Hang in there, Kira," he whispered to himself. "We're coming for you."

CHAPTER 71

Kira Shelton felt numb, down to her very soul, her last shred of hope extinguished. When they had been dropped off in the middle of nowhere in Nasavi, awaiting another ship, Kairos had delighted in telling his two prisoners that *Tala* had been shot down, *obliterated*, and that Robert and Matt were dead.

He went on to boast how he had learned he was a wanted man from a trusted spy, and that they were about to be retrieved by a private army completely loyal to him. Most importantly, he had gloated that he had no need to return to the tunnel system at Nexus Prime to activate his weapon.

And now they were here. On the island that possessed a facility that could remotely trigger Nexus Prime to unleash absolute devastation. A facility that he alone knew about. Even now, his soldiers still weren't sure why they were ushering him to the bunker, but once he used the weapon, it wouldn't matter if they knew. It would be too late.

In less than thirty minutes, they'd arrive at the facility, and it would all be over. She'd be imprisoned for life, or killed, and history would proceed the way it had before.

But nothing mattered to her now, anyway. *Nothing*. Robert and Matt were dead. She had come to care dearly for the young Hopi and mourned him greatly. But a world without Robert? This was too much for her to bear.

She was unprepared for how devastated she was by this news. His death, along with the certainty that Kairos would win, had sapped her will to live. She was now nothing but the husk of a woman, not caring what happened, wanting to curl up into a fetal position and make the world go away.

The forest was an oxygen-rich maze of towering trees and dense underbrush, the air thick with the scent of damp earth and pine. She loved the forest, but not today. Not now.

Kairos and the two guards at his side continued to shove their prisoners forward, their grip bruising Kira's arms. Kairos had made sure the kit of every commando with him included a tranquilizer gun so that if Aethor escaped, they wouldn't have to use lethal force. Instead, they could bring him down with a neurotoxin dart that would knock him out for an hour or two.

Kairos had also removed the comm from his ear and affixed a different one to his lapel, and she and Aethor were close enough to hear his communications through a speaker. Kira suspected he had done this to impress his son with his command acumen.

Not that this had any chance of working. Aethor had protested his father's actions so often and so fervently, Kairos had made it clear that if Aethor spoke one more time without being asked, he would have him gagged.

Two scouts had been deployed to the north ahead to take out a pride of four American Lions, although Kira realized this wasn't the name the Atlanteans used. The lions had been seen moving north, toward where Kairos wanted to go, and the soldiers had just called in to say they had found these lethal predators and were tracking them farther north.

Kira had almost been devoured by beasts such as these, but she was rooting for them to survive and kill Kairos before he could make it to the facility, even if she had to die too.

Suddenly, the rustle of leaves underfoot was interrupted by a low, unnatural thunder that tore through the canopy, and her head snapped up. A searing orange glow erupted in the distance, about a hundred yards ahead, where the trees seemed to convulse in a wall of flame. The fire was alive, a writhing beast devouring the forest in a jagged line.

She glanced behind her and to the skies just in time to see a battle-scarred *Tala* darting away. The ship's identity was unmistakable.

Tala. Not destroyed, after all. Kairos had *lied*.

She suddenly felt an overwhelming certainty that Robert and Matt were also still alive. Kairos had told her otherwise out of sheer cruelty. But now her friends were here, just in time to work one final miracle.

Hope surged back into her like water from an exploded dam. If the trio of time-travelers were together, nothing could stand against them. Robert would find a way to come to her rescue and defeat Kairos once and for all. Her eyes had widened upon first spotting *Tala*, but now they narrowed defiantly, and she flashed a broad grin aimed straight at Robert.

The fire continued to rage ahead, spitting embers that moved like malevolent fireflies. Black smoke billowed and the air reeked of charred timber. The heat pulsed against her face, even from this distance, a suffocating wave making her skin prickle and her eyes sting.

Kairos and his men were caught completely off guard and lost their composure. Everyone spoke through the comms at once, an incomprehensible jumble as they tried to adjust to this new reality.

"Cut the chatter!" Kairos barked into his comm. The channel went silent immediately. "Disregard the aircraft. Automated sentry will force it groundside. Once down, expect enemy deployment. Maintain dispersal and do not cluster. Watch your sectors for movement in the treeline and monitor for enemy transmissions. Stay sharp."

He paused in thought. "Also, expect reconnaissance drones in the area. Forest density requires close-range surveillance, making them vulnerable to our short-range jammers. Deploy countermeasures immediately. Radio discipline from this point forward. Contact only for enemy sightings or critical intel. Out."

"This is Captain Malto," came a pained voice through the comm, one of the two men sent to clear predators from the perimeter. "We were . . . tracking the lion pride . . . got caught by the fire's edge. I'm badly burned. Blasreth is . . . he's dead. Need immediate . . . medical extraction—"

His voice trailed off, and it was clear he had fallen unconscious or dead.

Kairos gazed at the monstrous wall of flame and seemed unconcerned by the horrible fate of his two underlings. The fire was spreading, but the lack of wind, and the high humidity, were limiting its growth. Even so, he had their small group retreat fifteen yards farther south.

Kairos called a halt and turned to one of the soldiers beside him, who had just activated his datapad. "Get me a read on that fire."

The man frantically pored over his device. "Sensors indicate the fire stretches almost a quarter mile on each side of us in the east-west direction. They must have known we were heading north and wanted to discourage us from trying to go around it. It's only fifty yards thick, and growing quite slowly. Weather stations report a recent rainstorm across the island, leaving the forest damp and slowing the fire's spread, though pockets of drier underbrush still fuel a steady advance. It's burning at a temperature of five hundred degrees near the ground. About twice that higher up."

"How many thermochromic jumpsuits do we have with us?" he asked the soldier.

The man consulted his datapad. "Eight. They're being carried by Lieutenant Bartus."

"Get them!" said Kairos. "Bring them back here as soon as you can."

The soldier rushed off to carry out his orders while Kairos turned to his son. "How can your comrades know about this place?" he asked. "Was it *you*? Did you somehow manage to piece it together?"

"If I had," said Aethor defiantly, "I'd have sent the Resistance to destroy it."

"They'd have failed. Regardless, you and your friends continue to impress. It's sad that they're wasting their considerable talents opposing me, instead of helping me create a stronger world." He shrugged. "So be it."

"Councilor," came a voice over his comm speaker, "this is Captain Cantos, Shield Team Actual. We caught a break on enemy comms. One of their two channels is running encryption we cracked recently. We've been intercepting transmissions for the past several minutes and have assembled their overall tactical plan."

"Report."

"Their force consists of sixty Lemurian soldiers, including eight Protectorate. They're splitting into two elements, approaching from east and west simultaneously in a classic pincer movement. Objective is to compress us into a kill zone, then eliminate us with plasma rifles, laser rifles, and explosives. With enemy walls east and west, and a fire wall to the north, survivors will be channeled south, straight into the guns of their grounded starship."

"Solid tactical assessment," said Kairos, almost in admiration. He glanced north as the hellish fire raged on, and small animals continued rushing past, fleeing the inferno. "Countermeasures?"

"Affirmative. Digital terrain maps show their western element has to transit a narrow ravine, a natural choke point, half a mile out. We position at the exit and engage them as they emerge."

"Eastern element?"

"Three-quarters of a mile east, there's elevated terrain overlooking their likely route. We take the high ground and engage from a superior position. Since we're intercepting their comms in real-time, we'll know their moves before they execute. Should be able to neutralize the force despite being outnumbered. Only drawback is we'll need most of our personnel, so we can't provide adequate security for your position."

"Understood. Execute immediately. Send three men to me, split the rest into two forces to engage the incoming hostiles. I'll be transiting the fire wall and proceeding north. Be advised, after I advance another half-mile, comms will be down. Once you've neutralized the Lemurians, maintain alert status. I'll issue further orders when I'm back in range. I need every last hostile eliminated."

"Consider it done. I'll ensure our comms stay configured to intercept and decrypt Lemurian transmissions the moment they're issued."

"Good. I'm counting on you," said Kairos, signing off.

Kira was her determined self once again, and her agile mind was fully engaged. It was horrible luck that Lemurian comms had been compromised, but these soldiers had no idea that Robert carried a Vesh'tar, nor its extraordinary destructive capabilities. She was confident he'd win the day, despite the traps being laid for him and his comrades. She had to stall Kairos as much as she could until the cavalry arrived. Every second counted.

Over the next seven minutes, the soldier returned with the heat-resistant jumpsuits, and the requested reinforcements arrived, giving Kairos five soldiers at his side. The six donned jumpsuits while being sure at least one soldier was always able to train his rifle on the prisoners. Each suit also had a spacious outer compartment, extending nearly its entire length, large enough to hold a rifle and other weaponry and protect its contents from blistering heat.

When Kairos finished putting on the ultra-thin garment, he turned to Aethor and Kira. "Now it's your turn. Put on the suits. Quickly!"

Kira snorted. "You're out of your diseased mind, Kairos. Just kill us. Don't roast us to death in your flimsy little pajamas."

"Not pajamas," said Kairos. "Thermochromic nanofilm. Just four millimeters thick, but capable of protecting a wearer from temperatures up to eight hundred degrees for short durations. The molecular structure reflects radiant heat at the same time it dissipates thermal energy, preventing burn-through. The mask removes smoke and particulates from the air while letting in oxygen that has been flash-cooled to breathable temperatures."

"Wow, you're a natural salesman," said Kira, her voice dripping with sarcasm. "If this High Marshall thing doesn't work out for you, you could get a job with the pajama company that makes these things."

"Put it on! Now! Or I'll have my men put it on for you. Your choice."

Kira complied, but as slowly as possible, still fumbling with the suit when Aethor was already entombed by it. The jumpsuit was a technical marvel, sporting a deployable hood and oxygen mask with a transparent, heat-resistant visor and sealed seams, encasing the wearer from head to toe. Thin gloves and boots were integrated, using flexible, graphene-reinforced patches for dexterity and durability.

Fully unfolded, the material shimmered like liquid mercury, with faint hexagonal patterns visible under light, hinting at its nanoscale engineering.

As Kairos and the soldiers marched their prisoners closer to the towering wall of flame, Kira's feet crunched against the scorched earth, each step kicking up ash that swirled like gray snow in the air. Air that would have been scalding if not for her mask.

The inferno loomed ever closer, a monstrous wall of flame now almost eighty yards wide that shot orange and crimson tendrils thirty feet into the sky like coronal mass ejections from the sun. Heat shimmered in waves, distorting vision, yet Kira's flimsy suit kept her skin eerily cool while heading into an apocalyptic hell. Her heart beat hard against her ribcage, not from the temperature but from the sheer, towering menace of the blaze, its glow reflected in her wide, unblinking eyes.

They passed the corpse of Captain Malto, just short of the fire line. He had managed to make his way far enough south before expiring to still be just beyond the blaze. Kira almost vomited upon seeing him. His skin was a raw, blistered red, with his tattered uniform clinging to gaping burns that had seeped a mixture of blood, plasma, and melted tissue.

Kairos passed him without a second glance, staring into the raging maw of the voracious inferno. As they came to within fifteen feet of it, Kira trembled before its unthinkable power. Before a primal force that could consume an entire forest as if it were a light snack.

Kairos had already outlined how they would proceed from here. He and one of his soldiers would go through first. Once they were safely on the other side, the remaining four soldiers would sprint through behind Kira and Aethor, whose bonds had been cut to give them better balance as they ran through the flames. The prisoners would make it through before the soldiers behind them, but Kairos and his underling would have their guns trained on where they would emerge, giving them no hope of escape.

Kairos and his hand-picked second wasted no time before racing off into the heart of the blaze, but even in their supreme athletic condition, given low visibility and falling, burning branches, it took them almost a full minute to make it through. Once they had, they alerted the soldiers on the south side of the wall to follow suit.

Kira quickly moved to Aethor and pressed her head against his. "Stall them," she said, loudly enough for him to hear over the cacophony of the blaze, but not enough to be overheard by their four chaperones. The soldiers shouted for them to go, and then shoved them into the flaming forest when they hesitated.

Kira had known terror before, but being in the heart of a bonfire fueled a visceral dread, and she ran for fifteen seconds before panic subsided enough for her to remember her plan.

When she did, she slammed on the brakes and sprinted back the other way, daring the soldiers to follow her, or shoot her, as they ran for their lives, dodging falling branches and being terrorized by the mother of all nightmares come to life. She raced by them, her heart pounding against her chest like a caged, feral beast. As she had hoped, they were too preoccupied to shoot her or even slow their frenzied race to get to the other side.

Seconds later, she was back on the south side of the flames and her heart began to slow from its runaway pace. She paused to catch her breath and then made a beeline for the burned, fallen soldier named Malto, quickly relieving him of his weaponry.

She had passed the baton to Aethor, giving him the responsibility of stalling his father.

But now, with the fate of worlds on the line, she had other plans for herself.

CHAPTER 72

The wall of flames roared, a living barrier that split the island's dense canopy into a hellscape of orange and black. *Tala's* Plasma Pulse Arrays had done their job all too well, and the inferno's heat pulsed through the air.

Robert, Matt, and a pair of Lemurian Protectorate commandos continued to work their way toward the blaze at best possible speed, all clad in thermochromic nanofilm jumpsuits. They should be arriving at the inferno just about when Ishar and Argo were completing their missions, ensuring no enemy soldiers could pursue them from the rear.

Not that they would delay their pursuit of Kairos, even if Argo and Ishar failed. They were out of options, and they couldn't let anything slow them down.

***

Farther behind them, to the east and west, the forest was still cool, and Argo and Ishar led their squads of five into position, moving like phantoms through the underbrush. Each squad consisted of three Lemurian Protectorate commandos and two Atlantean Sovereign Guards.

Their fake communications had worked perfectly. Kairos's forces had taken the bait, splitting into two groups to counter a nonexistent pincer movement.

Argo's team crept toward the western ravine. Thirteen of Kairos's soldiers waited in ambush position, as they expected a Lemurian force of thirty. The actual force was much smaller, and it wasn't moving to flank Kairos as advertised.

Ishar's squad, meanwhile, stalked the eastern hill, where another fourteen Atlantean soldiers prepared to snipe from elevated ground.

The Atlanteans would soon be part of an ambush, all right, just not in the way they expected. Kairos's men were walking into the same slaughter they planned to *deliver*.

Argo crouched low, his laser rifle whirring softly. He signaled his team to fan out. The ravine was a natural choke point, its narrow exit framed by jagged volcanic rock and dense vines. Kairos's soldiers had positioned themselves just beyond it, expecting to pick off a large approaching force. Instead, Argo and his five commandos circled around, using the forest's density and the enemy's misguided focus to mask their approach. Argo was acutely aware that the men he now intended to slaughter had been his comrades less than a day earlier. He vowed not to let that slow him down.

"Set the pulse mines," he whispered into the secure comm channel.

His team moved, planting four grapefruit-sized devices along the path the Atlantean soldiers were likely to take once they realized the tables had been turned. The mines were programmed to detonate when they detected multiple heat signatures, spraying plasma shrapnel when activated.

"Done," reported Lieutenant Vara.

Argo paused to gather his thoughts. It was time to reassure the enemy he and his men were in the ravine, so the focus of Kairos's ambushing force didn't stray. It was time to be certain that the blinders Kairos's men had on were *cemented* to their faces.

"Orange Team," he said, using the compromised comm channel, "this is Commander Sagus. This ravine is becoming more restrictive than I'd hoped, funneling us toward a blind egress. When you emerge beyond the ravine, be alert for drones or possible random hostiles."

Argo ended his communication and peered through his visor's thermal overlay. Thirteen red silhouettes glowed against the cool green of the forest, clustered behind rocks and trees, their rifles trained on the ravine.

He shook his head in disbelief. Knowing they couldn't be seen from the ravine, they hadn't even bothered to block their IR signatures, an unforgivable oversight.

"They're locked in," he whispered into the secure channel. "On my mark, we hit them from the rear. Vara, take the left flank. Joren, right. The rest, with me. We go stealthy and fast."

The commandos nodded, their movements fast, silent. Argo counted down. "Three . . . two . . . one . . . now!"

The forest erupted. Argo's team opened fire with both laser and plasma rifles, with the Atlanteans using the former and the Lemurians the latter. Two of Kairos's soldiers dropped, their chests vaporized. The others spun, caught off guard, their formation crumbling as Argo's men advanced. The pulse mines detonated in a chain reaction.

Geysers of molten plasma blasted into the air. Three more soldiers screamed as shrapnel tore through their armor. Their bodies collapsed into the undergrowth.

"Push forward!" barked Argo, firing a burst catching another soldier in the shoulder, spinning him into a tree.

Vara lobbed a plasma grenade, which exploded in a flash between two soldiers. Blood sprayed onto nearby trees. Two other Atlantean soldiers attempted to escape the reverse ambush but chose a predictable route and raced through an invisible net of monofilament wire Joren had strung, slicing them to shreds. Their faces turned into gruesome masks of crimson liquid, as if they'd run through a spider web spun from razor-sharp threads. They fell to the forest floor. Their lips, tongues, and mouths so butchered they couldn't even scream in agony as they died.

After less than a minute, only three of Kairos's soldiers remained, firing wildly into the trees. Argo had lost two men of his own. Still, he and his three remaining comrades were relentless and used the terrain to their advantage. Vara took out one soldier with a headshot, while Argo pinned the final two behind a boulder. A well-thrown plasma grenade ended the fight. The explosion shook the ground and sent a plume of dirt skyward.

"Clear," said Argo, scanning the carnage. Thirteen bodies lay scattered about in grisly poses. Some so dismembered by blasts they were barely recognizable as humans.

Given how rapidly it had happened, and how startled and preoccupied Kairos's forces had been as they battled for their lives, Argo doubted they had the time, or presence of mind, to warn their forces to the east. Even if they had, provided Ishar had begun his attack on schedule, the two attacks would synch up and the warning would come too late.

"Regroup on me!" said Argo into his comm. "We'll advance at best speed to the east in case Ishar needs backup. Be mindful not to hit any of our own mines or monofilament nets on your way out of the kill box."

Argo blew out a long breath. He'd lost two men. Good men. The Protectorate and Sovereign Guard commandos had fought like brothers, side by side, and they'd managed to take out a force almost three times their number. So far, so good.

Surely Ishar would soon be reporting success. Until that happened, Argo wasn't about to take anything for granted.

***

On the eastern hill, Ishar moved with the speed of an Anunnaki. Although they sported large frames, they were quick. His squad of five had scaled the rocky incline without a sound. Kairos's thirteen soldiers were spread along the hill's crest. Their sniper rifles were trained on the path below. There, they waited for a nonexistent Lemurian squadron. Ishar signaled his team to prepare.

"Thermal decoys, now," said Ishar into the comm. The soldiers activated and released the small, automated bots. Since they weren't controlled remotely, they were immune from the countermeasures Kairos had used to take out *Tala's* recon drones. The bots had been programmed to project holograms of Lemurian soldiers and emit false heat signatures, mimicking a force of thirty soldiers moving quickly through the forest below. The enemy snipers took the bait. Their laser rifles flashed as they fired at ghosts.

Ishar's team struck. He led the charge, a rifle in one hand and his curved, vibro-molecular battle knife in the other. The first sniper never saw him coming. The man's head rolled into the underbrush before he could scream. Blood spurted from his neck.

The others turned. Ishar's squad was already on them. Plasma and laser bolts lit up the hill, searing through armor. Through flesh. One of Ishar's commandos, Kael, triggered a micro-explosive trap they'd planted on the hill's slope. It sent a cascade of rocks and shrapnel onto three snipers, crushing them instantly.

The remaining hostiles tried to fall back. Ishar hurled a disruption grenade. Its electromagnetic pulse fried their comms, disrupted their targeting systems. Disoriented, five more fell to perfect shots from Ishar's team. An Atlantean survivor shouldered his rifle. Ishar surged forward in a blur. His long arm lashed out. His blade cleaved through the rifle, and then through the man's neck.

The last three soldiers attempted a desperate counterattack, but Ishar's four remaining commandos finished them with a barrage of laser and plasma fire.

"Area secure," he reported to Argo as blood dripped from his blade.

Ishar sighed. He and Argo had done their part. Now, it was all up to Robert, Matt, and two Protectorate commandos. The ambush teams had killed twenty-seven enemy fighters. *Tala* had reported that two more had been caught in the blaze that *Tala* had created, just before her recon drones had been disabled. Out of the thirty-seven humans *Tala* had identified upon arrival, only eight were left—Kairos, his two prisoners, and five Atlantean soldiers.

Robert and Matt should be reaching the fire any minute. Ishar desperately wanted to help them, but the fire would be impossible to cross. The only four fireproof suits available were all made for tiny humans.

Still, he had confidence in this small group. Protectorate commandos were unequaled, at least in the human sphere. And while Robert and Matt lacked experience, they also had hearts the size of *mountains*. If anyone could prevail through force of will alone, it would be them.

***

"Argo to fire team," said a familiar voice in Robert's ear as he and his team neared to within fifty yards of the wall of fire. Exactly where they suspected Kairos had crossed. "Mission complete. All hostiles eliminated."

"Outstanding," said Robert. "Congratulations to you, Ishar, and your ambush teams."

"Thank you. We took out twenty-seven men in total. Which means that Kairos is making his way to his destination with five Sovereign Guards and two prisoners. Unfortunately, the fire is wreaking havoc with *Tala's* IR sensors, and she won't be able to locate their positions."

"Understood," said Robert. "Can't be helped."

"Kairos may have left some traps behind," added Argo. "Consider moving east or west along the firewall before crossing."

Robert glanced at his companions questioningly and wasn't surprised to see them all shake their heads. "Negative, Argo. Any movement east or west will cost us time, which we don't have. I assume a straight line is still the shortest distance between two points, even here. Plus, the terrain is rough and unpredictable, so what seems like a small detour could lead to a large time sink."

"I figured that would be your response, but I felt I had to offer the choice. Stay alert. And good luck."

"Thanks," said Robert, just as he reached the edge of the inferno with Matt and the two Protectorate commandos. All four stood facing the flaming leviathan, bracing to charge through it. Robert's heart thumped wildly. Not from the thought of entering the blaze, but from the thought of Kira on the other side at Kairos's mercy. He cursed again that he'd lost his Vesh'tar. Its absence felt like a missing limb. With the ancient marvel in his hands, nothing could have stood in his way.

Robert exchanged an anxious glance with the young Hopi at his side. "Let's do this," he said. "Talk about jumping out of the frying pan and into the fire. I always thought that was just a metaphor."

He turned to the two Protectorate commandos, Toren and Syla. "Matt and I will take point. You two can cover our flanks."

Both shook their heads simultaneously. "That isn't happening," said Syla, the more senior of the two. "Command or no command. You're civilians. I don't care how talented you are, you won't be leading the charge into possible traps while I'm around. We'll go first. Wait thirty seconds and follow."

Robert opened his mouth to argue, but Syla wouldn't have it. "You're in command, but this isn't up for debate."

"Okay," said Robert grimly. "You win. See you on the other side."

Syla nodded, and then he and Toren charged into the flames, quickly disappearing from sight. Robert and Matt waited the allotted time and plunged into the fire, their suits deflecting the searing heat as flames roared around them. Visibility was nearly zero, and the air was a haze of smoke and embers. The fire had scorched away much of the underbrush, simplifying their path, but the ground was uneven, littered with smoldering branches and hidden roots.

They ran blindly, weaving through the blaze accompanied by the crackle of flaming trees. Robert's lungs burned from the exertion. Matt's heavy breathing echoed beside him. The fire-wall stretched on, nearly two hundred yards wide now, a relentless gauntlet of heat.

Syla's voice boomed through their comms as they ran. "Warning! You're moving into an ambush! Four hostiles west of the fire's edge, concealed behind treeline! Hold position before exit to clear your weapon from storage. After exiting, engage targets, find cover, whatever it takes to stay alive. We're engaging now, but they're entrenched!"

Robert's stomach lurched as shock spiked through him. Argo had warned of booby-traps. Not soldiers lying in wait. Kairos was even more cunning than they'd feared, leaving a rear guard to slaughter anyone who made it through the blaze.

He and Matt slowed as they neared the fire's northern edge. They halted, fumbling to remove their plasma rifles from the sealed outer compartments with hands still encased within thin, protective gloves.

Through the thinning smoke, Robert glimpsed bursts of blue-white plasma bolts and the flashes of laser fire. Syla and Toren were already locked in combat, their silhouettes darting between trees. The ambush had caught even the elite commandos off guard. The enemy's position was strong.

Robert nodded at Matt, still gasping for breath. They ran through and then out of the fire zone and into the still-intact forest. Robert darted left, Matt right, weaving between trees. Shouts and laser rounds echoed to the west, where the Protectorate commandos continued to draw enemy fire.

As Matt sprinted away from the flames, a root snagged his foot. He stumbled. His momentum slammed him head-first into a thick trunk. He went listless, unmoving, his rifle skidding across the forest floor.

"Matt!" yelled Robert. He scrambled to his young friend and dragged him to cover behind a massive trunk. He checked his pulse. Steady. But Matt was out cold, a bruise blooming on his forehead.

The situation was spiraling out of control. Their two elite allies had somehow managed to avoid getting killed immediately and were keeping the enemy occupied. But they were outnumbered, and with so many trees for cover, this was a battle that could remain a stalemate for some time. Kairos was too far ahead for them to waste another second. They needed to flush the enemy out somehow. They needed to do it *now*.

Robert hit his palm against his forehead. Of course. He was being an idiot. He shouldn't need a neon sign to see the obvious.

He switched to the compromised comm channel. "Toren, Syla," he said, still breathing hard. "What is your precise position with respect to the hostiles?"

There was an extended pause. Robert prayed this meant they remembered they were being overheard and would respond accordingly.

"Four hostiles, all to our west, concealed behind boulders and trees," said Syla. "Toren and I have ceased fire, hoping they'll think we're down and drop their guard. We're maneuvering around to their rear now and will be in position in under a minute. Keep laying down suppressing fire in their direction. Make sure they stay focused on you until we can neutralize them."

"Will do," said Robert. "Alert me when you're in position."

Robert fired blindly in the direction of the Atlantean guards, but high enough to avoid hitting his allies. Since they'd said they were circling to the west of the Atlantean soldiers, that meant they were really circling to the east, waiting for the enemy fighters to train their focus in the wrong direction so they could emerge from behind and take them out.

"We're due west of them now," whispered Torren through the comm. "Working our way toward their backs. Keep them facing your direction."

The two Protectorate commandos advanced on their quarry from due east, crouching low in the underbrush and remaining perfectly stealthy. They soon had a pair of hostiles in their sights. Firing simultaneously, they dropped the two.

But they had miscalculated. Kairos's forces had split their focus. Two faced west as expected. But two others faced east, watching Robert's position.

Which meant they were now facing Syla and Toren.

When the Protectorate Commandos had fired, they had given away their positions. Both surviving enemies returned fire instantly. Syla crashed to the ground, dead. Toren's knee exploded.

Toren ignored the agony. Grunting through the comms, he went to the ground, rolled, and lined up his targets in the blink of an eye. He fired twice. Two kills.

But it was too late. Syla was gone, and he was crippled.

"All clear," Toren managed to spit out, his voice reflecting his agony. "Can't . . . walk."

"Coming to you," said Robert, lifting Matt in a fireman's carry and joining Toren less than thirty seconds later. He set Matt down and bent low to examine Toren's knee and administer first aid.

"Go!" said Toren. "I can patch myself . . . up . . . and watch your friend." He gritted his teeth, doing his best to manage the pain. "No one else is . . . coming. I have a rifle in case predators . . . stop by. You need to stop Kairos. Now!"

"I have to move both of you farther away from the fire."

Toren shook his head. "We're far . . . enough, and still in protective . . . suits. I can drag us both away if I have to." He fumbled at his belt, pulling off his last grenade, seeming to manage his pain better the more he spoke. "Take this. Hook it here . . ." He tapped Robert's belt. "Press the activation stud with your thumb one second before you throw. The proximity sensor . . . calculates the perfect . . . detonation point. Smart little bastards."

Robert clipped it on. Cold weight against his hip.

Toren unholstered his sidearm. "Extra firepower." Robert secured it in his chest holster. Two guns now. He'd need them both.

"Go! Get that bastard. Make this all worth something."

"Count on it," said Robert.

He quickly unsealed his suit, and it collapsed to the ground. He pulled the thin fabric of the built-in gloves and boots from around his hands and shoes. "Hang in there," he said to Toren, and then raced off to the north, plasma rifle in hand, driven by his hatred of Kairos and his fear of what this tyrant had planned.

But as he dashed through the thick forest, an epiphany hit him. He realized he was fooling himself. Because he wasn't thinking of Kairos at all. He was thinking only of *Kira*.

He had to save her. Nothing else mattered.

His fatigued legs weren't churning out of hatred. They were churning out of *love*.

He was in love with Kira Shelton, he suddenly realized. *Madly* in love. Hopelessly, passionately, *desperately* in love. And this had come about even though he'd never truly held her, or kissed her, or shared any type of true physical intimacy.

They'd stood shoulder to shoulder in life-and-death situations. Had battled together in the face of impossible odds, as they were facing now. When they'd partnered before arriving in this time, he'd only seen a *shadow* of Kira's true qualities. Yet, here he'd witnessed it all. Her comradery, her sense of humor. Her intelligence, her drive. Her spirit, her indomitable will. And her incredible courage.

This was a stunning, accomplished woman whose smile, whose laughter, could light up a city.

The question wasn't, how could he have fallen in love with her? The question was, how could he *not* have?

It was now clear that he'd been suppressing his true feelings for some time. But no longer. He felt himself finally surrender to a love that refused to be denied. He allowed it to penetrate every atom of his heart, soul, and mind as he ran, and a renewed strength surged into him.

A strength he doubted even his Vesh'tar could have provided.

CHAPTER 73

Aethor stumbled through the forest, prodded forward by his father and a single Sovereign Guard. He was horrified that Kira hadn't made it through the fire. If her suit had malfunctioned, he couldn't think of a more terrible way to die.

The small party of three had long since shed their fireproof garments, and Aethor's hands were bound behind his back once more. The wall of flames roared to the south, blackening the sky, but his focus was on his father, Kairos, marching beside him toward the bunker.

Kira had asked him to stall his father. That's exactly what he planned to do. Kairos had already shown he wouldn't kill his son, even going to the trouble of ensuring his troops carried a non-lethal weapon. The man saw his son as too much of an extension of himself. Saw qualities in him that he admired, and even had a twisted respect for Aethor's defiance.

Aethor closed his eyes for a moment and braced himself for what was to come. He was about to demonstrate his defiance yet again.

He pretended to stumble. Collapsing to his knees in the damp underbrush. Shouting out in pain.

"Move!" barked the Atlantean soldier at his side, jabbing him with the butt of his rifle.

Kairos turned, eyes narrowed. Aethor seized the moment. He rolled sideways, kicking out at the soldier's legs, sending him stumbling. Before Kairos could react, Aethor scrambled to his feet and bolted away to the south through the ever-present forest, weaving between trees.

"Stop him!" roared Kairos. "Remember, tranq gun only!"

Aethor was fast, despite his bound hands. He ducked under low branches, his breath ragged, but he slowed down on purpose. His goal wasn't to escape. It was to remain just out of reach for as long as he could, tempting his father to backtrack for an extended period of time.

The soldier gave chase first. Boots crunched through the undergrowth, with Kairos close behind.

"Aethor!" his father bellowed through the trees. "Stop this idiocy! You have no chance of escape."

"What's the matter, old man?" shouted Aethor as he moved. "Worried a High Marshall can't keep up with a bound physician?"

Aethor hoped that would be enough to keep his father motivated, because he couldn't waste either time or energy on further shouts. He channeled all his focus into running, into staying at large for as long as he could. Kairos and his lone soldier got off several shots with tranquilizer guns but missed wide each time.

Aethor somehow managed to keep ahead of his pursuers for almost ten minutes but was beginning to falter. It was tough going, and the two men chasing him moved faster through the challenging terrain than he did. He only managed to stay ahead because he'd often disappear from sight behind thick tree trunks, causing them to have to momentarily pause to regain his trail. But he was now gasping for breath with every step and couldn't remain clear much longer.

Still, any delay he created was multiplied. Once he was recaptured, they'd have to return to where they'd begun, and in their fatigued state, the return trip would take much longer than the outgoing one.

A petrifying, primal growl stopped Aethor dead in his tracks. In a small clearing ahead, a massive, short-faced bear lumbered into the shadows. Its dark eyes gleamed. Aethor had never seen one in person but instantly recognized the giant figure, looking like a wildly overgrown grizzly with a short snout and sunken face. A solitary hunter, it was the largest and most powerful predator on Earth, and it looked *hungry*.

Its hulking frame tensed. Lips peeled back to show bone-crushing teeth. Aethor's blood turned to ice, his veins like mini glaciers. He'd meant to delay Kairos, not die in the jaws of an unstoppable beast.

The bear rose on its hind legs to its full height of over twelve feet and then dropped down again and charged, barreling toward Aethor at more than thirty miles per hour.

Aethor dove aside, slamming into a tree as the beast's claws swiped the air inches from his head. The Atlantean soldier caught up, raising his rifle, but instead of targeting Aethor, he fired at the bear. The creature bellowed, the shot grazing its side, and it wheeled on the soldier, who fired again and again, having to strike the beast in the chest five times to put it down. The bear fell in a heap, its bloody carcass twitching before going still.

Aethor struggled to his feet, panting. The soldier was on him in an instant, slamming him to the ground.

"Enough!" shouted Kairos, his voice cutting through the forest as he approached, a small stun pistol in his hand. "I wanted to keep you awake, Aethor. To witness the activation of the Nexus Prime weapon, a triumph I know you'll come to appreciate in the fullness of time. But I can't have you slow me down anymore. You're more trouble than you're worth."

With that, Kairos fired a dart into Aethor's neck, who was still pinned down. Aethor's world blurred as the neurotoxin took hold. Aethor's limbs grew heavy, his vision darkening.

***

Robert raced northward alone, his plasma rifle gripped tightly, its weight a poor substitute for his lost Vesh'tar. Matt was back there, wounded but alive, as was their Protectorate ally.

Love, and the abject terror he felt at the thought of losing Kira, spurred Robert on, allowing him to exceed his own physical limits by a considerable amount, maintaining a pace he would have bet his life he couldn't maintain.

He stopped and peered into the distance. The trees were thinning considerably as he approached the crater, and he could finally make out the facility at the outer boundary of his vision. A flicker of motion caught his eye. Through a break in the foliage, he spotted Kairos as he marched toward the bunker, just fifteen yards ahead of him!

Incredible. He'd caught up in time. A miracle.

The High Marshall carried a pistol in his hand. Beside him, a single Atlantean soldier carried Aethor's limp form across his shoulders, a laser rifle slung behind his back.

Robert's heart caught in his throat. Where was Kira? Had Kairos shot her? Had she fallen in the blaze?

He sank to his knees, and for precious seconds, his mind was on fire. He couldn't think, couldn't function. Panic. Anguish. Both mixed to form a debilitating miasma, his eyes suddenly unable to focus.

Finally, as a tear rolled down his cheek, he used his last ounce of will to push her from his mind. He didn't have the luxury of becoming paralyzed, of torturing himself by imagining horrific ways she might have died.

Kira must have escaped. He refused to believe otherwise. Knowing her, it was a wonder Kairos had managed to keep her contained for as long as he had. By now she was probably back with Ishar and Argo, or safely aboard *Tala*, devising a strategy to save the day—one they'd missed, entirely.

After five more minutes of slow going, largely due to Aethor needing to be carried, Kairos called a halt. Robert crept forward all the while, maintaining his distance, and the bunker was now close enough to see clearly. Its silhouette loomed through the ever-sparser tree cover, a large, one-story obsidian building, a hundred feet on a side, sitting in a pool of volcanic rock at the crater's edge. Its surface shined unnaturally, reflecting the orange glow of distant flames. Robert crouched behind a gnarled tree and considered his next move.

Kairos walked forward again and stopped ten yards from a whirring energy shield surrounding the entire facility, where it protected multiple entrances. He barked an order and his Sovereign Guard set Aethor down, propping him against a large, volcanic rock, while Kairos pulled a datapad from his belt and began tapping. Minutes went by as he entered codes, likely clearing nested authentication protocols. Finally, the shield's hum intensified before abruptly ceasing, the blue shimmer collapsing around the extensive structure like a falling curtain. Kairos dragged Aethor's unconscious body onward. The three crossed the threshold into the bunker's perimeter.

Robert braced himself for action. The shield would likely reactivate soon. He had one chance.

A rustle behind him made him spin, rifle raised. Matt stumbled into view, his face pale, a welt on his forehead. "I woke up just after you left," he said. "And followed you. Can't let you have *all* the glory." He forced a smile. "Damn, you're fast for an aging professor."

Matt looked terrible, barely hanging on, but too much was at stake to refuse his help. "Stay sharp, Matt. And stay behind me."

They sprinted from cover, legs pumping, plasma rifles and pistols bouncing against their chests. The Atlantean soldier with Kairos glanced back, eyes widening, but Robert and Matt were already halfway across the clearing. A laser bolt screamed past Robert's ear, scorching the ground. Robert dove, rolling behind a boulder as another shot vaporized a chunk of rock inches from his head. Matt ducked beside him, firing a wild plasma burst forcing the soldier to take cover.

Kairos now stood over his son's body at one of the facility's entrances. He glanced back, his face a mask of cold fury, and hoisted Aethor to his shoulders, entering the building. The Sovereign Guard retreated toward the door Kairos had used, firing to keep Robert and Matt at bay. The shield's whirring sound began to build again, a low whine signaling its imminent reactivation.

Robert gnashed his teeth. They had seconds. He unhooked the grenade from his belt, pressed the button, and let it fly. The device arced high as Matt fired another plasma burst, the blue-white bolt grazing the soldier's leg. The grenade erupted, a shockwave of sound and force sending the soldier staggering, his rifle clattering to the ground. Matt surged forward, firing a plasma burst. The beam punched through the soldier's chest, and he crumpled, lifeless, just outside the door Kairos had used.

The shield's whine intensified. Robert and Matt ran faster than ever, lungs burning as they dove through the closing gap. A crackle of the shield's energy grazed Robert's back, but they were through. The shield snapped back into place behind them with a loud whir, sealing them inside the perimeter.

They ran toward the door and found it wasn't locked. The energy shield had been designed to keep trespassers out. The door, on the other hand, had not been. They rushed inside, but no sign of Kairos. He'd disappeared into the depths of the facility, presumably still carrying his son.

Matt swayed, his eyes fluttering. "Can't . . . keep up," he mumbled, collapsing against a wall, his weapon slipping from his hand. "Go," he whispered faintly before his eyes closed.

Robert checked his pulse. Faint, but steady. A good sign. No lethal wounds or injuries. Matt was unconscious, but likely only because he had pushed his battered body beyond its current limits.

He gave his young friend one last look, and then, steeling himself, stepped farther into the facility.

Inside, the bunker stretched ahead like a hospital corridor. Blue conduits pulsed along the walls and cast everything in a sickly light. The air hummed with the low thrum of machinery. Robert took one silent step after another, plasma rifle ready, tracking the echo of Kairos's boots somewhere in the depths.

The passageway opened into a central chamber, a large circular room dominated by a towering control console, with several pillars rising from floor to ceiling around the perimeter. Aethor was slumped against a wall, still unconscious. Holographic displays flickered, showing maps of Atlantis, Lemuria, and Nexus Prime. Kairos stood at the console where he'd likely been for minutes now, carefully inserting the palm-sized core processor, the quantum crystalline matrix he'd removed from Robert's pocket fairly recently, but also a lifetime ago. A glowing red lever hovered at Kairos's eye level, which Robert was certain activated the Nexus Prime weapon.

It was a low-tech control, but Robert understood why this would be. A holographic control could be activated by accident. A lever that needed to be forcibly pushed upward could not be.

"Move away from the console!" shouted Robert, stepping into the chamber, his rifle trained on the High Marshall's chest.

Kairos turned slowly, his right hand still very near the lever. He shook his head as if unable to believe that a Sovereign Guard had been bested by a civilian. "Where's your little friend?" he said. "He looked like he was about to drop dead at any moment. I suppose he finally did."

"He's alive and well. Sleeping off a minor concussion. *Tala* will have him back to normal in no time."

"You really are something," said Kairos. "As tenacious as a salmon fighting against the current. Your determination is beyond compare. But no matter, like the salmon, you'll still end up in the jaws of a predator in the end."

"You really like hearing yourself talk, don't you?"

"You're too late. You've come closer than I thought an entire army could ever get, but you've still fallen short." His hand inched toward the lever. "I push this up, and the Nexus Prime weapon blasts Lemuria. Total destruction. Mayhem. Few survivors. And that's just for starters. A new world will rise from the ashes. One *I* control."

"Where's Kira?" demanded Robert.

Kairos chuckled. "Did you not hear what I said? Your precious Lemuria is about to die and all you care about is this . . . *Kira*?"

"Where is she?" he screamed.

Kairos studied Robert for several seconds. "You're madly in love with her, aren't you? I can see it in your face."

Robert didn't bother to respond or deny the man's words.

"I can understand why you've fallen for her," continued Kairos. "She's a beautiful, extraordinary woman. Too bad she was lost in the fire. Or perhaps she made it back to the south side of the forest and she's cowering there, a broken woman. Either way, she's irrelevant now."

Robert was barely able to stop himself from issuing a primal scream. Instead, his finger tightened on the trigger, but he held back, wary of the console. Kairos was baiting him, trying to provoke a mistake. "You're outnumbered, Kairos. Argo and Ishar have taken out your men. Surrender now while you can."

"Argo?" said Kairos angrily. "I should have known he'd jump at the chance to betray me. How did you team up with him?"

Before Robert could reply, Kairos quickly moved his hand toward the lever. Robert fired multiple shots, causing the High Marshall to miss the lever altogether as the plasma rounds forced him to duck behind the console. Kairos returned fire with his laser pistol as Robert dove behind a large metal crate. The chamber erupted into a deadly exchange, beams and bolts crisscrossing the air. Robert shot cautiously, mindful of Aethor's position. Kairos fired with ruthless abandon, each blast shaking the crate.

Robert needed a plan. He was pinned down and had used his only grenade. If Kairos pushed that simple lever, all was lost. Robert peeked out, firing a burst to keep Kairos pinned, then rolled to a new position behind a pillar. A laser strike grazed his arm, searing through the outer layers of his skin. Pain lanced through him, but he refused to falter.

"You can't win," taunted Kairos, his voice reverberating off the walls. "You're fighting for a world that's weak and vulnerable. I'll make it unified. *Strong*. I'm not the monster you think I am. I'm humanity's salvation."

Robert's eyes darted around the chamber, searching for an advantage. The console was too far, and Kairos's position gave him perfect cover. Robert's heart sank. He was losing, and Kira was gone. He'd failed her. Failed *everyone*.

Kairos stepped out, laser pistol raised, and fired a quick shot. Not at Robert. At the pillar he was hiding behind. Several more shots. The pillar cracked, and one more direct hit caused it to buckle and fall. Robert jumped out of the way and into the open as the pillar crashed to the floor, pieces breaking off and careening through the air in all directions. Kairos had anticipated this outcome and rushed over to Robert on the floor, savagely kicking his fallen pistol away.

"You made a valiant effort," said the High Marshall, "You were a surprisingly worthy opponent. But, as I told you, your time has come to an end."

He extended the laser pistol, and his finger tightened on the trigger.

A sharp crack split the air. Kairos staggered, his pistol clattering to the floor as he clutched his neck, where a dart protruded. His eyes widened in shock before rolling back, and he collapsed, unconscious. Robert froze, holding his breath, practically paralyzed while he struggled to process what had just happened.

Kira Shelton stepped from the shadows of a side corridor. She gripped an Atlantean tranq gun in her hand, her face smudged with soot, eyes defiant.

CHAPTER 74

Kira glanced at Kairos for just a moment and then rushed over to Robert, who lay sprawled on the floor, dazed, speechless. Tears began streaming down his face. Not because he'd cheated death. Because Kira was alive and well. His relief was immense. Beyond anything he'd ever experienced.

Kira began shedding tears of relief and joy as well. She hugged him on the floor as if she'd never let go. Her touch felt electric, invigorating, like a long draw of spring water for a man dying of thirst.

They separated and she helped him up off the floor.

"How in the world?" he said in dismay. "How are you here? How did you do that?"

She wiped away tears with the back of her hand. "I could ask you the same. Why didn't you take him out with your Vesh'tar?" she asked, quickly surveying the room. "Where is it?"

He cringed. "I lost it in the Nexus Prime tunnels."

Kira was taken aback. "But Kairos's men intercepted your comms. They had you dead to rights. How did you win the day without it?"

"Long story. Why don't you start yours, and I'll chime in as needed."

She nodded. "Pretty simple, really. Kairos dressed us all in fireproof jumpsuits to move through the fire-wall. I was able to flee, and I doubled back through the blaze and relieved a fallen Atlantean of his weapons. Including a tranq gun. I knew I might be our only hope of stopping Kairos, but he had five Sovereign Guards with him."

"How'd you beat him here? He was ahead of you."

"A single person moves faster than a group of seven. And I asked Aethor to stall his father just before I escaped." She gestured toward her unconscious ally. "Looks like he came through."

Robert quickly explained about the ambush on the north side of the fire, and how he and Matt had arrived at the bunker. She listened with rapt attention.

"I didn't know Kairos had set up an ambush," she said. "But I didn't want to run into him, either. So I took a different route. I went through the fire a few hundred yards east, then straight north to the crater. Gambled I could beat them here and lie in wait."

"Then what? You expected to be up against Kairos and five elite soldiers."

She cringed. "Yeah. It was a suicide mission. My goal was to kill Kairos with the laser rifle before his men could kill me. Stop his weapon, even if it cost me my life."

Robert stared at her. This woman was *amazing*. In every way.

"When I got here, the terrain was mostly open rock," continued Kira. "Bad cover. So I hid behind a large boulder near the second entrance, waiting for Kairos to arrive and lower the shield."

She paused. "Then you and Matt showed up. I was too far out of position to help with the firefight, so I rushed the door the moment the shield dropped."

"And found it unlocked."

"Yes. Kairos relied on that energy barrier too much. I hid near the control room, had a shot lined up, but you entered and made him move. Had to wait for a cleaner angle. Figured it was best I use the tranq instead of the laser rifle."

"So let me get this straight," said Robert in amusement. "Because I lost my skirmish with Kairos so completely, I flushed him out into the open, which gave you the clear shot you needed."

"Pretty much. You provided the perfect distraction."

A broad smile spread across Robert's face. "Well, yeah. That was my plan. No way he could have beaten me otherwise. *Obviously*."

"*Obviously*," she repeated, matching his smile.

"I can't believe it's over," he said as the enormity hit him. "You did it."

"*We* did it. All of us." Kira's expression suddenly turned anxious. "Speaking of which, you told Kairos that Matt was alive and well. Please tell me that's true."

"It is. Thankfully."

Relief flooded her face. Then her expression grew serious. She looked down before looking back up. "You know . . . " her voice quieted. "I heard your entire exchange with Kairos."

"Yeah, the man is still as delusional as ever."

She stared into his eyes. "Was he delusional when he said you were madly in love with me?"

Robert nearly coughed on his own breath, if that was possible. He felt heat rush to his face. He opened his mouth, closed it, tried again. "I . . . that's . . . this is really . . . ."

"Robert?"

The words stuck in his throat. Everything he wanted to say, needed to say, but not here. Not now. Not with two unconscious men and a weapon of mass destruction surrounding them.

A nearby groan cut through the moment. Aethor was stirring.

"We need to move," said Robert, grateful for the interruption. "We need to disable the weapon and get the hell out of here. And get Matt treatment."

Kira nodded, though her eyes lingered on his face. Business first. The rest could wait.

"Right. I'll keep my rifle on Kairos," she said. "You wake up Aethor. We need him conscious to extract the crystalline matrix."

Robert moved to the doctor while Kira positioned herself with a clear shot at the High Marshall, still motionless.

"Aethor." Robert shook the man's shoulder. "Come on, wake up."

Aethor's eyes fluttered open. He gasped and jolted upright, eyes darting everywhere. "Where are we?" he mumbled in confusion. "How are you here? Where's my father?"

"What's the last thing you remember?"

Aethor paused in thought. "I was creating a distraction. Stalling my dad. Almost got killed by a bear. And then my father shot me with a knockout dart."

"Well, your stall tactics worked. You bought us enough time to catch up with him. We're in Kairos's remote facility. Kira managed to hit him with a tranquillizer dart before he could activate the Nexus Prime weapon."

Robert helped his dazed colleague into a sitting position. "Your father got close," he said. "Too close. He installed the quantum device into the system. Can you remove it?"

Aethor nodded. "Absolutely."

"How long until Argo gets here?" asked Kira.

"He'll be here as soon as he can," replied Robert. "As soon as that wall of fire dies down."

He turned to Aethor. "This site contains an automated anti-aircraft sentry. And is currently surrounded by an energy shield. Do you think you can disable both?"

"Yes. Easily. These defenses are nearly impossible to disable from the outside, but child's play to disable from within. Like a dead-bolt lock. I'll have both turned off in no time."

"Great," said Robert. "Then I'll leave you to it." He picked up Kairos's fallen rifle. "I need to see how Matt's doing."

Robert strode to where he had left Matt, glancing over his shoulder as he moved. Kira had settled in to wait with a weapon aimed at the most dangerous man on the planet, while Aethor had already begun walking toward the console to remove the crystal before lowering the energy shield surrounding the bunker.

Just another day in ancient civilization paradise.

A few more steps down the passageway, and Robert stole a glance back at Kira. The question she'd asked hung between them like smoke. When this was over, when they were safe on the ship, they'd need to finish that conversation.

His pulse spiked like a fever just thinking about it.

***

Just over five hours later, Robert sat on *Tala's* bridge, watching Matt do his best to sprawl across one of the seats. *Tala* had helped revive the young Hopi, but he still looked like he'd been hit by a freight train, his face a roadmap of bruises.

Aethor sat across from them, turning the quantum crystalline matrix over in his hands. The palm-sized device looked innocuous enough. Hard to believe something so small was instrumental in getting the gargantuan Nexus Prime to unleash a fury that could destroy continents.

"The Lemurian Circle will secure this properly," said Aethor. "My father's weapon will die with his ambitions."

Robert nodded.

Ishar sat silently off to the side, having made it clear that he wanted to be left alone to mourn his fallen comrades. The surviving Guards and Protectorates had made their way to the cargo bay, most likely sharing war stories about the firefight they'd just survived.

Kairos was being held in *Tala's* brig, soon to be turned over to Atlantean authorities to face justice for his treason.

Clean operation. No loose ends.

Everything was under control. Mission accomplished.

Robert winced. At least the mission affecting the fate of worlds had been accomplished. But there was one mission left. The daunting task of revealing to Kira exactly how he felt about her.

He glanced toward the crew quarters, knowing Kira was inside her room. He had deposited her there and asked her to give him five minutes to check on Matt, Aethor, and Ishar on the bridge before he returned to have the conversation they had put off until now.

Robert finally gathered enough courage to leave the bridge. The short distance he travelled to Kira's crew quarters felt like miles, and his head was spinning as he reached her open door. She was sitting on the bed. Their eyes met. He gave her what he hoped was a casual smile, which probably looked more like a grimace.

The room was average-sized. Just a bed, a locker, basic amenities. Every wall closed in on him. A least it felt that way. The door automatically shut behind him, as if *Tala* knew they needed privacy.

He sat on the edge of the bed next to her, careful to leave space between them. The silence stretched like a taut wire. "Okay," he said with a sigh. "I'd better get right to it, or I might just lose my nerve. Let's start where we left off. You overheard Kairos say that I'm madly in love with you."

"I did," said Kira softly. "So, was he delusional? Or was he right?"

The question floated. No escape route this time. No unconscious Councilor or doomsday weapon to interrupt. Robert stared back and winced. "I am *so, so* sorry," he began, trying not to stammer. "This is really awkward. *Really* awkward. But you deserve the truth. He wasn't delusional. Not about *that*. I am in love with you, Kira. Madly in love. Despite my best efforts to push these feelings away."

He had never felt so helpless. So vulnerable. "I just realized the truth today. I've been fighting it with all my might for some time now. But once my feelings finally escaped, they all but consumed me.

"I love you, Kira. I love you more than I thought I could ever love anyone. You're in my thoughts almost every waking moment. And now you're even in my dreams. I am so sorry. I tried so hard to fight it, but I couldn't. You're beautiful, and brilliant, and engaging, and fun, and . . . *amazing*. In every way. How could I *not* be in love with you? Have you *met* you?"

Kira nodded slowly, taking it all in. "Why do you think you've been fighting it?" she asked.

Robert ran a hand through his hair. "First, because I know you wanted to keep our relationship professional. Second, because our lives have been on the line constantly since we got here. The more I cared about you, the more terrified I became of losing you. When I thought you were dead . . ."

"You were afraid it would paralyze you."

"It *did* paralyze me. When I couldn't see you with Kairos and Aethor, I could barely function."

She was quiet for a long moment. Robert's pulse pounded in his ears. "I'm sorry to spring this on you like this," he said finally. "I just hope it won't ruin our friendship."

Kira had been poker-faced throughout, but now she issued an impish, radiant smile. "*Never*," she said, almost looking giddy. "Because I feel the exact same way about *you*. We were *both* fooling ourselves. The professional relationship we pretended to have had been over for quite a while now."

Robert felt his breath catch. He hadn't dared hope his feelings would be returned.

"Before you arrived on the island," she continued, "Kairos convinced us you were dead. It was the cruelest lie he could have told. I was *devastated*. Beyond words."

Robert flashed back to the drone footage of her on the island when they had first arrived. She had looked like she had given up—like she had wanted to die. Now he knew why.

"It turns out I've been fighting the same feelings you have. And losing."

Kira stared deeply into his eyes. "I love you too, Robert," she said softly. "Like you, I tried to suppress it. But like you, I failed. You're truly remarkable, Robert Shaw. Exceptional. Unlike any man I've ever met. When I thought I'd lost you, none of our professional concerns mattered anymore. All I could think about was how I should have told you how I felt. You have this way of being wonderful and irresistible when I least expect it."

"Irresistible, huh?"

"Don't let it go to your head."

They sat there grinning at each other. The tension that had been building finally had somewhere to go.

"I can't even imagine my life without you," said Robert softly.

"Then don't." Kira's voice was barely a whisper. "We don't have to fight ourselves anymore. Don't have to hide from each other."

Robert reached out and cupped her face with his hand. She leaned into his touch, her eyes closing for a moment.

"So what now?" he asked.

"Now we stop pretending we don't feel this way."

She leaned forward and pressed her lips to his. The kiss was gentle at first, tentative, like they were both afraid it might shatter. Then something burst open between them.

Robert pulled her closer as the kiss deepened. Her hands tangled in his hair, and he could feel her heart racing against his chest. It was like touching a live wire, electric and overwhelming.

They kissed with desperate intensity, making up for all the words they'd held back, all the moments they'd fought against this. Her lips were warm and soft, and when she made a small sound against his mouth, Robert thought his heart might stop entirely.

When they finally broke apart, both breathing hard, Kira smiled that radiant smile that lit up everything around her.

"I've wanted to do that for so long," she whispered.

"Me too." His voice was rough. "Though I have to say, your timing is perfect. Nothing like surviving mortal combat to put things in perspective."

She laughed, and the sound sent warmth flooding through him. "We should probably get back before they send a search party."

"Probably." Neither of them moved. Robert traced his thumb along her cheek, still hardly believing this was real.

"Robert?"

"Yeah?"

"I'm glad Kairos was finally right about *something*."

He grinned and kissed her again, slower this time, savoring it. When they separated, he rested his forehead against hers.

The ship whirred around them, carrying them toward whatever came next. But for the first time since arriving in this ancient world, Robert wasn't worried about the future.

They had each other now. And when they were together, there was nothing they couldn't achieve.

CHAPTER 75

Six Days Later

Robert shifted in the crystal-inlaid chair, still processing the grandeur of the Lemurian Grand Chambers. The dome soared more than eight stories overhead. Its translucent panels let in diffused light that played across the mushroom-like walls.

Were they really made from mushrooms? Robert didn't know, but it sure looked that way. The surface had an organic quality, and was a little fungal in nature, a bit alien-looking.

The past six days had been a whirlwind of activity. On the ship, he and Kira had allowed themselves maybe ten minutes to kiss, hold each other, and luxuriate in their newfound intimacy. And after that, they found many ways to privately celebrate their love. Matt had made a full recovery. Kairos had been imprisoned, and Aethor had returned to Atlantis. Who knew where the heck Ishar went.

Once the High Councilor had learned of Aethor's role in stopping his father, he'd been impressed beyond measure and was sizing Aethor up for significant roles in Atlantean government, if the young physician could be persuaded to serve.

Finally, they had turned over the island and the facility there to Lemurian authorities. To study and dispose of as they pleased.

And now all the parties involved in stopping Kairos sat among hundreds of dignitaries and officials in a truly magnificent venue, with Robert sitting next to Kira and Matt on one side and Elowin on the other. Floating camera orbs drifted through the air, broadcasting the proceedings to all of Lemuria.

The chamber stretched before him, dominated by a raised podium and stage draped with banners. A wide aisle bisected the tiered seating, where Protectorate warriors and Lemurian soldiers stood at attention alongside Elders wearing autumn-colored leaf headdresses cascading down their backs like feathers.

The head of the Lemurian government, Huku Nali, stood at the podium. His voice resounded through the space as he droned on about unity and cooperation between all nations of the world. Robert was surprised to find that proximity to Elowin Balivae still somehow triggered him to have an almost supernatural attraction to her.

But this knee-jerk response, this uncontrollable subjugation to irrational emotion, had lost its grip. Because what he had felt for Elowin was largely the result of a kind of chemically induced anomaly triggered by her mere presence. The love he felt for *Kira*, on the other hand, was *real*. It was a love she had *earned*.

And a love they had recently disclosed to their friends, although they strived to maintain professionalism while interacting with each other around others. Behind closed doors, on the other hand, things were dramatically different.

But what would the future hold? Not for them as a couple, but for the world?

He, Kira, and Matt had done what *Tala* had hoped they would do, and the ship was ready to return them to their own time. This had raised a host of mixed emotions in each of them, ranging from sadness to abject terror.

Sadness, because they had forged such close bonds with any number of people here, whom they would miss dearly. And terror because of what they might find when they did get back to their own time, with the expectation that *nothing* would be recognizable. That no one or no thing they had known would still exist.

Time travel and its rules were likely to be exceedingly complex and unknowable. It didn't take a logician to realize they hadn't just made a *negligible* change in the past, such that the tides of time would eventually recover their intended flow.

They had made an *epic* change. A *gargantuan* change.

Civilization here was so hyper-advanced it put the one they had come from to shame. Before they had changed things, the Nexus Prime weapon had been used, plunging humanity back to such a primitive state of science and technology that it hadn't fully recovered, even after almost thirteen thousand years. And, at a minimum, tens of millions of people had perished.

No longer. Now, these people *wouldn't* perish. They would go on to have offspring, and their offspring would have offspring, and so on, with billions of people ultimately descending from them. This would change the human gene pool beyond recognition, such that no one who had existed when they left their time would exist any longer.

It was a wonder *they* still existed. Robert theorized that they were somehow grandfathered in, having existed at the point of the change, so immune from it, even though they would never be born in the new timeline they had helped create.

And now, instead of humanity falling back into chaos and barbarism, the Atlanteans and Lemurians would have thirteen thousand years to advance their science and technology beyond its already extraordinary level.

So, what would Robert and his companions find when they returned to their time? Humanity that had achieved transcendence, with technologies and genetic enhancements that had turned them into veritable gods after thirteen thousand years of progress? Would human beings have achieved a state of perfect harmony with each other and the universe?

And where would Robert, Kira, and Matt fit in? Would they be so out of their depth they'd feel like amoebas trying to understand the mind and insights of Albert Einstein?

On the other hand, the aliens in the galactic community had yet to fully transcend. So perhaps there were limits to just how far science and technology could take a society. Even so, humanity in this new future would be far more advanced than it had been, and Robert, Kira, and Matt would still be the only three who remembered the people and reality of the world they had come from, making them the ultimate strangers in a strange land.

The trio had discussed staying here, in this time, which was especially appealing to Robert, who had spent a lifetime studying the faint echoes of the world he now inhabited.

In the end, they each decided they had to return. They had to know how it had all turned out. They had to see the future they had wrought, no matter what.

And through it all, Robert's biggest source of regret was that Matt wouldn't have the opportunity to have the long, heartfelt discussion he was so eager to have with his father. To regale him with all that had transpired and apologize for turning his back on him and Hopi traditions.

"And we must acknowledge Elowin Balivae," continued Huku, his eyes narrowing momentarily. Robert caught the flash of tension between Huku and Elowin before she rose gracefully to thunderous applause. Huku's voice grew stronger as he continued, "Without her courage and wisdom, we might still be locked in conflict. It was Elowin who exposed the truth to High Councilor Nereus Pyralis, revealing how certain members of his own Atlantean Council had poisoned his mind with lies. And it was Elowin who went on to quickly negotiate an end to the war with the High Councilor, ushering in a new era of peace, cooperation, and prosperity between our two great nations. Finally, because of her actions, Kairos Daedalus, the man who manufactured this war, now sits in a cell, his schemes exposed, his power broken."

The applause grew even louder as Robert thought back to his recent meeting with Huku Nali.

When Robert, Kira, and Matt were about to meet the Lemurian leader, they had spoken with Elowin about whether they should disclose their true origins. Despite Huku's vaunted position, they had collectively decided against it. Most of those who knew their secret were now dead, including Alara, Ishar's Anunnaki comrades, and numerous members of Thoth's Underground, and they had sworn the few still alive to absolute secrecy.

In the final analysis, the truth of their origins, and what this might portend, was too explosive, too extraordinary, for general consumption, and would raise far too many questions. Questions about their truthfulness and sanity for one. And if they *were* believed, questions about destiny, fate, the consequences of altering the timeline, and the mechanics of time travel—which, in many cases, *Tala* herself had no answers for.

Perhaps even worse, they couldn't risk panicking leaders or the public, who would fear that anyone could come from the future to meddle with their present—especially the three who had done so already—potentially rewriting history and erasing millions from existence.

So Elowin had publically released a sanitized account of their role in stopping Kairos, listing them as operatives from a tiny, sparsely-populated country located where Costa Rica was in their time. According to the account, this trio of unusual but highly-effective operatives had monitored the coming conflict between Atlantis and Lemuria, had feared their country might be swept up in a possible escalation, and had come to investigate. According to Elowin, they comprised a team of operatives so clandestine that not even their own government was aware of their existence.

As these memories flashed through Robert's mind, the entrance doors to the chamber swung open with a sharp clack. The celebration halted at once as a figure glided into the room. The being moved with confidence and almost seemed to be floating rather than merely walking. The alien's head was bald, with a blue tint to it, and it wore a gold headdress and a white robe that rippled like holographic water. Large almond-shaped eyes with violet pupils surveyed the crowd as it approached the podium. Huku bowed as the being took his place at the podium.

Matt gripped Robert's arm. "Is that a Kachina?" he whispered in awe.

"It sure looks that way," Robert whispered back.

Kachinas were the spirit guides of the Hopi people, and many Hopi Elders portrayed them as teachers from the stars able to show the way to truth and harmony. From what Robert could tell, this one was a female of the species.

Robert blinked as he struggled to process yet another extraterrestrial. First the Anunnaki, and now this? The Kachina's head was shaped like an elongated egg, with a face that was overly wide around the eyes. There was something mesmerizing about the being, an energy so radiant it seemed to vibrate with pure love, pure peace.

While her appearance wasn't particularly appealing to human beings, her energy, her aura, was incredible. Transformative. Just being in her presence could make someone question their entire understanding of existence.

The extraterrestrial closed her eyes and bowed her head, placing both palms on the podium. Although her mouth remained still, words resonated through hidden speakers, filling the chamber with a voice somehow bypassing Robert's ears and speaking directly to his mind.

"The threads of destiny have shifted," said the Kachina. "Through the actions of a few brave souls, the great curtain of time has been rewoven. Yet darkness lurks always at the edges of light, seeking to unravel what has been mended."

The Kachina shifted, her eyes still closed. "You must remain vigilant, never allowing fear or hatred to seep into your souls. Guard your minds. Guard your hearts. Guard your inner ways. The strength of Lemuria lies not in weapons or aggression."

The alien paused as if letting that point burrow into the heads of all in the room. "No, your strength lies in the wisdom of your healers, the vision of your futurists, the creativity of your artists, the dedication of your teachers, and the insights of your philosophers. Look to them for guidance, and to the eldest among you who carry centuries of hard-won wisdom."

The Kachina opened her eyes, and her gaze settled on Huku for a quick moment before continuing. "Through peaceful means, you can illuminate the shadows that threaten to blanket humanity. Where force fails, understanding prevails. Where hatred divides, compassion unites. The darkness cannot comprehend the light, and so light shall always triumph—if you but keep its flame burning in your hearts. Remember these words, Huku Nali, for all the days of your life."

The alien gestured toward Robert, Kira, and Matt. "Along with the brilliant Elowin Balivae, this truth was recently demonstrated by these three visitors. Through their courage and sacrifice, they altered the course of history itself. They risked their lives, and so much more, to preserve the harmony of Lemuria and her people. Their actions ripple through time like waves across water, touching shores yet unseen."

The Kachina nodded at Robert and his two traveling companions as she said this last, a veiled reference to changes to the future that made it clear to him she was well aware of their origins, but had decided not to out them. The Kachina equivalent of a knowing wink.

She turned once again to stare out over the gathering. "I give you this sacred charge: become the keepers of Earth's wisdom. Not through dominion or force, but through stewardship and teaching. Guide humanity toward enlightenment, but never conquest. Let your greatest legacy be the seeds of knowledge you plant in the hearts of those who will follow.

"The greatest challenge faced by humanity is to guard the ancient wisdom while embracing new understanding. Share your knowledge freely, but remember always that without spiritual awareness, even the most astonishing technology brings nothing but destruction. This is your sacred duty, to show humanity a better way forward.

"We, the Kachinas, do not come to forcefully alter your path or interrupt your evolutionary process. Your politics, your wars, your loves, your healing—these are *your* choices. They are your journeys, not ours. We are here as guides, understanding that you are on an evolutionary path just as we once were. Our role is not to eliminate the obstacles you face, but to offer wisdom, to illuminate potential, and to hold space for your growth. We cannot do the work for you, but we can shine light on possibilities."

The being stepped back, bowed deeply to the assembled crowd, and glided toward the exit. As silence fell over the chamber, the alien left the building. Minutes later, a deep rumble shook the walls. Through the glass-like ceiling panels, a ship wreathed in a blue aura flew upward, vanishing into the sky with a thunderous roar.

CHAPTER 76

The ceremony was soon over, and the crowd began to exit the magnificent Grand Chambers. The trio of visiting humans were among the throngs of people who'd chosen to remain in the chamber a bit longer. Robert exchanged brief words with Elowin, and both thanked the other for their part in stopping the war.

Elowin was truly remarkable. Absolutely dazzling. But she still wasn't Kira.

"*Tala* awaits," said Matt, although with mixed emotions. "I guess it's time to go back to our . . . *time.*"

Aethor, who'd been elsewhere in the crowd, now strode toward them, lugging a plastic case with him that was fully five feet long, reminding Robert of a cello case, but much thinner, without the bulge designed to accommodate the cello's guitar-like main body.

Aethor greeted his three friends warmly and then gestured at the case. "Open it, Robert," he said with a mischievous glint in his eye. "I think you'll be glad you did."

Robert laughed. "No need. Not to spoil your attempt to surprise me, Aethor, but you can't surprise a man with his own Vesh'tar. I've felt its presence since you first arrived."

"So, you were just waiting for me to drag it over to you?"

Robert beamed. "Pretty much. There's no way I can thank you enough. You played perhaps the biggest role of all in stopping this war. Your world, and mine, will be forever in your debt. And then you topped it off by returning my lost Vesh'tar to me." He grinned. "Now you're just showing off."

Aethor chuckled.

"Let me guess," added Robert, arching an eyebrow. "You found it in the caved-in room we fell into?"

"Exactly," said Aethor. "Where circumstances forced you to abandon it. Although, I have a feeling it will forgive you. There was quite a lot going on at the time."

Robert nodded. Given how clearly the Vesh'tar could make its presence known, could communicate directly with his mind, he had a feeling that it had abandoned *him*. Perhaps it wanted to see what he could do on his own, make sure that its presence, and capabilities, wouldn't become a crutch. If so, it had learned what it had set out to learn.

Regardless, all he knew for certain was that his Vesh'tar, like God, worked in mysterious ways.

While the trio of humans continued to speak with Aethor, Ishar approached them. "*Tala* is ready and waiting on the landing pad," said their towering Anunnaki ally. "She's ready to take you back to your time."

Robert swallowed hard. It was time to find out what the future held. And not just their future. *Tala* had finished repairing her stardrive days earlier, along with her hull, and she was now in the same full health as she was when they had first seen her.

Ishar nodded at each of the four humans in turn. "It was an honor fighting alongside you," he said with great sincerity. "You fought with ferocity, poise, and intelligence. No hesitation. No outward fear of death. Just the courage to stand together against impossible odds. You truly represent what's best about your species. You know," he added with a smile, "as pathetic as it is. In fact, the four of you, combined, are almost as impressive as a single, subpar Anunnaki warrior."

Kira laughed. "Coming from someone as delusional about the merits of his own species as you are, Ishar, that's the best compliment I've ever gotten."

"Yeah, thanks Ishar," said Robert. "One-fourth as impressive as a subpar Anunnaki Warrior. That's *so* beautiful. I think I'm starting to tear up."

Ishar grinned.

They made their way outside and climbed the spiraling steps toward the roof access. The stairwell opened onto a large landing pad where various craft sat against the backdrop of the ocean crashing against the cliffs below. As they approached *Tala*, her entry ramp lowered and thudded against the stone.

Ishar clapped Robert on the shoulder hard enough to make him stagger. "Farewell," he said. "May you find even greater battles to wage in your own time."

Robert nodded, not wanting to tell the alien that most humans would consider this sendoff a curse, since he knew the alien had meant well.

Aethor chimed in. "I'll keep the memory of Thoth alive, and those who died in the Resistance fighting for peace. And I'll make sure all of you become legendary for your actions, as you so richly deserve."

He gazed at the trio of travelers with great affection. "Do you think I'll ever see you again?"

"I suspect not," said Robert. "But as my Vesh'tar might say, *ever* is a very long time. I'm sure we'll meet again, in this life or the next."

As Ishar and Aethor continued to bid them farewell, Robert was stunned by how much these two had come to mean to him in such a short time. They would be sorely missed.

Finally, the time travelers ascended *Tala*'s ramp, with Robert clutching the Vesh'tar he'd long since removed from Aethor's case. Silently, he thanked Aethor for retrieving it, and Thoth for teaching him some of the ways of the Emerald Order. He imagined he'd need both to navigate the unknown waters ahead.

Robert sat with his two companions at a table on the bridge, and his stomach was churning. "Are you ready?" he said to his friends. "Are you ready to see how the future unfolds if Atlantis and Lemuria had never sunk beneath the waves?"

It would likely be an amazing future, one beyond their wildest dreams. But the absence of their friends and families would be devastating, and this paradise would likely be lonely, requiring more adjustments than they might be capable of.

"*No!*" said Kira emphatically. "I'm not ready. Are you kidding?"

"Yeah," said Matt, gritting his teeth. "This is as scary as it gets. But no use delaying anymore. I've always believed in pulling a Band-Aid off quickly."

Robert chuckled, despite his emotional turmoil. "Another example of your great wisdom."

He glanced down at the Vesh'tar lying near his feet, blew out a long, tense breath, and squeezed his eyes shut. "*Tala*," he whispered. "Take us back to our time. To three hours after we left. Let's find out what awaits us."

CHAPTER 77

Advisor Elowin Balivae
City: Sholani
District: Loma'i Shores
Location: Northwest Lemuria

The memorial garden sat behind the Lemurian Grand Council building. It was a private sanctuary where ocean waves crashed against the cliffs below. Stone paths wound through well-tended beds of traditional healing herbs and meditation spaces, all covered by transparent domes.

Elowin stood in front of the memorials, her focus on Elder Kona Makelo's monument. The newest addition towered above the others, its surface etched with flowing Lemurian script: "Here rests Elder Kona Makelo, Keeper of Ancient Wisdom, Guardian of Peace. His sacrifice lights the path forward. May his courage inspire generations."

After several minutes of mourning and meditation, Elowin's thoughts drifted to Robert Shaw. To the strange pull she felt toward the foreigner. Something in his spirit had caught her attention, despite all logic saying they could never be more than brief allies in a desperate time. Her heart belonged to Lemuria first. To its people, its children, its future. She'd chosen this path long ago and found peace in it, but more importantly, truth.

But, strangely, while the chemistry she had with Robert Shaw was undeniable, whenever she imagined her own future, it wasn't Robert who was in it.

It was Jalon Kiva.

Right on cue, the man in question approached. She recognized his measured footsteps, the same footsteps she'd heard often during their escape through Atlantis. When they hid in corridors while guards passed. When they sprinted across exposed walkways as laser bolts seared the air around them. When he always found a way to protect her, and Lemuria.

Bringing down Kairos had taken the heroic efforts of any number of people. The Resistance. The three visitors from the future. Aethor. Thoth. Ishar and his warrior friends. And Elowin herself.

But while Jalon didn't get the same credit, he'd been at least as instrumental as the others. Remove any one of them from the equation, and Kairos would have prevailed. The world would have burned. Or burned and then drowned, as Robert had insisted.

If not for Jalon, Elowin would have died on a rooftop, murdered by the Atlantean High Marshall. Without him, even alive, she couldn't have possibly achieved her objectives. Couldn't have possibly navigated the shark-filled waters to eventually arrive in the quarters of the High Councilor with the information needed to convince him of Kairos's treachery.

And she was convinced that no other member of the Protectorate could have done the same. No other member could have possibly been as devoted to her as Jalon had been.

He finally joined her and gave her a quick hug, which sent electricity coursing through her body. His mere presence made her feel alive. Feel safe. Was she falling in love with him?

Was she *already*?"

So much had changed since she had ventured into Atlantis on a mission to stop the war. It had only been weeks, but it seemed like lifetimes ago. And here she was with Jalon, a man as extraordinary as he was humble. A man who'd remained with her in Atlantis while she'd hammered out the details of a peace treaty, as indispensable as ever.

How many times had she found herself wanting to hold him? To abandon all caution and lose herself in his arms? To make love to him as if he were the only man who had ever lived?

"Hello, Jalon," she said warmly. "Thanks for stopping by. How are things going?"

They'd returned to Lemuria just two days earlier and had parted, but she'd been suffering from his absence in a way that truly shocked her.

He gazed at her with adoration, something that had failed to register with her until quite recently. How could that even be? She was the vaunted Elowin Balivae, considered almost superhuman in her ability to read people, read situations. So how had she failed to read that Jalon's actions, his never-ending support and praise of her, and the way he looked at her, were so much more than just the actions of a soldier doing his duty?

How had she failed to realize that he likely was in love with *her*? In retrospect, the signs were unmistakable.

"The Council has asked me to train the next generation of Protectorates," said Jalon in reply to her question. "We lost a lot more than we'd like to admit. We're at about 250 now, and they want that number to double, at minimum."

Elowin couldn't help but wince. Jalon was perfect for this job, but the thought of him working apart from her, being apart from her, somehow made her feel queasy, unbalanced.

"They couldn't have chosen any better," she managed to force from her mouth. She hesitated. "Did you . . . " She stopped, unable to finish. She'd faced dangers that could have easily ended her life, her nation, without flinching. But now she was terrified of asking a simple question, knowing the response she was likely to get. "Did you," she began again, forcing herself to spit it out. "Did you, ah . . . *accept* their offer?"

Jalon sighed. "Not yet, no. I told them I was honored, but requested a day to think it over."

A wave of relief washed over Elowin, like a blast of frigid air hitting her after she had been roasting in the desert.

"Interesting," she said, trying hard not to show her elation. "I must confess that I'm glad you didn't accept immediately. I wasn't aware this offer was coming, or I would have acted sooner."

He raised his eyebrows. "Acted sooner?"

"Yes," she said. "I was planning to make you an offer of my own. To ask you to be my personal guard. More than that, actually. My advisor. Confidant. All the things you've been since you carried me off that roof."

She paused. "I understand if you think this is somewhat selfish of me, wishing to monopolize the most exceptional soldier, the most exceptional *human being*, in our entire military. I understand if you want to serve your country more comprehensively, take a position that is far more important than helping just one woman. So, while I'm selfishly hoping you accept my offer and not the Council's, I'll totally understand if you don't."

Jalon beamed in delight. "That request is anything but selfish, Elowin. And I'm overjoyed that you asked. In fact, I came here to ask you to put me in the very position you just offered. To *beg* you. It's the only reason I asked for more time."

He shook his head. "As for the importance of the position, I truly believe that nothing I could ever do could be as important as continuing to work with you, the woman who saved our entire nation, and no doubt will again if it ever becomes necessary. In my view, I'll have a greater chance of helping Lemuria thrive if I'm by your side than if I were to replace Huku Nali himself. To say that we make an unbeatable team is an understatement."

Elowin smiled, and a herd of elephants stepped off her chest. "I'll take that as a yes," she said giddily, relishing the prospect of having him officially by her side as a friend and advisor. And, hopefully, *so much more.*

"My answer is more than a yes," he replied, unable to stop smiling. "It's an *emphatic* yes."

"Then welcome back to our team," she said. "I've missed you the past few days. I mean, *really* missed you. Almost painfully so."

"Yeah, tell me about it," he said, looking like he might float up into the sky upon hearing such a strong admission of Elowin's feelings for him.

"You know what," he added. "I just came up with an idea. Why don't I take you to dinner tonight to celebrate this new phase of our, uh . . . relationship. What do you think?"

Elowin beamed. "Now that, Jalon Kiva, might just be the best idea you've ever had. And I'd like to think that dinner will be just the *beginning.*"

CHAPTER 78

Councilor Kairos Daedalus
Former High Marshall of the Atlantean Military Forces
Location: Og City, Atlantis

The screams reverberated throughout the chamber. Another scream. Then again. How many shrieks had there been? Kairos vaguely realized that the screams were his own, issued as a release when he couldn't take the lights, the noise, the sensory overload that pounded into his brain any longer.

He sat on a stone bench, trying not to pull out his hair. Shaking his head, he looked around the small room. It was enclosed by three glass walls. Glass that was filled with static-like projections covering every centimeter of the transparent surfaces. The projections never ceased, just kept going, and going, and going, penetrating his skull like a hot needle, a flaming dagger, intended to drive him just short of mad.

But he wouldn't cooperate. He intended to keep all his wits about him. Not just his sanity. He was sure to need his full brain capacity when this torture was through.

He leaned back against a single concrete barrier. Time had lost all meaning under the constant glare of the excruciatingly intense lights, which penetrated even his closed eyes and the arm he put over them, but somehow didn't blind him.

It was Argo who had dragged him here in handcuffs, at the High Councilor's order. If he could slit Nereus's throat, he would do so now. Although, to be fair, that had been his intent all along, even if Nereus had treated him like a king.

The High Councilor's plans were clear to him. He would soften Kairos, weaken his mind and psyche, and then put him on trial. A show trial, regaling the nation with Kairos's crimes against Atlantis, against humanity.

But Nereus hadn't thought it through, and Kairos vowed to make sure his plan backfired in glorious fashion. Kairos had spent years weaving his influence through every media channel, every political network. His influence with the right people rivaled the High Councilor's own, and he had made lavish promises to those who held immense hidden power. Those able to pull all the levers of legitimate authority in a way that wasn't obvious to politicians or the public.

And Kairos could produce more evidence of the *High Councilor's* corruption, of *his* evil intent, than the High Councilor could produce when it came to Kairos's misdeeds. To be fair, Kairos's evidence would be completely fabricated. But that didn't matter at all. Not when key players would become rich by testifying to the veracity of Kairos's fabrications, and the media would report them as true, questioning only the High Councilor's evidence against Kairos, and not the other way around.

Truth could be manufactured on demand if one was clever enough, and if the media and political class were corrupt enough, which was the case here. So, the actual, real evidence Nereus had on Kairos would be discredited, and the fake evidence he had on the High Councilor would be supported.

If the High Councilor was competent, he would have killed Kairos the moment he had the chance. That's what Kairos would have done in his place. Nereus's problem was that he was weak, and naïve. For all his success, his climb to the highest position in the land, Nereus couldn't imagine just how many powerful men and women would turn on him, spread horrible lies without a single pang of guilt in pursuit of more power.

Ixra had already begun orchestrating these elements while Kairos was in prison. She was his most trusted lieutenant who controlled the back-channel business networks, the secret funding streams keeping some of these political parasites breathing. One word from her and those funds would dry up at once. Any politician foolish enough to speak against Kairos would find themselves professionally and financially gutted.

Within days, his political machine would grind into motion. They'd question Nereus's motives, suggest political persecution. They'd leak documents showing Kairos's brilliant handling of a variety of crises and tout his unquestioned bravery. They'd get testimony from his troops about how he insisted on going into battle with his men, against the wishes of the High Council, and had nearly been killed because of it.

Then they'd paint him as a victim of Nereus's desperate grab for more power. The media would run story after story about Nereus's failing leadership, his paranoid witch hunts against respected citizens.

And slowly, methodically, they'd reveal evidence of Nereus's own questionable political maneuvering, how he'd used Kairos's arrest to distract from his own failing policies and corruption and to shore up his crumbling support base.

They'd hammer it home until the public saw only what Kairos and his supporters wanted them to see, an innocent person scapegoated for the failures and corruption of a failing regime. The truth would be buried under an avalanche of lies.

The lights continued to penetrate his retinas, stabbing into his brain, making each second of the torture seem like forever. The irony was that he'd designed these chambers himself, the entire prison facility, while working with the Dracs, the reptilian aliens who had guided his rise through Atlantean politics. They were always in the background, unseen. They'd insisted on the constant blinding, stabbing lights in these cells, claiming they would break subjects faster, make them more pliable.

They'd been right, of course, as Kairos could now personally attest.

Reality blurred for him now. Dreams bled into waking moments. Finally, the lights ceased, and a man stood before him, studying a datapad.

"Who are you?" gasped the former High Marshall, his weak voice barely audible, and his mind screaming, unable to focus on what was right in front of him.

But with the lights no longer slicing through his eyes and psyche, his mind recovered quickly, and he finally remembered. This man, this attendant, was responsible for wielding the soft torture protocols that Kairos himself had developed. A man tasked with making sure the duration of the torture was just enough to soften the victim, to cloud his thinking, but not enough to turn him into a raving psychotic, a mental vegetable. The High Councilor wanted Kairos tortured to punish him for his plan to take Nereus's crown, and his life, but not so much that it would leave an obvious mark, either physical or mental.

Kairos needed to stand trial, after all, so Atlantis and the world could see what a true monster he was. At least that was Nereus's foolhardy plan. For his part, Kairos knew enough to pretend the torture was impacting him far more severely than it was, resulting in shorter and shorter durations.

The attendant didn't reply. Instead, he activated a small device that would take Kairos's vital signs remotely, gauge how quickly his heart rate slowed when the lights were off, ensure his blood pressure wasn't at dangerous levels.

As the attendant studied his datapad, the man suddenly gasped and then toppled forward as half of a fourteen-inch blade shot through his chest from behind. Blood pooled beneath his corpse, and the hilt of the dagger could now be seen shoved into his exposed back as he bled out.

The instant Kairos saw the knife explode through the attendant's chest, he realized he was a dead man. That the High Councilor must have finally decided to make the smart move and kill him, although it wasn't clear why the attendant had to die as well.

This conclusion was quickly proven wrong as he glanced up to see three giants who'd been responsible for the killing. *Draconians.* Nine feet in height, their muscular reptilian bodies were draped in purple and gold robes. Jewels crowned their scaly heads. Their long, thick tails swept the floor.

Despite their prehistoric appearance, their arms, hands, legs, and feet retained a human quality, though their black boots trimmed in gold did little to soften their presence. One gripped a ceremonial staff while the others carried rifles and curved daggers.

Drool trickled down Kairos's chin as he stared at them. "Why have you come?"

"Don't be stupid, Kairos," said the Drac in the middle, their leader. "It doesn't suit you." The alien extended his hand, helping the human prisoner stand. "You didn't think we'd leave our most valuable asset to decay, did you?"

"I thought my arrest might lead you to believe I was no longer useful. Which couldn't be further from the truth. I'm pleased you recognize the immensity of my continued value."

The Drac in command snorted. "*Immensity* of your value? That's quite the overstatement, Kairos. I see these setbacks haven't diminished the immensity of your *ego*. Still, it's good that you haven't lost your swagger. But, yes, we still recognize your skills and potential. While the disruption of your plans and your capture have been setbacks, they're nothing we can't recover from."

Part of Kairos was furious that the Dracs had intervened. He had the situation well in hand, and he'd be far more powerful once he'd turned the tables on the High Councilor and returned to full legitimacy than he would be as an escaped convict. Now he had no choice. The Dracs had no doubt left a long trail of savagely murdered corpses behind, so escape had become his only option.

"I assume there will be no record of your involvement here," he said.

"Of course not," said the Drac in charge. "Which is why we provided so much input on the construction of this facility and its security. Just in case we ever needed to free a high-value prisoner. We disrupted all cameras and other sensors on our way in. And while some of the guards did see us, they didn't live long enough for that to be a problem."

They exited the cell and walked past the bodies of fallen Atlantean security guards lining the corridor. Through a massive breach in the wall at the end of the hallway, tall grass swayed beneath the moon. Rolling hills stretched into darkness. A massive triangular ship waited beyond.

"We still expect big things from you, Kairos," said the Drac leader, motioning toward the ship.

"Good," replied Kairos with an arrogant smile. "Because I expect big things from myself. So have no fear. I won't fail you. And I won't fail Atlantis."

CHAPTER 79

The three passengers aboard *Tala* held their breath as they returned to their own time and raced toward the magnificent blue orb below them, their eyes locked on *Tala's* viewscreens.

"No noticeable changes so far," said Robert to his two fellow travelers seated across from him at the table.

"We're still in space," noted Kira. "What were you expecting?"

Robert shrugged. "I don't know. Scores of impossibly advanced starships clogging the space-lanes. An energy collector built facing the Sun, so vast it can be seen from where we are. You know, that sort of thing."

As they spoke, *Tala* screamed into Earth's atmosphere, slowing from the mind-boggling speed she used in space to a relatively snail-like velocity of eight times the speed of sound. But, as the Earth seemed to zoom in to greater clarity, everything below still looked the same as it always had.

"*Tala*," said Robert, "search for some equivalent to our Internet. Something you can access remotely to get information."

"Done," said the ship. "And what I've found isn't the *equivalent* of the Internet. It *is* the Internet."

"How can that be?" mumbled Robert, blinking in confusion. "Access it and compare this world to the one we left. Summarize the most salient changes in a few hundred words."

"Done," said *Tala* again. "I'm detecting no changes whatsoever. *None*. Everything reads the way it did when we left. The same nations and technologies. Your University of Arizona biography is still online and reads the exact same way it did when you left. Your friends and loved ones are all alive and living exactly where they were when you left earlier today."

The three travelers exchanged incredulous looks. The only thing more terrifying than an incomprehensibly changed future was one that hadn't changed at all.

"What does that even *mean*?" whispered Kira.

Robert shook his head. "I don't know. Maybe when we changed the past, time branched into two separate realities. The other branch is experiencing the changes, while *Tala* brought us back to the branch we were originally on. The branch where Atlantis and Lemuria were still destroyed."

"I don't believe that to be true," said *Tala*. "I don't understand everything about time travel, but I do understand a considerable amount. And I'm as certain as I can be that there was no branching. We remain on the one and only timeline."

Robert's eyes narrowed, deep in thought. "If that's the case, there's only one other explanation." He scowled. "We didn't stop the destruction of Atlantis and Lemuria after all."

"But we *did*," insisted Matt. "The weapon was disabled. Peace was forged. And Kairos was imprisoned."

"All that is true," began Robert. "Still, if you—"

"Sorry to interrupt," said *Tala*, "but we're being hailed. The hailing entity is asking to deliver a pre-recorded holographic video."

"*Hailed?*" repeated Robert in disbelief. The shocks just kept coming. "Aren't you in stealth mode? No one here has the tech to even know you exist, let alone the ability to hail you."

"Be that as it may, I am, in fact, being hailed."

Robert stared questioningly at his two companions, who both gave him a quick nod.

"Answer it," he instructed *Tala*. "Let's see this message."

A holographic image of Thoth materialized before them, wearing his familiar flowing robes, and carrying his ever-present Vesh'tar. It was him. In the pre-recorded holographic flesh. There could be no mistake.

All three passengers gasped at the same time upon seeing him, and the holographic video of Thoth seemed to wait patiently for their shock to subside.

"A fond greeting to my three friends, Robert, Kira, and Matt," began the hologram pleasantly. "And to you, as well, *Tala*."

The three-dimensional video of Thoth paused, and it was so real it was as if he were in the ship with them. The fall and rise of his chest, his breathing, so real it seemed as though they could reach out and touch him, interact with him.

"I can only imagine what must be going through your minds right now," continued the Hierophant. "Your confusion and dismay. But I think I know the questions you'll have, and I'll do my best to answer them.

"First and foremost, by now you've probably realized that your brilliant triumph in preventing the destruction of Atlantis and Lemuria didn't take. Everything still happened the way your original history records it to have happened. Just the way you foresaw it. Perhaps the original timeline is more stubborn, more intent on reasserting itself than we realized. Or perhaps human nature is so flawed it's uncorrectable, though I don't believe that myself.

"Regardless, the peace didn't last, and the war ended up happening the way you know it from your history. I am so sorry to deliver this news, but you've no doubt figured it out, anyway, given the unchanged state of the world you've just returned to."

The recorded Thoth paused to catch his breath and gather his thoughts.

"Another question I'm sure you have," he continued finally, "is how I managed to deliver a thirteen-thousand-year-old holographic message to you just after you arrived back in your time. That part is much less complicated than you'd imagine. During one of our discussions, Robert, you described the approximate location where *Tala* was buried for all those millennia, where you first found her. Inside a cave in a region you called Arizona. So, I planted a computer crystal in sleep mode close by.

"Well," he added with a smile, "just how close remains to be seen. But I'm confident I was able to get it within five hundred miles, which is all I needed.

"The computer crystal was covered by long-range sensors. Sensors that were set to awaken a hundred years before the approximate time you told me you came from. Once active, the sensors waited to detect *Tala*'s electromagnetic energy signature, which they would do once your past selves activated her in the cave.

"Since I knew *Tala* would return you home shortly after you left, this timing should work well. When the sensors detected *Tala's* awakening in the cave, they activated the crystal computer, which is programmed to broadcast this hail, this message, repeatedly, until it's received. But not until waiting an hour to make sure the *Tala* you had activated was safely back in the past, and *wouldn't* receive this message, which is intended only for *you*, the crew of the *Tala* who just returned to your time."

Robert nodded. Thoth's strategy was ingenious, and he had really thought things through. And he was right. What had seemed miraculous at first was surprisingly simple to explain.

I'm recording this message eighteen years after the last time we saw each other," continued the Hierophant. "I suspect you assumed I'd been killed during Kairos's raid on the Underground. I'm so sorry that I didn't contact you and tell you otherwise. But Kairos despises me above all others and would have never rested until he found me, no matter what tortures he had to inflict on my friends and allies.

"So I decided it was best for all involved if he thought me dead, and I disappeared. But there is something else. Something I didn't tell you or anyone else in the Resistance, just in case the organization ever became compromised. I had tasked a small team of brilliant scientists to develop an energy shield that would protect nations from the Nexus Prime weapon. Something that would require vast improvements to the energy shield technology already in existence. My hope was that if we couldn't prevent Kairos from using this weapon, at least we could render it impotent. After I survived Kairos's attack on our base, I joined the shield team, who I had stationed far enough from both Atlantis and Lemuria to be able to survive the promised cataclysm if it were to come."

Thoth issued a heavy sigh. "Two things are obvious from the fact that I'm delivering this message. One, the defensive shield wasn't ready in time. And two, I survived the cataclysm."

He paused, and expressions of both weariness and triumph crossed his face. "But now—*finally*—the shield is ready. Although long after it was needed. Which is the reason I'm sending this message.

"Even though I was in hiding when you were still here, wishing to be thought dead, I was well aware of what was happening in Atlantis and Lemuria. I was well aware of your heroic efforts, and those of the others involved. The three of you handled yourselves as magnificently as I knew you would. As *Tala* knew you would. Robert, you even found a way to triumph without the use of your Vesh'tar toward the end. All remarkable feats. You've gone beyond the call of duty a thousand-fold."

He blew out a long breath and lowered his eyes. "Which is why it so pains me to ask even more of the three of you. But I have no choice. I'm still convinced you, and only you, can rewrite history.

"As you know, as the Lemurian descendants you call the Hopi know, history repeats itself. It can be, and is, cyclical. Unless you break the chain, it won't just repeat, it will worsen. We've had these discussions. Your own world is on the brink of catastrophe. Humanity will be condemned to a never-ending series of ever-worsening cataclysms, *genocides*, until this cycle is finally broken. Or until humanity extinguishes itself from Mother Earth. As has been mentioned many times, I believe your talents and efforts, alone, can break this cycle, allowing humanity to achieve its full potential and prevent the deaths of *billions*!

"Here's what I'm asking of the three of you. First, while still in your time, retrieve the perfected shield technology. Embedded within this message are geographic coordinates for where I've stashed it. I buried it on land that is considered sacred to the people I'm currently among, so nothing should be built on top of it, even thirteen thousand years later, making it a simple matter for you to obtain it."

He sighed. "I wish you could just go back to the time I'm recording this message and pick it up directly from my hand, but *Tala* is very finicky about how often she uses time travel, as we all know. Time travel is finicky in itself, and I don't grasp its intricacies the way *Tala* does. Just asking her to go back to Lemuria at the moment you just left is pushing things, but my gut tells me she'll agree to that. She chose you for this mission, and I know she's just as heartbroken that it failed, in her own way, as we are."

"So, once you retrieve the shield technology from the coordinates I've provided to *Tala*, still in your own time, I'd ask you to return with it to Lemuria, to just after you left, and stop the devastation we thought you had stopped already."

He stared at the trio for an extended period, as if he were actually present in the room and able to study their body language, which, of course, wasn't the case. Finally, he spoke again. "I am so sorry. You've earned the right to be treated like heroes, like kings, for the rest of your lives. Instead, all I'm offering is more struggle, more responsibility, more peril. I can't be certain you'll even get this message, or how you'll respond. But knowing you all the way I do, I feel certain you'll agree to shoulder this burden in order to ensure the survival of our species.

"I wouldn't be asking so much of you if humanity didn't need your help so badly. But, without hyperbole, the three of you could prove to be some of the most consequential human beings who ever lived."

Thoth closed his eyes and nodded slowly. "It has been the honor of my long life to have met you all. It is my ardent hope that we will meet again someday."

And with that, the Hierophant of the Emerald order vanished, and *Tala's* bridge was silent once again.

CHAPTER 80

The three time-travelers didn't speak for some time as they digested the astonishing holographic video they had just witnessed, yet another entry in their list of experiences that would have seemed impossible only a short time ago, or at least surreal, but which now seemed par for the course.

Of course a wise, ancient emissary of the Emerald Order whom they thought dead—capable of wielding great powers using hyper-advanced tech embedded within a staff—had left a video for them. One that had been in hibernation for nearly thirteen thousand years.

By now, this was just another Tuesday.

When they finally did begin speaking, it wasn't long before they unanimously agreed to proceed as Thoth had requested. So did *Tala*. As the Hierophant had guessed, the ship had only been willing to take them back to when and where they had left Lemuria, rather than act as their personal time machine. There were reasons for that, reasons *Tala* explained in a cryptic manner. The temporal displacement technology was tied to specific genomic algorithms. Markers in the ship's DNA. These genetic sequences created a quantum resonance window only aligned under precise temporal conditions. All in all, *Tala* wasn't created as a recreational vehicle for temporal tourism. She was only willing—and able—to travel through time in the direst of emergencies.

In the end, there was no way they could refuse Thoth's pleas. When they had first taken off from the cave in Arizona, riding the mother of all untamed and unpredictable bulls, they had been an unlikely trio thrown together by what they thought was pure happenstance. They had no idea they were about to travel to the distant past. No idea how their destinies would be intertwined, with their convergence at a buried starship apparently anything but random.

At first, nothing could have convinced them that they could be critical in rewriting history and staving off disaster for the human race. Nothing. But after all they had been through, all they had seen, how could they not be more receptive to this possibility?

And how could they turn their back on Atlantis, and Lemuria, which they had come to love? On humanity itself?

It was horrific to learn that they'd failed in their mission, or, rather, that their success had only been temporary. But as maddening as the thought of going back was, it was also *exhilarating*.

As brutal as their battles had often been, they'd also forged undying friendships. They'd captained and crewed a *starship*. They'd seen and experienced different alien species and had undeniable proof that mankind wasn't alone in the Universe.

They'd been seduced by hidden history coming to life. By advanced technology. By gained knowledge and wisdom. By the challenge of surviving and saving the world. And by the growing awareness of their possible importance in the scheme of human history.

Robert had been in life-threatening situations before while gathering artifacts around the world. But being fully immersed in countless lethal situations in the ancient past had further cemented what he'd already begun to appreciate: that exposure to these types of challenges made ordinary life *pale* by comparison. Made it trivial and unfulfilling.

So they agreed to go after the shield technology Thoth had left them to find, and then back into the eye of the storm in ancient times. But only after spending a day in their own time, so Matt could seize on the opportunity to set things right with his father, and Robert could see his mother and introduce Kira.

While Robert hadn't seen his mother for over a month, as far as she'd be concerned, he hadn't been absent at all.

Tala flew them in stealth mode to the Arizona desert, to within two miles of where they'd found her in the cave system, right next to the SUV Robert had hidden over a month ago. Or just a few hours ago, depending on one's perspective.

The trio now stood together, watching a dust cloud approach. Gray Eagle's battered pickup truck bounced over the desert terrain, heading toward the location Matt had given him when he called his father just after arrival in this time.

The truck lurched to a stop fifteen yards from where they'd landed the starship. Gray Eagle climbed out slowly, appraising the ship with awe, as Matt, Kira, and Robert descended the ramp. When he saw Matt, the old man's composure cracked. Tears streamed down his cheeks as he rushed forward, pulling his son into a fierce embrace, and Matt's tears soon matched his own.

"I knew it!" he said ecstatically. "I knew how special you were the moment you were born."

"You aren't furious with me?" said Matt in surprise.

His father smiled serenely. "I was when you invaded the sacred cave, tried to steal the ancient tablet, and trespassed on this ship." He shook his head in awe. "But then it lifted off, a vast tunnel emerged, and it disappeared. That's when I realized the truth. You weren't trespassing. The ship *wanted* you there. It wouldn't have carried you away if it didn't."

He paused. "You must tell me all about your journey, Little Owl. You left just hours ago. But tell me, how long were you really gone?"

Matt's eyes widened. "How would you know to even ask that?"

"I can see it in your face. Hear it in your voice. You aren't the same son you were when you left. You're confident. Self-assured. Poised. I sense immense wisdom in you that wasn't there this morning. You couldn't have possibly changed this profoundly in less than a day."

"Your insight, father, is extraordinary. A quality you've always possessed, but one I failed to notice until just now. I've been a fool. I am so sorry that I turned my back on you. On our traditions. So sorry that I scoffed at your beliefs. Can you ever forgive me?"

"There's nothing to forgive," said Gray Eagle. "It was all part of your journey. The Great Spirit had bigger plans for you, and this was part of it. Tell me your story."

Matt spent hours telling his father everything, with Robert and Kira chiming in, often detailing Matt's valor at great length.

Matt told his father about the cities, the technology that sang with life, the great teacher who'd tried to guide humanity away from destruction. Gray Eagle listened without interruption, nodding at details confirming stories passed down to him through generations.

Finally, Matt gave his father a tour of the ship and introduced him to *Tala*, who appeared in her spectacular crystalline form.

Robert and Kira left in the SUV to give them time alone together, agreeing to return by midnight with food and supplies to load onto *Tala*, and gear they would need to retrieve the energy shield.

Tala recommended they bring a variety of items to the past that operatives from their day might use on a mission, simply because they had no idea what was in store for them. This list included guns and bullets, which would be undetectable by sensors scanning for Atlantean or Lemurian energy weapons, along with comms and listening devices. Whereas the ancient versions of these devices operated using advanced crystals, the ones from their time were electronic, which *Tala* believed would make them immune from detection.

Robert drove straight home and introduced Kira to his mother. He then announced that they had fallen in love. This came as quite a delight to the older woman, but also quite a shock, as he had never even hinted at having feelings for Kira before.

After an hour's visit, they left, and Robert tried to hide his tears as he said goodbye to his mother, knowing he might never see her again.

After filling the SUV with supplies, they returned to meet Matt and his father, who had spent many hours together, cementing their newfound bond. The four of them loaded supplies onto *Tala* and then it was time to leave.

Matt and his father were teary-eyed again as they said their farewells. "I couldn't be prouder of you, son," said Gray Eagle. "I always knew you would walk an important path, one the ancestors laid out for you. But I never would have guessed that you would be destined to play a critical role in ending the cycles of destruction. Nothing could be more important."

"Thanks," said Matt. "That means a lot to me. But you do realize that if we succeed, no one alive right now, including you, will have ever been born."

"I do, Little Owl," said his father with a weary smile, one transforming his lined face. "But in their place, many billions of others will have been born instead. Born into a better world, a better humanity. The Universe is vast, my son. What matters is that we serve something greater than ourselves."

Matt embraced his father again, understanding finally why the man had been given the name Gray Eagle. He soared above ordinary concerns, seeing patterns others missed.

Robert and Kira said their goodbyes to the great man and *Tala* once again lifted into the star-filled night sky.

"That was amazing," said Matt wistfully when they had lifted off. "I never thought I'd see the day when my father and I could have such a deep understanding."

"I'm so happy for you, Matt," said Kira gently.

The trio made their way to *Tala's* bridge in silence. "So, what now?" said Matt. "Onward to the Yucatan Peninsula?"

"That's right," replied Robert. "I'll have *Tala* go slowly so we can get some sleep along the way."

Thoth had told them he'd hidden the advanced energy shield on sacred land. If so, his strategy had backfired badly. Instead of the sacred nature of the land preventing it from being built upon, just the opposite had occurred, although not for at least eleven thousand years after it was buried.

The coordinates the Hierophant had given placed the shield right in the middle of the Ek Balam archaeological site in the Yucatan Peninsula of Mexico. The site was first built upon more than two thousand years earlier, and over the next thousand years had eventually come to cover almost five square miles. Its sacred core, the spiritual and physical heart of the city where Thoth's energy shield was buried, covered over fifteen square acres, encircled by concentric walls. At the center stood its Acropolis, a colossal ten-story limestone structure almost five hundred feet long, known for its well-preserved stucco relief sculptures and elaborate tombs, with a pyramid nearby rising even higher.

"Okay then," said Matt. "Let's go get ourselves an energy shield. Piece of cake, right?"

"Sure," said Robert in amusement. "I only wish Thoth hid it under Fort Knox. You know, because we love challenges so much."

Both of his companions smiled. "I'm pretty sure we'll have our fill of challenges no matter what," replied Kira.

"In that case," said Robert. "Before we start that phase of our lives again, I'd like to take a little detour."

Matt looked intrigued. "What did you have in mind, Professor?"

"I'd like to pay a quick, stealthy visit to a colleague of mine. One who's been a thorn in my side for years. Well, to be more accurate, a giant pain in my ass. Alan Donovan. Obnoxious, pompous, narrow-minded, incompetent, and always wrong."

"Yeah, you've told us all about him," said Kira. "He's the one who takes great joy in disparaging anything you say and has tried to get you fired."

"That's the one."

"Why didn't you mention this little detour to me earlier?"

"Here's the thing," he replied sheepishly. "I'd actually decided not to go through with it. But just before we boarded, just for the hell of it, I checked his address. It turns out he lives in a small, isolated home, on many acres of open land. Too good to be true, right? Would fate allow him to live in such a secluded place if it didn't want me to pay him a visit? I think we all know the answer."

"No, we don't," said Kira. "So, what's your plan? Prove to him that you were right about everything?"

"Sure," said Robert with an impish grin. "Let's go with that. I was thinking of vaporizing him into paste, actually. But proving I was right works too."

Matt laughed again. "I say you should do it."

"See," said Robert, turning to face Kira. "We wouldn't want to disappoint the young lad, right?"

"Okay, fine. Are you really sure you want to be this childish?"

"Of course I am," he replied with an impish grin. "It's like you don't even *know* me. Besides, *am I* being childish? Or am I giving Alan Donovan the ultimate gift? I'll be teaching him a lesson. Opening his mind. You'd think a professor would do *anything* to gain a higher perspective. I'm doing him a favor. He'll thank me one day."

"No, he won't," said Kira. "More likely he'll turn out to never have been born one day."

"Well, when it comes to Alan, either way works for me."

With *Tala's* cooperation, they were hovering above the sprawling property in front of Alan Donovan's one-story home less than a minute later, with stealth mode no longer engaged.

Robert asked *Tala* to extend the ramp and make sure she hovered completely motionless while it was open. He stood at the top, at the opening into the ship, while his two human companions and a crystalline *Tala* stood behind him out of sight, observing.

Robert took a deep breath, savoring the moment. "*Tala*," he said. "Can you detect Alan's cellphone and place a call for me?"

"I can detect his phone, but it's in silent mode, most likely because he's still sleeping."

"Can you change the settings from silent mode to the loudest volume possible? Unlimited rings?"

"Done," said *Tala*. "Placing the call now."

After six rings, Alan answered. "Hello," he whispered, his voice groggy and still half asleep.

"Hello, Alan. Do you know who this is?"

"What?" he said, still sounding dazed. "What's going on? Who *is* this?"

"Come on, Alan. Wake up. I know you recognize my voice."

"*Robert?*" said Alan, his brain finally beginning to come alive. "Robert Shaw? Is that you? Why did you wake me? *How* did you wake me? My phone should have been silenced."

"Come now, Alan, we have much more important things to talk about. Why don't you come outside. I'm at your front door. Well . . . sort of. You've ridiculed my theories. You've called me incompetent—an embarrassment to my profession. And worse. So, I've come to show you absolute proof that I've been right all along. Proof that even someone as pig-headed as you can't possibly ignore."

"What? You've lost your mind, Robert! I mean, even worse than usual. If you've deluded yourself into believing you finally have absolute proof, just send me an email and attach it. No need to deliver it in person. Go away and let me get some sleep."

Robert smiled. "I'm in a working Lemurian starship, Alan. Which isn't something I can attach in an email. Go outside and look up. You're really, really going to want to see this."

"You need help, Robert. Don't make me call the police."

"Really, Alan? Too stubborn to even spend a few seconds to see this for yourself? My evidence is so close it could, *literally*, fall on your head."

"You're having a nervous breakdown, Robert. A psychotic episode."

Robert laughed. "If there isn't a starship overhead when you come out, I swear on my mother's life that I'll resign my post and publicly denounce all of my theories. Just look up for five seconds, Alan."

Alan moved over to the front window, switched on outdoor floodlights, and peered out. "I don't see anything."

"Wow. You're thicker than I thought. Did you not get that you need to be outside so you can look straight up?"

Alan swore profusely, but seconds later emerged from his front door wearing plaid pajamas and gripping a phone firmly in his right hand. He looked up as though in protest, sure there would be nothing there, and his mouth dropped open upon seeing the hovering starship, along with Robert Shaw, standing at the top of a ramp lowered into nothing but air. Robert smiled and gave him a wave, and for the first time in his life, Alan Donovan was rendered speechless.

Robert had *Tala* amplify his voice from the ship. "What you're gawking at, Alan, is a Lemurian starship. It can also travel through time, so I've had the chance to visit both Lemuria and Atlantis for the past month or so. You've called my theories about such a starship delusional. If so, Alan, then you're the one having delusions at the moment, wouldn't you say?"

Alan's eyes bulged out, but he remained too paralyzed to speak.

"Look, I'm not trying to make you wet your pants here," said Robert. "Okay, maybe I am a little bit. But I really just want to open your mind. To get you to see that maybe you *don't* know everything. That there just might be more going on in this world than meets the eye."

He paused. "For example, you wouldn't think a staff well over thirteen thousand years old, with a crystal at its end, packed with advanced tech, could help me channel enough energy to defy gravity."

He raised his Vesh'tar and extended it toward Alan, who gently rose twenty feet into the air, too terrified, too petrified, to even scream.

"But then again," said Robert. "You never know."

"Let me down!" demanded Alan, finally finding his voice. "Please," he said, this time more meekly.

"Of course," said Robert as he lowered the man to a gentle landing. "And as fun as this has been, I really do have to be going. But from now on, Alan, it might be wise to keep an open mind the next time someone challenges your precious academic orthodoxy."

Robert paused. "To be fair, I do get that a starship is quite a stretch, so I can forgive your skepticism. What I can't forgive is your role in spreading rumors about me, trying to demean and humiliate me in front of my students, and filing false reports with the Dean. So, get your act together, *quickly*, or next time your return to earth might not be so . . . *gentle*."

And while Alan Donovan was still stunned out of his mind, his mouth still agape, Robert motioned to *Tala*, who closed the ramp. Thirty seconds later, she shot into the sky while keeping cameras pointed in Alan's direction.

A full minute later, just before they traveled beyond *Tala's* camera range, Alan was still standing outside his open front door in his pajamas, frozen in place, muttering incomprehensibly to himself and looking white as a ghost.

"Happy?" said Kira on the bridge as the image of Robert's nemesis disappeared from the main viewscreen.

"Very," said Robert. "I think it's safe to say I've expanded his horizons."

"That was truly epic," said Matt. "But all kidding aside, I'd have given anything if someone had done that for me. I wasted so many years fighting something I should have been embracing."

"Everything you've done has led to the man you are right now," said Robert. "I wouldn't change a thing. Although I'm glad I was able to perform a public service for Alan Donovan, so that he, too, can become his best self."

"I'll admit I enjoyed that," said Kira. "But now that you've gotten it out of your system, are you ready to get serious again? We have our work cut out for us from here on out. Who knows what the future has in store for us. Or rather, what the past does."

Robert nodded, becoming fully serious once again. She was right. And perhaps he was minimizing the challenges in his head because he was so ecstatically happy, so much in love with Kira Shelton that he felt in a constant state of euphoria.

But he'd better sober up quickly. Fate may have chosen them to play instrumental roles, but it certainly didn't guarantee their success. He couldn't let himself start believing they were invulnerable, because they weren't. Their experiences in the past had proven that repeatedly.

He believed in free will, and if fate had intended their success to be inevitable, they would no longer have any. Since their choices were still their own, success was anything but preordained. If they chose to walk into a hailstorm of weapons fire, no supernatural destiny in the universe would save them.

Robert couldn't let his newfound happiness prevent him from facing this stark reality. They had been tagged as the only three *capable* of catalyzing the changes needed. Whether they would ultimately succeed would depend on their skills, their courage, their determination, as well as considerable luck.

No matter what happened, Robert was at peace. His cherished theories had all been proven true, his life's work validated in a way he never thought possible. And if he was going to captain a starship into the bowels of hell, which might well be the case, there were no two people he'd want by his side more than Kira Shelton and Matt "Little Owl" Jones.

Kira was a woman of staggering competence and beauty, full of surprises, with a courage and sense of humor that were unsurpassed. A woman who'd shown him he was capable of love.

And Matt was a young man who'd become like a son to him. A young man of enormous hidden potential, who'd grown into this potential before Robert's very eyes. Who'd evolved from frivolous to wise beyond his years almost overnight.

Robert might well die on the coming mission. If this happened, he would die fulfilled, knowing he had loved, and that he had done everything in his power to change humanity for the better.

Everyone died. It was miraculous that he had the chance to die in service to the grandest of all causes. An honor beyond measure.

Not that he would welcome death. He'd do everything in his power to accomplish their mission. He'd fight to his last breath and maybe beyond. And he knew that Matt and Kira would fight for the cause just as hard, as they'd already demonstrated.

While the mountain they needed to climb was higher than Everest, and covered in razor-sharp, poisoned-tipped spikes, he considered himself the luckiest man who ever lived. He'd been given the chance to achieve something monumental with people he loved by his side.

No matter what might happen, he couldn't possibly ask for anything more.

"*Tala,*" he said, his voice resolute and determined, "take us to Ek Balam in full stealth mode. An energy shield has been waiting for us for almost thirteen thousand years. Let's not keep it waiting a moment longer."

DOUG AND BRANDON'S DISCUSSION OF THE NOVEL

CONTENTS

1) **Notes From Doug**
   - Introduction.
   - How this collaboration came to be.

2) **Notes From Brandon**
   - How I became obsessed with ancient civilizations.
   - What on Earth really happened 12,900 years ago?
   - Why did the "flood" catastrophe really happen?
   - Why haven't we found clear evidence of advanced ancient civilizations?

3) **Notes From Doug (round 2)**
   - All about crystals:
     - What, exactly, is a crystal?
     - Why are crystals so prominent in science fiction, fantasy, mysticism, and new age healing?
     - Can crystals really form the basis of advanced technology?
   - Nanotechnology and the miracle of birth.
   - Starships were meant to fly.
     - Just how vast is our galaxy?
     - How to beat Einstein's speed limit.
   - Is time travel possible?

4) **Douglas E. Richards Author Biography and list of novels**

5) **Brandon Ellis Author Biography and list of novels**

NOTES FROM DOUG

Introduction.

Thanks for reading *Echoes of Time*. We hope that you enjoyed it. If so, we hope that you will check out the other novels in the *Epic of Atlantis* series, beginning with Book 2, *Echoes of Deceit.*

If you are interested in reading other novels Brandon or I have written, we've included a complete list of our books, embedded with links to their Amazon pages, at the end of this section, along with our author bios.

At the conclusion of most of my novels, I include a section detailing what in the work is real and what isn't, along with a few personal anecdotes—and these sections have been very well received. So I thought I'd do so again here, but I asked Brandon to do most of the heavy lifting, since he's the one with the encyclopedic knowledge of lore, mythology, archaeology, and ancient civilizations.

But before I go any further, if you enjoyed *Echoes of Time*, Brandon and I would be grateful if you'd recommend the series via word of mouth and social media posts. Also, if you could take a few minutes to give this novel however many stars you think it deserves on Amazon, or even write a sentence or two about it in a review box, that would be super helpful.

I'll be handing off to Brandon soon, but before I do, I wanted to write a bit about how this collaboration came to be. Then, after Brandon's done tackling the areas he's most expert in, I'll finish with an abbreviated version of my usual notes on the science and technology elements of the novel.

How this collaboration came to be.

I've written numerous science-fiction thrillers, but all share the same DNA. Along with breakneck action, twists and turns, and intricate plots, I extrapolate current technological trends and include epic, mind-blowing ideas whenever I can. But, I have to admit, it's become ever more difficult for me to find major themes I haven't yet tackled.

I've often said on podcasts and radio appearances that I put every good idea I've ever had into each novel I write, but then I have to come up with the next novel. And the next one.

So how was I able to do this for so long? By reading endlessly about human behavior, cosmology, nanotechnology, futurism, scientific trends, quantum physics, and so on. Basically, if you use up all your good ideas on each novel, you need to reload your brain so you can come up with *others*. Even then, I had to strain my poor brain to its breaking point to come up with novel takes, unexpected, mind-blowing premises, and so on.

After about twenty novels, it occurred to me that there is also another option for generating new ideas: collaborating with another writer.

I don't play well with others, in general, but I decided I could use an infusion of fresh ideas, different perspectives, and a change of pace.

I can discuss plot ideas with myself, but that can be limiting. Which is why brainstorming sessions usually require more than one person. Or, to put it another way, I wanted to stop living the famous poem: Roses are red, Violets are blue, I'm schizophrenic, And so am I.

I remembered that Brandon Ellis had proposed a collaboration many moons earlier, but at the time I hadn't been ready to consider one. Now I was. So I called him and asked what ideas he had for a novel or a series.

He told me.

I was blown away. What he had been working on in his mind for some time was something I couldn't have dreamed up in a thousand years. Hopi legends about starships? Connections between lore and what I thought were mythological advanced civilizations like Atlantis and Lemuria? A sentient starship that takes an expert and his comrades back in time to stop an ancient war?

Fascinating stuff.

I quickly learned that Brandon has a deep, encyclopedic knowledge of all areas instrumental to the story. He knows the history and proclivities of numerous alien species thought to have visited Earth, which have appeared in drawings, writings, and lore throughout the ages. His expertise when it comes to all things Atlantis, and countless other ancient civilizations is also unmatched. And don't get me started on his knowledge of the Hopi, archeology, mythology, history, geology, and so much more. After all the years I've been doing research for my novels, all the books I've read, I consider myself fairly well-versed in a huge variety of fields—but there was *zero* overlap between my knowledge and Brandon's.

A marriage made in heaven. New blood. New ideas to play with. The ideas were so fantastic, so staggering, I was convinced they must be based solely on a series of fever dreams that Brandon had. But after vetting his claims with AI, they checked out every time.

That's what really made it special. My forte is taking accurate science and writing compelling fictional stories around it. But this would give me the chance to write compelling fictional stories about mind-blowing lore and mythology. Lore and mythology that really could be actual history, based on some of the evidence Brandon described, and which he wanted to include in these novels.

So I jumped at the chance to collaborate. He had much of the general premise worked out, and I offered my plotting and logic skills to help pull it all together. We have also come to believe that our combined writing skills are better than either of ours alone.

In any event, it's been great fun to explore different horizons and leave my lane a bit for once. But I didn't leave it too much. The series is still science fiction. Still action-packed, mind-blowing, and as scientifically and historically accurate as we could make it. Yet still different enough from my usual fare to be a breath of fresh air.

I guess the old adage is wrong. Apparently, you *can* teach an old Doug a new trick J

So that's it. The story behind the collaboration. And now, without further ado, I'll turn this over to Brandon, as promised, so he can take it from here.

NOTES FROM BRANDON
How I became obsessed with the ancient past.

Back in 1997, when I was a teenager, I read a book that put me on the path to where I am now: someone obsessed with ancient civilizations, archaeology, and mythology. The book was *Fingerprints of the Gods* by Graham Hancock. You might know Graham from his Netflix series, *Ancient Apocalypse*.

I dove deeper. Throughout my teens and twenties, I co-hosted several Near Death Experience groups. Some group members said they'd been shown visions of the distant, ancient past. Of Atlantis. Of Lemuria. And glimpses of what happened to them. What struck me was how often their stories matched up, down to specific details. These people didn't know each other before the group, yet their accounts were remarkably similar. It surprised them as much as it surprised me. But I needed more than visions. I needed to know if any of it could be real.

Since then, I've been driven to uncover the unknown about our past. It's just something inside me, pushing me to discover. What do I do with what I learn? I write it into some of my science fiction novels, including this one.

Mainstream archaeology claims to know the truth, even though their "facts" constantly change with new discoveries each decade. After extensive research and discussions with scholars and fellow researchers, I've reached a conclusion: no one knows the complete truth.

The truth emerges gradually. One dig, one translation, one eye-opening discovery at a time.

Regarding our ancient past, current humans simply don't know because we weren't there. But clues abound: archaeological finds, myths from cultures worldwide that somehow connect despite oceans between them, geological evidence science can't ignore, and more, and more, and more.

I've been thinking about a novel that covers the basic ground covered by *Echoes of Time* for about five years, but didn't feel I was getting it exactly right and continued to be distracted by a very busy writing schedule.

Finally, I realized why I couldn't get the story to work. I had been intent on making the main character an FBI agent, or a Special Ops agent, or even a pilot. It seems so obvious in retrospect, but it was only when I realized I should just make the main character an archaeologist that everything clicked.

What on Earth really happened 12,900 years ago?

But why this particular story? What drove me to explore these ancient mysteries? The answer lies in what actually happened to our planet 12,900 years ago. Events that science has documented but still can't fully explain.

I'll keep this general to avoid getting bogged down in complicated terminology and specific dates, but what I'm going to tell you below actually happened. Science agrees it happened. They just can't figure out exactly how or why.

But let me start a little later than 12,900 years ago.

About 19,000 years ago, Earth started shaking off the deep freeze of the Ice Age, inching toward the warmer Interglacial Age we're in now. Those big shifts from an icebox to a warm spell in Earth's history can take anywhere from 10,000 to 20,000 years, give or take, with ice melting, seas rising, and the whole planet reshuffling. Around 14,500 years ago, as the ice kept melting and the world warmed up, a massive event called Meltwater Pulse 1A sent oceans surging up about 260 feet. Beaches drowned. People migrated inland. Animals retreated.

As I briefly wrote above, this happens regularly throughout Earth's history. A normal cycle. The planet moving from an Ice Age to an Interglacial Age, and then from an Interglacial Age to an Ice Age. Water levels rising and falling massively. Over and over and over. Each age takes around 10,000 to 20,000 years to transition into and out of, give or take a few thousand years here and there. Again, I'm being general, so I don't bog you down too much with the complicated details of how and why this happens.

Now, during this last transition from the Ice Age to the Interglacial Age, something unbelievable happened to Earth that hadn't been recorded in the last 5 million years of geological history. This event was so incredibly huge that science not only named it, but scientists and historians were beyond perplexed by it. They still can't figure out what happened, how it happened, or why. They have theories, but they remain theories.

Almost exactly 12,900 years ago, Earth did something unprecedented during said transition from Ice Age to Interglacial Age. Science has labeled this event the Younger Dryas. To put it simply, all hell broke loose. An event blasted Earth so intensely that it stopped the Atlantic Meridional Overturning Circulation (the major ocean current system that keeps things temperate), and we plunged into another major ice spell.

Whatever hit Earth slammed it so hard that massive wildfires erupted across much of North America. The northern plains and forests went up in smoke, along with parts of Europe and Siberia. In what's called the "black mat" layer from that exact time, found worldwide, there are nanodiamonds, iridium spikes, magnetic microspheres, and other materials you'd only get from something huge slamming into Earth. Like a comet impact or something releasing energy on the scale of a nuclear explosion. High temperatures, high pressures, spread across continents as evidence of this global catastrophe. The impact melted the Laurentide Ice Sheet over North America rapidly, sending colossal floods across the continent, especially the central and eastern parts. All that meltwater dumping into the oceans disrupted the Atlantic Meridional Overturning Circulation (AMOC) so severely that temperatures dropped almost overnight by about 10°C (18°F), lasting for over 1,000 years. The sudden disrupted currents led to torrential rainfall for months as the atmosphere went haywire from the sudden cooling. Biblical amounts of water caused even more flooding. The impacts or airbursts or whatever it was that occurred triggered tsunamis along the coasts, swallowing lowlands in monster waves.

So, what *did* happen? Some scientists believe it was a massive influx of freshwater from melting glaciers that shut down ocean currents, but that doesn't explain half of it. Others think a comet or large meteor broke up in our atmosphere and peppered the planet with fragments, hitting multiple spots at once. Nonetheless, a catastrophe happened, and it killed off around 35 genera of megafauna in North America alone: woolly mammoths, mastodons, saber-toothed cats, giant ground sloths, short-faced bears, American horses, American camels, different elephant species, and more. It totally disrupted human life, as well. The Clovis people pretty much vanished from the archaeological record right at the start of this mess. Their culture collapsed or adapted so drastically that we can barely trace what happened to them.

Since I'd been studying ancient cultures for so long, I knew of Hopi stories and lore. I'd read several books on the Hopi, particularly the work of one Elder from the Coyote Clan, Oswald "White Bear" Fredericks. He shared his lineage's stories based on interviews with over 30 Hopi Elders. Some of this was published in books like Frank Waters' *Book of the Hopi* and Oswald's own *The History of the Hopi From Their Origins In Lemuria*.

Cultures worldwide speak of floods in our recent past that completely altered humanity. The Sumerian Epic of Gilgamesh, where Utnapishtim survives a god-sent deluge. Plato's tale of Atlantis sinking beneath the waves. The Mayan Popol Vuh describing a flood that wipes out people. The Hindu Matsya Purana, where Manu is warned by an avatar of Vishnu about a great flood. The Greek myth of Deucalion and Pyrrha repopulating the earth after Zeus floods it. The Aztec story of the Fourth Sun ending in a flood that destroys humanity before the current era. In the anthropological records, there are 1,000 flood myths globally, all suggesting a restart to humanity. That can't be a coincidence.

All these stories tell of a major catastrophe displacing everyone, including ancient technology, ancient symbols, ancient everything. It knocked us down to the Stone Age almost overnight. Continents sank. Massive technological cities found the bottom of the seas. Geologically speaking, Earth shook mightily, and changed so much, it was unrecognizable from before. People literally had to start over.

Why did the "flood" catastrophe really happen?

While we can't know for sure why this happened, I thought working from what Hopi Elder Oswald "White Bear" Fredericks taught served the best. Plus, in my heart, though I may be wrong, I believe there's truth in his words.

In Hopi lore, there are five worlds, cycles of creation and destruction. We're in the Fourth World now, called Tuwaqachi, which started after the Third World, Tokpa, was destroyed. The Third World was a time of advanced people who forgot their spiritual ways, became corrupt, and waged wars with flying machines and advanced technology. The gods sent floods, earthquakes, and fire to end it. The survivors, guided by prophecies, emerged into this Fourth World through the sipapu, the sacred emergence point. But the warning is clear: if we don't learn from the past, we're doomed to repeat what happened in the Third World.

Oswald believed, based on ancient lore he was taught, that Lemuria (Kasskara in his language) and Atlantis (Talawaitichqua, the "Land of the East") were real. They existed and were highly advanced, more so than we are now. A war between the two destroyed the Third World, sank both continents, and mass migration began because the world changed so drastically that survivors had to find safe places to live.

We can look at many interpretations of Atlantis and Lemuria through Edgar Cayce, Debbie Solaris, Madame Blavatsky, Rudolf Steiner, and works from the Theosophists. Each describes how Atlantis fell throughout thousands of years, spanning roughly 50,000 to 10,000 years ago. Atlantis had three major cataclysms: one around 50,000 BC that split it into islands, another around 28,000 BC that wrecked more of it, and the final one about 12,000 years ago that left just a few remnants before it was swallowed by the sea. An island empire at the end, warring for the last time and sinking into the ocean.

For this story, we chose to simplify things. Rather than show Atlantis as the fragmented island chain it likely was by 12,900 years ago, we kept it as a mostly intact continent alongside Poseidia, one of the mythical main islands. This gave us a cleaner narrative and let us focus on the final war between two great civilizations without getting bogged down in the complex geography of Atlantis's earlier breakups.

Why haven't we found clear evidence of advanced civilizations?

Okay, so, by this point, I know what you're thinking. If there were advanced civilizations in the past, why haven't we found them?

Good question.

The thing is, we have found them in the form of pyramids aligned with impossible precision, megalithic structures like Göbekli Tepe that our best engineers still puzzle over, hints of ancient technology in myths, and out-of-place artifacts that don't fit the timeline. As for the rest, time and nature are brutal. Most technology, structures, bones, just about anything, turns to dust, gets lost in jungle, buried under sediment, or eroded away.

Give it 100 years without us, and cities are already a mess. Vines strangling buildings, roots busting through concrete, and floods or earthquakes starting to topple stuff. In 500 years, wood is rotted to nothing, most metals are rust flakes, and even plastics are breaking down into brittle bits. By 1,000 years, roads are gone, swallowed by forests or deserts.

Fast forward to 12,000 years, about the time since Atlantis might've existed, and almost everything's erased. Skyscrapers? Crumbled into vague mounds under layers of soil. Cars, machines, tech? Reduced to dust or buried so deep you'd need a miracle to find them. Coastal cities like Atlantis might have been submerged under oceans, ground up by waves, or buried under sediment from rising seas. Even bones don't last, most turning to dust unless they're fossilized under rare conditions.

After 12,000 years of rain, wind, glaciers, and geological churn, only the sturdiest stone structures, like the pyramids or something like Stonehenge, might leave faint traces, and even those are weathered, some of them near-unrecognizable lumps. Our current civilization? If we all vanished tomorrow and nature took over, by 12,000 years, you'd be hard-pressed to find any sign we were here. Almost nothing survives the eons.

So, to wrap up this long note, Douglas and I put this all into one series. I hope we do it justice. This story, told through the lens of Oswald's ancient lore on the fall of two great civilizations, Atlantis and Lemuria, explores echoes of time most have forgotten. Whether you believe any of it or not, I hope you enjoy the journey.

NOTES FROM DOUG (round 2)
All about crystals

What, exactly, is a crystal? We chose to use crystals to form the bulk of Atlantean and Lemurian advanced technology, as well as the most critical component of the mysterious Vesh'tar technology.

One hears the word *crystal* bandied about all the time, but what, exactly, is a crystal, and why did we think this was such a good choice for the novel?

Everyone knows that quartz is a crystal, but many other examples aren't so obvious. Salt and sugar are crystals. So are snowflakes, graphite, and diamond.

But while I pride myself on having some scientific acumen, as I did research for this note, I was stunned to learn that *metals* can also by crystalline in nature. *Metals*! The aluminum foil in our kitchens and the steel in a car are made of crystalline grains, detectable through X-ray diffraction. Chalk is made of calcite, a crystalline form of calcium carbonate, with a trigonal crystal structure. Both bone and tooth enamel contain hydroxyapatite, a calcium phosphate mineral that forms tiny crystalline structures within organic matrices. Even rust can form crystalline structures, such as hematite.

So what makes something a crystal? Simply this: a material is a crystal if it has a highly ordered, repeating atomic or molecular structure that extends into three dimensions. This leads to characteristic physical properties like symmetry and defined shapes. In essence, a crystal's defining feature is its organized, repeating atomic lattice, which governs its shape, properties, and behavior.

Why are crystals so prominent in science fiction, fantasy, mysticism, and new age medicine? I'm not an expert on *Superman*, but I'd venture to say that the science on planet Krypton was based largely on crystals. Any tech that can produce a crystalline *Fortress of Solitude* in the Arctic, one made of crystals, powered by crystals, and controlled by crystals, must really have a thing for crystals. And I think we all know that without Dilithium Crystals the Starship *Enterprise* could never get to warp speed.

Crystals are also very popular in new age healing, meditation, chakra balancing, aura cleansing, and so on.

But why? What about crystals makes them so irresistible in so many settings?

First, they have unique physical properties, and can be quite rare and beautiful. Their clarity, color, and geometric shapes can make them striking, which in a fantasy setting can suggest magical or divine significance. Then, too, their ability to refract, reflect, or emit light evokes a sense of otherworldly power, often tied to magic or energy. Their connection to nature can also be used to tie them to natural or cosmic forces.

Crystals also have a long and storied history. Ancient civilizations like the Egyptians, Greeks, and others also used crystals in rituals, healing, and adornments, believing they held spiritual or protective powers. Medieval alchemists and mystics associated crystals with celestial forces or elemental energies.

But beyond all this, the flawless structure and beauty of many crystals can symbolize purity, perfection, or hidden power, making them ideal as sources of magic for fantasy uses. In addition, as outlined in the next section, since crystals are also capable of scientific marvels, they're ideal for science-fiction uses as well.

Can crystals really form the basis of advanced technology? Short answer: Yes. Long answer: *Absolutely*, yes.

Crystals have *already* played a significant role in advanced electronics and computing. In fact, I purposely left a few crystals off my previous list, silicon and gallium arsenide, which have been integral drivers of the computer revolution. These are used in microchips and transistors due to their precise electrical properties. Their crystalline structure allows for controlled doping—the addition of impurities such as boron or phosphorus to introduce extra electrons or create electron vacancies—which makes them ideal semiconductors.

Silicon wafers form the substrate for CPUs, GPUs, and memory chips. Gallium arsenide is used in high-speed, high-frequency applications like RF circuits and optoelectronics. These work because their regular atomic lattice of crystals enables predictable and controllable electron flow.

Quartz also plays a huge role in computing, as it possesses piezoelectric properties. That means it can generate an electric charge when subjected to mechanical stress. Or, conversely, it can deform or vibrate when an electrical field is applied. For this reason, quartz crystals are used in oscillators and clocks to generate precise frequencies, essential for timing in computers and communication devices. Quartz crystal oscillators also provide the clock signals that synchronize operations in microprocessors and other digital circuits.

Which brings us to photonic and optoelectronic crystals such as lithium niobate and others. These crystals manipulate light for applications like optical computing, lasers, and high-speed data transmission. Photonic crystals can guide light in optical circuits, potentially replacing or supplementing electronic circuits for faster, lower-power computing.

In addition to the uses described above, several emerging crystal-based technologies are now on drawing boards around the world. Crystals such as diamond, with nitrogen-vacancy centers, or rare-earth-doped crystals, are being explored for possible use as quantum bits, a fundamental building block of quantum computers. Other crystals, like transition metal oxides, mimic neural networks by retaining memory of past electrical states, potentially enabling brain-like computing. Finally, some researchers are exploring exotic crystals, which can act as topological insulators, for next-generation electronics with ultra-low power or high-speed properties.

So, in the end, given the versatility and narrative power of crystals, choosing to base the advanced technology of Atlantis and Lemuria on these marvels was an obvious choice.

Finally, it's been said that the famed crystal, diamond, is a girl's best friend. While Brandon and I don't know if this is true, we do know one thing for certain: the crystal sitting atop a Vesh'tar staff is definitely a *Hierophant's* best friend.

Nanotechnology and the miracle of birth.

In *Echoes of Time*, the characters continue to encounter advances that seem impossible, yet have obviously come to pass, so I thought I'd comment on this in the context of the miracle of biological reproduction. For my fans who have heard me speak about this on the radio and on podcasts, and have read about it in the notes of several of my books, my apologies. Save yourselves. Skip ahead to the next section. This is written more for Brandon's fans, who likely haven't heard or read my musings on this subject.

So here I go again.

Early on in my science-fiction writing career, I'd ask myself if I was going too far with an invented technology. Take self-replicating nanites, for example. I wanted to create a nanite technology that could basically 3-D print anything, instantly, by assembling it atom by atom. As if atoms were simply Legos and the nanites were master builders. But most critically, I envisioned nanites that could make exact copies of themselves.

For example, you could drop a single microscopic nanite on the ground. It would dig down, convert minerals and soil and such to whatever material it needed to make copies of itself, and make a copy. These two would then make four. These four would make eight. Then sixteen. And so on.

After only forty such doublings, you'd have over a trillion of them. These trillion would then dig in the earth and find what they needed to create a fully functioning plasma television, or a Gulfstream jet. These items would seem to just grow up from the ground, and would be completed in minutes.

I hesitated. Too much like magic. How could anyone believe technology this extraordinary could ever be created, even in a million years?

That's when it hit me. What I was envisioning is exactly what life does *already*. With *human* life being even more of a marvel because humans are imbued with sentience.

Many years ago, I was working toward a PhD in molecular biology (aka, genetic engineering), utterly fascinated by the field. I eventually changed course, earning a master's degree instead, because, while I loved the science, I was horrible at lab work. Horrible. I was impatient and sloppy. And sloppy isn't a great thing to be when one is working with high levels of radiation and potent carcinogens like ethidium bromide, whose sole purpose in life is to mutate DNA.

But in any event, my first graduate-level course in Developmental Biology (i.e., how an egg transforms into an adult) blew my mind. Nothing in all of biology is more fascinating and miraculous to me. How can a single fertilized egg cell possibly contain all the instructions required to construct an entire human, and then be able to carry out these instructions with such perfection?

And this process operates precisely the way I was envisioning the nanites operating. A single fertilized egg cell finds building material in its environment and makes an exact copy of itself. The copies do the same. In forty doublings you have a trillion cells. But during the process of creating life, the cells somehow differentiate along the way. At some point, obeying complex instructions, some of the cells become heart cells. Others lung cells. Or skin cells. And so on.

Or, most profoundly of all—some of the cells become *neurons*.

Just like the nanite I was envisioning, which I thought to be utterly impossible, a single cell ends up single-handedly constructing an entire human being. And this is a construction, and a feat, far more impressive than a plasma television. Yes, it takes nine months rather than minutes, and the process is limited to creating human babies only. But while this system can't be reprogrammed to create a Gulfstream Jet (which would be a tight squeeze for a womb, anyway), creating life from inert matter is a pretty good trick. And finding a way to produce a baby that possesses hundreds of billions of neurons wired in precisely the right arrangement to create consciousness? That's an even *better* trick.

Talk about your miracles. And the process isn't quite finished. The newborn grows from an infant to an adult by converting food into more of itself. Once again, our bodies must extract the raw materials we need for construction from such sources as ice-cream, meatloaf, and pasta, and then rearrange these raw materials into muscle cells, heart cells, brain cells, and so on.

The idea that a single fertilized cell can successfully transform itself into an adult human, including a conscious brain with many billions of neurons, is utterly preposterous. *Impossible.* There is no way this could ever succeed.

And yet, all of us are living proof that it does . . .

Starships were meant to fly.

Just how vast is our galaxy? Interstellar distances are vast beyond imagination. The fastest human-made object that remained Earth-bound was NASA's X-43A Scramjet, which reached a speed of 12,144 mph—over three miles a *second*.

Now that's hauling ass.

Still, at this speed, it would take 234,000 years to reach the nearest star, Proxima Centauri. And this star is only a measly 4.2 light-years away, or about 25 trillion miles.

So what's the fastest human-made object that *has* left the Earth? That would be the NASA Parker Solar Probe. On December 24, 2024, this probe reached a peak speed of 430,000 mph following a gravity assist from Venus. (Thanks, Venus!).

Yet, even at this incomprehensible speed, it would need 6,600 years to reach the nearest star.

And that's the *nearest* star, only 4.2 light-years away. We're a very backwater planet, situated twenty-five thousand light-years away from the center of our galaxy—where most of the action is taking place. Twenty-five thousand light-years away from where the density of stars is more than a million times greater than it is in our neighborhood.

Put another way, if the center of the galaxy were Manhattan, Earth would be a farmhouse in the middle of a thousand-acre turnip farm.

How to beat Einstein's speed limit:

Einstein's equations show that nothing can travel faster than light, which is a problem if you want to build a starship, since light plods along at a snail-like 670 million miles per hour. As previously mentioned, if you could travel at Einstein's speed limit—which you can't—even then it would take you four years to reach our nearest neighbor, and twenty-five thousand years to reach galactic center.

Note: When I was done with the notes, I pasted them into an AI and asked it to check for accuracy. Below I've copied what it said about a sentence you just read (and I am not kidding, it really said this). Specifically, it was referring to this sentence: "Einstein's equations show that nothing can travel faster than light, which is a problem if you want to build a starship, since light plods along at a snail-like 670 million miles per hour."

AI: Calling the speed of light "snail-like" is subjective and misleading.

Yikes. Sorry AI. I guess I've misled my readers. Perhaps snails *can't* travel at 670 million miles per hour, after all. Who knew? Thank you, AI, for the correction ☺.

Anyway, where was I? I think I was saying that the universe is large and requires faster-than-light travel for a species to get anywhere. The good news is that there are cheat codes that might make this possible. Not to break the speed limit, but ignore it entirely.

The two ways to do this that scientists are exploring the most both require exotic matter, which can create anti-gravity-like effects. Such exotic matter was long thought to be impossible, but like creating a human being from scratch, impossible events occur all the time. The good news is that scientists have discovered a force which is pushing galaxies apart at a much greater rate than should be happening, which has been deemed *Dark Energy* for want of a better term.

A repulsive force that pushes mass apart rather than an attractive force that brings it together? If that isn't a type of anti-gravity, I don't know what is.

Once you have exotic matter, you can use it to anchor a traversable wormhole. And by traversable, I'm not talking about the better-known Einstein-Rosen Bridges or Schwarzschild wormholes formed by black holes. I'm talking about hyperspace tunnels through spacetime that can connect remote regions of our universe. If you can manipulate spacetime in any way you want, you can create these shortcuts and stabilize them. This would allow you to pop through a wormhole and reach a planet a thousand light-years away in seconds.

The second possibility exotic anti-gravity producing matter might open up is a warp drive. While it's true that nothing in space can go faster than the speed of light, space itself can do so. In fact, during the cosmic inflation that started our universe, space expanded at a thousand trillion trillion trillion trillion times the speed of light, and not even the speedy *snail* can move that fast.

Bottom line, if you could speed up space and stick to it like glue, you'd come along for the ride. Like a stationary passenger on a moving walkway. Or a surfer, with space being the wave. You and your surfboard don't move much, but if you ride the right wave, you can get to shore in a hurry.

And exotic matter would make this possible. The US government is exploring both of these possibilities quite extensively. In fact, there is a Defense Intelligence Agency report that was declassified a few years back entitled, "Traversable Wormholes, Stargates, and Negative Energy." If you Google it, you can find it instantly and read it for yourself. I'll end with a few passages from this report that speak to the material I just covered.

WORMHOLE EXCERPT: "Implementation of interstellar travel via traversable wormholes generally requires the engineering of spacetime into very specialized local geometries. Analysis of these via the general relativistic field equation, plus the resultant source matter equations of state, demonstrates that such geometries require the use of "exotic" matter, which includes anti-gravity, in order to produce the requisite FTL spacetime modification."

WARP DRIVE EXCERPT: "The warp drive involves local manipulation of the fabric of space in the immediate vicinity of a spacecraft. The basic idea is to create an asymmetric bubble of space that is contracting in front of the spacecraft while expanding behind it. Using this form of locomotion, the spacecraft remains stationary inside this 'warp bubble,' and the movement of space itself facilitates the relative motion of the spacecraft. The theory of relativity places no restrictions on the speed of motion of space itself, thus allowing for a convenient circumvention of the speed-of-light barrier."

Is time travel possible?

In a novel named *Echoes of Time*, I'd be remiss if I didn't touch on time-travel science and theory. This being said, these notes have gone much longer than I intended, so while time travel is a subject I could write twenty pages about (and for which I've written four other novels about), I'll keep it super short.

Time travel isn't pure fantasy. According to relativity, time isn't a rigid, universal metronome. It's stretchy, like a rubber band, and can bend under the influence of gravity or speed. If you travel close to the speed of light, time slows down for you compared to someone lounging back on Earth. At the speed of light, time stops altogether. In 1971, scientists tested Einstein's equations by flying atomic clocks on airplanes and found they lagged behind clocks on the ground—by *precisely* the amount Einstein predicted.

Wow! That was one impressive physicist. I don't want to go overboard here, but in my view, Einstein was almost as smart as a *snail*. (If you've read the previous section, you might laugh here—if not, you won't have any idea what this means).

So, time travel into the future is possible, at least if you could travel very near the speed of light. Thousands of years could pass on Earth for every one second that passes for you.

What about travel back in time? It turns out, the laws of physics work equally well in either time direction, so it should, in theory, be possible. While no one has built a time machine quite yet, certain experiments in quantum mechanics and relativity show that time travel, along with retrocausality—where the future influences the past—are both very real possibilities.

I'll end this section by pointing to a few resources you might consult if you'd like examples of how a measurement in the future can affect the past. These theories and experiments are quite complex and require a solid grasp of quantum physics. In my view, the writings of Cambridge professor Huw Price are a great place to start.

For example, in Price's 2008 paper "Toy Models for Retrocausality," Price describes simple mathematical models showing how retrocausality emerges from global constraints in quantum systems. His 2012 paper "Does Time-Symmetry Imply Retrocausality?" argues that time-symmetric quantum theories necessarily involve retrocausal influences under certain ontological assumptions. Price has also co-authored a 2013 paper with Peter Evans and Ken Wharton entitled "A New Slant on the EPR-Bell Experiment," which proposes retrocausal explanations for existing quantum experiments.

Finally, I'll leave you with the words of David Deutsch, an Oxford physicist who laid the foundations for quantum computing. "I myself believe that there will one day be time travel. Because, when we find that something isn't forbidden by the overarching laws of physics, we eventually find a technological way of doing it."

Douglas E. Richards Author Biography and list of novels

Douglas E. Richards is the *New York Times* and *USA Today* bestselling author of science-fiction thrillers that have sold more than three million copies (see list below). Richards has been celebrated for his gripping, thought-provoking works that blend cutting-edge scientific concepts with heart-pounding narratives.

Richards burst onto the literary scene with his debut novel, *Wired*, published in 2010. The novel garnered widespread acclaim for its ingenious combination of scientific speculation and thrilling storytelling. This success set the stage for a series of bestselling novels, each marked by meticulous research, riveting plots, and characters that resonate with readers.

Known for his ability to translate complex scientific concepts into accessible and engaging narratives, Richards has become a go-to author for readers seeking an intellectually stimulating and adrenaline-fueled reading experience. His works delve deeply into the ethical dilemmas posed by scientific breakthroughs and the potential impact of technology on society.

A former Director of Biotechnology Licensing at Bristol Myers Squibb and a former biotechnology executive, Richards earned a BS in microbiology from the Ohio State University, a master's degree in genetic engineering from the University of Wisconsin—where he engineered mutant viruses now named after him—and an MBA from the University of Chicago.

The author has two grown children and lives in San Diego, California, with his wife and dog.

Richards loves hearing from readers and always replies, so feel free to write to him at douglaserichards1@gmail.com and address him as "Doug". You can also Friend Richards on Facebook at Douglas E. Richards Author, or visit his website, DouglasErichards.com, where you can sign up to be notified of new releases.

Near Future Science-Fiction Thrillers by Douglas E. Richards (Series)
WIRED (Wired 1)
AMPED (Wired 2)

MIND'S EYE (Nick Hall 1)
BRAINWEB (Nick Hall 2)
MIND WAR (Nick Hall 3)

SPLIT SECOND (Split Second 1)
TIME FRAME (Split Second 2)

THE ENIGMA CUBE (Alien Artifact 1)
A PIVOT IN TIME (Alien Artifact 2)

(Standalone novels)
QUANTUM LENS
GAME CHANGER
INFINITY BORN
SEEKER
VERACITY
ORACLE
THE IMMORTALITY CODE
UNIDENTIFIED
PORTALS
THE BREAKTHROUGH EFFECT

Kids Science Fiction Thrillers (9 and up, enjoyed by kids and adults alike)
TRAPPED (Prometheus Project 1)
CAPTURED (Prometheus Project 2)
STRANDED (Prometheus Project 3)

OUT OF THIS WORLD
THE DEVIL'S SWORD

Brandon Ellis Author Biography and list of novels

Brandon Ellis, an Amazon Best Selling and Amazon All-Star author, hails from the charming community of Gladstone, just outside Portland, Oregon. Graduating from the local high school and venturing into higher education, his journey took an unexpected turn when he excelled as an All State Baseball and All League Basketball player.

Beyond the world of sports, Brandon embarked on a path that led him to obtain state and federal Therapeutic Massage Licenses, ultimately becoming a successful Sports Massage Therapist and Instructor. This endeavor allowed him to help countless individuals regain their optimal health, showcasing his deep-rooted commitment to wellness.

With a family of five and an unwavering dedication to both his loved ones and his craft, Brandon Ellis is more than just an author; he's a storyteller. Drawing inspiration from literary giants like Michael A. Stackpole and Michael Crichton, and his extensive travels around the world, he weaves narratives that resonate deeply with readers.

His writing style and themes are a captivating blend of science fiction wonder, adventure, and a profound connection to history, archaeology, ancient tribal legends, and the mysteries of ancient civilizations, all in the realms of a future world. Brandon's extensive experience in health and wellness adds authenticity to his storytelling, making his books not only thrilling but also enlightening.

Influenced by literary luminaries like Jason Anspach and J.N. Chaney, Brandon has carved his own unique niche in the literary world. His bestsellers include the riveting Atlantis series, the enthralling Star Guild series, the action-packed Jackson Stone series, and the immersive Martian Colony Chronicles series. Among his notable works, the Shadow Watch series and the Blink series have earned significant acclaim and a dedicated following.

As Brandon Ellis continues to craft tales that transport readers to realms of imagination, history, and reflection, stay tuned for his upcoming projects, promising more adventures and insights for his growing fan base.

Near Future Science-Fiction Thrillers/Ancient Civilization books by Brandon Ellis
(Series)
Veil Rising (Star Guild 1)
Backlash Rising (Star Guild 2)
Alliance Rising (Star Guild 3)

Project Atlantis (Ascendant Saga 1)
Destination Atlantis (Ascendant Saga 2)
Colony Atlantis (Ascendant Saga 3)
Beyond Atlantis (Ascendant Saga 4)
Enigma Atlantis (Ascendant Saga 5)

Horizon Protocol (A Jackson Stone Thriller 1)
Dove Sequence (A Jackson Stone Thriller 2)
Lotus Gene (A Jackson Stone Thriller 3)

Space Opera/Ancient Civilization books by Brandon Ellis (Series)
Farthest Reaches (Farthest Reaches 1)
Starship Arcadia (Farthest Reaches 2)
Jump Trap (Farthest Reaches 3)

Martian Plague (Mars 1)
Martian Ark (Mars 2)
Martian Insurrection (Mars 3)
Martian Earth (Mars 4)
Martian Legacy (Mars 5)

Shadow Watch (Shadow Watch 1)
Frontier Worlds (Shadow Watch 2)
To Save an Emperor (Shadow Watch 3)

Alien Invasion/Alternative History books by Brandon Ellis (Series)
Alien Incursion (Blink 1)
Alien Dawn (Blink 2)
Alien Fall (Blink 3)

Military SciFi books by Brandon Ellis (Series)
The Intus Invasion (Battles of the Republic 1)
Battle for Intus (Battles of the Republic 2)
Battle of Shadows (Battles of the Republic 3)

Printed in Dunstable, United Kingdom